MARPLE

The Marple Collection

The Murder at the Vicarage
The Body in the Library
The Moving Finger
Sleeping Murder
A Murder is Announced
They Do It With Mirrors
A Pocket Full of Rye
4.50 from Paddington
The Mirror Crack'd From Side to Side
A Caribbean Mystery
At Bertram's Hotel
Nemesis

Short Stories

The Thirteen Problems
Miss Marple's Final Cases

Agatha Christie®

Marple

TWELVE NEW STORIES

Naomi Alderman
Leigh Bardugo
Alyssa Cole
Lucy Foley
Elly Griffiths
Natalie Haynes
Jean Kwok
Val McDermid
Karen M. McManus
Dreda Say Mitchell
Kate Mosse
Ruth Ware

HarperCollins*Publishers*

HarperCollins*Publishers* Ltd
1 London Bridge Street,
London SE1 9GF

www.harpercollins.co.uk

HarperCollins*Publishers*
Macken House, 39/40 Mayor Street Upper
Dublin 1, D01 C9W8, Ireland

First published by HarperCollins*Publishers* Ltd 2022
1

A catalogue record for this book is available from the British Library.

ISBN: 978-0-00-873816-7

Printed and bound in the UK using 100%
Renewable Electricity at CPI Group (UK) Ltd

FSC
www.fsc.org
MIX
Paper | Supporting responsible forestry
FSC™ C007454

This book contains FSC™ certified paper and other controlled sources to ensure responsible forest management.

For more information visit: www.harpercollins.co.uk/green

Contents

Miss Jane Marple, literature's pre-eminent amateur detective and one of Agatha Christie's finest creations, first appeared in print in December 1927, in a short story called 'The Tuesday Night Club'. Christie returned to this intriguing character – with the intention, as she herself put it, 'to give old maids a voice' – in 1930's *The Murder at the Vicarage*, which was followed by eleven further Marple novels, and several collections of short stories featuring St Mary Mead's sharpest mind, with the very last novel, *Sleeping Murder*, appearing posthumously in 1976, the year Christie died.

Christie had noticed that women, especially those in their later years who remained unmarried, were often patronised, overlooked and underestimated, but the world's bestselling novelist knew well how little escapes such village stalwarts, that underneath demure lace caps could lurk the shrewdest of brains, capable of outsmarting even Scotland Yard's finest. Evil, after all, is just as easily found in the most picturesque corner of England as in the meanest city streets – human nature is human nature, wherever you are. And so one of her most unforgettable characters came into being.

Evil in Small Places

Lucy Foley

'I wonder, sometimes, if there isn't a concentration of evil in small places.'

'What *do* you mean, Jane?' Prudence looked across at her former schoolfriend, who sat in the armchair opposite with a small glass of cherry brandy. In the kind, warm glow of the fire the marks of old age were flatteringly blurred. Jane Marple was so little changed, in the important details, from her girlhood self. The quick, birdlike manner, the bright, inquisitive eyes, the sense of a quiet, perhaps even formidable intelligence.

Just as Miss Marple opened her mouth to answer, a firecracker exploded in the darkness outside, followed by a series of shrieks and howls that might have come from the mouth of hell itself. Someone had begun to beat a drum. The two women could not see out as all the curtains had been drawn by Prudence's maid at four p.m. sharp. Fairweather House – imposing, Georgian – faced on to the main street of Meon Maltravers. And outside in the gloaming, just beyond the windows, a pagan-looking throng was mustering.

As the clamour from outside faded a little, Miss Marple spoke again. 'One is aware there is a great deal of wrong-doing in cities and larger towns, of course. The newspapers are desperate to make sure that we do not miss a single grisly detail. But I wonder if there aren't more terrible things happening in England's villages and hamlets than in its metropolises.'

Prudence pursed her lips. 'Well, it's not true of Meon Maltravers. This is a highly respectable place.'

Meon Maltravers was a small town with red-tiled, flint walled buildings built hugger-mugger across the centuries along its sloping, cobbled streets, with soaring views over the South Downs towards the coast. It had certainly had the appearance of a respectable place when Miss Marple had arrived earlier, in the light of day. But now darkness had fallen. And just at this moment came a new round of caterwauling and shrieks from the street.

Miss Marple raised her eyebrows. 'Are you sure?'

Prudence waved a hand. 'Just some local high jinks. Perfectly harmless. But you always *did* have a dark imagination, Jane.'

'This isn't imagination, dear. I've borne witness to it—' Miss Marple had been about to say 'first hand' and speak to some of her experiences over the last few years, but, again, there was another small explosion outside. Perhaps it was no bad thing. Too much talk of evil had a way of discomfiting one's companions, even those with constitutions as strong as Prudence's.

Instead, in the next window of relative calm, Miss Marple

said: 'People knowing one another's business, that's part of it. It gives rise to all sorts of misunderstandings and resentments. Boredom too: that's another thing. No cinemas or theatres or restaurants to take people out of the humdrum. The terrible acts that are likely committed due to a simple lack of other things to do—'

Prudence frowned and said, in her best head-girl voice (she had in fact been head-girl, all those years ago): 'I've been made to feel very welcome here since I lost poor George fifteen years ago – which is no given thing, considering he lived here alone as a bachelor for so many years before Alice and I joined him.'

Miss Marple looked to the mantlepiece. 'That's from the cruise, isn't it?'

The photograph showed a younger Prudence, alongside Alice, Prudence's daughter from her first marriage, and the late George Fairweather. It had been the last time Miss Marple and Prudence had met: on a tour of the Norwegian Fjords. George Fairweather, considerably Prudence's senior, had been a frail figure of a man, unsteady on his feet, with the mottled complexion of a windfall apple. As for Alice, she remembered a pretty girl dressed in clothes that seemed a little too luxurious for one so young.

'Where is Alice now?' Miss Marple asked.

'Oh, just outside the village. We've always been closer than most mothers and daughters. She married a local landowner, Sir Henry Tyson. They are quite the toast of Meon Maltravers—'

Miss Marple gave a small cough. 'And you really are *part*

of things here? In my experience, in such places one is often considered a newcomer for several decades before being truly accepted into the fold. Fifteen years is like the blink of an eye.'

Prudence drew herself up. 'I'm head of the Parish Council, Jane!' she said, as though that settled everything. 'And I'm certainly *vieille garde* when compared to our latest newcomer, the new choir mistress. She has been renting Badger's Rest, an Arts and Crafts monstrosity on the outskirts of town, and there is *much* speculation about her.'

Miss Marple leaned in. 'Of what kind?'

'She's foreign, for one thing. French. Young, or less than forty, anyhow. Near to Alice's age, in fact. And she used to be a rather successful opera singer, but the story is that she had some trouble with her vocal chords and had to leave the stage. Anyhow. She has ruffled a few feathers. An unaccompanied woman, you know how it is. Of course, I don't give in to gossip.'

Miss Marple nodded. 'Of course.'

'But Christopher Palfrey, our resident poet – and a very talented tenor – just published his latest collection, dedicated to "The Enchantress of Song". You can only imagine how that went with his wife, Annabelle – who's not what one would have in mind for an "enchantress" of any kind. She's something of a Socialist, you know – always making a nuisance of herself, opposing some of the most sensible suggestions on the Parish Council, which I find very tiresome. Anyway, she must be spitting feathers over the book, no one has seen her smile for weeks . . . though that isn't entirely unusual.'

'I wonder why she'd choose to come and live here?' Miss Marple mused, apparently lost to her own line of thought. 'The choir mistress, I mean. An unmarried, foreign woman? To come to such an out-of-the-way place – it seems strange, doesn't it?'

'It's not so out of the way as all that,' Prudence said, crisply. 'We have a direct train to London, a mainline station. As you have seen yourself.'

Miss Marple had wanted to visit the gardens at Honnington Manor – she'd had a rave review from Bunch Harmon about the Japanese maples and their astonishing autumn display at this time of year. It was too far to travel in a day. But Miss Marple had remembered, from their meeting on that cruise, that Prudence lived not far away. She had written to suggest a reunion. The two women hadn't been exactly bosom friends at school, but Miss Marple had always been rather intrigued by her and thought it would make for an interesting visit.

'Anyway,' Prudence continued. 'You shall meet Celia Beautemps – the choir mistress – tonight. The rehearsal will be at her house; the church roof is being repaired. And hopefully you'll see Alice again: she sings alto too. If she can get away, that is. She and Henry keep some animals – a few sheep and pigs.' And then, lest Miss Marple should look down on this enterprise, 'Henry is very much a gentleman farmer, of course. But one has to find a way to make all that land pay.'

'Tonight?'

'Yes! Choir practice, of course. I *did* mention it, surely? We have so much to rehearse before Advent and it's just around the corner now.'

It was not at all what Miss Marple would have preferred. A quiet sit by the fire, some knitting – she was just beginning on an Argyll jumper for her nephew Raymond's Christmas present.

'Besides, I remember you having a lovely soprano, Jane,' Prudence said. 'Clear as a bell. So if you wanted to join us—

'It's quite some time since I sang in the school choir, dear. I shall be perfectly happy to watch.'

At this moment a gust of wind funnelled down the chimney and a shower of sparks exploded on to the hearthrug. Miss Marple stared deep into the flames as though seeing something in their midst. Prudence caught the direction of her gaze. 'It's far too low! I'll ring for the maid immediately!'

'No, no,' Miss Marple put up a hand. 'I'm warm enough.'

But Prudence had turned to ring the bell. A few seconds later the maid had appeared. 'New logs! And be quick about it, girl.' Miss Marple watched as the flames took hold of the firewood, piled on top of everything below. She would now be far too hot. Here was the problem with staying in other peoples' houses. Miss Marple didn't do it, as a rule. Nothing was quite as you would have it yourself.

'She's rather a fool, that girl,' Prudence sighed, when the maid had retreated. 'It's so difficult to find good maids these days.'

'I remember you saying the same thing last time I saw you, Prudence.'

'I'm sure. George was always rather silly about the servants. He gave the house boy driving lessons, and even though he could be extremely parsimonious at other times, he paid for the former housekeeper's daughter's tuition; thought she was too gifted to spend the rest of her life as a scullery maid. He paid for our butler's holiday to Brighton too. That sort of thing gives them ideas above their station, if you ask me.'

Miss Marple couldn't help but be a little amused by this Lady-of-the-Manor act from Prudence, a greengrocer's daughter who had been on a full scholarship at school. Miss Marple also knew that after leaving she had worked for several years in various rather humble positions: a governess, a librarian. She had met her first husband, a pharmacist almost twice her age, while working as his assistant – and had met George as a young widow, while working as his secretary.

'Of course,' Prudence said, 'I let quite a few of them go when George's heart troubles began and never rehired as it was simply too much to keep on a full staff— Goodness!' she cut herself off mid-sentence, with a glance up at the clock. 'We better be going, or we'll be late.'

A few moments later they stepped out into the crisp November air, drawing their coats closely about them. Here they were confronted by a stream of masked figures, marching past the front door to the house. They were like something from a medieval painting; demons and fiends come to carry the sinners away. The acrid scent of burning paraffin caught at the back of the throat. Several of them were beating drums. All carried lighted torches and several groups had hoisted aloft life-size, papier-mâché figures with hideously distorted features: oversized heads and bulging eyes, clad in the red robes and caps of Catholic cardinals. There was a strange hum of energy about them. It felt dangerous, even flammable – as though any second the very air might ignite. Miss Marple paused, staring: at once fascinated and repelled.

Prudence beckoned, in her head-girl manner, taking no notice of the throng. 'This way.'

They had to push their way through the crowd. Several times Miss Marple felt herself jostled – once she could have sworn that a hand reached out to give her a rather hard shove out of the way, and she struggled to regain her footing. It didn't seem to matter a jot to these people that there were two elderly women in their midst. She heard the *whoomp* of the paraffin torches as they swayed above the masked heads, felt the heat of the flames on her cheeks, felt a little frisson of disquiet at being caught among these intent, anonymous figures who moved as one, like a herd or a marauding army.

'I don't understand,' Miss Marple said to Prudence, after they had managed to ford the flood of bodies and were standing on the other side of the road. 'Guy Fawkes' Night was two weeks ago. They had a bonfire in the fields by St Mary Mead. Dr Haydock contributed some Roman Candles and Griselda Clement – the vicar's wife – produced some sort of spiced wine . . . what was it called? Something foreign. *Glühwein*, yes: that was it. Delicious – perhaps a touch too much cinnamon. Of course, I didn't stay for long. Far too cold.'

'Ah,' said Prudence, 'but they do everything rather differently in Meon Maltravers, a little like the Cornish. Tonight's revels commemorate not the death of a band of Catholic rebels but the immolation of seventeen Protestant martyrs at the town cross. It's why they burn the cardinals – the figurines, you know. I suppose you could say it's a sort of revenge, albeit several hundred years later.'

'Revenge,' said Miss Marple, almost to herself. 'Revenge and settling of scores. That's another thing one finds a great deal of in small, out-of-the-way places.'

'Well, though the score here is so many centuries old, it's predominantly the youths of the town that are involved. And let me tell you,' Prudence said, casting a disapproving eye over the revels, 'religion has very little to do with it at all. In fact, it feels rather apt that we should be going to choir practice tonight. We will form a bastion of Christian righteousness in the midst of these pagan goings-on.'

They walked down the high street, away from the crowds and noise until they were on the outskirts of town.

'This way,' Prudence said. 'We'll cut through the woods and it'll take us the quick route to the back of the property.' She took out a small torch and switched it on.

Now the street had dwindled to little more than a path between a black thicket of trees. The light from the streetlamps behind them was almost lost but the full moon filtered down in fingers of light between the tangled branches and the beam from Prudence's torch bounced in front of them. It was only about five o'clock or so but it felt much later. It was hard to believe that only a hundred yards or so away were crowded streets and shops, noise and light. Every footstep was audible, every snapped twig. From the undergrowth around them came the secret rustlings of nocturnal animals.

'How much further?' Miss Marple asked, stepping carefully

over a tree root that had erupted up in the centre of the path.

'Only a little way along here. We're going via the back entrance, as it's quicker. There's a long driveway, but you reach it from the other end of the high street. You'll see the house lights shortly. Madame Beautemps keeps them on all night, which has caused some controversy with the local bird-watching group; they're convinced she's frightened away all the screech owls. She really has set the cat among the pigeons.'

'Or the owls,' Miss Marple said.

'No, Jane,' Prudence said, 'that's not how the saying goes at all—' she stopped short as a terrible, unearthly, animal screeching split the air in two. For a long time afterwards, the echo of it seemed to ricochet among the trees.

'How odd,' Prudence said. 'There must be a few screech owls about after all. Where was I? Oh, yes. Celia Beautemps has made enemies of most members of our choir too. I told you about the Palfreys before, didn't I? Then there's Colonel Woodage – who sings bass – hates all the French; had a son who lost both legs trying to rescue a band of Gallic deserters in the war, you know. And she's upset Mrs Prufrock – the former choir mistress for the last three decades – for obvious reasons. We think Reverend Peabody must be in thrall to her, because he ousted poor Mrs Prufrock from her position with no warning.'

'I'd say her quarrel is with the Reverend, then, rather than with her replacement.'

'Perhaps. But to add insult to injury, Madame Beautemps

has insisted that Mrs Prufrock shouldn't be singing soprano, because she's no longer able to hit the top notes. And there's Gordon Kipling, master of hounds for the local hunt – also a bass – who is convinced she killed three of his animals: two days after she complained about their barking (he lives just a little way over there, beyond those trees) they ate rat poisoning and perished. And then—'

Suddenly Prudence gave a very uncharacteristic scream. It happened so quickly. They didn't spot the figure until it was almost upon them, as though it had sprung from the darkness itself. Mask-clad, moving towards them at speed from the opposite direction. Prudence was standing plumb in their way. There was a moment's pause, in which the stranger seemed to hesitate, as though deciding whether to step around her. Then Miss Marple saw a hand shoot out; a second later, Prudence had fallen to the ground, the torch flying from her grip, the light going out with a little 'pop'. Another few seconds and the figure had disappeared. They were alone again.

'Prudence!' Miss Marple went to her friend and, with some difficulty, helped her to stand. 'Are you all right? Are you hurt?'

'I— I don't know,' Prudence said, a little shakily. I mean: yes, I think I am – all right, that is. I just . . . just need to catch my breath. He pushed me, Jane! Did you see?'

'Yes, yes. I saw – a frightful thing! Should we go to the police? I noticed we passed the station on the high street—'

'No,' Prudence said, bravely. 'I don't want any fuss. Nothing's broken. And he'll be long gone by now, into the crowd. They'll never find him. Just take my arm. It's only a little way now.' She seemed miraculously unperturbed by the whole affair, but then Prudence had always been made of stern stuff.

Miss Marple stooped to pick up the torch. As she did, she found something beside it, lying in the path: what appeared in the gloom to be a tiny, pale pebble. She picked it up and pocketed it.

Soon they had reached the back of the house. Strains of music floated towards them: Madame Butterfly's famous aria, 'Un Bel Di', if Miss Marple was not mistaken. All the lamps – including the outside lights – were on and blazing out into the darkness. A pair of French doors hung open and someone stood there stitched in silhouette against the brightness behind, featureless, still as a statue. As they drew closer, Miss Marple could make her out. A maid, a young girl, her face a mask of horror. She knew at once that it hadn't been a screech owl they had heard.

'Oh, missuses. Missuses . . . something terrible has happened.'

'What is it, girl?' Prudence was suddenly all practicality. Miss Marple remembered her words before. *You have to be firm with them. Show them what's what.* 'Come on. Out with it.'

The girl pointed a trembling finger towards the room behind her.

'I know not to disturb her when she's in the study. And the music was playing so loud on the gramophone – I didn't hear anything. They must have come through the French doors. I— I can't believe it.'

A large walnut desk hid half the carpet from view. All they could make out at first was one small foot, clad in a green suede shoe. Then, as they rounded the desk, the rest became visible. The woman's shawl – a theatrical affair in emerald cashmere – was spread all about her where she had fallen. On first glance the shawl appeared to have a burgundy-hued pattern – on a second glance it became clear that this was in fact blood, a great deal of it, which had soaked into it from a vicious slit just above the woman's clavicle. She was evidently very dead indeed.

There was a moment of silence as the three of them stared at the fallen form. In one hand, Miss Marple saw, the dead woman clutched a note. In the other a blank envelope. From here she could read the words, printed in capitals:

I KNOW YOU.
I KNOW WHAT YOU REALLY ARE.
PAY WHAT YOU OWE OR EVERYONE
WILL LEARN THE TRUTH.

Miss Marple couldn't help but notice the hand clutching the envelope. She always noticed hands. Fingernails too. There had been an incident she had been involved in a little while ago and fingernails had come into it. She saw that Celia Beautemps' fingernails were ugly, misshapen affairs, thick and yellowed. She'd seen such a thing before – she simply had to remember where.

The hair was in disarray, half-escaped from its chignon. Miss Marple could make out the mouse-coloured roots beneath a layer of black dye.

'Have you called the police, girl?' Prudence demanded.

The maid wrung her hands. 'No, ma'am – I didn't think. I was so shocked . . .'

'Go and do it immediately. We must have them here at once.' Prudence glanced up at the clock in the study. 'Five thirty. The rest of the choir will be here soon too.'

As if in answer, there was a sudden sharp rap on the door. Prudence sent the maid to answer. 'I'll ring the police.'

For a few moments Miss Marple was left on her own with the body. There was just time, she calculated, to make a quick study of the room, undisturbed, before chaos descended. She took another look at the note – the envelope too. She wandered over to the desk. Another stack of envelopes, these unopened, several stamped with the words FINAL REMINDER. A book of poetry, lying open on a poem entitled 'My Lady of Shalott'.

She moved to the wall hung with photographs of Celia Beautemps in her prime, performing on various different stages, alongside framed certificates from the Guildhall School of Music. On the mantelpiece sat a small, rather cheap-looking tin urn and next to it a small photograph of a woman wearing what looked like a white cap – though it was difficult to be certain because the image was old and foxed.

Suddenly she became aware that she was no longer alone in the room. The little maid had returned. She saw now that the girl looked not just shocked and upset by what she had found. She looked truly grief-stricken.

'Who could have done this?' she asked, plaintively.

'I don't know, child,' Miss Marple told her. 'But we will find out.'

'She were a good mistress. Not like others I've worked for. She treated me like a person. She bought me special gloves for cleaning and all.'

'It sounds as though she was very kind to you.'

'She was a kind lady, ma'am. But that's not how they talk about her in Meon Maltravers. All sorts of horrible things they say. She thought someone was spreading lies about. Things to make people turn against her. But she said she'd get even in the end—'

She stopped talking: someone had just burst into the room. It was a youngish man, pale and rather beautiful. He stopped dead at the sight of the body on the floor. Miss Marple suspected this might be the poet, Christopher Palfrey. Hot on his heels came a tall woman with angular, rather fierce looks. This had to be the wife, Annabelle. Just behind them followed a trim, grey-haired gentleman with a thick moustache and military aspect, a faded little woman in the clothes of a previous decade and, finally, a floridly handsome middle-aged man in a smart tweed jacket that was straining slightly at the buttons. All of them seemed to be peering over one another's shoulders with a rather horrid, prurient interest.

The faded woman – presumably the former choir mistress – let out a little cry. It was no doubt meant to signify horror but it sounded oddly like the cries of excitement Miss Marple had heard from the children watching the fireworks in St Mary Mead.

'Christ Almighty,' exclaimed the tweed-clad gentleman, who Miss Marple guessed to be Gordon Kipling, master of hounds. 'Someone's killed the bitch!'

'Steady on, man,' said the moustachioed man.

'Very sorry, Colonel,' Kipling said, quickly – seeming as appalled by his own outburst as the rest of them. 'Damned shocking thing to see, though.'

No doubt to his relief, the room's attention was quickly caught by another commotion: a sudden, low groan, more animal than human; a sound of great pain. Christopher Palfrey had fallen to his knees in front of the body. 'She's dead,' he moaned, words muffled through the hands he held over his mouth. 'She's dead and I killed her.'

A stunned hush settled over the room. And then: 'For God's sake,' Annabelle Palfrey said. She stepped towards him and put a claw-like hand on his shoulder, knuckles showing white. 'Get up, you bloody fool,' she hissed. 'Get up this second. Remember your heart. No over-excitement, Dr Briggs said.' She hauled him to his feet. There was a flush high on her cheeks: from the cold, perhaps, or some recent physical exertion – or maybe just anger.

Then she herself knelt over the body, felt for a pulse at both neck and wrist. 'Medical training,' she threw back to them, by way of explanation. 'Drove an ambulance in 1918.'

Yet these ministrations might also, Miss Marple thought, be a way to account for any of her fingerprints appearing on the corpse.

'I've called the police,' Prudence said, striding into the room. 'They should be here any moment – the station's only a couple of minutes' drive away. And come out of here, all of you. It's positively morbid.'

A few moments later there was the sound of a car drawing up in the driveway outside and, in a couple of minutes more, two policemen had joined them inside. The taller man was clearly the more senior of the two. He looked rather like a policeman from a Raymond Chandler novel or an American noir film: the lantern jaw, the overcoat, the hat pulled low over his dark-shadowed eyes. Miss Marple suspected he might have dressed specially to create this impression. The overall effect was marred slightly by the fact that, when he opened his mouth, he had a broad Sussex accent. 'I'm Inspector Eidel,' he told the assembled company. 'And I'd like to ask you all a few questions.'

A little while later, Miss Marple – nearly the last of the company to be interviewed – was led into a small sitting room by the more junior of the two policemen. He indicated an armchair opposite Inspector Eidel.

'Jane Marple,' Inspector Eidel stated, then paused – perhaps because Miss Marple was looking beyond him, through the window towards the woods – and said, in a louder voice, 'CAN YOU HEAR ME, MADAM?'

Miss Marple gave a little start, then fixed her eyes on him. 'Perfectly well, thank you.'

'Your friend told me that you had an altercation with a masked man in the woods this evening. Coming in the other direction – from the house, along the path that leads from the back entrance. Correct?'

'Not *quite* correct,' Miss Marple answered, brightly.

'Pardon me?'

Miss Marple tilted her head to show that he was, indeed, pardoned. 'You see, it wasn't the evening. It was a little past five o'clock – though at this time of year, when it gets dark so quickly, it's so easy to forget, I do understand . . .'

Inspector Eidel cleared his throat rather violently. 'Apologies, ma'am, just a figure of speech—'

'But it does seem *so* important to get these things right from the outset, doesn't it? You as a policeman will know this, of course. Words are words but they can be so dangerous, so misleading. So: yes, I was there this afternoon. And we encountered a masked figure. My friend was pushed roughly to the ground – a very shocking thing. Almost, one might say, gratuitously so.'

'What do you mean?'

'I'm not sure exactly. Merely that it seemed particularly vicious. To push an old woman to the ground like that when they could simply have stepped around her. As though they were trying to make a point. What that was, of course, I cannot say.'

'Well, ma'am,' Inspector Eidel said – a little patronisingly, Miss Marple thought – 'we *are* talking here of the sort of person who had in all likelihood just murdered a woman. So perhaps it's no great surprise. Unfortunately, whoever it was, they'll be long gone by now into that crowd marching to the town cross. We'll have to—'

'I'm not so sure,' Miss Marple interjected. 'That's what they would *want* you to think, of course. But if we assume that masked figure was our murderer – and I do agree with you that it is an assumption we can hazard – then, from what Prudence says, many of the people who had a real quarrel with the victim are here in this very house. Don't you see? It would have been a rather clever conceit to costume themselves as one of the revellers. And then it would have been the work of a moment to shrug off the disguise, conceal it in the woods, and return here in their ordinary clothes, ready for the choir practice – as though none of it had happened. So my two pennies' worth, if you would like to hear it, Inspector,' Inspector Eidel seemed to understand he didn't have much of a choice in the matter, 'would be to search the woods near to where Prudence and I met our masked assailant, search for any signs of them: clothing, for example.'

Inspector Eidel turned to the junior who sat perched on the edge of a chaise longue holding his notebook. A wordless exchange passed between them. The junior nodded. 'I'll put in a call to Honnington station, see if they can spare some chaps.'

Eidel turned back to Miss Marple. 'There was a note found in the dead woman's hand.'

'I know. I saw it. A rather threatening message.'

'You aren't from these parts, are you, Miss Marple?'

'No, I live in St Mary Mead. Have you heard of it? It's not a very well-known place. A small village, rather charming—'

'So,' Eidel cut in, 'I suppose, not being from around here,

it would be difficult for you to make a guess as to who might have sent it to the victim?'

'Oh, but of course I know the answer to that. No one!'

'Pardon?'

Miss Marple tilted her head again. 'The envelope tells us everything, of course.'

'The envelope was blank, Miss Marple.'

'Precisely! More than blank, it was pristine. It was *unused*. Which I believe tells us that *nobody* sent it. It had not yet found its intended recipient. The victim was the author of the note. She was blackmailing someone. And when she was killed, she had clearly been preparing to send it.'

There was a longish silence. Miss Marple could hear Eidel breathing rather heavily through his mouth. Finally he spoke again.

'One other thing. We have heard from several others that Christopher Palfrey said—'

He looked to the junior, who cleared his throat and spoke, reading from his notebook: '"She's dead and I killed her."'

Eidel turned to Miss Marple. 'Is that—'

'Correct. Indeed. He did say those words.'

'Thank you, Miss Marple.'

'But I don't think it was a confession at all. These creative types – my nephew Raymond is one, you know – they do have a habit of making everything about themselves and their work.'

Eidel frowned. 'And how exactly do you make all of this out?'

'Palfrey recently dedicated a collection of poetry to Celia

Beautemps. One of the poems was entitled 'My Lady of Shalott'. A nod to Tennyson, I imagine – I am so fond of Tennyson, I do like a poem that actually rhymes . . . perhaps that rather marks me out as the Victorian I am.' Miss Marple frowned. 'Where was I? Oh yes! In the old tale the Lady of Shalott dies, as you'll know, of course. I think that this is where Palfrey's artistic egoism comes in – he no doubt believes that because he *imagined* Madame Beautemps dead in verse, he somehow visited the Fates upon her. The arrogance of the artistic temperament, you know: my nephew has it too, and I say that as his loving aunt.'

'The artistic temperament,' Eidel repeated, a little weakly. 'The . . . Fates?'

'Besides, Palfrey couldn't have been your masked figure.'

'He couldn't?'

'No, because of his heart, of course!'

'His heart?'

'Annabelle Palfrey reminded him of his heart when he got so upset over the body. And I spoke to Colonel Woodage about it while we were waiting to be interviewed: he says Palfrey was exempted from active service because of it. I would be very surprised if he had been able to tear through the woods like that as a result.'

There was another long silence.

'Thank you, Miss Marple,' Eidel said, finally. 'I think we have everything we need now. If you could send in—' he turned to his junior.

'Gordon Kipling,' the other clarified.

*

Miss Marple joined the group in the dining room. Like the sitting room – and indeed any parts of the house that Miss Marple had glimpsed – it had an uninhabited, provisional look to it. In contrast to the sumptuous furnishings of Fairweather House, for example, there didn't seem to be quite enough furniture for the space, few pictures on the walls and no carpet upon the wooden floorboards. Around the table sat Prudence, the Palfreys, Mrs Prufrock, Colonel Woodage, Gordon Kipling and the maid.

Christopher Palfrey looked just as agonised as he had when confronted by the scene in the study. He sat white-faced and trembling slightly, slumped over to one side. His wife, her posture ramrod straight, seemed to be supporting him, the only thing preventing him from sliding off his seat and on to the floor.

Miss Marple took the seat beside Prudence and, because no one seemed to be talking, took out her knitting.

'I didn't like the woman,' the Colonel said, suddenly, into the silence. 'I'll be the first to say it. Cards on the table. And not, before any of you say it, because she was French. In fact, I don't think she was any more French than I am. Something off about that accent. Some dodgy vowels in there. No, I didn't like her because there was something . . . crooked about her, something false.'

Miss Marple noticed a little nod from Mrs Prufrock, the former choir mistress, in response to this. She was reminded of the words on the note. *I know what you really are.* But if her hunch was correct, and she was sure it was, then Celia Beautemps had been calling someone else out on a deception.

Colonel Woodage went on: 'I like people to represent themselves honestly. I didn't trust the woman. But I wouldn't wish her dead. I hope they find the scoundrel that did this.'

'She killed three of my hounds,' Gordon Kipling said. 'I'm certain of it. So some might say it's only just deserts—'

He stopped as the door to the dining room swung open. The junior policeman stood in the doorway.

'We would like to conduct a search of all your effects,' he said, a little nervously – as though he were asking a question rather than making a statement. 'If you'll submit to it. You don't have to agree, but . . . ah . . . your refusal will be taken into account.'

Miss Marple leaned towards Prudence. 'That means they've found the disguise, I think. In the woods. But *not* the murder weapon.'

'What do you mean, Jane?'

'Oh, I think our murderer – and your assailant – is here somewhere. I think Eidel does too.'

One by one they were called into the sitting room again. Miss Marple passed over her handbag to the policemen and waited as the contents were searched. She knew there was little in there beyond her knitting, her purse and some smelling salts – as a late-Victorian, she took them with her everywhere, since you never knew when such things might come in useful – but it did feel rather lowering, even violating, having these men paw through her personal effects. Afterwards, she waited outside while Prudence underwent the same treatment. Finally, they were free to go. But just as they were leaving through the front door, they heard a sound that seemed half shriek, half howl. 'Get your hands off me! How dare you! Unhand me, you fools! This is an outrage!'

'That's Annabelle Palfrey,' Prudence said, stopping in the entranceway.

Miss Marple inclined her head. 'Yes. I expect they found the knife in her handbag and are making their arrest.'

Prudence turned to her. 'Jane! Could *that* be what Palfrey meant, when he said he'd killed her? He'd realised his wife had found out about their affair and murdered his lover?'

Miss Marple was about to answer when they were caught in the beam of a pair of headlights, approaching fast. The car slowed and stopped. Prudence's daughter, Alice, looked out, as pretty as Miss Marple remembered, and the picture of a gentleman farmer's wife in silk scarf and pearls and smart country tweed. Prudence and Miss Marple went to greet her.

'Have I missed the rehearsal?' she asked. 'Sorry I'm late, our Persian hurt her paw—' A rather pathetic mewling sounded from a wicker carrier on the passenger seat.

Her gaze took in the parked police cars – several now – and her eyes widened. 'What on earth's going on?'

'Madame Beautemps has been found dead,' Prudence told her.

'*Dead?*'

'It's a terrible thing,' Prudence said, sombrely.

'And the police . . .' Alice asked, 'do they have any idea who did it?'

'We believe Annabelle Palfrey has just been arrested. Jane is convinced they must have found the knife in her handbag.'

At this moment the woman herself was led from the house, wrists handcuffed behind her and two policemen flanking her. She walked with surprising poise and dignity, even when one of the officers put a hand on her head to steer her into the back seat of the car. The three women watched silently. 'Annabelle Palfrey,' Alice said, after the police car had left. 'Just imagine! But you somehow *can* imagine it, can't you? There's something so . . . ruthless and calculating about her. Something rather masculine.' Then she turned to them. 'Do hop in. I'll give you both a lift back to Fairweather.'

'No, thank you,' Miss Marple said. 'I'd like to walk back. To clear my head.'

'But it's so cold! And besides, there might be a murderer on the loose!' Alice looked at her mother, questioningly, then back to Miss Marple.

'If Jane is walking, I'll go with her,' Prudence said.

'I'll be perfectly all right on my own,' Miss Marple told her.

Prudence shook her head. 'Well, I must insist.'

Alice left in the car and the two women made the long walk back along the main drive – considering they'd met a murderer via the other route, they weren't going to risk the dark shortcut through the trees this time. Miss Marple stopped a couple of times to make an inspection of the woods on each side while Prudence stood and waited, a little impatiently. Back at Fairweather House, they shared a light supper and went to bed early. But Miss Marple didn't sleep. She spent the next few hours thinking, until a weak dawn showed itself through the curtains. Then she asked for a restorative pot of tea to be sent to her room.

'Would you take this note to Inspector Eidel at the police station?' she asked the girl, the same one who had tended to the fire the previous day. 'Tell him it's urgent.'

'It really is shocking,' Prudence said at breakfast, buttering a slice of toast and then spooning a small dollop of marmalade on top. 'I have never seen eye to eye with Annabelle Palfrey, I'll admit. But I wouldn't have had her pegged as a murderer. You were right, Jane! Evil does happen in small places after all.' She took a neat sip of tea.

'It does indeed.' Miss Marple carefully buttered her own slice of toast. 'Yet I don't believe Annabelle Palfrey had anything to do with that woman's death.'

Prudence put down her teacup. 'You don't?'

Miss Marple frowned. 'Firstly, you see, what I don't understand is why one would go to all the trouble with the disguise, hiding it in the woods, etcetera, only to leave the murder weapon in one's handbag. I suppose it would have been *possible* to conceal a handbag under the cloak. But why not dispose of the knife too? It all seems rather foolish – and not at all in keeping with the woman I met last night. She seems altogether too intelligent for that.'

'So what are you saying?'

'I think I am getting ahead of myself. It seems important to start with the victim herself. You see, as soon as I saw those fingernails, I knew that something was amiss.'

Prudence's mouth twisted in distaste. '*Fingernails?*'

'I knew I'd seen something like them before. Those ugly, thickened nails, the reddened cuticles. Then I remembered that a maid of mine once suffered from the same condition. I sent her to Dr Haydock for treatment. Paronychia: common among domestic servants, the kind who spend a lot of time with their fingers in hot soapy water. Left untreated the condition can become chronic, can last for years. It's less common among famous sopranos, I imagine. But what if Celia Beautemps had had another life, before she became a singer? What if she had even, at one stage, worked as a domestic servant? And, perhaps, some kind benefactor had paid for her tuition. There was also the fact that Celia Beautemps went to the Guildhall School of Music and Drama, in London. That in itself seemed strange to me – why would a Frenchwoman not have learned her craft in her own country? The French are so snobbish, so particular about that sort of thing.'

Prudence picked up her teacup and took another sip of tea.

'Shall I go on?' Miss Marple said.

Prudence inclined her head.

'So, you see, I posit that the French persona was part of the disguise. The Colonel made that comment about her "dodgy vowels": still, much easier to disguise one's working-class origins with a French accent than with the pretence of an upper-class English one.

'I think Celia Beautemps – if that was indeed her born name, which I don't believe for a moment it was – was a domestic servant who learned her craft with the generosity of a wealthy patron. Didn't you mention yesterday that your own husband, George, paid for just such a thing to take place, despite being rather parsimonious in his other dealings? The former housekeeper's daughter, you said. And from Meon Maltravers, of course, with its fast train to London, it would have been easy for a girl to travel up there in her free time.'

Prudence put the teacup back down. The saucer rattled a little as she did so. 'What exactly are you suggesting, Jane?'

'What I am saying is that I believe Celia Beautemps was a figure from the past. From *your* past, in fact, Prudence. Someone you hoped had disappeared – especially after her mother's death. I think she came back here, after the issue with her vocal cords cut her career short, in the hopes of extorting a living out of you, via blackmail. That note, in her hand? I saw something like it in the fire last night. And you seemed so very eager, all of a sudden, to have the fire built up – to conceal what you hoped I hadn't spotted in the flames.'

'This is absurd,' Prudence said, in her most ringing head-girl tones. 'What reason could anyone have for blackmailing me?'

'Oh,' Miss Marple said, 'the fact that you'd killed your second husband – and her former employer – I suppose.'

Prudence opened her mouth in outrage, but Miss Marple continued.

'Seeing that photograph of the three of you – it reminded me of how frail George had seemed. The blemished, almost bruised-looking skin, the digestive complaints. And the eventual heart failure. All signs of chronic arsenic poisoning.'

'But how—'

'Those dyed flowers one used to wear in one's hat: I remember asking the milliner in Much Benham where the lovely green foliage had gone: Scheele's green, the colour was called. She told me about the poor girls in the factories, dyeing the things, getting sicker and sicker. They were slowly being poisoned by the stuff. The patches on the skin, the gastric complaints, the heart trouble – just as it was with George. A one-time pharmacist's wife! You'd know exactly how to do it.

'And you spoke of getting rid of the staff when George got sick. To ease the burden of keeping the household, you said. Or to rid yourself of potential witnesses.'

'This is preposterous. And you're saying I had something to do with Celia Beautemps' death too? I was with you when we heard her scream – when the poor wretch was killed. You saw me pushed to the ground by the murderer!'

Miss Marple nodded. 'Indeed. And a knife wouldn't be your style, Prudence. Poison is much more your thing. And how clever, to put yourself out of suspicion! To have been attacked by the murderer – it would seem to sever any connection that might be made between the two of you. But it was also a way, I believe, to achieve a transfer of the weapon. You wanted to plant it on Annabelle Palfrey. You told me she crossed you in the Parish Council – oh, I remember you at school, Prudence, and you never liked dissent. It would be a killing of two birds with one stone, as it were. When that masked figure pushed you, I think they were actually passing you the knife. To dispose of when you sat next to Annabelle Palfrey in the dining room, waiting to be questioned. What was it? Something small and neat – I suspect the woman's own paper knife.'

'This is utter nonsense—'

But Miss Marple was all ruthlessness now. 'And now I come to your accomplice. What was it you said about your daughter? "We've always been closer than most mothers and daughters." Alice is tall – a good fit for the masked figure we saw in the woods – who you were careful to describe as a "man" in your account to the police. She'd also make a good killer – a pig farmer's wife, gentleman farmer or no, would know how to slit a throat.'

'Alice arrived after everything had happened, in her car!'

'She arrived in her car, certainly. But I checked the woods on each side of the drive. Plenty of dark, relatively open spots for her to hide in the parked vehicle, once she had rid herself of her costume and crossed through the woods on foot to the driveway, with the headlights off, concealed from sight. It was a risk – the police who found the costume might have stumbled upon her. But it was far enough away – and the costume poorly enough hidden – that it didn't come to that. And then she could glide up the drive with her story about the cat, knowing it wouldn't be properly investigated.'

Miss Marple had said it all now.

There was a long silence. A very long silence that seemed to gather shape and weight.

Then Prudence rose from her chair. She was holding the knife she had used for spreading butter on her toast. Miss Marple sat very still. They were alone in the room. And Prudence kept so few staff . . .

Prudence was rounding the corner of the table now, the knife clenched in her hand. A knife might not be her preference, but Miss Marple was beginning to suspect that under duress she might not be so particular. She began to realise, as she rose and took a step backwards and Prudence continued to advance, that she might have done something rather foolish.

The doorbell rang. Then the sound of broad Sussex in the hallway. Prudence froze. Miss Marple let out the breath she had not realised she had been holding. The little maid opened the door to the breakfast room and showed him in.

'Good morning, Mrs Fairweather.' Eidel doffed his hat, revealing the heavily Brylcreemed hair of a noir lead. 'I'd like to invite you to the station to answer a few questions, if you don't mind. Your daughter is already in the car. And if you could put that down.' He gestured carelessly to the knife.

Prudence drew herself up.

'You have no evidence for any of this,' she said.

Miss Marple spoke up now: 'The victim herself is evidence. I have no idea what her real name was, though I'm sure it wasn't Celia Beautemps. But Beautemps means "fair weather" in French. A clue to her origins, to this very building: Fairweather House.'

'Wild, unfounded speculation,' Prudence said.

'And I have Alice's pearl stud,' Miss Marple said. 'From where she dropped it in the woods after she "attacked" you last night.'

'You could have found that anywhere!' Prudence said. 'Really, Jane, I always knew you were envious of me at school, but this—'

'I took the note,' the little maid said, suddenly. 'The one in the fire, the one the French woman brung here, yesterday morning.' She looked at Prudence. 'You're always threatening to turn me out if I' – she mimicked Prudence's ringing tones now – '"don't buck your ideas up, you silly girl!" So I snatched it out before I put the new logs on, thought I'd keep it, in case it came in useful.'

She handed a sooty scrap to Inspector Eidel, who read it and then turned to Prudence. 'George Fairweather was your husband, I presume? You know, ma'am' – the next words were spoken with the faintest hint of an American drawl, as though repeating a line from a film – 'you can't just go round killing people whenever the notion strikes you.'

For once, Prudence Fairweather seemed lost for words.

'And there you have it, Prudence,' Miss Marple said, into the silence. 'One mistreats or underestimates servants at one's peril. But I would have thought you'd learned that lesson already.'

When Prudence had been led away, Miss Marple reflected on the fact that evil hadn't been out there in the street amidst the pagan throng last night. No: it had been right here, inside in the cosy, well-appointed sitting room of this elegant home. Now she had yet another reason to avoid staying in other people's houses. The Japanese maples had indeed been glorious, but not altogether worth it in the end.

The Second Murder at the Vicarage

Val McDermid

To have one murder in one's vicarage is unfortunate; to have a second looks remarkably like carelessness, or worse. It was to no avail that I protested that the dead maid in the kitchen was not *our* maid. The unfortunate fact that she had formerly occupied that role was enough to set the tongues of St Mary Mead wagging more eagerly than the tails of a pack of hounds catching the scent of a fox.

To make matters worse, my wife had made no secret of our delight at Mary's departure from our employ. Dear Griselda has many fine qualities but the discretion that befits a vicar's wife is not among them. In fairness, however, anyone who had ever dined with us could bear testament to the literally diabolical nature of Mary's cooking.

On one occasion, she put a pan of eggs on the stove to boil and promptly forgot about them. The pan boiled dry, the eggs exploded, filling the house with a dark sulphurous reek. 'I imagine this is how the outskirts of hell will smell,' our neighbour, Miss Marple, remarked with a twinkle when she arrived later for lunch. It took three coats of paint to restore the kitchen ceiling.

So we felt no sadness when, on hearing that my wife was with child, Mary announced she was leaving us because she couldn't abide children in general and babies in particular. Miss Marple, who has an admirable record in training young women for domestic service, came to our rescue. Flora has all the qualities Mary lacked. She is reliable, capable and devoted to our son David. She is a good plain cook and an even better baker. Griselda further maintains she has a face like a policeman's boot, which she claims will discourage back-door suitors like Bill Archer, who courted Mary until his death only a week ago.

According to Miss Hartnell, the heartiest of our village spinsters, Archer had been hoist by his own petard. That he was a poacher was no secret – but then, there are few secrets in a village like St Mary Mead, thanks to what Griselda calls 'the clowder of old cats', who are swifter with the news than the BBC, though on occasion less accurate.

But I digress. Archer had cooked up a stew of one of Colonel Bantry's pheasants bulked out with wild mushrooms. Although he was an experienced forager, somehow he managed to incorporate sufficient poisonous fungi to have fatal effects. A passing farm labourer was alerted by the anguished barking of Archer's Jack Russell terrier. He peered through the kitchen window and saw Archer lying on the floor amidst a scatter of broken crockery and a smashed beer bottle.

Despite Archer's well-known proclivity for helping himself

to other men's produce, the local police did not take his death lightly. Inspector Slack – a misnomer if ever there was one – arrived from Much Benham with his usual flurry of self-importance. He bossed everyone around for the best part of a day, then locked up the cottage and placed a seal on the door.

'A fat lot of use that will be. Any idiot could get inside that ramshackle hovel of Archer's in a matter of minutes,' observed my nephew Dennis, whose year as a probationary police constable has rendered him an expert on all matters criminal.

It seemed, however, that even Inspector Slack could find no grounds for suspecting foul play. Only that morning, Miss Marple had stopped me as I passed the bottom of her garden. 'Have you heard when Archer's funeral is to be held?' she asked.

'I'm afraid his family can make no plans until the police release his body.'

'Had you not heard? The coroner has concluded his death was from natural causes. They removed the seal on his cottage yesterday morning. I believe Mary has already visited. It was her afternoon off.' Of course, Miss Marple *would* know the schedule of every domestic servant in the village.

But even Miss Marple could not have predicted that I would walk into my kitchen after our conversation to find the self-same Mary lying on the flagged floor, her head in a pool of blood, a cast-iron omelette pan discarded next to her. Though I feared she was dead, I did crouch beside her and feel for a pulse in her wrist. Not only was there no flutter, her skin was cool to the touch.

I straightened up and made for the phone in the hall. Much to the chagrin of Mrs Price Ridley, Miss Hartnell and Miss Wetherby, we have no village bobby here in St Mary Mead. (Just as well, says Dennis, who is already the perpetual target of their complaints.) So I was obliged to ring Much Benham, where Inspector Slack holds sway. I had hoped he might be out on an investigation, but as soon as I said 'dead body' I was transferred via a series of clicks and buzzes to the man himself.

'Mr Clement?' he snapped. 'What's this about a dead body in your kitchen?'

I explained what I had discovered. There was a long silence then Slack harrumphed down the line. 'I'd have thought one murder in the vicarage would be enough for any man of the cloth.' He paused. I had no idea what he expected me to say so I remained silent. Eventually he sighed. 'Don't touch anything. We'll be with you shortly.' The bang of the phone receiver hitting its rest reverberated unpleasantly through my head.

Slack was as good as his word, arriving with Dennis and another uniformed constable in tow. I was shooed out of the kitchen and into my study, where Slack soon joined me. 'PC Hurst tells me the dead woman used to be in service here,' he began without preamble.

Before I could reply, there was a tap at the French windows leading into the garden. There stood Miss Marple, carrying her gardening gloves and a pair of secateurs. In spite of Slack's tutting, I opened the door. In the absence of a lawyer, I felt the need of some moral support. 'I couldn't help noticing the police arriving,' she said, stepping inside. 'So indiscreet, those Black Marias.'

'No need for discretion when a woman's been beaten to death,' Slack said shortly.

Miss Marple's expression reflected surprise but none of the tremulous horror one might expect in an elderly spinster. My neighbour is made of sterner stuff, as I had discovered after Colonel Protheroe's murder in the very room we stood in. 'How distressing,' she said. 'But who has been murdered? I know it can't be dear Griselda or Flora, for I saw them driving off earlier this morning.'

'They've taken David to Chipping Marlbury to visit Griselda's parents,' I said automatically.

'According to PC Hurst, the victim is Mary Hill,' Slack interrupted in his most brusque manner.

Now Miss Marple did look shocked. 'Mary? But what was she doing here?'

'That's what I'd like to know.' Slack turned to me. 'Had she made an appointment to see you?'

I shook my head. 'No. She didn't even come to church, not since she handed in her notice. She went to work for Miss Hartnell and I've only ever spoken to her since when she answered the door there.'

'Was she a friend of your maid? Flora, is it?'

'Not that I'm aware.'

Miss Marple nodded. 'Flora is far too sensible a girl to waste her time with Mary. Why Mary should be murdered in your kitchen is indeed a puzzle.'

Slack circled the subject for a few minutes, getting no

further forward. He asked where I'd been before my discovery and I was able to provide a list of parishioners I'd visited. He made a great performance of noting their names and addresses, which served to make me feel guilty even though I knew myself to be entirely innocent of any assault on Mary.

At last, he left us alone. 'I think I should pay a visit of condolence to Miss Hartnell,' I said.

'Indeed, vicar. But she may not know about Mary's death yet.' Miss Marple stood up. 'If you don't mind, I should like to accompany you. Sometimes another woman's presence helps in the breaking of tragic news.'

I have always found Miss Marple impossible to refuse. She is never bossy, like Miss Hartnell, nor autocratic, like Mrs Price Ridley, nor guilt-inducing, like Miss Wetherby. But when she wants something, she has the knack of making it seem inevitable. 'I think, vicar, we should leave by the garden and take the back lane,' she continued. 'The police car on your doorstep will have roused the curiosity of everyone in the village and we should have to satisfy that several times over before we could draw close to our destination.'

As we approached Miss Hartnell's garden, I could see that she, like Miss Marple, was using the cover of pruning her roses to keep the vicarage under scrutiny. No sooner had we come into hailing distance than she popped upright with a speed usually only called into service to terrorise the local youth. 'Vicar,' she boomed. 'I see the constabulary are at your door. Has there been a burglary?'

Miss Marple put a hand on the garden gate. 'Might we

come in, my dear? I think we could all do with a cup of tea.'

Miss Hartnell snorted. 'You may have to make it yourself, Jane. Mary seems to have flounced off in one of her sulks. She's been nowhere to be seen since she cleared away the coffee cups after Matilda Merchiston dropped by. You know Matilda, vicar? The romantic novelist? I've no time for that nonsense myself, but the young women seem to swallow all that nonsense wholesale.'

'I'm afraid . . .' I stopped, not feeling entirely comfortable delivering my news among the gladioli and the dahlias and the talk of romance.

I often underestimate the steel under the tweeds when it comes to my older female parishioners. 'Mary's not sulking, my dear. Mary's been murdered,' Miss Marple said, her tone entirely lacking in drama.

Miss Hartnell's jaw dropped, revealing large yellow teeth that would have been more at home in the mouth of Colonel Bantry's favourite hunter. 'Mary? Murdered? There must be some mistake, Jane. What motive could anyone have for murdering Mary? It's not as if she's got the brains to be a threat to anyone. Or enough personality to provoke a murderous thought.'

It appeared that the concept of never speaking ill of the dead fell into abeyance when the dead were of the servant class. 'Nevertheless,' Miss Marple continued, 'murdered she has been.'

'Good lord.' Miss Hartnell harrumphed again. 'I think this calls for something stronger than tea. A small sherry, anyone?'

Before I could refuse, Miss Hartnell had swept indoors, her neighbour at her heels. She headed for the decanter and glasses that sat on the sideboard, but, as she poured, Miss Marple spoke again. 'Might we take a quick look at Mary's room?'

Miss Hartnell frowned. 'Isn't that the police's job?'

'Of course. But Inspector Slack won't look at it with a woman's eye. It may be that you and I might notice something he'd overlook.' Miss Marple was at her meekest. If Griselda had been present, I knew she'd have been struggling to keep a straight face.

'Brilliant, Jane. You have such a sharp mind. Come, let's take a look.'

Miss Hartnell led the way down the hall and through the kitchen to a tiny room I suspect may once have been a pantry. Between the single bed, the single wardrobe and the bedside chest of drawers there was scant room for the two women, so I stayed on the threshold. Miss Marple studied the room, taking in the clumsy watercolour of a woodland glade and the small mirror. She opened the top drawer of the chest and took out a bundle of picture postcards. All but the topmost were held in place by an elastic band.

She turned the bundle over. Even from where I was standing, I could see the cancelled stamp and the ill-educated hand. 'From Bill,' she said. 'Presumably Bill Archer?'

Miss Hartnell stuck her chin out defensively. 'I refused to allow Mary to speak to him on the telephone. Instead he sent her postcards confirming their meetings and passing on news.'

'You read them?' I asked.

'One could scarcely avoid it.' Miss Hartnell was frosty. 'And they were delivered to my house, after all.'

Miss Marple paid no heed to this exchange. Instead, she was frowning at the loose card. 'Most interesting,' she murmured, replacing them all in the drawer. There was apparently nothing else of interest in the drawers for she turned next to the wardrobe, going through all the pockets methodically. Apart from a couple of handkerchiefs, her search revealed nothing. 'Thank you, my dear,' she said, moving inexorably towards the door, causing Miss Hartnell and me to reverse clumsily. 'And now for the sherry, if you please.'

We returned to the sitting room. I'm not in the habit of drinking before lunch, but the prospect of that meal seemed to have disappeared from the agenda, so I took what was offered gladly. 'Who would do such a thing?' Miss Hartnell said at regular intervals, between sips.

She seemed to require no answer, but Miss Marple did inquire as to whether there were any other men who came calling for Mary.

Our hostess snorted in derision. 'Hardly, Jane. What Bill Archer saw in her was a mystery to me.'

'Bill was hardly a great catch,' I dared to point out.

Miss Marple gave me an indulgent look. 'You are quite unworldly, vicar.'

Before I could argue the point, the doorbell pealed. Miss Hartnell sighed deeply and got to her feet. 'I shall have to find another maid now,' she complained.

She returned with Inspector Slack bustling at her back. 'Vicar! What are you doing here?'

'Conveying the tragic news of Mary's death to her employer,' I said.

He glowered at Miss Marple. 'And you, Miss Marple? I hope you're not interfering with police business again.'

'I came to pass on my condolences,' she said sharply. She swallowed the last of her sherry and got to her feet. 'And now I will be on my way.'

I was torn between waiting to hear whether Slack had made any progress and the desire to discover what had so interested Miss Marple about the loose postcard in Mary's drawer. But I could attempt to draw Miss Marple out at any time, whereas Slack was a very different proposition. So I followed him and Miss Hartnell to Mary's room. I glanced back at Miss Marple, who seemed to be gazing into the middle distance towards the bow window that gave on to the street.

On the threshold of Mary's room, Slack brusquely dismissed us both. 'There's no need for you to be interfering with the scene of the crime. Don't you have parishioners to visit, vicar? Or did you manage to squeeze them all in this morning?'

I caught up with Miss Marple on the path to the gate where she had paused to admire the late bloomers in the herbaceous border. Once we were clear of Miss Hartnell's cottage, I ventured to ask what she had found so interesting in Mary's room. She smiled sweetly. 'Dear vicar, little escapes you. What struck me was that the stamp on the card had not been franked.'

'You mean, it hadn't come through the post?'

'It would appear not. It's my guess that Archer had written it but not posted it before he died and that Mary found it yesterday afternoon when she visited his cottage for the first time since his death.'

'What did it say?'

She closed her eyes, as if summoning the image up before her. '"Big surprise in the woods today, might be we can turn it to a profit."' She blinked and smiled.

'And that's all? No clue as to what he meant?'

'One can speculate. I can think of at least three or four possibilities, can't you? But no, there was nothing more specific than that.'

We had almost reached Miss Marple's gate when something dawned on me. 'But if that was all it said, why would anyone feel sufficiently threatened by it to kill Mary?'

'That is the question, is it not?' And so saying, she turned in at her gate and left me none the wiser.

Griselda returned shortly before six, accompanied by an exhausted and fractious David. I ruffled his hair affectionately as Flora whisked him off to bath and bed. 'How are your parents?' I asked.

'They grow duller and more narrow-minded with age,' she sighed. It unnerves me somewhat when Griselda says such things; it's as if she forgets that I am significantly closer in age to her parents than to her. My perennial fear is that she will come to think the same of me.

She caught my moment's apprehension, read my mind and leaned in to kiss my cheek. 'Don't be silly, Len. You know it's my mission in life to keep you for ever young.' She yawned. 'I'm worn out,' she complained. 'My father excites David so with his model soldiers and then my mother fills him with sweets and lemonade till the poor boy is beside himself. Once he gets to fever pitch, they can't cope and suddenly find something terribly urgent that must be done elsewhere and leave me to deal with the child.' She made for the study door.

'Where are you going?' I demanded, more sharply than I'd intended.

Griselda stopped and stared at me. 'To the kitchen, to heat up the pie Flora prepared for dinner.'

'You can't. You mustn't. You can't go into the kitchen. It's . . . it's out of bounds.'

My wife looked at me as if I was mad. 'Why ever not? How can we have dinner if the kitchen is out of bounds?'

Before I could reply, Flora's scream answered for me. Griselda raced to the kitchen, where Flora stood wailing, her apron over her face. 'The blood, the blood,' she hiccupped.

Griselda looked at the puddle of congealed blood on the floor then looked at me. 'There's blood all over the floor.'

'I know. That's why I was trying to stop you going into the kitchen.'

'Len – what on earth has been going on here?'

It took some time to explain what had happened; to persuade Flora not to hand in her notice on the spot; and then to calm David, who was near hysterical at the non-arrival of his bedtime milk and biscuits. The person apparently least affected was Griselda, whose ill-suppressed excitement was only augmented by the return of Dennis from the Much Benham police station at the end of his shift.

'Have you arrested anyone?' Griselda demanded.

Dennis threw himself into an armchair and shook his head. 'No. Not likely to either. Slack is beside himself. We've not turned up a single clue or a single witness who saw either Mary or her killer enter or leave the vicarage.'

'That's hard to credit,' Griselda remarked. 'Given the old pussies' network of observation posts.'

'It must have happened at that point in the morning where they're all busy making sure their maids polish the lightbulbs,' Dennis said.

'More to the point,' I said, 'it seems impossible to imagine who could have had a motive for murdering Mary.'

'Except possibly Miss Hartnell,' Griselda said. 'But if she wanted never to have to face one of Mary's cremated roasts again, she could simply have given her notice.'

'This is not a matter for facetiousness,' I scolded. 'Mary has been brutally despatched in the very kitchen she once counted home.'

Griselda had the grace to look ashamed. 'I'm sorry, Len, it's my way of coping.'

Before I could accept her apology, Flora showed in Miss Marple. She fluttered on the threshold for a moment then stepped inside. 'My dear Griselda, how terrible for you.'

'More terrible for Mary,' Griselda said. 'And for poor Flora who's on her knees trying to scrub the bloodstain off the kitchen floor.'

'Of course. And quite disturbing for you, Dennis. Your

first murder.' She paused and frowned. 'At least, I suppose it is your first?'

Dennis straightened in his seat. 'It brings home the importance of what we do.'

'Indeed.' Miss Marple turned back to Griselda and smiled apologetically. 'I'm sorry to intrude at a time like this, but I wondered whether you were still planning to go into Much Benham tomorrow? Only, I had rather counted on being able to visit the chemist.'

'Good heavens, yes. I don't think Mary would have expected us to go into formal mourning.'

Her mission achieved, I showed Miss Marple out through the study. 'By the way, what was it that caught your attention through the window at Miss Hartnell's?' I asked as I wrestled with the awkward bolt.

A momentary look of puzzlement was followed by the dawning of comprehension. 'Oh, but vicar, it wasn't the window I was looking at.' And without further ado, she was gone.

I stared after her, trying to imagine what she had noticed that had escaped both me and Inspector Slack. To one side of the window was a small mahogany bookshelf holding a dozen or so volumes. To the other, a console table with a shallow bowl containing a few calling cards. Surely even Miss Marple could not have managed to decipher any of those at that distance?

As was so often the case with my neighbour, Miss Marple had mystified me again.

*

Astonishingly, life at the vicarage appeared to have returned to normal by the next morning. Flora served breakfast, David recounted a somewhat confused version of a Rupert Bear story and Griselda complained about having to make jam for the next meeting of the Mothers' Union. I retired to my study to labour over the week's sermon and no police officers interrupted our day.

Over lunch, Griselda entertained me with her outing to Much Benham. 'One curious thing,' she said. 'Miss Marple disappeared into Goodenough's for at least fifteen minutes and came out without a book. That's odd, don't you think? To visit a bookshop and come out empty-handed?'

'They're not always well-stocked. I tried to buy you the new Matilda Merchiston the other week and they didn't have it, even though she's a well-known local author. I was quite taken aback. It's not as if she's a shrinking violet. She always seems to be giving talks to one organisation or another and those pugs of hers must have chewed half the rugs in the shire. Perhaps Goodenough's didn't have what Miss Marple was looking for. Did you ask her?'

'She was very evasive.' Griselda helped herself to a second serving of the chicken pie we should have had the previous evening. 'Oh, by the way, in all the kerfuffle yesterday, I forgot to tell you I ran into Jeremy Jenner in Chipping Marlbury. He was delivering election leaflets to my parents. You know he's standing in the by-election there next week?'

I could hardly have failed to know. We'd recently had Jenner and his wife to dinner at the vicarage out of obligation and he had spoken of little else. He claimed his experience in business had led the Prime Minister to promise him a cabinet post if elected. 'Do your parents think he'll win?'

Griselda pulled a face. 'A Gloucester Old Spot with the right party rosette could take that seat.'

As Flora came in with the apple crumble, Dennis slipped in behind her. 'Greetings, family. I'm supposed to be checking whether there's any sign of Mary having left a note for the vicar, but I thought I might seize the moment and grab some pudding.'

'On duty?' I said.

'He's entitled to a lunch break, surely, Len?' Griselda gave Dennis a conspiratorial wink.

I gave in and gestured to his usual chair. He'd started pouring the custard on to his heaped bowl when Flora returned with Miss Marple once more. She apologised profusely for interrupting us at table; Griselda told her she was always welcome, with a slight trace of grit in her voice; and Dennis carried on eating regardless.

'I know it's very rude of me, but when I saw Dennis go in at your gate, I thought I should take advantage of the opportunity to share my discovery.'

'A discovery? How exciting,' Griselda said. 'Is it to do with the murder?'

'It's certainly to do with *a* murder. I happened to take a walk in Old Hall Woods before lunch and I came upon something I think the police ought to see. And you know, vicar, how hard it can be to capture Inspector Slack's attention.' She twinkled at me, reminding me of previous experiences with the inspector. 'So I thought I might direct our very own constable to what I'd found. Best to leave it in place, you see?'

Dennis regarded his half-full bowl with regret, wiped his mouth with his napkin and pushed his chair back with a sigh. 'No time like the present.' With a last look of regret, he led the way out of the room.

'Poor Dennis, missing out on his treat,' Griselda said

'He doesn't know it yet, but his standing is about to rise,' I told her. 'Miss Marple is the last person I'd accuse of wasting police time.'

'It was the book that set me on the right track,' Miss Marple said, sipping a post-prandial cherry brandy in the vicarage sitting room later that evening. Events had proceeded at a remarkable rate after she'd shown her find to Dennis; two people were already under arrest.

'But you didn't *buy* a book,' Griselda said.

'I didn't buy a book because Goodenough's had already sold the only copy they'd had. *Native Fungi of the Home Counties*. I'd spotted it in Miss Hartnell's much-neglected bookcase and it struck me as very odd, since she has never shown any interest in unregimented nature. It looked very new, and I noticed it had Goodenough's sticker on the base of the spine. It made me wonder.'

'You wondered about Archer?'

She smiled. 'Exactly, vicar. Archer had been living off the land all his life. The idea that he would pick poisonous mushrooms for a stew seemed absurd. But to add them to his stew after the fact would be easy, I thought. His cottage is not in the best repair, and it would take little effort to get inside via one of the windows. The card he wrote to Mary but failed to post clearly indicated a plan to blackmail someone. But to do that effectively, you must be sure your victim lacks the courage – or the desperation – to put a stop to you. And that's where Archer went fatally wrong.'

'But who? And why?' Griselda demanded.

Ignoring her, Miss Marple continued. 'One would have to be certain of the poison. So the killer had to consult a reliable guide. Once it had served its purpose, his accomplice secreted it in Miss Hartnell's bookcase. If any suspicion had arisen, placing it there would have pointed straight at Mary.' Miss Marple pursed her lips. 'Such wickedness.'

'But who bought the book?' Griselda's voice was noticeably higher in pitch now.

'Jeremy Jenner.'

I had no difficulty believing Jenner capable of almost anything in defence of his seat. But Griselda frowned. 'He can't have killed Mary. We spoke to him in Chipping Marlbury yesterday morning. He was canvassing for the by-election. He couldn't possibly have been attacking Mary in the vicarage.'

'No, dear, Jeremy Jenner is not the kind of man who does his own dirty work. That fell to his partner in crime. And, I venture, his partner in adultery. I imagine Archer came upon them in the woods and thought, as he said in his card to Mary, that there might be some profit in it. I imagine that Jenner and his lover decided murder was preferable to having the sword of Damocles dangling perpetually over their heads and so they hatched their plot. His accomplice poisoned the stew and they thought that was the end of it.'

'Who was it?' Griselda demanded.

'And why kill Mary? Surely they were safe with Archer dead?'

Miss Marple shook her head sadly. 'Mary was struggling to believe Archer could have made so stupid a mistake, and his message convinced her he'd been killed. She wondered whether she'd be able to convince the police to take her seriously. So she sought advice. From the wrong person. The woman she spoke to tried to persuade her not to go to the police, but Mary still had her doubts.' She gave me a kind glance. 'I believe she came here to ask your wise counsel, vicar. And that she was followed by her killer.'

Griselda was literally on the edge of her seat. 'Who was it?'

Miss Marple raised her index finger. 'All in good time, Griselda. I believed I had unravelled the plot, but there was still no direct evidence. I wondered whether there might be something apparently insignificant at Archer's cottage that the police had missed. Something that might not seem meaningful to a man.'

'Something a woman might leave behind?' I asked.

'Something a woman might not notice she'd left behind. Archer's pantry has a small window that's hidden from view by a *rosa rugosa*. And, on closer inspection, I noticed a strip of fine cotton muslin had snagged on the thorns. I recognised the distinctive fabric at once, for I'd been in Miss Politt's sewing room only a couple of weeks before when its owner happened to pick her dress up. It is, I expect, unique. Not least because it has a strip torn from its very full skirt. I pointed it out to Dennis, and Inspector Slack whirled into action. Now Jeremy Jenner and his mistress are occupying cells in Much Benham police station.'

Griselda groaned. 'Stop torturing me, Miss Marple. Tell us who murdered Mary.'

'Matilda Merchiston.'

We both stared open-mouthed at our neighbour. The local celebrity author, doyenne of the romantic novelists, famously devoted to her husband and her pugs – a cold-blooded killer? It was beyond belief. I almost said 'There must be some mistake.' And then remembered just in time who I was dealing with.

Miss Marple drained her glass and stood up. 'This has been a shocking and tragic affair, dear vicar. Let us hope this will be the *final* murder at the vicarage.'

Miss Marple Takes Manhattan

Alyssa Cole

Miss Marple wore a serviceable dark blue wool coat paired with a thick cream scarf. Her gloves, kid leather softened by decades of use, were folded neatly in her pocket, and her bare fingers flexed at their knobby knuckles in the frigid air. She was very far from the village of St Mary Mead; she was, improbably, standing on a traffic island in the centre of Herald Square, Manhattan. A sea of New York's distinctive yellow taxi cabs roared by on either side of her, their exhaust matching the soft grey puffs of air that punctuated her exhalations of delight.

Despite being warned against such a circumstance by her nephew, Raymond West, and his wife, Joan, who had flown her out to the United States with them, she was standing alone.

She was supposed to be in her hotel room at the Martinique New York Hotel; in fact, she could see the window of her room from where she stood. Like most old women, Miss Marple was often *supposed to be* in one place, as if she were a candlestick or a sofa cushion; however, she had the oddest habit of ending up exactly *where she wanted to be* instead.

She assuaged her guilt with the fact that she wasn't alone, really; the idea was preposterous given all of the people bustling around her, just as in the films about this vibrant city. In fact, in addition to the people passing back and forth at every change of the traffic light, and sometimes in between, there was a bearded homeless fellow, and the pigeons he was feeding, sharing the pavement with her. He was good company, as he hadn't bothered her beyond a gruff hello, and a good host to boot, as he clearly saved only the best breadcrumbs for his feathered friends.

In truth, Miss Marple had initially resisted accompanying her nephew to America for the Broadway debut of an adaptation of one of his novels. He already did so much for her, kind boy that he was, and she'd reasoned that New York City was possibly a bit much for an old woman such as herself – one who encountered odd occurrences and mysteries wherever she went. Why, Manhattan was the crime capital of the world, wasn't it? Miss Marple had worried about what might go awry, and how she might be drawn into anything that did, but Raymond and Joan had promised a grand tour of the fancy American department stores, and curiosity had prevailed over practicality.

Yet, since they'd arrived in the city three days ago, Raymond and Joan had seemingly forgotten the most important stops on the proposed itinerary, as their excursions led everywhere but to a household goods department – St Patrick's Cathedral and the top of the Empire State building were fine indeed, but one couldn't purchase fine linen or an exquisitely crafted tea service at either location. Dinners had been taken at posh restaurants with trendy people who talked *at* her as if she was a drooping old spaniel whose ears must be scratched every now and again to check for signs of life. Worse, Raymond was convinced that she would come to harm if she ventured out by herself, so her choice had been either to tag along on their adventures or to stay in the hotel suite. She had travelled through locales more dangerous than an American shopping district, but she kept her thoughts on that to herself; Raymond only worried because he cared for her after all, and she couldn't begrudge him that.

That morning, when she'd raised the matter of the department store, Raymond had chided her for clinging to the familiar as, to his mind, the bric-a-brac in America was the same as that back home, and just as boring. Then he'd invited her to the Metropolitan Museum of Art, where the Mona Lisa was on loan. Of course, Joan being an artist, they'd already seen the piece several times at its home in the Louvre, but apparently it was different to her own desire to peruse china patterns and tea towels, despite the painting having markedly less functional value.

Miss Marple had politely declined, implying that it might be a good idea that she rest before the play's debut that night. Truth be told, she'd had her fill of the Italian masters when studying in Italy as a young woman, and she didn't consider a museum packed with sweaty people vying for a glance at a glorified postage stamp the height of excitement. After Raymond and Joan had left, she'd perched primly on the velvet-clad chaise longue in the parlour of their suite, musing that the Martinique was nothing at all like the traditional hotels of her youth – it was no Bertram's, for instance. The Renaissance style was gaudy, worse for wear if one had a keen eye for a well-kept home, and, overall, gave her a bit of a headache. She wasn't fond of most things French, apart from their porcelain and their pastries, and this American iteration of Frenchness was even less endearing.

While her eyesight wasn't what it used to be in her hawk-eyed youth, it was still quite good and had been drawn again and again to the room's large window, where the signs for Gimbels and Macy's had beckoned. When she'd looked down at the street below, she'd seen a stream of customers passing from the incivility of winter weather and into the warmth behind the doors of the grand department stores, looking alternately eager to browse or, as they passed out again, delighted with their purchases. The windows of the stores were dressed meticulously, beautiful displays that seemed to show the changing of seasons with a transition from snow-frosted glass into a riot of paper crocuses and daffodils.

Eventually, Miss Marple had placed her knitting aside and announced, 'After some reflection, I don't believe I have a dress appropriate for tonight', as if trying to convince the gauche décor around her that anyone cared what an old spinster wore while attending the technical rehearsal of a Broadway show. Then she'd stood gingerly, nodding along to the symphony of joint cracks and pops that come from a life of quiet but continuous adventure. 'They don't think leaving the hotel is safe, but the stores are just across the street. After all, I can't embarrass dear Raymond by showing up looking like some dowdy relic of the past. I should at the very least look like a *present-day* dowd.'

With a pleasing course of action thus decided, she'd gathered her coat, gloves and scarf. An hour had now gone by since she'd skulked out, glancing about as if Raymond and Joan might appear and drag her back to the room like a naughty child, and yet she still hadn't gone into any of the shops.

Miss Marple wasn't a woman who impressed easily, as a rule, and she should have found Manhattan a filthy and overcrowded cesspool compared to the simple charms of St Mary Mead – which was still relatively quaint even with the arrival of the Development People – but impressed she was. There was an energy and vitality to the city that seemed to match the same quality that vibrated in her old bones and always had. And there was so much to *observe.*

A taxi driver lowered his window and shouted at a cyclist who was darting through the intersection against the traffic light, uttering a nasal string of expletives that reddened Miss Marple's cheeks as much as the cold. A well-dressed businessman kindly stuffed a wad of bills into the homeless man's paper coffee cup with a tip of his hat. A couple walked hand in hand across the pedestrian crossing, past the fracas, the woman staring down at a ring on her hand with tears in her eyes and the man looking at her with pride. She thought they very much resembled Mr and Mrs Brade, the Montserratian musician couple Raymond had introduced her to, but Raymond had told her she mustn't tell coloured people they resembled one another, for some odd reason. Another incomprehensible modern change.

After absorbing the sights, sounds and smells of the city a moment longer, she finally decided to take leave of the traffic island and make her way inside the store. It was at this moment that she almost made a fatal error that would have proved Raymond's fears well founded – despite having watched the flow of traffic for so long, she looked the wrong way when stepping into the street and didn't see an errant bicyclist barrelling toward her. She was pulled back just in time by the homeless man who'd been feeding the birds – in addition to pigeons, he apparently also looked over old British hens.

'Thank you,' she said, and received a rough sound in return.

Having made it safely inside of Gimbels at last, she promptly decided that she didn't need a new dress after all, but since she had taken the trouble to get to the store, she'd have a look around. She rode the wooden escalator up to the household goods section and was met with the beckoning gleam of porcelain and familiar scent of silver polish – a much more agreeable olfactory experience than the perfume the sales girls had sprayed furiously in her direction as she'd entered the department store. It was a good thing her reflexes hadn't entirely quit her, or she'd have smelled like a 'sexy, youthful bouquet' when she returned to the hotel, which would have been sure to attract questions from Raymond and Joan.

She made a slow circuit around the displays of Wedgwood

and Noritake, admiring some pieces and looking with disdain upon others. The perusal wasn't quite as enjoyable as back in England, not so much because of the quality of merchandise but what was missing – nostalgia. She'd thought she enjoyed department stores by their very nature, but this place had no fond memories of her younger years or familiar markers of home, even if it sold the same brands. It was quite shocking to discover she possessed such a streak of sentimentality – she averted her inward gaze, not wanting to be rude to herself during such an unseemly show of emotion.

A bit disappointed with the excursion she'd built up in her mind having been a bust, she wandered down to the store's discount basement, a new experience for her that had the potential to make the trip worthwhile. Although it was novel, to be certain, she found nothing she'd bother transporting back across the Atlantic. Fifteen minutes later, she was standing half-heartedly stroking some dreadfully shiny tablecloth as she built up the fortitude to go back out into the cold, and was almost relieved when it was snatched from between her fingers.

'Oh, this is *it*!' a fire-haired woman, wearing a lipstick of an even deeper red, said in a voice that gave no indication of knowing it wasn't being used inside of a stable. 'This is it, Davey!'

'Are you kiddin' or what? It's a tablecloth, Serena,' the man beside her said in a low, frustrated voice. He had a thick moustache and thicker brows that rendered him surprisingly handsome; Miss Marple took an instant dislike to him. She didn't tolerate handsome men, at all. Rarely had she met one that wasn't up to no good, though usually their activities veered toward mischief that didn't require police intervention.

'So what if it is?' the woman held up the tablecloth as if it were a fine tapestry. 'I refuse to wear that hideous dress Carl insisted on, just to make a fool of me. If Estelle can pin and drape it, this'll be perfect for the final scene.'

'You think she'll defy Mr High-and-Mighty?' Davey asked.

Serena rolled her eyes. 'She'll love it. She told me he always *accidentally* rubs against her when she's dressing him, and she hates the dress he chose too. He thinks he can bully me out of this production, but I've held on this long, and I'll win in the end. I refuse to step on stage looking like, well – like her!'

Miss Marple looked up into the woman's face after some animal instinct alerted her that she'd been gestured at. The woman had slight pouches of skin beneath her wide brown eyes, and deep laugh lines bracketing her mouth. She was a young thing, not a day over fifty, and Miss Marple thought she was gloriously beautiful. Serena had the air of someone who thought mostly of themselves, but still paid enough attention to her surroundings to notice an old woman who, indeed, might have been mistaken for a pair of drab curtains by less observant passers-by and not given a second thought.

'Wouldn't want that,' Miss Marple said, with a twinkle, knowing full well what she looked like and not at all bothered by it. 'I should say that I doubt any dress could make you look as unremarkable as me. I have decades of experience at it, young lady.'

'You're British!' Serena crowed, the skin at the corners of

her eyes crinkling in delight, and when she spoke again, her accent had changed from American drama queen to East End urchin. 'I'ms an actress, I am. Nothing I loves more than an accent, 'cept a spot o' tea.'

The store was near the theatre district, of course, and now Miss Marple could imagine set dressers and stage designers popping in to grab last-minute items or unconventional additions. How splendid.

'You're very good,' Miss Marple replied carefully, when she realised Serena was waiting for her assessment. The accent was *not* good, but Miss Marple doubted she herself could pull off a convincing American accent and thus applauded the effort if not the result. She gestured toward the tablecloth. 'And you're going to wear this as a theatrical costume? I do think it's very . . . eye catching.'

'See?' the fire-haired woman said, shooting a look at Davey before turning back to Miss Marple. 'The dress that *creep* made them give me looks like a tablecloth covered in mud – because he wants me to *feel* like a tablecloth covered in mud. He's mad he didn't get a young ingénue as a co-star, one who'd bat her lashes at him and make him feel like something more than a washed-up hack. It'll be a gas to use a *real* tablecloth to show him that he can't shove me out of the spotlight!'

'Oh! Yes. Quite,' Miss Marple said. 'I do love such ironies.'

Serena turned, fanning the cloth dramatically behind her as if it were a fine cape – her physical acting was better than her accent, for in that moment, it *became* a fine cape, flowing majestically. She glanced back at Miss Marple and inclined her head, regally, then turned and walked towards the register of the discount department.

Davey – assistant, lover, or both – trotted behind her, jester to a queen.

'And I suppose I'm gonna pay for this?' he muttered.

Miss Marple smiled. Going to Gimbels hadn't been all for nothing. She'd met someone interesting, and wasn't that what she lived for? The myriad ways you might cross paths with another human? A slight chill went down her spine at that thought; she hoped for the fire-haired woman's sake that they didn't cross paths again. It was during a second meeting with Miss Marple in which other people didn't fare very well.

She ventured out into the cold and back to the hotel, where she found Raymond assailing the doorman for letting a frail, helpless and easily confused old woman wander out into the mean streets of New York City by herself. She wondered who the helpless old woman was for a moment, and then realised it was her.

'Tourists usually come to Manhattan to do just that, sir,' the doorman said. 'It would be bad for business if I tried to stop every old broad that left the place – it's a hotel, not a prison.'

'Well maybe you should add a prison wing!' Raymond retorted. 'You Americans are thrilled with the concept, shouldn't be too difficult to implement.'

'I'm all right, Raymond,' she said, grabbing his arm. He looked down at her with his face as pink and sweaty as when he'd thrown tantrums over not having enough sugar in his tea as a boy. He had always been excitable, her dear nephew.

'There you are, ma'am, safe and sound,' the doorman said with a nod, and pulled the door open, ushering them both into the lobby. 'Have a good afternoon.'

'I thought you were lying in a gutter somewhere!' Raymond exclaimed.

'The sewer system here wouldn't allow for that,' she said, then looked back at the doorman. 'He's just nervous about tonight,' she explained kindly, 'we're going to a rehearsal that he's quite anxious about. Don't mind him. And the gutters here are quite the feats of city planning, he meant them no disrespect.'

After a tense elevator ride, where Raymond expounded on the many calamities that might have befallen her – including being hit by a bicycle – they reached their suite, where Joan soothed her fretful husband and Miss Marple adjusted her ruffled feathers.

'Well, everything is fine now, isn't it?' Joan asked, handing Raymond a drink to calm his nerves. 'We'll rest and then get ready for tonight. They're sending a car to bring us to the rehearsal. I suppose we could walk over to the theatre district, since we're already on Broadway, but these streets are frightfully long – I doubt you and I would make it to Times Square without keeling over first, Aunt Jane.'

'If one is going to keel over anywhere, Broadway would be the proper place to do it – it would all be very dramatic,' Miss Marple mused, then recalled something. 'Are you quite sure about the location of the theatre? I asked that nice young fellow at the door about the address earlier, and he said—'

'The car has already been arranged by one of the actors as a welcome gift for Raymond, Aunt Jane. Please don't worry about a thing; you've been through enough today.'

'Why, I haven't been through anything at all,' she said, with just a bit of peevish bristle in her tone.

'Let's just rest,' Joan said, rubbing her hands reassuringly over Miss Marple's shoulders as she helped her out of her coat. 'It's going to be an exciting and exhausting evening. If you think our artist friends are unconventional, these Broadway people are mad – who knows what we'll get into?'

Miss Marple got another one of those brief chills down her spine and hoped it was from the cold, though a woman of her age knew intuition was far more reliable than hope.

'You're quite right,' she said. 'I do need to rest up. One never knows what the night will bring.'

Over the course of his illustrious writing career, Raymond West had come to understand how creative endeavours might fall short of their initially proposed scope. However, as he took in the decrepit theatre he'd been deposited in front of – located on a lower Manhattan street that looked like something out of the pulp novels he so disdained – he couldn't help but feel that this was quite beyond the average idea-to-completion miscalculation.

When Raymond's most popular novel, *Sordid and Unpleasant*, had been licensed for theatrical adaptation 'across the pond', he'd taken the news as an affirmation of his under-appreciated genius. That it was being produced by theatre legend G. Gregory Stapleton, who'd snagged the infamous Carl DeVoe as the male lead, had, to his mind, been a harbinger of his long-awaited ascension from 'successful English writer' to 'international literary giant'.

His aunt had often asked in her naive way whether his novels would ever be adapted for the West End, but who needed the Royal Court when his characters were about to surge up Broadway and make a splash on the Great White Way? When he'd regaled her with the news of the production, received via his agent, she'd congratulated him and then hesitated.

'This Stapleton fellow. His name does seem familiar, doesn't it? And it's being adapted and directed by a Ms Prince, is it? Are you certain this is all on the level? I'm certain I've heard those names before . . .'

'Why should *you* have heard of them, Aunt Jane?' Raymond had asked, amused that a spinster who rarely left her small English village might think herself familiar with movers and shakers of the American theatrical variety. 'Maybe you're mixing them up with other people. Perhaps Mr Stimpleton, the butcher? And Mrs Price, the new hairdresser over in the Development?'

'I'm probably mistaken, dear. You're right,' Miss Marple had said, and taken up her knitting, squinting at her work to avoid dropping a stitch, which happened more often these days.

It was because of things like that – dropping stitches and walking more slowly and generally being a woman in the winter of her life – that Raymond had convinced her to take leave of St Mary Mead and travel by plane from London to New York City. He'd wanted to make sure that Aunt Jane lived the remainder of her years to their fullest, but now he wondered if he hadn't actually brought her closer to an untimely demise.

'I believe there's been a misunderstanding,' Raymond protested, reflexively tamping down his agitation – it was a skill he'd honed over many years of dealing with writer's blocks, rejections and eviscerating reviews.

His statement was directed at Michael, the driver who'd been sent to fetch them from the hotel to the theatre, but Raymond's gaze was fixed on the marquee sign above him. It was lopsided and rusty, fashioned from scavenged metal and affixed to the front of what had clearly once been a factory, though quite a nice one, to be fair. The street was lined with these looming buildings of cast-iron design – the entire neighbourhood was one that had seemingly gone to rust. The few bulbs around the borders of the marquee were burnt out – some had been shattered, the spiky remnants cradling wisps of filament. The name of the show, *SORDID*, which had been painted in slapdash red, seemed more like a descriptor of their environs than anything else.

'Misunderstanding indeed,' Joan said, clutching his arm and looking suspiciously at a man vomiting into the gutter a few feet away from them. While they wore simple but elegant evening wear befitting a meet-and-greet at the theatre, the sallow, retching man wore a paint-spattered apron over denims – sans shirt – and matching paint-spattered boots. A couple walked past them, the woman looking like an inverted-mirror version of Jackie Kennedy, with her high bouffant and a minidress paired with pearls.

'This can't be the right theatre,' Joan said. 'This isn't even the right neighbourhood. Perhaps it's some kind of joke? American humour can be so crass and perplexing.'

Michael, a tall, pale man with the hunched shoulders often seen in the wards of canine humane societies, blinked in their general direction. When he spoke, it was with an accent much like a gangster out of a film, a voice that had seemed quite silly to Raymond upon their introduction but which now seemed somewhat menacing. 'I was told to bring you here, to the theatre, and here to the theatre is where I brought you. I did what I was told. I always do what I'm told.'

Joan looked at him askance.

'Run the errands, Michael. Clean the floors, Michael. Work the lights, Michael. See about Serena, Michael.' The man looked tormented, and Joan shuffled a step away from him.

Raymond was half-listening. Being a writer, he was always ready to fabricate a story that might explain situations both marvellous and unsatisfactory, and so he was doing just that.

'Are you certain?' he ventured, tone ingratiating. New Yorkers had a bit of a feral quality to them, in his experience, and were likely to lash out at the slightest provocation – with sharp wit, scathing reviews, or, judging from the cheap shine of Michael's ill-fitting suit, perhaps something a bit more dangerous. 'Perhaps you took a wrong turn, or we've entered some kind of alternate dimension? I do know the American space agency gets up to all sorts of things,' he joked.

Michael frowned at him.

Joan gasped at another heave from the man being sick, her elbow jabbing into Raymond's side. 'Look, I'm no expert on New York, but this is most certainly *not* Broadway,' she said. 'You expect me to believe that *this* is the home of *Guys and Dolls* and *My Fair Lady*? More like *Guys and Degenerates* and *My Fair Lush*.'

'West Broadway,' Miss Marple said, and Raymond jumped, having almost forgotten that his aunt was on his other side. His aunt – elderly and used to a sedate life, not the hustle and bustle of the Big Apple or the vice found in its wormier locales. This was supposed to be a stimulating but safe trip for the old lady, but he'd dragged her into much more dangerous territory than anticipated. A group of rough-looking young people approached from the end of the street in a bright, loud cluster like a swarm of post-modern bees.

'Aunt Jane,' said Raymond, taking her by the arm with his free hand, 'I'll sort this business out later. We must get you back to the hotel and away from these vagrants. I'm ever so sorry about this.'

'Now, now, dear,' replied Miss Marple, smiling up at her rattled nephew and resisting his pulling. 'There are no vagrants about – well, except for the one.'

Raymond glanced at the man who had been vomiting, who was now standing upright, laughing and wiping his arm over the back of his mouth as he fell in with the ruffians. One of them pulled a bandana from his pocket and tossed it to the drunk, who didn't seem quite so drunk any more.

'You mustn't apologise about these kind of mix-ups,' Miss

Marple continued. Her gaze went unfocused and the hint of a smile nudged at the wrinkles around her mouth. 'It's quite humorous, in a way, how perceptions can change things. It reminds me of when Mr Smith voted "nay" at the meeting about renovating the vicarage, and Mr Naysmith voted "yea", yet when the votes were tallied, everyone believed Mr Naysmith had voted against it.'

Joan West leaned forward, past her husband, to look at Miss Marple. 'Are you very tired, Aunt Jane? Raymond, let's get her back to the hotel. The jetlag must be muddling her thoughts.'

'West Broadway,' Miss Marple said again, more firmly, looking around the street lined with old factories that had fallen on hard times and been converted by artists and bohemians. She could see a certain beauty in these brick buildings and their large glass windows; there was a certain continental European appeal to them. Even the burnt-out craters that they'd passed during their drive might have been the result of the Blitz, though an arsonist high on paint fumes was more likely in this neighbourhood.

She wasn't sure why Joan was so upset – while their setting was a bit déclassé, they were clearly in some kind of artists' quarter and Joan herself was an artist. However, their surroundings made her look more kindly on the Development that had sprung up in St Mary Mead; the people who lived there at least wore shirts when venturing out of doors and hid their drunken sick in the privacy of their home, as was respectable.

'Oh!' Raymond grimaced as his aunt's nonsensical words

found meaning for him. 'West Broadway. Not Raymond West *on* Broadway. I'd assumed there was some sort of typo . . .'

'You can't be serious,' Joan cried in disbelief. 'Raymond, I told you to let me handle the correspondence, but, no, of course you had to—'

Just then, a door creaked open and a middle-aged black woman, wearing a long, loose-fitting patterned dress, stepped through it. Her hair was cut short in a style not very dissimilar from Miss Marple's, though the woman had no need of a permanent to give her curls.

'Mr West and family?' she asked, in an accent that Miss Marple found delightful – she sounded quite like a take-no-nonsense heroine from an American film. In fact, Miss Marple was immediately aware that this particular American actually *didn't* take any nonsense.

'Might you be the playwright and director, Ms Prince?' she asked, savouring the momentary surprise that crossed the woman's face.

'Aunt Jane?' Raymond asked tentatively, pulling her aside, as if worried she might say something offensive. 'Remember what I told you—'

'No, I'm quite sure it's her. I knew her name sounded familiar – during the Marina Gregg situation I found myself studying magazines about American celebrities, and there were articles about her,' Miss Marple continued, then glanced at Raymond and lowered her tone a bit further. 'Ms Prince was being prevented from doing her job, by people who dislike those of her background. You see, my dear, she's a—'

'Aunt Jane!' Raymond exclaimed.

'—a communist,' said Miss Marple, looking up at Raymond with worry. 'Are you all right? Perhaps it's you who should return to the hotel?'

Raymond ran a hand over his face, hand settling over his mouth as he shook his head. He muttered something, but Miss Marple's hearing was not as good as her eyesight.

'Come on in,' Ms Prince offered. 'The rehearsal is about to begin, and I'm so thrilled the writer himself is here to see how we've done. I hope I've been able to capture the unique brilliance of your novel.'

Raymond's spirits revived at that, and they all followed her inside.

As they entered the theatre, Miss Marple took the time to appreciate the rustic American architecture – bare brick walls with the occasional metal hook embedded, a remnant from its past existence as a factory. The lights overhead flickered in the high ceilings, and the huge windows let in the dim light from the streetlamps. Rows of seats had been installed on the flat surface of what had once been the shop floor, and a stage with minimalist set dressing had been constructed at the front of the large room.

It had likely not been a munitions factory during the war; from what Miss Marple could tell, perhaps a textile plant. There was a possibility it had produced uniforms, and then garments for everyday use. That was one kind of art, mechanized as it had become, and now the space was being used for another art, one that rejected the notion of assembly-line production.

All remnants of eras past must evolve and adapt, or

crumble; even Miss Marple herself. She knew that the younger people around her assumed she had already crumbled, and it did appeal to her, as it would be so much easier than changing. But she was self-aware: Miss Marple understood that she wasn't the crumbling type. She would have to go eventually, as all people do, but she hoped it would be in a blaze of glory, like the burnt-out buildings they'd passed.

'Your aunt is quite right, by the way,' Junie Prince said, as she pushed aside a bundle of electrical cords hanging from the wall. 'In fact, my political leanings are why your play is being put on here instead of on Broadway. Have you heard of the House Committee on Un-American Activities?'

Raymond stepped over a dubious puddle on the cement floor, and attempted to lighten the moment. 'I have, but in discussions with friends over what could get us called up on charges of being unBritish. Mostly tea-related offences, as one might imagine.'

Ms Prince laughed and then turned to face them as they manoeuvred down the centre aisle. The high-ceilinged warehouse floor wasn't the kind of theatre Miss Marple was used to, but it did remind her of adventures she'd had outside of St Mary Mead. She remembered how earlier, in the department store, she hadn't enjoyed it because it had been similar but not the same as the stores back home; this theatre reminded her that sometimes there was a thrill in the unknown as well.

'Well, apparently addressing racial inequality in one's work is un-American, so I was hauled before the committee.'

Raymond cleared his throat.

'I was quite shocked to read what had happened to you,' Miss Marple said, stepping over one of the many lengths of electrical wiring snaking around their feet. 'Have you considered coming to England to work? Such a thing would never happen there. We don't have racial inequality, and, if we did, we'd never be so blatant with it. It'd be terribly improper. You'd at least be *quietly* repressed, instead of hauled before cameras and all of that hullabaloo.'

Junie Prince gave her a look that managed to convey 'I'm quite all right, thank you', and then continued with what she was saying.

'I was found innocent, but after that, the project that was supposed to premiere on Broadway was scrapped, and no one would touch me with a ten-foot pole. My friend Mr Stapleton was already blacklisted, and he'd purchased this old building after seeing artists were moving into the area. It's been a warehouse and a factory and something not spoken of in front of our elders, but he's now converted it into a theatre where we persona non grata can still ply our craft. We chose your play as our first production because of its powerful meditation on injustice.'

Raymond's shoulders dropped back in pride. 'Injustice! Meditation! Yes, that's exactly what I was aiming for when writing; it's lovely to meet people who truly understand the deeper meaning of my work.'

'Isn't this the book you wrote to spite that reviewer who kept calling your prose bloviated nonsense?' Joan whispered.

Raymond gave her a wounded glance. 'Is being unappreciated not injustice?'

'Junie! Junie!' a shrill voice called out from behind the stage's curtain. 'He's at it again. Please, can't you make him stop?'

The corners of Ms Prince's mouth turned down as she glanced at the source of the noise. 'What's happened now, Serena?'

From one side of the stage, a woman wearing a drab grey dress stormed out. Her hair was dark brown, or one would have thought so if you didn't note the red whisps poking out from her slightly askew wig. In her hands, she held a shredded bundle of fabric in a pattern that was familiar to Miss Marple.

Miss Marple clutched her hands together. 'Oh dear.'

'He ruined it! I know it was him!' The actress shook the remnants of what had once been a cheap tablecloth with an eye-catching pattern. 'I just wanted this *one thing*, but no, everything has to be done Carl's way. It doesn't matter that we've caved to almost every one of his ridiculous peccadillos, he wants *all* of them catered to.'

Junie Prince kept her expression neutral as she repeated, 'What's happened now, Serena?'

'You know the dress I showed you? The one that I said was a better reflection of Trudy's character as I embodied her, instead of how *Carl* perceived Trudy?' She jerked a thumb back over her shoulder at the curtain behind her. 'He saw me getting it fitted and said I couldn't change things last minute, because his precious little ego wouldn't be able to tolerate it. His acting ability is disturbed by a new dress, but *he's* the stoic headliner and *I'm* the washed-up diva?'

At that instant a clean-shaven grey-haired man walked

out on to the stage behind her. He walked calmly, every bit the eye to Serena's storm. His expression was slightly bewildered, his hands in his pockets and slightly hunched shoulders conveying that he hated this conflict and that everyone was having to witness it.

He was handsome in the way of movie stars, with a shining inner charisma that both attracted and repelled, like a lighthouse beacon. Miss Marple gave a polite sniff of disdain.

'Serena, I simply said that it would throw me off to see you in something so different from what you've been wearing in dress rehearsals.' He turned to Junie Prince, 'And we've already checked the lighting – that'd have to be adjusted again, for some whim of hers. The point of dress rehearsals is for us to get habituated, isn't it?' He paused, very much like a barrister who's just asked a crucial question to a jury, then looked back at Serena. 'Yes, I asked that you not make an impulsive and unnecessary change. No, I didn't shred your dress.'

'They don't look at all how I envisioned William and Trudy while writing the book,' Raymond whispered to Joan. 'He's much too short and she's much too—'

'What?' Joan asked archly.

Raymond wiped at his brow nervously and fell silent.

'If it wasn't you, then who was it? The only other person who knew besides you was Estelle, and she wouldn't rip up her own work given how little she's paid.' Serena's voice was shrill; it reminded Miss Marple of a very small dog that has quietly growled as it was prodded by every guest at a party, and is then chastised when it finally breaks into a flurry of yipping barks. 'Carl wouldn't have known about the change at all if he hadn't barged into the dressing area because he thought my understudy, who might I add is twenty-five years younger than him, was getting changed in there!'

Carl's expression altered the tiniest bit, Miss Marple thought. There was a slight strain at the eyes – perhaps caused by tensing of his jaw – and his gaze sharpened into an ice pick. It was the expression a certain kind of man got when he encountered a woman too coldly proud to be affected by the heat he passed off as charm, but which was more akin to brimstone. It was a look that said, 'If you won't melt, I'll shatter you.'

'Lying is unbecoming, Serena. A woman your age should try to keep one of the few remaining assets she's got to recommend her.'

'Remaining assets? Oh, is that supposed to hurt my feelings?' Serena held a hand to her mouth and, instead of crying, began to slowly and methodically laugh. It was a laugh designed to act like salt on a snail, and even Miss Marple found herself shrinking from it. 'You think a crack like that is hurtful, but only because you're old and afraid of getting older. Of being an impotent, withered little man – I hate to break it to you, Carl, honey, but dipping your limp carrot into the dressing of any twenty-something who'll entertain you doesn't stop that.'

'You entertained that carrot quite happily when *you* were twenty-something,' Carl sneered. 'Or are you the only pretty young thing allowed to sleep her way on to the stage?'

Serena sucked in a breath and sent a desperate, plaintive

gaze toward Junie Prince, her face suddenly pale as she turned towards the small audience watching the theatrics play out, even though rehearsal hadn't even started. 'He's lying. I never did anything like that . . . I—'

'I'll take care of this, Serena. Don't worry.' Junie Prince looked unfazed, but her hands had tightened into fists.

'Please do! Or I will.' Serena sent Carl a dark look as she flounced past him, and at the last moment, tossed the ribbons of fabric into his face. He grabbed them in a reflexive rage, seething as she walked away from him, and then strode after her.

Junie looked down at Miss Marple. 'In case you ever got the idea that being a director is glamorous, we also get babysitting duty when co-stars don't get along. And tantrum duties when one actor seems set on making everything harder than it has to be.'

'At least you don't have to change nappies,' Miss Marple said. 'I had to change Raymond's when he was a wee one, and, I can tell you, it wasn't at all pleasant. I wondered if he didn't have some kind of ailment of the intestine.'

Junie Prince broke into a peal of laughter, and at the same time Raymond expostulated 'Aunt Jane!' once again. Perhaps the American penchant for loudness was catching, because he'd been shouting her name all day. His face was crimson, and for no reason at all too; when they got back to the hotel, she'd suggest he see a doctor before they boarded the plane back to England.

Ms Prince hopped up on to the stage, dusting her hands as she followed her two wayward leads.

'Well, they've certainly got the character dynamics down pat,' Raymond said, and then gave a sort of nervous chuckle. He looked around the shabby theatre and heaved a deep sigh. 'This will make for quite the dinner-party story one day, don't you think? I'm tempted to say we should all just stretch the truth and say it was a smashing success that lit up Broadway, but I invited all my American friends to opening night so—'

Two things then happened at almost the same time – the electricity surged in a sharp stab of light, then went dark, and a chilling scream, straight out of a fifties monster film, filled the entire theatre from floor to rafters. The fading echoes of the terrifying sound still lingered as the lights slowly blinked back on.

'What happened?' Joan cried out.

Miss Marple stayed quiet, determined to go see what could be divined from the unpleasant situation that surely awaited them.

Michael, the driver, came tearing out from behind the curtain, shouting, 'Someone's been injured! There's no phone here; I'm going to call the police at the bar down the street!'

Raymond stood frozen for a moment longer, then seemed to come back to himself. He began making his way up the stairs alongside the stage, with Joan and Miss Marple lagging behind him at a slower pace.

Joan's hands shook as she held Miss Marple's arm at the elbow and the wrist, guiding her on to the stage. 'What do you think—'

'Murder, dear,' Miss Marple pronounced, hating that bit

of herself that was already anticipating figuring out the hows and the whys. It was all a bit morbid but . . . some people knew things, and Miss Marple knew murder. There was no more point in being upset about it than a sparrow being sad that it knew how to build a nest.

They made their way into the chaotic backstage space, a labyrinth partitioned by strips of fabric. All kinds of odd items lay about on the floor, ready to trip one up. The ever-present loops of electrical wire, of course, plus various sorts of tools that might be needed at a moment's notice in set changes. Props too: a walking stick, a tea kettle, and what appeared to be a rubber chicken.

Now they passed between racks of clothing – the dressing room, perhaps – drawing closer to the source of the scream. Miss Marple steeled herself.

'Oh my! The show cannot go on, then,' Raymond cried out from somewhere just ahead of them, the words followed by a trilling laugh that she had only ever heard when he'd had a fright.

They passed through the next partition to find Serena standing with her face covered by her hands and Junie Prince sporting an expression of resigned horror. They were flanked on either side by a young black woman holding a pair of sewing shears and a Puerto Rican woman with full stage make-up – Estelle the set dresser and the unnamed young understudy, Miss Marple supposed.

Carl lay face down on the floor, unmoving.

Junie shook her head.

'This . . . is . . . exactly the last thing this production needs.'

She looked hard at Serena and, when she spoke again, her question was impressively direct. 'Did you kill him? If so, please make it known before the police get here. I've already been falsely accused of a crime once, and I'd rather not have another go at it for murder.'

'Attempted murder,' Miss Marple corrected. 'That man isn't dead.'

Indeed, if one looked very closely, Carl DeVoe's back was slowly rising and falling.

'Not yet at least,' Raymond said, approaching the body.

None of the people who actually worked with Carl moved toward him.

'Like the Naysmith incident in more ways than one,' Miss Marple murmured, though no one paid attention.

'It was an accident!' Serena said. 'I came into my dressing room to get away from him! I wanted to calm down and try to get ready for the final rehearsal, but he stormed in after me. He stepped on one of the wires and—'

She mimicked, with what Miss Marple assumed was great accuracy, a man with a quantity of electricity coursing through his body.

'And then you all came running in,' she finished.

Miss Marple glanced at Carl's feet – he was clad only in thin house slippers, which were wet. There was a puddle beside him, and a cord that had frayed through. She wasn't entirely certain the puddle had been there before the electrocution or that the cord had frayed naturally; she'd leave the former detail to someone else to verify.

'And why didn't *you* step on the wire?' Junie Prince asked.

'And before you get upset, I'm asking because the police will be here soon and they're gonna want to know too.'

Serena pulled the wig off in frustration and tossed it across the space. Then she sighed and headed after it, the poise in her steps making it appear that she almost floated.

'How is it that I have to answer for Carl's carelessness on top of everything else? Will I end up in jail because I'm not some actor with his head so far up his own rear end that he doesn't pay attention to his surroundings?' she bit out over her shoulder, expertly navigating the loose wires and various detritus on the floor as if it was a game of elastics while barely looking down.

'Dancers,' Miss Marple ventured, 'do seem to have a kind of sixth sense in their feet. I remember a young woman I met after the war; she said that because of her dancer's reflexes she had never once tripped over a pile of rubble while working the tea canteens.'

Serena picked up the wig and moved towards Miss Marple, glancing down at the old woman gratefully before hanging the distressed brunette locks on a hook next to various other faux hair pieces.

'I have no idea what most of that means, but yes – I've trained for years to be able to naturally avoid anything that I might trip over while onstage. I do it while dancing forward, dancing backwards, and even while trying to evade a pest of a co-star.'

Junie sighed. 'I believe you. You would have throttled him, if anything, and not stopped until the light left his eyes. You're thorough, not someone who leaves things up to chance.'

Serena smiled at the compliment. 'Thank you, Junie. Whatever else happens, it's been lovely working with someone who sees the best in me.'

Junie sighed, and turned to the dresser and understudy. 'And what about you two? Estelle, those scissors could fray up some wire nice and easy.'

Estelle snorted. 'Junie, you would have to be out of your mind to think I'd risk my life trying to take out either of these two.' She jerked her chin toward Carl's prone body and then Serena.

Serena made a small sound of realisation. 'Me?'

Estelle's expression softened. 'This is your changing area. If that little trap was meant to take anyone out, it was you.'

All eyes turned toward the understudy. The young woman was dark-haired, with freckles smudged across the light brown skin of her cheeks. Miss Marple hoped it wasn't this girl, who probably felt all grown up but whose life was just beginning. It was almost worse than seeing someone die, seeing a young person throw their future away for murder when there was almost always some other solution.

Serena's voice was genuinely hurt for the first time that evening. 'Vera . . .'

'It wasn't me,' Vera said, her large brown eyes filling with reactive tears. 'I love Serena – worship her. You all know that. As for Carl . . . he kept bugging me. Kept telling me if I just . . . did him a favour, he would do one for me. Help my career.' A sudden fierceness came into the young woman's eyes. 'But I wouldn't do all this if I wanted to hurt him. This whole set-up? When he could just get pushed in front of a subway car with no possibility of being linked to me? What do I look like?'

She shook her head ruefully and Miss Marple smiled. The girl was young, but she had a good head on her shoulders.

'So it was an accident,' Raymond said, finally feeling at Carl's neck for a pulse. 'There are wires everywhere since this is a converted factory, and that seems enough to prove that it was simple bad luck. Accidents happen in factories, and in theatres, all the time.'

Raymond wasn't fazed by the fact that someone had possibly tried to kill the man; he'd met enough men like Carl, and had been told about enough of them by Joan, that he was certain electrocution was a gentle attempt compared to what he might deserve. But having a show cancelled due to accidental electrocution was a great cocktail-party story; having one cancelled due to murder was drama of the lowest kind.

'That's even worse,' Junie said. 'Who's at fault for an accident? The theatre company. Everything we're trying to build . . . all our hard work . . . it's not fair!'

'Shouldn't the police be here already?' Joan asked. 'Michael should be back at the very least.'

'With the way he jumps every time Carl snaps his fingers, I'm surprised he didn't carry him to the hospital himself,' Estelle said.

'Oh. Oh, I see,' said Miss Marple, running her fingers lightly over the front of her coat. 'Not quite the same, but very much so. Naysmith.'

Raymond looked up at his aunt, dread forming a familiar

knot in his belly. 'You don't think this was an accident, do you?'

Miss Marple looked around, her expression contemplative and calm. 'Oh, I do, but not quite how everyone else is imagining it.'

'Is your aunt a medium?' Serena looked at the old woman with renewed interest. 'Is that why you were there at Gimbels earlier? You knew handing me that tablecloth—'

'No, no, I do not adhere to any of that sort of thing. Our meeting earlier was simply a delightful prelude to the current unpleasantness.' Miss Marple sighed. 'But . . . Naysmith. After Mr Smith was outvoted on the matter of the vicarage, he let everyone believe that Naysmith had voted against it, even though it was he himself who'd voted against it. Some assumed he disliked Mr Naysmith – not sure why, perhaps they thought it was a simple matter of feeling slighted by his name? But I always thought that Mr Smith was against the plan for the vicarage and Mr Naysmith was simply a convenient target.'

'I'm not sure what you're talking about,' Serena said, lost.

'Me either,' added Estelle.

'I . . . think I'm beginning to pick up what you're putting down,' Junie Prince said, taking a step closer to Carl DeVoe.

'After the vote failed to go in his favour, Mr Smith even went so far as to claim Mr Naysmith was embezzling church funds,' Miss Marple continued. 'It was all a lie, you see. Mr Smith, in fact, had been part of a group trying to buy the land the vicarage was to be rebuilt upon in order to construct new houses – I believe some of them went on to be partners in the Development, but that's neither here nor there.'

'The development?' Vera asked, and Miss Marple shook her head in apology.

'Oh, never mind that, dear. It took some time to untangle the lies, but Mr Naysmith was very much discredited in the eyes of others who had respected him, and some people never believed that he'd done nothing wrong. It was all quite unseemly.'

'Get up, Carl,' Junie said, nudging him gently with her shoe, then not so gently. 'Now, or I'll hit you with a real live wire and tell them I was trying to jump start your heart.'

Carl didn't move . . . then rolled over slowly, eyes open and sparkling with a mischief that was so inappropriate it bordered on perverse.

Serena let out a shriek that was several decibels lower than her initial one, and Junie crossed her arms over her chest. 'George said you were trying to be supportive, but I knew there was something off about you badgering us to be part of this production even though you weren't blacklisted – you're a mole. And one digging away at our foundations.'

Carl looked up at Junie, giving her a winning smile. He was back to being charming and engaging. 'Aw now, Junie, who'd believe some bunk like that? No one, that's who.'

'What on earth do you mean?' Raymond asked, unsure whether to be relieved or upset.

'I mean, he's been undermining this play – we're doing this our way, unsanctioned, and with people who have been blacklisted. Except for Carl.' Junie shook her head in frustration. 'All that arrogant behaviour, and demanding things that lowered the quality of the production, and trying to drive Serena up the wall, was just to make sure we failed. You set us up.'

'Was he going to fake his death?' Vera asked.

Carl shook his head, and when he spoke he was absolutely earnest. 'I couldn't fake my death. I'm Carl DeVoe.'

Junie sighed. 'But tabloids love reporting on intrigue. A theatre run by blacklisted communists is one thing, but a theatre run by blacklisted commies that led to the near death of all-American darling Carl DeVoe would have been *actual* death for our careers.'

Miss Marple gave a nod of agreement. 'I believe that before Michael ran out so quickly – too quickly to have checked what had occurred – he used the lightboard to create the illusion that Carl had been electrocuted. Then he ran out under the pretence of making a phone call, when he was actually going to get other participants in the charade.'

'But how did you figure any of this out, Aunt Jane?' Joan asked. 'You've just met these people.'

'As I said earlier, there was only one vagrant outside with us tonight.' Miss Marple walked over to where the hairpieces hung and pointed at a beard, plucking a grey pigeon feather from it. 'I met Serena earlier today, and apparently Michael as well. He was in disguise as a homeless man. I recognised him after we arrived here, but assumed his crime had been panhandling under false pretence, not spying on Serena.'

She considered mentioning how he'd saved her, but decided it wasn't relevant to the situation at hand.

'Someone rewarded him handsomely for his spying – quite a lot of money shoved into a beggar's cup and passed off as kindness. Michael reported what he saw to Carl, which was how Carl knew about the dress. It must have sparked this idea of how to anger Serena and also give the show one last push off the rails in one go.'

'Are you saying that the adaptation of my play is a casualty of American political intrigue?' Raymond exclaimed, sounding not at all put out by the notion. '*This* will make me the toast of all of literary England!'

'It would if anyone believed you,' Carl said, standing up by himself, since no assistance was offered. He grimaced at the dust that had accumulated on his clothes, then looked up at Junie with his ice-pick expression. 'I'll be going now. I'm sure the play will flop and be forgotten once it's announced that I'm no longer the lead. It will still die, but with a whimper instead of a bang.'

'You can't just leave. Wait until the police get here!' Vera said, as Carl brushed off his trousers.

He laughed. 'I haven't done anything illegal, darling. Maybe if you'd waited until after I'd hammed it up at the hospital to figure this all out you could have had me at misuse of public services. But since you didn't . . .'

At that moment Michael rushed back in with two paramedics. All three of the new arrivals looked harried and heroic as they ran in, but their demeanour changed quickly as they took in the scene.

'Jig is up?' Michael asked miserably, and Carl nodded.

With that, Carl, Michael and the faux paramedics all simply left; the anticlimactic nature of it was so startling to Miss Marple that it nearly circled back around to exhilarating.

Serena, Estelle and Vera huddled together, rehashing what had just occurred. Junie Prince left to find Carl's understudy and to contact George Stapleton.

'I'm so glad you convinced me to come with you,' Miss Marple said delightedly. 'What a marvellous evening.'

'Why are you in such high spirits?' Raymond asked.

'Because, dear Raymond, I got to solve a murder with no murder having been committed,' Miss Marple said, as if the answer should be evident. 'New York really is a city where one's wildest dreams might come true.'

The Unravelling

Natalie Haynes

'I don't see how that would explain anything,' said Susan Goldingay. 'And there's no point in having a haberdasher's if they aren't ever open.'

Miss Marple nodded gravely. 'Well, yes,' she said. 'But I'm sure Mrs Weaver will open up again in the morning.'

'Did you see the—' Susan broke off and eyed the tables around them. But the tea-room was bustling on this rainy autumnal day, and no one was eavesdropping. 'The brawl?'

'Oh, dear me, no,' replied Miss Marple. 'I heard about it from Florence. And she heard about it from Williams, when he delivered the post.'

'So he saw them?'

'Oh yes,' Miss Marple raised her cup and took a delicate sip. As she returned it to its saucer, she leaned slightly closer. 'He saw the whole thing. The farmer and his man arrived in the square just before three o'clock. He was quite sure of it because of the bells and the pigs, you see.'

Susan frowned but didn't interrupt. She had been friends

with Miss Marple for too long not to know the story was coming, one way or another.

'Syme went into the butcher's and left the new man – Martin, I believe – in charge of the pigs. Williams told Florence that he was waiting for Syme quite calmly. The pigs weren't causing a nuisance at all.'

Susan wrinkled her nose. She had always found pigs to be nasty creatures, their sharp teeth like shards of broken crockery.

'And Martin was no trouble until Mr Weaver came out of the shop and told him to be on his way.'

'How odd!' said Susan. 'The man could hardly leave without Syme, could he?'

'No, dear,' replied Miss Marple. 'But when he refused to move on, Mr Weaver became agitated and began to shout.'

Susan raised her eyebrows. 'He's usually so quiet!'

'As you know, I don't like to criticise a man who had a difficult war,' said Miss Marple. 'But Williams was quite sure about what he'd seen. He said this Martin tried to keep calm even while Weaver was shouting. He was darting nervous glances at the butcher's, but Williams couldn't tell if he was afraid Syme would come outside, or afraid that he wouldn't, if you see what I mean.'

Susan nodded. 'Poor man,' she said. 'He must have been worried about losing his job.'

'Yes,' Miss Marple said. 'Syme only hired him a week ago, Florence said. So no wonder he was anxious. But I wonder if that explains . . .' Her voice tailed off and she frowned. 'I'm really not sure it does, you know.'

'What happened then?' asked Susan.

'Williams said that Mr Weaver raised his fists,' said Miss Marple. 'And Martin stepped back and tripped on the kerb-stone.'

'Oh dear!'

'Yes,' Miss Marple nodded. 'So the poor man was lying on his back among the pigs when Syme reappeared and Mr Weaver started shouting at him too.'

'No!'

'Which was lucky, in a way,' Miss Marple continued. 'Because it meant Syme could see Martin wasn't at fault, since he blamed Mr Weaver straightaway.'

'I see.'

'But then Martin jumped up from the pavement and began waving his stick in Mr Weaver's face. Williams said he'd been provoked enough to excuse it, but he'd have certainly lost his job if Syme hadn't been so angry with Mr Weaver, and if he hadn't also needed help to round up the pigs, which had run all over the square when Martin fell.'

'And this was when Sergeant Dover arrived?'

'Precisely.'

'I still don't understand about the bells?' said Susan.

'Oh, well, the bells chimed three as three pigs ran past him,' said Miss Marple. 'That's how Williams could be so sure of the time.'

'And what did Dover say?' Susan asked.

'Well, he was all ready to keep Martin in the police station overnight, but Syme persuaded him that the poor man was hardly at fault. So, in the end, Dover let them take the pigs back to the farm and told Mr Weaver to speak to the police next time he was concerned about livestock in the square.'

'Well, that's an end to it,' said Susan.

Miss Marple frowned. 'Perhaps,' she said.

But the Weavers did not open again in the morning. Nor did any of the little shops in the square, leaning higgledy-piggledy against each other. The whole row kept their doors locked while the police searched for the weapon used to kill Martin, whose body – brown eyes clouded and sightless – had been discovered by the milkman just after dawn. At first, they thought the old man must have died from the stress of his argument with Weaver. Then they wondered if he had hit his head on the stone step of the haberdasher's as he fell. There was a small dark stain on the edge of the lowest step, which Dover was sure must be blood.

But when the doctor felt the back of the man's head, he pronounced it uninjured: not even a bump. And, besides, there was no doubt about what had killed him when they turned the body over. The broken shaft of an arrow was still protruding from his chest.

Susan felt no need to wait for the village telegraph to convey the tidings when she could take news of the man's death to Jane herself. To give herself an excuse for calling in the morning, she wrapped some rock cakes in waxed paper, twine sliding to and fro as she tried to tie it in a rush. But, honestly, it was bad enough that she had missed the fight over the pigs the previous day because she had been arranging flowers in church, and so she refused to be cut out of the most extraordinary incident in the village for as long as she could remember. She knew she was due at the vicarage to discuss choir practice, but she was confident that, if God was pleased with her endeavours on His behalf, He would spare her from another church meeting this once so she could have the pleasure of talking murder with Jane. And if He didn't appreciate yesterday's dahlias, she could make amends another day, when less important things were going on.

She hurried up the hill, her stout walking shoes squeaking as she went. But as she rounded the bend, she saw Williams, the postman, sailing downhill on his bicycle. She gritted her teeth with vexation as she returned his cheery wave. Surely the man spent some time delivering letters, and not simply acting as a personal messenger service for Jane? It was – she reflected, as papery leaves crunched beneath her feet – typical of Miss Marple to have found a housemaid who was walking out with the postman. And if the village had no postman, she would doubtless have acquired a gardener who was brother to a delivery boy. News always reached Miss Marple, one way or another.

'Oh!' said Miss Marple, as Susan bustled into the sitting room. 'Are those some of your delicious rock cakes, Susan? How kind.'

Susan smiled as she handed the parcel to Florence the housemaid, along with her hat and coat.

'You are too bad, Jane. You've already heard it from Williams, haven't you?'

'About the dead man? What an awful thing. A bow and arrow, he said?'

'That's right.' Susan was determined to be the authority on something. 'I spoke to Sergeant Dover myself before I came up to see you.'

'Had the arrow been snapped off?' Miss Marple enquired.

'Yes!' said Susan. 'Dover thought it had broken under him when he fell, but they couldn't find the rest of it anywhere.'

'I see,' said Miss Marple. 'That does make things more complicated.'

'It's quite mad. Who would shoot a man and then come and try to take the arrow back?'

Miss Marple nodded slowly. 'Who indeed?' she murmured.

The answer – as far as Sergeant Dover was concerned – was obvious. The pigman had only arrived in the area a few days earlier and no one knew where he had come from. Syme said he had knocked at the door and offered to work for food and a dry barn to sleep in. The farmer was short-handed and, although he was usually suspicious of strangers, his dog had shown an uncharacteristic fondness for this man, Martin. When he arrived, the animal had pelted across the farmyard, barking loudly. But as soon as the animal approached the stranger, the man had reached down to scratch the dog's ears and it had wagged its tail as though they were old friends. Syme considered his dog's judgement sound as a rule, so gave Martin the benefit of the doubt. But he was not a man to make idle conversation, so he knew little more about the stranger than anyone else.

Sergeant Dover began and ended his investigation in the haberdasher's. He was apologetic in his manner and mild in his questioning: the Weavers were a popular couple in the village. As Miss Marple had put it the previous day, they had endured a difficult war. Mr Weaver had signed up, patriotically but reluctantly, as he was rather too old and his eyesight was poor. And Mrs Weaver had run the shop on her own for years, never complaining that she had no help, or that she was trying to bring up her son Eric on her own, or that so many items they used to sell – wool winders, sewing machines – were impossible to source these days. She was practical and kind: as Susan noted, she would always hold wool for her customers so they could buy a jumper's worth at a skein a week when their wages came in. Miss Marple agreed this was the mark of an excellent shopkeeper.

Mr Weaver, meanwhile, had found himself in the navy. At first, the village heard plenty of his exploits: he had fought in one battle after another, always managing to avoid serious injury, although, alarmingly, he was reported dead more than once. But as the years dragged on, things went quiet. No one liked to ask Mrs Weaver too much, because bad news travelled more quickly than good, and no news was often the cruellest kind of all. More than one person speculated that Weaver was working with the French Resistance, others had him in North Africa. There were reports of almost everyone else in the village who'd gone off to war, yet never news of him.

Once the war was won, the men drifted back to the village. Not all of them, of course: many were lost and some were damaged beyond return. But, one by one, they were all accounted for, with one exception. Weaver had disappeared. And so things remained – Mrs Weaver running the shop, no one remarking that her husband was still missing – for several more years. And then, one day, he came home.

That – Susan reflected, as she collected five new skeins of wool for Miss Marple and carried them up the hill – had been the last time something dramatic had happened in the village. Normally the place was so sleepy and pleasant. But when Mr Weaver returned, Mrs Weaver had cried out in shock and delight.

'Do you remember, Jane?' Susan asked, as Miss Marple compared the dye lots of each skein, nodding as they all matched.

'Remember what, dear?' she said. Her spectacles were perched on her nose as she consulted her pattern. She had knitted this baby's blanket pattern many times before, but she still liked to refresh her memory on the number of stitches each repeating motif required.

'When Mrs Weaver saw her husband again after all that time?'

'Of course I do,' said Miss Marple. 'One could hardly forget such a scene.'

Susan smiled. 'She was so happy, do you recall? She dropped a great basket of cloth and screamed for joy.'

'Oh, do you think so?' Miss Marple picked up her knitting pins and checked the gauge.

'You said you remembered! A great squawk of delight, it was.'

Miss Marple looked up and frowned. 'I do remember he

was exhausted, poor man. It looked as though he'd been travelling for months.'

'Years,' Susan agreed. 'And it must have been so strange for him to be alone after so long living and fighting alongside his men. He looked lost.'

'Indeed he did,' said Miss Marple.

'I suppose he must have been to so many places.' Susan prided herself on her imagination.

The villagers had welcomed back their long-lost neighbour with kindness and some curiosity. But only children were blunt enough to ask Weaver where he had been for so long, and they received no answer beyond a clip round the ear from the nearest adult. Weaver's pale eyes told their own truth: wherever he had been, it was not for sharing. And if the haberdasher's was somehow quieter with two people working there than it had been when it was just Mrs Weaver, the villagers still felt lucky to have it.

But as they muttered to one another over the coming days, what was Sergeant Dover to do? The ruckus in the square had been witnessed by several bystanders and they all agreed: Mr Weaver had been the aggressor. And since no one else admitted to any connection with Martin – beyond Syme's cursory exchanges – Dover had little choice but to speak to the haberdasher.

The questioning took place behind closed doors, with no one present but the sergeant, his constable, Weaver and Mrs Weaver. Yet the details of this interview – such as there were – flew around the village without delay.

'Was Martin known to you before this week?' asked the sergeant. His round face was reddening and he glanced down at the constable's notebook to avoid making eye contact with anyone. The constable had written 'WEAVER' in block capitals, before drawing a double line underneath it.

Weaver shook his head.

'Why were you so angry with him?'

Weaver shrugged. 'I would like an answer, sir,' said the sergeant, unhappily. He was more accustomed to resolving neighbourly disputes and helping to find missing cats. Murder was not something he had ever expected to deal with. He waited, hoping the haberdasher would yield first.

'I was angry about the mess, I suppose,' said Weaver. He sounded so weary that neither policeman could imagine him shouting. But Dover had heard the fracas himself. He had seen its immediate aftermath, and he wasn't going to be put off.

'It was just a few pigs, sir.'

'He shouldn't have left them right outside the shop,' snapped Weaver. 'It puts off our customers. Who wants to walk through a farmyard to get to the door?'

'Has this been a frequent problem?' Dover raised his eyebrows. Syme brought his pigs into town two or three times a year at most.

'That's not the point,' the man replied. Sweat was beading on his brow. 'If my customers wanted to work on a pig farm, they would.'

'So you told him to move along?' asked the sergeant. 'And he refused?'

'Yes,' said Weaver. 'And he was insolent about it.'

'How so?'

'He said he wanted to see my wife.'

'Your wife, sir? What for?'

'I don't know,' he replied. 'I didn't ask him why he wanted to speak to her. I told him not to be so damned impertinent.'

'I see. And did your wife know what he might have wanted from her?'

The haberdasher's eyes bulged. 'Why don't you ask her? Penny! Penny!'

Mrs Weaver appeared in the doorway so quickly that the sergeant knew she had been listening behind the door.

'Forgive me, madam,' Dover said. He thought it best to pretend Mrs Weaver hadn't heard every word spoken so far. 'We wondered if you might have any idea why the dead man wanted to speak to you?'

Mrs Weaver was a handsome woman with long, dark hair plaited and pinned tight. Her bright blue eyes glinted with suspicion, though Dover half-remembered her as a young girl and he fancied those eyes had once glinted with laughter. When Weaver had left for the war, their son had only been a babe in arms. And what was he now? Twenty? Twenty-one? Old enough to be working as a junior master at the local school anyway. So perhaps it wasn't suspicion he saw in her expression, but the weariness of age.

'I?' Her voice was richly melodic. 'Why would I know, sergeant?'

Dover found himself stumbling over his words. 'I – we – I hoped you might have recognised him.'

'No,' she said. 'I don't believe I did.'

'Had he been here before?' the policeman asked, hopelessly. To his surprise, a flicker of emotion appeared and disappeared on her face. 'No,' she said.

But this time he knew she was lying.

Miss Marple raised an eyebrow an eighth of an inch and the waitress rushed to their table. Susan – who had been trying to catch her eye for five minutes – tried not to sound irritated as she ordered afternoon tea for the pair of them. Miss Marple wrapped her shawl a little closer around her shoulders: the door kept opening as customers came and went.

'I've never seen it so busy!' Susan said, turning in her seat to get a better view. 'We were lucky to find a table. And I don't recognise half these people.'

Miss Marple nodded. 'I wonder if the inquest has attracted the attention of the newspapers,' she said.

Susan's eyes widened. 'Murder tourists!' she hissed. 'Is that what they are?'

'I think they might be,' Miss Marple replied. 'Yes, certainly a possibility.'

'Will they leave when the inquest is over, Jane? I don't think I like it.'

'They may do,' Miss Marple replied. 'Yes, once the sergeant has made his arrest, they may leave.'

'Arrest? Who is he going to arrest?'

'Mr Weaver, of course,' said Miss Marple.

'Oh no!' Susan put her hand to her chest so emphatically that her pearls jumped. 'He couldn't have.'

'Couldn't have what, dear?'

'Murdered the pigman,' Susan whispered. She didn't want other people to think that she was a murder tourist too.

'No, he didn't murder anyone,' said Miss Marple. 'You can see the poor man couldn't harm a fly. He shudders when a dog barks.'

'But you said—'

'I said he would be arrested. But he certainly didn't do it. The man was killed – rather theatrically – with a bow and arrow.'

'I know,' said Susan.

'Mr Weaver has the shakes, dear. He came back from the war like that.'

'Does he?'

'Yes. That's why Mrs Weaver has to do the weighing and cut the cloth.'

'But the dead man wasn't stabbed. Or hit with scales.'

Miss Marple did not sigh, but she exhaled with commitment. 'He couldn't have held an arrow still, dear. Let alone aimed it.'

'Then he mustn't be arrested!'

'I'm afraid the sergeant will be expected to arrest someone,' Miss Marple replied.

And as so often, she was right.

The morning light was soft and grey and Susan collected Miss Marple in her car, so her friend wouldn't have to walk to church on the slippery pavement. The cake sale planning committee was abuzz with rumours, as Sergeant Dover and

Constable Jebb had taken Mr Weaver away. The two men must have known each other in the war, it was thought, and Martin had come back to settle a long-held grievance. Or Mrs Weaver was involved in some way. Certainly, Martin didn't seem like the kind of man she would know, but there was no telling, was there? If she hadn't known him, why did he want to speak to her? And why was Weaver so angry, unless he knew something the rest of them did not?

Miss Marple listened attentively to each question and suggestion but said nothing. Since she had been driven to the meeting, she had brought her knitting. The blanket had grown a little, Susan noted, but surely not as much as it should have.

'Did you run out of wool, dear?' she asked.

Miss Marple smiled as she counted the stitches along the knitting pin. 'No, I dropped a stitch,' she said. 'And I didn't notice for rows and rows, so I had to unravel inches of work.'

'How annoying,' Susan sympathised. She had never really understood the appeal of knitting. 'Yes, of course,' she added, this addressed to the chairwoman of the committee. Mrs Wilson wanted Susan's rock cakes for the sale and no one would be able to say that she had let the church roof fall into disrepair for want of her baking a batch or two.

'Did it take a long time?' she asked Miss Marple, now Mrs Wilson's sharp gaze had turned in another direction.

'The knitting? Yes, dear. But not the unravelling. It takes longer to pick the stitches back up and—' Miss Marple broke off. 'Oh,' she said. 'I suppose that could be it, couldn't it?'

'What, Jane?' Susan had known her friend for many years, and she recognised the signs of Miss Marple realising something important: her eyes almost glazed as though she were mesmerised.

'But it doesn't tell us who killed him, of course,' said Miss Marple. 'Although perhaps it narrows the field.'

'Jane!' Susan was trying to be discreet, since they were in a room filled with people who knew the Weavers, so she whispered urgently but as quietly as she could. She nonetheless drew a hard stare from Mrs Wilson.

'Are you volunteering, Susan? Marvellous, thank you.'

Susan nodded weakly, wondering what she had just agreed to do. From the grateful expressions on the faces of the other committee members, she had no doubt she would regret it.

Once Mrs Wilson had declared the meeting finished, Susan and Miss Marple walked slowly out into the square. The rainclouds had melted away and skeletons of damp leaves lay imprinted on the church path.

'I'm not sure what I promised to do,' Susan murmured, as the two of them eased away from the other committee members.

'Teas at the school play, I'm afraid,' said Miss Marple.

'Oh no.' Susan rolled her eyes. 'Is it soon?'

'Tonight, I believe.' Miss Marple twinkled at her. 'I could help you, if you like.'

The two women arrived at the school hall at four o'clock precisely. A rather battered box of cups and saucers was perched on the edge of a trestle table, and the urn was already warm to the touch. Miss Marple laid out the saucers in neat rows, while Susan mixed orange squash in a large jug and poured it out into paper cups. By the time the audience started arriving, they were ready to serve tea and biscuits to all who wanted them.

A handsome young man – barely older than the children, it looked to Susan, but carrying himself with an air of authority and wearing an academic gown to boot – appeared from behind the stage curtains and frowned as he scanned the school hall. It was not perhaps quite as full as he was hoping. Susan waved at him before she realised who it was.

'Jane!' she said. 'It's Eric! I mean, young Weaver.'

'Oh, yes,' said Miss Marple, as the young man waved back rather self-consciously and began walking towards them. 'He teaches here, does he not?'

'What can we ask him?' Susan muttered, as Eric drew nearer.

'Nothing at all,' said Miss Marple firmly. She held out a cup of tea and Eric seized it.

'Thank you so much,' he said. He had light brown hair and chestnut eyes, a small shaving cut healing on his left cheek. Susan thought how lucky it was that he favoured his mother, with her strong jaw and straight nose. The same features made mother and son handsome in different ways.

'Were you looking for someone?' asked Miss Marple.

'My mother,' the young man explained. 'She was hoping to attend tonight's performance.'

'I'm sure she knows how much work you've put in to rehearse a whole play,' Miss Marple said.

His face broke into a smile. 'She has witnessed it first-hand! She's watched me wrangling with the script and the rehearsal schedule for weeks.'

'I'm sure she'll be here soon,' Susan said.

The children were all filing in now: how tidy they looked, Susan thought. Their navy blazers had the school crest on the pocket, and they walked in pairs to their seats.

'Your pupils are very well behaved,' she said.

He nodded. 'They've really taken to drama. As soon as I realised the only way to get boys interested in a play was if it was full of violence, they became really keen.'

'Oh,' said Susan, rather faintly. 'What is the play?'

'Aeschylus,' he said. 'Wives murdering husbands. Never fails.' He wandered off, still looking for his mother.

'How very modern, Jane,' Susan said.

'In a way,' she replied.

Mrs Weaver appeared just before the lights dimmed, walking straight past their table without pausing. If her face was rather drawn from worry, she nonetheless wanted to support her son.

At the end of the play – having understood no more than one word in five and wondering if anyone was left alive – Susan nudged Miss Marple. Mrs Weaver was seen hurrying out of the hall before the smattering of applause was over. Susan tried waving to catch her attention, but without success: Mrs Weaver did not lift her pale gaze from the floor.

'I suppose she doesn't want to talk to anyone,' said Susan, as she ferried cups and saucers from beneath the wooden seats and Miss Marple stacked them neatly on the table.

'No,' said Miss Marple. 'I imagine she has been trying to avoid questions from all sides.'

'Do you think the police have interrogated her?' Susan was shocked.

'The police, and her son, of course.'

'Why would her son be interrogating her?'

'Because he's afraid she's done something quite awful,' said Miss Marple.

'Not murder?' whispered Susan.

'No, I don't think so.' Miss Marple stacked the last of the saucers on top of one another. 'Something he will find rather harder to forgive, perhaps. But she may be able to keep her secret, if she is lucky. Although, of course, she hasn't been terribly lucky before now, has she?'

But the following morning, it seemed as though the Weavers' luck had changed at last. Mr Weaver was released from custody, after witnesses had come forward to say they had seen him walking by the mill pond at the hour in question. Even if he had been able to fire an arrow – as Miss Marple had observed he could not – he certainly couldn't have fired one from half a mile away. Why hadn't the witnesses come forward sooner, everyone asked one another, and who were they? The police were not prepared to answer idle gossip and speculation, so the village came to its own conclusions, which happened (in this instance) to be accurate. Weaver had been spied by a couple having an illicit meeting that neither wanted to become public. Nonetheless, they were unwilling to see an innocent man hang for their indiscretion, so they separately made statements to Sergeant Dover.

'The oddest thing about it, Jane, was that I saw Mr Weaver when he came back to the shop from the police station,' said Susan, as the two of them sat in Miss Marple's sitting room. Susan's hands were a foot apart as she held the skein of wool for Miss Marple to wind. 'And he didn't look happy at all.'

'Oh, that is interesting.' Miss Marple wound the wool so quickly that it seemed to leap from Susan's outstretched hands. 'How did he look?'

Susan thought for a moment. 'Weighed down,' she said. 'If you'd seen him and not known, you'd have guessed he was walking into prison, not away from it.'

Miss Marple didn't slow down. 'Then it is just as I thought,' she said. 'He let himself be arrested because he was protecting someone.'

'His wife?' Susan let her hands drop a little, but the wool snagged and jerked them back up again.

Miss Marple looked at the wool, and looked at the baby's blanket that she had carefully unravelled a second time to eliminate another mistake she had made by trying to knit without enough light. So trying, to drop a stitch right near the beginning, impossible to pick it up without tugging the fabric too tight on either side. She had backed the work as carefully as she could, so that she didn't have to begin the whole thing again.

'I do wonder if that is it,' she said.

'What?' asked Susan.

'I think we've all been looking at weaving when we should have been thinking about unweaving. Even me, who should know better,' Miss Marple replied, absently.

'Unweaving?' said Susan. 'Is that even a word?'

'There is one easy way to confirm it, of course.' The ball of wool in Miss Marple's hands grew as the skein in Susan's hands shrank.

'Confirm what? How?' asked Susan.

'Did you see Martin?' asked Jane.

'Yes, I walked past him and Syme on my way to church that day, before the argument with Mr Weaver.'

'Were you close enough to notice the colour of his eyes?'

'Yes,' said Susan. She screwed up her own in an effort to remember what she had seen. 'Brown,' she said. 'I think they were brown.'

'And Mrs Weaver has blue eyes,' said Miss Marple. 'I noticed them at the school the other day.

'Yes, that's right,' said Susan. 'She wears that lovely crimson dress and it brings out the auburn in her hair.'

'I see,' said Miss Marple. 'Well, that changes everything then, doesn't it?'

'Does it?'

'Yes, dear. I've been so foolish. I've been looking at them the wrong way round.'

'At who? Honestly, Jane, I do pay attention to everything you say, but sometimes you might as well be speaking in another language.'

'I am sorry, Susan, I don't mean to irritate you. But I really have been looking at this puzzle from the wrong perspective. And if I'm right, Mrs Weaver will be arrested before the end of today.'

'No!' said Susan.

'We need to speak to Sergeant Dover,' Miss Marple continued. 'Or he'll make a terrible mistake, and I don't know what might happen after that. Although I suppose it's too late now to save him.'

'Save her,' said Susan.

Miss Marple finished winding the ball and dropped it into her workbox. 'I beg your pardon, dear?' she said.

'Save Mrs Weaver,' Susan repeated.

'Oh,' said Miss Marple. 'I'm not sure she would want to be saved. I think she plans to do exactly what Mr Weaver tried to do.'

'I don't know how you think I can help you,' said Sergeant Dover. He had been the village policeman for many years now, and he was fond of the majority of its residents, even the ones who seemed to take up most of his time. He did wonder if things had become rather more difficult when Miss Marple moved into her cottage at the top of the hill. She was, he admitted, a model citizen: helping out at the church, the school, supporting the local shops and so on. And yet, somehow, her presence made him feel less of a model citizen himself. Which was ridiculous, since he was the police sergeant. But something about the old lady in her neat tweeds and carefully positioned hat, hands resting lightly on the wooden handles of her bag, made him feel as though he was eight years old again, and had been caught stealing sweets.

'Mrs Weaver,' said Susan. 'She's made a terrible mistake.'

'I rather think you're underestimating the seriousness of murder, Mrs Goldingay,' said the sergeant.

'She hasn't committed murder, sergeant.' Susan was beginning to find him rather irritating. 'That's what we've been trying to tell you.'

'She has confessed to murder.' Sergeant Dover placed his elbows on his desk and clasped his hands. 'As a general rule, that means someone has committed murder.'

'Ah, but, you see, she has committed a sort of murder,' said Miss Marple. 'But not the kind she could be arrested for.'

The policeman sighed and turned his attention fully to the white-haired old lady, who seemed so patient and never gave in. 'What kind of murder would that be, then, Miss Marple?'

'Well, it's rather difficult to give it a name, isn't it?' said Miss Marple. 'I suppose she helped to murder her husband, in a way. But only because she believed he was already dead.'

'Her husband is very much alive, Miss Marple,' Sergeant Dover sighed. 'He was in my cells until two days ago.'

'No, Sergeant, I'm afraid you're mistaken. He was found dead in the street with an arrow in his chest,' Miss Marple replied.

'Miss Marple,' said the policeman, 'I think you must be confused. Mr Weaver is at home in their flat above the haberdashery shop. Mrs Weaver has confessed to murdering the stranger, Martin.'

'Well, of course she has,' said Miss Marple. 'But she didn't kill Martin, and he wasn't a stranger.'

'I'm tempted to call them both to the police station to explain things to you slowly,' he said.

'Oh, but I don't think they would want to,' said Miss Marple. 'Their lives together have been built on a lie, so I doubt the truth would come easily to them now.'

'I have a dead body that has been identified as Mr Martin,' said the policeman. 'And a murderer who has made her confession.'

'What reason did she give for killing him?' asked Susan.

'She didn't have to give a reason,' said the policeman. 'She admitted to it. She admitted to shooting him. She even confessed to breaking off the arrow.'

'But she didn't give a reason, of course,' said Miss Marple.

The policeman narrowed his eyes. 'She did not,' he said.

'A decent lawyer will see her leave the court a free woman,' said Susan. 'Which she should, because she's not guilty.'

Sergeant Dover thought for a moment, and relented. 'We're visiting Mr Weaver this afternoon,' he said. 'To collect some necessities for Mrs Weaver. If you choose to visit the haberdashery at four o'clock, you can put your questions to them yourselves.'

'I think half past four would be preferable,' said Miss Marple. 'If you want the murderer to attend as well.'

The policeman began to laugh. 'Does he have something else to do first?' he asked.

'Yes,' said Miss Marple. 'And he won't be able to leave until four o'clock.'

The church bell chimed twice for the half hour as Miss Marple and Susan climbed the steps to the haberdashery shop. Inside, they found Mr and Mrs Weaver, standing awkwardly behind the counter as Sergeant Dover and Constable Jebb looked on. Mrs Weaver's hair was tied back simply, and she looked younger than she had in years.

'Good afternoon,' said Susan, brightly. 'We wondered if you might answer a few questions?'

'I don't know what you want,' said Mrs Weaver. 'Or what you hope to achieve.'

'I think the truth might be useful, don't you?' said Miss Marple.

'Why do you think I'm not telling the truth?' she replied.

'Because we don't think you're a murderer,' said Susan. 'And Jane knows who did it.'

Mrs Weaver looked rather pale, and held on to the ladder she used to reach the higher shelves. 'I killed him,' she said. 'I'll plead guilty.'

Miss Marple shook her head sadly. 'That won't save him,' she said. 'He won't let you take the blame for what he did. You know that he'll be here any moment to confess.'

Tears sprang from Mrs Weaver's eyes, and her husband moved to comfort her.

'Who's confessing now?' asked Constable Jebb. The sergeant shook his head.

And then the door behind them swung open, and Eric Weaver burst into the shop.

'But how did you know, Jane?' asked Susan, as they sat together in the tea rooms, restoring their equanimity with sandwiches and scones.

'Well, because he couldn't be Mr Weaver's son, of course,' said Miss Marple. 'I mean, the new Mr Weaver. I suppose we'll never know what his real name is.'

'How do you mean?' Susan poured tea into both cups, frowning at its colour as she did so.

'Eric Weaver has brown eyes,' Miss Marple explained. 'Mr Weaver – the new Mr Weaver – has blue eyes.'

'Do you mean Mrs Weaver . . . ?' Susan looked appalled and couldn't finish the question.

'I mean the Mr Weaver who came back from the war wasn't the same man as the one who went away to fight in it,' said Miss Marple, firmly. 'I imagine they were comrades. Mr Weaver has confessed as much to Sergeant Dover. He saw the first Mr Weaver injured and then captured. In North Africa, I believe, near the end of the war. It never occurred to him the man might have survived. Meanwhile, Mrs Weaver received notice that her husband was missing in action and obviously feared the worst.'

'So the man who came back to the village as Mr Weaver wasn't him at all?' Susan asked. 'But she must have known!'

'Perhaps,' said Miss Marple. 'But we expect men to change during a war, don't we?'

'You said it yourself, Jane: his eyes were a different colour!'

'Yes. But if you were Mrs Weaver, running a business, bringing up a boy on your own for all those years, do you think you would have asked that question?' Miss Marple's eyes glittered. 'Or might you have simply accepted that a man was standing before you, claiming to be your husband and offering to share the work?'

Susan looked uncertain. 'I suppose I can just about imagine that,' she said.

'The man who had left her wasn't ever coming back,' said Miss Marple. 'Or so she thought.'

'And so Mr Martin, Syme's new farmhand, was the original Mr Weaver?' Susan asked. 'But where had he been all this time?'

Miss Marple shook her head. 'I don't suppose anyone will ever know that,' she said. 'Whatever he went through must have been truly terrible, for him to come back changed beyond recognition.'

'Yes,' said Susan. 'Although the new Mr Weaver recognised him, didn't he? That's why they had the fight in the square.'

'I think so,' said Miss Marple. 'Recognised him or at least recognised something about him. Perhaps his conscience did the rest.'

'And Eric Weaver recognised him too?' Susan asked.

'I wonder,' Miss Marple said. 'He was just a baby when his father went away. And I don't think he ever questioned that it was his father who had returned. Would he even remember what his real father looked like?'

'But if he didn't, then why did he . . . ?'

'I think he saw the fight and drew his own conclusions,' said Miss Marple. 'Eric is an educated man, and he would know a blue-eyed father and mother would be very unlikely to have a brown-eyed son. I think he believed his mother had had an affair with a stranger and that the stranger had returned – after many years – to throw his family into chaos. That's why he shot him.'

Susan placed her hands over her mouth. 'No,' she whispered. 'He killed his own father without knowing? That's too awful.'

'Mrs Weaver took the arrow, of course, when he panicked and told her what he'd done. She was worried there would be fingerprints on it and didn't know what else to do. Mr Weaver agreed to be arrested, and they hoped to have the case dismissed through lack of evidence. But when the witnesses came forward to say he couldn't possibly have committed the crime, they had to come up with another plan, and quickly.'

'Which was Mrs Weaver taking the blame?'

'Exactly.'

'But Eric wouldn't have let his mother hang, surely?'

'No,' said Miss Marple. 'I don't believe he could have. They were hoping the case would fail in court.'

'I almost wish we hadn't interfered, Jane.'

Miss Marple nodded. 'I understand, dear. But a man cannot kill his father and go unpunished. Not when that father has done nothing wrong except to be unfortunate.'

'How did you work it all out?' asked Susan.

'It was the unravelling,' said Miss Marple. 'It reminded

me of Penelope undoing her funeral shroud every night for years, because she believed her husband would come back to her.'

'Does anything ever surprise you?' Susan smiled.

Miss Marple shook her head. 'Not yet,' she said.

Miss Marple's Christmas

Ruth Ware

'So, *dear* Aunt Jane . . .' Raymond West's voice came over the telephone wire with more than his usual dose of cajoling charm. 'What do you think? A real old fashioned St Mary Mead Christmas?'

Miss Marple suppressed a wistful little sigh. What she was thinking was that no modern Christmas could possibly live up to the Christmases of her youth, and certainly not one spent crammed into her little cottage with Raymond and his wife. Christmas, in Miss Marple's childhood, had been an affair of blazing log fires, stockings full of sweets, nuts and trinkets, crackling chestnuts, and a Christmas dinner to rival that of Henry VIII's court, with sirloin, ham and turkey, potatoes both roast and boiled, and not one but two helpings of Christmas pudding.

The rambling country house had been full of children her own age, as well as a plethora of aunts, uncles and assorted relations all now sadly departed, and they had played the kind of games modern parents frowned upon as far too dangerous.

Snapdragon had been her own favourite, which had involved snatching burning raisins from a flaming dish of brandy – great fun and accompanied by many shrieks and scalded fingers, she remembered, and very difficult it was for the poor maids to remove the burns from the nursery rug.

Christmas with Raymond and Joan would no doubt be very pleasant, and would probably involve a good deal of listening to music on the wireless, playing bridge with the Bantrys, and a great many cocktails, but a real old fashioned Christmas it very much would not be.

'Of course we can go to an hotel if it's any trouble,' Raymond added. 'I hear the Savoy does a very creditable Christmas spread. But Joan's rather against the idea – and I thought perhaps you'd like the company?'

'Oh, I shouldn't dream of letting you do such a thing,' Miss Marple said, a little shocked at the suggestion. 'Hotels are all very well in their way, Raymond dear, but Joan is quite right – *not* for Christmas. And think of the expense. No, I should be delighted to have you and Joan to stay while your plumbing is put right. But I must warn you, it will be very quiet.'

'Peace and quiet is just what the doctor ordered,' Raymond said cheerfully. 'I've got my novel to finish, and Joan – well, Joan's been a bit pulled down recently, so a dose of the old St Mary Mead pond water will be just the ticket for her. Walks in the country, plenty of fresh air – that sort of thing. If you're quite sure, we'll see you on the 22nd.'

'I shall look forward to it,' Miss Marple said, truthfully.

*

'So that makes seven now,' Mrs Bantry said to her husband, putting down the telephone receiver and counting on her fingers. 'No, six. No – I was right the first time. It *is* seven. Nine, including you and me.'

'What's that? Seven? Seven what?' Colonel Bantry's voice emerged from behind the morning paper.

'Seven guests, for Christmas dinner. I shall have to tell Cook to order a larger turkey. Or do you think two small ones would be safer in case the range is playing up again?'

'Seven?' Her husband folded the paper and stared at her, nonplussed. 'What d'you mean, Dolly? You've invited seven people for Christmas? What possessed you?'

'Arthur, how many more times? We've discussed this. You invited those friends of yours the Dashwoods to stay when you went grouse shooting with Major Dashwood, don't you remember?'

'Hardly friends,' the Colonel said, a little grumpily. His wife continued as if he hadn't spoken.

'And then *they* asked if they could bring their nephew, Ronald. And I invited Jane Marple, and now *her* nephew and his wife are staying with her over Christmas because of their drains, or perhaps it's their electricity, I can't quite remember, so I've had to invite them too.'

'Oh dash it, Dolly. Not that West chap, the one who writes those frightful books?'

'Yes, and you're to be *polite* to him, Arthur. I don't see how you'd know whether they were frightful or not, you never read novels anyway.'

'Well, I still don't see how that makes seven. That's only six.'

'Sir Henry Clithering.'

'Oh.' Colonel Bantry was mollified. He liked Sir Henry – the former commissioner of Scotland Yard was a man after his own heart; traditional, fond of his after-dinner pipe, and not too talkative. 'Oh yes, I'd forgotten that. Well, he's all right, but do we really have to put up with all the rest of 'em in the house?'

'They won't be *in* the house, Arthur, not all of them anyway. Raymond and Mrs West will be staying at Miss Marple's cottage – they're only coming here for Christmas Day. And the Dashwoods are nobody's fault but your own. *I* didn't invite them.'

'Well, the rum thing is,' Colonel Bantry said ruminatively, 'I don't quite know what possessed me. I certainly didn't *mean* to invite them, if you know what I mean. But Major Dashwood was so dashed friendly, and somehow the subject came up and I found I'd extended the old hand of hospitality, don't you know.'

'No, I *don't* know, Arthur, I wasn't there. All I know is that you telephoned in a great panic saying had we room for two more at Christmas, and here we are. And now,' Mrs Bantry stood, smoothing down her skirt, 'I had better go and break the news to Cook. I only hope we're in time to speak to Footit about putting in an order for another turkey.'

'I can't tell you what a treat this is, Mrs Bantry,' Joan West said again. She stirred her cocktail and gazed admiringly around the drawing room at Gossington Hall, from the blazing fire in the hearth to the massed holly and ivy trailing across the mantlepiece. 'A real old-fashioned Christmas. And such a lovely tree.'

'Collins has outdone himself this year,' Mrs Bantry said. She put her sewing basket aside and looked with satisfaction at the tall Norwegian Spruce standing in the corner of the drawing room. 'He's our gardener, you know – although these days he's more of a director of operations. We've had to hire a new under-gardener, Bertie Finch, as poor Collins can't manage the heavy digging any more. Bertie's a little—' She stopped, caught Miss Marple's eye, and coughed, then said, 'Well, in any case beggars can't be choosers and I must say we've had no complaints with his work. And it is *so* difficult to get staff these days, and we do have a *lot* of garden.'

Joan followed her gaze out of the drawing-room window, across the admittedly expansive lawns. 'Oh! It's snowing again! How perfect.'

White flakes had begun to fall on to the thick blanket of unbroken snow already covering the sculpted yew trees and hessianed rose trees of the terrace.

'A white Christmas,' Raymond said with a wry smile. 'Quite the picture postcard cliché.'

'Yes, dear, most picturesque,' Miss Marple agreed placidly. She was sitting in a tall armchair beside the fire, very much the Victorian old lady with her lace cap and gloves, and she was knitting something snowy and white that frothed over her lap. 'Although very inconvenient for the car drivers, or so I have always heard.'

'Blasted inconvenient for everyone,' Major Dashwood put in. 'Heard on the wireless that the train line from London is blocked. Seems like we were bally lucky to get through before the snow started.'

'I do hope we won't be trapped, Carlton,' the lady opposite said, her blue eyes widening. Mrs Dashwood was a pretty, rather vacant-looking woman in her early thirties, with a face that was both mobile and yet strangely devoid of emotion. Her eyes, now, were open as wide as they could go, rather in the manner of a china doll, but the expression in them seemed to Joan like a sort of pantomime alarm.

'Don't you worry, Esmé, m'dear,' her husband assured her, patting her arm. 'We've no reason to hurry back to London, and Arthur and Dolly won't throw you out into the snow, ha ha!'

'What's that?' Colonel Bantry said, looking up from where he was cleaning out his pipe into the fire. 'Throw you out into the snow? I should think not, no question of such a thing.'

'Arthur!' Mrs Bantry's voice cut into the conversation from the centre of the room, where she was standing under a huge bunch of mistletoe suspended from the chandelier. 'I have been standing under this mistletoe for quite ten minutes waiting for you to notice me.'

'Well, we can't have that!' Major Dashwood said, putting down his whisky and soda and heaving himself to his feet with a show of gallantry. 'May I, Mrs B?'

Mrs Bantry presented a powdered cheek – rather reluctantly, it seemed to Miss Marple – and Major Dashwood planted a whiskery kiss upon it and then bowed.

'Too late, Bantry, what what!' the Major said with a chuckle, returning to his seat.

'My turn, Raymond,' Joan said. She set down her glass by the big scarlet poinsettia and moved to stand under the arrangement. Her husband smiled and stood up to join her.

'Of course, it's all very pagan,' he remarked, as he kissed his wife's cheek. 'It's a good thing the vicar isn't here – I'm not sure what he'd think of these survivalist vestiges of the old gods. Your pretty little Christmas customs,' he waved a finger at the room, encompassing the Bantrys, Dashwoods and his aunt, 'are very far from Christian, in fact they're something of a druidical wolf in sheep's clothing. The Norse Gods would have recognised all this holly and ivy for what it was – symbols of fertility, plant worship and renewal. Kissing under the mistletoe is the modern, watered-down remnant of what were once some very earthy customs indeed.'

'Ha, steady on now, old chap!' Major Dashwood said with his short barking laugh. 'Let's not shock the women and children, what?'

'I don't think your nephew is listening, Major Dashwood,' Joan said, with a nod to the far side of the room where Ronald sat droopingly over a book. 'He seems far too interested in his book. And speaking for myself, I'm an artist, and I assure you it takes a great deal more than a few Norse Gods to shock *me*.'

'Oh, but you're married, Mrs West,' Mrs Dashwood put in, with a significant glance at Miss Marple. 'And that makes a difference, doesn't it? I doubt dear Miss Marple is used to talk of – what was it? Norse fertility rituals?'

'Oh, well,' Miss Marple murmured, picking up a stitch. 'I wouldn't say – I mean, in a village one is not nearly so protected as outsiders perhaps assume. Fertility . . . birth . . . I can assure you these are hardly matters unknown in St Mary Mead. Only the other day, Mrs Clyde's girl, Dora – but there . . . I mustn't gossip.'

'I rather like the old traditions,' Sir Henry Clithering said from his seat by the fire, with a smile. 'When I was a boy, the tradition in our village was to break off a berry every time one kissed a girl, and when all the berries were gone, so were all the kisses. What do you think, Miss Marple? Shall we?'

He rose and stood beneath the mistletoe, hand outstretched.

Twinkling, the old lady laid aside her knitting and moved to the centre of the room, presenting her pink cheek for Sir Henry's kiss. Sir Henry, for his part, reached up to pluck a berry, but then withdrew quickly, sucking his finger.

'Ouch! I'd forgotten how prickly greenery can be. Well, dash it, the berries will have to stay. But I'll claim the kiss.'

He bent and kissed the old lady's cheek, and Miss Marple gave him a rather mischievous smile.

'Not my first kiss beneath the mistletoe, Sir Henry. It always reminds me of hat pins, you know.'

'Hat pins?' said Sir Henry, rather bewildered. 'I'm afraid you've lost me with the association there, Miss Marple.'

'Oh yes, indeed. Young men used to loiter beneath it at Christmas parties, and if a girl came past that they liked, they would claim a kiss, and *sometimes* they were rather insistent. But my dear mother always used to advise all the young ladies to keep a hat pin in one's bodice. There's nothing like a hat pin to provide a little discouragement to an unwanted suitor. Railway carriages too.'

'Railway carriages?' Colonel Bantry sounded disconcerted. Across the room Raymond shot his wife a look of slight concern. Really, his aunt was becoming more than a little scatty these days.

'Oh yes,' put in Mrs Bantry from her seat at the other side of the room, '*I* remember that quite well. The train would go into a tunnel, and all the lights would go out. And the young men would seize the chance to kiss the girl sitting opposite them, complete strangers sometimes. And if it was a long tunnel, of course, they would sit down before the train exited and then, when the lights came on, you would be glaring at a row of young men, quite unable to tell which of them it had been. But if you kept a hatpin to hand, you could jab them with it, and *that* soon sent them scurrying back to their seat.'

'Dear me, Dolly,' said her husband, looking quite astonished. 'I had no idea you were so very fierce.'

'Well, Arthur, only if one didn't *like* the young man.'

Just then the gong rang out. The drooping young man in the corner raised his head from his book.

'I say, is that dinner ready? I'm starving.'

'It's the dressing gong,' Mrs Bantry said briskly. 'Not that I shall bother.' She picked up her mending again, and smoothed down her rather serviceable dark brown lace dress. Mrs Dashwood, however, rose and left the room murmuring something about powdering her nose.

'I say, Clithering,' Major Dashwood stood and stretched. 'Fancy a spot of billiards before lunch?'

'I don't play, I'm afraid,' Sir Henry said. 'But perhaps Bantry would indulge you in a game and I'll come and keep score?'

'I'll join you for a cigarette,' Raymond West said, and the four men departed for the billiards room, leaving Joan, Miss Marple and Mrs Bantry alone with the listless Ronald.

'I wish he'd put down that book,' Mrs Bantry muttered to the two women, sticking her needle into her mending with a restrained ferocity. 'It's so extremely rude, reading in company. I would have my novel confiscated if I'd behaved like that as a child. Oh blast. I've run out of pins.'

'Yes, dear, but it's an awkward age,' Miss Marple whispered. Then, more loudly, she said, addressing the boy, 'Do tell me about yourself, Ronald. You are staying with your aunt and uncle?'

'Yes,' the young man said. He looked, Miss Marple thought, a little old to be a student, although it was hard to tell with young people these days. His mannerisms, however, were more that of an awkward schoolboy. Now he flushed an unattractive beet purple and fell silent.

With the air of someone valiantly wringing conversation out of a stone, Mrs Bantry remarked, 'Your book seems to be very engrossing. What is it?'

'Detective stories. *Hangman's Holiday*.'

'What a ghastly-sounding title,' Mrs Bantry said, but Miss Marple shook her head.

'Oh no, dear. Miss Sayers, you know. Lord Peter Wimsey is her detective, a very glamorous young man. I read that one myself last year from the circulating library at Much Benham. Her plots are *so* very clever, and full of literary quotations, although I must confess I don't always understand the Latin. Raymond is very kind about translating for me, but I fear he disapproves of crime fiction.'

'Raymond would,' Mrs Bantry said, a little tartly.

'I think it's simply that Raymond is more interested in the *psychology* of the crime than the allocation of blame,' Joan put in. 'So many crime writers concentrate on *who* did it at the expense of *why*. What Freudian inadequacies lie at the root of these criminal urges?'

'I'm sure you're right, Joan dear,' Miss Marple said, her needles clicking placidly. 'But you know, although people are very wicked, I am not sure if there are quite so many *sexual neuroses* involved as Raymond seems to believe. So frequently I find the motives are much more mundane. Money, for example, comes up sadly often.'

At the mention of the word *sexual*, the young man flushed an even darker shade of beetroot, muttered something about washing his hands, and left the room.

'Who *are* the Dashwoods, Dolly?' Miss Marple asked, as the sound of Ronald's footsteps died away up the corridor. Mrs Bantry put down her mending, and poked the fire with rather evident ill-temper.

'Oh, really such *awful* people. I have no idea what Arthur was thinking. It's quite unlike him – he's the most unsociable person usually. Well, I mean not with people like *you,* and Sir Henry. People that he likes, I mean. But with people he doesn't really know, he's normally positively antisocial. And then he goes and invites the Dashwoods! *He's* Coleton or Carlton or something – a retired major, and a brother of Lord Archibald Dashwood. Or maybe a cousin. I can't quite remember, they're such a big family. And she's – well, I think she used to be some kind of actress. Her name is Esmé, if you please. And as for their nephew, he's been absolutely tiresome ever since he arrived. Wouldn't even come to church this morning. On Christmas Day, for goodness sake! I thought Arthur was going to threaten him with a horsewhip.'

'He's probably bored,' Joan said, thoughtlessly, and then flushed, perceiving her faux pas. 'I mean, for us it's different, of course! But you know, at that age . . .'

'Of course he's bored,' Mrs Bantry snapped. 'Any boy his age would be bored, cooped up in the country with a lot of middle-aged people. But that's hardly my fault, or Arthur's. From what I understand, he's been packed off with his aunt and uncle as some kind of punishment for being sent down from Oxford. Gambling or something. Result, they don't want him here, and he certainly doesn't want to *be* here. And the trouble with young people today is that they don't hesitate to show that. No consideration for Arthur or me. Just sits around with his arms folded giving monosyllabic answers to questions. I'm afraid I've put him next to Raymond at dinner. I thought he might be able to get something out of the boy.'

'Oh Dolly, do you think that was wise?' Miss Marple asked. 'Raymond is a dear boy, but he can be – forgive me, Joan dear – but, well, just a touch cynical at times. And children that age are so very susceptible to influence.'

Joan laughed.

'Well, I'm beyond caring,' Mrs Bantry said with finality. 'I've put up with him for long enough, and so has Arthur. As far as I'm concerned, Raymond is welcome to him and perhaps he can turn him into a character in one of his novels. He likes unpleasant people, doesn't he?'

'Dear Raymond—' began Miss Marple, but her remark was cut short by a piercing shriek from upstairs.

'What was that?' Joan said, frowning.

'Oh, probably that awful Dashwood woman's seen a mouse,' Mrs Bantry said. 'I told Lorrimer only the other day we needed to set some traps on the upper landing.'

'Oh, Carlton!' The cry came again, this time unmistakeably the voice of Mrs Dashwood. 'Carlton, come quick! They're *gone*!'

The three women turned to each other, and then, with one accord, rose and moved out into the hallway, where Mrs Dashwood was standing at the foot of the staircase, holding a green morocco case and remonstrating with her husband.

'Carlton, they're *gone*.'

'Gone? What d'mean *gone*, Esmé? What's gone?'

'My pearls! I put them in here last night, but then I thought it would be nice to wear them for Christmas dinner. And now—' A sob rose in her voice. 'Now they're *gone*.'

'Arthur!' Mrs Bantry said, her voice filled with alarm as she turned to her husband. 'Arthur, what is going on? Have we been burgled?'

'Burgled? Impossible,' Colonel Bantry expostulated. 'Don't believe a word of it.'

'My dear Mrs Dashwood,' Sir Henry Clithering's manner was soothing. 'Please don't distress yourself. I'm sure there's a perfectly reasonable explanation. Perhaps the pearls have fallen out into a drawer, or you didn't put them away as you thought?'

'If you're calling my wife a liar—' Major Dashwood said stiffly. Sir Henry looked taken aback.

'Not for a moment, Major. But it seems to me far more probable that this is all an unfortunate misunderstanding. Mrs Bantry,' he turned to his hostess, 'will you summon the housemaid and I'm sure we can have this sorted out.'

'Yes, yes, of course,' Mrs Bantry replied distractedly. 'Perhaps— oh dear. Why don't you all go back to the drawing room and I'll ring for Mary.'

The little group filed away and Mrs Bantry turned despairingly to her friend.

'You see, Jane? Didn't I tell you the Dashwoods were insufferable. And right before Christmas dinner too. Cook will be *so* upset and it's so difficult to keep sirloin *warm*, you know.'

Some ten minutes later, Lorrimer, the butler, accompanied by a red-eyed but composed Mary, the housemaid, were standing in the corner of the drawing room, Lorrimer drawn up to every inch of his impressive height and radiating an aura of stiff correctness.

'I have spoken to Mary and she is quite certain, ma'am, that she never touched the green case, nor saw any pearls when she was putting the room to rights this morning. However, if you will give me leave, perhaps a search of Mrs Dashwood's room would be in order?'

'I tell you, the necklace isn't *there*,' wailed Mrs Dashwood, from her reclining position on the chaise longue in the corner. She was holding a glass of brandy and looked quite distraught.

'I've searched and searched. Do you think I didn't search? I'm not a complete fool, you know!'

'Of course they have to check, Esmé,' her husband said gruffly. 'Only thing to be done. The question is, who's to do it?'

'I think,' Sir Henry put in, gently, 'that we should entrust the search to Lorrimer and Mary, but that it would be as well for one of the Bantrys and one of the Dashwoods to be present.'

'Excellent idea,' said Colonel Bantry. His expression was grim. 'Shall we, Dashwood? And I'd like you to come too, Clithering. Third party. Disinterested and all that.'

Sir Henry nodded, and the three men stood up and followed Lorrimer and the housemaid up the stairs.

'Well, I *say*,' Raymond West drawled, as silence fell on the drawing room. 'This is a turn up for the books. I can see the morning papers: "Christmas Jewel Heist in Sleepy St Mary Mead!"'

'Heist!' moaned Mrs Dashwood from the corner of the sofa. 'Oh, don't even say such a thing! The pearls belonged to Carlton's mother, you know – they're priceless, quite priceless. At least three thousand pounds. Probably five! If they're gone— well, I simply don't know how I'll bear it.'

Raymond let out a little whistle and shook his head.

'Insured?'

'Heavens, how should I know! Carlton takes care of all that – but even if they are, these companies always find some way of wriggling out of paying up!'

'Oh dear, oh dear,' Miss Marple put aside her knitting with an expression of concern. 'I know quite well what you mean, Mrs Dashwood. Mr Blair, that clever young solicitor in Much Benham, had his motorcycle stolen three times in two years, and the last time the insurance company declined to pay out, you know. He made quite a fuss about it. But then it turned out that his friend had borrowed it and parked it in the wrong garage, so it was all to the good in the end, as I do understand the insurers are very strict about fraudulent claims and, indeed, he might have found himself in a very difficult situation had the claim actually gone through. In fact, *some* people thought the friend— but there. I mustn't gossip.'

Mrs Dashwood turned a tear-stained face to Miss Marple.

'Why on earth are you going on about motorcycles? I haven't lost a motorcycle! And I highly doubt my pearls are going to turn up in somebody's garage.'

'No, no, indeed,' Miss Marple murmured apologetically. 'I'm so sorry, I'm afraid my mind was wandering. You're quite right, Mrs Dashwood. Most distressing.'

'Come now, let's not write the pearls off just yet,' Joan said, comfortingly. 'There's every chance they've just slipped into a drawer.'

But when Sir Henry Clithering returned to the drawing room some twenty minutes later, it was with a grave face, and he shook his head slightly in reply to Raymond West's interrogatively raised eyebrow.

Mrs Bantry stood at the sight of him, with the air of someone who has reached the end of their tether.

'I must go and speak to Cook, she'll be simply beside herself. Jane, will you come?'

Miss Marple nodded and, setting aside the fleecy white

wool, she followed her old friend down the hallway. She did not say anything for the first few minutes, but as they turned the corner to the library she ventured to speak.

'Surely, Dolly dear, the kitchen is in the opposite direction?'

'I know that perfectly well,' Mrs Bantry said frankly, opening the library door and sinking into a leather armchair with a martyred expression. 'I simply had to get out of that drawing room. I couldn't listen to that blasted woman sighing and groaning for another minute. Oh Jane, it's too bad. And on Christmas Day! Arthur was looking forward to his sirloin *so* much – and there's simply nothing worse than dry turkey.'

'I suppose she *was* wearing the pearls last night?' Miss Marple asked. 'I mean to say – it's not possible that they were left at home or mislaid on the journey down here?'

'Yes, she was wearing the things,' Mrs Bantry said crossly. 'In fact, she never stopped going on about them. Made quite a to-do about the value. Arthur said afterwards it very nearly put him off his soup. Rather vulgar, I call it. It's hardly surprising they've been pinched if she goes about boasting how much they cost. It's probably that sulky nephew of hers. Or his. Whichever he is.'

'So you *do* think they've been stolen?' Miss Marple enquired. Mrs Bantry threw up her hands.

'Heaven knows! But if they don't turn up, I don't see what other explanation there is. I utterly refuse to believe Mary has anything to do with it, though! Or any of the staff, in fact. They've been with us for years. But if they aren't found, there will always be that nasty, nagging suspicion. Oh Jane, I could strangle the woman, I really could.'

'Strangle who?' said a deep voice from the doorway, and Mrs Bantry turned with a guilty jump, laying a hand on her breast.

'Arthur! How could you give me such a fright? I quite thought you were one of the Dashwoods. How are things? Any sign of the necklace?'

'Not a bit of it,' her husband replied lugubriously. 'Mary and Lorrimer have been through the Dashwoods' room with a fine-tooth comb, and now they're starting on the servants' rooms. It's dashed difficult, Dolly, I don't mind telling you. I came down to telephone for Constable Palk in the village. Nothing else to be done at this point.'

'Oh Arthur, must we? If we get the police involved . . .'

'Nothing else for it, m'dear.' Colonel Bantry's expression was grimly resigned. 'Mrs Dashwood is quite adamant they've been taken, and probably sometime this morning, either while everyone was at church, or while we were all having drinks. She put them away in her jewel case last night before she went to bed, and she's quite certain no one could have come into her room overnight. And she breakfasted in her room too, which gives a window of about 10 o'clock onwards. Clithering is questioning Collins as to whether he saw anyone sneaking about the grounds, but I think it's a long shot.'

'Oh dear,' Mrs Bantry said distractedly. 'Then I suppose there's no alternative to ringing up Palk. But the turkey will be dry as a bone by the time *he's* finished.'

Alas, Mrs Bantry's worst fears came about. It was almost three o'clock by the time Police Constable Palk struggled through the snow to Gossington Hall, and later still when he finished interviewing the Bantrys' servants and turned his attention to the guests. Rather than the sumptuous Christmas repast they had been expecting, the little group in the drawing room dined on cold roast beef sandwiches and hot tea. Very good in their own way, as Raymond pointed out, but *not* quite the same as a full spread of sirloin and turkey, with wine, pudding, cheese, and port to follow.

Mrs Dashwood had retired to bed with a sick headache after her own interview with Palk, and Colonel Bantry was to be seen pacing the snowy terrace with his pipe clenched between his teeth and a face like thunder, when Palk entered the drawing room and said, 'Miss Marple, if I may?'

Miss Marple nodded composedly, folded her knitting, and followed the constable down the corridor to Colonel Bantry's study, where the interviews were taking place.

Sir Henry Clithering was seated in an armchair in the corner, and raised one eyebrow, rather amused, as the old lady entered and sat, very upright, in the straight-backed chair in the centre of the room.

'Detective Inspector Slack wasn't able to make it through the snow,' he explained, as Miss Marple arranged her knitting composedly across her lap and folded her hands. 'The road from Much Benham is completely blocked. So Palk here invited me to sit in on the interviews. I presume you don't mind, Miss Marple?'

'Oh dear me, no. No indeed. Two heads are better than one, as my dear mother always used to say.'

'Or even three?' Sir Henry said, with a little smile. 'Do today's events remind you of anything, Miss Marple?'

'Oh dear.' Miss Marple became at once a little flustered. 'Well, yes and no. But it's so difficult to be *sure*, you know, and I don't quite like to *say* anything. I suppose they found a window open?'

Sir Henry's other eyebrow rose at that, but he gave a nod.

'As a matter of fact, yes. The one in the little boot room by the back door. But what made you say that?'

'Well, of course there would *have* to be a window open – to give an opportunity. I suppose it was forced?'

'Yes,' Sir Henry said dryly. 'And not very expertly. Looks like some kind of trowel was used. Together with the snow, which effectively rules out any outside intervention, I'm very much afraid this looks like some kind of inside job – but searching for the pearls in a house of this size is proving to be something akin to looking for a needle in a haystack – to say nothing of the grounds.'

'Oh dear, yes, I know *quite* what you mean. And the grounds, so very difficult. There were no visitors at all?'

Sir Henry shook his head.

'None. Lorrimer was quite clear on that. And we would have seen the tracks, you know, coming back from church. No, much as I would like to believe in an outside agent, I'm afraid there's no help on that score.'

'Oh dear, that poor young man. It is so *very* difficult to shake off a past. And that can lead one to make, well, *foolish* decisions.'

'Poor young man?' said Sir Henry, frowning.

'Can I ask where you were between the hours of ten a.m. and half past noon, Miss Marple?' put in Constable Palk, evidently doggedly determined to stick to his brief of obtaining a statement from everyone present. 'I'm sorry to ask, but it's purely routine, as I'm sure you understand.'

'Oh, but of course,' Miss Marple said earnestly. 'I do *quite* understand. And I can tell you quite well, I was in church, along with the Bantrys, Joan, Raymond and the Dashwoods. At least, the two older Dashwoods. The nephew, I think, was *not* there.'

'No, he stayed here,' Sir Henry said. 'And I don't mind telling you, Miss Marple, we're looking into his background. He was sent down from Oxford for running up some quite considerable gambling debts.'

It was at that moment that the door to the study opened and Mrs Bantry came in.

'If you'll excuse me, ma'am,' Palk began, stiffly, but Mrs Bantry cut him off.

'Oh, don't give me that, Palk. How could you upset Collins? I don't know what you said to him, but he's very much put out, and Bertie Finch, the under-gardener, is threatening to give notice. It's too bad, it really is.'

'My dear Mrs Bantry,' Sir Henry said, 'Constable Palk is only doing his job. If Finch has nothing to hide, then he has nothing to fear.'

'Poppycock!' Mrs Bantry said, turning on him angrily. 'You know as well as I do how gossip gets around in a place like this. Collins says that Palk as good as accused Finch of forcing the boot-room window with a trowel. He says he found chips of paint on one in the potting shed.'

'I have reason to believe that young man may not be all he says he is,' Constable Palk said, with a touch of pomposity. 'You might do better to take up references next time, Mrs Bantry.'

'I know quite well who he is!' Mrs Bantry snapped. 'He's the nephew of the baker in Market Basing and he went to prison for petty theft for two months. That's why we were able to get him for a post no one else wanted, and a very good under-gardener he has been!'

'A very good under-gardener, but a rather foolish young man,' murmured Sir Henry Clithering, tapping his empty pipe on the table and looking thoughtfully at Miss Marple. 'Isn't that right, Miss Marple?'

'Oh dear, oh dear.' Miss Marple said, with a worried sigh. 'So *much* foolishness in the world, and so very difficult for a young man trying to make his way. Dolly, if you will forgive me, I need to speak to Constable Palk and Sir Henry Clithering for just a moment. And then I will join you in the drawing room. I think we all need a spot of hot tea.'

'You'd better all stay the night, Jane,' Mrs Bantry said resignedly, over the promised tea. 'It's much too dark out, and Arthur says the road to the village is quite blocked.'

'Oh, thank you, Dolly. I am sorry to put you out, but I do think it would be for the best. Dear Raymond was talking about walking, but I don't think he's quite used to our country lanes, and as for Joan—'

'As for Joan?' said an inquiring voice from behind them, and Miss Marple turned to see her nephew and his wife standing behind them. Joan laughed. 'I'm sorry, Aunt Jane, I didn't mean to eavesdrop, but I couldn't help overhearing my name. Are we quite snowed in then?'

'I'm afraid so,' Mrs Bantry said. 'Even Palk hasn't been able to get back – he's bedding down in the empty room above the scullery. I've asked Mary to make up the blue room for you and your husband, Mrs West. Jane, I've put you in the room over the porch. I dare say you'll all be horridly uncomfortable, but it can't be helped – Mary's usually so efficient, but she's been quite put out by all of this business, and the second housemaid, Dorcas, has gone to bed with hysterics. Hysterics, I ask you! When I was a girl, housemaids didn't have hysterics.'

'Yes, indeed, Dolly,' said Miss Marple gently, 'but, you know, Bertie Finch is her young man, so it's understandable she would be very much upset by the whole affair.'

'She's not the only one.' A gruff voice came from over Miss Marple's shoulder, and the little group turned to see Colonel Bantry standing behind them, with a very grim expression on his face. 'Absolutely damnable business.'

'Oh Arthur, they haven't arrested him, have they?'

'Taken for questioning, but I think it's only a matter of time until he's charged. Looks pretty bad for the boy. The pearls are nowhere to be found, but Palk found a piece of the clasp in the flowerbed outside the boot-room window. And the worst of it is that Dashwood has been on to his insurance company and it looks like the blasted things weren't insured properly – the policy ran out last month.'

'Oh Arthur, no!' Mrs Bantry's face was a picture of horror as she put down her teacup. 'So what does that mean?'

'Mean? Means I'll have to pay for the blo— I mean the blasted things. Can hardly refuse to, considering it seems to have been one of *my* servants who took the pearls. I'm going to have a word with Barlett and Mundy when they reopen, see if we can claim on our policy perhaps, but I'm not hopeful, Dolly, not hopeful at all.'

'How much were they worth?' Mrs Bantry asked.

'Between three and five thousand pounds,' Colonel Bantry replied, in a voice of deep disgust. Raymond West gave a whistle.

'I say! So La Dashwood wasn't exaggerating. That's a pretty cool sum. I can't see your insurers being too happy, Colonel.'

'Nor I,' Colonel Bantry said gloomily.

'Oh dear.' Miss Marple's expression was one of deep distress. 'Oh dear, that poor young man. So *very* foolish. And so difficult to know what to do for the best.'

'What on earth d'you mean, Miss Marple?' Colonel Bantry said, his voice gruff. 'Nothing to be done apart from take his medicine.'

It was five minutes past two in the morning, and gentle snores were coming from the bedrooms all along the east corridor when a stealthy footstep might have been heard on the staircase at Gossington Hall. Softly, very softly, someone was coming down the long flight of stairs in stockinged feet, and padding quietly along the corridor to the drawing room, where a low fire still burned in the grate, sending the shadow of the tiptoeing figure lurching across the hearth rug to the corners of the room.

Softer still, the figure picked up one of the upright chairs from beside the fire and placed it gently in the centre of the room, beneath the huge bouquet of mistletoe that hung from the chandelier. With a slight grunt, the figure climbed up on to the chair, and reached up – only for a voice to speak from the deep shadows beside the fireplace.

'Oh, do be careful, Mrs Dashwood. Those pins are really very sharp.'

The woman standing on the chair gave a little scream and staggered to the ground, peering into the shadows with her hand over her heart.

'Oh! Miss— Miss Marple, isn't it? You gave me a simply frightful shock. What in heaven's name are you doing here? And why on earth are you talking about pins?'

'The pins in the mistletoe,' said the old lady earnestly. 'I should be very careful if I were you. Sir Henry pricked his finger quite nastily.'

'I have no idea what you're talking about,' Mrs Dashwood said, rather flustered. 'I— I had asked that poor under-gardener for some mistletoe – we live in London, you know, and it's rather difficult to find, so I thought I'd try to start some of our own on the apple tree in our garden. Only then, with everything that happened – and I didn't like to bother the Bantrys, considering everything – so I thought I'd just slip down and help myself.'

'I don't think that's quite true,' said Miss Marple gently. 'I think, you know, you have come for the pearls. It's why I waited. I couldn't be *sure* who would come for them.'

The woman standing in the centre of the room said nothing, but her face and demeanour changed with a suddenness that was almost bewildering. Her hand dropped from her heart to her side, and the foolish, rather vacant expression had vanished, replaced by a kind of hard cunning. She looked at Miss Marple rather appraisingly, as if sizing up the old lady's strength and constitution.

'I shouldn't, you know,' said Miss Marple, with equanimity. 'I am a good deal tougher than I look, and I chose this chair because it was *very* close to the servants' bell. I have my finger on it now.'

'And who's to say *I* didn't ring it after you wandered down in the night and had a bad turn?' said the woman standing in front of her, her voice hard and cold.

'I am,' said a voice from behind her. The woman whipped round, and the lights came on. Constable Palk was standing in the doorway, his expression very grim. 'Put that pin cushion down, Mrs Dashwood. You're under arrest.'

'So their name wasn't Dashwood at all?' said Colonel Bantry, rather astonished, over eggs and bacon the next morning. Miss Marple shook her head.

'No. But it's so very easy to take a name like Dashwood, someone with a large sprawling family, and claim to be a distant relation.'

'But I don't understand,' Mrs Bantry said plaintively. 'The pearls were real. They had a certificate of authenticity and everything.'

'Oh yes, *quite* real, that was why it was quite imperative that she got them back.'

'And what put you on to the Dashwoods?' said Sir Henry, mystified.

'Well, dear Sir Henry, it was really you,' Miss Marple said, with a twinkle. 'Or rather your remark about the prickly greenery. Because, you know, mistletoe doesn't *have* prickles. And that made me wonder.'

'But the pearls hadn't even gone missing then,' Raymond West said.

'No, indeed. And that was all part of their plan. They displayed the pearls as prominently as possible at dinner the night before, and then the next day they disappeared off to church, leaving that poor foolish boy in charge of what I believe thieves call *the handover*. I don't know what they told him. I dare say the police will get to the bottom of it. But of course he was very badly off, having run up considerable gambling debts and young men will do *very* foolish things for money.'

'Ah, the handover,' Raymond West said. 'And here we come to Bertie Finch, I presume?'

'No, dear. Not Bertie. The problem was, the snow made everything so very difficult. I don't know *when* Ronald discovered that the accomplice wasn't coming – the news of the road closures were on the wireless – but he must have had a very nasty moment when he realised the plan had failed and he could not get the pearls out of the house. Of course the sensible thing would have been to simply call the whole thing off, and somehow intercept his aunt before she could raise a hue and cry. But I think he panicked. And put together with the book he was reading . . .'

'So the original plan was to hand the pearls over to an accomplice?' Mrs Bantry asked. 'And make it look like a break in?'

'Yes. *That* was why the nephew had to remain at home. Then, on return from church, Mrs Dashwood would raise the alarm and insist on a very thorough search of their belongings, so as to make it *quite* clear that the pearls were not in the possession of the Dashwoods. I think, you know, Sir Henry, you will find that they have done this before. But there is a very great difference between staging a robbery in a place like London, with many people coming and going at all hours, and St Mary Mead, where every visitor is remarked upon.'

'Well, I have to hand it to him,' Raymond West said, magnanimously. 'He may have panicked, but that was a pretty clever idea about the mistletoe. I wonder how he came up with it?'

'Well, my dear,' Miss Marple said, colouring a little. 'I don't know whether it really *was* his idea, you know.'

'Not his idea?' Raymond looked puzzled. 'Whose idea was it then?'

'Dorothy L. Sayers,' Miss Marple said simply. There was a moment's puzzled pause and then Mrs Bantry spoke.

'The author? That's what the boy was reading, wasn't it?

'High-society crime,' Raymond said. 'But I don't see—'

Miss Marple flushed again.

'I know, dear Raymond, that you do not really approve of detective stories. But I must admit to having rather a weakness for them. Lord Peter Wimsey is so *very* dashing, and Miss Sayers' plots are really extremely ingenious. There is a story in *Hangman's Holiday* where a thief hides some unstrung pearls in a bunch of mistletoe and I think when poor Ronald realised he was not going to be able to dispose of the necklace as planned, the inspiration proved irresistible. He snipped the string, took the pins from your pin cushion, Dolly – you remember, you found you had run out – and hastily fastened the pearls into the arrangement. It was a risk – but not such a big one as all that. The servants were all either at church, or occupied with preparing the Christmas dinner. I would imagine he burned the string in the drawing room fire, and that left only the clasp to dispose of – which he dropped out of the boot-room window.

'What I do not know is whether he meant to incriminate poor Bertie Finch. I rather think not – it was simply bad luck that the snow prevented an outsider from being blamed, and of course Ronald was *rather* foolish to use a trowel from the potting shed to force the window. That meant the evidence pointed to Bertie in a very unfortunate way.'

'Well, bravo, Aunt Jane," Raymond said, with the air of one magnanimously accepting a point scored against him. 'That's one up to you and your lending library. Never again will I cast aspersions on your reading taste! But I must take issue with your theory that they'd done it before – I don't see how that could be. They could hardly keep claiming on their insurance for the pearls. The insurance company wouldn't put up with it for a moment.'

'I don't think there ever was an insurance company, dear. *That* was just to make it clear to the Bantrys that if they did not take responsibility for the theft, the Dashwoods would be out of pocket. No, I think they were a rather clever pair. Major Dashwood – although, you know, I am not quite convinced that he is a real major – travelled the country looking for likely, I believe the term is *marks*, for their little game. Upright, honourable types like Colonel Bantry, who could be relied upon to pay up when their own servants were thrown under suspicion.'

'Dash it, I *said* the fellow forced himself upon me,' muttered Colonel Bantry, rather chagrined. 'Couldn't even remember inviting him for Christmas, and then suddenly there we were, lumbered with them.'

'Quite right on all counts, Miss Marple,' Sir Henry put in, buttering his toast. 'I spoke with Detective Inspector Slack in Much Benham this morning. Our so-called Major Dashwood wasn't a major at all – plain Mr Philip Rider from Friern Barnet, with two outstanding warrants to his name, if you please. He lost his head completely when they took him in. Confessed everything. *She*, on the other hand, was a very cool operator and, I rather think, the brains behind the operation. Quite the contrast from the fluffy-headed type she made herself out to be. The inspector still hadn't got to the bottom of her real identity when I last spoke to him, but I've no doubt he will. They'd run the scheme very successfully in London, Manchester and Leeds, but the last time there were some difficult questions asked about the Major's whereabouts during the window of time when the pearls disappeared. Poor Ronald – his name really *is* Ronald, by the way – must have seemed like a gift from heaven in that respect – someone they could saddle with the risk of the handover, while they were unimpeachably attending church with alibis up to the hilt.'

'What *I* want to know,' Mrs Bantry said, with some acerbity, 'is whether they'll be able to charge them with anything. Is stealing one's own pearls actually a crime? Especially when *they* weren't the ones who made the insurance claims?'

'Well, that is the question,' Sir Henry Clithering said, thoughtfully, stroking his moustaches. 'But Inspector Slack's a clever chap, and I rather think he may be able to get them on misrepresentation or obtaining goods by deception or something. Mark my words, he'll make sure they're locked up one way or another. And, at the very least, they'll have said goodbye to those pearls – apparently the insurance companies are already fighting over who owns them.'

'And good riddance!' Mrs Bantry said, with satisfaction, sawing at her bacon in a manner suggestive of unspent vindictiveness. 'By the way, Mr West, did your wife hear the breakfast gong? I'm afraid we keep country hours, and the breakfast things are usually cleared by nine o'clock.'

'Oh,' Raymond said vaguely. 'We're not really morning

people, you know, and I think perhaps she had one or two too many cocktails last night. She's having coffee in her room. I dare say she'll be down later.'

'Ah, the artistic life,' said Sir Henry with a twinkle.

A few hours later, Inch's taxi was sitting outside the front door of Gossington Hall while Miss Marple fluttered around, packing her knitting, writing out the recipe she had promised Cook, and bidding goodbye to the Bantrys and Sir Henry. As the taxi drew away down the newly shovelled drive, Sir Henry looked after it indulgently.

'You would never think that that lace cap hid one of the finest crime-solving brains in all of Christendom, would you? Mind like a bacon slicer, and there she is fussing about Dundee cake. I doubt we would have caught them, you know, if Miss Marple hadn't tipped Palk to the pearls being hidden in the mistletoe. The Dashwoods would have retrieved them, changed their name, and been off to the next victim, and none of us any the wiser.'

'You see, Arthur,' said Mrs Bantry, with a touch of triumph in her voice. 'It was a lucky day for you when I invited Jane Marple to Christmas dinner. A lucky day for you,' she repeated, with satisfaction.

'Oof!' Joan said with a sigh, sinking back into the armchair in Miss Marple's little cottage. 'I feel absolutely beat! I've no idea why.'

'Don't you, my dear?' Miss Marple said, giving her a rather curious look.

'I suppose it takes it out of you,' Raymond said. 'Crime and skulduggery, I mean! Really, Aunt Jane, that was a frightfully lucky guess you made about the mistletoe. The Bantrys would have been in the soup without that.'

'Yes, dear, very fortunate. Not to mention poor Bertie Finch.' The old lady settled herself in the armchair on the other side of the fire, and shook out her knitting. 'Now, if you'll excuse me, I must sort this out. I'm very much afraid I dropped a stitch earlier at the Bantrys, and my eyes are sadly not what they were. Dolly and I were gossiping – *most* reprehensible, but, really, it's only human nature – and I was not concentrating properly.'

'What *are* you knitting, Aunt Jane?' Joan asked, looking curiously at the snowy white pile trailing across the old lady's lap. 'You've been clicking away all the time we've been here. Is it a shawl?'

'A shawl? Not quite, my dear,' Miss Marple said, her cheeks going a little pink. 'No, not a shawl, but, indeed, I don't quite like . . .'

'What on earth?' Raymond said, looking astonished. 'Don't go all Victorian on us, Aunt Jane, and tell us you're knitting underclothes or something? Though I don't believe that even in St Mary Mead people wear knitted bloomers.'

'Not underclothes, dear, no.' She shook out the snowy white square across her lap. 'It's, well . . .' She shot a sharp, penetrating look at her nephew's wife. 'Well, it's a baby's blanket. But I didn't quite like . . .'

'A baby's blanket?' Raymond said, and suddenly it was his own cheeks that were flushed, as he looked from his aunt to his wife, for the first time almost, in Miss Marple's long experience of her nephew, lost for words.

There was a long pause, and then Joan burst out laughing, and threw up her hands.

'I declare, Aunt Jane, you must be a witch. However did you guess?'

'Well, my dear, when one lives in a village like St Mary Mead, one becomes well acquainted with human nature in that regard. And Raymond did say you had been rather pulled down recently, so I confess I wondered before you came down here, and, of course, once I was looking out for the signs . . .'

'And I thought I was being so clever pouring my Gin and It into the pot plants and stifling my yawns. I couldn't very well tell anyone that cocktails make me feel quite sick these days.'

'Yes, dear, and, if I may suggest, in future it would be better *not* to choose a poinsettia. They are rather sensitive to over-watering. And then, of course, when Raymond said that you were late to breakfast because of too many cocktails, I'm afraid I knew that to be an untruth.'

'Well, we're rumbled,' Raymond said with a laugh. 'Joan and I had wanted to keep it to ourselves for a few weeks more, but I suppose the whole of St Mary Mead knows by now?'

'Oh no, dear,' Miss Marple said, looking a little shocked. She folded the knitting neatly in her lap. 'No, I shouldn't dream of breathing a word until you and Joan are ready to announce her—' she gave a little deprecating cough, 'her *condition*, you know. No, my dear,' she turned to Joan with a smile. 'Your secret is *quite* safe with me.'

The Open Mind

Naomi Alderman

At the far end of the Fellows' Retiring Room, as the pre-dinner sherries were passed around, Professor Cuthbert Cayling, the Master of St Bede's College, Oxford, was holding forth, as he so often did.

'Of course, this college would have collapsed after the Restoration had it not been for the intervention of the family of which I have the honour of belonging to a cadet branch . . .'

Miss Marple watched him with interest. She had seen Professor Cayling, expert on constitutional history and politics, on the small black-and-white television set in her parlour. He was a frequent guest on the type of angry discussion programme that she often felt tended a little more towards entertainment than enlightenment. She had had the impression before that he rather enjoyed the sound of his own voice, and everything that she'd seen so far this evening tended to bear that out.

Professor Cayling's voice boomed from the depths of his

enormous beard. 'Edward Bedlington, the fifth duke, felt a connection to the college owing to the family seat being fairly near Jarrow, you see: the location of the Venerable Bede's abbey.' The bored-looking young woman he was addressing suddenly went wide-eyed.

'Look, the poor girl's trying to keep herself awake,' Sir Aaron Kahn muttered, in an aside to Miss Marple. 'Who is she? Elspeth Something. Works for the BBC, I think. Bloody Cuthbert does this every chance he can get. Just show him a pretty girl and he's off.'

'Yes,' said Miss Marple, 'it does look as if he's trying to impress her. I wonder whether he's succeeding.'

Sir Aaron laughed under his breath.

Professor Cayling was now explaining the arcane rules according to which, even though he descended from the Bedlington-Bomarsands via the female line, he was still given access to the family estate at Seaham Ryhope. Elspeth Something of the BBC was feigning interest, nodding and smiling. She wants something from him, thought Miss Marple, I wonder what it is.

It was Founder's Day at St Bede's College, in the freezing early January of 1970, and Sir Aaron Kahn – retired judge and an honorary fellow at the college – had invited Miss Marple to be his guest at high table. They were celebrating the successful end of a particularly difficult case – the Quaverley choir murders – which had had the police baffled. The solution was only uncovered when Miss Marple, who'd happened to be visiting her dear friend Ruth, a stalwart of said choir, had pointed out the crucial importance of the reversed oil painting. Sir Aaron, having jumped at the chance to be partners in detection, had suggested they could toast the end of that investigation at St Bede's. The Founder's Dinners were legendarily sumptuous.

'Just don't mind Cuthbert Cayling,' Sir Aaron had said, 'he's a brilliant scholar and a very ambitious man, only . . . his manners.'

Sir Aaron had been right. He had very kindly motored Miss Marple up in his own racing-green MG Roadster, and as he and Miss Marple had pulled up in the college-allotted parking space half an hour earlier, Professor Cayling had been waiting for them.

His first words to Sir Aaron had been: 'Pretty little car. Well, I suppose you can spare the shekels, old man.'

Sir Aaron introduced Jane Marple – 'the genius who puts the bench to shame' – with all politeness, but Miss Marple saw that the casual anti-Jewish insult rankled, and noted an expression she'd never seen before on her friend's face – a flash of pure dislike. Even hatred.

Although the buildings were a glorious mix of High Medieval and Gothic, the event so far was a touch less grand than Miss Marple had anticipated. The leather of the high wing-backed chairs was cracked, the sherry was good but rather frugally poured, and the staff seemed to her less well-trained than her own maids. But, of course, she reminded herself, standards now were not what they once were, and one must permit the permissive society to live by its own lights.

'Budget cuts,' said Sir Aaron, noticing Miss Marple's surprise, 'it's all "Open University" now and "flinging the doors open". Modernisation and "serving the great unused reservoir of human talent and potential" are *not* well-represented by the dons of this college supping on honeydew and the milk of paradise, according to Mr Wilson.'

'I notice Harold Wilson doesn't intend to return his Oxford degree and take an Open one instead,' laughed Dr Agnetha Strom, mirthlessly. 'Hypocrisy is everywhere.' Her English was very mildly accented with traces of unplaceable Northern European. 'Not least over there,' she indicated Professor Cayling with her pointed chin. 'Look at him cosying up with that BBC producer. He thinks he'll be the next Kenneth Clark. A ten-part lecture series on democracy through the ages. Pay lip service to the masses but don't give up your own luxuries. Typical.'

Sir Aaron chuckled warmly, 'Miss Marple, Agnetha hasn't forgiven Cuthbert for taking her place on one of those late-night arts discussion programmes.'

'He knew less than nothing about Schopenhauer,' Agnetha hissed.

'But he was fit and well for the discussion with Huw Wheldon and you were . . . indisposed. It's not Cuthbert's fault that one appearance has turned him into an academic celebrity.'

'I wouldn't put it past him to have slipped some senna into my soup,' said Dr Strom darkly.

'Oh,' said Miss Marple, 'oh dear.'

On this unappetising note, the butler appeared at the door of the Fellows' Retiring Room and declared in a loud voice, 'My lords, ladies and gentlemen, dinner is served!'

St Bede's College's fifteenth-century dining hall was renowned as one of the most beautiful in Oxford. Tiled in black-and-white chequerboard, lit by hundreds of fragrant beeswax candles in sconces, and furnished in five-century-old dark polished wood, it was all Miss Marple had hoped for. She couldn't prevent herself from murmuring 'Oh my' under her breath as she and the other guests were ushered to their tables. The linen was white as a snow-covered hill, the silver gleamed like a lake in moonlight. Each place-setting was written in swooping calligraphy – as she found her place, Miss Marple noted with relief that Sir Aaron was to her right hand and, with surprise, that 'Miss Elspeth Hearken' was to her left. Opposite Miss Marple, a dour, long-faced, rather thin and pale man was swooping toward the seat labelled 'Dr Eammon McManaway'.

Dr McManaway immediately introduced himself, as grim as if they were attending a funeral not a celebration feast: 'Eammon. Ancient Languages. What are you? New Medievalist at St Cross? I hear they're having a bad time there with rats at present. Have you rats? In your rooms?'

'Oh,' said Miss Marple, scarcely able to know how to respond to this, 'No, no, I don't have . . . rats.'

'You will,' said Eammon darkly, 'that's what I hear. On the subject of rats, look at that.'

He pointed towards the top of the table, where Professor Cuthbert Cayling was engaged in a dispute with a shortish red-faced man with luxuriant brown-gold hair.

'You know who that is, don't you? Medievalist, like you. Simon Skipper. You've read his monograph on Mathilda. Seminal. Bursar of the college. Thinks he should have been Master at the last election. Takes any opportunity to undermine Cuthbert. What's he on about now?'

Miss Marple strained her ears but only caught a few snippets of the conversation. Certainly both men seemed extremely angry. The staff were trying to indicate that it was time to sit down for the meal, but neither man took much notice. The undergraduates, who were already seated, were mostly busy with their own boisterous conversation, but a few had started to notice that something was going on at high table.

Without warning, the golden-headed Simon tipped over the Master's half-empty crystal glass of wine, staining the white linen red as blood. He stormed away from high table, his face a dark cloud.

'Bloody hell,' said Eammon, 'it's never gone that far before.'

Professor Cuthbert Cayling looked about, bemused, as the staff covered the stain with fresh linen and set him a new place. Once this was done, Cuthbert ceremoniously and rather pompously tapped his fresh glass nine times precisely, and waited until there was total silence in the hall, until each undergraduate had stopped whispering to his neighbour or shuffling on his chair. He stood ponderously and declaimed the words 'Benedictus Benedicat', before sitting back in his chair with great solemnity. That, it appeared, was that for speeches.

Elspeth Hearken, the producer from the BBC, had taken in the drama unfolding at high table with raw curiosity. She was a modern young woman, with long brown hair and a deep fringe, wearing a black-and-white polka-dot long-sleeved dress in the fashionably short style that showed most of her dimpled, slightly mottled legs. These fashionable styles didn't quite *suit* everyone, Miss Marple thought, and Elspeth Hearken seemed rather a victim of the current trend, as she self-consciously pulled the hem of her dress to try to get it a little lower when she sat.

'I should have worn tweed, like you,' said Elspeth, half apologetically, 'only I didn't want to seem to be trying too hard to fit in. Tell me, do you know what's going on at the head of the table?'

'Professor Cuthbert Cayling never makes a friend if he can make an enemy,' Eammon McManaway answered her. 'He beat Simon Skipper in the election to be Master. You'd think that victory would make a man magnanimous. But, since then, Cuthbert has gone out of his way to humiliate Simon at every opportunity. Last week at college council, he asked him to bring the tea and biscuits. As if he were a scout! And he's trying to get Skipper out of his rooms – he has rather a nice set on staircase five that Cuthbert wants to use as a second office.'

'On these tiny differences, academic life is built,' said Sir Aaron, pleasantly.

'*Is* it tiny?' asked Elspeth. There was something forceful in her manner that Miss Marple had to respect even if she couldn't quite like it. An ambition. 'I do think one must keep an open mind about everything. Hasn't the college received a large bequest? One which the Master can decide what to do with, as long as he has approval of council? Don't you think Professor Cayling might be trying to force Simon Skipper to leave the council – or make it so unpleasant for him here that he leaves college? Isn't it possible that's what's going on?'

'Oho,' said Eammon, 'we should watch what we say, with a journalist in our midst.'

Elspeth continued: 'Well, isn't it? Can't you acknowledge that possibility?'

She seemed scarcely able to let the matter lie, but, propitiously, the man on her left asked her about her own academic interests. They set about discussing them with fervour.

The first course, partridge stuffed with prunes on a bed of wild mushrooms – was placed before them all. Miss Marple suddenly felt rather tired. It happened more and more these days that, at a large event such as this, a wave of exhaustion would sweep over her. She found herself longing for her quiet parlour in St Mary Mead. These young people, she said to herself, have no interest in you any longer, Jane, nor any need for you. To them, you are a Victorian relic; ancient history, just like the manuscripts they study. Snippets of conversation swirled around her: Sir Aaron's stories of his time on the bench, the academic discourse of these terribly intelligent people.

'Do you know, he had been using that baker's shop as a front for his drug-dealing business?' said Sir Aaron conversationally to the young don sitting next to him, 'The chicken pies were stuffed with it.'

'In a way, one can't help admiring Chatterton for his daring. All those forgeries, took everyone in,' said Elspeth, to the man to her left.

'I've heard people say that, but, honestly, what would most of us *do* with a computing machine at home?' said Eammon McManaway. 'I can't even work my Goblin Teasmade. I keep putting the wrong liquid in the wrong place.'

From two places down the table, the oddly accented tones of Dr Agnetha Strom could be heard: 'Of course there are ways for him to use it for himself. Every trust needs a generously-paid president, didn't you know?'

Miss Marple's mind snagged on something she'd just heard. She couldn't think which part it was, only that someone had just said something very unexpected. Something that suggested . . . what was it? She thought of Jim the butcher's boy in St Mary Mead, who'd bet he could jump the mill race. Something . . .

She jumped in her seat as a hand gripped her left shoulder. The thought was gone.

Professor Cuthbert Cayling squeezed Miss Marple's arm with a painful over-familiarity.

'You don't mind, do you?' he peered at the place-setting card, 'Jane, my darling. Only Elspeth and I were rather in the middle of a conversation earlier.' He chuckled. 'I asked Simon Skipper in the friendliest possible way whether he'd mind changing places with you, Elspeth, and he got in a frightful bate.'

'Oh,' said Elspeth, 'but I'm halfway through my meal.'

'Don't worry about that. The college staff will deal with it. I was rather interested by what you were saying about a new *political* lecture programme on BBC2.'

'She's fine where she is,' said Eammon.

Professor Cayling's eyes were pure fury.

'She can decide for herself,' he said, 'can't you, my dear?'

Elspeth looked around nervously.

'You don't have to go,' Eammon said softly, 'he can't make you.'

And yet, with an appearance half of modesty and half of what seemed to Miss Marple something like fear, two points of high colour on her cheeks, Elspeth Hearken stood up, her short dress barely covering her bottom, and walked up the table to take her place at Professor Cayling's side.

There was a strange silence around Miss Marple. The main course had been served: racks of venison with roast parsnips, blackberries, and a chestnut stuffing. Eammon dug into his meat viciously. Agnetha Strom moved along a few places from her seat to take Elspeth's place. She and Eammon exchanged a dark glance. Even Sir Aaron seemed subdued.

'Forgive me,' said Miss Marple, 'but I do wonder whether Professor Cuthbert is quite *safe* with young women.'

Eammon gave a hollow laugh.

At the far end of the table, Professor Cayling was whispering something into Elspeth Hearken's ear. She looked nervous. She seemed about to refuse, tucking her chin into her chest and making a little frightened shake of the head, but Professor Cayling's arm was around her shoulder, squeezing with that vice-like grip.

'Safe?' said Eammon. 'It's going to be that Harrison girl all over again.'

'Harrison girl?' prompted Miss Marple mildly.

Even from this end of the table, everyone could tell what Professor Cayling was saying to Elspeth. What a pretty girl she was, and surely she didn't wear a dress that length not thinking that people would look?

Agnetha Strom said, 'I told Elspeth about her earlier. She was rather a good friend of mine. Cuthbert touched her up. Everyone said she ought to keep quiet about it. But she made a fuss, went to the University. Of course, Cuthbert said she'd been as keen as he was and just regretted it afterwards. He said, she said. And she *had* been caught in bed with a boyfriend after curfew a year earlier, so it all looked rather bad for her. She was passed over for a Junior Fellowship after that.'

Professor Cayling's squeezing hand went lower down Elspeth's arm, the back of his hand almost grazing her breast. He tapped the pocket of his jacket and whispered something in Elspeth's ear.

'Quaaludes,' said Eammon, 'he gets them from a doctor on Harley Street, to help him relax. He gave them to Harrison. Look,' he said to Agnetha, 'I know she was your friend, but you haven't heard the half of it. I had the room next to hers. I was the one who heard her crying in the night. I used to sit and talk to her when she was too frightened to sleep.'

Miss Marple watched Professor Cayling and Elspeth

Hearken. He handed her a small white pill and she dropped it into her wine glass. He did the same with his own glass. They each swirled their glasses and drank them down.

'But Cuthbert has no control over Elspeth, does he?' said Sir Aaron with mild alarm. 'She's not a postgraduate. She works for the BBC. She's a free agent and can do as she pleases.'

'You say that,' said Eammon. 'I believe she applied for a PhD here a year or two ago. Some theory she has about Oliver Cromwell and Lady Sarah Bedlington, Charles II's mistress. Got turned down. A lot of people would like to live this rather sybaritic lifestyle.' He paused and glanced up the table again. 'Look, I have to say something.'

A formal dinner is a difficult place to interrupt a seduction, but Eammon McManaway made a bold attempt. Under cover of speaking to one of the butlers about a rickety chair, he edged closer to the head of the table where Professor Cayling's hand was massaging the small of Elspeth Hearken's back, straying closer to her bottom. Eammon picked up the carafe of wine and offered to pour both of them an extra glass, just to be friendly. Then he suggested that Cayling had taken up quite enough of Elspeth's time and perhaps she might return to her original place. Elspeth shook her head, mutely. Cuthbert Cayling laughed uproariously. Squeezing Elspeth tightly, he said, loud enough for everyone at the table to hear, 'Now, before the toasts and the pudding, my dear, perhaps you'd like to freshen up in my rooms.'

Elspeth, large eyes gleaming, followed Cuthbert Cayling out through the back of the dining hall.

'Perhaps she actually fancies the old goat?' said Agnetha, watching them depart.

'No one fancies Cuthbert Cayling.' said Eammon, returning to his place, 'She's too frightened to say no.'

'Are we sure something untoward is going on?' asked Sir Aaron, 'Perhaps she really does need a moment to freshen up? It is awfully hot in here.'

Miss Marple was overcome with a creeping sense of trepidation. Something untoward was certainly happening. Something terrible had been happening at this table all evening. If only she hadn't taken two glasses of sherry before the meal, she would know what it was. She had the sense that they were all chess pieces at this dinner, moving over this chequerboard floor in a pattern already ordained by someone. But who?

It was no more than thirty minutes later that Cuthbert and Elspeth returned to the table. Both of them, to Miss Marple's eye, had clearly taken some sort of drug. She had learned the signs of the new drugs from her friends in the police force over the past decade, and also learned that she was expected by many to disapprove. Drug-taking that had once been considered rather demeaning and low-class in 1959 was now, in 1970, seen even among intelligent people as a sign of an adventurous spirit and a nose for fun. But Miss Marple remembered a time before there were any laws at all about the taking of drugs. She recalled that, during the Great War, one could buy 'A Welcome Present for Friends at the Front' at Harrods – cocaine, morphine and all the accoutrements. Young people always thought they'd invented everything.

Elspeth and Cuthbert both looked to Miss Marple to have taken rather a lot of whatever it was. Quaaludes, Eammon McManaway had said. And they had missed their main course. The staff were patently eager to start clearing and serving pudding, but there was the formality of 'the address' to get through. Elspeth swayed and stumbled as she took her seat, looking drowsy and confused.

Professor Cayling didn't look much better. Despite this, he stood up again, his face glowing, his eyes very bright, and began the formal address that marked Founder's Day, declaiming the Latin words with which the college's original benefactor had asked to be remembered. But something was wrong. The words were increasingly slurred. He lost his place repeatedly, and muttered 'Forgive me' several times. His eyes closed and opened again. And he slipped slowly forward, landing face-first in the remains of the roast venison, sending wine glasses spinning to smash on the floor.

At once, Sir Aaron leapt up. He had had a little medical training during his time in the army, so hauled Professor Cayling bodily out of the venison, felt for his pulse, and looked in his mouth.

'Call a doctor!' cried Sir Aaron. 'For God's sake, call a doctor!'

Cuthbert Cayling was still drawing slow, choked, bubbling breaths.

Elspeth Hearken, beside him, fell slowly sideways from her chair. On the floor, her face mashed into the crumbs and fragments of dinner on the polished wood boards, she began to shake and fit, jerkily.

The last voice Miss Marple remembered hearing in that terrible moment was Eammon McManaway's, shouting, 'What the hell are you all standing there for?! Call a bloody doctor!'

Miss Marple and Sir Aaron sat together the next morning at breakfast in the spacious dining room of the Randolph Hotel, overlooking the Georgian grace of Beaumont Street and the Martyrs' Memorial. Sir Aaron had thought it unwise to attempt to motor home, nor had either of them wanted to take up their respective guest rooms at the college. Much of the college, in fact, was currently being combed by police for any evidence relating to the taking of illegal drugs and the subsequent death. All the attendees at the dinner had been warned to stay in Oxford for the next few days, until enquiries could be concluded.

Sir Aaron said: 'Elspeth Hearken, at least, is out of danger.'

'Yes,' said Miss Marple, 'that is a great relief.'

Elspeth Hearken and Professor Cuthbert Cayling had both been taken by ambulance to the Radcliffe Infirmary. Elspeth, younger than Cuthbert by more than thirty-five years, had had – according to the report Sir Aaron had managed to have sight of that morning – a bad night. But after having her stomach pumped, she was now resting easily and was expected to spend only another night or two in hospital before being sent home.

But the late morning copy of *The Times* spread on the

table between Miss Marple and Sir Aaron carried a full-page obituary of Professor Cuthbert Cayling. His education at Eton and Balliol, his ancestry in the Bedlington-Bomarsand family, whose vault would be opened for the funeral, his PhD work at Harvard. The obituary listed his considerable achievements in political history, his popular book on democracy published in 1965, his talents as Master of the college, his two wives and two divorces. His face – younger by a couple of decades but still engulfed in his luxuriant beard – stared out from the page, his gaze piercing.

'Tell me,' said Sir Aaron, 'honestly, how does it smell to you?'

Miss Marple's eyes took on an intelligent gleam.

'Well, I must say,' she said, 'one must keep an open mind, but there are one or two matters that trouble me.'

'All right,' said Sir Aaron, 'let me guess before you tell me everything. It is a *little* odd that Cuthbert, whose quaaludes they were,' Sir Aaron said the word with some distaste, 'and who had taken them many times before, managed to take so many on this one occasion that he overdosed and died. And, moreover, that he put Elspeth Hearken in danger.'

'Yes,' said Miss Marple, 'that is one problem. One would have thought that he would know precisely how much to take. It does seem unlikely that that could have killed him. And one notices,' she glanced out of the window, still seeming to be shy of her own perspicacity, although Sir Aaron was well aware of it, 'one can't help but notice how very easy it would have been for someone to tamper with the drinks.'

'I did think of Simon Skipper tipping over that wine glass.

He might have been trying to pour away a poison he'd already dosed Cuthbert with.'

'Yes, quite. And tipping *over* the glass might have been intended to make everyone think he couldn't possibly have given the Master anything – whereas, of course, it would mean that all traces would be immediately removed and the linen laundered by the staff. And then Professor Cayling *did* have quite a number of enemies around the table. He really had quite a talent for making enemies. He made a grotesque anti-Semitic remark to you when we arrived, for example.'

'You can't think that *I* killed him.'

'Oh, no, no. It would have been rather extraordinary for you to invite *me* to witness you committing a murder. I just mean to say that he was an easy man to dislike. His stance on the college bequest was unpopular. Agnetha Strom believes he deliberately undermined her. Dr Eammon McManaway can't bear him. Did you happen to notice that Dr McManaway also picked up the wine carafe at dinner? It would have been easy enough for him to slip pills or powders into it.'

'Or the Master's wine or his meal could have been doctored by someone who distracted any of the college staff. The Chief Constable here is a friend of mine. I must tell him to make sure all the serving staff are interviewed thoroughly with that question in mind.'

'Yes,' said Miss Marple, 'that's very wise, of course, very wise. I can't help feeling, though, that there are undercurrents here that I haven't quite understood.'

A polite cough interrupted their conversation. A waiter in Randolph livery stood by their table, holding an envelope.

'Just delivered for you, Sir Aaron.'

Sir Aaron tipped the waiter and waited for him to leave before tearing open the envelope.

'Analysis of the stomach contents. I asked to see a copy as soon as possible. Now we'll know what Cuthbert and Elspeth were poisoned with.'

As he read the document, his curious and intelligent face took on a puzzled expression. He passed the report to Miss Marple in silence. She read it carefully, twice through.

The hospital report stated unequivocally that there had been no additional drugs in Cuthbert Cayling's system; wine and the quaaludes prescribed by his private doctor in Harley Street were the only intoxicating substances.

'Oh,' said Miss Marple, 'Well then. That makes it all very clear. Very clear indeed.' She helped herself to the final crumpet on the rack in front of her, 'The only difficulty will be proving it.'

Three weeks later, Miss Jane Marple and Sir Aaron Kahn took their seats in the great family chapel on the Bedlington-Bomarsand estate on the Seaham coast a few miles south-east of Jarrow. The marble vaulted ceilings were ribbed and fanned – it was a bit like looking up at the sky through the branches of a great tree, Miss Marple thought. The wooden benches were well-cushioned with hand-embroidered pads and the congregation was made up of famous faces from the academic world, the world of the media, the aristocracy and even two minor members of the royal family. There, too, were many of the people Miss Marple had met and seen three weeks earlier at St Bede's College: Agnetha Strom in an austere black ankle-length dress, Eammon McManaway in a rumpled suit, Elspeth Hearken still looking a little pale and unwell in black lace, the angry Simon Skipper wearing an extraordinarily moth-eaten black jumper and slacks, defiantly casual. Several of the college staff and servants were there as well.

'I very much suspect, Sir Aaron,' murmured Miss Marple, 'that the murderer – and I do think a murder *was* committed, whatever the police say – won't be able to stay away from this, don't you agree? This moment, I believe, is the reason for everything.'

The choir's voices were raised in the 'Dies Irae', the haunting music filling the huge echoing space, resounding from walls, floor, ceiling, seeming at times to come directly from the carved angels above them or from the glowing stained-glass image of Mary Magdalen above the altar. The Magdalen was the patron saint of the Bedlington-Bomarsand family, someone had explained, in a rather knowing nod to the family's having originally been raised to high estate because the first duchess had been one of Charles II's many mistresses. The family's marble busts lined the wall; and, to honour their founding matriarch, the line of Bedlington-Bomarsand descended through the female as well as the male line. Thus, Professor Cuthbert Cayling, to his immense pride, was considered a Bedlington-Bomarsand too by the wider family, because his mother had been a daughter of the duke, even though she had married a Mr Cayling, a humble industrialist with a fat wallet.

'The women of the family have always been rather formidable, I'm told,' said Sir Aaron, 'going right back to the first duchess. Look at her there. One can't help imagining the intellect behind those fine eyes and that enormous nose, can't one?'

'Yes,' said Miss Marple, 'there's a certain kind of mind that is drawn to imagining the past. Even imagining friends among the dead. That kind of person can begin to feel they have more in common with the past than the present.'

Professor Cayling's Aunt Constance, the dowager duchess, was a woman in her mid-nineties. She retained an upright and unyielding bearing, and walked with great dignity from her seat at the front of the chapel before taking a great iron key from her beaded bag. Slowly, she walked to the leather-studded, iron-banded great oak door to the left of the altar, inserted the key in the lock and turned it. The door opened slowly, and a chill wind blew from the vault, making the candles sputter in their sconces. There was something grand and glorious about it. The great vault of Bedlington-Bomarsand was open.

'The family vault,' said Sir Aaron, 'by family tradition it will stand open for seven days and seven nights while Cuthbert lies at the altar, before his coffin is placed in the tomb with his ancestors and the vault is sealed again.'

'Ah, yes,' said Miss Marple, 'I rather thought it must be something like that. I suppose it's been a great many years since it was last opened?'

Sir Aaron frowned at her, 'Yes, extraordinary, isn't it? Twenty-two years, I think, since the last Bedlington-Bomarsand died.'

'That would make perfect sense,' Miss Marple said.

The music rose once more, the choristers of the Seaham Ryhope school melding their voices with the cello, thc oboc and the bassoon, the notes plashing on the eardrum like the falling of soft rain.

'I do hope it isn't too cold, that crypt,' said Miss Marple.

'The corpses scarcely mind,' said Sir Aaron.

'No,' said Miss Marple, 'but we shall.'

Past midnight that night, Miss Jane Marple and Sir Aaron Kahn sat in the dark. It was, in fact, exceedingly cold. Sir Aaron had loaned Miss Marple his own fur-collared driving coat, and he sat there in the lighter Macintosh he kept in his car, shivering.

'Do you think we shall have to wait long?' he asked.

'No,' muttered Miss Marple, 'I believe the person we're expecting thinks they have waited quite long enough. You've seen the painting *The Death of Chatterton*? I saw it at a summer exhibition some years ago and was very struck by it. The brilliant young poet and forger, flaming curls of red hair, lying amid his papers, which would win him lasting fame even after his death. Only seventeen when he died, in 1770. An extraordinary evocation. Well, you do see, Sir Aaron: an admirer of Thomas Chatterton is someone who thinks that the world ought to take notice of the genius of the very young. That any need to wait for approval or affirmation is too much to bear. An admirer of Thomas Chatterton is impatient.'

'Chatterton, the poet?' said Sir Aaron, 'What does Chatterton have to do with it?'

'Well, you see, it was the mention of Chatterton at dinner

that put me in mind of Jim the butcher's boy. How he couldn't wait for Betsy to notice him of her own accord. Had to jump the mill race to prove himself – and, of course, he tumbled in. Impatience, that's the link. Afterwards, Jim accused one of the farmhands of having greased the rocks, but . . .'

'Sorry, I still don't quite see . . .'

'Shh!' said Miss Marple.

For someone was descending the steps into the family vault. A light and careful tread. And there was a beam of torchlight sweeping over the vault where the coffins sat in their marble niches. Sir Aaron and Miss Marple were well-concealed in a side chamber and the torchlight passed by without touching them. From their viewpoint in the chamber, they saw a figure in a hooded coat bend over one coffin in particular – the ancient oak coffin in the central niche. The figure pulled a long object from their coat and began to methodically wrench the coffin open.

Sir Aaron gasped in disgust, but quickly muffled the sound. He patted Miss Marple's shoulder, as if to say 'Surely, now we act', but Miss Marple indicated that they should both remain silent with a tiny shake of her head.

The figure at the coffin had it open now. There was a smell – not entirely unpleasant – of old musty rooms, of faint decay. The figure was bending over the body, the coat concealing what it was they were about. They turned from the coffin, their posture confident, almost exultant.

'Now,' murmured Miss Marple.

Sir Aaron turned on the beam of his torch. The figure was a young woman.

'Stop right there,' he said, in the commanding voice that had won such acclaim in his years as a KC.

The figure turned to run, but from the chapel above six police officers were already descending the steps. In defeat, the grave robber turned her face at last fully to Miss Marple and Sir Aaron. She pointed a trembling finger at the coffin where a packet of letters was clasped between the fingers of the mouldering skeleton.

'Look, I've found them. I've really found them. You can say what you like about what I've done, but I've found them,' said Elspeth Hearken.

'What exactly were the letters, after all that?' said Miss Marple, 'That's the one part of the thing that I didn't know. Something about Cromwell?'

'Good grief, how did you know that?' Sir Aaron looked baffled, as did the local police inspector and the current duke. All of them were seated around a roaring fire in the library at Seaham Ryhope. Tea, whisky and thickly buttered crumpets had been provided to take the chill of the crypt from their bones. Miss Marple was ensconced in front of the fire, a heavy rug over her knees, and Sir Aaron rather suspected she was enjoying her momentary position as the centre of attention.

'Oh, don't you remember that remark of Dr McManaway's at dinner? That Elspeth Hearken had been turned down for a PhD and that she had a theory about Oliver Cromwell and Lady Sarah Bedlington, Charles II's mistress?'

'Good lord. Yes. Well. She *did* have a theory. And, as you say, she had a very single-minded and impatient way of pursuing it. The letters are extremely interesting, in fact. I've been allowed a brief chance to look them over – and, of course, I'm no expert in the period – but they are letters between Lady Sarah and Charles II that suggest that Oliver Cromwell was actually in favour of the restoration of the monarchy. That he had secretly worked to undermine his own protectorship and not to provide a successor, so that the rightful king could be restored to the throne after his death. They're certainly going to provide plenty of evidence for academics to chew over.'

'Yes, I expect they will,' remarked Miss Marple a little tartly, 'I quite see that that is the sort of theory that might have caught the attention of a woman like Elspeth Hearken. She's rather earnest, almost painfully sincere in a certain way. Trying to dress like a modern girl, but she'd have been happier in an earlier age. She must have latched on to that theory as a sign of a secret continuity in the world; that even people who were trying to change things might secretly be in favour of the status quo, perhaps? I think she chewed over it, thought about it constantly, in fact. Yes, I can quite see that, having been rebuffed for her PhD on the subject, she might have become so obsessed that she'd kill to prove her point.'

'Are you suggesting she plotted to murder Cuthbert Cayling purely so that the crypt would be opened and she could get to these letters?'

'Plotted? No. No, I merely think she saw her chance. She may not even have known Professor Cayling was part of the Bedlington family until he mentioned it at dinner. And, of course, she hadn't brought a murder weapon with her, let alone a poison. No. He told her of his links to the subject of her obsession, and she realised that, if he died, the family vault would be opened and she could show her theory was correct. She'd heard enough of the gossip about him at the college to know he would have any number of enemies who'd be suspected of the crime before her. And then *he* offered *her* drugs. Well! The chance was too good to miss, I suspect. Impatience, you see. It must have seemed that she would never be caught.'

'But how on earth did she get so much of the drug into Cuthbert?'

Miss Marple raised an eyebrow.

'Come now, Sir Aaron, how does a pretty young girl get a foolish older man to do anything? She dared him, I expect. She took some. She said she'd taken them before and she preferred the effect if one took five or six. Perhaps she concealed some in her cheek and spat them out later. He was already drunk. Who would possibly suspect the man's own drugs as a murder weapon?'

'Except you,' said the duke, 'you're quite an astonishing woman. It's going to be dashed hard to show it was murder even so, I'd think. I must say, though,' he sat back, hands folded over his stomach, 'while I shall miss curmudgeonly old cousin Cuth, I am rather delighted by the light she's thrown on the history of m'own family. Imagine being secretly involved in a plot orchestrated by Cromwell to bring the king back to the throne!'

He poured himself another generous measure of whisky and offered the decanter around.

'Oh, I'm so sorry, your grace,' said Miss Marple, 'No, no, I have not explained. The letters aren't real. They're forgeries.'

Around the room a short stuttering breath emanated from three men simultaneously.

'Yes,' said Jane Marple mildly, 'this is exactly the sort of strange theory people *do* get obsessed with. Everything was intended. There was a great conspiracy. There are secret powers moving behind the scenes. No, no. Jim the butcher's boy all over. No one had greased the rocks. Things happen. There is no great secret that everyone knows but you. They happen because they happen. That's why she spoke so highly of Chatterton; he was a famous forger, you see. She was thinking through what she could do, even there at the dinner. Telling herself that if Chatterton could do it, she could do it. If she could somehow get this one man out of the way, and then forge the letters she needed, she could prove her own theory true. I suppose,' mused Miss Marple, 'that she intended to break the coffin open by night and leave it to be discovered the next day. It wouldn't matter to her that *she* discover the letters, only that someone should and she should be proved right.'

'I don't quite follow,' said Sir Aaron.

'She didn't *discover* the letters in the coffin. She forged them, like Chatterton. And she planted them there.

'Bless my soul,' said the duke.

In the following week, the letters were examined by an expert from the British Museum, who pronounced them very clever forgeries indeed. Written on old paper cut from the backs of books from the period, they would have been virtually undetectable. Elspeth Hearken would have been vindicated; her PhD work would have been accepted by any college in Oxford. Miss Marple felt rather sorry for her, in a way – she remembered Jim the butcher's boy pulling himself bedraggled from the mill race – but as Sir Aaron reminded her, this was a woman who had deliberately killed a man by an overdose, so one needn't feel too sorry for her.

Beside everything else, Simon Skipper, the new Master, had invited Miss Marple back to dine at college.

'The college fellows rather want to befriend you, I think. Moving with the times,' said Sir Aaron, 'the new open and egalitarian society.'

Miss Marple smiled and said she would consider it.

The Jade Empress

Jean Kwok

Miss Marple was mildly surprised to find herself waltzing. She had always admired it as an elegant dance, but given little thought to doing it herself. However, after several weeks aboard the cruise ship *Jade Empress* on its way to Hong Kong, where she was to meet her nephew, the successful novelist Raymond West, she found herself succumbing to the enthusiastic cajoling of the ship's ballroom-dancing instructor.

'If you can walk, you can waltz,' the attractive young woman had said, holding her head with its smooth dark chignon high. Like many of the staff on board, she was Chinese.

What Miss Marple liked about the waltz was that a person was allowed to remain dignified, unlike those Latin dances where one was expected to contort oneself into a pretzel. Her elderly dance partner, Mr Pang, who had a cabin in her corridor, was also a reasonable height. Most young people these days seemed to shoot up to ridiculous lengths that seemed quite inconvenient for fitting through doorways and the like. Mr Pang was, in fact, short and stocky, and Miss

Marple was relieved to feel no resultant pain from the rheumatism in her neck as she gazed at him.

'The Jade Empress is the Queen Mother of the West, did you know that?' said Mr Pang, huffing a bit from the exertion. 'They say she holds the elixir of life. One swallow and you could live for ever and never grow old. That would be something for the likes of us, eh? When a man gets on in years, he wants to—'

It was fortunate that Mr Pang only knew a few dance steps, Miss Marple thought, or it would be even more difficult to follow his rambling stories than it already was. Since the two of them had neither the knowledge nor desire to waltz around the upper deck as some other, more adventurous and foolhardy dance couples did, they revolved gently in the corner, like a carousel, only intermittently punctuated by an underarm turn, which Miss Marple executed quite gracefully.

She allowed her mind to wander. It was a lovely afternoon on the top deck. She enjoyed the clear and mild spring weather, as well as the deep blue ocean around them. They'd just left Singapore – such a long way from her own village of St Mary Mead! – and would be at sea for a few more days before arriving at their ultimate destination. Raymond was truly so kind. He was to be there for a year, producing a play set in China while also serving as some sort of cultural ambassador, waving the flag for Britain, and he'd insisted that Miss Marple join him for a month. He stressed it would be good for her health and mental faculties, as if she were becoming *senile*. But her dear nephew had taken care of everything, and so Miss Marple found herself with little to do but admire the waters of the South China Sea while listening to the lilting strains of 'The Blue Danube'.

'I haven't seen my son since he was a child,' Mr Pang continued, oblivious to Miss Marple's inattention. 'I didn't want to leave him and his mother, you understand, but I had no choice.'

'Of course not,' murmured Miss Marple, trying to piece the story together. 'Why exactly did you leave Hong Kong again?'

'To make a new life for us. Moved to Liverpool, took me years before I could scrape together enough to bring them over, and, by then, his mother had passed away and my son didn't want to come any more. Said he was happy in Hong Kong. In just a few days, I'll be reunited with him again after all these decades.' Mr Pang's eyelid was drooping a bit and Miss Marple politely ignored a tear that he quickly wiped away with a shrug of his shoulder.

'Is that your daughter who is travelling with you?' Miss Marple had noticed a large, rather shambling young woman, in addition to an older lady with a glass eye, who seemed to be some sort of caregiver to Mr Pang.

'Yes, from my second wife, who sadly also passed away last year.' Mr Pang abruptly jerked his left arm up in the signal for an underarm turn and Miss Marple swept underneath it. 'She loved to garden—'

When Miss Marple returned to the appropriate dance position, Mr Pang was saying, '—peony, treasure of my heart. The sight delights me every day.'

Miss Marple said, 'A lovely flower.'

'As important to the Chinese,' said Mr Pang, 'as the English rose—'

They were interrupted by the firm tones of the ballroom dance teacher as she called, 'ONE two three, ONE two three . . .' Over Mr Pang's shoulder, Miss Marple caught a glimpse of the instructor sweeping back and forth with a solid-looking young man who was intently staring at his feet. His neck was so red and blotchy from embarrassment that the dark colour resembled some sort of rash or birthmark. The teacher reminded him, 'Eyes up', but was ignored.

'Ah, there come your daughter and friend,' Miss Marple said, looking beyond the hapless man to Mr Pang's rapidly approaching companions.

Mr Pang glanced in the direction she indicated and froze. He stared fixedly over her shoulder. He seemed to have difficulty breathing for a moment, as his face turned a deep purple.

'Mr Pang,' Miss Marple said, slightly alarmed. 'Are you quite all right?'

She followed his gaze and found only the old man's companions, and a married couple in their mid-thirties whom she had met earlier – Victor and Ellen Richards. They were both lean and intense. Victor had an aquiline nose and deeply sunken eyes while Ellen's long face, framed by a curtain of light brown hair, had a morose quality. It seemed they owned a successful pharmaceutical company together, which, Miss Marple had understood from Victor, manufactured all sorts of important drugs, without which society would be quite crippled.

'Yes,' Mr Pang wheezed, after a pause. 'Just a bit too much waltzing, I believe.'

Seated at her little table at the corner of the ballroom after dinner, Miss Marple peered around with interest. Soft lamps glowed at each table while the sparkling chandeliers bathed the imposing room in golden light. The men were distinguished in their black tie and the women were mainly in colourful evening gowns. Miss Marple herself was tastefully clad in a grey lace dress. Her fellow guests were of all races, ages and sizes, ranging from a few families with small children to elderly couples with silver hair. Many were demonstrating the steps they had learned at the dance lesson that afternoon as the ship's orchestra played a slow melody. Others chatted or drank hot beverages or cocktails at the round tables scattered around the perimeter of the room, as Miss Marple herself was doing.

Ellen Richards, looking somewhat tree-like in a long green dress covered with a leaf pattern, paused by Miss Marple's table. 'May I join you?'

'Of course,' said Miss Marple. She took a sip of the excellent coffee, then set down her cup. 'Where is your husband?'

'Victor had a bit of a headache, so he's retired early.' Ellen waved at the waiter and a fresh pot was brought. 'I don't see your dance partner.'

'Mr Pang? Indeed, I was looking for him myself. He seemed a bit unwell earlier, so I hope he's all right.'

Ellen sniffed. 'It's no wonder with that companion of his. Aunt Faith, they call her. Well, you'd need to have faith in her strange ways to tolerate her, I suppose.'

'Do you mean the older lady?'

Ellen nodded and bent closer. Despite Ellen's serious demeanour, Miss Marple had discovered that she dearly loved to gossip. 'I believe she's become quite friendly with the crew. She actually uses the ship's facilities to cook extra for him, providing him with all sorts of traditional Chinese medicine. I shudder to think what she's been feeding him. Have you seen the outrageous things she's been doing? Burning incense at all hours of the night. Chanting to herself as she walks. There are rumours that she pokes him with needles. The other day, I actually saw her tossing live crabs and lobsters into the sea!'

Miss Marple raised her eyebrows. 'Where did she get them from?"

Ellen shook her head. She seemed surprised by Miss Marple's matter-of-fact reaction. 'The kitchen, I believe.'

'That *is* a bit odd, but quite refreshing for the crabs and lobsters, I'd imagine.'

Ellen lowered her voice, although the orchestra nearly drowned her words anyway. 'She's a Chinese witch.'

But instead of looking appropriately horrified, Miss Marple seemed quite fascinated. 'I wonder if any of her techniques actually work.'

'Of course not!' exclaimed Ellen. 'Superstitious nonsense, not based on any type of science at all.'

'Well, you would know better than I, I'm sure,' said Miss Marple modestly. 'I'm afraid I've led such a sheltered life.'

Ellen gave a smug little smile that made it clear no one could expect such an elderly and provincial woman to have any grasp of logic anyway. 'It will surely unsettle you, but I'm quite certain that witch only stays with the old man because of the treasure he's rumoured to possess.'

It would astound *you*, thought Miss Marple, what shocking events one can experience in such a small village as St Mary Mead, but, aloud, she merely said, 'What sort of treasure?'

'A piece of extremely valuable jewellery.'

Later that evening, Miss Marple lingered at Mr Pang's door, which was only a few cabins down the corridor from her own. She really didn't want to intrude, and he clearly had the help of both his daughter and care-giver, the one Ellen had called a Chinese witch. Yet, she felt a vague sense of disquiet. Earlier on, Mr Pang had seemed quite startled by something, despite his claims to the contrary.

As she was wondering if she should knock, the door opened. Miss Marple was startled by the surprised face of Mr Pang's daughter, who appeared to be in her mid-twenties. She was tall, with broad shoulders and large hands, and wisps of black hair that were falling out of a messy bun.

'May I help you with something?' the daughter asked politely.

Miss Marple blushed a bit, feeling like a meddling old busybody. 'I am sorry to bother you, but I danced with your father earlier and I was just wondering if he felt all right.'

The daughter smiled, her expressive dark eyes lighting up her pleasant face. 'I remember. My father was quite proud of his waltz with you. Miss Marple, yes? My name is Mudan and I'm grateful to you for caring about Pa's health.' She frowned. 'He did seem to have some trouble swallowing earlier, but I'm happy to say that he's asleep and resting now.'

She opened the door further to show Miss Marple a darkened cabin, from which the faint sound of breathing emitted. There appeared to be the remnants of a meal on the sideboard: a bowl of rice and a plate of hard-boiled eggs next to a vase of flowers. On a little table near to the door, Miss Marple noticed a faded black-and-white photo of a woman holding a small child in her arms.

Mudan saw Miss Marple looking and picked it up to show her. 'Pa mentioned he was telling you about my half-brother, Tao. The photo is of him as a toddler with his mother. This is the last time Pa saw him.'

Mr Pang's first wife had a serene, oval face that was visibly filled with love for the little boy in her arms, despite the dappled sunlight that cast shadows over them. One particularly dark patch obscured a part of the child's face and neck, which made it difficult to make out his expression, but Miss Marple noted his neatly pressed sailor's outfit and jaunty hat. He appeared well-cared-for. A beam of light cascaded off the sparkling brooch pinned to his mother's blouse.

Mudan's expression was sad as she gazed at the photo. 'My father can't wait to see him again in Hong Kong. He's been talking about it for years.'

Miss Marple understood. It was a little like the school-teacher Mr Murray back in St Mary Mead, who pined after his long-lost love, a girl who had moved to London years earlier, while his wife languished from lack of attention. Miss

Marple said gently, 'It's hard to compete with a fantasy, isn't it?'

Mudan's fine eyes flew to Miss Marple's face, surprised. 'How insightful of you, but, of course, the elderly are known for their wisdom.'

Mudan gave Miss Marple a little bow, hands clasped together in a gesture of respect, then stepped out of the cabin, closing the door carefully behind her. After wishing Miss Marple a very fine evening, Mudan went into her own room across the hall from her father's.

Miss Marple was blushing. The reverence Asian cultures held for older generations was unexpected and very welcome.

The next morning there was a great deal of commotion in Miss Marple's corridor. She poked her head out into the hallway to see Dr Grant, the ship's doctor, striding into Mr Pang's room. Miss Marple had met the kindly and rotund medic once when her rheumatism was acting up. Even more alarmingly, Dr Grant was quickly followed by Chief Webster, the ship's security officer, a tall and imposing figure.

Miss Marple got dressed quickly. She was coming out of her cabin just as one of the ship's stewards, a gentle young man, approached. Instead of his usual calm demeanour, he seemed agitated. His tanned face was white against his black hair, his lips pale as wax, and his dark brown eyes were wide with fear.

'What has happened?' Miss Marple asked. She had become quite friendly with this particular steward ever since she'd complimented him on the lovely shapes he created using the cloth napkins in her cabin: a crown, a double star, and, once, even a bird of paradise. Sometimes she came across him in other parts of the ship, serving cocktails on the top deck, for example, or handing out cards for bridge lessons.

The steward hesitated, then said, 'I am so sorry to tell you unfortunate news, but the older gentleman down the corridor passed away in the night.'

'Mr Pang?' At the steward's nod, Miss Marple felt sad for her friend, who would now never see his son again, and for Mudan. 'But he was *waltzing* just yesterday. He might not have been feeling entirely well, but not in a way where one would expect him to die.'

The steward's hands were visibly shaking. He whispered, 'There have been some strange goings-on in that cabin.'

'Oh?'

'Very bad omens there.'

'What in the world do you mean?'

The steward leaned in. 'Terrible things. For a Chinese person, anyway. Other people wouldn't even realise anything was wrong. I once found a bowl of rice with a set of chopsticks stuck right in the middle, like we Chinese only use for burials. Duck eggs, which are very unlucky because they're associated with death. And pure white flowers, also a symbol of funerals. I've seen them in his cabin several times, including just yesterday. Each one of these items invites death into your house.'

'Why would Mr Pang have kept such unlucky things in his cabin?'

The steward shook his head. 'That's just it. Mr Pang was

a very superstitious man. I'm sure he didn't bring those objects into his cabin. He was being terrorised.'

When Miss Marple reached Mr Pang's open door, she paused. Now that daylight was streaming into the room, she could see the sideboard clearly. It was empty. Had someone removed the ill-omened items? Miss Marple thought back to her last glimpse inside the cabin. There had definitely been rice, eggs and flowers, although they'd been hard to see clearly in the semi-darkness. Had some mysterious person been frightening Mr Pang? For what possible reason? Had Mudan or Aunt Faith simply cleaned those things away?

As Miss Marple prepared to walk on before she was noticed hovering in the doorway, she realised something else: the photo of the first wife with the little boy was also missing.

Then the murmur of voices alerted her that the room was occupied. Miss Marple peered inside to find Mudan perched on the bed her father had died on, now stripped of its sheets and bedding, and Aunt Faith sitting in a chair. Chief Webster and Dr Grant stood facing them. Mudan's eyes were red and puffy from weeping while Aunt Faith was white-faced and defiant, her hands clenched into fists. Miss Marple took a step back into the shadows of the hallway to avoid being noticed. She knew she should move on, but she couldn't help feeling that Mudan might need her help at some point. Fortunately, they were so intent upon their conversation that no one glanced in Miss Marple's direction.

'We just need to get a brief statement of what happened,'

Chief Webster said. 'Can you tell us how you found your father?'

Mudan took in a gasping breath. 'I— I went in—'

'It's all right,' Aunt Faith said, patting Mudan on the arm. 'You did nothing wrong.'

'Of course not!' Mudan said, shocked. She inhaled and tried to calm herself. 'I b— brought Pa his morning cup of tea b-but he didn't respond.' She broke out in deep shuddering sobs again.

'I am truly sorry we need to do this,' Dr Grant said gently. 'It's just that there are a few irregularities.'

At this, Mudan's head reared up while Aunt Faith focused on him with her good eye. 'Wh-what do you mean?' asked Mudan.

Chief Webster gave Dr Grant a quelling look. Miss Marple understood no information was to be given to the witnesses or suspects before getting their statements. 'Please know that the best way you could help your father now is to tell us everything you saw, in as much detail as possible. Did you notice anything unusual about Mr Pang last night?'

This concept of being useful seemed to steady Mudan. 'Pa wasn't feeling well last night, but I thought perhaps he'd eaten something that didn't agree with him. He had some difficulty swallowing and didn't speak much as the evening progressed, but finally he settled down and went to sleep.'

Dr Grant said, '*Did* he consume anything unusual last night?'

'Just his normal Chinese medicine,' Aunt Faith said. Her glass eye glittered in the light.

'What would that consist of?' Dr Grant asked in a mild voice.

'He has been very nervous these past weeks, so I have been giving him a strengthening brew to build up his courage: ginseng and ground cobra,' Aunt Faith said calmly.

Chief Webster straightened abruptly. 'You fed Mr Pang cobra?'

'Surely, they removed the venom,' Dr Grant said.

'Oh no,' Aunt Faith declared. 'The venom is the best part! Fear is a poison and you must fight poison with poison.'

Dr Grant raised a bushy eyebrow. 'Ah, similar to the concept of fighting fire with fire, I imagine. But don't you think that adding poison to poison could go terribly wrong?'

'Oh no,' Mudan interrupted. 'Aunt Faith is the best healer we know. She's famous within the Chinese community at home and has been with our family since before I was born. She only gave Pa a tiny bit of cobra each day, not enough to poison him. She would never make a mistake like that. Not enough to kill Pa.'

At that, she broke down and buried her face in her hands. Aunt Faith crossed over to her and lay her hand on her shoulder while glaring at the two men.

Chief Webster cleared his throat. 'That's enough for today.'

A moment before the two women exited the room, Miss Marple stepped away from the doorway and busied herself with her purse, pretending she was looking for her cabin key. Mudan stiffened when she saw her, but then surprised Miss Marple by giving her a weak smile. Aunt Faith didn't even acknowledge her presence. After Mudan and Aunt Faith were out of sight, Miss Marple resumed her position by the cabin.

Chief Webster turned to the doctor. 'What do you make of all that?'

Dr Grant ran a hand down his face. 'It would make sense. A small amount of snake venom can be ingested – not that I would ever recommend doing such a thing – but it would be broken down by stomach acids and digestive enzymes. However, higher amounts could make its way into the bloodstream, which could lead to an attack on the nervous system. Symptoms might include droopy eyelids and difficulty talking and swallowing, leading to the inability to breathe. As you know, I've already determined that the cause of death was suffocation.'

Chief Webster said in his deep voice, 'Manslaughter then, or murder.'

'I'm surprised you didn't arrest her immediately.'

'I want to go through Mr Pang's possessions and papers first to try to determine if there might be a motive. After all, we're on a ship. There's nowhere for Aunt Faith to go.'

Miss Marple pressed her lips together. First Mudan's father had passed away, then his companion was suspected of murder. What a terrible time this was for that gentle young woman.

Miss Marple did not see any sign of Mudan or Aunt Faith the rest of the day. The other passengers seemed unsettled by the sudden passing of Mr Pang but not unduly worried. He had been quite advanced in years, after all, and there were rumours that he'd had some sort of nervous condition, which had surely led to his sudden expiration, as if all anxious elderly people were liable to drop dead at any moment, Miss Marple thought.

At dinnertime, Miss Marple stepped into the dining room, deep in thought. Mr Pang and his stories . . . He'd spoken of his first wife and son. He loved peonies and delighted in them. Then he'd become quite agitated at the sight of either his daughter and care-giver, the so-called Chinese witch, or Victor and Ellen Richards. And there was what the steward had believed about someone trying to scare him on purpose. Miss Marple couldn't quite put her finger on something unusual about that moment on the dance floor. She was missing something. Furthermore, what could the connection be to the missing bad-luck items or photo? There was also that rumour about a fabulous piece of jewellery owned by Mr Pang. Was that still in the cabin? And now he was dead. *She didn't like it any of it, not one bit.*

There was still no sign of Mudan or her companion when the time came for the evening meal, but Victor and Ellen spotted Miss Marple and waved for her to join them.

As soon as Miss Marple sat down, Ellen said, 'Have you heard the awful news about your friend?'

Miss Marple noted Mr Pang's elevation in status from being her *dance partner* to *friend* in Ellen's depiction, but merely nodded. Many people found a vicarious thrill in being close to death. The closer the better, until death invariably came for them.

Victor added, with relish, 'Well, clearly the cause of his

passing wasn't natural. They're planning to arrest that strange Chinese woman, Aunt Faith, tomorrow morning for poisoning Mr Pang with ground cobra. She admitted to it herself.'

'What?' said Miss Marple, feigning incredulity.

'Oh, the medical staff on board are very chummy with us,' Ellen preened. 'After all, we supply them. *They* believe she thought she was helping him . . . You must admit that she had some very suspicious practices.'

When the waiter approached to take their order, Miss Marple was surprised to recognise her own steward. 'I haven't seen you in the dining room before.'

He gave her a little bow. 'We have a small crew on this ship, so we all have various duties, and, tonight, they needed help here.'

Miss Marple hesitated a moment, then pressed forward. 'Would you mind explaining a few things to us?'

Victor and Ellen stared at her with alarmed expressions, apparently appalled that she was conversing with the Chinese waiter.

Victor exclaimed, 'This is hardly proper—'

Miss Marple ignored him. 'Can you tell us why a person might poke another with needles? Or toss live lobsters and crabs overboard? Or why they might consume ground cobra?'

The young steward flushed a bit but endeavoured to give Miss Marple her answers. 'The use of needles is called acupuncture. It is an ancient Chinese treatment that alleviates pain and has been used effectively for thousands of years. Some believe in releasing animals like lobsters and crabs as an offering to the gods, a sort of cosmic gift to bring good fortune. And a small amount of medicine like cobra is given sometimes as a restorative, but the quantity has to be carefully controlled by the practitioner.'

'Thank you for that enlightening explanation,' Miss Marple said, smiling at the steward. 'Do you know Aunt Faith at all?'

'Yes, somewhat. She often comes into the staff area. In fact, she was there earlier today because she needed some boiled water, but something seemed to startle her and she wound up spilling it all over the floor. The supervisor was quite cross.'

Ellen then said, quite rudely, 'Can we order now?'

As Miss Marple ate her dinner of succulent carp steamed in soy sauce, she felt disturbed. From her own knowledge of plants, she knew that a number of Chinese herbal treatments had merit. Despite the common mistrust of Aunt Faith on board, Miss Marple didn't believe Mudan would allow a charlatan to treat her beloved father. And none of this explained the missing items or photo.

She couldn't help but feel that there was more here than met the eye.

Miss Marple felt too agitated to go to the ballroom after dinner and so she headed back to her cabin. The peace and quiet might help her clear her mind and concentrate her thoughts about this suspicious death.

She had just made the turn on to her corridor when she heard a high-pitched scream.

Mudan came staggering out of one of the cabins, hugging herself with her hands. She was breathless and sobbing.

'What is it?' Miss Marple cried.

'A-Aunt Faith! Sh-she's dead!' Mudan swayed as if she might faint.

Miss Marple grasped her arm and then caught her breath as she saw the dark stains on Mudan's blouse and hands. Blood.

There was much gasping and talk around her as other inhabitants of the cabins opened their doors, drawn by the commotion. Someone ran off to fetch the doctor and security officer.

'You poor dear,' Miss Marple said. 'Come, you need to sit down.'

Miss Marple led the young woman to Mudan's own cabin, where the door was ajar, and brought her to the bed. Mudan sat down heavily. She buried her face in her hands, not realising that she was smearing her cheeks with blood. Miss Marple poured her a glass of water and patted her on the back.

When Chief Webster and Dr Grant came through the door several minutes later, Mudan's blood-streaked countenance was the first thing they saw.

'Goodness!' exclaimed Dr Grant, stopping short.

'If you'll excuse us,' Chief Webster said to Miss Marple, but Mudan clutched Miss Marple's hands.

'Please stay!' she begged. 'I'm all alone now. P-please let this kind lady stay.'

Dr Grant and Chief Webster exchanged glances and, with a tiny nod, Chief Webster decided to allow Miss Marple to remain. 'Can you tell us what happened?'

Mudan pressed her fingers against her closed eyelids as if

she wanted to erase the images she'd seen. 'S-she wasn't feeling well. She said she was seasick. I went to check on her and s-she was covered in b-blood.'

'Did you touch the body?' Chief Webster asked.

Miss Marple cast her eyes over Mudan's blood-soaked fingers and wanted to sigh. Of course she had.

'Y-yes,' said Mudan. 'I checked for a pulse. I-I was hoping—' She stared at the floor and said nothing more.

'How was Aunt Faith killed?' Miss Marple asked.

Dr Grant said heavily, 'A knife. The murder weapon is missing but she was stabbed quite recently, within the past hour, I'd say.'

Here Chief Webster glowered again at the talkative doctor, but before he could say anything, Mudan wailed, 'Papa! Aunt Faith!' She broke out in great, heaving sobs.

Miss Marple wrapped a bracing arm around Mudan's shoulders. 'Gentlemen, are you finished? This poor young woman has been through a great deal.'

'I'm afraid this matter is far from finished,' Chief Webster said grimly. He stood up. 'But we shall leave you for tonight.'

After the men had left, Miss Marple helped Mudan clean herself up and get into bed. 'Don't think too much. There's time enough for that tomorrow.'

She stayed by the young woman's bedside holding her hand until Mudan drifted off into an exhausted sleep. Although she had advised Mudan to rest, Miss Marple couldn't do so herself.

There was a murderer on board the *Jade Empress*.

*

'Why hasn't that daughter been arrested yet?' Victor hissed. 'The safety of all of us is at stake! Is that her sitting by the window?'

Miss Marple took a bite of her pineapple bun, which, ironically, did not contain any pineapple. It was still sweet and delicious, however, and she took some comfort in it at breakfast after her restless night. 'That's a different woman. I believe Mudan is taking her meals in her cabin. There's been no evidence found against her.'

'Well, they all look alike anyway,' Ellen said, taking a sip of her black coffee. 'Of course it was her. Who else could it be? She found both bodies. I heard she was covered in blood. Everyone on board is riled up. And here we are, stuck at sea, with a murderer running loose. You can't trust those people.'

Miss Marple looked up. 'Which people?'

'Foreigners,' Victor answered for his wife.

'In Hong Kong,' Miss Marple said, 'I believe we will be the foreigners.'

When Miss Marple returned to her cabin after breakfast, she was surprised to find Mudan waiting by her door.

The young woman was pale and visibly shaking, but she managed to give a wan smile. 'I wanted to thank you for your kindness last night.'

'It was nothing. Are you all right?'

'No. I don't suppose I'll ever be all right again. Not in the same way, anyway.' Mudan gave a little sniff.

'Why don't you come inside?' Miss Marple suggested, as she opened her door.

Mudan nodded and followed her into Miss Marple's tidy cabin. She sank into a chair by the table as if completely exhausted. Miss Marple took the seat next to her.

Miss Marple said, 'The night your father passed away, did you notice anything strange in his cabin?' At Mudan's confused shake of her head, Miss Marple continued, 'Food items, like rice or flowers?'

'Possibly? I was worried about Pa. I didn't really look around.' She wrinkled her brow. 'Although someone seems to have taken the photo of Pa's first wife and Tao.'

'Yes, I had noticed that.'

Mudan gave her a sharp look. 'You are very observant.'

There came a hard knock on the door. Miss Marple opened it to find Chief Webster, a number of security officers and her steward standing outside, the latter wringing his hands.

Chief Webster's face was hard and forbidding. 'We thought we might find her here. Mudan Pang, you are under arrest.'

'What? Why?' cried Mudan, leaping up from her chair.

The other security officers quickly entered the room and surrounded her, grabbing her arms on both sides.

'We found the murder weapon, a steak knife, hidden in a cloth napkin in your room, which had been folded into the shape of a tall, furled tower.'

'But I didn't do anything. I would never, ever hurt—' wailed Mudan. She looked around wildly, settling on the steward. She pointed at him. 'I saw him! He was leaving the hallway as I approached Aunt Faith's room. He must have done it just before I arrived and he hid the knife in the napkin in my room.'

The steward's face turned ashen.

Chief Webster shook his head. 'He's already been questioned. At the time of death, he was on duty in the dining room in front of many of the guests. And it seems quite suspicious that you didn't mention this before.'

'I was distraught! Everything fled my mind. Please—'

'Why would she do such terrible things?' Miss Marple asked mildly.

'It appears her father had a large life insurance policy,' Chief Webster said.

'She was the beneficiary?' Miss Marple asked.

'Yes, she and her half-brother. It appears upon closer investigation that she owns a bakery in Liverpool, and it hasn't been doing well.'

'Business always goes up and down,' Mudan said.

'We've asked around and it was no secret that the father greatly preferred the son. Perhaps it was envy as well.'

Mudan staggered back as if he had struck her. She raised a trembling hand to her mouth.

'What would be her motive with regard to the second murder?' asked Miss Marple.

Chief Webster said, 'That remains to be determined.' He shrugged. 'It is possible Aunt Faith found some proof of her wrong-doing.'

Mudan moaned, 'But I loved my father and Aunt Faith.'

'You must believe me to be a silly old woman,' Miss Marple said, 'but my instincts tell me that she *did* care about them very much. Furthermore, my steward mentioned that a number of items had been put in Mr Pang's cabin, possibly to terrorise him, such as white rice with chopsticks stuck straight up in it. There would have been no reason for Mudan to do such a thing since she had access to his food anyway.'

The steward nodded.

A glimmer of respect entered the chief's eyes. 'I have learned never to underestimate instinct. However, I cannot form a case based on that alone.' He handed Miss Marple his business card. 'If you should remember anything more concrete, day or night, please let me know. I will be returning to my position with the Hong Kong police after this cruise.'

He turned to his officers and they marched a protesting Mudan out of the door. She gave Miss Marple one last pleading look as they took her into custody.

A few days later, Miss Marple was doing Tai Chi in the park in Hong Kong with a group of other elderly practitioners. She had had a troubled mind since disembarking from the cruise ship, puzzling over the details of what had happened on board. Raymond's house was lovely, but he did tend to sleep in, while Miss Marple preferred an early start. She had been delighted to find a group doing this gentle but invigorating exercise every morning.

Although she'd never done such a thing before, she found the simple exercises to be soothing. Together, they stretched their linked hands high in a movement she'd learned was called Lifting the Sky to get their energy flowing, then moved into the Crane, where Miss Marple held her arms out like an ascending bird, with her left knee raised. Her mind was free to fly while her body engaged in the meditative activity.

The murders on board the *Jade Empress* left her extremely unsettled. Had Mudan's innocence been an act, designed to beguile an elderly lady? Or could it have been the steward after all? It might have been possible for him to slip away during his dining room shift, although rather unlikely, Miss Marple had to admit, and it did not seem to be in character for him either. Perhaps even Victor or Ellen was involved. With their knowledge of and access to pharmaceuticals, it would have been very easy for them to poison Mr Pang, and anyone could have obtained a steak knife. However, the bitter truth was that no one on board the cruise ship, except for Mudan, had a possible motive for those murders.

Miss Marple was paired up with another elderly lady for an exercise called push hands. As she mirrored her partner's movements, she noticed a large red birthmark on the side of the woman's face.

Suddenly, everything became clear.

'It is very good of you to join me on your day off,' Miss Marple said. 'These barbecue pork buns are excellent. May I tempt you with one?'

'Delicious,' said Chief Webster. He surveyed their table, which was crowded with sweet lotus seed buns in bamboo steamer baskets, rice noodle rolls filled with beef on tiny plates, and small bowls of congee, a savoury rice porridge. Waiters and waitresses pushed carts filled with delicacies around the restaurant and the guests picked what they desired.

'I have recently learned that "dim sum", which I believe

is what this style of food is called, means "touch the heart",' Miss Marple said. 'That's lovely, isn't it?'

'Indeed,' answered Chief Webster. His brows were furrowed, as if wondering why she had invited him to join her. She had worried that he might refuse to come, but she could tell from the way he now bit into a crystal prawn dumpling with relish that he clearly appreciated a good meal.

'Answers to such mysteries as murders are always linked to matters of the heart, aren't they?' she said.

Chief Webster stilled as he chewed, shifting his focus from his food to Miss Marple.

'There were at least two items missing from Mr Pang's cabin,' she said. 'A valuable brooch and a photo of his first wife and son.'

'Such items were not found, but there is no proof they existed in the first place.'

'That is the reason I did not mention this before,' Miss Marple said. 'However, I believe they are key to solving this mystery. On the evening before Mr Pang died, I was waltzing with him and I noticed he became quite agitated when he saw something over my shoulder. I saw only Mudan, Aunt Faith, and Victor and Ellen Richards, but I was guilty of a fault that many of us share: *I didn't notice the staff*. They were invisible to me. The ballroom dance instructor was also dancing with a young man. It took me a long time to remember that there was something unusual about him, something quite obvious, because he kept looking down at his feet. At first, it appeared his neck was flushed with embarrassment, but it was more than that. He had a red birthmark on the side of his neck.'

Chief Webster's eyes wandered back to the tender egg tart on his plate. He must have been wondering if there was a point to her story.

'I was reminded of an incident I had heard of,' said Miss Marple, omitting the fact that she had in fact solved this particular mystery, 'in which a woman disguised as a chambermaid had committed a murder, yet no one noticed her because all they saw was the uniform, rather than the person inside.'

'I must admit I have no idea what you're trying to say,' Chief Webster confessed.

'Why, it's all very simple,' Miss Marple said. 'You said yourself, there were two beneficiaries to the life insurance policy: Mudan and her half-brother, Tao. Tao is the young man with the birthmark on his neck. In the photo of Tao with his mother, his birthmark was visible but appeared as a dark spot due to the dappled sunlight. I suspect he came aboard the cruise ship as a passenger, then disguised himself as the steward. Since many people think all Asians – and servants – look alike, they didn't look to see that the steward going in and out of their cabin was not always the same person.

'Thus, our actual steward was innocent, but Tao pretended to be him at times. And while disguised as a steward, he had access to the keys. He placed frightening items in Mr Pang's cabin to drive Aunt Faith to feeding him cobra, then ensured that Mr Pang overdosed. His father must have recognised him during our waltz and so Tao had to strike that evening. That was relatively easy with his access to Mr Pang's meals.

'I imagine he wanted Mudan to be accused, because that would invalidate her claim to the life insurance pay-out and he would be the sole beneficiary. Also, I was told that Aunt Faith was often in the staff area, and the *real* steward mentioned to me an incident in which she had been startled by something. I believe Aunt Faith recognised him because of the birthmark on his neck; she had been with the family for a long time. So that gave Tao a reason to get rid of her too. While the real steward was in the dining room, Tao stabbed Aunt Faith. Afterwards, he planted the knife in Mudan's room.'

Chief Webster's mouth was hanging open. He closed it with a click. 'What of the rumours about the priceless piece of jewellery in Mr Pang's possession?'

'I believe that was the brooch. Tao's mother was wearing it in the photo. I think you'll find it when you search his home. He must be on your passenger list and the ballroom dance teacher will be able to help you identify him if he used a fake name.'

'What sort of brooch should we search for?'

Miss Marple answered, 'The image was unclear, but it was a flower. I suspect a peony, because Mr Pang spoke of how much he delighted in seeing his peony every day. At first, I believed he had a plant in his room or perhaps some cuttings from Singapore, but then I remembered that it is impossible for a peony to bloom in the tropics. They need a hard winter. Therefore, he must have been referring to something else.'

Chief Webster shook his head. 'Why did you keep pursuing this matter when it appeared to be such a cut-and-dried case?'

Miss Marple took a sip of oolong tea, delighting in its smokey flavour. 'It didn't make sense to me that Mudan would kill two people she clearly loved. As I said, murders are always linked to matters of the heart. Now, would you care for a wonton?'

Miss Marple had to blush when she read the newspaper. Chief Webster had given her full credit when the priceless peony brooch and the photo of his mother and himself were found in Tao's house. Tao made a full confession. It appeared that Tao had hated his father, because, contrary to Mr Pang's assertions, he hadn't had a first and a second wife. Rather, Mr Pang had been a bigamist. He left Tao and his mother in Hong Kong while he went to Liverpool and then married Mudan's mother. After his mother had died in poverty, Tao was deeply resentful of his father's second family, and especially of his half-sister. He wanted the full inheritance and the peony brooch for himself.

A Mr and Mrs Victor Richards from the cruise line were quoted as being 'absolutely astounded' that Miss Marple had solved this case, but her favourite part of the article was the end, when, upon being told that her father had spoken of his peony being the treasure of his heart, the newly-freed Mudan said, 'That's my name. Mudan means peony.'

A Deadly Wedding Day

Dreda Say Mitchell

One

Even murder wasn't enough to make Miss Marple interrupt a tender moment between a bride and groom, as she arrived – vexingly but unavoidably – late for the strangest wedding reception she had ever attended. Slipping quietly into the room where the wedding breakfast was to be held, she couldn't immediately put her finger on why it was so strange. There was nothing wrong with the venue, of course. A banqueting hall in a stately home was clearly a suitable place to celebrate the wedding of a baronet's son. The walls were lined with paintings of the groom's ancestors, and the furniture, fittings and dinner service had the heaviness of centuries' use. Everything brass and gilt sparkled. All was well with that.

Nor was there anything jarring about the guests, who were all respectable and well dressed. And the doting groom and his bride were playing their part as the happy couple on their wedding day too. Peter Apfel-Strand wore the traditional morning suit, while Marie Baptiste, his bride, looked a picture in a white chiffon gown. Though her dress was perhaps a touch too modish for Miss Marple's taste.

No, it was the collection of individuals seated at the top table that was baffling, resembling as they did a scene from one of those modern New Wave films that critics seemed to enjoy so much but which left their audiences thoroughly confused. The bride's end of the table was deserted, apart from Miss Marple's close friend, Miss Bella, the bride's aunt. Marie's family were from St Honoré, a beautiful island in the Caribbean where Jane Marple had recently been on holiday. Maybe the distance between St Honoré and England was the reason more of Marie's nearest and dearest couldn't attend? When Miss Marple had enquired after Miss Bella's niece's other relations, mildly surprised to merit an invitation, the answer had been the politely evasive 'Families can be very complicated.'

Indeed they can.

If the bride's side was almost empty, the groom's was crowded. There was Peter's father, Sir Herbert Apfel-Strand, his mother, Lady Margaret, and his maternal uncle, Bishop Ambrose, who had officiated at the ceremony. Other family members seemed to proliferate wherever one looked, and the groom's parents were wearing rictus grins as they greeted everyone, clearly determined to keep up appearances; like a family of vultures that had descended on a victim only to discover that the hyenas had got there first.

There was an unavoidable and unpleasant explanation for

their obvious discomfort: while one might hope that, in the England of the 1960s, racial prejudice would be a thing of the past, sadly that was not the case. Was the fact that their son and heir was marrying a black woman from St Honoré perhaps the reason for the Apfel-Strands' gloom? Miss Marple's lips compressed with disapproval.

'Jane! I'm so glad you could come.' Miss Bella greeted Miss Marple with a warm hug, having temporarily excused herself from her place along from the happy couple.

'I'm sorry I'm late.' Miss Marple had missed the wedding ceremony. 'I'm afraid two trains from St Mary Mead were cancelled. That will be something to do with Lord Beeching and the axe he has taken to the railway service, no doubt.'

Miss Bella's statuesque figure towered over her much smaller friend. She wore a no-frills mauve dress that offset the gloss of her brown skin, and a smart hat was perched atop her head. Miss Bella never left home without a hat. Although the women had last seen each other only recently, when Miss Marple had been holidaying on St Honoré – a trip that had included the nasty business of the loss of a hotel guest – they had actually first become acquainted within the confines of an air-raid shelter during the Blitz. While bombs dropped on London, Miss Bella had whiled away the time explaining to Miss Marple, up for a brief visit to the metropolis, how she had not been allowed to serve in the Auxiliary Territorial Service, as the then young Princess Elizabeth had, but how she had recovered from that knock-back, and fought tooth and nail to be admitted to the Women's Auxiliary Air Force instead. The unit had contained other Caribbean women like her, who had answered the call to help the 'Motherland', as they had been brought up to think of England. Miss Bella had then, post-war, stayed on and become a nurse in Britain's new National Health Service.

'Has Marie no friends she could invite?' Miss Marple asked.

'She keeps to herself. In fact, I don't know too much about her life in England at all. She only arrived from St Honoré just over a year ago. I believe she has some type of office job.'

'Do you know how she met the groom?'

'No. She is always vague about how it happened.' Miss Bella added, 'We don't know each other very well, what with my residing for so much of my adult life in England. I don't want her to think I'm sticking my nose into her business.'

'Are you staying locally?' Miss Marple asked.

'I'm sharing a room with Marie at the Fruit Pickers Arms in the village. But I'm returning home tomorrow, while Marie and Peter are leaving on honeymoon this evening. At least I assume they are; Marie was rather fuzzy about that too.'

Marie Baptiste appeared to be vague about many things.

Miss Marple's keen eye noticed someone else at the high table. 'It appears your niece has a guest after all.'

The newcomer was a woman in her early twenties, a few years younger than the bride, willowy tall, sporting a blonde Vidal Sassoon bobbed haircut and a tan, as if she had recently returned from warmer climes, and she was standing over Marie. She wore what was known in the more salacious newspapers as a 'mini-skirt'. It was immodestly short and certainly not the kind of attire you would expect a respectable young lady to wear to a wedding reception. Marie and her guest were exchanging what looked like terse words, and their exchange ended with a long pause and then Marie shrugging her shoulders. The woman then seated herself in the chair Miss Bella had vacated.

Miss Marple and Miss Bella weren't the only ones watching this curious exchange it seemed. Bishop Ambrose, the groom's venerable uncle, was carefully studying the woman's legs, and his expression suggested that he might well be considering a sermon railing against the sins of the flesh.

'Do you know that young lady?' Miss Marple asked Miss Bella.

Her friend shook her head. 'I think I saw her briefly at the Fruit Pickers Arms at breakfast. Perhaps she's staying there too? Marie must know her well or she wouldn't be invited to sit at the top table. Oh, I see Sir Herbert is about to call everyone to their seats. I'd better go and find another for myself before he starts.'

While Miss Marple wove through the mingling guests and found her allocated table, the doughty peer of the realm got to his feet, a stiff grin still carved into his stony face. 'My wife and I would like to welcome everyone to Strand Hall on the happy occasion of the wedding of our son, Peter. The wedding breakfast will be served now, before the speeches.'

A chilled asparagus soup, followed by salmon and vegetables, and then a fruit salad for dessert, were complemented by an agreeable white wine, with champagne provided for the toasts. All good English fare, and, a little over an hour later, with everyone replete, Sir Herbert rose again and tapped his wine glass with a spoon. But before he could speak, there was a commotion on the bride's side of the table.

Marie's mysterious guest struggled to her feet, gulping for air. She clutched her chest in apparent agony, then her belly, before finally her hands desperately grabbed and clawed at her throat. Her chair tumbled backwards, crashing to the ground as she staggered past the horrified bride towards the father of the groom.

She rasped out: 'Stra . . . Strand . . . B . . . B . . . Ap . . .'

Then she collapsed into the arms of the astonished baronet.

Instinctively, his arms cradled her twitching and jerking body. Then she was still. Sir Herbert appeared on the verge of panic, until his wife stepped into the breach with phlegmatic upper-class sangfroid.

Lady Margaret addressed the guests. 'Ah . . . this young lady seems to have fainted. It *is* dreadfully stuffy in here. Perhaps someone could open a few windows?' She turned to her husband, her voice tight, delivering her words through clenched teeth, 'Let me help you escort our guest to the salon, where she can lie down and recover.'

Quickly waving away the staff who had rushed forward to help, Lady Margaret took one of the woman's limp arms and draped it over her shoulder. The baronet and his wife then gamely half-carried, half-dragged the young woman through a door at the back of the banqueting hall.

Miss Marple and Miss Bella exchanged knowing glances. Miss Bella was a retired nurse, while Miss Marple, too, had seen much in her time.

Both women were certain that the unfortunate stranger was dead.

Two

'Did you establish that the young woman is indeed dead?' Miss Marple asked Miss Bella, as they both loitered by the door through which the baronet and his wife had disappeared.

Miss Bella had just that minute returned, after attempting to offer her services as a trained nurse. 'I didn't get a chance. Sir Herbert and Lady Margaret wouldn't let me see her. They insist they don't need any help.'

Just like Miss Marple, Miss Bella had something of a reputation as an amateur detective amongst London's Caribbean community. It was she and she alone, after all, who had deduced what had really happened in the infamous and so-called 'Steel Pan Murders' in Notting Hill.

Miss Bella's expression was severe. 'I don't know what they're playing at. . . Why don't you go and see for yourself?'

Miss Marple did exactly that. Through the door was a hallway with a number of closed doors. But there was no need to guess behind which of them the Apfel-Strands happened to be; their raised voices carried clearly along the corridor.

'I'm telling you, Herbert, for the final time, that we are *not* cancelling this reception. You know how much it cost.' Lady Margaret sounded like a bulldog on the attack. 'Don't you remember the grin on the face of that nasty little banker when we asked for an extension to our overdraft? With a stately home like this, there's no way we could have ducked out of providing the venue for the wedding. If we hadn't, everyone would've have guessed our situation. We can't afford to abandon this reception and then potentially have to pay for another one. It's not as if the bride's family are likely to come up to scratch, and appearances *must* be upheld.'

Miss Marple stopped and listened.

'You're not seriously suggesting we leave this dead girl on a pile of orange boxes while we go and celebrate our son's wedding?' Sir Herbert rallied, 'I'm calling the police and an ambulance. Right now.'

'You'll do no such thing.' His wife's response cracked in the air. 'We'll wait until all the guests have departed and *then* we'll call them. We can easily explain the delay.'

When Herbert Apfel-Strand spoke again, it was in a much softer, more wheedling tone. 'Is it so bad that our son has married for love, Margaret? Marie is such a lovely girl.'

'Marrying for love?' his wife sneered. 'You sound like a chambermaid. We don't marry for love in this family, as well you know. If your son had done his duty and married a suitable *and monied* spouse, we wouldn't be in this mess. Or would you have preferred Peter to get hitched to a woman like this strumpet you invited to the wedding?'

The baronet remained silent, provoking her ladyship to even greater rage, 'I see you don't even have the good manners to deny it.'

Her voice then came to an abrupt halt, maybe sensing that someone was hovering outside of the door. Miss Marple thought it prudent to knock, and the door opened a few inches wide to reveal a sliver of Sir Herbert's deeply furrowed face. 'Oh, Miss Marple, is it not? How may I help?'

'I was just wondering whether I could be of any assistance with the young lady who was taken ill. I'm an experienced first-aider, you know.'

Apfel-Strand gave a light and not completely convincing laugh. 'You'll be happy to hear the patient is upright and drinking a glass of water.' He turned his head, calling out, 'Isn't that right, Louise?' He turned back. 'She's rather embarrassed, to be honest, and doesn't want any further fuss. We'll be back in our places shortly, so if you would be so kind as to return to the wedding party?'

The door closed firmly in her face. As it did so, Miss Marple heard a further snatch of their conversation.

Lady Margaret was saying bitterly, 'Is that Jane Marple? My godmother lives in the same village as her, St Mary Mead, and claims she's an interfering crackpot. Losing her marbles more likely, in her old age.'

Miss Marple sighed. It wasn't the first and it wouldn't be the last time she was dismissed as a silly old woman with one foot in the grave, and, she reflected, it was in such strong contrast to the way Miss Bella was treated by her Caribbean community. Her friend was highly esteemed, and no one would ever dream of calling Bella Baptiste by her first name only. The honorific 'Miss' was considered a mark of respect for her age and life experience.

Wandering back down the hallway, Miss Marple noticed that one of the other doors that led off it was ajar. Out of idle curiosity, she pushed at it and stepped inside. The room, which had clearly once been a rather grand drawing room, was now bare. In contrast to the opulence of the banqueting hall, the walls here showed marks where pictures had once hung. What appeared to be the last remaining contents of the room were now packed away in wooden boxes, stacked in haphazard piles on the now bare floorboards, seemingly awaiting collection. The Apfel-Strands had clearly fallen on hard times – what else might they be hiding?

Miss Marple and Miss Bella conferred together in a quiet corner. Miss Bella muttered to her friend, '"Alligator lays eggs but it's no chicken", as we say back home.' For the avoidance of doubt, she elaborated further, 'Things are not always as they seem, are they? Healthy young women don't drop dead at wedding receptions, and the family certainly don't then pretend a dead guest is alive. I don't need my years of nursing to know that her symptoms were those of someone who has been poisoned. Perhaps we should call the police ourselves?'

Miss Marple considered this but shook her head. 'I fear the police would be sent away with a flea in their ear, should Sir Herbert and Lady Margaret want to deny there's a dead body on the premises. The provincial constabulary tend to be rather deferential where the gentry are concerned. I suggest we see if we can shed some light on the matter ourselves for the time being.'

'The trouble is we don't even know who she is, much less who might have a motive for poisoning her, if that is what has happened. We need to speak to Marie and find out what she knows.'

'We might already have a clue to her identity. Sir Herbert called her "Louise". He was too flustered by all that was going on to make that up, so that is quite probably her real name. And his wife as good as accused him of having an illicit liaison with "this strumpet", which I'm assuming is also a reference to the dead and, if we're correct, murdered young lady.'

Miss Bella nodded in agreement. 'To my ears, it sounded like she was trying to say his lordship's surname before collapsing into his arms. That looks *very* incriminating.'

'Maybe not,' Miss Marple countered, after a few seconds of silent thought. 'In moments of medical distress, it is often natural to call out the name of the person in front of you for help.'

'Except,' her friend persisted, 'Louise staggered past Marie to get to his lordship.'

With so much unexplained, Miss Marple and Miss Bella proceeded to organise their plan of action with almost military precision. Miss Marple would use her eyes and ears, speaking to the bride for a start, and Miss Bella would attempt to track down the source of the poison.

After a short search, Miss Marple found Marie out on the lawn at the edge of the grand formal gardens. Several other guests were having a post-prandial stroll, but Marie was alone, and the newlywed woman's arms were wrapped tight around her middle. Miss Marple approached and said kindly, 'I'm so sorry that your friend Louise was taken ill.'

'I beg your pardon?' Marie's lashes fluttered wildly. 'Who?'

'The young lady seated next to you? Who fainted. Louise?'

Marie looked off across the vast, manicured gardens. 'She's not my friend. I've no idea who she is. Or what her name is. I didn't get much say in the guest list, I'm afraid.'

'It still seems rather unusual to ask a stranger to sit next to you on your wedding day, dear.'

'Oh, she told me she was a friend of Tante Bella's,' Marie explained. She used the French for aunt, emphasising the long ee sound at the end. Though St Honoré was English speaking, the odd French word remained. 'Or maybe it was someone else in the family. I can't recall. She asked if she could join us, and I felt it would be rude to turn her away.' She turned her face back to the older woman, her eyes wide, goosebumps rising on her bare arms in the cooling wind. 'Is she all right?'

Miss Marple decided to play her cards close to her chest for now. 'Your in-laws are taking care of her.' Quickly, she changed the subject. 'How did you and your delightful new husband meet?'

Marie stammered, looking flustered, and replied with what seemed to be her habitual vagueness, 'I can't remember.'

Before Miss Marple could press her further, the groom appeared. He was attentive, sweetly grasping hold of his wife's hand. 'Sorry to cut you both short, but I think my parents will be back shortly and the speeches will begin at last.'

Miss Marple left them to have a quiet moment together and returned to the wedding reception. After all, she had another witness she particularly wanted to interview.

Taking advantage of the disruption to proceedings, she took the spare seat next to Bishop Ambrose at the top table. She didn't know him personally, of course, but was familiar with his voice and opinions. He was a regular guest on the wireless, particularly the BBC's Home Service, where he was known to hold forth on the evils of 'the permissive society'.

'Bishop Ambrose, please forgive the interruption, but I just thought I'd take this opportunity to say how much I enjoyed your talk warning good Christian folk about the dangers of listening to those young men from Liverpool – The Beatles, is it?'

Ambrose was flattered enough to forgive her mistake. 'It was The Rolling Stones, madam, but thank you.'

Miss Marple knew any attempt to interview the bishop would have to be brief, as the reception was about to resume with the return of the Apfel-Strands, so she proceeded with alacrity. 'That young lady who was taken ill, do you know her, by chance?'

Ambrose pursed his lips with disapproval. 'Regrettably, yes.'

'Oh, is she not quite the thing?'

Bishop Ambrose confided, 'I'm not one to cast the first stone, but my eyes know what they saw. I will merely say this. You can hardly expect the lower orders to behave properly when their social betters set such a bad example.' With that, the bishop cast what might be considered an accusatory glare at his brother-in-law, Sir Herbert, who entered the room at that point. 'A fish rots from the head.'

Three

'Kitchen Personnel Only' warned the notice attached to the kitchen door below stairs. In normal circumstances, Miss Bella would have returned to the reception on sight of it; she was a stickler for the rules, especially where kitchens were concerned. However, a determination to get to the bottom of what had happened to that poor unfortunate girl drove her on. Inside there were plenty of staff rushing about, and orders being shouted every which way. No one noticed Miss Bella, but she spotted what looked like the staff cloakroom and ducked inside. There she found one of the grey smocks everyone seemed to be wearing and pulled it on, hoping that, as several of the catering team were also black, she would pass without comment. She replaced her hat with the white bonnet that came with the uniform and then headed off to the enormous butler's sink, where tray after tray of plates and bowls that had been cleared from the banqueting hall were stacked high. Her aim was to first examine the food for any evidence of anything unusual, anything that might suggest poison, and, if that yielded no results, to check the remnants of the drinks that had been served.

But there was only one way to examine the plates without drawing attention to herself, and that was to pretend to wash up. Miss Bella, ever indomitable, rolled up her sleeves, put in a plug, and began to fill the sink with soapy water. Putting on a good show of washing the dishes but never actually plunging them into the water, she carefully examined each plate for any sign or smell of foul play. She was focusing on the fish course to begin with, when one of the bowls of half-eaten fruit salad caught her eye.

'And *what* are you doing here?' a voice demanded.

Miss Bella turned to find a chef in his tall white hat looking at her with deep suspicion. His cheeks were ruddy, giving him the appearance of someone who maybe guzzled the cooking brandy on the quiet as he commanded the *batterie de cuisine*. Nevertheless, she couldn't fault his commitment to getting the food for the reception right, because she noticed he had the roughened hands of someone who worked hard for a living.

Quick off the mark, Miss Bella replied, 'One of the waiters was asked what was in the fruit salad, and he asked me if I knew when he brought the dishes in. Delicious, apparently. I know how busy you chefs are, so I was checking myself.'

With pride, the chef lengthened his neck, making his hat wobble. 'My *salade de fruits*? A sprinkling of exotic spices and my special ingredient. You must tell them that it is a secret!'

He flounced off, and Miss Bella turned back to the fruit salad bowl that had caught her attention. Using a spoon, she pulled out a piece of the fruit and stared at it in horror.

What was it Marie Baptiste was hiding? Why was she pretending not to know Louise? And why did the bride become so ruffled and evasive when asked how she had met her groom? These questions plagued Miss Marple as she sat back at her table in the banqueting hall, waiting for the groom to commence giving his speech. Miss Marple's sharp mind ticked over, trying to think of a subtle way to somehow provoke Marie into talking about her relationship to the dead woman, as she was certain there was more to it than Marie had let on. Miss Marple smiled with satisfaction as she suddenly hit upon just the thing.

She turned to the other guests at her table, mildly observing: 'I do so often think it's rather a pity that the bride doesn't get to have a speech at her own wedding, don't you? That it's just the groom and his best man and the rest of the men in this day and age?'

The ruddy-faced, balding man opposite her didn't agree. 'Brides making speeches at weddings? What are you, a radical or something?'

Happily, however, his attractive and much younger wife was quick to pick up the baton. 'Don't be rude, Giles. She's quite right. Why *doesn't* the bride get a chance to say a few words? Women do have tongues as well, you know.'

Giles rolled his eyes, but he softened, demonstrating an indulgent affection for his wife. 'I don't know, dear. I only deal with the law, I don't make it.'

Their attention was then caught by the top table as the groom, Peter Apfel-Strand, rose to his feet and cleared his throat. He told several stories, but not the one Miss Marple had been hoping to hear: how he had met Marie. So, when he finished, she sighed to the attractive women at the table, 'Oh, I would so like a few words from the bride about how they met. I am *such* a romantic.'

On cue, the woman, who had maybe imbibed more of the wine than was wise, called out, 'What about a bit from the bride about how you met!'

Some of the older guests looked a tad scandalised by her behaviour; shouting out at a high society wedding like a stallholder at Petticoat Lane Market just wasn't the done thing. However, a number of the younger women were firmly nodding in agreement. This was the 1960s; the world was swinging, and changing fast.

Gamely, Peter rose to the occasion. 'We met in a solicitor's office—'

'No, we didn't,' Marie interjected with a touch of alarm, then, softening her voice, she continued, 'It was at a party.'

'Was it?' Peter appeared thoroughly confused by his bride's assertion, but whatever he read in her face made him swiftly change tack. 'Of course . . . of course, it was a party! How could I forget?'

Miss Marple acknowledged wryly that her ploy had failed, and she was about to leave the table to go find Miss Bella and see how she'd been getting on when Giles, the red-faced husband of the vocal woman, suddenly spoke up. 'I know how they met.'

Miss Marple paused momentarily and then seized the moment. 'Really? Do tell.'

'I'm the family solicitor. Peter and his father were in my office one day discussing some financial business. My next two clients were seated outside and, out of the blue, started having a bit of ding-dong. Anyway, Peter, Sir Herbert and I broke up the dispute. One of the women was Marie. That was how Peter met her. He took her outside to calm things down and that was the start of their courtship. Meanwhile, Sir Herbert took the other young lady elsewhere to do the same.' He coughed. 'Calm her down, I mean.' But he looked significantly at his wife and winked.

Miss Marple was all ears. 'And who, may I ask, was this other young lady in the waiting room?'

He seemed rather surprised at the question. 'Why, Louise McCracken. That woman who fainted at the top table.'

Miss Marple hurried away, big with news, but stopped in her tracks as soon as she came across Miss Bella in the hallway and saw her stricken face. 'What is it? What's happened?'

Bella opened up the folded napkin she held. Inside was what looked like half of a baby-sized green apple, but she batted Miss Marple away when she reached out for a closer look. 'Don't touch it, Jane!'

'What on earth is it?'

Bella was terribly distressed. 'It was in a bowl of fruit salad that must have been given to Louise—'

'McCracken. Louise McCracken.'

Miss Bella continued. 'They're called the Little Apples of Death. Highly poisonous. They can be deadly. There must have been more of them in her fruit salad, which she ate. They're said to have a very sweet, seductive taste.'

Noticing her friend was deeply shaken, nearly in tears, Miss Marple said, 'I don't fully understand. Why are you so upset?'

'Because they are the fruit of the Manchineel tree, which is native to the Caribbean. They grow in St Honoré, not here.' She looked Miss Marple squarely in her eye. 'There are only two people at this wedding who come from St

Honoré and would know about this tree. And *I* didn't put these apples of death in Louise McCracken's dessert.'

That only left one other person. The bride.

Her beloved niece, Marie Baptiste.

Four

'Your niece is innocent, I'm sure of it, and we're going to prove it,' Miss Marple asserted as they sat in the back of the taxi on their way to the Fruit Pickers Arms. 'I'm sure, once we've had a good look in Miss McCracken's room, we'll get to the bottom of this. But we'll need to find the real killer as quickly as possible, or they will vanish like that golden eagle everyone made such a fuss over.'

Miss Bella nodded at the reference to the now notorious Goldie, who had recently escaped from London Zoo and remained at large for thirteen days.

Miss Bella spoke with passion. 'One of the reasons I fought long and hard, all those years ago, to gain admittance to the Women's Auxiliary Air Force was to pave the way for the next generation of black women, like my beloved niece, Marie, so that, when *her* time came, she could walk, head held high, right through the door.' Bella Baptiste gave herself a shake and then straightened her shoulders with determination. 'There is no way that my youngest sister's daughter could have taken another's life.'

In that moment, Miss Marple understood. Their investigation was no longer just about who had killed Louise McCracken. For Miss Bella, this was about exonerating

Marie, who she was certain could not be guilty of such a wicked crime. She was already facing deep-seated prejudice by marrying into the aristocracy, so the last thing she needed was any shadow attached to her name. But who could the guilty party be, and why did it seem that they were trying to frame the bride?

Sir Herbert was an obvious suspect. It was pretty clear he was involved in an illicit liaison with the unfortunate Louise. But it was surely highly unlikely he would have invited his paramour to his son's wedding. Of course, if it was indeed true that they were carrying on, then Lady Margaret would potentially have a motive. Or was Peter Apfel-Strand maybe exacting revenge against Louise for whatever she had done to his Marie, which was presumably the cause of the fracas at the solicitor's office? And what about Bishop Ambrose? Had his eyes lingered rather too long on the legs of the very tall and willowy Miss McCracken? Was he, secretly, a bit too fond of the sins of the flesh he so condemned? There was no greater hypocrite than one with a high moral tone, Miss Marple reflected.

'Tell me about the Manchineel tree, Bella.'

'You probably saw them in St Honoré on your recent holiday. The tree grows along the beach, a natural defence to keep the coastline safe from erosion. Unfortunately, everything about the tree is dangerous. It's not only the fruit of the tree that can be deadly, but so is the bark and leaves. The tree produces a milky sap that will burn skin and, if ingested, burn the throat and cause terrible stomach trouble. I have also heard that if the bark is lit, the fire produces poisonous fumes that can blind and kill. The authorities paint white crosses on them to warn people to stay clear. The toxin it produces is powerful and still very much a mystery.'

She continued to speak looking down at her clenched hands. 'Although most on St. Honoré know to stay away from this terrible tree, every now again there are deaths. Sadly, usually children. I remember one case where a child fell asleep under one of the trees on the beach. The sap from the bark and leaves dripped on their skin with the quiet of a silent killer. He was rushed to the local hospital, but there was nothing anyone could do.' A wave of memory dulled the usual sparkle in her brown eyes. 'The howl of grief from his mother will stay with me for all my days on this earth.'

Frowning, Miss Marple racked her brains, trying to recall if she had ever heard of the Manchineel Tree or its poisonous fruit. As a keen gardener, she made it her business to increase her knowledge of the flora and fauna of the world, including the deadly varieties. And surely, if this tree was so harmful, there must be records of it causing deaths. Rightly guessing what her dear friend was thinking, Miss Bella raised her head, the tips of her mouth turning down. 'The death of us native people on St Honoré wasn't of much interest to the authorities, so why bother keeping records when one of them dies from an encounter with the malevolent Tree of Death?' Her brow pleated. 'What is strange, though, is that Louise McCracken died so quickly.'

'What do you mean?' Miss Marple pressed.

'All the cases I know of people sickening from eating the Manchineel's apple have either lingered long enough to receive treatment and have survived or died hours later because they had no access to medical intervention. There must be another explanation for why Marie's guest died so quickly.'

The English countryside, so seemingly benevolent compared to such Caribbean dangers, flew by as the taxi carried them back to the local village, where the Fruit Pickers Arms stood part way along a mediaeval high street. The inn itself was the picture-book image of an English country hostelry, half-timbered, but with some Georgian brickwork here and there, and luxuriant ivy insinuating itself where it was most needed to round off the overall effect. Dappled with early evening sunlight, the ancient sign swung in the breeze.

Miss Bella grimaced. 'I should warn you now that the landlord isn't an overly sympathetic person. A perpetual grouch and growler. When Marie and I arrived, he reminded us that he didn't get many "guests from the Commonwealth" staying at his establishment. He made that sound like a good thing.'

'Did he indeed?' Miss Marple felt vexed that her wonderful friend and her beloved niece had had to deal with such blatant prejudice, especially compared to the warm welcome she herself had received in St Honoré.

The whiskery old duffer behind the reception, whose clothes appeared to be wearing him, instead of the other way round, levelled them with a suspicious, bleary eye.

'Ladies. How may I help?'

Miss Bella stepped forward. 'I'm afraid one of your guests has been taken ill and we're here to collect her belongings. Her name is Louise McCracken.'

The landlord was very firm. 'That's out of the question. In situations like that, we can only offer keys to the police or ambulance staff.'

Miss Marple squeezed her friend's arm and stepped forward. 'We quite understand. Normally we wouldn't dream of asking, but if you recall the young lady in question, you'll understand why her family wants to keep the authorities' involvement to a minimum. She will have left these premises in an ensemble some might conclude was more suitable for retiring at night rather than outdoor wear. . .'

The landlord sniffed. 'You mean the young lady in room six?' He then took malicious pleasure in scoffing, 'Come to some sort of sticky end, has she? I can't say I'm surprised, by the look of her. We get that kind of carry on even in a sleepy village like ours. Young men with long hair and females of questionable reputation driving around in open-top sports cars, blasting their horns at all hours of the night.'

Miss Marple drew close. 'Louise is from a very upright family, so, as you can imagine, they're anxious to avoid any scandal. If you could permit us to collect her things, they would be for ever grateful.'

The landlord considered the situation for a few moments before his sympathy for the parents won out. As he handed over the key, he grumbled another complaint. 'That Louise wouldn't stop chit-chatting with Elsie, my chambermaid, distracting the girl from her work. I'm not paying her to be idle and to cosy up to the clientele.'

In room six there was very little sign that anyone had occupied the room at all. Some make-up sat on the dressing table along with an overnight bag that only contained a change of clothing.

Miss Marple sighed. 'Disappointing.'

But as they started to leave, Miss Bella retraced her steps and picked up what looked like a jewellery box. 'This is a rather unusual item, don't you think? And it's got a crest engraved on it.'

Miss Marple explained, 'I think it's what the Scottish call a "snuff mull", which is a type of large snuff box.' Her finger smoothed across the top. 'Scottish snuff mulls were made of animal horn, like the top of this one, and very often they were left in the shape of the animal's horn. This is an antique and rather expensive item.' A close inspection allowed Miss Marple to disentangle some of the details of the crest, which was expertly carved. 'Cross of St Andrew . . . a Stag . . . a mountain peak . . . definitely Scottish, if rather stereotypically so.'

Miss Marple opened the box inside, which revealed a few scratchy leaves and a small piece of wood, which was chipped, with shavings lying beside it. Urgently, Miss Bella snatched the box back.

'Don't touch them, Jane.' She emptied the leaves and wood on to a piece of paper on the writing desk. She examined them under the desk lamp. 'These are the leaves and bark of the Manchineel tree. They will be coated with the toxic, milky sap.' Her gaze flicked to Miss Marple. 'Did someone deliberately leave them in there, knowing she would place her hands in the box? Was this another way of trying to poison Louise McCracken?'

They left the room and locked the door. Miss Bella headed for the stairs, but her friend hesitated. 'No, Bella, dear.'

'Surely we're finished here?'

It had to be said. 'We need to check Marie's possessions too. The police will be investigating shortly and its better we get some answers before they do.'

Once inside the room, Miss Marple conducted a thorough search of Marie's suitcase, where, in a side pocket, she found a slim, folded silver photograph frame. When it was opened, it displayed two black-and-white photos, one on each side. One was of a white naval officer with a black woman in a smart suit, her arm linked with his. In the background was a white clapboard church with a mountain in the background. When pulled from its frame, a pencil inscription on the back read '24th June 1940'. The other picture was of the same woman, lovingly cradling a baby.

'Do you know who these people are, Bella?'

Her friend's hand shook as she took the photos. 'The woman is my youngest sister, Colette, and the baby is her daughter, Marie. It must have been taken on St Honoré, because that's the extinct volcano that dominates the island behind them.'

She peered hard at the uniformed man. 'I've never seen him before. There was a naval base on the island during the war, hunting U-Boats, that kind of thing. Perhaps he served on one, met my sister and, as these things happen, a baby was born. I was in London, but I am sure I heard she married. By the time I finally returned home after the war, there was the child, Marie, but no husband, and I asked no questions.'

Without a word, Miss Bella took the twin photo frame and left the room. A few minutes later she returned with the snuff mull from Louise McCracken's room. She showed Miss Marple the crest on it and then the one, worn by time, on the silver photograph frame.

They were the same.

Downstairs, Miss Marple used the pay phone to call her old friend, Sir Henry Clithering, a retired former commissioner of Scotland Yard. She spoke quietly and quickly to him. After she finished the call, she and Miss Bella partook of some refreshments while they waited for Sir Henry to call back, which he did in less than an hour. Furnished with the information he provided, Miss Marple and Miss Bella finally alighted on the truth of the murder committed earlier that day.

Miss Bella shared another of her shrewd Caribbean sayings: '"Before a monkey buys trousers, he has to know where to put his tail".' She explained, 'This crime was carefully planned every step of the way.'

Before they left, the landlord told them one thing more. 'The girl in room six was a very busy bee yesterday.' He squinted at Miss Bella. 'In the morning I saw her talking to the young woman who travelled with you. And later that night I saw her deep in conversation with his Lordship, from up at the Hall.'

Five

'Louise is dead?' Marie slumped back against the burgundy Chesterfield, tears springing to her eyes. Miss Marple noted she was no longer keeping up the falsehood of not knowing the other woman.

The reception was still in full swing in another part of the Hall. On their arrival back at Strand Hall and, after another visit to the kitchen, Miss Marple had discreetly gathered all the relevant parties, in a room she suspected Lady Margaret had chosen, because it was one with furniture still in it. It was here that Miss Marple revealed the tragic news of the unfortunate death at her wedding to the bride.

Peter protectively drew his wife close, snapping at Miss Marple, 'What do you mean dead? She fainted, and I assumed by now she was on her way home.'

Miss Marple's shrewd eyes rested on his parents. 'She is lying dead in another room on the ground floor, isn't that correct, Sir Herbert?'

Herbert Apfel-Strand had the grace to look away, but his wife was another story; she mutinously compressed her lips. Then again, no answer was necessary; the silence of the truth was as loud as a scream.

Miss Marple began. 'The young woman who died here today, as some of you will already know, was Louise McCracken. In her room at the Fruit Pickers Arms, we discovered an item that displayed the crest of a very wealthy Scottish family. Clyde McCracken, laird of Clan McCracken, recently passed away, which left his daughter, Louise, a very rich heiress.

'During the last war, however, Clyde McCracken had been a naval officer stationed in the Caribbean, on St Honoré, where he met and fell in love with a local woman—'

'My younger sister, Colette,' interjected Miss Bella, the emotion in her shaking voice audible for all to hear.

'They had a daughter, who they named Marie,' Miss Marple pressed on. 'When Clyde came back to England, it was to find that his father had ploughed the family finances into some very unwise investment ventures. In the tradition of the upper classes, Clyde had to marry for money, which he did within the year. The heiress was from another landed Scottish family. And he worked hard to re-establish the family finances,' – Sir Henry had, in fact, estimated that he had tripled them – 'as a tough businessman, on both sides of the border. But Clyde McCracken was hiding a secret.

'As a young naval officer, he had not only fathered a child with Colette Baptiste, but had also done the honourable thing and married her, in a ceremony at the local church in St Honoré. This meant his marriage with Louise's mother was bigamous, and that Marie, his first and only legitimate born child, was his true heir, not Louise.'

Peter looked down in astonishment at his new wife, 'Darling, is this true?'

Marie gazed back up at him, clearly distraught. She trembled slightly in his arms, and was about to speak, when his uncle's voice boomed out into the room.

'Eh?' Bishop Ambrose spluttered in clerical outrage. 'Impossible! The church keeps meticulous records of all marriages. If he had tried to get married while he still had a wife, he would have been found out.'

Miss Marple had already considered this. 'The marriage records for Clyde and Colette were in the Caribbean, on the other side of the world; well out of the reach of anyone in England. This wouldn't be the first time such a thing has occurred. During and after the war, getting married twice was not unheard of, I'm sorry to say, whatever the Church might like to think.'

Finally, Marie quietly spoke up. 'I knew that Clyde McCracken was my father. But I didn't know that he was married to my mother until this nasty business with Louise started.' Peter's embrace tightened. 'Clyde bought a holiday home on St Honoré, where he would bring his *wife* and Louise for the summer, while paying furtive visits to me and mummy on the other side of the island. He paid for me to have a good education and helped me get a good job when I came to England.' Fire lit up her eyes. 'But I was always a dirty little secret. I never asked for any of this. I did *not* murder my half-sister.'

Miss Marple then settled her inquisitive gaze on Sir Herbert and his wife. Lady Margaret scoffed, 'You're not suggesting that *we* had anything to do with her death?'

Miss Marple focused on the baronet. 'Were you having an illicit relationship with Louise McCracken?'

It was Miss Marple who answered, however, without waiting for Sir Herbert to speak, but with another question, this time directed at Marie, who remained notably silent, strain tightening her face. 'But you know this not to be true, don't you, my dear? Your father-in-law wasn't having an affair with your half-sister. He was helping you.'

'Marie is such a lovely girl.' Miss Marple recalled Sir Herbert's words to his wife earlier. The words had been

spoken with such tenderness that it was clear that he not only wholeheartedly approved of his son's choice of wife, but he also held a great personal affection for her. Enough to help her when she found herself in a troubling situation.

Her voice barely above a whisper, Marie said, 'My father's solicitor summoned me to his office in London and this is where I met my half-sister for the first time. We were both informed of my parents' marriage and that I was the legal heir . . . We argued.' Tenderly, she turned to her new husband. 'And that's where I met Peter. He came to my rescue, but he didn't overhear the heated discussion I had with Louise, so was ignorant of the details. After that, Louise wouldn't leave me alone. She kept threatening me to stay quiet about my mother and father's marriage. And then Sir Herbert found me very distressed one day . . .'

'And decided to warn Louise off,' Miss Marple finished. Her gaze turned to Marie's father-in-law. 'You visited Louise at the Fruit Pickers Arms and confronted her. Unfortunately, your brother-in-law, Bishop Ambrose, saw you both outside. He reported back to Lady Margaret, his sister, that you were in the company of an attractive young woman, no doubt succumbing to the vices of sinners.'

Looking sickly and stunned, Lady Margaret rounded on her husband, 'Is this true? Why didn't you deny it earlier?'

'Marie told me what was going on in the strictest confidence. After the wedding, I was going to explain it all to you.'

'But the girl collapsed into your arms and was trying to call out our family name, Apfel-Strand. *Your* name,' his wife accused. The shape of her mouth turned ugly. 'She was probably also trying to say "Herbert", but couldn't get it out.'

'She was attempting to call out his Lordship's name, but not for the reason you think,' Miss Bella informed the group. 'Miss McCracken died by poisoning. Someone placed a potentially fatal fruit in her dessert. Earlier, the chef told me that when he arrived in the kitchen, he found a bowl of fruit salad carefully covered on a counter. There was a handwritten note stating that it contained a certain delicacy from St Honoré that Marie loved. The note was from Sir Herbert, and the special dessert a surprise for his new daughter-in-law.'

Herbert Apfel-Strand was outraged. 'That's preposterous. I requested no such thing.'

'We know,' Miss Marple affirmed. 'In a box in Louise McCracken's room we found leaves and the bark of a very poisonous tree.'

'The Manchineel tree from St Honoré,' Miss Bella explained. 'It can be deadly.'

Leaning forward, following all that was said avidly, Bishop Ambrose gasped. 'Are you saying—?'

'Yes,' Miss Marple confirmed. 'It was Louise McCracken who placed the murder weapons, the poisonous fruit known on St Honoré as the Little Apples of Death, into Marie's dessert. But that wasn't enough for her; she had to make sure that Marie died, and died quickly, so she also placed bark and leaves from the tree in the dish too. This would increase the potency of the poison in the fruit salad. She disguised the bark by chipping it to make it appear like a spice, something akin to ground cinnamon or grated nutmeg, along with leaves, which were shredded. You see, sometimes eating the apple is not enough. Marie's half-sister knew that she had to use other parts of the tree that had sap on them too to be sure.'

Jane continued, 'Marie has confirmed that Louise holidayed with her parents on St Honoré as a child, so she will have known all about the Manchineel tree. And she appeared very tanned today, which suggests she had recently returned from somewhere with a very hot climate.'

Hugging his bride even closer, a confused Peter said, 'But Louise McCracken is the one who is dead and, thankfully, not my sweet Marie. I don't understand.'

Miss Marple slotted the final piece of the puzzle into place. 'Marie, your Tante Bella has told me that you don't like apples. I suspect that, when your dessert arrived, you swapped your bowl with Louise's because hers had no apples?'

Nodding, Marie shivered with the knowledge of how close she had come to her own death. On her very own wedding day.

Lady Margaret still wasn't convinced, 'Surely this McCracken woman would have recognised her own devious handiwork when the dessert was placed in front of her?'

Miss Bella held up a cautionary finger. 'Marie's half-sister hadn't reckoned with the artistic eye of the chef. He did not like the overall presentation of the dish he found waiting with a note for him in the kitchen, so he cut up the apples and mixed the ingredients, inadvertently incorporating the bark and leaves deeper into the fruit salad. When I first saw him, his palms were deep pink in colour, which I assumed was a sign of work-worn hands, and his bloodshot eyes I mistook for an overindulgence of drink. I was wrong. Both his hands and eyes were irritated from touching the apples. Louise McCracken ate the fruit salad because she did not recognise it as the dish she had prepared.'

'But how did she know what food was being served at our wedding breakfast?' It was Peter who asked this question.

'The landlord at the Fruit Picker's Arms was very displeased that Louise kept speaking to the young woman who cleaned the rooms,' Miss Bella explained. 'But Miss McCracken knew exactly what she was doing. She had discovered that Elsie, the chambermaid, was also one of a number of additional staff taken on to work in the kitchen during the wedding at Strand Hall. It was through Elsie that Marie's half-sister found out what the menu would be. The fruit salad was the perfect dish to hide her lethal culinary cocktail.'

Miss Marple picked up the tale again, 'When Miss McCracken realised she had been poisoned, she staggered to her feet, her throat burning, her airways closing up. She stumbled, looking for help, but faced a dilemma. The nearest people to her were both her enemies, Marie on one side and Sir Herbert, who had confronted her at the inn, on the other. She chose the lesser enemy, the baronet. Miss McCracken was indeed calling out his Lordship's surname, Apfel-Strand, but not how you think. Apfel is the German for apple and strand is the old name for a beach, as in 'Apple-Beach'. The poisonous fruit of the Manchineel tree is not only called the little apple of death; it is also known as the beach apple. In her distressed state, Louise was trying to tell everyone that she'd eaten the beach apple, but she couldn't get the words out, so was also pointing to Sir Herbert, indicating his name. She even managed to say the word 'strand'.

Miss Marple caught the eye of everyone in the room. 'This is not a case of murder but that of the perpetrator and victim being one and the same, dying from the murderous malice of their own hand.'

In a sorrowful voice, Marie murmured, 'I told her I would share all our father's wealth with her. That maybe we could get to know each other as sisters. But that wasn't good enough for her. She wanted it all for herself. And me dead.'

Miss Marple looked kindly at Marie. 'Your half-sister was a desperate, greedy person.'

Miss Bella quietly added one of her sage Caribbean sayings. '"Crave all, get none."'

It wasn't until a week later that Miss Marple and Miss Bella, along with the Apfel-Strands, loudly cheered the happy couple off on their honeymoon. Their honeymoon had understandably been delayed due to the police investigation. But Sir Henry Clithering had assured the officer in charge that he could trust everything that Miss Marple told him, as she was a woman who conducted a meticulous investigation and understood the grave failings in human nature better than anyone else, in his experience.

Now, outside Strand Hall, Marie gave Miss Marple and Miss Bella an especially big kiss and hug. Wearing a huge grin, she joined her new husband in their super sleek E-Type

Jag. The two women watched as it drove down the road, tin cans tied to the rear bumper and clanging after them, with a 'Just Married' sign hanging from the boot.

Turning to her great friend, Miss Bella whispered with an amused twinkle, 'It would seem that Sir Herbert and Lady Margaret's wish has come true. Their son has indeed married an heiress.'

Miss Marple nodded, but added, with a returning twinkle, 'More importantly, two young people have found each other and found love.'

Murder at the Villa Rosa

Elly Griffiths

It's not necessary to travel to a beautiful place to commit murder, of course, but sometimes it does help. I thought this several times as I drove the hired car along the vertiginous Italian road, each corner revealing a scene of almost unbearable beauty and, at the same time, bringing me infinitely closer to my own demise. It was all too much: sea, cliffs, blue sky, white houses, the prospect of the afterlife. Now and then, with no warning, a tunnel would plunge me into darkness and, by the time I'd located the headlights, I was out in the blazing sun again, swerving to meet another hairpin bend. The worst moments were when I'd meet a car or a bus driving in the opposite direction. These vehicles showed no sign of slowing down and I soon learnt that the only option was to steer into the hedge and let them thunder past. Sweat poured from under the brow of my newly acquired Panama hat and my hands were rigid on the wheel.

I'd thought about killing Ricky for years. At first I loved

him, of course I did. We've come a long way together and he's been a big part of my success. Everyone likes Ricky and I suppose that's part of the problem. I grew tired of him, every mannerism grated, every apparently spontaneous joke seemed signalled years ago, in the ice age of my memory. But still people laughed at those so-called witticisms and seemed never to tire of his company. The only answer, as I came to see it, was to kill him.

But how and where? It was too difficult to do it at home. My house in Battersea was large and comfortable. I had a book-lined study in the attic from which I could see the curve of the Thames. I also had a charming wife and two intermittently charming children. But the trouble was that No. 5 Waterway Drive was full of Ricky. I'd already had a few disconcerting experiences where I'd seen Ricky in places where he couldn't possibly have been; following me along the towpath to the pub or standing ruminatively on my balcony. No, I couldn't kill him there.

It was Paula, my wife, who first mentioned the Villa Rosa. She'd heard about it from Fran at one of Cassowary's cocktail parties. It was the perfect place, said Paula. It was on the Amalfi coast but not in a tourist trap like Sorrento or Positano. The photographs showed a dusky pink building, half hotel and half castle, on a rocky outcrop overlooking the Bay of Naples. 'You can get away from it all,' said Paula. 'Do some work or just rest. Whatever you feel like.' Paula knew that something was wrong. She just didn't know what. If she had known, she would have tried to stop me. And I didn't blame her at all.

I had the directions, typed by the travel agent, on the seat beside me. The trouble was, as the sun grew lower, I added blindness to my disadvantages as a driver. The sea sparkled on one side, the mountains loomed on the other, my hired Fiat ploughed into the hedge again and again to let the behemoths power past. It was lucky that I had memorised the instructions, partly because they sounded so picturesque. Past the shrine to the Madonna of the Rocks, past the umbrella pines, right at the ruined tower. These landmarks came in quick succession. I was now being followed by another monster bus, mooing impatiently, so I nearly missed the turning and only had time to wrench the car to the right, in the direction of the sea, and come to a shuddering halt under a canopy of vines.

Instantly the passenger door of my car was opened and a soothing voice said, 'Good evening, Signor Jeffries. I am Bertrando. Welcome to the Villa Rosa.'

I stepped out, swaying slightly after the long drive. It was blessedly cool in the portico and I listened to Bertrando telling me that 'the boy' would collect my bags and park the car. As he spoke, he ushered me inside. I was aware of a dark hallway, hovering staff and the scent of lemons. Then Bertrando opened another set of doors and I blinked in wonder.

We were on a terrace, a square of tables and umbrellas. But, beyond the stone parapet, there was nothing. Only blue. The waters of the Mediterranean stretched to the horizon. On either side, in the distance, I could see the curve of the bay, the multi-coloured houses clinging to the wooded shore, a golden dome glittering in the evening sunlight.

'Welcome,' said Bertrando again, 'to the Villa Rosa.'

My room was large and luxurious. The blinds were drawn but, opening them slightly, I saw that view again, almost sinister in its utter beauty.

'This is a wonderful location,' I said.

'There was once a Roman villa on this site,' said Bertrando. He spoke perfect English, his accent only noticeable on certain vowels. 'In the Renaissance, it was rebuilt for an aristocratic family. They painted the frescos on the walls. Then it was a monastery, and a hospital during the war. So many stories. So many secrets. Now, I will leave you to relax.'

I had my own bathroom (Bertrando had called it an 'en-suite') tiled in blue and yellow. There was a bath, shower and, apparently, two lavatories. On inspection I discovered that one of them was the Continental contraption called a bidet. I showered and changed into fresh clothes. Bertrando had explained that it was the tradition of the hotel for guests to gather on the terrace for pre-dinner drinks at eight. As it was now half past, I smoothed down my hair with bay rum, tucked in my shirt and headed downstairs.

The enchanted space seemed very full of people. A grey-haired couple, a young woman with an older husband, a middle-aged man of military bearing and an elderly lady, who was incongruously wearing a tweed suit.

Bertrando was at my side, murmuring introductions,

'Signor and Signora Martinelli, Lord and Lady Braithwaite, Colonel Peters, and Miss Marple.'

'Felix Jeffries.' I shook hands and bowed, as appropriate.

'The writer?' said Lady Braithwaite, the woman with the older husband. She had an American accent and was, I was realising slowly, quite staggeringly beautiful.

'Yes,' I said, feeling embarrassed as I always do when admitting to spending my days in this way.

'We just love the Ricky Barber books. Don't we, darling?'

Lord Braithwaite, 'darling', said, 'Terrific stuff.'

'Ricky Barber,' said Signora Martinelli, the grey-haired lady. 'I am a complete fan.' Ricky is translated into thirty languages. He gets everywhere.

'It must be such an interesting thing, to be a novelist,' said Miss Marple.

Something about the way she said it made me look at the last speaker more closely. She had an innocent pink-and-white face, untouched by the Italian sun, and white hair in a careful bun. Her eyes were pale blue and very bright. She looked at me for a second, an odd fluttery glance, and – maybe it was a trick of the light – it was as if she knew *just* how interesting I found my profession.

'I'm very lucky,' I said, as I always do.

'Luck,' said Colonel Peters, 'is only another word for cunning.'

Bertrando announced that dinner was served.

The food was absolutely sublime and seemed to go on for ever. Antipasti, pasta, chicken with green beans, fish in caper sauce, lemon sorbet, cheese, coffee in tiny brittle cups. By the end I was lolling in my chair, but Miss Marple, at the table next to me, was as upright as ever, still wearing her tweed jacket. After coffee, Bertrando offered us all a liqueur called limoncello, bright yellow liquid in miniature blue glasses. I accepted, feeling reckless, as did the Colonel and Signor Martinelli. The conversation became general and we discussed how we'd come to the Villa Rosa. I said that it had been recommended by my publisher. The Martinellis had stayed here the year before and 'fallen in love with the place'. Lord Braithwaite said that he'd had a special offer. He seemed pleased about this, which surprised me, because he was obviously a very rich man. He'd already mentioned racehorses and yachts. As for his beautiful wife, everything about her dripped luxury.

When second drinks were offered, the Braithwaites and Colonel Peters excused themselves. Lady Braithwaite said that she was tired after a day in the sun. Colonel Peters announced his intention of retiring with a good book. Something in his tone suggested that this tome would not be penned by Felix Jeffries or one of his ilk.

By unspoken consent, the remaining diners drew together on one table. By now it was nearly midnight and the candles were burning low. Occasionally we would see the glow of a firefly or the lights of a late-night fishing boat, but otherwise the bay was in darkness. All around us, the crickets were singing.

We talked about home. The Martinellis were from Milan and Miss Marple from a village called St Mary Mead. I spoke at length about the delights of Battersea.

'Of course,' said Elisabetta Martinelli, 'I lived in Sorrento once. When I was a nun.'

I didn't at first take in her meaning. For this, the limoncello was partly to blame. But Miss Marple said, 'The cloistered life must be fascinating.'

'Yes,' said Elisabetta. 'Although I wasn't always cloistered. When the war came, we were part of a group – the Assisi network – trying to help Jewish Italians escape persecution. We hid men, women and children in our convent and eventually I was captured.'

'What happened then?' I said. It was hard to reconcile this story with the grey-haired woman, elegant but unobtrusive in a green dress, who sat beside me. Luigi Martinelli was watching his wife, his gold-rimmed glasses glinting in the light from the candles, a gentle smile playing around his lips.

'I was taken to Naples and imprisoned there,' said Elisabetta. 'The fascists had recently arrested a young resistance fighter. They were going to shoot him. I stood in front of him and said, "You will have to kill me first." They were still too superstitious to murder a nun, so they reprieved the man.'

'What happened to him?' I asked.

Elisabetta waved a hand towards her husband.

'I am that man,' he told me gravely. 'We met again after the war. I'd become a doctor and I met Elisabetta when she was nursing in Naples. I knew her immediately and we fell in love. Well, I had always been in love with her. Ever since she stood in front of a bullet for me.'

'It was difficult,' said Elisabetta, in her soft voice. 'I had taken vows and I took those seriously. But love cannot be denied.'

'We've been very happy,' said Luigi. 'We have four children and a rich life. Of course, I can never repay her.'

'You repay me every day,' said Elisabetta.

Once again, I blame the limoncello for the tears that came to my eyes.

'That's a beautiful story,' I said.

'Just like a book,' said Miss Marple.

The next morning, when we breakfasted on the terrace, it was hard to look at Luigi and Elisabetta in the same way. On the surface, they were the same contented couple enjoying a holiday in the sun. But to think that their past held so much danger and tragedy, so much *backstory*, made me almost shy of them. We greeted each other with 'Buongiorno' and I sat down to eat melon and ham, an unusual but excellent start to the day. As I drank my coffee, I watched a lizard sunning itself on the white wall. I should go to my room and plan my murder, I thought. I'd requested a typewriter and it was now sitting accusingly on the desk in my bedroom, a brand new Olivetti. I'd told Fran that I would have a synopsis of the new book by the end of the week. Fran was my editor, one of the many young women at Cassowary who seemed to belong, not just to a different generation, but to a different world. She was in her late twenties or early thirties, unmarried, wore trousers and rode a small motorbike to work. A Vespa, I think it was called. My previous editor was a man called Martin, who took me for long lunches and spilled cigar ash on my manuscripts. I thought of Martin with nostalgia, even though he invariably called me Phil.

I should be writing. But suddenly I wanted to lie reptile-like on the sand.

A shadow fell over my *prima colazione*. It was Miss Marple, wearing a blue dress and a large straw hat.

'How do you plan to spend the day, Mr Jeffries?' she asked.

'Felix, please. I should do some work.'

'I thought I might explore the beach,' she said. 'Bertrando says the hotel has a private one. The steps are very steep but there's a sort of *ski lift*.' She made these last words sound very exotic, almost dangerous.

When Miss Marple had twittered away, full of her funicular adventure, I thought of my room: bed, wardrobe, desk, typewriter. And I decided that I too would visit the beach.

The steps were cut into the rock and, like the road yesterday, took several twists and turns, offering snapshots of the glittering bay. When I reached the beach, I found Miss Marple already established on a deck chair, sipping a lime cordial. The beach was just a triangle of sand (which, extraordinarily to me, was black) surrounded by rocks. Lady Brathwaite was there too, stretched out on a sun lounger and wearing a two-piece costume that left very little to my imagination.

I remarked on the sand and Miss Marple told me that it was volcanic. 'Of course,' she said, 'Vesuvius is not so very far away. I often think about those poor people in Pompeii. Such an *untidy* ending.'

I had to stifle a smile at this. The residents of the Roman town had died in agony, buried under burning ash. Untidy was not the word I'd use. But I found Miss Marple's company soothing and, before long, I was telling her of my plans for Ricky.

'I've come to hate him,' I said. 'And I can never be free of him unless I kill him.'

'It must be hard writing about a character you dislike,' said Miss Marple.

'I don't mind writing baddies,' I said. 'After all, I'm a crime writer. Murder's my business. I love being inside the mind of someone truly evil. That's the trouble with Ricky. He's too nice. He was all right at first, when he'd just left the army and joined the police force. He was full of interesting angst. He had unhappy love affairs, he was estranged from his son, he had a health condition. But, as people came to like Ricky, I've been scared to make him suffer. He just drifts along, solving crimes that don't really affect him. He's reconciled with his son, and everyone – including my editor, Fran – has forgotten about his health problems.'

'That reminds me of someone in my village,' said Miss Marple, rather to my surprise. 'Mrs Randall disposed of her husband because every night, at ten o'clock precisely, he always said, "I'm going up the wooden hill to Bedfordshire."'

'I can see how that would get on your nerves,' I said, 'but divorce seems an extreme reaction.'

'Oh, she didn't divorce him,' said Miss Marple. 'She killed him.'

*

The sun was hot and, after a while, I ventured into the sea. The water was wonderfully cool and clear, very salty, with hardly any waves. I swam a long way out, until I could see the misty shape of Naples, with Vesuvius looming in the background. 'Untidy ending,' I said to myself, floating on my back and feeling the sun beating on my face. Endings are vital for a crime writer. You have to solve the crime, identify the culprit, dispense justice and tie up any loose ends, all in the last fifty pages. Any sooner and readers will complain it's too easy. Any later and they will feel short-changed.

I swam back to shore and found that Louisa Braithwaite had joined Miss Marple, her ladyship now wearing a diaphanous pink-and-gold robe over her swimsuit. The hotel had constructed a small bar in the corner of the beach, with buckets of ice in which bobbed an assortment of bottles.

The young barman, who introduced himself as Carlo, said, 'Would you like a drink, Signor Jeffries? Soda? Wine? Beer?'

I should have opted for a soda, but the thought of drinking a cold beer was suddenly too appealing. Carlo placed the sweating bottle on a rush table by my deck chair. Louisa was telling Miss Marple that she was Lord Braithwaite's third wife. Miss Marple didn't contribute much to the conversation beyond a few soothingly phatic murmurs, but, as had been the case earlier with me, she certainly seemed to inspire a confessional spirit in her companions.

'It's a lot to live up to,' said Louisa. 'Marcus is very particular. And, of course, he likes a particular sort of woman.'

'What do you mean?' I said, entering the conversation rather abruptly. But I was intrigued.

In answer, Louisa delved into her expensive-looking handbag. To my surprise, she produced an envelope and drew out a newspaper cutting. Miss Marple and I leaned forward to examine it.

'Lord and Lady Braithwaite at Cannes,' read the caption. The picture showed the couple, dressed in pre-war fashions. This surprised me because Louisa didn't look older than thirty. Miss Marple said, 'Quite a resemblance.'

'Yes,' said Louisa. 'Number two looked like me too.' And, from the same envelope, she drew a black-and-white photograph of a man and a woman standing next to a racehorse. The woman was also extraordinarily like Louisa, except maybe taller. Even allowing for her big hat, she was at eye level with her husband. I'd noticed last night that Louisa was a head shorter than Marcus.

'I mean, he has a type, right?' she said now. 'I didn't realise it at first. I met Marcus in New York after the war. I was a dancer and he came to every show, sitting in the front row in his British pin-striped suit, staring straight at me all the time I was on stage. Someone told me that he was a lord but I didn't believe it. Eventually he asked me to go for a meal with him and we were married within the month. I didn't even know about the other wives until we were on honeymoon. It was at the Villa Rosa, as a matter of fact.'

'Must be the perfect place for a honeymoon,' I said.

'I suppose.' Louisa looked out at the sea, glittering gold in the midday glare, but I got the impression that she was seeing something else. 'I didn't mind that much about being wife number three. I mean, Marcus is older than me. You'd expect him to have some past. It was just, when I saw the photographs, I thought . . . what happens when I no longer look like this?' She tapped the Cannes picture, as if it really did display her likeness and not that of the first Lady Braithwaite.

'Lord Braithwaite reminds me of a dear friend in St Mary Mead,' said Miss Marple. 'She's had three dogs since I've known her. All black-and-white cocker spaniels called George.'

'Gee, thanks,' said Louisa. 'Cute analogy.'

'You don't need to worry,' I said, rather hurriedly. 'Lord Braithwaite dotes on you. I noticed that immediately.'

'He doted on the others too,' said Louisa. 'Until they died.'

'They died?'

'Yeah,' said Louisa. 'Unlucky, right?' And she lay back in her sun-lounger and shut her eyes. I thought of what Colonel Peters had said last night.

Luck is only another word for cunning.

Carlo produced an extraordinary lunch from nowhere. I picked at salami and mozzarella. Miss Marple ate heartily, a napkin spread over her knees. Louisa did not open her eyes. Maybe it was the food, maybe it was the sun, maybe it was the beer (I had a second), but I started to feel very sleepy. I decided to go to my room for a siesta.

The stairs seemed incredibly steep going in this direction. When I reached the top, I swayed and almost fell.

'Signor?' came a woman's voice.

I opened my eyes. It was one of the maids. Simonetta, I think her name was.

'Are you all right?'

'Yes,' I said. 'It's just the stairs and the heat.' And the beers, I added silently.

Simonetta seemed to be flickering in and out of focus like an old film. 'Did Bertrando offer you his special limoncello last night?' she asked.

'Yes,' I said.

'It can be very strong if you're not used to it,' she said. 'It can make you see things that aren't there.'

When I opened my eyes again, she was gone.

I continued up to my room. The shutters were closed but I could see the typewriter shimmering in the gloom. I ignored it and lay down on the bed. A mosquito buzzed somewhere high in the rafters. *Zanzare* in Italian. A wonderfully onomatopoeic word. Suddenly I thought of Fran's motorbike. *Vespa*. A wasp. Another perfect name.

I thought I'd sleep immediately, but words and images whirred like insects around my head.

The cloistered life must be fascinating.

It must be hard writing about a character you dislike.

Vesuvius glimmering on the horizon.

Such an untidy ending.

Louisa proffering a photograph. He has a type, right?

Before I slept, I had one last, coherent thought: Simonetta looked very like Louisa Braithwaite.

At dinner, it transpired that Miss Marple's nephew had paid for her holiday. 'He's very generous,' she said.

'It is a wonderful thing to be an uncle or an aunt,' said

Bertrando. 'My nephew Carlo works with me. I speak to my niece Francesca on the telephone every week.'

'Can't stand my nephew,' said Colonel Peters. 'He killed my sister.'

This remark was made to the company in general. Not surprisingly, a silence fell after these words. Elisabetta whispered something that sounded like a prayer.

'How did he kill your sister?' asked Miss Marple, looking up calmly from her risotto.

'He worried her to death,' said the Colonel. We seemed to release our collective breath. 'With his drinking and womanising and gambling. Well, I've had my revenge in my book.'

Yes, the Colonel was another author. When he retired to bed with a good book, he meant his own. It turned out that he'd written two well-received military memoires but now he was embarking on a new venture. 'It's a crime novel,' he told us, becoming expansive over the limoncello. 'Hope it's the start of a series. I'm putting all my enemies in it and killing them off one by one. Fancy that I've got a very good plot too. A killer hook, I think they call it.' He leered around the terrace, showing yellowing teeth.

'A killer hook,' repeated Elisabetta, rather nervously.

'Felix here could advise you,' said Marcus Braithwaite.

'I don't need advice,' said the Colonel. 'In fact, I'm off to write another chapter.' He marched, rather unsteadily, into the hotel.

Miss Marple and I found ourselves seated side-by-side on a wicker sofa, looking out over the blue-black sea. Lord and

Lady Braithwaite had gone for a stroll on the beach and the Martinellis were talking to Bertrando in Italian.

'It sometimes seems as if all the world is writing a book,' I said.

'I always feel that it must be a very hard thing to do,' said Miss Marple. 'Much more difficult than it seems.'

I warmed to my elderly companion. It's surprising how many people think that being an author is easy. 'I've always wanted to write,' they say, 'if only I had the time.' As if time is all it takes.

'Maybe it's easy if you have a killer hook,' I said.

'I suspect there's no such thing,' said Miss Marple. 'Perhaps it's lots of little hooks, like crochet. When you put them together, it's a complete tapestry. I do like crochet. Knitting too. It's more of a winter pastime, though.'

A woman passed from the light of the terrace into the dark of the hotel. A few minutes later, I saw her taking the stairs to the beach. She had long dark hair and, for a second, I thought she was Louisa Braithwaite.

'Simonetta looks very like Lady Braithwaite,' I said to Miss Marple.

'Beautiful people do often look rather alike,' she replied.

'That was quite a story she told us on the beach,' I said. 'About the three wives.'

'Yes,' said Miss Marple. 'A modern-day Bluebeard.' She laughed but the words made my skin contract, as if a mosquito had landed there. I thought of Lord Braithwaite. He seemed like a typical upper-class Englishman, rather reserved and aloof, perhaps not very bright. But who knows what lies beneath? Murderers aren't always evil geniuses like Moriarty. They are people you meet at parties, people with whom you share a meal, who you pass in the street or sit next to on a London omnibus. I thought of Bertrando saying, "So many stories. So many secrets."'

Then a scream cut through the night.

I sprang to my feet, but Bertrando was quicker. He hurtled down the steps. I followed as fast as I dared. I saw the black sea breaking in white waves on the black sand. I saw Lord Braithwaite, his face pale in the moonlight. And a woman lying at his feet, her hair as dark as death.

Then I saw no more.

When I came to, I was lying on a sofa in the hotel lobby. I could smell lemons and Italian cologne. Blearily I focused on a ceiling fan and the terracotta shades of a fresco. Then a man's face, eyes intent behind gold-rimmed glasses. Luigi Martinelli was bending over me.

'Just a slight concussion,' I heard him say. I'd forgotten that he was a doctor.

'What happened?' I struggled to sit up. 'Who died? Who was killed?'

'Nobody died.' Bertrando's voice seemed to come from a long way off. 'Simonetta saw a . . . what do you call it? . . . a jellyfish . . . on the beach. She screamed, ran for the steps and fell. She is very embarrassed.'

That makes two of us, I thought.

'Why did I faint?' I said.

Dottore Martinelli put a glass of water in my hand.

'You fell down the steps. Easy to do in the dark. You hit your head on a rock.'

'How did I get here?' I took a sip of the water. It tasted odd, sulphuric.

'Bertrando and Signor Braithwaite carried you. But you should be in your bed. Are you able to stand?'

I was, with help. Bertrando on one side, the doctor on the other. As we reached the stairs, I saw my fellow guests gathered in a concerned group by the French windows. Lord Braithwaite with his arm round his wife. Elisabetta comforting Simonetta. Miss Marple standing sightly apart, the electric light gleaming on her white hair.

Apart from a slight headache, I felt fine in the morning. Bertrando himself brought me breakfast in bed: small croissants that he called 'cornetti', unsalted butter, jam, orange juice and coffee.

'Dottore Martinelli said to take it easy today,' he said.

'Take it easy,' I said. 'How come you speak such good English?'

'I spent some time in London after the war,' said Bertrando. 'My brother lives there. It's where I learnt to be a hotelier.'

'You're very good at it,' I said. 'How's Simonetta this morning?'

'She is well,' said Bertrando. 'Just embarrassed to have caused such . . . such commotion.'

'Tell her not to worry,' I said. 'I blame it on the limoncello.'

I thought that Bertrando looked slightly guilty as he bowed his way out.

After breakfast I showered, dressed and decided to walk into Priano, the nearest town. It wasn't far but the route took me along the coastal road, which felt almost as frightening on foot as it had behind the wheel of my hired Fiat. How long ago was it that I'd negotiated those hairpin bends? Was it really only two days past? And I'd got no further with killing Ricky. I thought of Colonel Peter's smug retort last night: 'I don't need advice.' I rather thought that *I* did.

The road led though one of the sudden tunnels cut into the cliffs. It felt very cold and dark after the heat of the day, but, as I progressed farther, I saw that it was lit with a faint phosphorescent glow. In the eerie light I made out a strange adornment. On a rough shelf cut into the stone wall was a model village: houses, domed church, ruined tower and a pink building that looked very like the Villa Rosa. There were lighted candles by the church and the tower, and it was these, reflected against the rocky roof, that gave out the ominous green light. I walked on quickly.

Priano was beautiful, all white-washed houses and winding steps. Apparently the church contained some important paintings, but I was happy just to sit outside a café with a *spremuta di limone* and a two-day-old copy of *The Times*. I asked the owner, who spoke English, about the model village in the tunnel and he said it was a *presepio*, a kind of Christmas nativity scene. It had been created by a local artist two years ago and no one had wanted to remove it. Instantly the candle-lit houses seemed quaint rather than sinister. I had a sudden desire to write about it. Perhaps I should send Ricky to Italy, I thought, before remembering that Ricky was not going anywhere, except to his doom. I would make a start that evening.

The walk back was hard work, as the sun was at its hottest. The sky was a bright hard blue and the cicadas were like voices in my head. Maybe I had been too adventurous attempting such a trek. After all, the doctor had told me to take it easy. I remembered the day earlier, when I'd felt dizzy climbing the stairs from the beach. Maybe I was sickening for something? The tunnel was a relief and I stood for a moment, breathing in the clammy air. When I stepped out into the daylight, it was as if the sun were directing its rays directly on to my head. I wished I'd worn my Panama hat.

It was then that I saw a man walking in front of me. I thought it was odd that I hadn't seen him in the tunnel, but maybe he had joined the road from one of the coastal paths. He was tall, with greying dark hair, and he walked with a slightly uneven gait. I thought of Ricky, who used to limp in the early books, the result of a wartime injury, but now seemed to be as spry as an eighteen-year-old. I thought of the times I'd seen Ricky at my house in London. Maybe he had really been there all along? It suddenly seemed important to catch up with the Ricky walk-alike. I quickened my pace, although it made my heart beat faster and the sweat run into my brows.

At last, there was the Villa Rosa, its pink walls seeming almost red in the midday sun. I thought of the cool lobby, the jar of lemons that stood on the front desk, the fresco showing the judgement of Paris. I would sit in the dark and drink a glass of water before attempting the stairs to my room. Then I stopped. The limping man was also turning to go into the hotel. For some reason, I felt that I had to stop him. I ran forwards and lurched through the double doors.

Once inside, I was aware of several things simultaneously. The tiled floor was pulsating in an unpleasant way. The ceiling fan was circulating dust motes that looked to me like the keys of an Olivetti typewriter. I heard laughter. Then the voices of the cicadas formed a name.

Ricky Barber.

I saw a familiar face.

And I rushed forward, intent on murder.

This time, when I woke, I was lying on my bed. A woman's voice said, 'How are you feeling?'

'Fran! What are you doing here?'

For a moment it seemed incredible that my editor should be sitting by my bedside in an Italian hotel. She belonged in London, part of another life. But, in another way, she looked oddly at home in this setting. She also reminded me of someone.

'I'm sorry,' she was saying. 'I just wanted to help.'

I struggled to sit up. The shutters were closed and the fan was whirring in the ceiling.

'What happened?' I said. 'Did I faint again? I thought I saw Ricky. He was walking just ahead of me.'

'That was Salvatore,' said Fran. 'He works in the kitchens.'

'I thought it was Ricky,' I said, feeling very foolish. 'I thought I had to stop him going into the hotel.'

'You sort of lunged forward and fell to the floor,' said

Fran. 'It was very dramatic. One of the guests is apparently a doctor and he said it was probably heatstroke.'

'But I heard someone say "Ricky Barber".'

Fran looked perplexed for a moment and then she laughed, at the same time making a curious gesture of stroking her chin. 'You heard me say *che barba*. It means "how boring". Literally, you could wait for a beard to grow.' She made the gesture again. 'Carlo must have been talking to me about football.'

'You haven't said what you're doing here,' I said. 'Honestly, Fran. I think I'm going mad. This whole place is driving me insane. It's like something out of a book. You wouldn't believe the stories I've heard.'

'I would,' said Fran, 'because I've been telling them to you.'

'I don't understand.'

'I was worried,' said Fran. 'I knew that you wanted to end the Ricky books. That's fine by me. It was just that you hadn't got an idea for a *new* book. Or a new series. I thought you'd fallen out of love with writing. With storytelling. I spoke to Paula about it.'

'You spoke to Paula?'

'At the Cassowary author party. She was worried about you too. She asked if I could recommend a writers' retreat and I thought of this place. It's so beautiful here and there's so much history. I thought it might inspire you. Then, I thought, what if I filled the hotel with interesting characters? People who had stories to tell. My uncle suggested the Martinellis because they had stayed here before. He'd been very struck by them and by their history.'

'Your uncle?' I said.

'Bertrando.'

Then I remembered that Bertrando had once lived in London. Also that he had a niece called Francesca. That was the resemblance I had noticed earlier. They had the same dark eyes and high cheekbones.

'Lord and Lady Braithwaite had their honeymoon here,' Fran continued. 'Zio Bertrando remembered them well. He said that Lady Braithwaite had been rather disturbed to learn that her predecessors had looked rather like her. She even mentioned it to him. I thought, if she tells that story to the hotel manager, she'll tell it to anyone. I persuaded my uncle to give them a special offer. Rich people always like a bargain.'

'And Colonel Peters?'

Fran laughed. 'Terry is another one of my authors. There's nothing wrong with a bit of healthy competition. He's always going on about having a killer hook for his crime series. I thought that might spur you on.'

I shut my eyes. I could hear the *zanzare* buzzing.

'So this whole thing was for my benefit? I'm not being poisoned by the limoncello?'

'Zio Bertrando's limoncello is rather lethal. But you're not being poisoned. I just think you had a touch too much sun today.'

I thought of the tunnel with the candles burning, of the lights of the fireflies at night, of the ruins of Pompeii. Dust and ashes.

'Something's been happening to me,' I said. 'I'm not quite sure what.'

'There's an old lady downstairs called Miss Marple,' said Fran. 'She's very keen to see you. Shall I send her up?'

'Yes, do.' Suddenly I wanted to hear Miss Marple's gentle voice and see the world through her sharp blue gaze.

'Did you guess?' I said, as Miss Marple entered, neat and birdlike in a flowery dress.

'Not entirely,' she said. 'But that first night, Elisabetta's tale. You said yourself it was a beautiful story and I thought: just like a book. Then Louisa's performance on the beach. A fairy tale, a modern-day Bluebeard. I wondered if someone was collating these stories for you to find.'

'But what about the husband and the two wives who died? That actually happened.'

'Louisa made it sound very dramatic,' said Miss Marple. 'But I think that Marcus Braithwaite is just a man who likes a certain type of woman.'

'What about Simonetta?' I said. 'Was it a coincidence that she looked just like Louisa?'

'It's a vague resemblance,' said Miss Marple. 'That's all. As I said, beautiful people do tend to look rather alike. The three Lady Braithwaites are not really any more similar than my friend's three spaniels. It's just the name that makes them appear so.'

'What about you?' I said. 'Are you here for me too?'

'Oh no,' said Miss Marple. 'I'm just on holiday. Though I did meet Bertrando years ago in London. And my nephew did pay a very advantageous rate for my room.'

'My editor is Bertrando's niece,' I said. 'She set up this whole thing to give me an idea for a new book.'

'And have you got one?'

'Maybe,' I said. 'I'm thinking about what you said about lots of little hooks, like crochet or a tapestry.'

'That's right,' said Miss Marple. 'I'm no author, but that's how I imagine you might put a story together. Especially a crime novel, where you need so many threads.'

I looked towards the Olivetti on the desk. My fingers ached for the keys.

Miss Marple said, in a diffident voice, 'If I might make a suggestion?'

'Please do.'

'Don't kill Ricky. Do you remember what I said about Letty Randall and her husband?'

'Up the wooden hill to Bedfordshire?'

'That's the one. She was acquitted of his murder, but she was never free of him. Now, if she'd just left Arthur, she would never have had to think of him again.'

'You think I should divorce Ricky?'

'In my experience,' said Miss Marple, 'nothing puts a stop to curiosity quite like happiness. Could you give Ricky a happy ending?'

'I could certainly try,' I said.

The Murdering Sort

Karen M. McManus

'Aunt Jane, this is *perfect*.'

The words come out with a contented sigh as I fling myself on to what appears to be a plush velvet sofa across from my aunt's rocking chair. Appearances are deceiving, though, and I land uncomfortably on rock-hard cushions. 'Well, nearly perfect,' I amend, sitting up with the straightness the sofa demands. 'How did Granddad manage to find a cottage that looks like something from the Home Counties in the middle of Cape Cod?'

'Raymond has always been so clever,' Aunt Jane murmurs, eyes on the white fleecy wool that she's knitting into . . . something. A baby's blanket, probably. If you've met my great-great aunt even once, you can be certain of receiving a blanket in the post no more than two weeks after your baby is born. 'And wonderfully generous too. Really, Nicola, I have never known why he should take so much trouble about his old aunt.'

'Because he knew I'd like to see you,' I say affectionately, although I'm sure that's only half the reason. St Mary Mead can be cool and damp even during summer, and my grandfather is always on the lookout for drier climates to help with Aunt Jane's rheumatism. It's a bonus that I was already here, spending the summer with a school friend.

'And I you,' Aunt Jane says, resting her knitting on her lap in order to give me her full attention. It's the first time we've seen one another since she arrived here in Chatham yesterday, and I'm suddenly aware that the patchwork shorts I borrowed from Diana don't blend particularly well with this time-warp room. 'You look very. . .'

'American?' I break in. It's what my parents have been saying ever since I started hanging out with Diana. She was the talk of school when she showed up at the beginning of fifth form – the glamorous New York heiress whose English mother whisked her off to the countryside after an acrimonious divorce. I never expected her to notice me, but she'd tapped me on the shoulder her second day and said, 'Nicola West, right? I'm Diana Westover. We have matching names, so we're destined to be the best of friends.'

And then, like magic, we were. We became Di-and-Nic, together so much that our classmates called us by a single name. When school ended and I knew Diana would soon leave for her grandfather's beachfront estate in Cape Cod, the approaching summer felt endless and empty until she invited me to come along.

'I was going to say *grown-up*,' Aunt Jane says diplomatically. 'Though I still think seventeen is a bit young to spend the summer away from home. Of course, your father's generation has different ideas than mine. And David assures me the Westover family is *quite* above reproach.'

'Quite,' I echo. Then I clear my throat, a nervous childhood habit that even being one half of Di-and-Nic hasn't cured.

Aunt Jane looks up sharply. I don't know how old she is, exactly, but one thing's for sure: no matter her age, nothing gets past her. 'Are they not?' she asks.

'Well—'

The doorbell rings before I can figure out how to start. 'Why don't I let Diana explain,' I say, hurrying for the front door. When I pull it open, I find myself saying 'Hello' to an enormous flowering plant.

'Nic, hi!' Diana calls happily, as though it's been half a year since she's seen me rather than half an hour. 'Sorry I'm late, but I didn't want to arrive empty-handed.'

'Mission accomplished,' I say, stepping back so Diana can sweep inside. Somehow, she manages to make carrying an oversized plant look graceful, as though it's the latest must-have accessory. Her long dark hair is so perfectly straight and shiny that I wish I'd taken her advice and tried using her new Vidal Sassoon conditioner on my own unruly curls. Then I wrinkle my brow and add, 'You changed?'

As soon as I say it, though, I realise that *of course* Diana wouldn't meet my aunt in shorts and a peasant blouse. She's a pro at matching her outfit to the occasion. Sure enough, even though Aunt Jane looks baffled by the plant, her expression softens into approval when Diana places it on the floor to reveal a sedate, perfectly tailored summer dress. 'Hello, Miss Marple, I'm Diana Westover,' Diana says warmly. 'I brought a potted hydrangea for the yard.'

'How kind,' Aunt Jane says. She's far too polite to mention any of the drawbacks to this gift, including the fact that the yard in question isn't hers. That's Diana for you, though; rich enough to assume that everyone owns multiple houses, and so passionate about the environment that she thinks the more usual gift of *cut* flowers to be an abomination.

'I'll just take this into the kitchen for now,' I say.

By the time I've settled the pot beside the sink – Aunt Jane's companion, Cherry, will know what to do with it when she returns from the shops – Diana is perched on the edge of the sofa, talking animatedly. 'And have you visited the seashore yet, Miss Marple?' she asks.

'We tried yesterday when we first arrived,' Aunt Jane says. 'But there were some rather large construction vehicles blocking the view.'

Diana exhales in frustration. 'Oh, it's awful, isn't it?' she asks. 'They're putting in *condominiums*. Absolutely ruining the shoreline! It makes me miss being at school in Banbury, where everything was so wonderfully green. Nic says you live in quite a picture-perfect village, Miss Marple?'

'Not any more,' Aunt Jane says with her own little sigh. 'St Mary Mead also has a . . . Development.' In response to Diana's raised eyebrows, she adds, 'All sorts of new, modern homes. It's progress, of course, and young people must live *somewhere*. But I do miss the old days.'

'Me too,' Diana says fervently, earning a smile from my aunt.

'You're far too young to remember them, my dear.'

Diana laughs. 'I suppose you're right, but even ten years ago I could hear frogs singing from the pond across from Grandfather's house when I went to sleep, and now? I don't hear anything.' She catches my eye and winks. 'Other than Harry hacking away at that guitar. He's a charmer, my cousin, but a terrible musician.'

I don't want my eagle-eyed aunt to notice that the name *Harry* makes me blush, so I quickly say, 'Di has something she wanted to ask you, Aunt Jane. Because you're so, well, you know . . .' I clear my throat again. 'Good at murders.'

Aunt Jane blinks, startled enough to drop her knitting needles. 'I beg your pardon?'

'Well, not at *doing* them, obviously. At solving them,' I say.

It's an awkward start, so Diana tries to smooth things over. 'Nic's been telling us that you're practically a one-woman Scotland Yard, Miss Marple,' she says.

Aunt Jane's cheeks grow pink. 'I assure you, I am not. I simply have a certain knowledge of human nature that has, on occasion, proved helpful to the police.'

I poke Diana with my elbow. 'Told you she'd say that.'

I didn't think it was possible for Aunt Jane to sit up straighter, but she manages. 'Why on earth are you girls discussing something so dreadful?' she asks.

Diana winds a strand of dark hair around one finger. It's not as obvious as my throat-clearing, but it's a signal that she's uncomfortable too. 'Because of my grandfather,' she says.

'He's always been eccentric, but ever since the family arrived two weeks ago, he's been treating us like . . . well, like *criminals*.' She flushes. 'He's very rich, you know, and very old, and he's gotten it into his head that we want him gone so we can inherit his fortune.'

'It's so unfair!' I break in, cheeks warming at the memory of Josiah Westover's bitter accusations. 'Diana doesn't care about money at all! And even if she did, her father made an absolute fortune on Wall Street.' Then I worry that was terribly crass – none of the Westovers except Josiah like to talk about money – but Diana flashes me a grateful smile.

'Thanks, Nic,' she says. 'But I don't take it personally.'

'Oh dear,' Aunt Jane murmurs. 'Elderly gentlemen can be so difficult. It's hard to lose your health and your strength, and to feel that one is a burden on others.'

'It's not that, so much,' Diana says, tugging harder on her hair. 'The problem, really, is that Grandfather is convinced that we're trying to murder him.'

Aunt Jane's china-blue eyes widen. 'Indeed? And is there . . .' She gets a little pink again. 'Forgive the question, but is there evidence to support such an accusation?'

Diana and I exchange glances. Josiah Westover is one of the oddest, crankiest men I've ever met – but one thing he's *not* is paranoid. Two days after we arrived, the brakes on the car that only he drives failed, and could have caused a terrible accident if he hadn't noticed before leaving the driveway. A week later, the heavy vase on the shelf above his desk came crashing down beside his chair, missing his head by inches.

'There have been a couple of close calls,' Diana says. 'But

all accidents!' she adds quickly, as Aunt Jane gives a sage nod. 'You have to understand – my family is quirky, and, yes, some of them are a bit hard up, but they're not *killers*. It's been driving my father mad, and when he heard about you, he suggested we invite you to my great-aunt Edith's birthday celebration tomorrow night. Dad thought you might be able to reassure my grandfather. That you could tell him, perhaps . . .' Diana trails off, and I know she's worried that Josiah will be just as rude to Aunt Jane as he is to everyone else. 'That we're not the murdering sort?'

'Ah, my dear,' Aunt Jane smiles kindly, 'the problem with that, you see, is that no one is ever the murdering sort until they are. The least likely people can shock you. Young mothers, elderly clergy, esteemed businessmen. You can't rule out anyone, I'm afraid.' She picks up her knitting with a sideways glance toward me. 'Even charming guitar players.'

It's a little annoying, sometimes, how Aunt Jane never misses a thing.

When Josiah Westover throws a party – even a small one for his sister's birthday – he goes all out. The space that Diana calls 'the great room' – something of a giant sitting room with sliding glass doors that open to a deck overlooking the ocean – is filled with flowers and candles. The doors are open, framing the deep blue of the evening sky and allowing a salt-scented breeze to pass through. A musician seated at a grand piano in the corner plays soft classical music, while white-coated servers pass trays of canapes and drinks.

All this, for ten people.

I fidget in my borrowed dress at the doorway, wishing I hadn't listened to Diana when she told me to head downstairs while she finished her hair. Most of her family intimidates me, except for—

'Drink, Nic?'

As if I'd summoned him, Harry Westover appears by my side, holding two champagne flutes. He's wearing the dark suit his grandfather insisted upon, but no tie, his white shirt unbuttoned at the top and more than a little wrinkled. 'Go on,' he adds with a dimpled grin when I hesitate. 'No one cares that you're underage.'

I accept the glass with murmured thanks. I don't particularly like champagne, but I do like Harry. Probably too much. When I first got to Westover House, Diana warned me that Harry is incapable of talking to any woman under fifty without flirting. *Don't take him seriously,* she said. So I try not to, but it's difficult with those bright blue eyes fixed on mine.

Diana was right; Harry's guitar playing isn't great. But he's been practising 'Fire and Rain' nonstop for the past two weeks, and you can almost recognise it now.

'I see you've gone full Diana tonight,' Harry says.

I almost choke on my tentative sip of champagne. 'Pardon?'

'*Pardon*?' Harry repeats, still grinning. 'Everything sounds better with your accent.' Then he gestures to my nearly straight hair, which Diana tamed into submission with lots of conditioner and a blow-dryer. 'What happened to the curls?'

'I'm trying something new,' I say.

'You don't need to,' Harry says, sounding unusually sincere.

That ties my tongue, but fortunately Diana enters the room

then, grabbing a flute of champagne from a passing server. 'We'll need this tonight,' she says, clinking her glass against Harry's. 'What do you suppose Grandfather is up to?'

'God knows,' Harry says, then drops his voice into a raspy imitation of Josiah's peevish tone. '*I want to talk to each of you, alone.*' He gazes around the room at the rest of the guests – Diana's father, Michael, who's perfectly content to stand alone; Harry's father, Alan, deep in conversation with Josiah's assistant, Stephen Macfarlane; and Alan's second wife, Lucretia, gesturing dramatically as she talks with Great-aunt Edith. Those last two make an odd pair; the glamorous Lucretia is what Harry uncharitably calls a failed actress, while Edith is no-nonsense and still wearing her gardening clothes. 'Sounds different from the usual *you're all a deep disappointment* conversation.'

Diana raises her eyebrows. 'Even you? But you've fallen so beautifully into line. Heading to Harvard and majoring in economics like all the Westover men.'

Harry scowls. 'For now. I'll never last there, but Dad says we can't rock the boat. Not after his latest can't-fail business did, in fact, fail.' Then he drains half his glass before turning to me. 'What happened to that aunt of yours, Nic? Thought she was coming tonight?'

'She wanted to,' I say. 'But she gets so tired.'

'Good idea avoiding Grandfather, then,' Diana says, smoothing an invisible wrinkle from her dress. 'He's exhausting.'

'Speak of the devil,' Harry says, as his grandfather enters the room.

Everyone quiets in Josiah Westover's commanding presence.

He's small and wizened, his face a mass of wrinkles and his white hair nearly gone, but he has the energy and vitality of a man half his age. He's leaning on a gilt-topped black cane, head cocked to one side like a predatory bird as he surveys the room.

'Where's Sarah?' he demands.

'On her way,' Alan Westover replies instantly. Sarah is his daughter, granted, but it doesn't matter what question Josiah asks; Harry's father is always the first to answer.

'With her mysterious fiancé, or without?' Harry murmurs. He's insisted to Diana and me that he overheard his older sister whispering about an engagement over the phone, but if she was referring to her own, no one else in the family has mentioned it.

Josiah's assistant, Stephen Macfarlane, steps forward. He's about thirty, and might be handsome if he ever dropped the eager expression. 'Miss Sarah called before she left Boston and mentioned traffic might be difficult this time of day,' he says. 'Even so, she should arrive within half an hour.'

'Well, I can't wait any longer,' Josiah says, tapping his cane on the floor. He stares around the room until his eyes land on Lucretia. 'You first.'

Harry's stepmother puts a delicate hand to her throat. 'First for *what*?' she asks.

'You'll see,' Josiah says.

Out of the corner of my eye, I catch Diana's father heading our way. 'Excuse me, I need the loo,' I say, placing my champagne glass on an empty tray. I don't, really, but I can at least check how my hair is holding up – and maybe allow a few curls to spring back – while the Westovers discuss how to manage their patriarch.

I usually use the bathroom near my bedroom, but that's an entire floor and wing away, so I make my way down the hall and keep my eyes peeled for anything that resembles a powder room. I haven't spent much time in this part of the house, which is very much Josiah Westover's territory, and before I know it I've made a distinctly wrong turn. I'm in what looks like a small sitting room, and I can hear the sound of voices far too close. My heart starts beating uncomfortably fast; I don't want Diana's grandfather to accuse me of snooping. So I do what any normal, rational person would do and . . . dive for what looks like a cupboard door, shutting it quickly behind me.

Except it wasn't a cupboard door, after all.

I'm in an imposing room dominated by a mahogany desk positioned in front of the window. At least, I assume there's a window behind those richly patterned silk drapes. A leather sofa is on one side of the room, and two matching armchairs on the other. Three of the walls have floor-to-ceiling shelves, filled with leather-bound books and the kind of model airplanes Diana's grandfather likes to make. The plush rug in the centre of the room features the Westover family crest.

Oh no. I'm in Josiah Westover's *study*, aren't I?

The door opens, and before I can even think about what I'm doing, I've ducked behind one of the armchairs. Then I peer around its corner to watch Stephen Macfarlane stride across the room, reach out a hand to part the drapes, and step behind them.

What on earth?

Maybe the drapes cover a door, not a window? There's no sign of Stephen any more, and I'm about to rise and flee when the sound of footsteps keeps me in place. They grow nearer, and I watch in horror from my hiding spot as Josiah and Lucretia enter the room.

'Take a seat,' he says, and if she chooses this armchair I'm utterly doomed. How will I ever explain myself? But she lowers herself on to the leather sofa, and Josiah sits beside her.

'What's this about?' Lucretia asks.

'Just a little family business,' Josiah says.

'I'm all ears.' Lucretia's tone is neutral, but her jaw is clenched. I wish, desperately, that I'd stayed put with Diana and Harry instead of wandering in here, but it's too late now.

'Good,' Josiah says, taking a prescription bottle from his pocket and settling it on the table in front of them, beside a glass of water. 'You'll excuse me if I make sure my heart pills are handy. I've had palpitations lately, and you can't be too careful at my age.'

'Naturally,' Lucretia says.

'Here's the thing, Lucretia,' Josiah says. 'You've been a fine wife to Alan. I have nothing against you personally, but the fact is, Alan is never going to launch himself into the world when he knows he has my money to fall back on. So, tonight, I'm changing my will and leaving everything to charity. You and Alan get nothing, I'm afraid, except the model airplane of your choice.' He sweeps a hand around the room. 'You can pick one now, if you wish.'

'I have no need for a model airplane,' Lucretia says tightly.

'Wouldn't you like something to remember me by, though?' Josiah asks.

Lucretia's nostrils flare. 'Have you told Alan about this?'

'No. I thought I'd tell you first.'

'Why would you do that?'

'Because . . .' Josiah breaks off, inhaling sharply. 'Excuse me. Had a bit of pain just then. What was I saying? Oh, Alan. The thing about Alan is—'

He stops again, clutching his chest. 'Are you all right?' Lucretia asks, though she doesn't sound particularly concerned.

'Fine,' Josiah says, but the word comes out like a gasp. 'I'm fine.' Then he slumps against the cushions, his face a mask of pain. 'I think . . . I think I need my pills. Could you—'

'Of course,' Lucretia says. My eyes zone in on Josiah's face, and despite the way it's twisted in agony, I don't think I'm wrong in thinking that he's watching her carefully.

He's testing her, I think. It seems supremely obvious to me; so obvious that I'm not surprised when Lucretia calmly extracts a pill from the bottle and hands it over, along with the glass of water. 'Here you go,' she says.

'Thank you,' Josiah wheezes, gulping it down.

After Josiah 'recovers', he rings a bell and the butler opens the door. 'Roberts will take you to the east wing, where you'll be seated for dinner,' Josiah says. 'It will be served once I've had the opportunity to speak with the rest of the family.'

'So I'll be separated from the others?' Lucretia asks. 'How interesting.' She sounds frustrated, but leaves without further comment.

Once the door shuts behind her and Roberts, Josiah raps his cane on the floor and calls out, 'Well? What did you think?'

My heart drops. *He knows I'm here.* But before I can nervously clear my throat and try to explain myself, Stephen Macfarlane steps out from behind the drapes.

'That needs a *lot* of work, Mr Westover,' he says.

One thing you can definitely say about Josiah Westover is that he's a quick study.

He spends nearly fifteen minutes with Harry, skilfully needling him about Harvard and his musical dreams, before he starts to exhibit much more subtle heart-attack symptoms. When he finally collapses, it's so convincing that I have to dig my nails into my palm to keep from crying out. I can't help but be relieved when Harry springs into action, even going so far as to put the pill – which, I've now learned from the back and forth between Josiah and Stephen Macfarlane, is made from sugar – into Josiah's mouth.

Harry's father Alan is a different story, though. When Josiah goes into what's now a very convincing portrayal of a heart attack, Alan does nothing except watch him gasp in pain. Eventually, Josiah slumps against the cushions, perfectly still. Minutes tick by with agonising slowness, until Alan tentatively says, 'Father?' Then Josiah sits up so suddenly that Alan recoils and I nearly gasp out loud.

'False alarm,' Josiah says, eyes narrowed at his son.

Alan's thin face turns tomato-red. 'Oh, thank goodness!' he cries. 'I . . . I was frozen with shock, and—'

'And you can go now,' Josiah snaps, ringing for Roberts. 'I have everything I need from you.'

After Alan skulks away, Josiah confers briefly with Stephen, in such low tones that I can't hear them. Then Stephen heads back behind the curtains, and it's Diana's turn. 'Well, here she is,' Josiah says, when Diana takes a seat on the leather couch. 'Our little English rose. Abandoning her family the first chance she gets.'

Diana sighs. 'You know I had no choice. My mother insisted.'

'Nonsense. You're perfectly capable of getting your own way when it suits you,' Josiah says. 'And now that you're back, are you happy to see us? Hardly. All you do is complain about *frogs*. Ungrateful girl.'

He's being so awful that I'm almost relieved when he falls into the now-familiar rhythm of his performance. Diana reacts just as quickly as Harry did, giving the cap of Josiah's medicine bottle such an energetic twist that she nearly stumbles, and I feel a burst of pride for my friend. Sarah, Harry's older sister, who has now arrived from Boston, takes longer to react, but ultimately helps out too.

Then Aunt Edith enters the room. I don't think she cares about Josiah's money any more than Diana does, and I can't help wondering what she'll do.

What Aunt Edith does, as it turns out, is burst into incredulous laughter once Josiah goes into his act. 'Stop it, you ridiculous old crank,' she snorts, as Josiah writhes in supposed pain. 'Is that what you've been doing all this time? Happy birthday to me, eh?' Aunt Edith brushes at the knees of her practical trousers before adding, 'You ought to be ashamed of yourself. Your family are *people*, not puppets you can yank back and forth.'

'Edith, truly,' Josiah moans with convincing agony. 'Something's wrong.'

'What's *wrong* is that you've let your fortune warp you,' Edith says.

'Please,' Josiah wheezes. 'Call a doctor.'

It's those words – *Call a doctor* – that make me act. 'He's not pretending this time,' I cry out, springing to my feet and wincing at the ache in my legs from squatting for so long in one place. 'Something's wrong.'

'Good lord!' Aunt Edith stares at me, open-mouthed. 'Have you been there the entire time?' Then Stephen Macfarlane steps out from behind the curtains, and her jaw drops further. 'Have *you*? What on earth are you two doing?'

Stephen ignores us both to bend over Josiah. 'Mr Westover?' he says, pressing his fingers against Josiah's neck. 'Are you all right? Do you need your pills?' Aunt Edith grabs the bottle on the table and thrusts it toward him, but Stephen doesn't take it. Sweat beads on his forehead as he says, 'Not those.'

'What's happening?' Aunt Edith demands. 'What kind of sick game is this?'

I swallow hard, unable to tear my eyes from Josiah's rigid, deathly pale face. 'I don't think it's a game any more,' I say.

'So what do you think? Who did it?'

I gaze between Aunt Jane and Detective Laura Wilcox from the Chatham Police Department, seated side by side in deck chairs behind Aunt Jane's cottage. After Detective Wilcox questioned me about Josiah Westover's death the week before, I told her that all she needed to do to solve the case was speak with my aunt. She brushed me off and drove me home – to Aunt Jane's, who insisted that I couldn't stay at Westover House with a murderer on the loose. Although part of me hated leaving Diana, the rest of me was relieved.

Then, right after Aunt Jane and I finished lunch this afternoon, Detective Wilcox stopped by. She told us, her tone deferential, that when she mentioned Aunt Jane to her chief, he recognised the name from a police convention in New York where my aunt's old friend, Inspector Dermot Craddock, had been a featured speaker. 'I'm to provide you with whatever information you ask for, Miss Marple,' Detective Wilcox said. Then she'd been treated to nearly fifteen minutes of St Mary Mead gossip until I couldn't keep quiet for another second.

'Really, Nicola, I couldn't say,' Aunt Jane says mildly, her knitting needles clacking.

If Detective Wilcox thinks I've oversold my aunt's crime-solving abilities after that lacklustre response, she doesn't show it. 'It's tricky with these wealthy families,' she says, taking a biscuit from the plate Cherry left for us. 'They close ranks.'

'But it was definitely poison that killed him?' Aunt Jane asks.

'Oh yes,' Detective Wilcox says. 'The autopsy report was clear on that. Josiah had white baneberry in his system, which is highly toxic. It might not have killed a healthier man, but the plant's ability to sedate cardiac muscles is deadly for someone with a heart condition.'

Aunt Jane tuts. 'And you think this poison was administered through the pills that Josiah Westover had prepared for this little farce?'

'We believe so. It's possible more than one of the pills he took while speaking to his family were poisoned, but those remaining in the bottle were pure sugar.'

'Dear me,' Aunt Jane says. 'Josiah was playing a dangerous game, wasn't he? And for what? To test his family?'

'That's what Stephen Macfarlane says,' Detective Wilcox says. 'Josiah had become paranoid after a few too many suspicious accidents. He wanted to know who would come to his aid when they thought he was having a heart attack, and who would let him die.' She shakes her head. 'Which is foolish, because the way people behave in a moment of crisis doesn't always reflect their intentions or character. But, apparently, he put an idea into someone's head.'

'And yet, surely no one was meant to know about this plan except for Stephen Macfarlane?' Aunt Jane says.

'Yes, but Macfarlane admits that he and Josiah worked through the logistics in Josiah's study, which has a window overlooking a large flower garden,' Detective Wilcox says. 'The window was open to take advantage of the good weather, so it's possible they were overheard. Other than Sarah, the entire family has been at the house for the past two weeks.'

'Can anyone other than Stephen Macfarlane corroborate the open window?' Aunt Jane asks.

Detective Wilcox tilts her head. 'I'm not sure. Why do you ask?'

'Well,' Aunt Jane says gently, 'it seems the sort of thing one might say to divert suspicion off oneself. I'm not saying that Stephen Macfarlane is guilty,' she adds quickly. 'But he is, of course, the only person that you know for certain was aware that Josiah Westover intended to ingest multiple sugar pills over the course of the afternoon. Being in that position is nerve-wracking for even an innocent person.'

Detective Wilcox nods. 'Very true. Macfarlane, though, is the only person in the house who doesn't benefit from Josiah's death. He received a generous salary, but there's no provision for him in Josiah's will. He was well aware of that.'

'Was Josiah really going to change his will?' I ask. 'Or was that a lie?'

'He'd already had his lawyer draw up a new version,' Detective Wilcox says. 'Left everything to charity. But here's the kicker – he hadn't yet signed it. His old will remains legally binding, and his family will inherit his assets.'

'Who benefits most?' Aunt Jane asks.

'His sons, Michael and Alan. They split half the estate, and the other half will be divided between Edith, Sarah, Harry, and Diana.'

'So, really, *Alan* benefits the most,' I say. 'He's practically destitute.'

Aunt Jane frowns at a dropped stitch. 'And yet, he seems the least likely culprit, doesn't he?' she asks. 'One would imagine that, had he placed the poisoned pill in Josiah's bottle, he would have taken pains to appear as helpful and loving as possible during what he knew to be a false attack.' She sets her knitting aside with a sigh and adds, 'Although, if he were exceptionally devious, he might consider such inaction excellent cover.'

'I don't think Alan Westover is that smart, Aunt Jane,' I say.

'Well, I've never met him,' Aunt Jane says placidly. 'But perhaps, if he were the killer, he would *want* to give Josiah a pill. Since the more he took, the more likely he'd swallow a poisoned one.' She turns toward Detective Wilcox. 'How many pills were in the bottle?'

'According to Stephen Macfarlane, Josiah said that he prepared seven,' Detective Wilcox replies. 'One for each member of the family.'

'Michael never made it into the study to speak with Josiah,' Aunt Jane says. 'And neither Alan nor Edith gave Josiah a pill. But Lucretia, Harry, Diana, and Sarah did. How many were left in the bottle after Josiah collapsed?'

'Well, it's interesting you should ask that, Miss Marple,' Detective Wilcox says, shifting in her seat. 'Four were left. Not three, which is what you'd expect when you're starting with seven pills. Stephen insists that Josiah was definite about the number, but perhaps he counted incorrectly.'

'Perhaps,' Aunt Jane says. Her voice turns musing. 'Four left, all made of sugar. Potentially, Josiah could have missed the poisoned pill entirely. How odd that is. One would imagine that our murderer would not leave it to chance that the poison pill be the one ingested, and replace them all. Where was the bottle kept before Josiah brought it into the study?'

'Stephen Macfarlane says that the pills were on Josiah's person the entire time.' Detective Wilcox shifts in her seat. 'But, once again, we have only his word for that.'

'He'd be your top suspect if he had a motive, wouldn't he?' I ask.

'It wouldn't look good,' Detective Wilcox says wryly. 'It's lucky for him, I suppose, that Josiah's death makes him poor and unemployed.'

'Does it, though?' Aunt Jane murmurs, picking up her knitting once again. 'I wonder about that. Yes, I wonder very much.'

Later that evening, I'm helping Cherry clean up after dinner with Aunt Jane when the phone rings. 'Could you get that, love?' she asks me.

'Of course,' I say, plucking the receiver from its wall mount. 'Hello?'

'Nic, you won't believe what happened!' Diana's voice is breathless. 'You know my cousin Sarah's supposed secret fiancé?'

'Yes.'

'Well, he's real. And you'll never guess who he is.' She doesn't give me a chance to answer before adding, 'Stephen Macfarlane!'

The telephone nearly slips from my hand. 'Really? Are you sure?'

'Oh, yes,' Diana says. 'Somebody sent an anonymous note to the police, and Sarah broke down when she saw it. It's a proper scandal, let me tell you. Uncle Alan had no idea.

Stephen and Sarah are both at the police station right now. I wouldn't be surprised if he's arrested before the night is over.'

'Wow.' It's an inadequate response, but I can't think of what else to say. I should be relieved, but there's something not quite right about this news. I can't put my finger on it, though. 'That's unbelievable.'

'You think so?' Diana asks. 'I don't. Especially after how you said he acted in in the study. He didn't even try to help Grandfather, did he? You had to step in.'

'True,' I say.

'It's always the outsider,' Diana says. As if I'm not one too.

My aunt enters the kitchen as I hang up, an aspirin bottle in hand. 'Nicola, could you open this for me, please? I have a bit of a headache, and my rheumatism makes it difficult to manage these childproof caps.'

'Of course,' I say, twisting it open. 'Here you go. Aunt Jane, you won't believe what Diana just told me. It turns out that Stephen Macfarlane was secretly engaged to Sarah Westover, and now everyone thinks he's the one who killed Josiah.'

'Ah.' Aunt Jane looks troubled as she accepts a glass of water from Cherry and downs her aspirin. 'I did wonder if Stephen might be the secret fiancé. It's not uncommon for ambitious young men and heiresses to find one another irresistible.'

'You *knew*?' I gape at her. 'Why didn't you say anything?'

'I didn't know,' she corrects. 'It was simply a guess. And I didn't say anything because I don't believe for a moment that

Stephen Macfarlane killed Josiah Westover. If he wanted his employer dead, he could have devised a dozen easier ways of doing it – and none of those would have made him look suspicious.'

'I suppose so.' I put the cap back on the bottle, frowning as I think about Stephen slipping behind those drapes. Something is bothering me, tugging at the corners of my brain but refusing to show itself fully.

'I think we should arrange another conversation with Detective Wilcox tomorrow,' Aunt Jane says. 'In the meantime, Nicola, please keep your distance from Westover House. You were in the room with Josiah when he died, and saw things that nobody expected you to see. That's a dangerous position. So often, it's the tiniest observation coming to light that trips up a killer who thinks they're safe.'

I take her hands in mine with a rush of affection. 'You worry too much, Aunt Jane,' I say. 'I'll be fine. I promise, I'll stay right here.'

A few hours later, though, I've gone back on my word.

Diana called again right before Aunt Jane went to bed, utterly distraught. 'The police haven't charged Stephen. They just let him *leave*,' she said tearfully. 'He's gone to some hotel, apparently, but what if he doesn't stay there? What if he comes after us?'

'He'd be mad to do that,' I said, Aunt Jane's words echoing through my mind. *If he wanted his boss dead, he could have devised a dozen easier ways of doing it.* 'Please try not to worry, Di. The police must have let him go for a reason.'

'Because they're incompetent!' she wailed, and then her voice dropped lower. 'I'm scared, Nic. So horribly scared.'

I did my best to reassure her. After we hung up, I tried to distract myself with a book, but I couldn't concentrate. Eventually, I gave up and decided to walk back to the Westover's. I'd surprise Diana, cheer her up, and maybe we could have a late-night snack like we used to when she stayed over at my house in Banbury.

Now, as I approach the driveway, lights are blazing from every window in Westover House, making it look deceptively cosy. My steps slow as I get closer, and I find myself reluctant to ring the doorbell. When it comes to murder, there's no one on earth smarter than my Aunt Jane. If she thinks it's unwise for me to return to the scene of the crime, then maybe I shouldn't.

What had she said? *So often, it's the tiniest observation coming to light that trips up a killer who thinks they're safe.*

I stop in my tracks then, as the memory that had been teasing me at Aunt Jane's cottage hits me with full force. Maybe it's nothing. But it could mean . . .

I bypass the front door and head towards the back of the house. There's something Diana calls a *bulkhead* leading into the basement that, she told me, is supposed to be locked but rarely is. Sure enough, it pulls open with a loud creak. I step into a dim, musty space that leaves me completely disoriented; I've never been in this part of the house before, and I'm not sure how to get to where I need to go – Josiah Westover's bedroom.

Am I out of my mind, though? It's most likely locked, and even if it's not, what I'm looking for is probably with the police.

The police. *Right.* I feel around in my pocket for the card Detective Wilcox gave me right before she left. 'Call any time if you remember something else you'd like to tell me,' she said, writing her home number at the bottom.

I doubt there's a phone in the basement, but I know there's one in the upstairs hall. I inch my way through the darkened room, with only faint moonlight from a single window keeping me from bumping into walls and old pieces of furniture until I finally reach a staircase.

There's a sliver of light coming from beneath the door at the top, so I make my way up and grasp hold of the doorknob. Hinges squeak lightly as I push the door open and step into a hallway. I don't recognise where I am, but it's much less elegant and imposing than the rest of the house. More storage space, perhaps, or a place where the many employees who keep the house running spend their breaks? I don't know for sure, but it doesn't really matter. The most important thing, right now, is the phone on the wall.

I lift it and dial Detective Wilcox's home number. A woman picks up after the second ring. 'Hello?'

'Detective Wilcox? It's Nicola West.'

'Nicola, hi. Is everything all right?'

'Yes. I think so. But I have a question.' I grip the phone tighter, ears straining against the quiet surrounding me. Did I hear a creak of some sort?

'What's that?' she asks.

'Josiah Westover's pill bottle. Did it have a childproof cap, or the older kind – the ones that pop up?'

'It's the pop-up kind. Why?'

I close my eyes briefly and lean my head against the wall. Of course it is. I'd watched three Westovers open the bottle that way, without fully registering what they were doing. I probably wouldn't even have remembered if I hadn't opened Aunt Jane's aspirin bottle with a twist – the kind of motion you wouldn't need for Josiah's bottle.

But I'd seen one person make it.

'Nicola? Why are you asking?' Detective Wilcox asks.

I can't bring myself to answer her. 'Are you absolutely sure there were four pills left in the bottle?' I ask. 'Not three?'

'Yes, but—'

The creaking sound repeats, then morphs into footsteps. Someone's coming down the hall, and I need to get off the phone before they catch me talking to Officer Wilcox. 'Okay, Aunt Jane, I'll be right there,' I say hastily before hanging up.

Diana comes around the corner, a mug in one hand. 'Nicola!' she says, eyes widening in surprise. 'I thought I heard your voice. What are you doing here?'

'Oh, I just— I was worried about you, so I wanted to check in.' I attempt a smile, even though Diana is the last person I want to see right now.

Diana. Who twisted the bottle top. She made a great show of doing it, and yet – I don't remember seeing the cap come off. But Diana handed a pill to Josiah anyway.

'And you decided not to ring the doorbell?' Diana asks.

'It's late, I didn't want to wake anyone.' My fake smile stretches to its breaking point. 'But my aunt asked me to call when I got here, and she's so worried that I think I'd better go back. Sorry I disturbed you for no reason.'

'Oh, it's no trouble. It was sweet of you to think of me. You don't have to walk, though. We can have a car take you. Here.' She places the mug in my hands. 'Have some of my tea while I arrange everything. You look cold.'

'Okay, thank you.' I clutch the mug, waiting for her to leave so I can take off.

She doesn't, though. 'Go on, Nicola, take a sip.'

I gaze down at the shimmering brown liquid. *What's in there?* 'I'd better not,' I say, backing up a few steps. 'It keeps me up too late.'

'You're such a little bit of a thing, Nic,' Diana says, in her usual affectionate tone. 'I think, you know, that if it comes to that – I could *make* you.'

She reaches for me and I don't have time to think – I drop the mug with a loud clatter and run for the stairs behind me. Diana's on me in an instant, though, knocking me heavily to the ground. 'I saw you,' she hisses in my ear as I struggle. 'Coming up the walk, and then sneaking around the back. I heard every word you said. You should have left well enough alone, Nicola.' She has me on my back now, straddling me, one hand clamped over my mouth as I flail uselessly at her. 'It's a shame you ruined my tea, but I have backup. One has to be prepared for anything.'

I keep thrashing about, fighting to free myself so I can scream. Diana's twisting too, reaching for something, and then her hand lifts from my mouth. Before I can take a breath, she's pinching my cheeks to keep my mouth open, and attempting to shove something white past my lips. 'Rat poison,' she hisses. 'Fitting, since you turned out to be such a rat of a friend.' I manage to clamp my mouth closed and turn my head away, but Diana grabs hold of my nose, making it impossible to breathe. I'm going to run out of breath soon, and when I do . . .

'Stop!' calls a commanding voice. And then Diana's weight comes off me as she's yanked roughly to her feet by a man I've never seen before. 'That's enough, Miss Westover,' he says, pulling her backwards as I struggle into a sitting position. 'More than enough.'

I can barely catch my breath, but manage to ask, 'Who are you?'

'Officer Peter Graves with the Chatham Police,' he says. 'Once your aunt heard that Stephen Macfarlane had been released, she made arrangements for me to be on site tonight. She thought Josiah's killer might turn desperate.' He tightens his hold on Diana. 'And I guess she did.'

'But what was her motive?' I ask Detective Wilcox. We're back on Aunt Jane's deck, two days after the night Diana tried to poison me. 'Did she need the money after all? Has her father gone bankrupt?'

'Why are you asking me?' Detective Wilcox asks with a smile. 'Surely your aunt has figured it out by now.'

'If she has, she hasn't told me,' I say, unable to keep the annoyance out of my voice. 'She keeps saying I need *rest*.'

'Well, you do,' Aunt Jane says calmly. 'And of course, I don't know for sure, but I rather suspect that Diana and her grandfather clashed over a passion of hers. Perhaps . . .' She gazes at the hydrangea bush Diana gave her, which Cherry planted discreetly among several others in the yard. 'Perhaps it had something to do with frogs.'

'Frogs?' I echo. 'I don't understand.'

Aunt Jane inclines her head. 'They don't sing any more, you see. Which is the sort of thing that happens when land is overdeveloped and species are displaced.'

'Goodness, Miss Marple, you don't miss a trick, do you?' Detective Wilcox says admiringly. 'That's exactly it. Diana was furious that Josiah planned to develop an enormous parcel of what she thought should be conservation land. She was eavesdropping at the window below his office, trying to understand the timing, when she heard about Josiah's plans with the sugar pills. She decided to make up her own pill, but couldn't figure out how to get it into the bottle – Stephen Macfarlane was right that it never left Josiah's possession – so she simply carried it with her. Pretended to open the bottle and handed over her pill instead. It was hastily done, and she was taking a risk that Josiah might have noticed. But, clearly, he didn't.'

'What about the car, and the vase?' I ask. 'Was that Diana too?'

'She says no,' Detective Wilcox says. 'But we certainly wonder.'

'Why didn't Diana just slip poison into Josiah's tea, like she tried to do with me?' I ask.

Detective Wilcox's expression darkens. 'We haven't gotten her to admit this yet, but I suspect she's the one who sent the anonymous note about Stephen Macfarlane and Sarah's engagement. She saw Josiah's plan as the perfect opportunity to frame Stephen, and she took it.'

'How did she learn so much about white baneberry and . . . rat poison?' I ask with a shudder. *Fitting, since you turned out to be such a rat of a friend.* It's ridiculous, considering what Diana did, that her words have the power to sting. What hurts, I suppose, is that I never actually knew the girl I thought was my friend. Di-and-Nic wasn't real, and maybe I should've taken a clue from the fact that Diana's name came first. *Diana* always came first.

Today my hair is back to its usual curls, and I'm wearing my own clothes. But I can't shake the memory of how eager I was to be exactly like Diana.

'She's very knowledgeable when it comes to plants,' Detective Wilcox says. 'Especially ones that grow locally. She knew white baneberry would likely kill her grandfather, but not a healthy young person. As for the rat poison, that was initially intended for Harry.'

'For *Harry*?' I ask, aghast.

'Oh dear,' Aunt Jane murmurs. 'A second victim.'

'Exactly so, Miss Marple. Diana was frustrated that we hadn't arrested Stephen Macfarlane, and hoped we'd believe he wanted to increase Sarah's share of Josiah's fortune with another death. But when she saw Nicola heading for the house and overheard her conversation with me, plans changed.'

My stomach rolls. 'What will happen to her?'

'That's to be determined. She's still a minor. And her father has engaged the best lawyer possible for her,' Detective Wilcox says. 'But her actions have been quite cold-blooded. The Chatham Police would like her off the streets for a very long time.'

'Good,' Aunt Jane says crisply. 'It's a shame, of course. She's a charming young woman in many respects, and almost as clever as she thinks. I could see she was reluctant to share her father's invitation to me, but I put that down to embarrassment. She played that part well. I thought we had some views in common, particularly when she spoke so glowingly of simpler times.' She sighs. 'I hadn't fully connected the dots, but thank goodness I listened to my instincts. It's a pleasure, Detective Wilcox, to work with someone who respects intuition.'

'I'm grateful for your involvement,' Detective Wilcox says. 'When Nicola hung up so abruptly that night, I feared she was in immediate danger. If we'd waited until then to send someone, it might have been too late."

'So, essentially, Aunt Jane, you saved my life,' I say. My spirits rise a little as I add, 'Maybe Granddad will finally admit that you're the criminal mastermind of the century.'

'Goodness, Nicola, the nonsense you talk,' Aunt Jane says reprovingly. 'I'm sure Raymond would think no such thing.'

'You're right,' I say. 'But that's only because he's never understood you. Now, me, on the other hand – I want to learn your ways.' I press my hands together in an act of mock supplication that's only half-joking. 'Teach me, Aunt Jane, how to spot the murdering sort.'

'Murderers are few and far between, thankfully. It's much more important to spot trouble of the *everyday* sort.' She gives a prim little cough and adds, 'In that vein, perhaps this would be a good time to tell us about the note you received from the Westover boy this morning?'

I drop my hands into my lap as Detective Wilcox blinks. 'Note?' she asks.

'Aunt Jane, really, how could you know that?' I ask, flushing.

'It was a *most* high-quality envelope you opened, and you blushed quite a bit as you read it,' Aunt Jane says serenely. 'Just as you are doing now. I assumed the handsome young cousin had been in touch and, perhaps, extended an invitation of some kind?'

'You're not supposed to use your detecting skills on *me*!' I protest. Then honesty compels me to add, 'All right, yes. It was Harry, apologising for what happened and asking if he could visit the cottage some day this week.' I'd been desperate to say yes, and now that I know Harry was meant to be another one of Diana's victims, I'm even more so. But I don't trust my own judgement any more, after Diana fooled me so completely. 'Should I tell him no?'

'A visit?' Aunt Jane asks. 'I was concerned he might want to whisk you off to some sort of *club,* but that sounds perfectly proper. I should be glad to meet him.'

'Really?' I ask, smiling for what feels like the first time in days.

'Really,' Aunt Jane confirms. 'But do ask him to leave the guitar at home.'

The Mystery of the Acid Soil

Kate Mosse

One

There is nothing quite like being settled comfortably in a railway carriage in good time, one's luggage stowed, ten minutes before the train is due to depart.

Jane Marple was sitting in a first-class compartment of the Southern Railway service, or whatever it was called these days, the bustle of the concourse and the ticket office quite behind her. There had been no shortage of porters at Victoria Station, her suitcase was on the rack above her head, and the guard had let down the window to let in a little air. Her faded leather handbag and travelling gloves were on the seat beside her and there was a trail of grey wool in her lap, the beginnings of a pullover for a great-nephew.

It was a gentle afternoon in late August, that shimmering time of day when the air is heavy with heat. She had spent an enjoyable two days in London with her nephew, Raymond, and his wife Joan, a painter who was making quite a name for herself. Raymond had taken her to see the new comedy at the Vaudeville Theatre, they had dined at Simpson's and taken their boys to London Zoo to see the lions. She had stayed in a sister establishment to Bertram's Hotel, which, despite everything that London had put up with during the Blitz, seemed little altered: the same kind of people, the same steady pace, colonels and black-corseted widows and the memory of an older England, now swept away. Were it not for the shadows of bombed-out buildings, or notices in shop windows apologising for shortages, it might have been as if the past eight years had never happened.

Miss Marple had enjoyed herself, but she was rather tired. London was loud and noisy, so very many people rushing about. The air seemed all used up. A peaceful holiday in Sussex with her dear friend Emmeline Strickert would be most welcome. Her visit to Drovers had been originally planned for the autumn, but Emmeline had been operated on for a contracture in her right palm and so had invited her to come earlier to help her in what might be an uncomfortable convalescence. There were so few people who belonged to the old days, who knew the girl she had been. So, Miss Marple had had no hesitation in putting her maid on board wages, sending her plate and King Charles tankard to the bank for safe-keeping, and making arrangements to spend the last three weeks of August in the country. Her only concern was that her jasmine hedge might run riot while she was away.

The whistle blew.

Two

As they were pulling away, the door was flung open and a young man all but threw himself into the carriage. He sank into a seat opposite, his face red with exertion, the hem of his cassock rimmed with the dust of London streets.

'My apologies,' said the curate, catching his breath. 'I was anxious to not miss the train.'

'I assumed as much,' she replied, her faded blue eyes twinkling.

Miss Marple returned to her knitting; her travelling companion wiped his face with a handkerchief as the train jerked its way out of the terminus and stared out of the window. The sound of metal on the tracks, the hiss and steam of the engine. Over the Thames and past the grimy backs of the tenement buildings of Victoria and Battersea, into the leafy suburbs of Clapham and Streatham. Although he did not say anything, Miss Marple could not fail to be aware that the young man was in the grip of some strong emotion. He picked at a loose thread on his cassock until she thought the button would fall off, and bounced the toe of his shoe anxiously on the floor.

The suburbs gave way to countryside. Green fields and a heat haze over the river valleys. Lulled by the rhythm of the tracks, she found her hands growing heavy in her lap. In the distance, the South Downs came into view.

'But if only I knew for sure,' he muttered.

Her eyes snapped open. 'I beg your pardon?'

The curate flushed. 'I'm sorry, I didn't realise—'

'It is so easy, if one fancies oneself unobserved, to speak one's thoughts out loud.'

'I suppose it is.' He made an effort to pull himself together. 'Are you travelling far?'

Miss Marple smiled. 'To Fishbourne, beyond Chichester.'

His face lit up. 'That is my parish. It's my first post and where I . . .' He stopped.

She wondered what he had been about to say.

'I had an uncle who was a canon at Chichester Cathedral,' she said. 'My sister and I used to stay with him before the War – before the Great War, that is. It is a beautiful part of the world.'

'It is, at least . . .' He broke off again, the frown back on his face.

Miss Marple waited, but he had once more retreated into his own thoughts.

'I am to stay with a friend from my school days,' she offered. 'We were together at a *pensionnat* in Florence when we were girls, so very many years ago now. We had so many ideals. I was going to nurse lepers and Emmeline was going to . . .' She shook her head. 'Do you know, I can't remember.'

The young man looked as if he was about to speak, but then he put his hands over his face.

'Forgive me,' she said quietly, 'but is something the matter, Mr . . . ?'

'Kemp,' he replied, looking at her with despairing eyes. 'Ernest Kemp.'

'I am Jane Marple. It is none of my business, of course,' she said, 'and perhaps I have misunderstood – I so often do

– but you said you wished you could be sure. I wonder what you meant?'

For a moment, she feared she had presumed too much, but then she saw him straighten up. She resumed knitting and listened.

'There is a girl,' he said. 'I'm awfully fond of her and I thought she was of me, but . . .' He took a deep breath. 'She has vanished.'

Her eyes sharpened. 'Vanished?'

'Her father – that's to say, her stepfather – says she simply upped and left. Gone to London to join a theatre company.'

'Oh dear,' Miss Marple murmured.

'I know what you're thinking,' he said quickly, 'but she's not that kind of girl. And when I went to the theatre near Waterloo today, they had never heard of her.'

Many thoughts were going through Miss Marple's head, none of them, she thought, would be welcome.

'It's utterly out of character,' he continued. 'Elizabeth is unhappy at home, although she never complains. Her mother died two weeks ago, at the beginning of August – and she was devoted to her mother – but to leave without saying a word. Not even a letter.'

Miss Marple was sadly aware of how often girls acted out of character. Or, rather, how young men could be rather innocent about those they admired.

'How long has it been since you saw her?' she asked kindly.

'Two days. Her mother's funeral was on Monday, and so we arranged to go for a walk yesterday. I thought she might need a shoulder to cry on. When she didn't arrive, I was worried, so I called on her at home. That's when her step-father told me she had left that morning.'

Two days did not seem a very long time and, although she felt sorry for the young man, she thought it was possible that Elizabeth simply did not want to see him, but lacked the courage to tell him to his face.

'No doubt there has been some misunderstanding. You say she has recently lost her mother. Is there anywhere she might have gone? To relatives, perhaps?'

'There is no one else. She's alone in the world.'

'Except for her stepfather,' Miss Marple said carefully.

'Him! Cooper doesn't care about anyone except himself!' he said fiercely, then was instantly embarrassed at his lack of Christian charity. 'I apologise, I spoke out of turn. If only I could be sure she is all right.'

She took pity on him. 'If you are genuinely worried about your young lady, then why not speak to her neighbours. She might have said something to them. They have a daily, perhaps?'

Kemp shook his head. 'Mrs Hands was let go away after Mrs Cooper died. It's rotten if he expects Elizabeth to wait on him.'

The train began to slow. He looked out of the window, then made another effort to compose himself.

'We're coming in to Chichester, which is where I get off. Fishbourne is just a minute or two further on.'

'Do you not live in Fishbourne, Mr Kemp?'

'I do – I'm currently lodging at the rectory until I can find somewhere more permanent – but it's a shorter walk from Chichester than from Fishbourne station. Let me help you with your luggage.'

Kemp pulled the suitcase down from the rack, bracing his feet against the rocking movement of the carriage. 'You may need assistance when you get off, as it is quite heavy.'

Miss Marple flushed. 'It is rather. My friend is fond of both my damson gin and my cherry brandy. Of course it is so hard to get anything these days. Because I couldn't decide, I brought them both. I shall be there for three weeks, you see.'

Kemp smiled as he set her suitcase on the floor beside the door. He pressed in the window latch and pulled down the glass as the brakes began to bind.

'You have been very kind, Miss Marple. Perhaps I am over-reacting. I might have misheard the name of the theatre, or . . . Well, as you say, there's bound to be an explanation. I do hope you enjoy your stay and I'll hope to see you on Sunday, perhaps.'

'Yes, indeed,' she smiled. 'And I do hope your friend is in touch.'

Kemp nodded, then stepped down on to the platform, closed the door and raised his hat. Miss Marple watched the lovestruck curate grow smaller and smaller as he walked away. But, as she packed away her knitting, she was frowning. One or two things the young man had said had given her pause for thought.

There was no time to reflect further. Within minutes, they were pulling into Fishbourne Halt, a tiny branch station surrounded by fields and trees filled with nesting rooks. Miss Marple looked for the stationmaster, but he was occupied with the railway crossing gates and the signal. Before she could attract his attention, a big, florid man in a rather loud checked suit was reaching into the carriage and taking the case from her hands.

'Let's see if we can sort you out.'

'Oh, do take care,' she said, as he dropped it heavily on to the platform, fearing for her bottles and the jar of night cream Joan had given her as a gift.

'There we go!'

Miss Marple was not, she hoped, an ungenerous person. But although she was grateful, she did not like to be addressed in so casual a manner.

'Thank you,' she said, with studied politeness.

'Always happy to help a lady in distress,' he said, putting his finger to his temple by way of salute, then climbed into the carriage.

'Jane! Jane!'

Miss Marple turned in the direction of the voice with relief and there was her old friend, looking exactly as she always did, standing at the end of the platform and ordering the stationmaster to hurry along with his trolley.

Three

Drovers was a pretty flint-faced cottage with trailing roses around the door, a white gate and a path lined with lavender. It stood in a generous plot of land on a quiet road that led down towards the Marshes, used only by farm vehicles and the occasional delivery van.

By six o'clock, the two ladies were happily settled in wicker chairs in Emmeline's back garden, surrounded by rhododendrons, azaleas, clematis crispa and other acid-loving plants. The afternoon sun filtered through the waxy, dark-green leaves, setting bands of light on the lawn. Jane Marple had changed from her travelling clothes and into her reliable summer dress. Emmy, meanwhile, was wearing a voluminous cotton frock of her own and an untidy wide-brimmed straw hat that looked as if it had seen better days. The cherry brandy had been put on a slate shelf in Emmeline's pantry; the damson gin was with them on a cane table on the lawn.

The two old friends each sipped at their respective tiny crystal glasses.

'It's my grandmother's recipe,' Miss Marple said. 'It is so pleasant, don't you think, to be taken back in time?'

'I do,' said Emmeline, with a nostalgic smile.

'Of all our senses, it is smell and taste that seems to most capture – is that what I mean? – the past.'

Her friend laughed.

Two spots of pink appeared on Miss Marple's cheeks. 'Am I running on, Emmy? It's so easy to become rambling, isn't it, and one wanders from the point.'

'Not at all. I was only thinking how you don't change a bit, Jane. Listening to you, we could be back in our *pensionnat* in Florence. Do you remember Fraulein Schweich?'

'I do. Those boots!'

'Do you ever hear from Ruth or Carrie Louise?'

The American sisters had seemed much more glamorous than the other girls at their finishing school, and Emmeline, who was forever being told to sit up straight and pull up her stockings, had been in awe of them.

'I haven't seen Carrie Louise for, oh, it must be twenty years. She took me to the opera at Covent Garden. I can't remember what we saw, only the red and gold of the magnificent curtains,' Miss Marple replied. 'But Ruth and I correspond from time to time. She's on her second, possibly even third marriage by now, all very successful.'

The chair creaked as Emmy sat back. 'I'll never forget Ruth saying how extraordinary it was that, despite your innocent appearance, you always believed the worst. And weren't you cross with her!'

'I don't think we spoke for a week,' Miss Marple replied. 'But, you see, the worst is so often true.'

Emmy took another sip. 'On which point, I'm not sure we should tell anyone that you have arrived to stay with two whole bottles of macerated spirits. It will give the village quite the wrong impression.'

'I have never been an advocate of teetotalism,' said Miss Marple, primly. 'A little strong drink is always advisable on the premises in case there is a shock or an accident.'

'Have we had a shock or an accident?'

'No,' she twinkled, 'but travel is wearying, is it not?'

From inside the house, the sound of the maid preparing the evening meal floated out into the still August air. They talked for a while of the problem of retaining servants and the continuing frustrations of rationing. Beyond the garden,

Miss Marple could hear the sound of a tractor in the fields and the cry of gulls out at sea. It was all very soothing after the clamour of the city.

'I met a rather charming young man on the train,' she said. 'I believe he is your new curate, Ernest Kemp?'

'Oh, yes,' said Emmeline, leaning over and pulling a tiny weed from the otherwise immaculate soil beneath the rhododendrons. 'He's awfully young and rather athletic – he was in the Royal Sussex Regiment and fought at Arnhem – so he is already a firm favourite with the ladies who manage the flower rota!'

'That does not surprise me,' Miss Marple said with a wry smile. 'He told me a rather curious story.'

After she'd finished recounting Mr Kemp's tale, she looked fondly at her friend. Emmeline still had a wonderful mane of blonde hair, with perhaps only a little recourse to science, and her slightly bewildered expression was barely altered by the passage of the years. Emmy had always worn her heart on her sleeve, and did so now.

'Emmy?'

'Well, it is rather odd, now I come to think about it. Elizabeth going away like that without a word to anyone.'

'Really?' She put her glass down on the table. 'You interest me very much.'

'Well, I'm not sure what to say. Or if I have anything to say. Only, that it *is* odd.'

Miss Marple picked up her needles and started to knit. 'Go on.'

Emmy rubbed her nose, leaving a smudge of earth on her

cheek. 'It is rather as our curate said. She isn't that sort of a girl. She's awfully bookish, serious-minded. It's true she has a lovely voice – she sings in the church choir – but not at all the sort who'd to want to be an actress, I'd have thought.'

'Where would she have met an acting company?'

Emmy waved her hand. 'There was a repertory company, playing the south-coast tour earlier in the summer. You know, Gosport, Portsmouth, Bognor Regis, Worthing. She must have gone to one of their shows.'

'Is she pretty?'

Emmeline looked doubtful. 'Well, I'm not sure I would say that. Handsome, in an old-fashioned sense. She was very much devoted to her mother, even though Mrs Cooper was rather a trying woman. Her only interests in life were her garden and her own ill health. Nothing was ever quite right.' Emmy frowned. 'Yes, it is peculiar Elizabeth should have gone off like that.'

The sun suddenly went behind a wisp of cloud and the garden, beneath its dark-green perimeter of waxy leaves, felt suddenly much colder.

'Mr Kemp also said that the Coopers had let their daily go. Are they perhaps in straitened circumstances? So many are these days.'

Emmy shook her head. 'Far from it. Cooper is one of those men who was, as people put it, "rather useful" during the war and did well out of it. Very jolly, hail-fellow-well-met, you know the kind. Over familiar. He always seemed to be able to acquire things that were in short supply.'

Miss Marple found it easy to imagine Fishbourne during the war. Coupons changing hands, meat and fish, black-market petrol, with Cooper at the heart of things. They had had a similar character in her own village of St Mary Mead, but then that was hardly surprising. Human nature was much the same everywhere.

'You said his wife was in poor health. Do I take it her death was expected?'

'Not at all. Dr Barden was of the opinion there was nothing actually wrong with her at all. No, she contracted tetanus.'

'How terrible.'

'Yes. You know how people put used razor blades around the roots of plants like rhododendrons and the like to acidify the soil?'

'It's a very foolish habit.'

'Poor Mrs Cooper cut her finger on a rusting blade in her garden and died within days. Such a tragedy.'

Miss Marple coughed gently. 'The doctor was a local man, I assume? Was he satisfied?'

Emmeline nodded. 'He was. I know, because there was talk and someone – I can't remember who – challenged him one evening in the public house. Accused him of not knowing what he was doing. Dr Barden was *adamant* it was tetanus.'

'I would like to know who challenged him,' Miss Marple said lightly.

Emmeline glanced at her friend. 'I will try to remember, though I don't know why you should be interested.'

Miss Marple was wondering. 'And what do you think of Dr Barden, Emmy?'

'He wasn't my doctor, I'm glad to say. He was set in his ways, terribly out of step with modern ideas. Very much opposed to the National Health Service.'

She leant forward in her chair. 'Was?'

Emmeline frowned. 'He died just a few days after Mrs Cooper.'

'Good heavens, of what?'

Emmeline flushed. 'I don't like to speak ill of the dead.'

'It might be important, Emmy. I would not be asking if I didn't think it mattered.'

Her friend sighed. 'He had a weak heart and . . . He was found dead in his chair by Mrs Hands – the same daily who did for the Coopers – with an empty bottle of whisky at his elbow. It was common knowledge he was much too fond of drink. What with that, and his heart . . .' Not wishing to be cast in the role of gossip, she started to get to her feet. 'Shall we go in? It wouldn't do to catch a chill, Jane, when you've only just arrived.'

Miss Marple didn't move. 'Where does Mr Cooper live?'

Reluctantly, Emmy sat down again. 'In Salthill Road, very close to the railway station. In point of fact, he was on the platform yesterday when I was waiting for you.'

'Ah, *that* was Mr Cooper,' she muttered, remembering the loud suit.

'What are you up to, Jane? Do you think there's something wrong?'

'Well,' she replied carefully, 'when three unusual events happen in close succession, one has to wonder. And the daily being let go, that is very suggestive.'

'Of what?' asked Emmy, confusion on her placid face.

Miss Marple did not answer. 'When a man is widowed, it is sometimes the case that his life goes on reasonably untroubled by grief. How did Mr Cooper respond to the twin shocks of bereavement and now his stepdaughter's desertion?'

Emmeline considered. 'I would say that the even tenor of his routine does not appear to have suffered so much as a wrinkle.'

Four

The next morning, Miss Marple rose at her usual time, having slept surprisingly well in an unfamiliar bed. She found Emmeline in the dining room, looking regretfully at a jar of shop-bought marmalade.

'Let me do that.'

With deft practice, she twisted the reluctant lid, which popped open with a snap. 'You should be resting your hand.'

Her friend pulled a face. 'I don't want to be a trouble.'

Miss Marple smiled. 'Don't be silly, Emmy. It's why I'm here.'

The two ladies sat down to breakfast in companionable silence. The only sounds were the rattle of cutlery against china and tea being poured from the pot. French windows gave on to the back garden and a light breeze was blowing in from the Marshes. Jane Marple read the obituaries in *The Times* and Emmeline opened her post.

'We are invited to tea with the rector this afternoon,' she

said, brandishing a letter. 'We don't have to go, of course.'

Miss Marple thought of the young curate. 'How very kind. I would be delighted.'

Emmeline raised her eyebrows. 'All right, I'll send a note. What would you like to do this morning?'

'Perhaps a walk before the sun becomes too hot? I'd like to get to know Fishbourne better.'

'I've been very happy here at Drovers. Were it not for the road . . .' Emmeline began a long story about how the steady increase in through-traffic was changing the nature of the village for the worse. 'But then things never seem to change for the better.'

'Oh, I don't believe that's true,' countered Miss Marple. 'Think of the extraordinary advances in healthcare, many of them, so I am told, the result of research carried out during the two World Wars. There is always good in bad, as there must always be bad in good.'

Looking unconvinced, Emmeline buttered a third piece of toast.

Jane chose an ash walking stick, Emmy stuck to her old faithful, and by nine-thirty they were setting out to explore the village.

The two ladies strolled gently along the main road, past the old bakery, the village school and the water treatment works. It was true that the traffic was depressing, the constant rumble setting up clouds of dust. Miss Marple thought of St Mary Mead and how lucky it was that the lane outside her door wasn't a through road to anywhere.

They reached the old laundry and she saw they were at the junction with Salthill Road.

'Might we go this way for a while?'

'There's not much to see,' Emmeline said, looking surprised. 'Just the railway station.'

Miss Marple was already walking north. They passed a lime pit and a row of modest new houses with long front gardens.

'Didn't you say that Mr Cooper lived somewhere on Salthill Road?' she asked casually.

Emmeline peered at her from under the wide brim of her straw hat. 'What are you up to, Jane?'

'Simply getting my bearings.'

'Hmm. Well, in point of fact, that is Mr Cooper's house opposite. Dr Barden lived a few doors further down.'

Miss Marple stared at the low brick wall topped with clay tiles, then crossed the road to take a closer look. The window frames needed attention, all the curtains were closed and there was moss in the gutters and growing thickly among the thatch. The garden was pretty, but it was unkempt. She fished her spectacles from her handbag and peered over the wall. 'That's Lily of the Valley,' she said, 'quite lovely. And there is Phacelia, usually planted for its ability to improve the soil, but with beautiful mauve blooms if you let it. And those ornamental clovers beside the front door are a picture.' She moved to the other side of the gate. 'Ah,' she said quietly, 'I did wonder.'

Emmeline looked rather fogged. 'Wonder at what?'

'There's wild marjoram, very popular with butterflies, and

Jacob's ladder with lovely blue flowers. And then the lawn, quite unusual and ragged, called, I believe, blue moor grass. They all go together.'

'You *are* clever, Jane. The only plants I can recognise are the lavender along the path and honeysuckle.'

'And what does that tell you?'

Emmeline shook her head. 'I'm sure I don't know. That Mrs Cooper had green fingers.'

'Yes, indeed, but—'

Before she could explain, the front door opened and Cooper himself was striding down the front path towards them.

'Perhaps we should move on,' Emmeline whispered. 'We wouldn't want it to be thought we were snooping.'

Miss Marple smiled. 'There is nothing more commonplace than two elderly ladies admiring a neighbour's garden. It would be much odder if we did not.'

Cooper was wearing a very white shirt with a red tie, and the same loud checked trousers she remembered from the day before. His eyes were slightly bloodshot. He did not, in her opinion, look like a grieving widower.

'Good morning, ladies. Miss Strickert, is it? Is there something I can do for you?'

His words were genial enough, but, instinctively, Miss Marple did not think he was a man to be trusted. He reminded her of a man she had met at a Hydro some years before the war. All bonhomie and nothing-too-much-trouble, but thoroughly wicked beneath the genial surface.

'My friend and I were admiring your garden,' Emmeline said, in a fluster.

Jane Marple watched as Cooper rearranged his expression. 'My wife was the gardener,' he said, dropping his voice to a suitably sombre note. 'Without her, I'm afraid it is running to seed.'

'Please accept my condolences,' Miss Marple said. 'It must be so difficult. And, of course, for a daughter to lose her mother so unexpectedly.'

Cooper's shrewd eyes narrowed. 'It is,' he said shortly. 'Now, if there is nothing else, I'm sure you ladies have plenty you need to be doing.'

Five

'Well!' Emmeline said, as soon as they were out of earshot. 'What a disagreeable man.'

Miss Marple was troubled. 'Yes, indeed.'

Her friend looked at her. 'I'm not sure I like the way you say that, Jane.'

She looked back at the Cooper house, then to the surgery three doors along, where a brass plaque glinted in the August sunshine: Dr J Barden MD.

'I wonder, dear Emmy, if you are not too tired, might we find time to call upon Mrs Hands before we return home? There are one or two questions I would very much like to put to her.'

Mrs Hands, who had previously done for both the Cooper household and for Dr Barden, lived in a brick-built house beside The Bull's Head Public House, one of a narrow row designed to serve only the most basic needs of agricultural workers – a roof over their heads and a single cold-water tap at a large kitchen sink.

Miss Marple had to bow her head when they were invited in, but the inside of the premises was spotlessly clean and furnished with an eccentric, though well-tended, collection of unmatched bits and pieces.

'It must have been a terrible shock,' she said, 'finding Dr Barden, as you did.'

Mrs Hands put her hand to her heart. 'Oh, it was. And then, to receive a letter from the lawyer saying the doctor had left me fifty pounds and any pieces of furniture I might choose to have. Well, I came over all somehow.'

She gestured round the room at a medical specimen cabinet, in which she kept her china ornaments, and a swivel desk-chair.

'And we are sitting on the chairs from the waiting room, I imagine?' said Miss Marple.

'That's correct. I prefer a straight.'

'So do I,' said Miss Marple, glancing at Emmeline, who looked like she didn't.

'Now then,' said Mrs Hands. 'What did you want to know?'

'We were just passing,' Emmeline said weakly.

'I mind there's more than that.'

Miss Marple's blue eyes sparkled. 'It seems you are a step ahead of us, Mrs Hands. To be candid, we would like to know more about the circumstances of Dr Barden's death.'

The charwoman folded her arms. 'It's about time someone

took an interest, though I expected the police, not a couple of old maids.'

'Mrs Hands!' Emmeline protested weekly.

'I say it like it is. Now, I won't deny he had let himself go, because he had. His heart was ever so weak. And I won't say as he wasn't too fond of the bottle, because everyone knows he was. But he always knew when to stop.'

'Do go on,' said Miss Marple.

'Well, Dr Barden and Cooper – I won't call him mister – they were friends, after a fashion.'

'After the fashion of drinkers?' asked Miss Marple.

'Jane!' cried Emmeline, 'how did you know?'

'A doctor's practice depends on his reputation, does it not? Particularly before the advent of the National Health Service that Dr Barden appears to have so resented.'

'He hated it,' exclaimed Mrs Hands. 'He said it "broke the bond of trust that comes from the exchange of honest payment for services rendered". I couldn't agree with that. What about them as couldn't afford the "bond of trust"?'

'Quite so,' said Miss Marple. 'Now, may I make an appeal to your candour, Mrs Hands? It will perhaps reassure you to know that I am lucky enough to count among my closest friends Sir Henry Clithering, formerly the Commissioner of Scotland Yard.' Mrs Hands looked suitably impressed. 'Wouldn't you like to tell me what you know – or what you think you know?'

Mrs Hands hesitated, then leant forward. 'Well,' she began, lowering her voice, 'there were two glasses on the table.'

*

Six

Three quarters of an hour later, Miss Marple and Emmeline were standing outside The Bull's Head on the main road. The early morning clouds had burnt off and the sun was now quite fierce in an intense blue sky. Miss Marple's face was sombre.

'Are we any further along, Jane?'

'Oh, I think so. After all, cases such as this are almost always the same. I know in books it is generally the most unlikely person, but I never find that rule applies in real life. Except . . .'

'Except?'

'It seems to me there is more to it.' Miss Marple frowned. 'It's the sequence of things all running together. There being two glasses, and Mrs Hands being dismissed from Cooper's service.'

Emmeline's eyes were bright. 'And what do you think?'

'That Dr Barden understood he had made a terrible mistake and regretted it, and Mr Cooper realised.'

'I can't begin to say I understand, but it really is most exciting.'

Miss Marple's expression grew even more grave. 'No, Emmy. Murder isn't a thing to be taken lightly.'

'Murder!' Emmeline wailed. 'Do you mean to say that Dr Barden was murdered?'

'Oh, I think so.'

Emmeline's eyes grew wide. 'Shouldn't we tell someone?'

'Having a suspicion is not the same as proof.' Miss Marple

glanced at her wristwatch. 'I wonder if the rector would forgive us for calling on him a little earlier than invited?'

Emmeline opened her mouth, then closed it again. 'I will see if Williams might drive us – he's by way of being the informal village taxi service. It's quite a step from here to the rectory.' She turned to knock on the door of a second cottage in the same row. 'Oh, I've remembered! It was Williams who had the argument with Dr Barden.'

'So much the better,' said Miss Marple, with a gleam in her sharp blue eyes.

Seven

Five minutes later they were heading east towards the rectory in Grove Park.

Pleading travel sickness, Miss Marple had contrived to sit up front with Williams, a lean country man who exuded a fragrance of bitter beer and pipe tobacco. It was the work of a moment to find out just why he and Barden had flung insults at one another in the saloon bar at the Bull's Head.

'He near as dammit – pardon me French – killed my little girl and I won't believe anyone who says the contrary. Impetigo, he said it was. Impetigo! I could see, and so could my wife, that it was the measles, and not the ordinary measles, it was the German measles, and nothing good's never come out of Germany that I can see.'

'I trust your daughter recovered?'

'Yes, but no thanks to him. Turning up smelling of whisky

and my little one almost gone because of it. Have you seen his garden?'

'I can't say I ever did,' Emmeline said, startled.

'Weren't much of a garden, because every minute he spent in it was in his summer house.' Williams snorted. 'At least, he called it a summer house, though it was little better than a shed for tools he never found the inclination to use. You know what he used it for?'

'Somewhere to sit in private?' replied Miss Marple.

'Exactly. That's where he kept his supply, out of sight – but I knew.' Williams put a leathery finger to his prominent nose and made a gruff noise in his throat, something between contempt and self-satisfaction. 'Roof was leaking and he asked me to come round and replace a few shingles. Not much of a job but he paid me handsome. You know why?'

'Alcohol can loosen the tightest purse strings, I believe.'

He graced Miss Marple with an admiring look. 'That's right. And I saw where he kept his tipple – in a tin chest brought back from the war, half buried in the dirt floor to keep it cool.'

'And you confronted him about Mrs Cooper in The Bull's Head?'

'Mrs Cooper? Who told you that? No, I told him that he didn't know a rhododendron from a lilac, so he wasn't fooling anyone. I told him how the NHS spotted it was the rubella and fixed my girl up for free, so that if he was thinking of sending a bill, he could . . .'

'Quite,' Miss Marple said hurriedly, seeing Emmeline's scandalised expression in the mirror. 'So, who was it mentioned Mrs Cooper?'

Williams put out his indicator and turned left into Grove Park. 'You know, I believe it was him. And he had a funny look.'

'Yes,' murmured Miss Marple, 'it is becoming clearer now.'

'Is it?' said Emmeline.

'Might you wait?' Miss Marple asked, as Williams opened her door. 'We might need your continuing services.'

'Right you are, madam.'

He helped Emmeline out of the back seat, then leaned against his bonnet and took out his pipe.

'I haven't the slightest idea of what is going on . . .' hissed Emmeline as they hurried up the path to the rectory.

'In the course of his conversation with Williams,' Miss Marple explained, 'Dr Barden realised he had taken too much on trust. Because Cooper and he had been friends, after a fashion.'

'But what does any of that . . .'

Miss Marple shook her head and pulled the bell.

Eight

The introductions dispensed with, Miss Marple and Emmeline Strickert were sitting in the rector's homely drawing room. If he was surprised the two ladies had arrived so very early, he had the good manners not to show it.

'Such a charming village,' said Miss Marple, giving no indication of the troubling thoughts racing round her head. 'But tragedy strikes even in the nicest of places. The death of Mr Cooper's poor wife, for example.'

'Indeed,' murmured the rector, with an expression of professional sympathy.

'And then his stepdaughter leaving – like something out of a penny dreadful. I imagine you advised him?'

'Well . . .' said the rector doubtfully. He looked surprised that this pink-faced lady should eschew the usual old-maidish small-talk of knitwear and flower-arranging. 'One does what one can.'

'Mr Cooper is an assiduous churchgoer?'

'No, I wouldn't say that. But Elizabeth is a most valued member of our choir.'

'Does he perhaps attend the midweek evensong?'

'Things are not quite what they were, Miss Marple. Mr Cooper has business interests that take him to Portsmouth in the afternoon, so—'

'Every day?' Miss Marple said quickly.

'I believe so.'

'And what of Mrs Cooper?'

The rector looked very uncomfortable. 'She did occasionally attend Sunday services, but she was something of an invalid. Devoted to her garden.'

'And she and Mr Cooper made for a well-matched couple?'

The rector screwed up his eyes as the bright sunlight struck his glasses – or, perhaps, it was the incisiveness of Miss Marple's questioning. 'I really couldn't say. *De mortuis nil nisi bonum*. I trust you will not oblige me to go further.'

'Of course,' Miss Marple said, but carried on regardless. 'Might I ask if Elizabeth was a happy girl?'

The rector fidgeted on his chair. 'I think things were rather difficult at home. After the funeral, Elizabeth asked if she might speak to me, but then Mr Cooper was in a hurry and he rushed her away. Grief affects people in different ways, Miss Marple, as I am sure you know.' He sighed. 'I regret that I did not insist.'

Miss Marple had heard enough. And having lived all of her life in a small village, she had a certain knowledge of human nature. With impressive agility, she stood up, taking both the rector and Emmeline by surprise.

'I wonder if your curate is at home and might spare me a few minutes?'

Emmeline and the rector both watched, bewildered, as Miss Marple stood in the garden talking to Ernest Kemp. His expression altered from astonishment, to concentration, to urgency.

After a few minutes, she came back inside.

'Mr Kemp has agreed to accompany us to Salthill Road,' Miss Marple said, looking at her clock on the mantlepiece. She nodded to the rector. 'Thank you for your hospitality, but I hope you will excuse us. We must hurry.'

'Good heavens, Jane, why?'

'To prevent a third murder.'

Emmeline opened her mouth but appeared to have nothing she thought adequate to say in reply.

Nine

Williams leapt to attention as the mismatched trio hurried down the path.

'To Drovers, Miss Strickert?' he asked.

It was Jane who answered. 'To Salthill Road, if you please. Just past the lime pit. As fast as you can.'

'Where are we going?' Emmeline asked, as they took the first corner at speed.

'To Cooper's house. The rector confirmed what Mrs Hands said, namely that he goes every afternoon to Portsmouth. If we assume he takes the same train from which I disembarked yesterday, we can time our visit for when he is away from the house.'

'But why—'

The car skidded to a halt.

'Force the door or break a window, if you have to, Mr Kemp, but find Elizabeth,' said Miss Marple.

Kemp ran up the path, his cassock flapping around his legs, with Williams following behind. The two ladies watched as Kemp knocked at the front door but received no answer. He bent down and called through the letter box, then stepped back and looked up at one of the curtained windows at the side of the house.

He called again and, this time, evidently had a response.

'She is here,' Kemp shouted back to Miss Marple. 'She's all right.'

Jane Marple had not been aware she was holding her breath, but now she exhaled. 'I am very glad to hear that.'

Kemp disappeared from sight, appearing moments later with a ladder. With Williams steadying the base, the curate hitched up his cassock and began to climb.

'Jane!' Emmeline said, pulling at her sleeve.

'Don't worry, Emmy. Things are going to be all right.'

'No,' she said, panic in her voice. 'Look.'

Miss Marple turned. Cooper was storming down the road, his face red with fury.

'The Portsmouth train must have been cancelled,' cried Emmeline. 'Williams, do something.'

But as Cooper pushed past them and thundered up the path, clearly intending to drag Ernest Kemp from the ladder, it was Miss Marple who thrust her ash walking stick between his legs and brought him crashing to the ground. Cooper roared and tried to throw a punch, but Kemp and Williams were on him in a moment. He was no match for the former soldier and the local man, and was quickly overcome. Williams removed his belt and tied Cooper's hands behind his back. Kemp went through his pockets until he found the latch key, and ran inside.

'Well, Emmy,' said Miss Marple, 'that was a close call, wasn't it?'

Ten

At the end of the long August day, the sun was sinking down to earth.

Miss Marple and Emmeline were back in the pleasant garden of Drovers, surrounded by acid-loving plants. Ernest Kemp and Elizabeth Cooper, none the worse for her ordeal, were sitting together on the bench. The rector sat in a wicker chair. The cherry brandy had been brought from the pantry and was on the table with three glasses. There was whisky and soda for the gentlemen.

'Now, Miss Marple, tell us everything,' the rector said. 'What made you suspect Mrs Cooper's death was not what it seemed?'

Jane Marple put her head to one side. 'There was never anything very clever. Complicated things only really happen in stories, not real life. This was a sadly commonplace story, driven by greed and the fact that Cooper clearly had had enough of his wife.'

'So Dr Barden was wrong?' Emmeline said. 'She didn't die from tetanus?'

'No, she did have tetanus. It is only that the *reason* Cooper gave about how she had contracted it could not have been true.'

Ernest Kemp leaned forward. 'I'm afraid I don't follow, Miss Marple.'

She smiled at the young curate. 'I have a lovely jasmine hedge at home. I ask the maids to put tea leaves around the roots to acidify the soil. The idea of using razor blades is, I suppose, possible, and would achieve the same results, albeit with a degree of risk of injury when weeding and—'

'Yes, we know all that,' said Emmeline.

'Cooper's garden was all alkali-loving plants. His cottage was next door to a lime pit, a source of alkali nutrients. Mrs Cooper was a keen gardener and would never have mistaken acid soil for alkaline. She would have known it would never be possible to acidify the soil sufficiently to grow rhododendrons, and would never have put razor blades in their garden.'

Emmeline sat back in her chair. 'When you put it like that, it seems so obvious.'

'So how did he do it?' Kemp asked.

'The rector, though of course discreet, intimated that Mrs Cooper was not an easy person to live with. Elizabeth says her mother cut her hand.'

The girl nodded. 'Quite badly.'

'I assume Cooper found some way of infecting the wound when helping her to dress it. It is difficult to attend to an injury to one's own hand, is it not?'

Emmeline considered her own bandage and nodded.

'That is what made me worry,' Elizabeth said. 'My mother was concerned always about her health. He had grown impatient with her. They rowed a lot, so it seemed out of character that he should suddenly be so solicitous.' She turned to the rector. 'That is why I tried to speak privately to you after the funeral, but he must have realised I was suspicious and hurried me away.' She took a deep breath. 'When we got home, he forced me upstairs, closed all the curtains and locked me in my room.'

'To think you were there,' Kemp frowned, 'and I didn't even know.'

Elizabeth smiled at him. 'But you went to London to try to find me.'

Kemp turned red. 'Well, I thought something was wrong. Why didn't you try to attract attention when he was out of the house?'

'I wanted to call out, but I was frightened. The house is so far back from the main road, and my room is at the side, so no one can see it. I didn't know how long he was intending to keep me there. Or what he was going to do.'

Miss Marple noticed Kemp reach out and take Elizabeth's hand, and she approved.

'I think Cooper would have waited until the fuss had died down and then I shudder to think. Wicked.' She shook her head. 'It is why he let Mrs Hands go, of course, so there would be no witnesses.'

'Why didn't you believe him when he said I had gone to London, Miss Marple? Everyone else did.'

'Mr Kemp didn't,' she replied with an indulgent smile. 'And it struck me as rather unlikely, as if he'd got the idea out of a book,' she paused. 'The writers of detective fiction have a great deal to answer for. Also, everyone said it was out of character.'

'It sounds so obvious now you say,' Emmeline said again.

'But why were you so sure Elizabeth was in the house?' Kemp asked.

Miss Marple inclined her head. 'I wasn't. But Mr Cooper was not a man to observe formalities. His attire, a matter of days after his wife's funeral, spoke to that. Such an inappropriate suit! That being the case, it seemed unlikely to me that he would observe the Victorian niceties of keeping all the curtains drawn after a funeral.'

Emmeline waved her hat in front of her face. 'Of course, that was odd too, especially in this heat.'

'Then there was Dr Barden,' Miss Marple continued. 'It was Williams who put me wise to that. When he confronted Dr Barden in The Bull's Head, the doctor suddenly realised – as I did – that the explanation of how Mrs Cooper had contracted tetanus could not have been right. And do you remember, Emmy, how Mrs Hands said she found two glasses on the morning she discovered Dr Barden?'

The rector looked appalled. 'Are you saying that Cooper also murdered Dr Barden?'

'A post-mortem will prove it one way or the other,' Miss Marple answered solemnly, 'but I fear so. I think Dr Barden invited Cooper to his house to discuss things. It is so easy to make murder seem like an accident. It would have been a simple matter for Cooper to introduce something into his drink. He was gambling on the fact that everyone would assume Dr Barden had, finally, drunk himself to death, so would not investigate properly.'

Elizabeth shivered. 'How awful.'

'But, why?' Emmeline asked. 'Why did Cooper do it? If he had simply grown tired of his wife – forgive me, Elizabeth – divorce is not such a scandal as it used to be in our day.'

The rector shook his head. 'I fear that is true.'

Miss Marple turned to Elizabeth. 'Money, pure and simple,' she said. 'Am I right, my dear?'

'You *are* clever, Miss Marple,' the girl replied. 'He had been pressurising my mother to sign a new will in his favour for some months – he has some business interest in Portsmouth and he needed money to invest. I don't know what he said to bring her round, but, at the beginning of August, she gave in. My father left my mother quite well off, so it would have been a tidy sum.'

Emmy finished her glass of cherry brandy. 'Well, Jane, you've only been here for twenty-four hours and already you've discovered two murders that no one else even realised were murders. And in Fishbourne, of all places!'

'You have lived a sheltered life, Emmy. But there is wickedness everywhere.'

Emmeline Strickert, who had driven an ambulance in France during the Great War, and tended to dying soldiers on the battlefield, wisely said nothing.

'And of course,' Miss Marple added, 'Mr Cooper reminded me of a man called Sanders. I met him at Keston Spa Hydro, some years ago. He was a similar character, genial and ruddy, but with something uncomfortable underneath, if you see what I mean. The moment I set eyes on him, the Sanders man, I knew he intended to do away with his wife.' For an instant, her blue eyes lost their sparkle. 'On that occasion, I did not act quickly enough. I have always regretted it.'

Emmeline shivered. The rector bowed his head. The curate squeezed Elizabeth's hand tighter, no longer minding if anyone saw. Beyond the garden, there was the sound of men coming home from the fields at dusk. A blackbird sang to her mate. The ordinary everyday world kept on turning.

'Well, we are very much in your debt, Miss Marple,' Kemp said, raising his glass to her.

Miss Marple flushed with pleasure. 'I am delighted to have been of service. Though, I do hope the remainder of my stay will be less eventful.'

The Disappearance

Leigh Bardugo

Miss Marple gathered one of her many woolly scarves around her narrow shoulders and considered another cup of tea. Despite what should have been the pleasant warmth of a London summer, her nephew Raymond's fashionable flat was forever drafty, owing to the large windows that stretched from floor to ceiling. They offered little in the way of privacy, but Miss Marple had been told they were *essential* and very much sought after.

'Glorious light,' Raymond's wife Joan had explained, as she bustled through on the way to her painting studio, but Miss Marple noted that she shivered.

'Glorious indeed,' murmured Miss Marple, tucking her knitting into her lap. 'But perhaps best enjoyed beside a fire.'

From somewhere in the library, the phone began to ring, just as the doorbell buzzed merrily down the hall.

'Won't someone answer the phone?' Raymond shouted from the kitchen, where he was assembling a cold lunch.

'I've got to get the door!' Joan cried, already whirring away in a cloud of artistically arranged silks.

Someone was always coming or going at the flat – artists, writers, deliveries of champagne or flowers. Ordinarily Raymond and Joan would have decamped to the country or the south of France for the warmer months, but Joan was busily working on a gallery show and Raymond was determined to finish what he claimed was not a novel but 'a collection of tone poems, quite revolutionary' in time for publication the following spring. It was all very lively, and Miss Marple was certainly grateful for the invitation to join them for the summer. Even so, she longed for the quiet of her cottage, the distant sound of Cherry humming in the kitchen, and the golden light that was perhaps not as emphatic as the determined sunbeams that pierced Raymond and Joan's fashionable windows, but that shone gently over her garden in the waning afternoon hours, so that each blossom glowed as if dipped in amber.

Raymond appeared in the doorway, breaking her reverie. 'Aunt Jane,' he said, his tone accusatory. 'It's for you.'

'For me?' A faint alarm sounded in her head. Had something happened at the cottage? She'd been worried the pipes wouldn't make it through another winter, but perhaps they'd decided to give up early.

'It's Dolly Bantry,' Raymond drawled, 'and she sounds even more breathless than usual.'

'What in the world could Dolly want?'

'I certainly don't know and I don't care to ask.'

Miss Marple knew Dolly had been restless ever since she'd

moved into the East Lodge, and it hadn't helped that her children and grandchildren had forgone their holiday visit this year. It was understandable, given how far away they lived, and Dolly had insisted she was relieved not to have to worry about meals and clean up for so many, but Jane suspected it had been a blow nonetheless.

Miss Marple bundled her knitting under her arm and joined Raymond in the library, where the telephone sat on a cluttered desk.

'Dolly?'

'Oh, Jane!' Dolly exclaimed. 'You must come home at once. I need your marvellous brain.'

'I'll be home at the end of August,' Miss Marple protested. 'Raymond and his wife are taking me to a most intriguing play next week. Very controversial.'

'Quite right,' said Raymond, lighting a cigarette and leaning against the mantel. 'The actors perform in nothing but red paint. Impossible to get tickets, even in summer.'

Miss Marple suppressed a shudder. 'What's wrong, Dolly?'

'I can't possibly explain it all.'

'You must try.'

Dolly took a deep breath. 'You know the family who moved into Gossington Hall? The Barnsley-Davises? Their son has disappeared and you *must* come home and find him.'

Miss Marple glanced at her nephew, who had crossed his arms and was looking at her with an air of bemused expectation.

'Disappeared?' she inquired.

'I knew it!' Raymond crowed. 'I knew something horrid was taking place in that little village of yours.'

'Yes, two days ago.' Dolly's voice dropped. 'Along with several pieces of jewellery from the Barnsley-Davises' guests, and my sapphire earrings.'

'Your grandmother's earrings?'

'The very ones! Jane, you must come home and fix this immediately. He's to be married next week.'

Raymond had sidled up to perch on the desk and eavesdrop. Now he laughed. 'Doomed to matrimony next week? No wonder he's done a runner.'

'I hardly see what I could do—' Miss Marple began.

'None of that, Jane. I'll expect you tomorrow.'

'But what about the play?' sputtered Raymond.

'What about it?' his wife Joan asked, entering the library with a bottle of champagne in one hand and a jar full of dirty paint brushes in the other.

'Saturday at the latest,' Dolly said. 'Please, Jane. His fiancée is in a state and we can't afford another scandal at Gossington Hall.'

Miss Marple considered. She knew Raymond and Joan would be disappointed, but she had to admit she wouldn't mind the chance to return home just a bit early.

'I'll see what I can do, Dolly,' she said at last. 'Now go fix yourself some tea with brandy in it . . . No, don't argue with me. Tea with brandy, and a good long rest. You'll feel much better.'

She set down the receiver.

'You can't possibly go hieing back to that village just

because something dreadful happened at Gossington,' Raymond complained. 'That happens practically every spring. What tragedy has befallen St Mary Mead this time?'

'The son of the house has gone missing,' Miss Marple said quietly.

Joan threw herself into an armchair. 'Didn't the Barnsley-Davises move into Gossington?'

'You know them?' Raymond asked, with some surprise.

'We met Michael Barnsley-Davis last summer, didn't we? In cote de something or other?'

'Oh, yes, golden hair, white teeth, disgustingly charming.'

Joan laughed. 'Raymond's just peevish because he likes to be the centre of attention.'

'I certainly do not. As a writer, it is essential I be free to observe and that is best done away from the spotlight.'

'Michael truly was a delight, though,' said Joan, 'and completely smitten with his fiancée. You mean to say he's really gone missing?'

'This is hardly worthy of Aunt Jane's talents,' said Raymond, searching for an ash tray, then settling for tapping his cigarette into a potted orchid on the mantel. 'Charming youth hides dark secrets behind handsome face, vanishes rather than risk exposure. Mystery solved.'

'Exposure for what?' cried Joan indignantly.

'Gambling debts, a secret wedding in some backwater, perhaps he was less smitten with his fiancée than we thought. She did seem dimmer than a dark theatre.'

'Pure speculation. None of that sounds like the Michael we met. Surely he's just been called away somewhere suddenly.'

Miss Marple cleared her throat. 'There is the matter of some missing jewels.'

'That might just be coincidence,' Joan offered doubtfully.

Raymond cast her a wry glance. 'There are no coincidences in St Mary Mead.'

'Dolly seemed genuinely upset,' said Miss Marple slowly. 'I don't think she'd make a fuss over nothing.'

'You can't fool me, Aunt Jane,' Joan said. 'You've tired of our London clamour and you want to be back in your garden.'

'I do find it harder to keep up these days,' admitted Miss Marple. 'And surely you'll want the guest room free for your dear friend, Juliette? The one married to the director?'

Joan blinked. 'What does Juliette Henderson have to do with it?'

'She'll need somewhere to stay when she leaves her husband, of course.'

Raymond nearly knocked the potted orchid from the mantel. 'When she does *what*? Why would she leave Ambrose?'

But Joan was staring at Miss Marple. 'Aunt Jane, how could you possibly know? She hasn't said a word to anyone but me and I haven't told a soul.'

'Well, my dear, if I'm not mistaken, you two made a little shopping trip to the jeweller – the same jeweller – this week and the last.'

'So?' demanded Raymond. 'Women like baubles. There's nothing sinister in that.'

'Yes, but they didn't buy anything, did they? I imagine Juliette knows she will be in need of money soon and left her jewels to be appraised, then had to return to retrieve them.'

'But . . .' Raymond sputtered. 'They were here for dinner only last month. She's head over heels for him, I saw it myself!'

Miss Marple looked dubious. 'No woman who has been married that long smiles at her husband so much. It isn't natural.'

Joan barked a laugh. 'And I thought Juliette did such a splendid job of covering it all up when she'd been crying only hours before.'

'Poor Ambrose,' said Raymond.

'I shouldn't worry too much about him,' said Miss Marple. 'I imagine he'll console himself with that actress, the one we saw in that most . . . interesting adaptation of Macbeth. He couldn't have cast her for her talent, so he must be very much in love with her indeed.'

Raymond threw up his hands. 'Send the witch back to her village. If she stays much longer, all of our secrets will be revealed.'

Miss Marple smiled and returned to her knitting.

'Come straight to me,' Dolly had insisted, when Miss Marple had called back to tell her she'd be arriving Saturday afternoon.

But Miss Marple was no longer of an age that accommodated such urgent demands. She wanted a chance to wash her face and perhaps eat a little something before she visited East Lodge.

At the first sight of her cottage and the heaps of purple clematis crowding the arbour, Miss Marple felt a sense of calm wash over her. Cherry waved at her from the doorway, her freshly platinumed hair swept up on her head and a tidy red apron tied around her waist.

'Did you take a cab, then? Terrible waste of money. I would have sent Jim to pick you up if I'd known you were coming,' Cherry chided, hurrying down the walk to take Miss Marple's suitcase from her. 'You got my letter, then? Or had you just had enough of . . . the city life?'

Miss Marple noted the pause. Cherry had never had much use for Raymond's snobbery or Joan's pretensions.

'I'm afraid I must have just missed your letter, Cherry.'

Cherry waved away her concern and ushered Miss Marple into the cool entrance hall. 'I'll catch you up on everything. I've got a nice little chop from last night's dinner I can heat up.'

'I did tell Dolly I'd go to the lodge straightaway.'

'Dolly Bantry can wait. Always so imperious, as if she was still the grand lady of the manor. I ran into her at the butcher's the other day and all she wanted to talk about was Michael Barnsley-Davis.'

'Oh?' said Miss Marple, eager to hear what Cherry might offer by way of village gossip. If she was to put her mind to this problem, she needed information and she was at something of a disadvantage having been gone from St Mary Mead for the better part of the summer. 'What did you think of Michael?'

'Handsome as the devil, but only half as clever.'

'I understand there's the matter of some missing jewels.'

Cherry set down the little chop arranged with a small stack of carrots and new potatoes. 'Now *that* I hadn't heard. Is that what you came back for? Missing jewels?'

'That isn't why you wrote?'

'Of course not! It's the poor girl, the student who went over the side of that bridge by the old mill. Police are saying she did herself in, just like they claimed with Rose Emmott, but . . .'

'But?'

'Well, there's been talk. She did quite a bit of work up at the Hall.'

Miss Marple was not the least bit surprised. 'Was she young? Pretty?'

'Young,' said Cherry, considering. 'But not pretty. You know the type. Couldn't be bothered with a scrap of powder or lipstick. Always mucking around the grounds in work boots and coveralls. Not the type to catch a man's eye. Here, I clipped the story out of the paper for you.'

The article was brief: Miss Genevieve Andrews, nineteen years old, of Lyndhurst, Hampshire, a student of botany at nearby Moorlands College, was staying in St Mary Mead for the summer to work on the grounds of a local estate. She had gone out for a walk on the evening of August 23rd and never returned to her rented lodgings. Her drowned body had been found the following day.

'So young,' said Miss Marple, peering at the blurry photo of Genevieve Andrews. 'She visited Gossington often?'

'Yes,' said Cherry eagerly. 'She was working on the grounds.'

'And she took her own life. Was this before or after Michael left?'

Cherry leaned forward, nearly planting her elbow in the leftover carrots. 'That was exactly my thought, Miss Marple. The Barnsley-Davis boy had something to do with that girl's death. He seduced her and she threatened to go to his fiancée or some such, he lost his temper, and pushed her right over.'

'That's quite a lot of supposition. Did he seem the type?'

Now Cherry frowned. 'I can't say that he did. He was always fussing over that fiancée of his, Lydia Adams. Truly devoted, not just for show. And Lydia may be the prettiest girl I've ever seen off the screen.'

'It's a most dangerous bridge,' Miss Marple observed, wondering why Dolly hadn't mentioned young Genevieve's death. She ate her lunch slowly, watching the clouds pass outside the window and listening to the clock tick.

'If you don't like it, I can fix you something else,' Cherry offered.

'No, it's very good,' Miss Marple assured her, but she was too distracted to do Cherry's fine cooking any justice.

'But what do you suppose happened?' Cherry demanded. 'Did he push her most cruelly into the river? Did he drive her to take her own life and then run off in shame? Or is he just an innocent lad, himself the victim of foul play?'

'Cherry, you really must stop listening to those lurid radio dramas. Tell me, would you rather Michael was alive and well but a rogue? Or that he was blameless but met a bad end?'

Cherry paused, picking up Miss Marple's still half-full

plate and setting it by the sink. 'I suppose . . . Well, I suppose I'd want him to be innocent, even if that beautiful Miss Lydia had to lose him. Then she'd know he always loved her true.' Cherry rested her hip against the counter and folded her arms. 'But what do *you* think, Miss Marple?'

'I think Jim had better get the car out and drive me over to the Lodge.'

'Jane!' Dolly exclaimed, throwing open the door to the East Lodge and hurrying down the path. 'Where have you been?' She'd clearly been watching from the window, awaiting Miss Marple's arrival.

'I came as soon as I could, Dolly. I would have thought I'd find you working in the garden. Your borders are coming along so well.'

'They are, aren't they?'

'Hollyhocks, delphinium, and are those asters?'

'I had to do something to fill all these empty hours this summer, with Bertram and Alice and the children off on their adventures. Now, let's go up to the house. I've secured us an invitation to tea.'

'And how did you manage that, Dolly?'

'Rather shamelessly, I'm afraid. I may have mentioned that you were the person who solved the mystery of the body in Arthur's library.'

'And did you perhaps suggest that two lonely old women had nothing better to do on a Sunday afternoon?'

'One does what one must.'

'Too true, Dolly.'

Dolly looped her arm through Miss Marple's as they headed up the slope. The day wasn't too hot, and despite the circumstances, Miss Marple couldn't help but rejoice in being away from London's smoke and bustle, strolling instead beneath a blue summer sky.

'Tell me about the family, Dolly, but don't do your usual job of it. I'll need details if I'm to see the situation clearly.'

'Can't you just figure it all out yourself? You know I'm hopeless with this kind of thing.'

'I know you can manage when you try.'

Dolly heaved a great sigh. 'Then try I shall. The mother is one of those hypochondriac women, always clucking over *dear Michael* and forever rambling on about her doctor's recommendations. I haven't seen much of the father. I think he made his money in spigots or widgets or something mechanical. I can't recall. Hard to say where the boy got his charm. Perhaps it skips a generation.'

'And the fiancée?'

'Lydia? Poor thing. A darling girl. Beautiful and always game for a chat or a laugh.'

'But not perhaps the brightest?'

'Now what makes you say that, Jane?'

'It was just the way you phrased that, Dolly. The way you described her sounded less like you than Arthur.'

'Well,' said Dolly, plucking the wilted head of a rose from a bush as they passed. 'I suppose she is the kind of girl Arthur might have found distracting. But that doesn't mean her fiancé is a thief.'

'Certainly not. And the other guests?'

'There's Vera Fowler. She's Lydia's best friend, down for the wedding. She's striking in her own way, and might be quite appealing if she didn't insist on drawling every word as if the mere act of speaking bored her. Then there's a professor and his nephew visiting, both archaeologists of some type. I can't remember if they dig up pots or people. I think they're hoping to get Mr Barnsley-Davis to invest some of his widget money in their next excursion.'

'Let's stop a moment, Dolly. I need to catch my breath.'

Dolly paused beneath the leafy branches of a yew tree. 'You're not unwell are you, Jane? London is no good for anyone's health, I always think.'

'Just old, and I'm afraid we cannot blame London for *that* fact. What a view this is. I forget how lovely the village looks from here.'

'If you squint and pretend you can't see the Development.'

Miss Marple turned to gaze up at Gossington's impressive brick facade. 'I see the new owners have made quite a few changes. It's almost as if . . .'

'I know. As if they've taken it back in time. When Marina Gregg bought the place, she made so many *improvements*. But I'm not sure they were entirely appreciated by the rest of the village.'

'No, this feels much more like your Gossington now.'

Dolly said nothing because of course it wasn't her Gossington any longer.

'I know you weren't sentimental about the place,' Miss Marple added. 'And the Lodge is so much more practical for heating and upkeep.'

'Oh yes. Infinitely so.'

'But perhaps not quite so convenient for larger gatherings?'

'No,' mused Dolly, as they continued on. 'I don't suppose it is. And people have so very many places to go these days.'

'Why didn't you mention the poor girl who went over the side of the bridge?'

'Genevieve?' Dolly said, in surprise. 'Very tragic, but I don't see what it has to do with anything.'

'She and Michael Barnsley-Davis weren't close?'

'I never saw them together, but people were bound to talk with Michael disappearing so soon after her death. It's unspeakably cruel to put Lydia through it.' Dolly bent to yank a weed from one of the flowering pots. 'Now Jane, do put your mind to the task at hand. Time is of the essence.'

'So you keep saying. Is there anyone else in the party at the hall?'

'Only a rather weaselly American friend of Michael's. I believe they went to school together and he just turned up one afternoon. Very rich, very loud, only . . .'

'Go on.'

Dolly rang the bell and lowered her voice. 'I don't think he's quite so stupid and crass as he'd have everyone believe.'

They gathered for afternoon tea in what had once been Dolly's shabby but comfortable drawing room. During Marina Gregg's tenure it had been transformed into a grand kind of salon peppered with modern art and bits of sculpture. But under the new owners' stewardship, it had reverted back to a traditional drawing room cast in dark wood, and matching sets of stately furniture, almost like a stage dressed for a play set in an English country house.

Tea itself was a generous if peculiar affair, served by a buck-toothed maid who set out dainty porcelain plates and cups. In place of scones or cake were biscuits made of shredded carrot, while the soft white bread that would usually be used for sandwiches and kept moist beneath a towel had instead been replaced by some kind of cracker composed of various nuts and seeds.

'My doctor,' announced Mrs Barnsley-Davis, clad in a lettuce-hued tunic and strings of coloured beads, 'keeps me on a very strict diet of roots, seeds and assorted legumes. Dr Martin Bickford, very sought after. Do you know him?'

'I can't say that I do,' replied Miss Marple, discreetly hiding her uneaten carrot puck beneath her napkin. 'But I am not well informed on medical developments.'

'Are you well informed on quackery?' asked Reginald Marsh, slouched in his chair by the window. This was Dolly's weaselly American and the description did seem rather apt. He wore disreputable trousers and some kind of blue chambray shirt. The effect was both unsavoury and artistic – and exactly his aim, Miss Marple suspected.

But Marjorie Barnsley-Davis didn't seem at all offended; in fact, she looked at Reginald fondly. 'Reggie has been such a comfort to me now that Michael has . . . well, with Michael not . . .' She took a handkerchief from her voluminous sleeve and wiped at her eyes. 'With Michael *away* for a bit. But Reggie does love to provoke. Dr Bickford says it's because he eats too many red foods. Bad for the spleen.'

'Spleen?' demanded Mr Barnsley-Davis, as he entered the room, rubbing his hands together, face red and moustache bristling. 'Nothing wrong with his spleen. Just doesn't care for work at all.'

'Don't be unpleasant, Lionel,' chastised his wife.

'Yes, Lionel, don't be unpleasant,' said Reginald Marsh. 'That's my job.'

'Your only job.'

'Nonsense. I'm also pursuing a full regimen of lying about and being good for nothing.'

Miss Marple was grateful for the opportunity to observe the house's occupants as tea was poured. Lydia Adams, Michael's fiancée, was just as beautiful as Dolly had said, her hair a warm honey-gold cloud that framed her cornflower-blue eyes, which would have been quite luminous had they not been red and swollen from crying. She sat with a plate on her knee, eating nothing, her gaze distant. Her friend Vera sprawled in a chair beside her, wearing a violently yellow frock, her head resting on her hand. Neither of them had said a word since they'd been introduced to Miss Marple.

Professor Helmut Roederer, Dolly's German archaeologist, rose awkwardly from the spot on the sofa he'd been occupying with his rather pallid nephew. 'Lionel, I wonder if I might bend your ear—'

'Vile!' Lionel Barnsley-Davis roared, ignoring the professor and chewing vociferously on one of the seed crackers. 'Can't one get a proper tea around this house?'

'Dr Bickford—' began Mrs Barnsley-Davis.

'Don't want to hear about that old fraud, Marjorie.'

'Lionel—' Professor Roederer attempted again.

'Helmut!' Mr Barnsley-Davis bellowed with such force that the professor toppled back on to the couch, as if blown over by a hard wind. The pallid nephew shrank into the cushions, blanching an even more milky hue. 'My son's vanished into the godforsaken countryside and you have the bad taste to badger me for funds? I'm not giving you another dime until you prove you can find something more than heaps of dirt and some fragments of old custard cups!'

'I know the timing is not, perhaps, ideal,' stammered the professor. 'But the pottery we've found is vital to understanding Second Kingdom—'

'Vital? Where's the gold? The jewels?'

'Oh, Lionel,' moaned Mrs Barnsley-Davis, '*must* you be so vulgar?'

Reginald Marsh laughed and said, 'Perhaps best not to mention jewels at this juncture.'

A vein pulsed alarmingly on Lionel Barnsley-Davis's forehead. 'You ungrateful little whelp. If you have the temerity to—'

At that moment, Lydia burst into tears and ran from the room, sobbing.

'Perhaps . . . perhaps we should go after her?' mumbled the pallid nephew, as her footsteps faded up the stairs. It was the first time he'd spoken.

'Won't do any good,' said Marsh, real misery in his voice as he rose, and headed out the doors to the garden. 'Nothing shall be right until the prodigal returns.'

'Prodigal?' Miss Marple queried, as the Barnsley-Davises

and their other guests made their exits, perhaps glad to put distance between themselves and the carrot biscuits. Only Vera Fowler remained, lounging in her chair, gazing disinterestedly at Dolly and Miss Marple, and the maid who had begun to clear the tea things.

'The Golden Boy,' Vera drawled, lighting a cigarette in the silence that had followed the exodus. 'Michael dearest.'

'You didn't like him?' asked Miss Marple.

Vera raised a brow. 'You don't stand on ceremony, do you?'

Miss Marple's cheeks pinked a little. 'Oh, you must forgive me, dear. Old women have so little occupation. We can't help but get wrapped up in the dramas and romances of the young.'

Vera shrugged. 'I couldn't find any fault with dear Michael, if that's what you mean. Rich, handsome, kind to orphans.'

'Did he ever . . . well . . .'

'My, aren't you the old voyeur? No, he never made a pass at me, if that's what you're hinting at. More's the pity.'

'Now, now,' said Miss Marple gently. 'You don't mean that. You aren't quite so callous as you pretend to be.'

Vera took a long drag on her cigarette. 'No. I suppose not. The truth is Michael seems to be a good egg and Lydia loves him dearly, and I don't understand what's happened at all.'

'You think he's been hurt.'

'I do. He didn't just run off with a wayward starlet or something. He's never put the make on me or any of our friends and he's certainly had the opportunity with every pretty girl from here to Devon.'

A loud crash of dishes and silver sounded and Miss Marple

turned to see the buck-toothed maid crouched on the floor, cleaning up broken porcelain and morsels of food with shaking hands. 'Very sorry, miss. Very sorry, madam.'

'Where do *you* think he went?' Dolly asked, leaning forward in her chair.

The girl stared out at the manicured grounds. 'I've wondered about that. I think . . . for all his charm, I think Michael made someone angry or jealous and something awful happened.'

Miss Marple studied Vera's profile, the dark slash of her brows. 'When I asked if you liked him, you didn't really give me an answer.'

'Didn't I? The truth is I had no reason *not* to like him.'

'But you didn't.'

'No. I don't know why. But I didn't trust him to be good to Lydia. And now . . .'

'And now you feel guilty because you think something terrible has befallen him.'

'I do. I feel like the worst sort of person.' She gave a brittle laugh. 'Isn't that absurd? As if it changes anything.'

'Dolly,' said Miss Marple. 'I think you and I should go speak to Lydia.'

'She's who I really care about,' said Vera, 'and she wants him back desperately. Do you think there's hope?'

'Of course there is,' Dolly replied. But Miss Marple said nothing.

'Strange girl,' whispered Dolly, as they left the drawing room.

'Perhaps,' said Miss Marple. 'But not a stupid one.'

'Going hunting for poor Lydia?' inquired Reginald Marsh, slouching his way up from the garden through a side door. He'd found a tennis racket somewhere and was swinging it rather aggressively through the air. 'No doubt you'll find her sobbing picturesquely in her boudoir. Not that dear Michael deserves such an outpouring of emotion.'

'I thought you boys were friends at school?' Dolly asked.

'And we're still friends now.'

'If that's the way you speak of your friends,' said Dolly, 'I'd rather not know how you hold forth on your enemies.'

'Look,' said Marsh, leaning against the wall and crossing his long legs in front of him, 'Michael was good fun, always flush, always up for a lark, but not the man you'd want at your back when the wind got rough, understood?'

'I don't believe you were invited to the wedding,' said Dolly coldly. 'In fact, I don't think you were invited to the house at all. You just showed up on the doorstep.'

'It's not your house any more, so what do you care?'

Dolly pressed her lips together.

Marsh swiped his tennis racket within inches of a nearby vase. 'I happened to be visiting this area of the country and thought I'd call in. Maybe you Brits stand on ceremony, but Michael was perfectly happy to mooch off my family in the States, so I thought I'd return the favour.'

'Michael Barnsley-Davis visited you in the United States?' Miss Marple asked.

'What about it? We have plenty of room.'

'How fortunate to have a large family,' Miss Marple

twittered. 'When one is alone in the world, it's a pleasure to hear of all these happy relations.'

'Not so large as all that.'

'But siblings certainly. A younger sister perhaps?'

Reginald Marsh pushed off from the wall. 'Perhaps. Now where's Vera? I'm sure I can offend someone else before dusk falls.'

'Such a rude, insufferable boy,' Dolly said with a scowl, as they headed up the stairs. 'Jane, what are you puzzling over with such fierce concentration?'

'Nothing really,' said Miss Marple. 'Only . . . did you see the way he was holding that racket, Dolly? His knuckles were positively white.'

'I did wonder if he might take a swing at one of us. Wretched creature.'

They found Lydia in her bedroom, curled into the window seat, surrounded by apricot cushions. She'd tucked her knees up and was resting her tear-stained face on her folded arms.

'Oh my dear,' said Dolly, going to her. 'You mustn't weep over him.'

'I don't understand it,' she said, fresh tears welling in her enormous blue eyes.

'How could you?' said Miss Marple, placing a clean handkerchief in her hands. 'Such things aren't really understandable.'

'He wouldn't just leave! He said he loved me. He told me he couldn't wait to be married to me.'

'When did you last see him?' Miss Marple asked gently.

'The afternoon of the garden party. He stayed until the

very last toast. He said I looked like a jonquil.' She dabbed at her eyes and added, 'I was wearing butter yellow.'

'Ah,' said Dolly.

'He had a train to catch to London.'

'Did he take a car to the station?' asked Miss Marple. 'Or drive himself?'

Lydia blew her nose. 'Neither. He said he wanted to walk.'

'Such a long way?' asked Dolly.

'He liked the exercise,' Lydia replied defensively.

'I see,' said Miss Marple.

'He has a flat in London,' Lydia continued. 'But the doorman never saw him that night and no one at the station could say for certain if he boarded the train.'

Dolly patted the girl's hand. 'The stations are very busy. He might easily have been missed.'

'But no one misses Michael. He's . . . he's magnificent.'

'You'll forgive me, my dear,' Miss Marple ventured carefully. 'But I must ask. Did he say or do anything out of the ordinary in the days before? Was there, perhaps, an argument or can you think of anyone who would want to do him harm?'

'No one!' cried Lydia. 'Everyone loved Michael!'

'Everyone?'

'That professor whatshisname was always dunning him for money, telling him to pressure his father for funds. And perhaps not Mr Marsh. But he doesn't like anyone.'

'I suspect that's not strictly true.'

Lydia burst into a fresh spate of tears. 'What should I do? The wedding is a mere week away!'

'I think you should go home to London.'

'But what if Michael comes back?'

Dolly gave her an encouraging pat on the knee. 'Then he shall call you on the telephone and you will make him apologise for behaving very badly and perhaps buy you something nice.'

They fetched Lydia a damp washcloth to place on her eyes and left her tucked up in bed, already snoring softly.

'Poor girl,' Dolly said in the hallway. 'Do you really think Michael is just off clearing his head and will turn back up when he's ready?'

'I do not. But I think Lydia is a very pretty girl and will do much better for herself surrounded by eligible fellows in London rather than moping around here. And I suspect she'll have Reginald Marsh for company soon.'

'Marsh?' Dolly asked incredulously, then seized Miss Marple's arm. 'But if he'd fallen for his best friend's girl, then he'd have quite a motive to make Michael disappear.'

'He would,' agreed Miss Marple. 'But I doubt very much that's what happened. Let's go back to the Lodge, Dolly, and we'll ring Jim to come get me. I need to put my feet up and have a think.'

'We could ring from here, Jane.'

'No,' said Miss Marple firmly, watching Reginald Marsh and Vera Fowler walking along the terrace above the garden. 'We've already stayed too long.'

That night, Miss Marple had her supper on a tray in her room instead of in the kitchen with Jim and Cherry. Ordinarily she welcomed their company, but she craved quiet tonight, a chance to watch the fireflies gather in the twilight.

Cherry managed to hold her tongue until after she'd taken away the tray and brought Miss Marple a glass of warm milk.

'You've been deep in your thoughts,' she noted.

'I have, Cherry. Getting old is a terrible thing.'

'You're not so old as all that, Miss Marple, and sharper than most people half your age.'

Maybe so, but tonight Miss Marple felt every year and every hour, heavy in her bones. Cherry bustled about the room, closing the curtains and straightening cushions, until at last Miss Marple smiled and said, 'Cherry, you must stop fussing. Speak your mind.'

Cherry planted her hands on her hips. 'I'll stop fussing when you put me out of my misery! Did he do it or not? Did Michael Barnsley-Davis kill the gardener girl?'

'It's funny you should call her that. But, no, I don't think he did.'

'Then why run off like that?'

'A very good question, Cherry.'

'And are you going to tell me the answer?'

'You presume I have one.'

'Because you always do!' cried Cherry in exasperation.

'What does Jim think?'

'Oh, you know how Jim is. He just laughs and says the butler did it and rolls over to go to sleep.' Cherry sighed. 'And I suppose I had better do the same.'

'Will you open the window, Cherry?'

'It's cool tonight,' Cherry said, as she obliged. 'Make sure you don't catch a chill.'

Miss Marple listened to the sounds of the garden, the summer insects buzzing, the soft rustle of something nesting in the hedgerow. She should shut the window. She should go to sleep. But she lay awake thinking just the same.

The next morning, Miss Marple rose and dressed, and ate a sparse breakfast of toast and tea. Then she asked Jim to take her to the Lodge.

'D'you want me to wait, Miss Marple?' Jim asked, when they arrived. 'Or would you prefer to ring round?'

'Go on about your business, Jim. I'm sure you have plenty to do today without worrying about me.'

'Mrs Bantry's garden is looking fine. She's always out there no matter the weather, looking like a flower herself in that big floppy hat.'

But Dolly was inside today, so Miss Marple made her way slowly up the path, noting the new plantings.

'Jane!' Dolly exclaimed when she answered the door. 'Have you solved it?'

'I fear I have,' Miss Marple said, happy to step out of the sun and into the cool front rooms of the Lodge.

'Well?' said Dolly. 'Is it the greedy archaeologist? The jealous American? The bitter best friend?'

'You could at least offer me a cup of tea, Dolly.'

Dolly cast her eyes heavenward. 'Very well,' she said, as she strode into the kitchen. 'But I expect a good story once the water boils.'

'You got rid of your lovely brass kettle.'

Dolly snorted. 'Bertram and Alice gave me no end of ribbing over it during their last visit. They said it was an antique and probably poisoning me and any guests. The new electric kettle heats up much faster and is far more hygienic.'

'Maybe so,' said Miss Marple. 'But we're not the type of people who cast off treasured things for the sake of fashion.'

'Jane, you're getting sentimental in your old age.'

Miss Marple smiled. 'There's no doubt about that.'

Once they were settled in the front room, Dolly in a comfortable armchair and Miss Marple on the sofa, Dolly could contain herself no longer.

'So which of them did it?' she demanded.

'None of them,' said Miss Marple.

'Then he just ran off?'

'No, not precisely.'

Dolly gave an unladylike grunt of frustration. 'Then did he push that poor girl off the bridge?'

'He didn't do that either. I'm sorry to say poor Genevieve took her own life. She was so young, you see, and so afraid, and I don't think Michael Barnsley-Davis treated her very kindly, not when he found out she was . . . well, in a family way.'

'But Vera said Michael wasn't that sort of man, that he'd never made a pass at her or—'

Miss Marple held up a finger. 'He wasn't interested in pretty girls. He sought out the shy ones, the plain ones, the ones everyone else overlooked. Girls like Reginald Marsh's younger sister, I expect. He knew they were more vulnerable and less likely to be believed. Didn't you notice the way the maid reacted to what Vera said? I suspect Michael had made love to her too. And Genevieve wasn't a pretty girl, was she?'

'No,' said Dolly quietly. 'I don't suppose she was.'

'But she had many other fine qualities, didn't she?'

'She had a real way with flowers. But that's not something men care about.'

Miss Marple watched her friend's face, wistful and caught up in thought. 'Did he threaten you, Dolly?'

Dolly looked up sharply. The clock on the mantel ticked and the shadows of the room seemed to deepen around them. She took a sip of her tea, then set her cup and saucer aside. 'I guess I should have known you would see through me, Jane. You always do.'

'I didn't at first,' Miss Marple admitted. 'I couldn't understand why you would call me back to St Mary Mead if you'd done something wrong. But then Cherry mentioned she'd run into you at the butcher's. She told you that she was writing to me about Genevieve's death, didn't she?'

'Yes,' said Dolly. 'I thought if *I* was the one to demand you come home, you might not suspect me. Genevieve was a dear girl, a very dear girl, so young and full of ambition, and so devoted to the garden. We talked whenever she came to work. When Bertram and Alice didn't visit this year . . . Well, I suppose I was lonely and she was kind enough to indulge an old woman.'

'And she killed herself because of Michael Barnsley-Davis. Because she was carrying his child.'

Dolly's eyes flashed. 'Do you think he cared? I saw him

in the garden the day after they found her body, whistling, face turned to the sun as if he hadn't a care in the world.'

'You confronted him.'

'I did. In this very room. I saw him through the window, walking to the train station. I waved him over, offered him tea. He didn't know Genevieve had confided in me, that she'd sat on that sofa and wept over him.' Dolly struck the arm of her chair with a small, clenched fist. 'But he didn't care. Not a wit. He said Genevieve had made her own choices, that some people weren't strong enough for this world. And when I called him cruel . . . He laughed at me. He asked me what I was going to do about it. So I told him I would tell Lydia, his mother and father, anyone who would listen.'

'That was very dangerous, Dolly. Men like that don't like to be told. Don't you remember the fishmonger's son, Ralph Wiles? All smiles and *good morning, ma'am* until someone questioned the receipts. Then he smashed clean through the display case and tried to pretend it was an accident.'

'No,' Dolly whispered. 'Michael certainly didn't like it.'

'You must tell me,' Miss Marple said, her voice firm. 'You must tell me all of it.'

Dolly hesitated. Then, with the air of a woman leaping off a cliff, she spoke. 'He changed . . . It was as if all his humour and handsomeness bled right out of him. I hadn't quite believed it when Genevieve said he'd threatened her. I thought he was just a rash young man, overcome by emotion. But now it was as if I was seeing him truly for the first time.' She took a deep breath. 'He said he could kill me right then and there, and that no one would ever suspect. They'd just think I'd taken a nasty fall, one more old bat whom no one would miss. He said . . . He said I could be dead for days and no one would know until I started to smell.' When she looked up, her eyes were full of tears. 'And do you know the worst part, Jane? He's right. Age is cruel, and crueller still to women. A woman becomes a ghost when she stops being worth looking at.'

'A ghost can be quite frightening,' murmured Miss Marple. 'A ghost might get away with anything at all.'

Dolly wiped her tears away brusquely. 'He put his hands on my throat. He was smiling. I think . . . I think he was enjoying himself. I was so frightened; I picked up the kettle and . . . I struck him.' She shuddered. 'He didn't get up.'

'It must have been quite difficult to move his body on your own.'

Dolly gave a brief nod, eyes dry, back straight. This was the woman who had raised four children, who had managed a crowded household, and who had seen her husband through what was nearly a charge for murder. 'I waited until dark and dragged him out to the garden. I'd been preparing one of the beds, but I hadn't decided what to plant yet. It took hours to dig the hole deep enough, working in the dark. And then I just . . . rolled him into it.'

'And you planted the bed with asters from up at the hall.'

'The gardener had bought far too many. No one would notice.'

'That's what made me wonder, Dolly. You've never liked asters. I knew you would only choose them if you needed to fill a space in a hurry. You hid the jewels too, didn't you? Your earrings and a few little items from up at the hall, to create a kind of motive?'

'My grandmother's sapphires. I loved those earrings.'

'I suppose they're all buried with him in the garden.'

Dolly nodded. 'Was it really just the asters that gave me away?'

'Not just that,' said Miss Marple. 'You'll pardon me for saying so, but Lydia isn't the kind of girl to elicit such compassion from you. And, of course, I noticed the kettle missing when I insisted on ringing Jim from the Lodge yesterday.'

'That's the problem with you, Jane. You always seem to *know*.'

'I wasn't certain,' Miss Marple said. 'Not until we sat down in the parlour. You took the chair facing away from the window. I've never seen you do that, Dolly. You always take such pleasure in your garden.'

Dolly glanced toward the window, her eyes sad. 'It's rather ruined now. But I don't suppose it matters. You'll have to tell the authorities, the poor Barnsley-Davises.'

Miss Marple was quiet for a long time, watching the flowers bordering the garden path bob their heads as if to say 'good morning'.

'It's unfortunate,' she said at last. 'That men hold so much power in this world. But you know, Dolly, it's not really strength that's necessary to survive. It's cleverness.'

Mrs Bantry held herself very still. 'Is it?'

'My nephew Raymond has invited me to winter in the Canary Islands. Such a generous offer. I hadn't planned to accept, but now I'm of a mind to spend some time in warmer climes. We might go together.'

Dolly's brows rose. 'Might we?'

'Yes. Who knows whom we may encounter in a crowded marketplace, maybe even a magnificent, golden-haired young man, seen at a distance. Nothing that can be confirmed, of course.'

'But nothing that can be denied either?'

'Precisely. Shall we go for a walk in the garden before it gets too warm?'

'I'd like that very much,' said Dolly.

Arm in arm, the two friends strolled out of the lodge to let the late summer sun warm their old bones and to listen to the bees hum. They kept their backs to the new beds, brimming with red asters, their green stalks bending gently in the summer breeze, their red petals the colour of blood.

About the Authors

Naomi Alderman's most recent novel, *The Power*, was the winner of the 2017 Baileys' Women's Prize for Fiction, topped Barack Obama's book list from 2017 and has been translated into more than thirty languages. Her first novel, *Disobedience*, was published in ten languages and was recently adapted into a feature-length film by Oscar-winning director Sebastián Lelio, starring Rachel Weisz and Rachel McAdams. Alderman has been mentored by Margaret Atwood and, in April 2013, she was named one of Granta's Best British Novelists. She is Professor of Creative Writing at Bath Spa University, is a Fellow of the Royal Society of Literature and is currently executive producer for the forthcoming television adaptation of *The Power* for Amazon.

Leigh Bardugo is the *New York Times*-bestselling author of *Ninth House* and the creator of the Grishaverse, which spans the Shadow and Bone trilogy (now a Netflix original series), the Six of Crows duology, the King of Scars duology, *The*

Language of Thorns, and *The Lives of Saints* – with more to come. Her short stories can be found in multiple anthologies, including *The Best American Science Fiction and Fantasy*. She lives in Los Angeles.

Alyssa Cole is a *New York Times* and *USA Today* bestselling author of romance, thrillers, and graphic novels. Her Civil War-set espionage romance *An Extraordinary Union* was the American Library Association's RUSA Best Romance for 2018; her contemporary rom-com *A Princess in Theory* was one of the *New York Times*' 100 Notable Books of 2018; and her debut thriller *When No One Is Watching* won the 2021 Edgar Award for Best Paperback Original. Her books have received critical acclaim from the *Washington Post*, *Library Journal*, *Kirkus*, *BuzzFeed*, *Book Riot*, *Entertainment Weekly*, and various other outlets. When she's not working, she can usually be found watching anime or wrangling her menagerie of animals.

Lucy Foley is a No.1 *Sunday Times* and New York Times bestselling author with over two and a half million copies sold worldwide. Her contemporary murder mystery thrillers, *The Hunting Party* and *The Guest List*, were shortlisted for the Crime & Thriller Book of the Year Award at the British Book Awards, were selected as one of *The Times* and *Sunday Times Crime Books of the Year*, and *The Guest List* was selected as a Reese's Book Club choice. Foley's most recent thriller, *The Paris Apartment*, was an instant *Sunday Times* bestseller and a No.1 *New*

York Times bestseller. She lives in Brussels with her husband and baby son.

Elly Griffiths is the author of the best-selling Dr Ruth Galloway books. Her first standalone, *The Stranger Diaries*, won the 2020 Edgar award for Best Crime Novel. The second, *The Postscript Murders*, was shortlisted for the CWA Gold Dagger. In 2016 Elly was awarded the CWA Dagger in the Library for her body of work. She also writes the historical Brighton Mysteries and A Girl Called Justice, a series for children. *The Locked Room* (Ruth 15) came out in February 2022 and was a *Sunday Times* No. 1 bestseller.

Natalie Haynes is a writer and broadcaster, and tours the world speaking on the modern relevance of the classical world, so far on three continents. Her retellings of Greek Myth, *A Thousand Ships* and *The Children of Jocasta*, bring women's perspectives to the fore, and *A Thousand Ships* was shortlisted for the 2020 Women's Prize for Fiction. Her non-fiction book on women in Greek myth, *Pandora's Jar*, featured on the *New York Times* bestseller list in 2022.

Jean Kwok is the international bestselling author of *Girl in Translation*, *Mambo in Chinatown,* and *Searching for Sylvie Lee*, which was an instant *New York Times* bestseller. Her work has been published in twenty countries and is taught in schools across the world. She immigrated from Hong Kong to Brooklyn when she was five and worked in a Chinatown clothing factory for much of her childhood. Kwok received her bachelor's degree from Harvard University and earned an MFA from Columbia University. She currently lives in the Netherlands.

Val McDermid is an international No. 1 bestselling author whose books have been translated into more than forty languages. Her multi-award-winning series and standalone novels have been adapted for TV and radio, most notably the Wire in the Blood series featuring clinical psychologist Dr Tony Hill and DCI Carol Jordan. She is the recipient of six honorary doctorates and is an Honorary Fellow of St Hilda's College, Oxford. Among her many awards are the CWA Diamond Dagger recognising lifetime achievement and the Theakstons Old Peculier award for Outstanding Contribution to Crime Writing. Val is also an experienced broadcaster and much-sought-after columnist and commentator across print media.

Karen M. McManus is a No.1 *New York Times*, USA Today, and international bestselling author of young adult thrillers. Her work includes the *One of Us Is Lying* series, which has been turned into a television show on Peacock and Netflix, as well as the standalone novels *Two Can Keep a Secret, The Cousins, You'll Be the Death of Me* and *Nothing More to Tell.* Karen's critically acclaimed, award-winning books have been translated into more than forty languages.

Dreda Say Mitchell is a bestselling and award-winning author who was appointed an MBE by Her Majesty Queen Elizabeth II for services to literature and education work in prisons.

She scooped the Crime Writers' Association's John Creasey Memorial Dagger in 2004, the first time a Black British author has received this honour, and is a cultural and social commentator, broadcaster and journalist, who has written for the *Guardian*, presented BBC Radio 4's flagship arts programme, *Open Book*, and appeared on BBC Television's *Newsnight*, *Question Time* and *The Late Review*. She is a trustee of the Royal Literary Fund and an ambassador for the Reading Agency. Her family are from the beautiful Caribbean island of Grenada and her name is Irish and pronounced with a long ee sound in the middle.

Kate Mosse is the multi-million bestselling author of ten novels and short story collections, four works of non-fiction and four plays, including the Languedoc Trilogy *(Labyrinth, Sepulchre* and *Citadel)*, *The Burning Chambers*, *The City of Tears*, and Gothic fiction *The Winter Ghosts* and *The Taxidermist's Daughter*. Non-fiction includes *An Extra Pair of Hands* and *Warrior Queens & Quiet Revolutionaries: How Women (Also) Built the World*, publishing in October 2022 and based on her global #womaninhistory campaign. The Founder Director of the Women's Prize for Fiction, she is a Fellow of the Royal Society of Literature, Patron of the Chichester Festival of Music, Dance and Speech and a Visiting Professor in Creative Writing & Contemporary Fiction at the University of Chichester.

Ruth Ware is an international number-one bestseller. Her thrillers *In a Dark, Dark Wood, The Woman in Cabin 10,*

The Lying Game, *The Death of Mrs Westaway*, *The Turn of the Key* and *One by One* have appeared on bestseller lists around the world, including the *Sunday Times* and *New York Times*. Her books have been optioned for both film and TV, and she is published in more than forty languages. Ruth lives near Brighton with her family.

THE AGATHA CHRISTIE COLLECTION

Mysteries
The Man in the Brown Suit
The Secret of Chimneys
The Seven Dials Mystery
The Mysterious Mr Quin
The Sittaford Mystery
The Hound of Death
The Listerdale Mystery
Why Didn't They Ask Evans?
Parker Pyne Investigates
Murder Is Easy
And Then There Were None
Towards Zero
Death Comes as the End
Sparkling Cyanide
Crooked House
They Came to Baghdad
Destination Unknown
*Spider's Web**
*The Unexpected Guest**
Ordeal by Innocence
The Pale Horse
Endless Night
Passenger To Frankfurt
Problem at Pollensa Bay
While the Light Lasts

Poirot
The Mysterious Affair at Styles
The Murder on the Links
Poirot Investigates
The Murder of Roger Ackroyd
The Big Four
The Mystery of the Blue Train
*Black Coffee**
Peril at End House
Lord Edgware Dies
Murder on the Orient Express
Three Act Tragedy
Death in the Clouds
The ABC Murders
Murder in Mesopotamia
Cards on the Table
Murder in the Mews
Dumb Witness
Death on the Nile
Appointment With Death
Hercule Poirot's Christmas
Sad Cypress
One, Two, Buckle My Shoe
Evil Under the Sun
Five Little Pigs
The Hollow
The Labours of Hercules
Taken at the Flood
Mrs McGinty's Dead
After the Funeral
Hickory Dickory Dock
Dead Man's Folly
Cat Among the Pigeons
The Adventure of the Christmas Pudding
The Clocks
Third Girl
Hallowe'en Party
Elephants Can Remember
Poirot's Early Cases
Curtain: Poirot's Last Case

Marple
The Murder at the Vicarage
The Thirteen Problems
The Body in the Library
The Moving Finger
A Murder Is Announced
They Do It With Mirrors
A Pocket Full of Rye
4.50 from Paddington
The Mirror Crack'd from Side to Side
A Caribbean Mystery
At Bertram's Hotel
Nemesis
Sleeping Murder
Miss Marple's Final Cases

Tommy & Tuppence
The Secret Adversary
Partners in Crime
N or M?
By the Pricking of My Thumbs
Postern of Fate

Published as Mary Westmacott
Giant's Bread
Unfinished Portrait
Absent in the Spring
The Rose and the Yew Tree
A Daughter's a Daughter
The Burden

Memoirs
An Autobiography
Come, Tell Me How You Live
The Grand Tour

Plays and Stories
Akhnaton
Little Grey Cells
Murder, She Said
The Floating Admiral†
Star Over Bethlehem
Hercule Poirot and the Greenshore Folly

* novelized by Charles Osborne
† contributor

Also available

The Last Death of the Year

By
Sophie Hannah

Hercule Poirot and his good friend Inspector Edward Catchpool arrive on the Greek island of Lamperos for a relaxing holiday . . . but is that really why they're there?

There's something sinister behind the scenes at The House of Perpetual Welcome. Is this group of very good friends as close as they seem or is someone hiding something terrible?

As the clock ticks towards the New Year and a festive guessing game takes a sinister turn, can Poirot stop a murderer who is determined to strike before midnight?

'I was thrilled to see Poirot in such very, very good hands.'

— Gillian Flynn, bestselling author of *Gone Girl*

'Sophie Hannah is genuinely Christie's heir.'

— *The Scotsman*

N. Alderman
Dreda Say Mitchell
N. Alderman
Dreda Say Mitchell

The Porcelain Poet

Joly Braime

Book Cover by JD Smith Design.

First edition, 2025.

For G

One

Four of us stood in the gents' latrines, staring down the row of stalls. The coat of pale green paint on each door was fresh and unsullied, spotless as a coffin-lining, and it was all wrong.

Arthur Letts, chargehand in the maintenance gang, raised his voice slightly over the gut-deep thump of the great steel presses outside.

'It's been four days, Mister Jonas. We painted them on Monday morning. Never stayed clean this long before.'

My father ran a finger down the glossy surface of the nearest cubicle door. Usually the first profane limerick was daubed over the paint while it was still wet. Today, his finger left a sticky mark, for the summer of 1909 was a fierce one and the heat in that place was ungodly. Out on the factory floor, most of the men were stripped to the waist as they skated across the melted surface of the oil-soaked floorboards.

'So it was him all along,' whispered Michael, my cousin. In the four months since Michael had started at Catcliffe Steel, the Porcelain Poet had quickly become an obsession for him – but it was not a sensitive thing to say in the circumstances, and I hoped Arthur hadn't heard.

Twice a year we had these toilet doors repainted, and by the time Arthur Letts and his boys returned with their brushes next time round, the green paint was always dense with scrawl. Some was the badly spelled anatomical slander you'd expect in any spot where working men have time on their hands, but a good portion of it was presented in verse, and in a single, recognisable hand.

The Porcelain Poet, they called him. He wrote neatly with black enamel paint and a fine brush, and he always underlined the title of each poem with a steady hand that made me wonder if he did fine work in his job. A machinist, perhaps, or one of the dextrous little chaps working the fly presses in the light press shop. His anonymous stanzas were witty, abusive and sometimes politically charged, but we had never troubled to clamp down on it – mainly because we wouldn't catch him anyway.

His identity was a closely guarded secret even among the men, and one summer the poet himself had neatly titled one stall door *'WHO IS THE PORCELAIN POET?'* Many helpful suggestions had been offered beneath – including my own father's name – but the exercise had really only muddied the waters, which presumably was the whole idea.

Except now, as Michael had observed, we all knew who he was, because the Porcelain Poet was not the only man who had failed to return to his work on Monday. A fact that solved one mystery but created another.

'Both shearmen still missing, you say, Arthur?' asked my old man, trying not to breathe too deeply. Even over the paint fumes, the smell in the gents was a bit sharp.

'Yes, sir,' said Arthur Letts. 'Not Abe nor Timmy seen since they left the pub on Saturday night. My wife's going spare over it. Abe's always been in and out of bother, but he's never been the sort to run off. And the coppers don't want to know, of course.'

Abraham Bickley was Arthur's brother-in-law; Timothy was both men's nephew. In British industry, dynasties ruled the gantry and the factory floor alike.

It was no surprise that mountains were not being moved to find them, for they were union men of the more vigorous sort, and had tangled with the police on several occasions.

Though two Bickleys were missing, the poet would almost certainly be Abe: shop steward at Catcliffe's, local branch secretary for one of the big metalworkers' unions, and general stirrer of pots great and small.

My old man paused for thought and pushed his untidy hair out of his eyebrows. The Bickleys had caused us a good deal of trouble over the years, but they were also among our best men. When the last-minute jobs came in, it was the shearmen who set the pace – roughing out the sheet steel into lengths that would then be blanked, pressed, drawn and punched into everything from motor car head-lamps to carpet sweepers. Abraham Bickley had been head shearman since the London factory had opened nearly ten years back, and he had never failed us when it counted, especially after his nephews Timothy and Alfred came to work with him.

Aside from his union work, Abraham Bickley was also a committed churchgoer. Every Christmas, around the time of the wage review, my father received a cheap Christmas card informing him pointedly that the congregation at St Matthew's were all praying for his soul. It was difficult not to like old Abe, however much he hated you in return.

My father fixed his eye on a tiny patch of old graffiti high up near the cistern, above the level at which the fresh coat of paint stopped. No doubt he was trying to ignore the fact that the initials

'HFHC' scratched into the wall undoubtedly stood for Harrison Francis Harding Catcliffe. Not exactly a bad apple, but certainly one of the more wasp-chewed in his family barrel, best suited for rotting down into cider.

'I tell you what, Arthur, this won't do. Since you first approached Mr Harrison about this, go to his office at lunch and tell him everything you can, then he'll see what we can do.'

'I know you're not busy, Harry,' he muttered to me as we climbed the stairs back to the offices. 'I've watched you spend at least half an hour this morning sharpening your pocketknife and shaving strips off your desk. Sometimes I wish our offices did not have glass doors.'

....

Come lunchtime, however, neither Arthur Letts nor I were to be found at Catcliffe's, because at around the same time we were inspecting our bog doors, a group of lightermen were dragging the mortal remains of Abraham Bickley out of the river at Black Eagle Wharf.

The full story was in the evening paper. When a crime was committed in London, it was always a toss-up whether the Metropolitan Police or the newspapers would be first on the scene, but it was generally accepted that only a fool gave a decent story to the coppers for free when you could sell it to a journalist for sixpence. For their part, the newspapermen liked to quip that it was the easiest way they knew of turning silver into gold – and a sack-suited chap from *The Evening News* certainly got his money's worth on the Wapping riverfront that morning.

According to those involved, retrieving Abe's body was not a straightforward task – wedged as he was under the wharf and tangled up with the old rope, flotsam and general filth that got trapped in the tight spaces of the bank – but lightermen always took the time to fish bodies out of the Thames, in the hopes that someone might do the same for them one day if the worst happened. They drew straws over who would go in the water, then the unlucky nominee was roped up and lowered into the river, swimming through the timber struts into the half darkness underneath as the others fed out the line a little at a time.

He wriggled gingerly through the unknown horrors that brushed and slithered against his body, gagging at the smell and keeping his mouth tightly shut. Among the mess of rope, fur and wood, the white, rubbery form of Bickley was unmistakeable, and the shivering lighterman eventually managed to hitch a second line underneath the corpse's arms. The head, mercifully, was looking away from him, but he shuddered even more violently as he touched a patch of cold flesh. He would buy none of his own drinks that night, and would have a good many – mostly thanks to the largesse of the man from *The Evening News*.

Raising his face as high above the sloshing water as he could, he risked opening his mouth to cry out, 'Pull!' and the line he'd just hooked round Bickley sprang out of the water, taut. Now for the worst bit. As the body lurched in the water, the lighterman worked his way around, his hands all over it, feeling for the places where it was caught on underwater obstructions. He kicked a leg free from a loop of metal and cut a rope that was wrapped round one arm, all the while praying that the burly men up above didn't pull too hard.

Finally, Bickley came free, and began to swim away in short jerks as they reeled him in. The movement turned him, and his head spun over suddenly, one milky eye barely two feet from the lighterman's own face. Even so long after his death, it was clear that he had taken the most horrendous beating before he entered the water. The lighterman fought to keep from crying out as the battered ghost drifted past, and he looked over his shoulder to see unseen hands hauling it out of the river. Water ran through the boards above his head, then he felt the rope around his own chest tighten. He clutched the back of his neck like a child as they pulled him back towards the sunshine.

Two

'Seen plenty like that before. Mermaids, we used to call 'em. Been down there long?'

'That's horrid, Jabez. And yes, since Saturday night, probably. I'm glad Arthur didn't see him.'

Jabez Potter was supposedly my manservant and general factotum, and I could never work out why I had employed him. We had fallen into company the better part of two years earlier, united by a misadventure that had not ended well for either of us. At least we had not died (a close-run thing, in Jabez's case), unlike eleven less fortunate souls.

An odd consequence of the episode was that whispers of it, heavily distorted, had made it into the public domain, and I was now regarded as the sort of man that fellows like Arthur Letts could come to in a pinch. A reputation that was as unwelcome as it was unjustified.

At the time, Jabez had been 'working' as a drayman for the Vauxhall Brewery. I had been amazed that anyone would pay him a wage to spend his days roaming round London attending to his own business while pub cellars ran dry – yet when the brewery ran out of patience and dispensed with his services, I had taken him on without a second thought.

This evening, as Great Portland Street basked in a rich summer glow outside my top-floor windows, the rat-faced little ghoul was in a state of great contentment at the news of the day's horrors. He sat sprawled in my favourite armchair, with one of my cigars in his yellowed teeth and his wooden leg stretched out on my coffee table. The original limb had gone astray in China during Jabez's previous career in the Royal Marine Light Infantry, but neither that nor a near-fatal pistol shot on Christmas Eve 1907 appeared to have diminished his speed and capacity for violence. It was true that he walked with a stout hazel stick, but he brandished it a good deal more than he leaned on it.

'Are we looking into it, then? Please say we are.'

'A good man is dead.'

'There's no need to be so delicate, it's only me listening. You're bored too, Harry. It's this heat.'

'It's more than the heat.'

He picked a scrap of tobacco from the tip of his tongue.

'It's the ghost of past failure, regrets over a long-gone girl you won't admit having felt soft about, and the lull of too much dead time after too much action.'

'You can be quite poetic when my brandy is good enough.'

My own glass of brandy was untouched on the side table. After the sight of Abraham Bickley on the slab earlier, I hadn't much stomach for it.

'I'm just putting it in terms a man with as many hats as you can understand. It's boredom, plain and simple. So I ask you again, are we on it?'

'Yes, Jabez. Yes, we are, in our own unofficial capacity. The police are investigating, of course, but with the Bickleys being union men, the old man wants us to ask around a bit.'

Jabez's grin widened around his cigar. I would not admit it to him, but I felt all the things he had just mentioned, along with a sense that I was marking time through life without finding anything worth doing with it. Perhaps he was right and that was boredom.

'When I went to identify the body, the police said he'd probably been beaten with something heavy and metal. Wrench, hammer, even a pistol... Broken bones, skull bashed in, the works. Could have happened anywhere, but the most obvious time would be the route home from the Two Brewers.'

'Big drinker?'

'People say not. Just a few on a Saturday with all the others. Though Arthur Letts mentioned that he didn't always go straight home after closing. Fond of a smoke and a think by the riverside.'

I thought of Arthur, sitting across from me in the pub earlier. When the news about Abraham came in, I'd given him the afternoon off to go and break the news to his wife while I went to officially identify the body in my capacity as Bickley's employer, but when I emerged from the police station I found him waiting for me, scrunching his cap in his hand. He was a gentle man – what you'd call a 'company man', unlike his brother-in-law. Out of his paint-splattered overalls, he was very neat and small, with more hair than a fellow of his age deserved. We had sat over a pint in the Griffin, and he had been so ashamed of his glossy eyes that he only looked straight at me once.

'You will still look into it, won't you, Mister Harrison?' he said. Outsiders were often surprised that our factory workers called us by our forenames, but there was a particular hierarchy to our forms of address at Catcliffe's. Workmen usually went by their first names, foremen and above by their surnames – Mr Petch, Mr Smith and so forth – which was fine until you got to management, where everyone was called Mr Catcliffe. So we kept the 'mister' but went back to forenames again.

'I'd ask around myself,' said Arthur, 'only no-one'll give me the time of day. Not the union men and certainly not the coppers.'

'So he thinks it's a union thing, then?' said Jabez.

'Maybe. I asked who might want Bickley dead and he said you could fill a notebook with the names. Foremen and factory owners right down to apprentices. Even some of his workmates on the factory floor didn't much like him.'

'Well they certainly won't like you, so why don't I handle them, eh?'

'If you promise not to be rude.'

Which meant that if the workmen were Jabez's then the bosses were mine, and I had a pretty good idea where to start. I would pay a visit to old Dick Fletcher.

....

Where it was unthinkable for me to start dropping in on wealthy industrialists at half past seven on a Thursday night, Jabez needed no excuse to find himself tipping back a mug of beer in the public bar at the Two Brewers that same evening. By ten o'clock he had drunk five pints, and by half past ten he was picking himself up off the cobbles outside, his knuckles bloodied and his purpose accomplished.

The Two Brewers was almost directly opposite Catcliffe Steel. It was a rare southern outpost of a Yorkshire brewery, and its flagship status meant that it was smarter than your average workmen's boozer.

It had tiled walls, curtains that still held a little life in them, and nicely executed window paintings in red and gold depicting the brewery emblem of a cavalier doffing his feathered hat.

That night the place thrummed with the anger of men and beer and injustice. The talk was all of Abraham Bickley and his grisly fate, embellished many times over in the retelling. Timmy was generally accepted to have gone the same way, washed out into the estuary or sunk into the mud. Virtually every man at Catcliffe's was in there that night, especially those who had locked horns with Bickley in life, fearing that any absence would be noted when the speculation and finger-pointing began.

Which it did soon enough. A local gang was suspected. Hardly a gang, really, just a group of lads who hung around the nearby streets and sometimes tried their luck robbing drunks. There were proper criminals about, too, but Abe Bickley had grown up with the Bagby brothers, and a couple of their representatives were standing drinks in his honour at the bar. Someone mentioned Bickley's landlord, with whom he had a fractious relationship. But then Bickley had enjoyed a fractious relationship with just about everyone, including many of those present in the Two Brewers.

'To old Abe.' The pottery mugs of beer clunked for the umpteenth time, and as inebriation set in, the more outlandish theories began to find voice. This time the previous week many had regarded Bickley as a stirrer and a troublemaker, but now he was a hero and a martyr, a champion of the working man murdered by unscrupulous bosses or those scabs at the National Free Labour Association. Perhaps even the government, come to that. There was talk of a deep rift with cowardly union leadership, and of a violent difference of opinion over strike action with the shop steward at Donaldson Mills. A tear-up with the blackleg labour lads some years earlier had put one of their lot in the hospital, and Abe was meant to have been the man who threw the fateful punch. Someone recalled that a man from Poultney's Cannery had threatened to bash Bickley's head in during a heated exchange at the local factory football league, but no-one could remember the man's name or what he looked like.

For much of the evening, Jabez Potter sat alone at the public bar, absorbing the conversations around him and presumably marvelling at the fact that the deceased had gone through life putting up more backs than even he himself had. He sank his pints at a steady but unhurried rate, his eye on a sallow-faced young man who always had at least two drinks in front of him. Each time the lad seemed on the verge of catching up, someone would gently place another pot of mild in front of him, but they rarely stayed for more than a word or two of commiseration before moving on. For the most part, the young man sat drinking in determined silence, kept company by a similarly taciturn but much older fellow.

By the time Jabez contrived to sit down with them, the pale-faced youth was verging on paralysis.

'Like to offer my condolences,' mumbled Jabez – never much of one for pronouns. 'Family member of Mr Bickley?'

'I'm Mr Bickley?' said the young man, uncertain whether he was articulating a statement or a question.

'I'm sorry, mate,' said the other man, 'Alf's had a few. But thank you for your concern. This is Alfred Bickley, Abe's nephew. His brother Timmy is still missing.'

‘That’s bad luck,’ sniffed Jabez. ‘Didn’t know either of ’em. I’m just in here wetting my whistle and I can’t help hearing what everyone’s saying. Hope the lad turns up.’

‘Abe was like… like the father I’ve…’ began Alf, the varnish on his eyes becoming more pronounced.

‘I know, mate,’ said the other, laying a hand on his shoulder.

‘Abe was a widower,’ he explained to Jabez, ‘and none of his own children survived. He was close to his nephews and nieces, especially Timmy and Alf, and my son Ben – he’s off in the army.’

‘You’re his brother?’

‘In-law.’

‘My brother,’ slurred Alf, earnestly, ‘ain’t dead. But he’s as good as.’ He widened his eyes, suddenly realising anew that he had no idea who the man in front of him was, then repeated with emphasis, ‘As good as.’

‘How’s that?’ asked Jabez, but Alfred was rising unsteadily to his feet, his eye on the toilet door at the far end of the bar.

‘Here, Alf,’ said a burly youth with sandy hair and heavy side whiskers, scooping the drunk into the crook of his arm and steering him through the crowded pub. The barman gave him a warning look, and the sideburned man responded with a brisk obscenity, as Jabez himself would have done.

‘I’d watch that one,’ said the older man. ‘In fact, I’d watch the lot of them if I were you.’

Jabez raised his eyebrows by way of query.

‘You might not remember me, and I don’t know your name, but I came out to fix the sash window at Mr Harrison’s rooms last year, and I’m minded that I saw you there.’

'Jabez Potter.'

'Arthur Letts. Look, Mr Potter, if you're here on Mr Harrison's business then that's good of you and him both, but this isn't the time and place. Plenty of lads here won't want to go home without a fight, and you're just about the only stranger in.'

'Appreciate your honesty, Mr Letts. But I'm just a lonely drinker looking for conversation, nothing more.'

'As you like, Mr Potter. But mind how you go.'

Arthur glanced around self-consciously, then rose, taking his cap from his coat pocket.

'I'm going to fish Alf out of the lav and take him home. Good to meet you, Mr Potter.'

Moments later, Jabez realised what had precipitated his departure, as the heavy-set lad with the sideburns and two others sat down around him.

'Not seen you in before.'

'First time.'

'Strange night to pick.'

'So it seems, mate. So it seems.' Jabez had finished his pint, and he picked up one of Alf Bickley's spares. The lad wouldn't be needing it.

'Thing being,' continued the young man, scratching his side whiskers, 'Alf says you been asking him questions about Timmy and Abe. Now why would that concern someone who doesn't know any of us?'

'I'm naturally curious,' replied Jabez.

The other man leaned in closer, beer and baccy on his breath.

'Let me tell you what I think. I think Abe Bickley ain't the first union man to go missing this past year. Not even close. I think chances are there'll be more of us turning up in the river before the year's out. And I think there's too many naturally curious men nobody knows hanging around in pubs asking questions.'

'Union man yourself, are you?'

'That's right. Don't like that, do you? What are you, Free Labour? Snitch for the bosses?'

He was getting uncomfortably close to the truth, and this – combined with an oily forefinger planted square in the middle of Jabez's chest, was just about as far as he was going to get.

'Fancy a bit of fresh air?' said Jabez.

Three

'Bickley, Abraham and Timothy. Ever come across them?'

Across his richly polished mahogany desk, Dick Fletcher picked at his stiff collar, his knuckles pressing into the loose skin of his neck where it hung slack like a turkey wattle.

'I have,' he rasped, pausing for breath. 'And it was not a pleasure.'

Some said that our ailing bon viveur of a king was the spirit of that changing age in which we lived, but for my money old Fletcher was closer to the mark. A shipping tycoon, grain merchant and latterly an owner of breweries, sugar refineries and chocolate factories. His wealth was vast but he made sure everyone knew he'd started out as a clerk on the docks. Fletcher was shrewd, greedy and charming – an old magpie in a morning suit – and I liked him very much.

Obvious as it may sound, I knew that the Catcliffe family hadn't arranged Abraham Bickley's murder – but it seemed quite possible that someone like us might have done. Bickley had been Deptford branch secretary for the Amalgamated Association of Toolmakers, Millwrights and Metalworkers. In that regard, his reach had extended well beyond Catcliffe's, and if I wanted to find out who else he had rubbed up the wrong way, Dick Fletcher was a good place to begin.

Where many mill owners were happy to stay in their offices and let the middle-men deal with the workers, Fletcher – like my own insufferably industrious father – was one of those nosey parkers who liked to know what was happening on the floor. He trod the decks of his steamships, peered into the foremen's kiosks in his factories, and fed apples to the dray horses at his breweries. He was known to shuffle through the clock card records and bonus sheets, and as I sat waiting outside his office at the Rotherhithe docks first thing on that bright Friday morning, the whispered talk among the secretaries was of how he had unexpectedly turned up with a cup of coffee and a raft of seemingly innocuous questions during his sales clerks' breakfast break. If Bickley's fingerprints were on his own workforce, he would know.

'Can't say I remember Timothy,' said Fletcher, 'but Abraham I've met a number of times. Stood in this very office more than once and told me what was what.'

'Despite the fact he didn't work for you?'

'Because of it, I think.' Fletcher coughed wetly. He never seemed to have enough breath to get through a whole sentence.

'I'm told my own lads are scared of me. God knows why, I'm not all that bad.' He allowed himself a wheezy laugh, presumably because he was all that bad.

'When it comes to negotiation, they're worried there'll be consequences for a man who sticks his neck out further than the others. So sometimes they use an outsider to handle the talks for them – someone grizzly who they *think* I haven't got any leverage over.'

He leaned on the word 'think' in a *little-do-they-know* sort of way.

'Someone like Abraham Bickley.'

'That's it. First time he came in here was about an overtime dispute with some of my engineers at Woolwich Syrup. I was getting beaky with them and they were on the verge of striking, but no-one wanted to come and have it out with me. Shop steward lost his nerve, so they called in the branch man – who was Bickley.'

He smiled at the memory.

'Stood right next to that chair you're sitting in now. Wouldn't sit. Gave me hell. Not a fool though. Canny enough to take a compromise when I offered it.'

I couldn't tell you why, but all of a sudden I felt terribly sad about Abraham Bickley. Fighty old sod scrawling his dirty poems on the bog doors. Had someone like Fletcher paid to have his head bashed in over money?

'I've heard a rumour, Dick.'

'You want to be careful of those. Did you hear it in a drawing room or a pub?'

'Pub. Well, I didn't hear it, my man Potter did. Got his eyebrow split open over it last night.'

'Ah, yes, your little terrier.' Another wheezy laugh. 'Well, in my experience the pub scuttle is more likely to be true than the drawing room scuttle.' As if you'd catch Dick Fletcher in a drawing room.

'The rumour,' I pressed on, 'is that Abraham Bickley isn't the only union man who's gone astray lately.'

'Now that *is* a good rumour.'

Fletcher reached into his desk drawer and withdrew a couple of cigars. There was a brief pause while we lit them, then a violent fit of coughing before his breathing settled down.

'Soothes the asthma,' he said with relief.

Conversation was curtailed while the horn of a steamship boomed through the room so hard that the sash window juddered, but Fletcher didn't seem to care. He owned the dock next door, and if he'd chosen to put his office here it was presumably because he liked all the clanking and crashing and shouting.

'My rumour, Dick?' I asked hopefully.

'Your rumour, yes,' he said, rolling his cigar in his bony fingers as he thought for a moment. 'Union men vanishing into the ether – or the Thames, in this case. And who do your rumour-mongers think is behind it all?'

'Oh, take your pick. Union management, gangsters, Free Labour, some bloke from the football. Mainly us, I think.'

He had a good chuckle at that.

'The wicked bosses, eh? Reckon your old dad's got it in him?'

'Not the old man, no. Reckon you might do though, Dick.'

He liked that even better, and I had to wait a little while for the laughing and coughing to subside.

'Consider, if you will,' he said, wiping his eyes, 'that you're young, and you haven't been doing this as long as me and Young Jonas.'

The older generation still referred to my fifty-six-year-old father as 'Young Jonas'. Back in the day it was how they had distinguished him from 'Old Jonas' – my shrewd, now-dead grandfather, who half a century earlier had sacked off horse doctoring and gone into steel.

'Thing is,' continued Fletcher, 'there's an order to things, and each man has his part to play. Including and especially the Abraham Bickleys of the world. To the outsider, they might seem like a thorn in our side, but the world of industry doesn't work without them. Tensions are always going to build where lots of men work under pressure, but boys like Bickley can perform a controlled bleed.'

The incomprehension must have been plain on my face, for he grinned, showing an incomplete set of mostly brown teeth.

'We don't value things we haven't fought for, but too much fighting does no-one any good. Say that, through a channelled release of anger and energy, the men who fix the machines at my sugar factory happen to come out with a better overtime rate – without actually striking, but nudging right up to the edge of it. They might have got their pay rise anyway – or they might not – but because of the way they've got it, several goals have been accomplished for a good number of different men. Bickley and I both understood that when we met, but it seems some people don't.'

'So what you mean is that getting rid of union men is bad for business.'

'I mean getting rid of the ones like Bickley is bad for business.' He had spent too much breath on his little monologue, and had to stop for a few slow puffs on his cigar.

'Look here, lad,' he said, 'have you heard about this bloke Osborne and his case at the High Court?'

'The chap from the Railwaymen's Union?'

'That's him. Head porter at Clapton Station, and branch secretary for Walthamstow. Dyed-in-the-wool Liberal, got fed up with his union subs getting funnelled into the Labour Party. So he's gone to the courts arguing that trades unions shouldn't be using their subscription monies to fund political parties. The High Court has already ruled in his favour, and a little bird tells me the Law Lords will too. He's going to win.'

'What's that got to do with Abe Bickley?'

'Keep up. It means that in six months' time the unions won't have the Labour politicians in their pockets any more. Take away their mouthpiece in Parliament, and you can bet they'll fall back on the old tried-and-tested tactics when they want to make a point.'

'Strikes, you mean.'

Fletcher tapped his cigar into a large silver ashtray with a sailing ship embossed on it.

'We're going to have a lot more of 'em, you wait and see. You won't remember the bad old days before Keir Hardie and his Labour boys set up in the Commons, but the unions used to call their members out at the drop of a hat. Bad for us, but bad for the working man too. My sailors strike, your German steel never turns up. Your lot are out of a job and so are the lot at Phoenix Motors waiting on your engine parts. Et cetera, et cetera. That's Latin, lad.'

'So I've heard.'

'Did it at school, I suppose.'

He flapped his hand dismissively but without unfriendliness, as if to say that school was fine if you liked that sort of thing.

'Some union men can see the bigger picture, some can't. Bickley was a lippy old bugger but he knew how to get what he wanted without calling the whole game off. You mark my words, come next year we're going to need all the Abraham Bickleys we can get.'

Dick Fletcher never told you something straight up when he could dance around it and leave you to draw your own conclusions, but the implication was that no businessman in their right mind would have had Bickley killed.

'I've heard your rumour,' said Fletcher, 'and you're right – something's off. More union men going astray than there should be, I'd say. Sailors and Firemen's Union lost a district official last month. Bloke called Newby – used to work for me as a coal trimmer. Vanished without a trace. Stories of others too. Shop steward at Duraweave, regional officer at the Metalworkers' union. I can't remember them all.'

'Is there going to be trouble?'

'Over Newby at least. Going to blow up if we're not careful. The men all think it's me and the other shipowners in the Federation did something to him, but I liked Newby – you could deal with him.'

'Maybe another shipping company didn't feel the same way.'

'Maybe. Probably, come to think of it.'

'How about Free Labour? Bit of murmuring about them.'

Strangely, Fletcher didn't like that. He wagged a finger at me.

'You want my advice, lad, you'll leave Collison alone if you can. You might need his lot one day.'

I saw his point. William Collison was the leader of the National Free Labour Association. He was the man who could get you workers when your own went on strike.

'I'm not saying they're clean as a whistle,' he went on, 'just suggesting that you dig around elsewhere before you point the finger at them.'

'Fair enough. Any idea where I might start digging then?'

'As it happens, I've been concerned enough about some fool upsetting the apple cart that I hired a man to look into it. Old friend of yours. Perhaps you can compare notes.'

Four

'Why do I always feel like there's trouble on the horizon when that cut-up face of yours comes through my door, Harry?'

Dawoojee Dukanwalla loved to mock the scars on my cheeks and forehead, which he knew stemmed from a bout of scrupulously safe academic fencing during my university days in Leipzig rather than from an actual fight. He leaned with his elbows on the bar, his shirt-sleeves rolled untidily to reveal sinewy brown forearms. It was barely eleven in the morning, but already his pub, the Saracen's Head, was half full with the human flotsam of the Limehouse riverfront.

'I don't know what you mean,' I began, removing my elegant hom-burg hat and gloves.

'So it's a coincidence, then, that yesterday they fished your shop steward out of the Thames, that twelve hours later Jabez was brawling outside the Two Brewers, and that this morning you're in here talking to me?'

'How do you know all that?'

'Because knowing what goes on along the river is my most valuable talent.'

This was true enough – and the wrong sort of people often paid him handsomely for his insights.

'Jabez does a good deal of brawling outside pubs.'

'True enough,' admitted Duke, who had served with Jabez in the navy, 'but not with men from Catcliffe's.'

He grinned. I might have known Limehouse's premier wharf-side racketeer would know all about my missing shearmen.

'Have you time for a drink, Dawoojee? It's about the work you've been doing for old man Fletcher.'

'He know you're here?' asked Duke.

I nodded, and he called out to a shifty-looking young woman who was flirting with a bunch of sailors in the far corner.

'Annie, mind the bar for me a minute?'

Annie reluctantly disengaged herself from the men but continued to give them the glad-eye from her stool behind the bar. The sight of her there felt wrong – it had always been Dawoojee's wife, Liza Dukanwalla, who had ruled the Saracen's Head. Her red hair and her tired smile.

Duke picked out two bottles of porter and a couple of cleanish mugs, and we took a seat out of the way. His arthritic old bull terrier waddled stiffly after him, pausing to leave an affectionate snail trail of saliva across my trouser leg before it flopped under the table.

'Good lad, Cap.'

Duke reached down and tickled what remained of an ear, shredded in a pit fight many years earlier.

'The children still in Ireland with Liza's family?' I asked cautiously.

'For now. Maggie wants to come back, but the boys like it out there, and little Millie doesn't really know anything else.'

Millie had been a babe in arms on the terrible night two years earlier when I had walked the four of us into an ambush in a derelict house in Somers Town. Liza had been killed and Jabez had very nearly gone the same way. Duke had walked away unscathed but not unchanged.

'And Thomas?' I always wanted to know about Thomas Edlington – squirrelled away from those who would do him harm and those who loved him, all of whom thought him dead.

Duke gave me a rueful smile as he poured out his beer.

'Little Lord Thomas is well, though he's just plain Tommy out in County Clare. I do believe my feral kids are turning that well-bred orphan boy into a right little savage.'

'Thank you, Duke.' Among the many things that were never said was that rescuing Thomas was just about the only good thing to have come out of 1907.

'That's all right,' he said, as if that was all it was. It hung there for a moment, then moving abruptly on, he asked me about Abraham Bickley.

'I don't know much more than you do. Quite possibly less. As a man, Abe Bickley could be devilish awkward but he was a good worker. Decent and bold with it. Went missing with his nephew on the way home from the pub on Saturday then turned up dead on Thursday morning. Still no sign of Timothy.'

Duke lit a couple of cigarettes from a battered pewter case and passed me one.

'Fletcher tell you much about what he's got me doing?'

'Just that Abe isn't the only union man to have gone missing lately. Jabez got the same thing out of those boys in the pub last night. Fletcher says he's got you looking into it.'

Dawoojee Dukanwalla was a fine fellow in his way, but in the twenty years since he had left the family home in Gujarat to sail the high seas, he had committed an unknown number of crimes –including but not limited to smuggling, blackmail, bribery and murder. It was just like Dick Fletcher to hire such a man.

'That's about the size of it,' said Duke, scratching at a stubbly cheekbone with his thumbnail. 'From what I can tell, there have been at least twelve unusual disappearances since March, but what sets your Mr Bickley apart is that he's the only one who's turned up again, dead or alive. The others might just as easily have vanished of their own accord, of course.

'Do you believe that?'

'Not really. Don't get me wrong, working men up and move on all the time, sometimes without telling a soul – particularly if they've got debts – but not usually loudmouths like these.'

'Any unions in common?'

'Now you're getting to it. Five were from the AATMM.'

'The Amalgamated Association of Toolmakers, Millwrights and Metalworkers. Abe Bickley's lot. He was branch sec for Deptford.'

'Right. Plus two from the Boot and Shoe Riveters, one from the Dockers' Union, two from Weavers and Allied, and one from Sailors and Firemen. Then there was one argumentative factory floor mischief-maker who spent his time shouting about how union leadership were as bad as the bosses.'

'Mixed bag then.'

'But not as mixed as it might be, given the number of trades unions out there.' He turned sharply. 'Annie! Customers!'

Sly Annie was back with the sailors, oblivious to two bearded gentlemen in cloth caps standing patiently at the bar.

'She's almost as useless behind a bar as I am,' said Duke without malice. 'Not her primary trade.'

Annie shot him a weary look and dragged herself back to the shelves of bottles and chipped pint pots. The beer mugs in Duke's establishment were almost all pottery rather than glass, presumably so you couldn't see how murky his beer was.

'What about the factories?' I asked.

'Two of the missing men are full-time union employees. That's the fireman and one of the metalworkers. Which leaves ten men spread across six workplaces.'

'So some of those factories have lost more than one man.'

'You mean apart from yours?' He took obvious enjoyment in that. 'Seems that way, yes. Two from Catcliffe's, two from Duraweave, three from J. F. Garrett and Son.'

'The boot people?'

'That's them.'

I tipped back the last of my beer.

'When Jabez was in the Two Brewers there was talk of Free Labour being involved. Anything in that, do you think?'

'The National Free Labour Association? Collison's lot? Sounds a bit obvious to me. Sworn enemies of every union man. If I were the coppers, that's the first door I'd kick down. Still, I thought I might talk to them anyway. Now I wonder if they might be friendlier with a man who owns a factory.'

'They just might be. None of it feels like much though, does it?'

But Duke did not share my insecurity. He picked up the empty bottles and mugs, and nudged the dog into life with his toe.

'Legwork,' he said. 'That's all that'll get you anything in this world.

‘The AATMM is a big coincidence – which doesn’t mean that it isn’t a coincidence all the same, but you’ll never know unless you start asking questions. I’d say you’re best placed to pull on that particular thread. Same goes for the Free Labour boys. I’m going to pull on some of my own. See you back here.’

I left him to his inexpert bartending and stepped out into the dank little yard that stank of piss and beer and the wet dog-ends of cigars. Duke persisted that the Saracen’s Head was the perfect base of operations for his work trading in information, goods and occasionally people, but even on a bright summer’s day there was a gloominess to Limehouse that made me feel depressed. Perhaps it was just the sight of dark-eyed Annie where Liza Dukanwalla should have been.

FIVE

The appearance of the welt above Jabez Potter's eye had not been greatly improved by the ministrations of my maid, Edie. A dyspeptic old crone trapped in the body of a twenty-one-year-old girl, Edie was the youngest daughter of my landlord and lady on Great Portland Street, and I was fairly certain they let me have the rooms cheap as compensation for employing her.

She disliked Jabez, and when I asked her to tend to the cut across his eyebrow, she had expressed her feelings about both man and task by doing a very poor job of it. The bandage resembled a sort of dishevelled turban, and the vision of him slumped asleep in my chair as I crept in was reminiscent of Jacques-Louis David's famous painting, *The Death of Marat.*

I sat quietly in my second favourite chair, my jacket and collar removed and my sleeves rolled, sipping a glass of sherry and contemplating a snooze. The dust hung lazily in the warm evening light from the window. It had been a long day of running all over London chasing Abe Bickley's ghost. After a few minutes, Marat spoke.

'Bloody racket you're making over there.'

His eyes were still closed and his voice was even more gravelly than usual with sleep.

‘Good evening, Jabez. How has your day been? Please tell me you have been out and about in London with that remarkable dressing upon your brow.’

‘Of course I have.’ Eyes still shut. ‘Had things to do, didn’t I?’

‘What things?’

One eye opened.

‘Never you mind what things. What about you? Been busy? I know you have. You’re dying to tell me.’

I had, and I was.

‘I, Jabez, have spent this afternoon talking to people who did not like me.’

‘You still are.’ The eye was closed again. ‘Go on.’

....

The headquarters of the Amalgamated Association of Toolmakers, Millwrights and Metalworkers was not quite so grand as one might expect for a national organisation with several thousand men on the books. Situated off Peckham Road, it had once been a couple of terraced houses with a ground-floor shop, and was now a warren of uncomfortable little offices, cluttered with second-hand furniture and groaning filing cabinets.

In common with its membership, the functionaries at the AATMM were mostly wiry little men in patched suits, but as I stooped to enter what had once been the shop, it was a severe woman in early middle age who glanced up from her desk. She took in my natty clothes and general air of undeserved privilege, then pointedly returned to her work shuffling through a pile of papers.

‘Take a seat,’ she said, apparently to herself. Her hair was extraordinary, like sculpted wire.

I perched on a wobbly wooden chair and waited patiently as she stamped and initialled her way through the stack. Finally, she picked up the sheaf of papers and tapped it several times on the desk to even it up.

'Yes?' she asked, as if I had just that second walked in.

'I'm looking for Mr Jacob Bell, please.'

'What's it concerning?'

'It's about one of his representatives, Abraham Bickley, Deptford branch sec and head shearman at Catcliffe Steel.'

'And whom shall I say wishes to see him.'

'Mr Harrison Catcliffe.'

The woman gave me a knowing look, presumably to show me that she had deduced who I was, then she rose and ascended the stairs with a good deal of swishing and creaking.

When the gorgon showed me into Bell's top-floor office a few minutes later, the man himself did not turn out to be quite so hostile. It still wasn't what you'd call a warm reception, but then I was hardly the right man in the right place for that.

'Mr Catcliffe, please...' He gestured towards a chair. 'What can I do for you? It is, I may say, somewhat irregular for you to be calling on me rather than the other way round.'

'In terms of union men I have known,' my father had told me over a late lunch in the directors' dining room at Catcliffe's, 'Mr Bell is the polar opposite of Mr Bickley.' I soon saw what he meant, for where Abe Bickley had been all sarcasm and balled fists, Jacob Bell had the instinctive caution of the career bureaucrat. No doubt he had at one time worked in one of the professions he represented, but I would have bet good money that he had stuck at it only long enough to lend credibility to his work at the AATMM.

'I apologise for the intrusion, Mr Bell, but I wondered if you might have time to answer a few questions about the shop steward at Catcliffe's, Mr Abraham Bickley. He was one of your branch secretaries too, and quite an active member by all accounts. As you may know, he was found murdered yesterday morning. We are concerned about what might have become of his nephew, Timothy.'

Bell looked sharply over towards the door, where the gorgon was still hovering. As her indignant footsteps receded down the creaky stairs, he took off his spectacles and polished them fretfully on his shirt.

'A tragic business, Mr Catcliffe. Indeed, we have already had a visit from the police. I can only tell you what I told them – that I consider it unlikely to be connected to his union work. I am afraid I can be of little help to you in tracing young Timothy.'

'You knew the lad, though?'

'Oh yes, he was a member too, and sometimes accompanied his uncle when he was working on our behalf.'

'Forgive me, Mr Bell, for repeating a question you have already been asked. But are you absolutely sure there can't possibly be any connection between the Bickleys' work for the AATMM and Abe's murder?'

'Well how could there be?' he asked. 'Our disputes with factory owners like yourself occasionally become heated, but I doubt any of you would stretch to murder.'

He laughed nervously, wondering if he had overstepped the mark.

'I should hope not.' I smiled with what I hoped was a dash of wickedness. 'Still, these questions must be asked – and we're not the only ones Mr Bickley tangled with in the course of his union work, are we? Were there any trade federations, free labour groups, anyone else he had particularly poor relations with?'

'You are quite right that these questions must be asked,' said Bell, 'But I cannot help wondering why it is you who are asking them, Mr Catcliffe?'

'Frankly, I'm worried we may get the blame. It will be easier to defend my own firm if I know the truth of the matter.'

It was a weak answer to a good question, but he let it pass.

'If I too may speak frankly,' said Bell, 'Mr Bickley had a way of lighting a fire inside people – friends as well as enemies. He had poor relations with many of the people he came into contact with. But there was never any hint of violence.'

'I heard he put a man from the National Free Labour Association in hospital,' I said, dredging up a titbit that Jabez had overheard in the Two Brewers. 'Sounds fairly violent to me.'

'That was different,' said Bell. 'He was on a picket line and the NFLA men tried to fight their way through. There were injuries on both sides, but it was a long time ago and both we and the Free Labour men have learned to manage these clashes better since then.'

'And everyone just walks away afterwards? No grudges?'

'Naturally there are, but working men do not murder each other over labour disputes, Mr Catcliffe. Criminals murder people to rob them. That seems much more likely in this case, wouldn't you say?'

'All the same, Mr Bell, an unusual number of your members have been vanishing of late.' He was not expecting this, and I could see he didn't like it.

'Can I ask,' he said, changing tack abruptly, 'why it is that you have chosen to speak to me in particular about this matter? I'm sure there are a number of men both at Catcliffe's and within the AATMM who could have aided you just as ably. I would also suggest that any query about a branch sec such as Mr Bickley should have been escalated in the first instance to a representative from the London regional office rather than going all the way up to national headquarters.'

He meant this quite literally, since the AATMM's regional office was on the lower ground floor of that same building.

'Forgive me if I have come to the wrong place, Mr Bell. It is simply that you have a reputation as an even-tempered fellow who deals well with management.'

I had always been a poor liar, but most of us will believe any old nonsense if it is cut with a dash of flattery.

In fact, I had got his name from a stocky, sandy-haired young die-setter called Mickey Helm – a fellow AATMM member who I had invited to my office when I returned briefly to the factory around lunchtime. Along with a pair of heavy sideburns and a mortal hang-over, Helm also displayed a good deal of facial bruising and an eye that was almost swollen shut.

Helm did not know why he had been singled out to help with my enquiries – and had told me so, because he was that sort of a man – but he was civil enough despite his night of boozing and scrapping with Jabez. He had plenty to say about Abe Bickley's relations with his union leadership.

'They're toothless, Mr Harrison,' he said. 'And old Abe he never let them forget it. They sit in their offices organising and filing and rubber-stamping, but it's us on the factory floor that leads the charge. They wanted Abe out but none of us here were having any of it. Wouldn't be surprised if they sold him out to the Free Labour lot.'

'Was there anyone at the AATMM who Mr Bickley clashed with above others?' I had asked him.

'Bell,' replied Mickey without hesitation. 'Jake Bell. Never liked the way Abe did things. Always pushing for him to step down as branch sec. Thinks he's all that, this Mr Bell. You mark my words, he's angling to end up in politics. A lion become a lamb,' he added with gravity, no doubt parroting something he'd heard Abe Bickley say.

The lamb sat across from me now, looking pleased with himself at my compliment.

'Very good of you to say, Mr Catcliffe. If only all our members felt the same way.'

'Not everyone understands what can be accomplished with a little diplomacy.'

'Indeed not,' he said, sighing. 'I'm afraid your Mr Bickley in Deptford was a case in point. He was popular with the men, but for him the threats always came too easily. Some of his attitudes were very close to outright syndicalism. In fact, I believe he was involved with syndicalist fringe groups in this and other unions.'

That was news to me. A syndicalist was to your average trade unionist what a crusader was to an Anglican churchwarden. The syndicalists believed – so far as I understood it – that industries should be collectively owned by the people working in them, rather than by some marbly-nosed plutocrat. The ultimate end was that an association of workers' organisations would replace conventional government – but of more immediate concern was the fact that they were not great talkers, preferring radical action and massive strikes.

One or two of them were occasionally to be found outside Catcliffe's handing out pamphlets with titles like *END THE EMPLOYER*. Fortunately for the employer, the British working man was essentially conservative, and syndicalism had never really taken off on the mainland – which didn't mean that it never would. Just two years earlier, across the Irish sea, the famous syndicalist Big Jim Larkin and four thousand unionised dockers had treated Belfast to a long summer of chaos and a police mutiny.

The fact that Bickley had been interested in this particular form of radical unionism came as a surprise, but on reflection it ought not to have done.

'Did these leanings ever carry over into his work for the AATMM?'

Bell was hesitant.

'It's difficult to say. He and I disagreed from an intellectual and pragmatic standpoint on the effectiveness of solidarity strikes, for example, but there's a difference between claiming to believe a thing and actually wanting to do it.'

'You knew him reasonably well, then?'

'Well enough.'

He pursed his lips, unhappy that his own person had been drawn into the discussion, but obviously feeling that he ought to clarify his position.

'We were never friends, but we wanted many of the same things. We just disagreed on how to get them.'

'Dick Fletcher told me he rather liked Abe Bickley's style.'

‘That’s as may be,’ replied Bell with a hint of defensiveness, ‘but Mr Fletcher is not most bosses.’

I smiled to placate him.

‘You’re right there. But what about Timothy Bickley? Was he cut from the same cloth as his uncle in that regard?’

‘You know, I’m not sure. To be honest with you, I barely heard the lad string two words together. He almost always attended meetings with Abraham, but he kept his own counsel as far as I know.’

I was getting nowhere, and I sensed that I was running out of time before Jacob Bell sent me packing.

‘I don’t suppose you could tell me anything about the other members who are missing? I gather there are two more, including a regional officer.’

Bell shifted in his seat and fidgeted with his glasses again.

‘The regional officer I assume you are referring to is a man who works in this building – or used to. You are correct that he went missing in the spring, but without wishing to be indelicate, there could be a number of reasons for that.’

‘It would really help me if you could be clearer.’

Bell looked at me with the beginnings of impatience.

‘He had family problems, Mr Catcliffe. And he drank. And I would appreciate it if you could keep both those facts to yourself.

‘As for the other two,’ he said, ‘they worked at Woolwich Syrup and Duraweave respectively – and I really think you’d be better off speaking to Mr Fletcher and Mr Garrett. What I can tell you is that neither of those men were shop stewards like Mr Bickley. Just rank-and-file members.

'Look,' he went on earnestly, 'this is London. Men go missing all the time in this city. So five of our members have gone missing in the last few months. The only remarkable thing about that is that you've noticed it.

'I daresay you'd find many more than that if you looked at the annual disappearances among the thousands of men who make up our membership nationwide. Really, Mr Catcliffe, it's a coincidence, that's all.

'We at the AATMM appreciate your concern for your workers all the same. I would suggest that if you really want to help them, the way to do it is by committing to better working conditions. I trust that we can rely on your support in the upcoming gas safety negotiations?'

Six

'Sounds like he was full of it,' grunted Jabez, tugging at the loose end of his bandage.

'I'm not sure. At any rate, it's odd that he didn't want to talk about the others.'

'How so?'

'Well, your friend Mickey Helm had a good deal to say about them.'

'How did his face look? Helm, I mean.'

'Terrible. Worse than yours.'

Jabez looked satisfied, and began unwinding his turban.

'What Mickey said,' I continued, 'was that the fellows who went missing from Woolwich and Duraweave were both militant types like Abe Bickley. Clashed with their own union representatives over taking too soft a line with management…'

'Hang on,' interrupted Jabez, a smirk beginning to play at the corner of his mouth. 'Are you trying to tell me that you think the AATMM top brass are skimming out piss and vinegar types who strike too easily?'

I sensed that the HMS Potter was wheeling broadside to rake me with a cannonade of scorn, so I said nothing.

Jabez suddenly roared with laughter, and had to take a huge slurp of sherry to steady himself.

'That is the biggest piece of mill-owner claptrap I've ever heard you come up with. Do you ever listen to yourself? Because I wish I didn't have to.'

'There's no need to be like that,' I said, stiffly. 'I'm just telling you what people told me today. Whatever conclusions you draw from it are entirely your own, I'm sure.'

'Harrison Catcliffe,' he went on, affecting a tone of rich pomposity, 'champion of the working man. Diligently protecting his workforce against malicious sods who want to get them better pay and working conditions.'

Jabez affected not to notice my indignance, merely draining his sherry glass in one swift movement.

'And then, I suppose,' he said nastily, 'the champion of the working man went straight to the enemy.'

....

William Collison was in his mid-forties, with a doughy face and round wire spectacles. Though originally a docker, he was emphatically middle class in much the same way as the officers at the AATMM were emphatically proletarian. He sported luxuriant curly hair, thinning considerably at the front, and a natty bow tie.

His headquarters stood in a townhouse on Kennington Lane – a few minutes' walk from Vauxhall Bridge. It was a smarter location than the AATMM's premises off the Peckham Road, but also an impeccable spot for a labour exchange, backing as it did onto the terraces and tenements of Lambeth.

The way into the labour exchange itself was down a side alley, and the smart high street entrance was strictly for the hiring classes. A large brass plaque gleamed next to the front door, and when a clerk directed me into Collison's office on the ground floor, there was a conspicuous smell of beeswax polish.

All of which belied the fact that his organisation was in decline. The National Free Labour Association had been born out of the bad old days of the 1890s, when the unions were drunk on their new-found power. Back then, they had called their members out over the tiniest slight – and when a strike was called, Collison's blacklegs were waiting in the wings.

There were a lively few years when strikers, free labour and police clashed enthusiastically at the picket lines until everyone eventually got tired of mopping up the blood. Since then, the bosses had come to realise it was easier to deal with the unions than to antagonise them – but it was an uneasy peace. If anyone was hoping for the strikes to ramp up again as Dick Fletcher predicted, it would be William Collison.

I found Collison with his coat on and his hat in hand, full of aggressive bonhomie.

'Mr Catcliffe, you say? Of Catcliffe Steel?' He worked my hand as if it were a village water pump in need of a good oiling. 'Very good to make your acquaintance, sir, very good indeed. Though I regret that you catch me on my way out to a meeting at the Roaring Meg. If only I had known you were coming. It is a gentleman of considerable influence and I fear I cannot keep him waiting.'

I wondered what sort of influential figure could be meeting the likes of William Collison in a back-street pub in Lambeth at five o'clock in the afternoon.

'My business will not take long. Perhaps I might walk with you?'

The Roaring Meg was only five or ten minutes away, over on the far side of Lambeth workhouse. To get there, we cut through the rookery of crumbling slum housing that no doubt furnished Collison with much of his casual labour. It was the sort of contradictory place where the bricks were rotting into powder in the blackened walls and yet immaculate semicircles of scrubbed pavement radiated from most doorsteps. In one window sat a chipped Staffordshire spaniel, in the next a geranium in a tea tin.

School had finished for the day, and the streets were full of shrimpy children, the boys playing a noisy game of hopscotch and the girls taking it in turns to mind a little pool of infant siblings while they each got a go on a skipping rope. Collison and I picked our way among them.

'Forgive our unconventional consultation, Mr Catcliffe,' said Collison as he puffed in the heat. 'Never rains, but it pours, eh? What can I do for you?'

'Take a guess, Mr Collison.'

'Men!' he said, beaming. 'Men are my business! Tell me how many you need, and when, and what you will pay, and you may consider it done.'

'That is good to know,' I said, having rehearsed my script in the cab. 'And how much notice might you need, should we require workers?'

Collison waved his hand impatiently as he walked, taking in the district around us.

'A day, no more. I can probably fill your empty presses in hours. No shortage of men looking for work here, and plenty keen enough to break a strike.'

And here my inference finally cut through his haste. He stopped, and cocked his head in query.

'Are you expecting a strike, Mr Catcliffe?'

'Maybe. We hope not, but we are worried enough about it that I would like to make sure we have alternative labour lined up if needs be.'

'What's the fuss about this time? Overtime? Bonus rates? Not this blasted gas safety? Bureaucratic nonsense!'

'Nothing so simple, I'm afraid. One of our shop stewards has been murdered and things look set to go very bad if the police don't get to the bottom of it. Nothing to do with us, but you try telling that to the crowd in the Two Brewers.'

And then, because I couldn't resist scattering a few cake crumbs on the goldfish pond:

'Man called Bickley, if you ever heard of him. Abraham Bickley.'

Collison betrayed no sign of recognition.

'Never come across him,' he said, a shade too quickly. 'Wouldn't, really, in my line of work. Dare I ask what became of him?'

'Pretty brutal, I'm afraid. Beaten to death and dumped in the river.'

I waited for him to say 'a bad business' like everyone else, but instead he shook his head sadly.

'Far too many ways to die in this world for a working man. You'll understand that I'm no friend of the shop steward as a species, but I wouldn't wish that upon any of them.'

He checked his watch, made a face, and commenced walking again at a fast clip that didn't sit well with his tight clothes and bullish physique. It took me a moment to catch up.

'Still,' he called back to me, 'sounds much more like something criminal to me. Why are *you* in the firing line?'

We both dodged into the roadway as a small boy came careering past on one roller skate. Collison smiled at him indulgently.

'Context, Mr Collison. Abraham is not the only union man to have gone missing lately, and there are cries of conspiracy. If it all goes down the pan, I daresay I will not be the only factory owner coming to you for extra men.'

We rounded a corner and I could see the Roaring Meg at the end of the street, sitting in the shadow of the railway line. I was running out of time.

'I am very grateful,' I said, 'for your reassurance that men can be made available if needs be – and I would be more grateful still if this conversation could remain strictly between the two of us.'

'Don't want to be seen talking to the wicked Free Labour chap, eh?' he said, grinning.

'It is not just that. I hesitate to say it, but there are wild accusations that your men may have been involved. Revenge, they say. The story goes that Mr Bickley was on a picket line some years ago during a bad clash with the NFLA. Hurt someone quite badly. Absolute nonsense, I'm certain – but you see how it might look if word got out I had been talking to you.'

Collison did his best to look affronted, but there was something else beneath it too. A flicker of genuine feeling that might have been anger or suspicion.

'As you can perhaps appreciate, Mr Catcliffe,' he said, 'these tales get exaggerated on both sides, particularly when drink has been taken. A broken eyebrow becomes a grievous head wound, a bruise becomes a break, and so on. I'm pleased to hear that you give the matter no credence. In fact, I was present at the incident you mention. Fisticuffs and a little claret, no harm done. Our man recovered. It was the sort of thing that used to happen quite a lot.'

By now we were standing outside the Meg, its peeling sign depicting a gigantic cannon surrounded by redcoats. Drawn up on the cobbles outside was a huge six-cylinder Belsize motor car with a limousine body. It was a very odd thing to be gracing a rough boozer under a railway line, made more conspicuous by the brawny chauffeur watching over it like a Dobermann pinscher.

'What a machine!' cooed Collison. 'Any Catcliffe parts in it?'

'Not that one, I'm afraid. I can recommend a Phoenix, if you're in the market.'

'I'd sooner have one of these, thank you,' said Collison with a broad grin. 'As you see, the gentleman I am due to meet has already arrived, and I would prefer not to keep him waiting. My apologies – I regret that we cannot talk longer.'

'Not at all, Mr Collison. I appreciate your making time for me.'

He extended a clammy hand.

'I hope you may feel more confident knowing that we are here. Just say the word, Mr Catcliffe, and we will bring your presses back to life again. Free labour is the future – I am absolutely sure of it.'

He paused to check his reflection in the front window of the Meg, then drew himself up and stepped smartly inside, leaving me standing on the pavement next to the Belsize.

'Lovely machine,' I said to the chauffeur as I passed, thinking to myself that whatever he had claimed, William Collison knew full well who Abe Bickley was.

....

Altogether, I considered it had been quite a productive day. I had covered a good deal of ground, tested the patience of several men – and spent scarcely any time at all at my place of work. What's more, even that negligible amount of time at Catcliffe's had produced an unexpected lead.

Before I left the factory to track down Jacob Bell, I had obliged my father by taking a turn around the works. It was a matter of principle with him that one or another of the five Catcliffes working in that grimy sweatbox should show their face on the factory floor or the gantry at regular intervals throughout the day – though it was never clear whether our presence was supposed to intimidate or reassure. Normally he undertook the task himself, and it was a commonly accepted fact of life at Catcliffe's that if you accidentally smashed a die by putting two sheets of steel in the press instead of one, Mr Jonas would invariably be standing behind you at the time.

'Harry, do the walk would you, before you bugger off again?' he said to me after lunch. 'I've got some technical drawings to finish off and it's clear you're not planning to do any work today.'

I opened my mouth to defend myself, realised he was completely correct, and closed it again. As the ladies stacked up the plates and empty cups, we parted outside the directors' dining room, my old man to his drawing board and my cousins to their files and ledgers. I set off down the shiny parquet corridor towards the oily end of things.

As I emerged through the double doors onto the gantry, the noise and heat were immense. Below me, nearly two hundred men toiled, mostly shirtless, their forearms blackened with oil and criss-crossed with scars from the sharp sheet steel. Steam-powered drive shafts ran parallel to my gantry down the long rows of presses, and pairs of men shuttled back and forth along the avenues in between, hauling away wheeled cages full of automotive parts or restocking the operators with stacks of steel blanks. To my left, the little fly presses of the light press shop chattered away excitedly, while over to the right, the hulking machines of the heavy press shop thumped with a deep bass note that you felt right down in the pit of your stomach. Most of these big boys were northern-built, and the three biggest had nicknames – Samson, Caesar and Blackbeard.

Brought in by ship a decade ago, these oily giants stood fifteen feet apart from one another – and it was a quirk of Catcliffe Steel that the feet in question were my father's. When he was installing new presses or equipment, the old man insisted on pacing all the measurements out himself, tottering heel to toe with his arms outstretched for balance like a burly ballerina. Over the years he had paced out the widths of the aisles, the turning circles for the trolleys and the foundations of the foremen's kiosks, until after a while the whole factory floor had come to be laid out in units of Mr Jonas's feet. He insisted that his shoes were exactly an imperial foot long, and by the time this was categorically proved to be untrue, it was too late to go back.

As it happened, this was one of the few things that made me a useful chap to have around, since our boots were exactly the same size (and somewhat dainty for our height). I was often called upon by exasperated workmen trying to convert imperial feet into Catcliffe ones, and I had paced out so many different areas of the factory that I fancied I could walk it in the dark if needs be.

It was a bit of luck that I'd ended up walking the gantry instead of the old man, because I could see Samson was out of action. The millwrights had their ladders up its side and various forged lumps of Samson's guts were laid out on the oil-slick floorboards. I descended from my perch to see what was going on.

The steps down from the gantry came out on the far corner of the factory floor. Not far off (roughly twenty-two Catcliffe feet, in fact), the small team of shearmen were busy chopping the sheet steel down into the right lengths for each job. They didn't look to be doing especially well. Abraham and Timothy Bickley had been temporarily replaced with a couple of lads from the heavy press shop, and they were struggling to keep pace. The shearmen also relied more than most on careful measurement and judgement, and we'd already had complaints from the foremen that they were getting steel through in the wrong dimensions.

Their work was no doubt hampered even further by the state of young Alfred Bickley, who looked just about as green as I'd ever seen an upright man. His pale torso was slick with sweat, and his jaw was slack as he heaved another length of sheet onto the trolley.

When he saw me, though, he stopped dead, as if he'd been caught doing something much worse than simply turning up to work with a raging hangover. He secured his piece of steel on the trolley, then removed his gloves and started to walk hesitantly towards me. One of the other men shouted at him angrily, but he didn't seem to hear.

'Mr Harrison?'

'Alfred. How are you? May I say again how terribly sorry I am about your uncle.'

'Thank you – it's been a terrible shock. I wonder, Mr Harrison, my Uncle Arthur says you're taking an interest in what might have happened to Uncle Abe, and Mickey says you had him in your office earlier asking questions about the union work.'

'You're correct, Alfred. I hope you don't mind. Mr Jonas is concerned about your brother and has asked me to do whatever I can to find him.'

Alf wiped the sweat out of his eyes, leaving a thin streak of blood. One of his gloves was brown with it where he'd fumbled a length of steel and sliced through the leather.

'Please don't take it the wrong way, sir, but I'd sooner you didn't. He's all right, I know he's all right, but you won't find him if he doesn't want to be found, and only bad things will come of trying.'

'I don't understand, Alf. If you know he's all right then why hasn't he turned up?'

'I can't explain.'

I swallowed my frustration and looked at him with as much kindliness as I could muster.

'Can't you at least try, Alfred? Should we keep his job open? He has worked well during his time here and I want to do the right thing.'

Alf glanced around him, at his fellow shearmen and at the nearby press operators.

'I can tell you something, but not here. Not in public. May I come to your office on Monday morning early before everyone's in? I can't say much, but maybe I can persuade you to leave Timmy be.'

'Very well,' I agreed, notwithstanding the fact that I loathed early starts. 'Six o'clock, in my office.'

He nodded mutely, then pulled his gloves back on and shuffled unsteadily back to his task.

Samson was knackered, and was going to be out of action for at least the rest of the day. I offered up a silent prayer that my father would lose track of the afternoon hunched over his drawing board, and set out for the Amalgamated Association of Toolmakers, Millwrights and Metalworkers without informing him about his broken machine or his under-par shearmen.

Seven

I could never quite get used to cemetery funerals. They felt progressive and pragmatic – the sort of thing that might have been imported from a more dynamic country like the United States or Germany.

Having grown up on the edge of Leeds, my idea of a funeral was a village parson droning on about the finicky theological subtleties of the afterlife, safe in the knowledge that he had all afternoon to do it. It was following the coffin solemnly out into the churchyard, where it would be interred within a hundred yards of the altar.

Not so the cemetery burial, where each departed soul was allocated a strict half-hour slot in the Anglican chapel, before a horse and cart whisked the coffin away to some remote corner of a fifty-acre park. Any mourner wishing to witness those final graveside devotions would require stout boots, a walking stick and sandwiches for the journey.

I understood why the realities of London life (or more to the point, London death) rendered the cemeteries necessary. They were, after all, vastly preferable to the putridly overcrowded urban graveyards of old. It just all felt rather industrialised – but then Abraham Bickley had been an industrial man.

At any rate, the efficiency of the cemetery system worked in Abe's favour. Having spent almost a week in the Thames in high summer, the police morgue was keen to be rid of him, and the London Cemetery Company obligingly took him on without delay. There had been no laying-out for old Abraham Bickley – and any grave robber thinking of disturbing his eternal rest would get more than they bargained for.

That Saturday morning, just two days after Abe had been found under Black Eagle Wharf, I approached the wrought iron gates of Nunhead Cemetery. Upside-down torches, winged hourglasses and snakes eating their own tails welcomed a steady stream of mourners to the village of the dead. Smoking as I waited, I wondered how many of them were for Abraham Bickley – and when his brief turn in the chapel came around, the answer was not many.

We worked Saturday mornings at Catcliffe's, which may have explained why there weren't more workmates there. Then again, it may just have been Abraham's particular personality. The only woman in evidence was Mrs Letts, the deceased's sister, who sat between Arthur and Alf on the front row. Further back, I was surprised to see Josiah Bagby, the older of the two brothers who oversaw most of the crime in our little corner of London. He was flanked by a couple of human oxen and behind him were four or five hard-looking lads who I took to be more of his crowd. You dark horse, Abe, I thought.

There were a few odds and sods – mostly whippety middle-aged men, mates from the pub or the football club – plus a handful of sober-looking old codgers from St Matthew's. There was a decent showing from the union, who could be relied on to turn out for one of their own. Among these was Jacob Bell, and the little bureaucrat seemed unaccountably grief-stricken by the proceedings. I distinctly saw him remove his spectacles as the priest intoned, 'O death, where is thy sting? O grave, where is thy victory?' He wiped his eyes with his coat sleeve, then fished down the front of his trousers for a corner of dirty undershirt to clean his glasses with.

As we left the cool of the chapel, the mid-morning sun was already high in the sky, and you could almost see the steam rising off the black-clad funeral procession. The hearse led us at a brisk walking pace for about fifteen minutes down Windsor Walk and onto the West Path, where a wooden stake marked the open pit where Abraham was to be laid to rest.

'Man that is born of woman,' began the priest, 'hath but a short time to live...'

I loitered near the back of the group as the undertakers lowered the coffin out of sight, getting the job done as speedily as they could while trying not to make it too obvious that they were on the clock. Holding my hat over my heart in the accepted fashion, I blinked sweat from my eyes and scanned the curious assembly of family members, union men, churchgoers, career criminals and unknown roughs.

Mrs Letts and Alf Bickley scattered the first clods of earth over the coffin, then others moved forward in turn with their own handfuls of bone-dry dirt.

'Lord have mercy upon us,' called the priest.

'Christ have mercy on us,' we all mumbled in return.

Except whichever one of you buggers knows what happened here, I thought to myself.

....

When it came to wakes, being the boss was a bit like being the officiating priest at the funeral. Which is to say that it was good manners to show up and bad manners to hang around. Not that the priest attended this one – he'd probably rattled through two more services before the tea urn started to steam in the upstairs room of a pub on Dennett's Road.

Abe's thruppence a week burial insurance had bought boiled ham with buttered teacakes, paste sandwiches and fruit loaf. It was a good spread and I was impressed the landlady had managed to rustle it up at such short notice, but perhaps if you were a public house within a quarter hour's walk of one of London's seven great cemeteries, you could safely assume you'd be doing a funeral tea most days.

I got a cup and lurked in a corner for a few minutes until I could catch Arthur Letts's eye. Though it wasn't much past midday, Alf Bickley was over by the window and he already had a mug of beer in one hand and a glass of the funeral port in the other. I wondered if he'd sobered up all week.

Eventually, a sombre delegation of trade unionists broke away from Arthur and his wife, and I slid into the space, ostensibly to offer my condolences but really to make my excuses so I could slink off without offence.

'Thank you, Mr Catcliffe,' said Mrs Letts. 'Have you had a piece of fruit cake? It's very good.'

I complimented her on the spread, as you were supposed to do at funerals, then told her I ought to be getting along.

'You'll be needing to get back to the factory, no doubt,' she said – inferring generously that my presence was somehow essential for the smooth running of that operation. Either Arthur didn't discuss his employers back home or she was a kind soul who didn't scruple over the odd white lie.

She was taller than her husband but almost as thin, and she had Abe Bickley's distinctive broad nose.

'Thank you, yes. And I really am very sorry about Abraham, Mrs Letts. I liked him. The rest of my family did too.'

She smiled.

'Gave you no end of trouble, I imagine.'

'Just a bit, sometimes.'

'Gave me no end of trouble and all.' She swirled the dregs of her tea in the bottom of the cup.

'Arthur says you'll look into what happened. See if you can't find out why someone killed him.'

I felt the weight of their expectation, heavy around my neck, and considered that I was really no closer to the truth of what had happened to Abe Bickley than I had been when I saw him on the slab two days earlier.

'I'll do my best, but please don't build your hopes up too much.'

I was surprised to feel her cool hand grip mine.

'You will try though, won't you?'

'Ada...' said Arthur, gently, and she glanced at him as if to say that of course she wasn't going to embarrass him.

'What I mean is, Mr Catcliffe, he gave everyone a hard time, and usually when he got into bother it was his own fault. And if it was his own fault this time then that's all right, but I just... I'd like to know, so as I can make my peace with it one way or the other.

'He was my last surviving brother, did you know? My parents had six of us kids and Abe and I were the only ones left.'

There was nothing to say. I squeezed her fingers, then nodded at them both and left as quickly as I could.

....

Walking up towards Queen's Road station, I felt the weight of Ada Letts's words heavy on my shoulders. Perhaps Jabez was right and I had started looking into Abe Bickley's death simply because I was bored, but I was well and truly tangled up in it now. It felt somehow unfair that these fine, grief-stricken people had placed their faith in me rather than in the police whose actual job it was, and I wallowed for a moment or two in the self-pity that always overtook me when anyone had any expectations of me beyond simply turning up in a good hat.

Coming up behind me, I heard the clopping of heavy hooves on the narrow street, followed moments later by the ungodly miasma of the glue-man's cart. I skipped into a side alley to let him pass, gagging at the stench of putrid horseflesh and butcher's waste heaped up on the back of his wagon. Brown fluid spattered from the tailgate as it juddered over the cobbles.

Fumbling for a cigarette to mask the smell and distracted on at least three counts, I never saw the punch coming until it cracked me squarely behind the ear.

There was an audible thump like two motor cars colliding inside my skull. I staggered and just about kept my footing, coloured dots suddenly bubbling up at the edges of my vision and surging towards the centre. I tried to blink them back, and I thought I'd just about managed it, but the black tide that followed snuffed me out and took my legs from under me.

I cannot have been out for more than a moment or two, because when I woke up someone was trying to pull my left boot off while someone else kicked his own hobnails repeatedly into my side.

Even through the shock, I recognised a strange mismatch between the violence of the assault and the fact that neither of them were shouting or swearing at me. Even if I were simply being robbed, I might have expected a bit of salty language to season the blows. I put my hands over my head and tried to curl into a ball, but it was difficult with someone holding onto my leg.

Then suddenly there was a voice, deep and with a pronounced Cockney accent.

'Bugger off, lads,' it said.

The beating stopped abruptly, and another voice, panting with the effort of laying into me, said, 'On your way. Or you'll get it next.'

There was the sound of a brief scuffle and a scream that sounded very much like someone having some smaller one of their bones broken, followed by footsteps running away. I only realised that the second man was still holding my foot when he dropped it abruptly and gave me a last good kick in the small of the back.

'Should have stayed well out of it, shouldn't you?' he spat at me, then I heard him running off too.

Slowly, gingerly, I opened my eyes and peered out through the gap between my forearms. The coloured dots were still there, fizzing and sparkling all across my vision, but nothing else was. I rolled onto my back and looked stiffly all around me, but there was definitely no-one there. My saviour, whoever he was, had vanished.

Nauseous with the effort of turning over, I rested my eyes for a moment, and I must have clocked out again because the next thing I knew someone was nudging my stocking foot roughly with their toe. I opened an eye to see a woman in a sackcloth apron looking down disapprovingly. Satisfied, presumably, that I was not dead, she shook her head and went on her way.

With some effort, I sat myself up against the wall and made a survey of the damage. My head throbbed mightily and there were more bits of me that hurt than didn't, but nothing seemed obviously broken. I felt sick and there was a dull pain in my chest when I breathed that made me wonder if I had cracked a rib. I found I was disproportionately concerned about my teeth, and explored each one carefully with my tongue to see if it wobbled.

I had obviously fallen in some of the effluvia from the glue-man's cart because I smelled abominable. As I sat there, dazed, a middle-aged man stepped carefully over my outstretched legs without looking down, but the next passer-by helped me to my feet and walked me to the station. He was an older chap in a threadbare black suit who looked like he might have been to a funeral himself.

'Tea with brandy when you get home,' he said, 'and you'll be right as rain.'

As he put me on the train, my good Samaritan presented me with my left shoe, which came as a surprise because I had forgotten I was missing it.

Eight

That night, Jabez and I dined off mutton and potatoes in an airless restaurant off Regent Street. I had a pounding headache and the egg on the side of my skull felt like it might explode every time I chewed. Jabez was characteristically unsympathetic.

'I don't know what you're fussing about. Look fine to me. They haven't even touched your face – not that another scar would make much difference.'

Jabez's own face still bore the bruises from his tussle with Mickey Helm and his mates. We must have looked quite the pair.

'How do I know my rib isn't broken?'

'Well does it feel like it's sticking into your lung?'

'No, it just bloody hurts.'

'Just bruised then. You'd know if it was broken.'

'How?'

'It would bloody hurt.'

He popped a boiled potato in his mouth and washed it down with a swig of beer.

'Sounds like they went easy on you.'

'Easy?' I hissed. 'What was easy about it?'

'Two blokes on one, and you down on the floor from the start? You shouldn't even be able to walk. I'd say they were just out to scare you. Knock you about a bit without doing any real damage.'

Once I had conquered my indignation, I wondered if he might be right. It was true that two fellows laying into an unconscious man ought to have done a lot worse. Nor had they robbed me, for that matter. They hadn't taken the trouble to relieve me of my pocket book, and when the passing Samaritan had helped me look for my silver cigarette and vesta cases, he found them lying where I had dropped them when the first punch hit.

'Curious business about the shoe,' I said, thinking out loud. 'They didn't take anything else, but he seemed very keen to get my boots off.'

'Maybe you were his size,' said Jabez, dismissively. 'Or maybe he just wanted to make a point.'

'What sort of a point?'

He mashed his last potato into the leftover gravy.

'Well you have to admit, making a man like you walk home across London in his stocking feet is a satisfying idea.'

'Not everyone is as chippy as you.'

'How would you know?'

Still a little queasy, I let Jabez finish up my potatoes, then we took a cab down to meet Duke in Limehouse. He sat as usual in a gloomy corner of the Saracen's Head with his ugly dog under the table. It being an evening, he had paid a couple of proper barmaids to tend the bar, though sleepy-eyed Annie was still there, plying her trade around the establishment along with several others of her profession.

When visiting London's less salubrious districts after dark, it was often my habit to wear a set of faded work drills that I had purchased from a millwright at Catcliffe's some years earlier. It became quite obvious as soon as I opened my mouth that I didn't belong in them, but equally I was hardly going to go swanking around the shadowy waterfront alleys at night in topper and tails.

'If there's one thing that really sets off your working appearance,' said Duke as we sat down opposite him, 'it's that cloud of Parisian cologne you waft around in.'

'Some of these boys in here will think you're touting for business,' quipped Jabez, and the two of them had a good old cackle at my expense.

A barmaid furnished us with a jug of beer, and Duke and I lit cigarettes. Jabez applied himself to stuffing the obscene little pipe he smoked almost constantly unless there were cigars on offer. It was made from some sort of rosewood, carved into a caricatured representation of a naked woman's torso, and it had been whittled for him by a now-dead comrade in the marines.

Duke tapped the side of his head and pointed at mine.

'What happened there then?'

I told him, and while his manners were better than Jabez's, the level of sympathy was about the same. This was the problem when you associated with human pit dogs.

'Might be a good sign though,' he mused. 'You're sure they told you to keep your nose out?'

'Past tense. More of an admonishment than a warning.'

'Sounds like you might have asked some questions someone didn't like. So who have you been talking to?'

I told him what I had discovered since we had last met, which as he pointed out to me was not a great deal.

'This meeting with the surviving nephew is interesting though,' he mused. 'I wonder what he's got to say that needs saying in such a publicly private way. Only time will tell, I suppose.

'As for why you got a kicking, I reckon you can probably track that back to Bell or Collison.'

'Something I've said to one of them?'

'Or someone who knows you've spoken to them and doesn't like the general idea of it.'

'But I haven't discovered anything,' I said despondently.

Duke grinned and pointed his fag at me.

'What would you say if I told you you've found something and missed it in all the fluff?'

I looked at him blankly.

'Duraweave.'

I remembered the name, but I still couldn't see what he was getting at.

'Yes, yes, the textile mill, two men missing. What about it?'

'That bloke at the union – Bell. When you mentioned Woolwich Syrup and Duraweave, he said you'd need to speak to Mr Fletcher or Mr Garrett...'

The penny dropped.

'J. F. Garrett and Son. The shoe factory that's lost three men. J. F. Garrett owns Duraweave too.'

He nodded.

'Actually it's the "and Son" who does. J. F. fell off his perch ages ago. The owner now is Piers Garrett.'

'So five of the missing workmen are his,' I said. 'Bloody big coincidence.'

'Just you wait – there are more coincidences where that one came from.'

As anticipated, Duke had done better pulling on his own threads.

'Paley's Wharf,' he said with meaning as another jug of beer arrived.

'What about it?'

'You remember I told you they were missing a labourer?'

I nodded as Jabez sloshed more beer into our pint pots.

'Well he might just be the odd one out. You're saying that the various men who've gone missing from the AATMM are all supposed to have been rabble-rousers. Now I can't speak for all the others, but I do know the steamship mate who's missing had a similar reputation. This docker at Paley's Wharf, though – he didn't. Seamus Dyer, his name was. He was in the Dockers' Union but he never made a real nuisance of himself as far as I can tell. Everyone says Dyer was a quiet, hardworking bloke, kept his head down. So why's he missing?'

'Not another bloody big coincidence?'

'Paley's Wharf, I think. It's a connection I hadn't spotted before. Piers Garrett...'

'...He of J. F. Garrett and Duraweave...'

'...Ships most of his goods out of it. Garrett mainly uses a line called Mercury Shipping, and they're also the company that happens to own Paley's Wharf itself.'

'So who's behind Mercury Shipping? Not Piers Garrett, surely?' I asked. I was struggling slightly to keep up, what with the beer and the beating.

'Man called Amos Patchard. I've never come across him – he lives in Hull. Mercury operates right the way up the east coast but it's based out of the Humber.'

‘Any connection between Patchard and Garrett?’

‘Well obviously a business one.’

‘Which isn’t to be sniffed at.’ I thought for a moment. ‘How many factories does this Piers Garrett have then?’

‘At least five that I know of.’

‘That’s an awful lot of freight.’

‘Much of which goes through Paley’s Wharf. And that’s where I think our Mr Dyer might be important.’

Jabez had been uncharacteristically quiet so far, suckling on his naughty little pipe and drinking faster than me or Duke. Now he jabbed his pipe stem triumphantly at Duke.

‘You reckon old Seamus is disappeared or dead because of something he saw at Paley’s Wharf.’

‘I do,’ said Duke. ‘Well, I might, anyway. So I did some asking around. Last time anyone saw him was the twentieth of June, when he arrived at Paley’s Wharf to work a night shift with a skeleton crew. Funny thing – no-one from Paley’s will say a word about it. I’ve asked some of the boys who were working that night and they’re keeping their lips tighter than a vicar’s knickers. Even to me.’

This last bit was significant, because Dawoojee Dukanwalla was not ordinarily a man to say no to.

‘In the end I had to check with the port authorities and the river police – and they told me the boat being loaded at the wharf that night was a big screw steamer called the *Clare Kelly*. Owned and operated by Mercury.’

‘Sorry, the river police told you this?’

‘They owe me a favour or two.’ He winked. ‘Anyway, some of the other soaks and vagabonds around here have heard an interesting rumour about the *Clare Kelly*, which is that Piers Garrett uses it to transport supplies to his country house in Cleveland, out on the Yorkshire Moors. You're a Yorkshire lad, aren't you, Harry?'

He knew I was. We did tend to tell people.

'West Riding though. Cleveland's in the North Riding, right up at the top. My aunt lives there, in a little port town called Whitby.'

'Well, that's where the *Clare Kelly* puts in. She stops at Whitby on her way up to Newcastle, at which point Garrett's cargo is loaded onto a smaller coastal steamer that drops it into a cove not far from his estate.' He waved his hand carelessly. 'Just coal and lamp oil, wine and table-linen, those sorts of things.'

Duke glanced across at Jabez, and they exchanged the broad grins of men well versed in illegality.

'It does sound odd,' I admitted. 'And what about this estate? Has he bought it, or is Piers Garrett actually Lord Something-or-Other? I didn't know there was much blue blood in the boot-and-shoe business.'

'Neither. It's not actually his estate. It's a place called Haydon Castle and it belongs to Lord Horncastle – but Lady Horncastle is Garrett's daughter. Garrett himself seems to spend a lot of time there.'

I had never heard of Haydon Castle or Lord Horncastle, but then I never was very well up on who was who. What concerned me a good deal more was that it looked distinctly like our London mystery had sprouted legs and toddled off to the other end of the country.

'It's a long way away,' I offered, truthfully but unhelpfully.

'Think I'll go anyway though,' said Duke.

'What if my shearman has something useful to say?'

He reached under the table and scratched behind the dog's ear. It made a most irregular noise in response.

'I've just been thinking about that. Maybe he'll give you the key to it all and maybe he won't – but I can feel things starting to get cold. There's enough pointing to Haydon Castle to make it worth the trip, so I'll get the train up tomorrow morning. The castle is on the edge of a village called Yattonby, in Birkdale. Sounds like it'll be a pig to get to.'

'That's the north for you.'

'You can talk to your man and see if he's got anything useful to say – and if it leads to Haydon then I'll already be there. Write to me at the main post office in Whitby and I'll make arrangements to have any post forwarded on from there.'

Nine

Six in the morning was an inhumanly early hour for slothful Harrison Catcliffe, who under normal circumstances rarely put in an appearance until mid-morning coffee was served in the directors' dining room at around nine. However, the rest of the workforce at Catcliffe's were commendably industrious. Work on the factory floor began at seven, and men in oily overalls usually began trickling in any time after about half six – sitting smoking on crates and drinking ersatz coffee that they bought from a stand outside the Two Brewers on the way in.

Earlier than that, however, and the place was deserted – save for two sleepy commissionaires clock-watching until the day shift showed up.

'Morning, Mr Harrison,' said George as I passed his little kiosk by the clock card racks. He was an elderly chap who had served about four hundred years with the Lincolnshire Regiment, and if he was surprised to see me in so early he certainly didn't show it.

I climbed the metal stairs to the gantry and slipped through the double doors at the end into the offices, pausing to switch on the electric light. As my boots clicked down the corridor, I noticed with great satisfaction that every single one of the glass-fronted offices was empty – including Young Jonas Catcliffe's.

At six in the morning on the dot, I sat down at my desk to await Alfred Bickley. I sharpened a pencil with my pocket knife, smoked a cigarette, and idly leafed through a folder of shipping paperwork. Discarding this, I burned the pencil shavings in my ashtray with a match then went through my drawers one by one to see if there was anything interesting in them. There was not.

At six twenty-five, there was the sound of hobnailed boots scrabbling at speed down the parquet floor of the corridor outside. A small man in an immaculate green shop coat skidded to a halt outside my office and began tapping urgently on the glass.

....

Down in the factory floor lavatories, all but one of the green-painted doors was still immaculate – an informal act of posthumous respect for the Porcelain Poet. The last cubicle at the end of the line bore the words 'I'M SORRY' daubed in spidery capitals with engine grease, and inside it, Alf Bickley hung by his neck from the cistern, quite dead.

The fellow in the green coat was foreman in our die shop, and held an exemplary record for punctuality. That morning he had been the first of nearly two hundred men to show up for work – at least so he thought – and had intended to make the most of the peace and quiet by attending to some personal business at his leisure. On discovering Alfred Bickley's body, he had run to alert George on the front desk then carried on straight up to me because George had bad knees and took a long time to tackle stairs.

For his part, old George the commissionaire had not experienced such excitement since gypsies had got in three years earlier and made off with two tons of sheet steel. He had not distinguished himself on that previous occasion, and now he finally had a chance at redemption.

A raft of garbled messages were dispatched to the police and the other directors, the crime scene was locked and guarded, and on their arrival the two day-shift commissionaires found themselves running circuits of the perimeter looking for signs of intrusion.

By the time Young Jonas Catcliffe's motor car drew up in the courtyard at seven, the ablutions block had already been sealed off by policemen, all four commissionaires were patrolling like mastiffs, and I was in my office giving a statement to a constable. My father tapped apologetically at the glass door, and I excused myself for a moment, explaining briefly to the copper that this scruffy old boy in a frock coat with shiny elbows was the organ grinder.

The old man had left home before George's message arrived, and had only the haziest impression of what had gone on.

'Harry, there is no-one in the commissionaire's kiosk, the lavatories are crawling with policemen and not a single press is going. Are things as bad as they look?'

It was midday before most of the police had left and the reassuring background thump of the presses had started up. Together with my middle brother and two of my cousins, I sat in my father's office drinking coffee. Of the London Catcliffe boys only young Michael was reluctantly missing, having been told to go and make himself visible on the gantry.

'Do we know what time he got in?' asked my brother, Gregory, licking coffee from his downy moustache.

'About ten minutes before me,' I replied glumly. 'If I'd just been a shade earlier I might have bumped into him on the way in.'

'You can't think like that,' said my father from behind his substantial leather-topped desk. 'If a man wants to do something of that sort then he will find a way.'

'At least if you'd bumped into him we might know why he did it,' said one of my cousins. 'It's ever so frustrating.'

My father shot him a testy glance. Andrew had a reputation for saying what everyone else was thinking, however inappropriate it might sound at the time. Fortunately, he was very good with figures, so this foible was usually overlooked.

'Who knew old George had such efficiency in him?' offered Gregory, trying to change the subject.

'Do you remember when the gypsies robbed us of all that sheet steel?' said my other cousin, John. 'Right under his nose, daft sod.'

Andrew affected a thick Irish accent.

'Sure we're workin' the night shift – can ye open up and let us in with these carts of ours?'

It was a valiant attempt to lighten the tone but none of us were in the mood and we lapsed back into silence. Finally, my father spoke.

'This business is getting out of hand,' he said. 'We'll have no shearmen left at this rate. Are you any closer to tracking down his brother, Harry?'

I shook my head, but I gave him the potted version of what we'd discovered so far, including Piers Garrett, Mercury Shipping, and Garrett's place in North Yorkshire.

The mention of Piers Garrett produced a curious effect on the old man, as if he had just bitten into a sausage roll and found a fingernail in there.

'Near Whitby, did you say?' he asked, the wheels of his industrious little brain evidently creaking round.

'That's right – Haydon Castle. I'm told the local village is called Yattonby, out in Birkdale.'

He thought for a moment, scratching at a scab on his knuckle where he'd cut it on some corner of sharp metal as he went about his daily business. Even management couldn't escape shedding blood in that jagged place.

'It won't do,' he said shortly. 'I don't know what's going on but it needs to stop, and if that old fox Garrett is connected to it then it's probably worse than it looks. Harry, I think it's time you went to see your aunt Diana.'

Reclusive Auntie Diana, living with her companion Clara up there in the wilds of the North East. On the one hand, I quite fancied the idea of a trip to the seaside, but also there was that old, persistent impulse towards an easy and uncomplicated life. This was not the first time I had got into something over my head, and I felt sure that poking around in Birkdale was pretty much guaranteed to make things worse rather than better.

'Don't worry, we can hold the fort here without you,' he said encouragingly.

Despite the solemnity of the conversation, there was a cough as some disloyal family member tried not to laugh and accidentally inhaled a bit of coffee.

I looked up at my father across the desk. It came to me that there was perhaps a reason I was being thrown this particular bone. Not all fellows get the sons they deserve, and my father was shrewd enough to know that sometimes the best way to keep his eldest out of trouble was to send a little my way.

TEN

To my immense satisfaction, my snickering blood relatives subsequently realised that they could not hold the fort without me – at least not immediately. At the time, German steel was outrageously cheap thanks to hefty subsidies from the kaiser's government, and we were on the brink of reaching a supply arrangement with a company from the Ruhr. The business was to be thrashed out on the Tuesday and Wednesday of that week. As the only man at Catcliffe's who spoke fluent German, I found myself suddenly invaluable to the firm. It was quite the novelty.

As far as I could see, the delay was also no bad thing for the other business either. Duke would have a few days' head start, and by the time I caught up with him, chances were he would have done most of the hard work for me.

It also gave me an opportunity for a meeting that I had both longed for and dreaded, but that I had known must come sooner or later. Crass nouveau riche industrialist as I was, the members of the aristocracy with whom I mixed were mostly London-dwelling rogues of about my own age, encountered over strong drink at second-tier clubs or short-handed dances.

However, there was a whole other category who lived their lives almost exclusively in the provinces – and who pretty much only ever came to the capital to broker marriages or show their faces in the Upper House when unfavourable land taxes were on the agenda. The Horncastles of Haydon were such a family, and while I knew nothing of them, there was someone of my acquaintance who would.

I was far from certain that Lady Halsingham would reply to my telegram, and still less that she would accept my invitation for luncheon on the Wednesday, but she did. We met at the Cordovan Hotel, overlooking Green Park – her favourite restaurant and also the scene of an argument from which our friendship had never recovered. She had chosen the spot, and as I rose to greet her, I saw her sister's Victorian star brooch pinned to her lapel. It was an unspoken signal that I was not to be given an easy ride, and I daresay this was no less than I deserved.

'Hello, Harry.'

It is a curious pain, love unrealised – even after such a long time. During the year and a half since I had last seen her, Agnes Cleveley had become Lady Halsingham, married with much fanfare to a man who I knew privately to be a murderer and a blackmailer. It had, briefly, been in my power to stop it, but I had chosen cowardice over honesty.

'Robert is still abroad attending to his business concerns in Rhodesia,' she explained primly as she sat, then looked up at me and softened a little. 'Perhaps just as well.'

She probably thought the mutual dislike stemmed from jealousy, and it did a bit. I wondered what Robert's 'business concerns' could be. Something shady, no doubt. I briefly considered asking her – just to make the point that she didn't know – but I recognised the impulse as misdirected unkindness and quashed it.

'And you, Agnes?' I asked. 'What occupies your days?'

'Never ask a lady that – didn't your mother teach you anything? No babies yet, if that's what you're getting at.'

It was, and my relief must have been obvious because she couldn't help slipping me a smile. She looked different. Not older, just tidier, her chestnut hair less rebellious and her manner altogether more poised. In former times she had never much reminded me of her deceased older sister, but she did now. Chief among the things Agnes hated me for was that I alone knew the circumstances of Henrietta's death, but I would not tell her. Could not, in fact – since Agnes's own life depended on my silence. But she was braver than I was, and would have risked it if I had given her the choice.

'I never see you these days,' she said, as if this were my fault rather than hers, 'but I hear of you sometimes.'

'What do you hear, I wonder?'

'Oh, you know, the odd mention. The steel factory man with the scars, not quite handsome enough to carry them off. Good dresser, entertaining in his way, drinks too much. Amelia Symes says you would be quite a catch for a girl who lives in a numbered house.'

'Amelia Symes talks a lot of rot. She also says she is going to marry Johnny Beaufort because he reminds her of her dead Pekingese. Anyway, you live in a numbered house when you're in town.'

'Belgravia address though – it hardly counts.'

There were so many things we could not say to one another that it was a relief to get onto the Horncastles, and Agnes visibly relaxed as I began to tell her about the dead shearmen and Piers Garrett. I remembered the nervous excitement of the murder case we had shared in 1907, and thought once again what a pity it was that she spent her days cloistered in drab wedlock instead of racing around London with me, getting into trouble.

'Do you know Lord Horncastle and his family, Agnes? I have never come across them.'

'Not invited to their sort of parties, I suppose.'

'Wouldn't go if I were.'

'Snob. Not everyone with a handle on their name is a bad lot, you know.'

In truth, I'd been invited to a good number of dances at one time or another, though usually only when they were short of guardsmen. Johnny Beaufort the Peke was a guardsman.

'I don't know them well,' she said. 'Old Yorkshire barons, been there since William the Conqueror, I shouldn't wonder. Mayhew is their family name. I remember the old Lord Horncastle being quite a charmer in an 1850s sort of way. He died a little while back.

'I didn't have a lot to do with Daniel, the son. He was quite a good-looking boy, a bit older than me. Sporty, I think. We girls always wanted to sit next to him at dinner, but when we did, we found he never had much to say. Of course, when you get older, you realise that a chap doesn't have to chatter on all the time to be interesting – but when one's younger, it seems unaccountably important.

'There are two daughters too, Anne and Delia. Both older, both married. Quite expensively, I should imagine. Anne is Lady Thirlstane.'

Forgetting herself for a moment, she leaned in conspiratorially as she had often done in other times.

'There was always a bit of chatter about how the former Lord Horncastle was on his uppers. Married for love, which people do say is a terrible mistake.' She suddenly caught herself and her enthusiasm faded.

'Old Lady Horncastle had a reputation for being clever with money but I don't think she came with much. Then again, you can never really trust the gossip because we all pretend we're richer than we are – apart from the really rich ones who claim poverty.'

'Well I should think there's plenty of money floating about Haydon Castle now,' I began, but she already knew that.

'Alice Garrett.'

'You know her?'

'Met her now and then. She's only a couple of years younger and her mother was always very keen that she did all the ladylike, countryish things. We went hunting together once and I got the impression she very much disliked it. No good at all on a horse. A wit in the drawing room though.'

She took a sip of her wine.

'I suppose you want to know if she's pretty.'

I grinned, despite myself.

'Why would you think that?'

'Because you won't be able to form a picture of her in your head until you know. You'll be fine to conjure up ideas of Piers Garrett or Daniel without knowing a thing about what they look like, but you won't be able to think anything about Lady Horncastle without knowing whether she's got sky-blue eyes and a bonny face.'

'You just told me Daniel was handsome.'

'So I did. And I bet you dislike him already.'

I did my best to ignore her, as I usually did when she was right.

'Have you ever met the father? Piers Garrett?'

'Goodness, yes. Shooting mad. And a real boor to boot. They used to have parties for Alice at their London house and I always got the impression he despised the lot of us. But then so do you.'

'I do not. I like you well enough… and several of the fellows at my club are all right.'

'High praise.'

'I don't suppose you know what sort of motor car Piers Garrett keeps, do you?'

I was thinking of that handsome Belsize with the fancy coachwork, parked up conspicuously outside the Roaring Meg in Lambeth. It was a long shot, but Agnes had a weakness for expensive motor cars, and if he had a particularly good one then she might know.

'What a strange question. I don't, I'm afraid. Hopefully not a Phoenix – I've heard they get their parts from a very disreputable East London steel firm.'

She smiled sadly.

'Harrison, you're not going to do anything silly, are you?'

I was glad the bruises from my beating after Abe's funeral were concealed beneath hair and clothing. There was a lovely greenish one on my leg.

'I'm not sure,' I replied honestly. 'Depends what I find.'

'You can't resist it, can you? Sticking your oar into another mess that's not yours.'

She wasn't criticising, just stating a fact, and she didn't wait for me to answer.

‘I sometimes think I don’t like you very much, but what I would like even less is if anything happened to you. We both know you’re frightfully bad at looking after yourself.’

‘I’ll have Jabez.’

‘Oh well that’s fine then. Definitely no chance of trouble with Rumpelstiltskin in tow.’

I saw no reason to tell her that Jabez was spending the afternoon buying a revolver from a Belgian in Lambeth.

Agnes lowered her eyes and returned to her fish, evidently having dispensed enough lukewarm affection for one day.

‘She is, by the way.’

‘She is what?’

Agnes didn’t look up.

‘Pretty. Alice Garrett.’

‘Oh good.’

‘Married to someone else, though.’

They usually are, I thought.

Eleven

There are only a handful of places in life where a man may reliably be left alone, and even those are hardly inviolable. The privy is one; the grave another. The sea, if one swims out far enough, but not too far in case some interfering soul decides to mount a rescue. In moments when I felt especially mithered, I used occasionally to think of those high Arctic trappers with their rotten teeth and soot-streaked faces, overwintering alone in a wriggly tin hut on Spitsbergen. Perhaps they had the right idea.

Mostly, when I was looking not to be bothered by anyone, I would skulk at the back of a church. Churches, after all, spent ninety per cent of the time empty, and whatever else you felt about them, there was a sense of being outside of the world that was difficult to find anywhere else. I had no real faith to speak of – though you wouldn't catch me denying the Almighty outright because the alternative provoked a sensation of existential vertigo too ghastly to contemplate.

Of the various London churches that occasionally played host to Mr Harrison Catcliffe in a bad mood, St Wulfram's – ten minutes' walk from my rooms off Great Portland Street – was my most regular refuge. I liked St Wulfram's, partly because it was so ugly when it had absolutely no need to be.

Outside it was mostly seventeenth century, and had probably been quite beautiful in an understated way until an extravagant remodelling in the early 1800s. Some wag with my own crass tastes had added cartoon battlements and modified the spire into a sort of balloon shape that gave it a dash of eastern Orthodox flair. They had then slapped pale grey render over the brickwork and cut lines into it to make it look like stone.

Inside, this majestic vision was not sustained, and someone – though I suspect not the same flamboyant vandal who had gussied up the façade – had lowered all the ceilings, added some plasterwork straight out of my grandmother's dining room, and painted the whole lot white. Lying as it did in the heart of central London, the once brilliant finish had darkened to a yellowish beige colour that was not unlike Jabez Potter's tobacco-stained fingers.

It was an amenable place, and somewhere I could think without interruption. If anyone did approach – say, the vicar or a nice older lady in a black hat hoping to get me to stay for the evening service – I would simply bow my head in prayer and be left reverently alone. A tortured soul, that one, they might think to themselves – and him with such fancy clothes on and all. It's true what they say, all the brass in the world can't buy you happiness.

This afternoon I badly needed a moment or two in St Wulfram's, so I stopped by on my way home. Partly it was Agnes – who always threw me off-kilter even before she was Lady Halsingham – but mainly I was there because I felt rotten about Alf Bickley, and because as usual I wondered whether it might have been my fault. I had pushed him to tell me what he knew despite his reluctance, and it was difficult not to read into the fact that he had been found dead at pretty much the exact time he was supposed to be in my office. Had I nudged him too far? It was obvious when I saw him on the factory floor that he was in a bad way, but in my curiosity and self-righteousness I'd been quick to overlook that.

There was an even more uncomfortable idea lurking in there too. Because if Alf had done for himself then you could argue that was his business – but if someone had seen him talking to me, put two and two together and made sure his confidences remained confidential, then I had even more to answer for. The fact that I myself had taken a battering just two days earlier was quite a coincidence. Would the truth – if I ever attained it – be worth the lives lost in its pursuit? I thought of all that business with Agnes's sister and brother-in-law a year and a half earlier, when it had certainly not been.

I closed my eyes, breathing in and out as slowly as I dared until I was in danger of passing out. '*The Ideal*,' wrote Thomas Carlyle in an impenetrable novel that we had been forced to do battle with at school, '*is in thyself, the Impediment too is in thyself...*'

The context escaped me, but I remembered the line well enough because that prattling old man in his wideawake hat was dead wrong. There was only impediment in me, the ideal was long gone. The man I wanted to be had been sabotaging himself for so long and so successfully that he had dwindled away to nothing, leaving only the saboteur.

I was interrupted in my melancholia by the ping of a coin ricocheting off the box pew in front of me. It hit the floor by my feet and bounced noisily behind the embroidered kneeler. Turning round sharply, I saw a man sitting two pews behind.

'Penny for 'em?' he said, nodding at the one he'd just lobbed.

Without invitation, he rose and sidled around to join me in my pew – if a fellow of such size could ever really be said to sidle.

The man was a human carthorse, over six feet tall and with shoulders like St Christopher. His head was razored smooth and freckled like an egg, but he compensated for his lack of foliage up top with a luxuriant chestnut moustache. To protect his suit from the smuts of soot that soiled just about everything in this filthy city, he wore a summer-weight brown duster, which he tucked carefully underneath himself as he sat down. With the addition of his considerable bulk, the pew suddenly felt quite cramped.

'Well then?' he said, without looking at me. His gaze remained reverently on the altar at the other end of the church.

'I'm sorry, do we know one another?'

'I know you, if that helps.'

'I see.' I paused, not quite sure where to go next. There was something about him – beyond his size – that made me profoundly afraid of him.

'No need to introduce myself, I shouldn't think,' said the man. 'I wouldn't give you my real name anyway, and all being well, you'll never see me again.'

'So really it's not worth it?'

'Exactly.'

He was polite and his clothes were of good quality, but his strong East End accent and the cloth cap tucked in his pocket told a slightly different story. I'd seen similar fellows propping up the bar in the Two Brewers, drinking a pint of stout very slowly and conducting brief conversations with deferential little men who flitted in and out of the pub bearing buff-coloured envelopes. The men in question worked for the Bagby brothers who ran that corner of London, and while I was a long way off their patch, my companion in St Wulfram's was definitely of such a type.

'Assuming, as you suggest, that it's best we don't meet again,' I began, picking my words with some care, 'what actions on my part might effect that?'

The gorilla pretended to consider the question, as if he hadn't wandered into the church and sat down next to me with any definite end in mind.

'Two things should do it,' he said. 'Firstly, I'd like to know your thoughts about your dead Bickley men.' He gestured under the pew. 'I've given you a penny for them, after all.'

'You can put it in the poor box,' I replied, more bravely than I felt. 'I don't know what's going on with the Bickleys. I wish I did. I'm wretchedly sad about Abe and Alf and I'd like to find Timmy before anything happens to him too – assuming it hasn't already.'

'Timmy Bickley's gone,' said the man. 'I'll give you that for free.'

'Dead?'

'Just gone.'

'Who made him be gone? And who killed Abe? You?'

'Doesn't matter. What matters is that you can't help the Bickleys, but you can help yourself and a lot of others – and the way to do that is to leave well alone.'

'Is that part two of the plan that means you and I never meet again?'

'It is.' He smoothed his moustache and for the first time looked away from the altar and directly at me.

'You're into something much bigger than a few missing men, and if you keep digging you're going to make a right bloody mess.'

'For whom? Piers Garrett?' If I hoped that was going to provoke a response, I was wrong. The man was a stone.

'Best keep away from that one.' His tone was firm but without any particular sense of malice.

'And let the men just keep on disappearing?'

He ignored that, instead affecting a long sigh that was entirely for my benefit.

'You wouldn't believe, Mr Catcliffe, how much of my time I spend trying to give people a sense of perspective. Explaining to them as best I can that things are bigger than them, and that by interfering they'll do more harm than good. To themselves, mostly.

'So just leave it. Stick that penny in the poor box, add one of your own if you like. Help who you can help. Help yourself. Let the dead lie. I'd tell you no-one can bring 'em back, but, well...'

He gestured towards one of the stained-glass windows where Jesus held up a bloodlessly perforated palm. Levering his heavy frame upright, he took his cap out of his pocket.

'Honestly, the way this story's going at the moment, the best way it could end – and I really do mean the best way, because there are worse options – is the lightermen fishing your bloated corpse out of the Thames in a couple of days' time. I know it sounds like I'm threatening you, but I'm doing you a favour – and it's not the first one I've done you either.

'But you can write a better story if you want to, and all it takes is cracking on with your life and staying away from Piers Garrett. I know what I'd choose.'

He let himself out of the pew and shuffled off up the aisle towards the doors, pausing to smile at an old lady who was switching the dead flowers by the font for some that were merely wilted. All of a sudden, St Wulfram's didn't feel like a sanctuary at all.

Twelve

Returning to my rooms in no mood for a night entertaining the German businessmen, I was surprised to find a pair of oily work boots sitting on a sheet of newspaper outside the door, and Arthur Letts waiting inside for me. He had evidently come straight from Catcliffe's, and he stood awkwardly by the window in my front room. Either he had decided not to risk getting oil on my armchairs, or more likely Edie had forbidden him to sit down.

So much for staying well out of it all, but I couldn't very well send him packing. Arthur wasn't to know what had just happened to me in St Wulfram's, and if I was going to back away from this business with Piers Garrett, it would need to be done sensitively.

The big fellow's warning – following as it did on the heels of a good shoeing – was a powerful motivation to pack it all in sharpish and return to a dull life. All the same, I had still not absolutely decided to do as I was told. I was frightened, but I had been frightened before and ploughed on regardless. For now, the decision could wait.

'I'm sorry if I've kept you waiting, Arthur. Only I wasn't expecting you. Do have a seat.'

He picked a hard wooden footstool – presumably because he thought it would not suffer too badly from any stray smears of paint or grease – and sat gingerly, lining his stocking feet up with the pattern on the carpet.

'No, no, forgive me. I've called unannounced – only, you see, I had to see you before you go away.'

'I take it this is to do with Abe?'

'It is, and I'm sorry to admit, Mr Harrison, that I've not told you all I should have done.'

He hung his head and scrunched his cap in his hands the way he had when I told him they'd found Abraham's body.

'Don't worry, Arthur, you're here now. Tea, please, Edie.'

Edie made to leave the room with her usual air of displeasure at domestic tasks, but Arthur held up his hand in protest.

'Please, no need for tea, I won't be a moment.'

Edie stopped, but I caught her eye and nodded at the door. I felt like he might be more forthcoming without her hovering impatiently in the background. She sighed to let me know how she felt about all this flip-flopping, then swept out and closed the door with an exaggerated gentleness that was somehow a good deal more aggressive than slamming it.

'What it is,' said Arthur, 'there's something about the night Abe died. I didn't tell you it because I didn't think it was anything, but after what's happened with Alf, well, maybe it is.

'The night Abe went missing, he and Timmy had a barney in the Two Brewers. All got quite ugly. They were good mates, Abe and Timmy – almost like father and son – but hotheads both, you see, and when they argued, my God did they argue. Young Alf was the peacemaker. Could usually get everything smoothed over, but he wasn't in the pub that night. Dicky tummy, Tim said.'

'Do you know what the argument was about?'

'Something and nothing. Abe was thinking of running for union leadership. Leaving Catcliffe's and going to work for the AATMM full-time. Timmy wanted him to stay a shearman, do what he was best at, maybe keep his head down a bit. I'd say they both had points worth thinking on, but it just blew up from there and soon they were saying all sorts about each other. Abe didn't care about his family, Timmy was a needy lad who'd been binned off by his own dad. You know how it can get.

'Eventually there was a bit of shoving and Abe gave Tim the back of his hand. Not too hard, like, just sort of to warn him off. Then he stormed out of the pub.'

'I see. What did Timothy do?'

'Just sat there for a minute or so, sort of collecting himself. I don't think he expected it. Then he got up and went after him.'

I suddenly realised what Arthur Letts was telling me.

'So you mean that the last time anyone saw either Abe or Timothy, one was following the other out into the night after a quarrel.'

'That's about the size of it, yes,' replied Arthur miserably, picking at the flecks of paint that always speckled his hands. 'I didn't say anything before because I knew how it would look and I didn't believe Timmy could have done it. I still don't. But for Alf to...' He lost himself for a moment and had to swallow down his emotions.

'For Alf to do that to himself,' he went on, 'I wonder if he did believe it. If he knew something that I didn't.'

Arthur Letts was a good man and I desperately wanted to lay a consoling hand upon his shoulder, but it wouldn't have been on. I offered him a cigarette instead, but he refused politely.

‘Do you have any idea what that might have been, Arthur? I’m so dreadfully sorry to push you.’

He shook his head.

‘I’m sorry, no. But they were always close, those two – Alf and Timmy. They had a room together in a boarding house not far from Catcliffe’s, and I went over there last night to clear their things out. Alf only had a week’s rent down and the landlady needed to let it out again.’

Arthur looked sadly at me.

‘Point is that when I paid the landlady her missing rent, she started going on about what trouble they’d been lately. I think she just wanted more money, but when I asked her what she meant, she said the police had been banging on the door late at night looking for Timmy.’

‘I suppose it will have been the first place they looked after he disappeared.’

‘No, you don’t understand. At least, I’m not explaining myself properly. The night the police came looking for him was the same Friday night that he and Abe went missing.’

I sat up sharply.

‘What? You mean, the police were looking for him before any crime had been reported?’

‘Exactly. Less than an hour after he left the Two Brewers, if you believe the landlady.’

It simply did not fit. I thought back to that fateful Thursday morning when Arthur had shown us the pristine lavatory doors at Catcliffe’s. ‘The coppers don’t want to know, of course...’ And yet here they were turning up on the doorstep the same night Abe was murdered. Had they been after Timmy for some other reason?

'Well, did they find him? Was he there?'

'Two different questions, Mr Harrison. Landlady says that when she knocked on the door to their room with the policemen, there was only Alf in there, but she swears she heard the two brothers talking just before that. Their window opens onto the outhouse roof and she says it was wide open when the police went in.'

'I suppose it would have been either way in this hot weather,' I observed.

'Maybe,' said Arthur gently, reluctant to disagree. 'But I think if my room backed onto the privy in high summer, I might have kept it closed and reckoned with the heat instead.'

I came with him to the door and waited with him as he laced his boots up.

'You needn't have taken them off, you know, Arthur. I never do.'

Arthur gave me a wan smile.

'Abe would've had a good laugh at that. He always teased me that I was a company man to the soles of me feet. Seems like he was right, doesn't it?'

After he had left – as I changed my shirt, doused myself in cologne and tried not to think about Agnes or the heavyweight in the duster – I considered this revised set of facts. So the Bickleys had quarrelled at the Two Brewers. Abe had set off to walk home, followed shortly afterwards by Timmy. In due course, Abe had been beaten to death and thrown into the Thames.

Within an hour of the argument in the pub, Timmy had arrived home and spoken to his brother, before the police disturbed them by turning up to ask about a crime that no-one yet knew had been committed. Instead of speaking to them, Timmy had run, which implied a guilty conscience.

Poor Alf had a guilty conscience too – but I couldn't help feeling that the guilt had to have been his own rather than Timmy's. A fellow might feel shame and horror if his brother committed murder, but would he really take his own life in an attempt to stop it coming to light? Especially when silence would accomplish the same object?

There was something more here than a family drama. The strange visit from the police, Alf's part in a murder for which he was not even present, and the sheer unlikeliness of Timmy Bickley bashing his uncle's head in over a featherweight bar-room dust-up.

For all I was trying to keep her out of my mind, there Agnes was, reminding me sharply of the time I had suspected her sister of murder simply because everyone else did. Agnes had told me that Henrietta wasn't capable of it, and she had been right. Which was to say in a roundabout way that character mattered more than appearances.

There was blind loyalty, and then there was sound knowledge of what someone would or wouldn't do. If Arthur Letts still didn't believe Timmy could have killed Abe, then nor did I.

THIRTEEN

At some point late on the Wednesday night, while well into our cups, I ventured to ask my father why I was going all the way to the North Riding of Yorkshire to snoop on Piers Garrett.

'Because he is a malevolent gnome,' he replied, reaching over to top my glass up.

'So really what you mean to say is that you are sending your oldest and dearest son – well, your oldest at least – half the length of the country because you don't like someone.'

One of the gentlemen from the Ruhr was singing, and cousin John was crawling around under the table looking for a dropped cigarette. My father had wanted to take everyone for another nice dignified night at his club, but the Germans had fancied experiencing the city and so here we were in a lively little place I knew off the Charing Cross Road. The old man hated it. Hated Piers Garrett too, apparently.

'I'm not sending you. You want to go – I'm just giving you an excuse. I was talking to Dick Fletcher over the weekend and he seems to have almost as much misplaced faith in you as I do. Good old Dick. I sometimes think he's about as close as an Englishman can get to being an American.'

‘He ought to play up to it. Call himself Richard and style his name with a middle initial.’

‘I’ll tell him that – he’ll like it. Probably doesn’t have a middle initial though.’

‘He can have one of mine. You gave me a spare.’

The old man smiled sheepishly. In our family we were stacked with middle-class affectations and he was the only one who never quite took them in his stride.

‘And it’s not just that I dislike Piers Garrett, though you’re quite right. It’s that I’m convinced he has a hand in it. Since the moment you told me most of the men were linked to his works. You haven’t met him, but he’s different – even in a field of cut-throats and show-offs like ours.

‘He and I both inherited things from our fathers, and I’ve always felt like the second generation in a successful family firm is a curious place to be. Men like Piers and I will never measure up to our fathers because they built up all that momentum from a standing start. Then it gets to our turn and we set off at a sprint and have to spend the rest of our lives trying to run fast enough that the rest of the pack don’t overtake us. It can make a fellow rather bloody, and you have to try quite hard not to be, except Piers has never made the slightest effort on that score.’

He was rambling a little, but I let him, perhaps because I was wondering if the third generation was where the pack finally ran you down.

‘I’m sure most of the rumours you hear about him aren’t true. I don’t really believe he had that clerk’s wife attacked after the fellow talked back to him, but I wouldn’t bet any serious money that he didn't. I knew him better when we were younger, and I do know that he once ruined a girl's reputation just because she rebuffed him. Made sure her brother lost his job too. She was no-one important, but powerful men can do that sort of thing.'

Loud squeals of laughter at the next table brought a momentary halt to the conversation. The Germans were getting especially drunk tonight. They had been cocky with their pitch but now they were being undercut by a Pole called Bobrowski and Andrew had deliberately let it slip, thinking it would make them up their game. It had, but not in the way he intended.

When my old man continued, it was in a more determined vein.

'Piers Garrett gets away with all these things because they seem small to those who could hold him to account about it, but if he has been involved in a man's death then that is different. That's why I want you to find out if it's true. You know how to take care of yourself. You have done this sort of thing before – that business two Christmases ago.'

'But I made an unholy mess of that, Father. A right cock-up. Four people died.'

'Did they? Oh well.'

FOURTEEN

On the Thursday morning, the long spell of hot, dry weather finally broke. Our friends from Dortmund packed up their hangovers and shuffled aboard the nine o'clock express to Dover, while I wrapped my own considerable suffering in a Norfolk jacket, topped it with a pearl grey homburg and transferred it gingerly aboard the ten forty-five Great Northern to York.

The journey north from King's Cross was one of those interminable crusades that continued well into the evening, accompanied by a biblical deluge that hammered us the whole way. We changed first at York and then at Scarborough, marshalling truculent porters and waiting on damp platforms as the rain splattered from the overflowing gutters. Jabez ferreted out an evening paper from somewhere, but it was a local rag with no news to speak of. A carriage had knocked into another carriage somewhere on the parade and a wheel had fallen off, that sort of thing.

My father often waxed lyrical about the elegance and distinction of Scarborough, calling it 'the finest watering place in the north of England', but I saw little of it in the grey evening light as we climbed northwards out of town on the Whitby line. Just blurred lights and the glow of high-gabled hotels through steamed-up windows. Soon we were labouring through drab, wild moorland, the rain lashing the train windows so hard that it seeped through the seals, soaking through to my shirt where my shoulder touched the sill. In an effort to lift his sodden spirits, Jabez poisoned our compartment by smoking endless fills of noxious twist, and Edie sat in disgust opposite, her knees drawn up to her chin and her face swathed in a shawl. It was the furthest north she had ever been, and it was clear she regarded anywhere above Epping as a sort of grim prison hulk moored up against England proper.

Finally, after dawdling for what seemed like hours in a string of seemingly derelict village halts at which no-one got on or off, the wretched train creaked to a standstill alongside the soot-stained brick-work of Whitby West Cliff station. It was almost nine o'clock at night, and no porters stood waiting – just a station master huddled in a great-coat with a small terrier shivering on a piece of twine. A handful of passengers made a dash through the rain towards the station building, and by the time we had struggled to shelter with our luggage, our fellow travellers appeared to have vanished into the ether. I enquired hopefully after a cab, and through his enormous moustaches, the station master told me that if I was Mr Catcliffe then there was a trap waiting outside for me.

'Not much of a summer, is it?' he remarked pleasantly, ignoring the fact – as people always do – that the country had been basking in an extended heatwave until the previous day.

Together, Jabez and I dragged our soggy trunks through the ticket office and out onto the street, where sure enough stood a small open carriage of antiquated design. Two stocky horses steamed and stamped in the mud, and a slightly built coachman in an oversized coat and a wide, floppy felt hat sat hunched over the reins. As we approached, the figure hopped down and dropped a slight curtsey. A pale hand pushed up the brim of the hat, revealing the face of a young woman, her dark hair stuck to her cheeks in lank strings.

'Hard to measure, boss!' she shouted over the din of the storm.

'Sorry?' I replied, baffled by this opening gambit.

The woman thrust her face right up to my ear, dislodging a good deal of water from her hat that ran straight down my collar.

'Artemisia Moss,' she cried. 'My name, sir, it's Artemisia Moss. I'm your aunt's housekeeper.'

The three of us struggled to lash the trunks to the back of the carriage while Edie stood under the eaves of the station building clutching a hatbox by way of contribution. Our clothes sopping wet and streaked with mud, we clambered aboard and the two ponderous horses moved unhurriedly off down a narrow lane lined with railwaymen's cottages.

Presently, we emerged onto a clifftop road, where the tarry expanse of the North Sea boiled far below. I clung to my homburg lest the howling wind might snatch it from my head, and looked out to where twin piers reached out from the harbour like pincers, a dim light smouldering on the tip of each one. High up on the east side of town, the spectre of a ruined abbey clung to the headland. It was a relief when we turned down a side street out of the gale, and pulled up outside a tall Georgian terrace with a light burning in the hallway.

'Home,' said Artemisia, simply.

Fifteen

Why my aunt Diana had chosen to pass her twilight years in one of Yorkshire's most remote and inaccessible coastal towns I had never quite fathomed, but she was a contrary old bird who mainly did things because she felt like it. Many older ladies, for example, would have had their maid open the door for a guest, but since Diana only employed a cook, an odd-job boy and the sopping wet housekeeper who was currently hefting luggage off the back of the trap, it was my aunt herself who cracked the door ajar and beckoned me in out of the rain with a jerk of her head. She did not wait to greet me, but scuttled off into the interior, leaving me to find my own way through into the sitting room, where a high fire glowed enticingly in the hearth.

'Let me have a look at you, young man,' she said briskly as I stood dripping in front of the hot coals. I had a look at her in return, noting how much stiffer her movements had become since I had last seen her at my grandfather's funeral in the Yorkshire Dales some years earlier. Diana had not ventured south in decades.

'You can look him over once he's got some dry clothes and a cup of tea,' scolded Clara, her companion, planting a swift peck on my cheek as she relieved me of my coat and hat and bustled out into the hall with them.

‘Lizzie,’ I heard her call down the stairs to the kitchen, ‘tea, if you please!’

Clara – or ‘Auntie’ Clara as we’d always known her – was a spry, birdlike woman, a good deal younger looking than my aunt Diana, though they must have been the same age because they had been at school together. Neither had ever married, and they had lived their quietly eccentric lives together for well over forty years.

Diana lowered her tall frame into a velvety green armchair, then mutely placed a forefinger on the thin skin that covered her cheekbone.

‘Hello, Auntie.’ I stooped to kiss the proffered cheek, then sat down opposite. Outside on the stairs there was a good deal of scraping and banging, which presumably meant Jabez was dragging my trunk upstairs with his usual degree of care.

‘Are you both well?’ I asked politely.

‘Of course not, dear boy. I sleep barely three hours a night and have very little appetite – even then only for the simplest of foodstuffs. Clara’s rheumatism, as you see, is a very great trial to her, and she struggles to hear the sermons in church. Both of us have very gloomy eyesight these days, and I have quite given up on novels, though Clara persists. I myself do battle with the *Gazette* once a week, but it is all I can do to get as far as the obituaries.’

I took a breath to speak, then paused, unsure of how to respond appropriately.

‘And the less said about our teeth, the better.’ She gave a twitch at the corner of her mouth which may have been a twinge of toothache or a smirk.

Clara came back in with a light smile, showing teeth which appeared in good nick for a woman in her sixties.

'I'm sorry to discover your hearing is causing you trouble, Auntie Clara,' I ventured.

'My what?' she said, turning away from me to sit down, and I saw Diana glance at her, the mouth performing its inscrutable twitch once more.

'It's very good of you to put me up like this,' I ploughed on, raising my voice just in case.

'That's quite all right, dear boy,' replied Diana with exaggerated quietness, as if implying there was no need to shout. 'Your father's letter intrigued me. His writing is as appalling as ever and is now quite beyond these old eyes of mine, but fortunately Artemisia was able to decipher it for me.'

'She reads ever so well,' interjected Clara. 'Especially bad handwriting. It is a wonder she has not been snapped up by the Egyptian expeditions to help them decode the writing of the ancients.'

I took out my cigarette case and proffered them to my aunt and her companion. My ladylike mother would never have dreamed of smoking but Clara and Diana both took one, as I knew they would.

'He was also deplorably light on detail,' said Diana as I lit her cigarette, 'and his lack of proper punctuation makes every sentence sound like a telegram.'

Diana had originally been six years older than my father, but the gap had widened with age. During her youth, before Grandpa Catcliffe had really started to make money hand over fist, she had worked for some years as a schoolmistress. I could only imagine what the experience must have been like for the tender young souls in her care.

I filled in the story for them, leaving out nothing – including the gorier details, which I could tell they relished. As we talked, a youngish woman who was presumably the cook brought in a tray of tea things.

'Artemisia is taking the trap and horses back to Faulkner's, ma'am,' she explained.

'Quite right,' said Diana approvingly. 'No sense paying for standing horses. Would you see about some supper for Harry, please Lizzie?'

'And something for Jabez and Edie too, if you wouldn't mind ever so much,' I added.

'He will be fine with a tray,' said Clara. 'Won't you, Harry?'

Lizzie nodded and withdrew, evidently a girl of few words.

By the time I'd finished talking, the teapot was empty and I was just about beginning to warm through.

'A queer old village, Yattonby,' mused Clara. 'It's up at the head of Birkdale – a devil to get in or out, even in summertime. There's mining up there – whinstone? Ironstone? – but it's never really flourished. Yattonby itself is really just an estate village for Haydon Castle, plus the miners, a handful of tenant farmers and quite a lot of gamekeepers.'

'You seem to be quite well informed about the place, Auntie Clara.'

'It so happens that it is where we found Artemisia,' she smiled. 'It has rather a notable ancient church – St Stephen's – so we rode over there five or six years ago. You know how Diana likes to sketch the misericords...'

'At least I did, before the arthritis became too severe,' interjected Diana.

'So Artemisia is from Yattonby then?' I was anxious not to reopen the cataloguing of ailments.

'Yes, dear, yes she is. We were in the church and the nice young rector was telling us about a local girl who had lost her father after a long illness. Mother dead a few years earlier, no surviving siblings. Very capable, by all accounts, nursed her father in his last years then worked at the castle for a spell. We took her on as a maid, and as you can see, she has become indispensable to us.'

As if to emphasise her indispensable nature, the domestic in question appeared in the doorway with supper on a tray. She had changed her wet outdoor clothes for a neat navy blue uniform but her hair was still damp and ratty.

'A glass of wine, Mr Catcliffe?'

'Harry will have a glass of beer at this hour, thank you, Artemisia.'

I chewed on my cold collation wearily – flattened by a combination of hangover, travel and heavy weather – until eventually Diana scolded me for keeping her up so late and packed me off to bed.

Artemisia showed me to a room on the second floor at the back of the house. Wind and rain rattled the windows and sent puffs of sooty smoke belching into the room from the smouldering fireplace. I looked down onto a pub yard, where a boxing match appeared to be in its final stages. In the midst of a howling crowd of soaking wet drunks, two great lumps of men swung exhaustedly at each other with fists like hunks of lead, their pasty white chests slick with rainwater and blood.

Pipe smoke and steam rose through the sheeting rain, and the patchy yellow glow of the hurricane lamps made demons of the side-burned men stamping their hobnails on the cobbles, fists clenched and teeth bared as they screamed encouragement. I was not especially surprised to spot Jabez jockeying for space near the front of the press.

Hasn't taken him long to find his feet, I thought, as one of the boxers finally lost theirs.

Sixteen

By morning, the storm had blown over and the shrieks of men had given over to the caterwauling of gulls. The birds and the smell of the sea air woke me sometime before seven – and even at that hour the golden light of what would become a beautiful summer's day was already seeping through the curtains.

It was at the breakfast table, in between leafing impatiently through the pages of the *Gazette* and picking at a plate of finely chopped boiled egg, that Diana informed me of the plan she and Auntie Clara had hatched at some unspecified point since bedtime. Clara, as was her custom, had taken her breakfast at around the same hour as the sparrows and blackbirds, and was already out conducting some obscure business at a coffee house over on the other side of the harbour.

'We consider it would be a great dereliction of familial duty to send you ill-prepared into the lion's den,' said Diana, her focus divided thirty–seventy between her beloved nephew and the obituaries page, 'so we have resolved that you will take Artemisia with you.'

I was certainly not prepared for such a generous offer. For the two of them to lend me their indispensable housekeeper – their woman Friday – was the equivalent of me letting someone else take Jabez.

Moreover, an obliging version of Jabez with a wide range of competencies beyond committing acts of violence and causing offence.

'That is ever so kind, Aunt. But what will you do without her?'

'It will be a hardship, that is true, but you could consent to lend us your maid in return.'

My heart sank. Could I truly do this to my own flesh and blood?

'I would caution, Edie's attitude to service is unconventional.'

'So is ours,' said Diana, dismissively. 'You'll have to find your own way to Yattonby, though. Artemisia can tell you how – I've a notion the train will get you most of the way there.'

'Are you absolutely sure?' It seemed unfair not to give them a last chance.

'It will be fine, Harry.' My aunt gave me that faint curl of the lip which passed for a smile. 'And you will need Artemisia if you are to get to the bottom of all this.'

I found Artemisia smoking with Jabez and Edie in the backyard. She alone rose hastily from her perch on the step and put out her cigarette when she saw me.

'Are you all done in there, sir? Miss Catcliffe gets irritated if I start clearing the breakfast things before she's finished reading the *Gazette*,' she explained mildly. No doubt my aunt had many such caprices, and I felt a guilty trill of delight as I imagined this well-mannered young woman temporarily switched for Edie.

'That's quite all right, Artemisia. Has she mentioned that she would like you to accompany us when we make our way to Yattonby?'

Artemisia nodded.

‘She has, sir. And Jabez here has been explaining the wherefores. I think I can help you, so long as you don’t mind Edie seeing to things here while I’m away.’

Edie bore an expression of profound ennui that made her own feelings on the subject clear.

‘I think you’d prefer to stay in town with Miss Catcliffe and Miss Wynnster than traipsing out all over the moors with me and Jabez, wouldn’t you, Edie?’ My maid nodded hesitantly, presumably considering Whitby the lesser of two abominable options, then flicked the end of her cigarette across the cobbles and rose stiffly to her feet.

‘I’ll clear the breakfast things,’ she said to Artemisia with a rare glimmer of friendliness. ‘You can sort these two out.’

....

It turned out my timing was poor – a fact of life that I had long since come to accept as inevitable. The previous day’s deluge had caused a sizeable landslip north of Whitby, swallowing up a section of the coastal railway line where it cut through an unstable moonscape of old alum shale dumps. The line would be out of action for days if not weeks, and the alternative rail route up to Middlesbrough was too far inland to be useful. There was a coach to Yattonby, but it had departed the day before and would not venture that way again for another week.

None of which seemed to faze Artemisia. She considered our best option for getting there without delay was to approach the mining company that quarried out low-grade ironstone in Birkdale.

‘They still ship most of their ore out by boat from Port Blyth,’ she explained. ‘It’s a little cove up the coast with a cliff winch. I shouldn’t think they’ll turn down a few passengers.’

Whitby was a town of two halves – a deep cleft in the coast separated by a busy harbour and a curious jointed bridge that swung open several times a day to let the tall-masted coastal freighters access the more sheltered waters of the inner estuary. The headland of the east side was dominated by the ruin of the ancient abbey and its associated church, with a ramshackle shanty town of fishermen's cottages and poky alleys crammed along a narrow strip of harbourfront – the whole lot wreathed in a blanket of coal smoke. Opposite, on the west side of the bay, was the smart Victorian resort, where the ranks of tall, elegant townhouses once owned by whalers and shipowners were increasingly occupied by refined seaside hotels catering to affluent smog-suckers from the industrial West Riding. It was here that one found the ballrooms and dance schools, the dining rooms, dressmakers and business concerns.

The Ross & Blayne Mining Company had an office on Flowergate – a smart, wide street that sloped steeply down from the mansions of the west cliff to the swing bridge. Nestled among shipping lines and solicitors, Ross & Blayne's premises were noticeably shabbier than their neighbours, but they were very helpful all the same, and a clerk called Cabourn offered us passage as far as Birkdale mine for a modest consideration. Ross & Blayne got ore out of Birkdale via a little coastal steamer with a shallow enough draught to use an isolated jetty below a clifftop hamlet called Port Blyth. The ore came across the moor from Birkdale by wagon, and was then winched down the cliff from the village. Happily, we could undertake the journey the other way.

'Most mining companies prefer rail transport to sea,' said Cabourn with a gappy smile, 'but it's times like this you can see why we don't. There's only us and the Garrett line using that jetty. If we cut our losses there to focus on our operations further north, it'll be hard on those folk at Port Blyth.'

'The Garrett line?' I asked with surprise.

'Oh, er, Mercury Shipping.' He waved his hand dismissively. 'We call it the Garrett line to distinguish it from the others – there are a few Mercuries about, as you can imagine. Shipping companies and newspapers.'

'Garrett as in Piers Garrett?'

'Well I don't know his first name. Him from London, up at Yattonby.'

'Does he own Mercury then? I thought it was a man called Patchard.'

'Couldn't say who owns it,' said Cabourn, grinning politely but obviously beginning to run short on patience. 'Everyone round here knows it as the Garrett line though. They mainly run a couple of big steamers called the *Sweet Heart* and the *Clare Kelly*, with a smaller one called the *Barbara* that works the shallower harbours.'

I emerged into the sunshine a few minutes later, having concluded our arrangements to sail the next morning on one of Ross & Blayne's own boats. Jabez was cackling over some dirty joke with a bloodstained lad outside a butcher's shop on the corner opposite. He looked ropier than ever, still sporting a mouse under his eye courtesy of Mickey Helm the die-setter.

Over on my side of the street, Artemisia was watching a juvenile gull following its mother slavishly along the cobbles, wheezing pitifully for attention. She tapped a cigarette on the back of her hand to settle the baccy, but began to put it back in her apron pouch when she saw me.

'Please, feel free if you like.' I took out my cigarette case and offered her one.

'Thank you, sir.'

She lit up then went back to watching the gulls, blinking slowly to feel the warm sun on her eyelids.

'I suspect we may rely on you quite heavily during this coming week,' I admitted. 'I could already do with some advice.'

She raised her eyebrows by way of invitation.

'Do you know anything about Piers Garrett, Artemisia? Jabez has told you our business here, I understand.'

She took a long pull on her cigarette.

'He has. And not much, I'm afraid, sir. His daughter didn't marry young Lord Horncastle until two years ago, and by then I was long gone. In fact, the old Lord Horncastle was still alive when I was last there. I haven't been back to Yattonby in nearly six years. No family left, you see. So all I've really got is gossip – and you should never believe that in a place like this.'

She allowed herself a faint smile. Her accent was thick but pleasant. I came from the West Riding of Yorkshire, where we rolled our vowels out like sausages then expelled them through our noses for good measure. Up here the sounds were rounder and softer, closer to Northern Europe.

'I happen to place quite a lot of stock in gossip...' I said, hopefully, thinking that it was mostly gossip that had brought me 250 miles north.

'Well, if you really want to know, I've heard odd things recently. Ran into one of the village boys working the boats in Whitby and he says there's a lot of locals been laid off on the estate. All the gamekeepers replaced with men from out of town, new butler, mostly new footmen and grooms. I saw Mrs Ewart the housekeeper in town a few months ago. She's still there, as far as I know. She was friendly but she wouldn't talk about any of it. Not at all like her.'

She dropped her cigarette end in a rivulet of something unmentionable running down the edge of the cobbles.

'The feeling I'm given is that Mr Garrett runs things there now. Lord Daniel was always a soft one and I shouldn't think he stands up to his father-in-law. The dowager was a force to reckon with in her day, but she had a seizure seven or eight years ago and she's not been right since.'

The sun was hot on my neck and I pulled at my collar to try and get some air down it. It sounded like our visit to Yattonby was not going to be a great deal of fun, and I told Artemisia as much.

'Oh I don't know,' she said. 'I haven't travelled much, but people say it's quite a beauty spot.'

'At least tell me there's a pub,' said Jabez, who had concluded his ribaldry with the butcher's boy and returned to join us.

'There is,' nodded Artemisia. 'The Bull. But can I suggest, sir, that we don't stay there?'

'As you recommend, naturally. But what's wrong with it?' I asked.

'Nothing wrong with the Bull. But I think you're better off asking to stay at the vicarage with the Reverend Wilkie.'

In my mind's eye, an unappealing vignette presented itself of a wire-haired old duffer with a gleaming pate and half-glasses, pouring out tiny thimbles of sherry. I didn't need to look at Jabez to know how aghast he would be at the notion of stopping in a vicarage, but Artemisia was quietly adamant.

'I know what you'll be thinking, Mr Catcliffe, but please trust me. You could do with a friend, and he will be a good one.'

Such praise from the understated Artemisia Moss was high admiration indeed – perhaps old Reverend Wilkie would be all right.

Seventeen

Our boat, the *Elsie Marley*, left just after first light as the tide turned. A scruffy little steamer with a high prow and salt-blistered paint, her deck space was mostly given over to big empty bays that Ross and Blayne would load up with iron ore at Port Blyth. As we cast off, large numbers of the local 'coble' fishing boats were already flowing in and out of the narrow harbour mouth.

The air at that hour was still cool, and the light breeze carried a heady cocktail upon it. Fish and sewage, brackish water and tar mixed with the salt smell of the sea, the coal smoke and the fresh bread baking in the big communal ovens over on the east side. Newly arrived boats of all shapes and sizes crowded the upper harbour, and stiff-limbed men in shirtsleeves hurried to unload bales of cargo while the tide was still high. Along the quay, the fish stalls were filling up with the morning's catch, attended mostly by square, middle-aged women in gut-smeared aprons and headscarves.

The *Elsie* chugged towards the harbour mouth, its crew exchanging yells with passing vessels in a dialect so impenetrable it was difficult to tell whether they were greeting or cursing each other. The boats in the harbour observed that principle common to all traffic on land or water – from ocean liners right down to pedestrians – that it is always the smaller craft that is in the way of the bigger one, rather than the other way around.

As we passed the bandstand at the base of the pier, a young woman who was perched on the wall knitting a long boot sock waved down to me, presumably tickled at the sight of some southern popinjay lounging against the railings at the *Elsie*'s bow. I took off my hat and waved it gallantly in return.

'Steady,' said Jabez.

He, naturally, was in his element, stretched out comfortably on a pile of sacking with his feet resting up against the anchor winch, filling his second pipe of the morning. After twenty years in the Royal Marine Light Infantry, Jabez appeared more at home on a boat than on dry land. Artemisia was a different matter. I could see her down on the main deck, where she had burrowed down into a corner like a sick cat, her arms hugging her knees. As we emerged from the narrow opening between the twin piers into the open sea, the tide and wind took hold of us with a bump, and the boat began to pitch gently in the swell. Artemisia curled into an even tighter ball and pulled her shawl over her head.

We turned north-west towards the tip of the next headland, looking back towards the small town clinging to its estuary. The bay was full of boats – it was high summer and the fish were running, so every man or boy fit enough to haul on a rope was making the most of the bounty. A good time for salters and smokers, I thought, catching a toxic wisp of Jabez's tarry twist on the breeze. Closer to shore, men in faded ganseys and long sea boots were rowing nets out from their cobles in little jolly boats.

'Sea trout!' shouted one of the crew, Billy, when he saw me watching them. Turning towards him, I noticed that we appeared to be running headlong into a similar-looking ship to ours coming the other way. We passed within about fifty yards of her – close enough that we could see a couple of crewmen standing watching us from the railings by the wheelhouse.

'We know that boat,' Billy explained, waving at them. 'She sometimes stops in at Port Blyth too.'

Oddly, neither man opposite waved back. From that distance, I could see them pretty clearly, and one of them – a rough-looking deckhand in a salt-stained black serge jacket – rapped his middle knuckle sharply against his crewmate's arm then pointed at me. Both of them treated us to a long, hostile stare that continued until we had passed them by.

We wallowed a little as we crossed the other steamer's wake, and I watched her stern as she continued away from us then turned south, aiming towards the harbour mouth.

'Don't know what's up with them lads,' said Billy, making a face.

'What's the name of that boat?' I asked him.

'The *Barbara*.'

'Garrett line?'

'That's the one.'

He tucked a loose skein of wool into the sleeve of his gansey and squinted out towards the headland. But I could no longer enjoy the view.

Eighteen

Lunch was well overdue by the time we reached Port Blyth, and I barely saw the place until we were almost upon it. It was a tiny inlet where the low tide had exposed a long slab of weed-strewn mudstone at the foot of steep cliffs, with a stone-built jetty reaching out into the grey-brown brine. Up top, overlooking the North Sea, was a single row of cottages and an engine house for the winching apparatus that hauled cargo up and down the cliff face.

We were obviously expected, and a few local men lounged smoking on the jetty among the heavy containers of iron ore waiting to be transferred aboard the *Elsie Marley* once her supplies had been unloaded. Behind them on the beach, four or five women foraged for winkles and limpets. Some way removed from the rest was a lone, barefooted fellow with a wide straw hat and a haversack, kneeling down by the rockpools.

Out of the wind it was baking hot, and I felt the sweat prickle under my shirt as we began to climb up to the clifftop. Thankfully we did not ascend via the rusty-looking winch cable, but by a narrow, zigzag track with ropes anchored at various points to help pull ourselves up. Jabez lagged behind the rest of us, slashing irritably at the gorse bushes with his stick. Even in the heat, he still wore his vast brown overcoat

– which in common with most of his clothes looked like it had been looted from the dead body of a man trampled by cattle.

Artemisia had recovered her composure more or less as soon as her boots touched dry land, and when we reached Port Blyth village at the top of the goat track she disappeared off to try and rustle up some food – having deposited her breakfast in the depths some hours earlier. The wagons for Birkdale mine were lined up by the winch engine, but ore was still coming down, and it promised to be a while before the *Elsie*'s cargo was raised up off the beach and onto the back of the carts. Jabez and I flopped on a patch of grass and opened up our collars as I told him about the men on the *Barbara*.

'It was almost like they knew who I was, Jabez. And yet I could swear blind I have never seen them before in my life.'

'And it was Garrett's boat?'

'The *Barbara*, yes.'

'Rather suggests some bugger's put word out that we're coming. Not to criticise, but if I heard that some bored busybody industrialist with more money than sense was on his way to cause trouble, then I saw you lounging on the deck of a working boat like a high-class prostitute, I think I'd put two and two together.'

He was rude, but it didn't mean he was wrong.

Artemisia returned with the news that one of the local wives ran a sort of simple hostelry for the workmen who passed through Port Blyth. We took ourselves off to the woman's little garden on the edge of the village where we enjoyed a good lunch of fried fish with bread and beer. By the time we had sopped up the last of the grease off our plates, the waggoneers had finished loading, and we climbed aboard for the journey across the moor.

There was a short delay while we waited for a missing passenger to turn up, and when he finally came puffing up the cliff path it turned out to be the man in the straw hat we had seen on the beach. As he approached, he removed his hat to wipe the sweat from his brow, revealing a sun-burned, clean-shaven face and a dense shock of reddish-brown hair.

'Reverend Wilkie!' cried Artemisia in delight, leaping down from the wagon.

'Missy Moss! Is that you?'

She dropped him an approximate sort of a curtsey and he gave her an exaggerated bow in return, as if they were playing at lords and ladies. Close up, he was about my own age and a touch on the portly side, in salt-crusted breeches and shirtsleeves with a faded jacket slung over the strap of his haversack.

'Well, young lady. What a joy to see you. How long has it been since those queer old girls spirited you away? Five years?'

Artemisia glanced up at me in embarrassment as I clambered down to greet the newcomer.

'Nearly six. I'm just visiting though, not back for good. This is Mr Catcliffe, nephew to Miss Diana, come to see Yattonby. Mr Catcliffe, this is Reverend Wilkie.'

'Harry, please.' I put out my hand and he reached up to shake it warmly.

'Peter Wilkie. I'm sorry to have held you up. Time always seems to run away with me when I'm fossicking by the sea.'

He boarded our cart with Artemisia behind him, and the train of wagons began its lumbering progress up onto the moor. It was July, and already the heather was beginning to glow purple with tiny, sweet-smelling flowers, occasionally shot through with yellow veins of coconut-scented gorse. Even Jabez could not bring himself to pollute such a heady fragrance by lighting up his vile pipe. At the edge of Port Blyth village we passed a line of bee skeps, their owners no doubt hoping that some of the perfume of summer might carry through into the honey.

'The perfect Amazonian commonwealth,' said Reverend Wilkie, smiling, gesturing towards the bees and quoting no doubt from some work of poetry that I had never read.

He and Artemisia were obviously overjoyed to see each other, she in her own understated way and he in an ebullient, high-spirited manner that made him beam from ear to ear. As I became better acquainted with Pete Wilkie, I was to learn that he spent a great deal of time beaming from ear to ear. That is not to say he was some grinning village idiot, just that he was a fellow who recognised happiness and enjoyed it where he found it.

I mostly kept quiet as the wagon pitched and rolled along the rapidly deteriorating moorland tracks, leaving the two of them to catch up on the years since they had last met. She asked after his sister, who had moved away three years earlier and was apparently now married to a publisher in London. Artemisia must have been scarcely more than a girl when she left the village to work for my aunt, and I wondered at the depth of their affection. Thus far she had struck me as one of those people who others liked because they were capable rather than charismatic, but it was different with Wilkie. Here was a proper friend.

As they spoke, Artemisia fed him snippets of our own business in visiting Yattonby, hinting at a deeper purpose beyond sketching the church's misericords and rambling upon the heather. It was not long before Wilkie invited us to lodge with him, as she had been confident he would.

I took the opportunity to ask after Duke, knowing that a six-foot Indian was unlikely to go unnoticed in a place like this. The Reverend Wilkie's cheeriness faded perceptibly.

'I wondered if anyone might turn up looking for him. Is he a friend?'

'Certainly. Saved my life once.'

'Then I'm glad you have come. I've seen him – not the sort of man you'd miss – but he hasn't been around for a couple of days. The strange thing is that he's left his dog behind.'

Jabez looked up from under the frayed brim of his bowler.

'That is most unlike him,' I said, thinking of Duke's rare affection for his grotesque old bull terrier. 'Are you certain it's Cap?'

'Dead certain,' replied Wilkie. 'We have our share of curs in the village but that beast is something out of the ordinary. They're looking after it at the Bull.'

He returned to his conversation with Artemisia and I sat back on a sack of something soft and hopefully not too fragile, troubled by the news of Duke but thinking that perhaps there might be an explanation. Dawoojee Dukanwalla was a wily fellow who had survived decades of criminality, not to mention a lengthy stint in the Royal Navy. Whatever Piers Garrett was or wasn't up to, it seemed unlikely that he would be the one to put Duke in a box where so many others had failed.

After a pleasant but seemingly endless climb, the wagon train picked up a line of scalloped flagstones cutting through the heather towards a huddle of barrows on the moortop. It was an old pannier-man's causeway, the rutted mud alongside it dry and cracked in the heat. As we passed the dimpled mounds, no doubt long since robbed of whatever calcined bones and ancient trinkets they might once have contained, Birkdale opened up before us – a deep green horseshoe stamped into the moor.

The dale was about three miles from foot to head, and running halfway down its centre was a slim, wooded ridge, falling away steeply on the left into dense woodland, and on the right into long, thin fields that were peppered with livestock and scattered with high-gabled stone barns and cottages.

Far away, among a curious bare landscape of warty hummocks right at the head of the dale, I could make out the untidy workings of Ross & Blayne's drift mines. Yattonby itself was just below us, where a slender river valley linked the right-hand tip of the horseshoe to the next dale along. It was a neat little place with one main street and a couple of more modern terraces in dark red brick like railwaymen's cottages.

Set slightly apart from the village was the Reverend Wilkie's sandstone church, and a little further up the dale towards the mine stood the long, pale bulk of Haydon Castle – a battlement-capped architectural mongrel surrounded by lawns and the usual cluster of stables, cottages and outbuildings. Even on a summer's day, smoke puffed lazily from the village chimneys, and a grey haze drifted across the castle grounds from a gardener's bonfire.

The other wagons continued their slow progress towards Birkdale mines, but ours had some cargo to drop off at the village grocer's shop, so we alighted there. A group of men awaited our arrival, smoking in the sunshine much like the chaps at Port Blyth – and almost before we had come to a stop they began pulling down crates and beetling off to their various establishments with bundles of brush heads, boxes of sheet tin and stacks of that morning's newspapers, the edges blistered with salt spray.

'Now then, Missy,' said a lad in an apron, stamping out a cigarette and offering her a hand down before he got to unloading the cart.

'Good afternoon, Lyle,' she replied politely, and I saw him suppress a smirk. Evidently the woman who had left Yattonby with Aunt Diana half a decade earlier was not quite the same one who now returned to it. Lyle disappeared inside the grocer's shop with his first tea chest of provisions, and moments later an older woman's face appeared in the window, nosy for a glance at the prodigal.

We carried our bags a few minutes down the high street, past old-fashioned croft-and-toft cottages in weathered sandstone. Alleyways led through to the long, thin back gardens where people grew vegetables and kept their pigs and chickens, but the boxy little front gardens were mostly given over to flowers. There were children everywhere, brown-skinned and ragged, their cheeks and ears scabrous from sunburn. It was a commonly accepted fact that miners bred like rabbits, which was probably just as well because the mines ate them up at a similar rate.

A couple of women called out friendly greetings to Artemisia or the Reverend as we passed. Missy seemed quite popular, though halfway down the high street a smartly dressed man on horseback pulled up his beast long enough to shoot her a glare of palpable hostility.

'Afternoon, Mr Chalmers,' said Wilkie brightly.

At the far end of the village, the vicarage sat in overgrown grounds, its walls mostly hidden by leggy roses and drifts of ivy. Jabez and Artemisia went to unpack our belongings, while Wilkie and I strolled out into the garden. A maid began setting out the tea things in the shade.

'Come and look at this,' said Wilkie, leading me round to the side of the house where a small conservatory glowed with a peculiar light. Inside it there was the usual array of ferns and dracaenas, but they were hardly its dominant feature. In the windows along the south side of the greenhouse were tall, free-standing shelves full of large glass jars. These were full of a purplish liquid that I guessed was methylated spirit, and piled up in them were loosely stacked mounds of pearlescent shells, fragments of sea glass, polished ammonites and large coloured pebbles made translucent and luminous by the strong light filtering through them. It was somewhere between a natural history display and a stained-glass window. Among the terracotta planters there was a table littered with paint boxes and jam pots of dirty water. One of his specimen jars sat in the middle, and the half-finished painting nearby appeared very inexpert.

'A fellow must have his hobbies, mustn't he?' said Wilkie, flipping a limpet shell into the air with his thumb like he was tossing a coin then failing to catch it. The shell clattered off into a plant pot somewhere. 'I've never grown out of rooting around for treasures on the beach.'

'Is that meths?' I asked.

'Yes, I tried it with water but it just turned green.'

'Goodness, Reverend. A spark in the wrong place and you'd have quite a bonfire. Don't smoke, do you?'

'I would remind you that I am on the side of the angels. But I don't, just in case.'

Nineteen

The vicarage, like many of its type, was just about as chaotic as the garden. An isolated parish like this was not what you would call a desirable living, and the people who ended up in such places were mostly either the dregs of the ecclesiastical barrel or wild-eyed missionaries – intent on bringing the good news of Christianity to pagan moorlanders who still buried aborted calves under the threshold of the cow byre to ward off the evil eye of Odin.

This sort of exile from modern Great Britain also occasionally attracted out-and-out eccentrics like Peter Wilkie, and several such men had evidently left their mark on the vicarage. There were collections of birds' eggs and insects in glass cases, and a whole wall was dedicated to small paintings of rectangular bulls that all looked identical to me but presumably represented some extraordinary achievement in longhorn cattle breeding. A discoloured beekeeping outfit hung on the back of the door in my room, and a suit of armour stood to attention on the landing.

Descending to dinner later, I paused and lifted the visor to peer inside the helmet. The visible surfaces had obviously seen an occasional application of polish, but inside it was spotted with rust and the leather was crumbling away. It had a rich, acid smell like corked wine.

‘It’s much smaller than it looks, that,’ said Wilkie, emerging from his bedroom and seeing me examining this sentinel of the staircase. ‘I tried to put it on once and I didn’t stand a chance.’

Dinner at the vicarage was simple and informal, taken as it was in the company of Jabez and Artemisia. It appeared that the Reverend Peter Wilkie was one of those men who did what he felt like instead of what he was supposed to, and fortunately he lived in the sort of place where no-one was likely to kick up a fuss about it. He was from Kent originally, and it was not clear how he had ended up three hundred miles away in Birkdale.

After dinner we moved through to the drawing room, where the walls were lined with framed maps. Wilkie went to pour out some tumblers of brandy and Artemisia stretched out on the hearth rug with the familiarity of old habit.

Possessing as he did the eye of a connoisseur, Jabez appraised the various chairs in the room, lighting upon one which – from the worn arms and greasy antimacassar – was obviously not only the most comfortable but also the Reverend Wilkie’s favourite. He ran his fingers around the edges of the cushion, fished out a few coins, then sank contentedly into the chair and began counting them.

Through politeness on both sides we had not yet spoken directly of our business in Yattonby, but the time appeared right, and I began to tell Wilkie about the murder of the Porcelain Poet half a world away in a factory in South East London. He listened quietly and drank his brandy, and when I was done he paused for a long time, as all good vicars and police interrogators are presumably trained to do.

‘I’m afraid for my own part I can’t give you much beyond what Missy has already told you. As she says, very few local staff still work there, and those that do are awfully tight-lipped. Most villagers were given their marching orders a while back – the Garrett family brought in their own people from London and they all live up at the castle and keep to themselves. You can imagine it hasn't endeared them to the rest of Yattonby.

'I can tell you they've become very protective of the estate, at any rate. The whole western arm of the dale is Horncastle land. It's all woodland over on that side and it used to be a lovely place for a walk, but it's strictly off limits now. Then they've fenced off the Ernecliffe – that sort of island that runs down the centre of the dale – plus most of the east side of the dale between my church and the outskirts of the mines.'

He cast his eyes in vain about the room for a map of the local area, but they all seemed to be of districts in Russia and the Far East.

'The miners can use the road to get to Birkdale Head,' he continued, 'but woe betide anyone who strays off it onto the estate either side. One young man got quite a bad beating off the new keepers a while back.'

'Any idea why?'

'The official line, as far as anyone knows, is that they're concerned about disturbing the game. Mr Garrett's a shooting nut, they say. Mostly deer and expensive birds, but rumours are he's got some odder quarry too. They say he goes out into the woods at night with his head gamekeeper knocking off badgers.'

Jabez snorted into his glass of brandy, though perhaps mainly to draw attention to the fact that it was nearly empty.

'I'm not saying it's true,' added Wilkie, hastily. 'The thing about a man like Mr Garrett is that he does tend to attract a lot of rumour, and I suppose you can't believe the half of it.'

'He certainly does not seem popular.'

'No.'

'My old man thinks he's a wretch.'

'Does he indeed? I daresay you'd find some round here who'd agree. Though in truth very few people have met him. I've only run into him briefly a couple of times. Not really long enough to form an impression. He doesn't come to church, though the Horncastles do.'

'I heard Horncastle is a bit of a wet fish.'

Wilkie glanced across at his old friend by the fire with a smirk. She had fallen asleep, though none of us had noticed.

'I suppose Missy told you that. She doesn't care for him, for various reasons. I suspect he's a more complicated fellow than people think he is. Whatever the case, I think he might be your way into Haydon Castle. He and Lady Horncastle will be at church tomorrow and I can introduce you.'

I thanked him. It was a good start but there was still something preying on my mind.

'I wonder, Peter, if we might not take a mug or two of beer at the Bull? I am keen to discover what they may know of our friend Mr Dukanwalla.'

'Best idea I've heard all day,' interjected Jabez from the vicar's armchair.

'By all means, though you may wish to temper your expectations, Mr Potter.'

I told him he need not fear, for the bar was very low.

'Just as well,' said Wilkie, lifting himself stiffly from his chair and smoothing the curled points of his waistcoat. 'When the prophet Isiah wrote so colourfully about the end of the earth, he spoke of a place where all joy is darkened, where the mirth of the land is gone, and where strong drink tastes bitter to them that drink it. Business as usual at the Bull, I would say.'

TWENTY

If Wilkie's appraisal of his village pub was not very charitable, it was at least accurate in one respect – since the Bull looked like it had been built to withstand the apocalypse. A squat droving inn of rough sandstone with tiny windows and walls three feet thick, it was a sort of miniature castle that reeked of dogs and coal smoke and the very roughest tobacco. The stocky, unsmiling men inside it spoke in such a rich and incomprehensible dialect that they sounded more Danish than English, giving the impression that they might have been a Viking garrison somehow overlooked during the Harrowing of the North. I thought it quite agreeable.

As we made our way to the bar, I heard Jabez cooing in a most uncharacteristic fashion at something under one of the tables. Sure enough, a lump of scarred canine muscle with a head like a damaged egg roused itself from the shadows and shuffled over to nuzzle affectionately at his hairy knuckles.

'Cap!' Somehow it was a joy to see Duke's old dog so far from home.

'Wandered in yesterday morning and just curled up under't table,' said the dour publican as he found us three pint pots. He was missing several finger joints on one hand and part of his face had been badly burned.

'Normally my lad chases 'em out but he were scared of that 'un. I quite like him though.'

I looked back to where Cap was wiping drool lovingly on Jabez's filthy trousers and remembered the appalling savagery with which I had once seen him attack a man. Duke had bought him in the first place because he lost so much money on him at the fighting pit that he became worried he would be fed to the more profitable dogs. Cap seemed to inspire this odd sort of affection in unsentimental men.

I asked the landlord what he could tell me of Duke, which was not very much. My friend had arrived with no luggage save a haversack and a rolled-up blanket, and had stayed the night in one of the rooms upstairs. He had made himself amenable in the pub that evening, striking up conversations and getting on quite well with several of the locals despite the twin shortcomings of being both cagey about his business and foreign. The next morning he had left after breakfast with his dog shuffling along behind, mentioning that he might be back in a couple of days. That was Thursday, the day of the rainstorm. The letter I had sent him from London after Alf Bickley died had been forwarded on from Whitby and was still waiting for him behind the bar, unopened.

'I will take the dog for the time being if you want rid of him,' I offered.

The landlord turned away and flicked some of his remaining fingers at me dismissively, so as not to reveal too clearly the pocket of softness that obviously lay somewhere within.

'No, you're all right. Leave 'im here. Just till t'Indian come back.'

Wilkie told me later that our host had formerly worked for Ross & Blayne until an accident had driven him above ground. Injury and industry, one being the hidden but inevitable consequence of the other – rather like one never sees a child in a whorehouse.

In fact, many of the men in there that night were miners. Strong little men of the sort that worked in the light press shop at Catcliffe Steel, only dusty rather than oily, with gaiters and stained beards and bad lungs.

'The mine pays better than the farms,' Wilkie said, 'but not much.'

We took a table against the wall and Wilkie greeted the drinkers next to us by their first names as we sat. It was a Saturday night – two weeks since Abraham Bickley had taken his ill-fated walk home from the Two Brewers – but the atmosphere was not especially cheerful.

'The mine's not doing well,' explained Wilkie. '"Loss and Pain", the miners call it. They've had to let eighteen men go since May. Ross and Blayne will be spitting feathers over the business – it's only five years since they paid old Lord Horncastle seventy thousand pounds to renew their mining lease, on top of tonnage royalties.'

'Hard-nosed old boy?'

'Not usually, but his health had been failing for a while and it was part of a very deliberate last-ditch stand to get the estate on a secure footing before I buried him. He'd already brought in a sharp new agent five years earlier – that chap with the horse we saw on the high street this afternoon – then he played it tough with Ross and Blayne and married his eldest son off to Alice Garrett for good measure.'

'And then fell off his perch, I imagine,' said Jabez.

'More or less,' said Wilkie. 'Perhaps no bad thing. It might have been crueller to live long into his dotage, gradually relinquishing his estate to the Garrett regime. They say he ought to have realised it would happen, but I'm not sure.'

He applied himself to his pint for a moment. The Reverend Peter Wilkie had an unusual and tremendously fast way of drinking. He would grip his pint pot between two fingers and thumb and sort of toss the beer at his face.

'For all his kindness, Lord Horncastle was a bit of a snob,' he explained. 'I imagine he thought he could handle the likes of Piers Garrett, but these industrialists are pirates.'

He realised as he said this that he was speaking to one – albeit a very low-grade buccaneer – and swiftly excused himself to replenish our drinks with an awkward smile.

In London pubs, the Cockneys liked to sing, and there was normally some veiny-nosed old boy with a rude nickname bashing out corny tunes on the piano. No such southern levity in the Bull – which at least meant I could eavesdrop on the neighbouring table while Wilkie was at the bar. They did not look like miners, and in fact one of them was the village shopkeeper we'd seen earlier when we arrived in Yattonby.

'Good-looking lass these days,' the man was saying. 'She were such a scrawny thing afore.'

'Parson'll be pleased, any road,' said another in an undertone, glancing up to where Wilkie was chatting to the publican. 'Allus did 'ave a soft spot for Missy Richardson.'

'Mrs Ewart from't castle saw her in Whitby a while back. Says she's calling herself Missy Moss now.'

'Aye, well I suppose there's no harm in it.'

Their conversation switched abruptly to another topic as Wilkie returned, but Jabez's beady little bird's eye remained on them for the rest of the evening and I could tell he had been listening too.

Wilkie was accompanied by one of the miners, a youngish man with rounded shoulders and hair that was thinning at the front.

'Harry Catcliffe, Sam Creedy,' he said, indicating us each in turn. 'I was hoping we might run into Sam in here.'

We shook hands and he sat. It turned out the reason Wilkie thought I might like to talk to Mr Creedy was that he had been a gamekeeper up at Haydon.

'Shifted out at end o' summer last,' he explained in his thick moorland accent, 'like everyone else. But I was born here, didn't want to leave, so I took a job off Ross and Blayne and went into the mine.'

'I see. And who replaced you?'

'Well, see, that's the funny thing. They've got more keepers now than they ever had before, but I'd say they don't know a right lot about game. I didn't see a single crow trap on the moor in spring. No corn stooks for feed, nor grit and water. Heather growing rank and woody. Boils my piss. The season's about to begin and I'll bet the grouse stocks are bloody rotten.'

According to Sam Creedy, the Horncastles had never enjoyed much success running the Haydon estate as a commercial grouse shoot. Even when the coastal train line wasn't buried in five feet of sludge, the nearest station was several miles away. The toffs and tycoons who could afford a fortnight's lease on a grouse moor in high season were sticklers for convenience, and a multistage journey involving two branch lines and a coach was far too convoluted. But then young Lord Horncastle had married Alice Garrett.

'Thought we were onto a winner that first year after Garrett came. He got a new head keeper in. American. Funny fish, but what he didn't know about game wasn't worth knowing. The castle took on extra staff, we ran that moorland better than ever, and had one o' t'best seasons anyone could remember. Shooting parties every week – Garrett was mad for 'em. Rich Europeans, industry men, politicians, the works.

'Then he just lost interest. Can't have been much past mid-September of last year. Plenty of the season left, but the parties stopped. He took to shooting deer and pheasant in the woods instead. Laid us all off – every last one except his American – and replaced us with these new lads. Rough bastards, not one of them with a family in tow. They live in a converted stable block at the castle and you never see 'em in here.'

'And you say they don't seem to do anything a normal gamekeeper would?'

'Oh, bits and bobs – but not what I'd be on with. Maybe they've just given up on the moors to work in the woods instead. But whatever else they're doing or not doing, they're hellish sharp on poachers.'

Mr Creedy was obviously a few drinks down, and I suddenly noticed he was speaking with a gloss on his eyes. This being the danger with stoic and plain-spoken men, that you never know you're winding them up until you've already done it.

Sam Creedy was upset because he wasn't the only one in his family who had been laid off, and it was this part of his story that really made me prick up my ears.

'My cousin, Tom. He was a keeper like me on the estate, only when they laid us off he went over to the other side. Took to poaching after his shifts at Ross and Blayne. I told him it was a bad idea but he was always too cocky.

'Wages round here aren't much good,' he explained. 'Can't make more than seventeen and six a week down the mine, and that's still better than farm work. You can get decent money selling a little fur and feather on the side if you're smart.'

Tom Creedy had gone missing one night a month or so earlier after dropping some cryptic comment about putting a feather in his cap. He had walked out of the pub with a grin on his face and they never saw him again.

'It was a full moon,' said his cousin grimly, 'and I know Tom wasn't the only one hunting in the woods that night. We heard gunshots from our house later on, and it wouldn't have been him. He used a longdog and an air gun, much quieter that way.

'Tried to ask at the castle but I couldn't get past the gate. Spoke to Chalmers, the agent, when I went to pay my rent, but he gave me the hard word – asked me what exactly I was implying – and I said nothing, and he said good, because he wouldn't be putting up with tenants imputing their betters.'

Impugning, I thought, but I resisted the temptation to say it.

The hopelessness of it took Sam Creedy to the bottom of his pint glass and back to the bar. Wilkie went with him. He bought him another, then left the man with his mates and returned to Jabez and me.

'You see why I wanted you to hear him out.'

'I do, Peter. Though I don't understand why he can't just tell the police about his cousin's disappearance.'

‘Because he was breaking the law,’ butted in Jabez. ‘Dead or alive, if they find him then it’s the poaching they’ll be bothered about.’

Jabez Potter had a low opinion of the police – a state of affairs that was entirely mutual.

‘You’ll find,’ said Wilkie, ‘that the law doesn’t really reach as far as Yattonby. We have a village bobby, but his authority is firmly in third place behind the castle and the mine.’

Twenty-One

Reverend Wilkie's rambling sermon about good trees and bad fruit seemed none the worse for all the beer and brandy he had drunk the night before, and the parishioners who packed out his pews sang as lustily as any Wesleyans. This was not ideal for one who felt so vinegary inside as I did, and I had ungodly thoughts towards a reedy tenor in the row behind.

The church – like the pub – looked to have been built to withstand direct assault by artillery fire, but inside it was in a state of pronounced dilapidation. The effects of long, damp winters were evident throughout, several of the windows were cracked, and the sandstone floor was so pitted and uneven that many a bride must have taken a tumble as she skipped down the aisle to meet her beloved. Parishioners were obliged to enter through the west door because the eastern one was stuck fast – and since it was out of commission, a vagrant had begun nesting in the porch outside, returning each summer like a house martin.

'How, then, does one tell the ravening wolf in sheep's clothing?' asked Wilkie, pausing for effect then slowly raising his forefinger. 'I'll tell you how, for it is written, "Ye shall know them by their fruits"...'

There was a commotion at the back as a bow-legged man sprang to his feet to chase out a couple of stray dogs, having already done so twice since the service began. It was evidently his particular job, and he was conscientious about it because his Lord in heaven was watching from above.

His lords on earth were watching too. At the back was a raised gallery in which Birkdale's more exalted residents looked down on the dog-whipper and his fellows. Glancing back from my pew near the front of the church, I could see a middle-aged man with jug ears and a large family – later discovered to be the mine manager – along with a variety of dishevelled old boys and their wives. The gentlemen looked like retired whaling captains and the ladies appeared to have bought their dresses when my aunt Diana was a rosy-cheeked schoolgirl, which perhaps they had. Set among this crowd, the Horncastles were not difficult to spot.

After the service they joined the general milieu swapping the pleasantries of the day in the churchyard, and Wilkie swiftly introduced us before billowing off to make sure no palm remained ungrasped.

Lord Horncastle appeared distinctly unlike my image of him. A fair, broad-shouldered fellow a little younger than myself and – I thought – rather well-dressed in the sort of dark brown striped three-piece suit that my father would have considered thoroughly inappropriate Sunday wear. He went clean shaven and sported a boater with a black silk band, his only sartorial crime in my book being that he wore it poker straight. He appeared robust, slightly dandyish and better looking than most – no doubt he had once been considered quite a catch for anyone with enough money to prop up his ailing estate.

The former Miss Alice Garrett had probably been quite a catch too, and aesthetically I thought her Roman nose particularly fine in a world obsessed with the daintier varieties. Wilkie told me they had been married somewhere impressive in London, which was a shame because for such an elegant couple to shackle themselves together in St Stephen's might have been rather a kindness to the shabby old church. Like her husband, Lady Horncastle wore an old-fashioned boater over her pinned-up hair, but hers was tilted well forward, presumably to emphasise that she was not a governess or an orphan. Her dress was an off-white affair with puffed sleeves, a pouched bodice and a good deal of lace about it. The waist had been let out some inches to accommodate what a few months down the line would perhaps be an heir to both the Horncastle estate and the Garrett fortune, if it were fortunate enough to be born male.

Lady Horncastle was one of those young women to whom you are either of significance or you are not. Having sized me up with some interest during Wilkie's brief introduction – presumably on account of my scarred face and good suit – she evidently decided I belonged in the latter category, and immediately assumed a vacant expression of polite boredom.

'You are in industry, then, Mr Catcliffe?' enquired Lord Horncastle pleasantly.

'Steel. Catcliffe Steel, of Leeds, Keighley and London.'

'My father-in-law is a fellow industrialist. No doubt you are acquainted.'

People who did not run factories always assumed all grubby plutocrats knew each other, in much the same way that Americans think everyone in Great Britain has met the King.

'Perhaps. What is his name?' I was a diabolical actor.

'Mr Piers Garrett.'

'Well, of course I know Mr Garrett by reputation, though we have not met.' This was easier, since it was misleading but technically true.

'Your father is a very successful fellow,' I said to Lady Horncastle.

'Yes,' she replied, her eyes half-focused on something about six feet behind me.

She was obviously in no mood to waste words, and left it at that.

'Well, we should see about introducing you, if you have the time,' said Horncastle. 'Do you shoot?'

'Dreadfully.'

This included having once shot a man and made a thoroughly bad job of it, but I didn't mention that. Horncastle smiled with a mix of indulgence and good humour. He himself was sure to be a crack shot.

'Dinner, then. Much safer for all concerned.'

We were interrupted by the arrival of the Dowager Lady Horncastle, who presumably had stayed behind in the gallery until the church was empty so that the indignity of being carried down the stairs would remain a private one.

A handsome couple Lord and Lady Horncastle may have been, but of the three of them it was the dowager who most arrested the eye. Though she cannot have been much older than my own mother, she seemed quite ancient. She defied the summery garb of the younger generation with a heavy black dress that must have been punishing to wear in that heat, and the wispy grey hair under her wide straw hat was like smoke streaming from her temples. At first glance her face seemed expressionless, but as I bowed in greeting, the edge of her mouth twitched in a gesture not unlike my aunt Diana. The dowager, or course, was half paralysed by a stroke, whereas Diana had no excuse.

She gripped a cane in one trembling hand – perhaps to make the point that she could walk if she chose – but was wheeled about in a chair by a prim lady's maid with shoulders like a boxer. Old Lady Horncastle did not speak, and I later learned from Wilkie that she could not. Some cerebral spring or retaining pin struck loose during the impact of her stroke, not yet repaired.

'My mother hears and understands perfectly well,' Horncastle reassured me.

I made some banal observations about the weather and how much I looked forward to visiting the castle, at which she nodded and looked slightly less bored than her daughter-in-law. I asked Horncastle if, during my stay at Yattonby, I might be permitted to do some sketching from the raised plateau of the Ernecliffe. This, at least, provoked a faint glimpse of interest from the younger Lady Horncastle, but it was directed at her husband instead of me, and he seemed to pause for just a moment under her eyes.

'Well, yes. I mean, I do not see why not. Though I would ask respectfully that you do not go into the woods on the west side of the dale.' He was talking to me but obviously making a point to his wife. 'My gamekeepers are trialling a new form of pheasant rearing and I gather the method leaves the birds very vulnerable to disturbance. Even we at the castle do not venture in there if we can help it.'

I gave him all the necessary assurances, then wished the Horncastles a good day.

'I shall send you a note at the vicarage,' promised Horncastle.

When we left the church, Artemisia had peeled off to talk to a group of local women. Now, as I made my way towards the lychgate, I found her standing over one of the newer gravestones at the end of a row.

It went without saying that Jabez had not accompanied us to church, since the sight of the cross might have sent him up in a puff of smoke.

'Renewing old acquaintances, Artemisia?' I asked as we walked out of the gate, passing a coachman in a cockaded silk hat who waited patiently for the Horncastles. 'Must be good to be back.'

'In some ways, sir,' she replied. 'I've been away a long time.'

Twenty-Two

I had told Lord Horncastle several lies, the biggest of which was that I would stay clear of the western woods. If his father-in-law's gamekeepers did not want us snooping round that side of the dale, then it was almost certain to be of interest. We were, however, not quite foolish enough to start trespassing upon the forbidden woods in broad daylight, so on that warm Sunday lunchtime we made a show of carrying our sketching materials up onto the Ernecliffe, as we had mentioned to Horncastle we would.

As a man who has always enjoyed dressing for an occasion, I put on a stout belt and rolled the bottoms of my trousers. I had neglected to bring a straw hat, but Wilkie had several – in various stages of disintegration – and topped off with one of the scruffier ones, there could be no doubt that I was a gentleman very seriously involved in leisure pursuits.

We loaded our haversacks up with paper, pencils, paint boxes and canteens of water, and with drawing boards and blankets under our arms we set out, skirting fields and clambering over fences towards where the Ernecliffe crested out of the valley floor like a hog's back. It was a steep climb but not a long one, following tunnels through the high bracken that seemed to act like greenhouses, trapping a tremendous amount of heat and deadening the air.

We emerged, panting and perspiring, onto the heathery spine of the Ernecliffe, and laid out our kit at the edge of a small hollow where a couple of straggly rowan trees provided a little shade. A warm breeze gave delicious relief after the sweltering doldrums of the bracken, chilling the sweat that had soaked through our shirts. To one side of us, the fields and farms rolled down into the hazy terraces of Yattonby, while on the other side, the woods filled the valley below us, dark and cool and inviting. Yorkshiremen have always liked to tell people that their territory is God's own country, but on such afternoons as these it truly did feel like the land of milk and honey.

Artemisia unpacked some sandwiches and bottles of beer, and the four of us lazed in the sun all afternoon, sketching and snoozing or just watching the world. Jabez disparagingly compared a protuberance on the horizon to something anatomical, and I could tell he was having a nice time because he was only ever so self-consciously crude when he felt suddenly in danger of happiness.

Eventually, when most of the heat had gone out of the day and the sun was well on its way down to nest in the moortops, I started to make a show of packing up my haversack.

'Come on then. If we're going to get a look in the woods while there's still a bit of light, now is the time.'

Jabez sat up with exaggerated slowness and a meaningful glare in my direction, while Wilkie continued to snore peacefully until Artemisia woke him.

'Time to be getting on, Reverend,' she said softly.

'Oh, yes, yes, right away.' He picked up the drawing he had been working on and appraised it with a critical eye. It appeared that sketching was perhaps not the Reverend Wilkie's chief talent. His depiction of Yattonby looked like a steamship being attacked by whales, but he seemed pleased with it all the same.

We left our gear under the rowan trees to retrieve later, and set off for the woods. Most of the western edge of the Ernecliffe was a sheer cliff dropping straight down into the tree canopy, so the path led us along to the southern end of the ridge, before taking a series of steep switchbacks down to join a narrow lane running along the valley floor. The cracked mud was rutted with cart tracks, terminating at a gate with a big black and white sign on it.

PRIVATE WOODLAND NO TRESPASSING

'As we forgive them that trespass against us,' said Wilkie, finishing the joke that I had considered too obvious to make out loud.

There were signs of considerable activity around the gate – foot and hoof prints, horse manure, bits of wire and empty glass bottles, but once we climbed over it and crossed into the trees, the place felt untouched save for the narrow footpaths that had been kept clear of vegetation.

Even on such a warm evening, it was damp and fresh in the western woods. The leaf litter under our feet was soft and springy, and I could hear a stream trickling away somewhere nearby. It must have been very ancient woodland, and the canopy was so thick that the forest floor was relatively clear of scrub – though some former Lord Horncastle had evidently seen fit to introduce rhododendron bushes, which in some places formed dense thickets of glossy, alien foliage.

'You can see why people in Yattonby are sore about not being allowed in here any more,' said Wilkie. 'It used to be a lovely spot for a Sunday stroll.'

The place was infested with pheasants – craven, stupid things that sprinted awkwardly away down the rides or burst noisily from the bushes, clucking hysterically. All apart from one, that is, which darted out from behind a tree, launched itself into the air and tried to bite Jabez. It was bigger than the others, with a long tail like a peacock, gold scales around its neck and a black and white face.

Plucky as it was, the bird had unfortunately picked on the only thing in the western woods more aggressive than itself, and it was forced to beat a hasty retreat, scuttling off into the undergrowth with a strange warbling noise.

'What the bloody hell was that?' barked Jabez.

'A Reeves's pheasant,' supplied Wilkie. 'They're Chinese.'

'Oh well that explains it then,' said Jabez with some bitterness. 'What's it doing here?'

'They put it in here for the shoots,' explained Artemisia.

'Sort of like a joker in the pack? Win the pot if you hit it, that kind of thing?'

'The opposite. Case of whisky for the keepers if you hit it.'

'Madness.'

'Not if you're a keeper,' said Artemisia. 'My father was one. Loved it when they put a Reeves's in the woods. Someone always got it.'

'No-one hit it last season though, did they?' I said thoughtfully.

I disliked shooting, probably because I was so poor at it, but I had done it quite a few times over the years – my old Grandpa Catcliffe, rest his soul, had been obsessed. I knew enough to recognise that most of the birds around us were last year's adults. If Garrett was really so mad on pheasants, his woods ought to have been swarming with newly released poults by now.

'I'd shoot it soon as look at it,' said Jabez, watching his attacker having a go at another cock pheasant instead. He did not care for anything Chinese, blaming the entire nation and a worldwide diaspora of millions for the loss of his leg at Langfang in June 1900.

Pleasant as it was, our search did not turn up nearly as much as we might have hoped. There was a scarred tree that had lately been used for target practice, a rotted cloth cap half buried in the muddy stream bank, and couple of neglected snares, one of which contained the remains of a fox. Strangely, the brush of its tail was still bushy and bright, while the rest of it looked like an old leather apron tossed over a tiny shipwreck.

As dusk started to close in, we turned our footsteps back towards home, and it wasn't long afterwards that Wilkie spotted something glinting off to the side of the path. Stooping to grub it out, he held up a large brass cartridge.

'Jabez, old boy. What do you make of that?'

The little ex-marine took it and inspected it for a moment.

'Must be bloody big badgers he's shooting.'

He passed it across to me.

'I've fired thousands of them. It's a .303. I was carrying a rifle that shot those cartridges when I fought the Boxers.'

'Might they be using it for deer, do you think?'

He stuck his nicotine-stained lip out.

'Couldn't say. Ask a country boy. It would do the job, though.'

We picked over the area again on the off-chance that there was anything else, but without any luck.

'That's enough,' I said, slipping the cartridge into my pocket. 'Let's get our gear and head home.'

It was peaceful in the woods, but I still didn't fancy getting caught in there by Horncastle's gamekeepers after dark.

Twenty-Three

Horncastle was as good as his word, and Monday morning brought a note inviting Wilkie and me to dine with them that night at Haydon Castle.

'You must be an important fellow,' said Wilkie, bashing in the top of his boiled egg with a spoon. 'It's been a long time since this humble country parson has darkened the door of the big house. Not since the old Lord Horncastle was still alive.'

We strolled over in the drowsy early evening, prickling with sweat inside our evening dress and harried by flies from the hedgerows. The castle gates were shut, but a man sitting outside the lodge was expecting us.

'It's a five-minute walk up the drive to the main door,' he told us in a Bristolian accent that felt distinctly out of place in a Yorkshire dale. I heard him lock the gates behind us once we were through.

So intrigued was I by the prospect of finally meeting Piers Garrett that it had not occurred to me that he would have a wife – but in hindsight the existence of Alice did make this likely.

Tall and extravagantly dressed in that unimaginative way very rich people often are, Ellen Garrett was of a type occasionally to be found among my mother's friends. She knew everything and everyone and her welcome as we entered the drawing room at Haydon was so expansive that you almost forgot the castle wasn't actually hers.

'How are your parents, Mr Catcliffe? I used to see them all the time at the opera but we have changed our night. Your mother and I both thought last year's Don Giovanni was very poor, but they will insist on trying to reinvent the wheel.'

I began to respond, but she had already moved on to Wilkie, commiserating brightly about how dilapidated his church was looking these days.

'Haydon's not far behind,' she added. 'But fortunately Piers has begun a schedule of renovations to the old pile.'

Horncastle stood quietly in the background as his mother-in-law explained how his ancestral home was going to be salvaged from his own family's long-term neglect. If he felt the implied criticism then he was polite or shrewd enough not to show it, and he smiled and nodded throughout as if he were very much interested in her plans. For my own part, conversations about other people's home improvement schemes usually hit me like chloroform.

What I *did* find interesting was that the great industrialist himself was nowhere to be seen. Presently, when a tray of drinks broke Ellen Garrett's flow, she explained:

'You must excuse Piers. He has some correspondence to finish. Business leaves him so little time for pleasure, but he will join us for dinner.'

It seemed, however, that Mrs Garrett had a consolation prize in store – and talk of Haydon Castle gave way to discussion of that lady's other passion – her kennels.

'Dog breeding,' she declared, 'is an art as much as it is a science. I have bred working spaniels since I was a little girl, and Haydon has given me plenty to get my teeth into.'

It turned out the Haydon Hunt had died the death a decade or so earlier – providing another passing opportunity for her to bash the old Lord Horncastle – but the castle still kept spaniels and Labrador retrievers.

'I'm sorry to say that the breeding here has not been of the best,' she lamented with some relish. 'I am sure Horncastle won't mind me noting that his father was not a stickler in that regard.'

For the first time, Horncastle's smile appeared briefly more genuine than well-mannered.

'He always kept lurchers lounging about the place,' he explained. 'Long-legged mongrels that got their noses into everything. It was one of his small eccentricities – he used to go rabbiting with them at dusk.'

'He bought them from *gyp-sies*, apparently,' said Ellen Garrett, pronouncing the word in two halves to imply a whole paragraph of subtext.

She shook her head in indulgent disapproval, then raised one finger theatrically.

'Though in some ways his fondness for high-performing cross-breeds continues at Haydon...'

There was a dramatic pause until I dutifully asked, 'How so?'

'Well,' she began with considerable pride, 'I am currently developing a new breed of hunting hound right here at the castle. Our head gamekeeper has been working on the mix for some years, and with the addition of my own expertise, the work has come on leaps and bounds.'

'Literally, I imagine.'

'We still have a little way to go, and have not yet finalised the name – but we rather like "the Haydon Courser". A nod to Horncastle *Père*'s mongrels, don't you see? Piers and I are confident that it will be one of the most outstanding and versatile hunting breeds in the country. Perhaps the world.

'Piers hunts with them regularly, and he pronounces them unrivalled in the pursuit of larger game. On a trip to Scotland in the spring, he told me that one of the girls, Heckie, brought down a *huge* red deer stag. I wish I could have seen it.'

I felt that same sense of inevitability as when a certain sort of man begins to talk about his art collection. That crescendo of increasingly insistent foreplay, at the climax of which you are supposed to request a viewing and be generously conducted to an underwhelming collection of paintings that are all 'after' someone famous rather than actually by them.

There seemed no sense in drawing the business out any longer, so I politely asked if we had time before dinner for a visit to the kennels. Ellen Garret made a show of checking the carriage clock, began to demur, then flapped her hand as if to silence her own fussiness. It was masterfully done.

'Would you be good enough to send word to McCrea?' asked Mrs Garrett, turning to the butler. 'Our guest would like to see my dogs.'

The fellow nodded in turn to a footman, who bowed obediently and withdrew.

'Mr McCrea is our head gamekeeper,' she explained, 'from the United States. We were really very lucky to secure his services, and he has bred and trained the doggies himself.'

Alice looked even more bored than usual.

'I shall stay with Mother-in-Law,' she announced sweetly, and swept across the room to where old Lady Horncastle appeared to be in no need of company. The dowager sat in an armchair by the open French doors, gazing out at the evening light on the lawn and drinking determinedly, her glass of gin clutched in a shaking fist.

Mrs Garrett led the assembled party out onto the terrace, around the side of the house and through a gate into a cobbled courtyard surrounded by rough stone outbuildings. As we approached, a booming bark issued from the nearest of these, quickly joined by a chorus of howling at various different pitches from several of the other buildings. Our arrival thus heralded, the stable door opened and a broad-shouldered, sandy-haired man emerged. He was dressed in shabby brown corduroy breeches and waistcoat, with heavy boots and high leather gaiters. His open collar and rolled sleeves showed skin burned brown and leathery by the sun.

'Please excuse Mr McCrea his working appearance,' said Ellen Garrett hastily – and unnecessarily, in fact, since no-one was really looking at the head gamekeeper but at the massive beast that plodded at his side on a thick length of rope.

The dog stood waist-high and must have weighed the same as a middleweight boxer, with a glossy, fawn-coloured body, a heavy neck and a long black muzzle that it carried low in an unusual, prowling sort of gait. The thing was muscled like a prize bull. Horncastle looked distinctly uncomfortable, but Mrs Garrett approached it with enthusiasm and it lapped a huge slab of tongue affectionately at the back of her slender hand.

I liked dogs well enough, but mainly the pet ones my extended family kept. Lazy greyhounds draped across the hearth rug or appealing little terriers that rolled over to show you their tummies then bit you for no good reason. Not these giant canine codpieces.

'Argo's grandparents were Turkish herding dogs,' she announced with considerable pride. 'His ancestors in Asia Minor have defended their masters' flocks from wolves and lions for thousands of years. Their intelligence and courage are just wonderful.'

She began to look misty-eyed, and I had that sensation – experienced so often in life – that it would be nice to skip forward a few pages.

'Consider,' she said, 'that the breed is largely unaltered since ancient times. When Agamemnon and Achilles first made landfall on Trojan shores – now widely accepted to be in modern-day Anatolia – they would have beheld virtually identical beasts standing majestically on the hilltops, guarding their flocks. Just think of it, a living link to the age of gods and heroes.'

'Of course, Mrs Garrett, that's only part of his story,' prompted McCrea with a cockeyed smile, his New World accent making him sound more polite than he looked.

'Well *yes*,' she said, scratching Argo behind his big drooping steak of an ear. 'You see, Mr Catcliffe, the Turkish shepherd is a livestock guardian, despite its size. To make them into hunters, Mr McCrea has crossed them with some of the fiercest and most powerful breeds in existence.

'We have four "Haydon Coursers" here – Argo here and three bitches: Iffie, Penny and Heckie. Properly Iphigenia, Penelope and Hecuba, but two syllables is about as long as you can go for training purposes. Sadly, our biggest boy, Ajax, died last month, but we plan for a litter of puppies when Penny next comes in season.'

Argo nuzzled her bodice adoringly, but I wouldn't have taken a step closer without a few more drinks in me.

'It is very unlikely that you will ever see another dog like this one, you know,' she continued with pride. 'The Turks value them so highly that they simply will not export them, and Mr McCrea had to spend a year on the Anatolian plateau gaining their trust before they would allow him to ship a single breeding pair to America. Their descendants are found only on the McCrea family ranch in Wyoming and here at Haydon.'

'What took you to Turkey, Mr McCrea?' I asked with genuine interest. 'I spent a little time there myself after university, though I confess I was more diverted by the tortoises.'

'Hunter,' said the American. 'Hunted all my life. My countrymen like to travel for exotic game, but to do that they need folk with local knowledge. That's what I do. A year or two here, a year or two there. Hunted most everywhere – Africa, Asia, Europe, America.'

'From the plains of the Serengeti to the grouse moors of Yorkshire.' I smiled, wondering just how much money it had taken to tempt him from the one to the other. Yank financiers loved the pomp of British driven shooting, but I couldn't see a career big-game man finding much satisfaction trapping crows and popping away at little brown birds.

'Argo's grandparents weren't the only dogs Mr McCrea shipped home from his travels,' interjected Ellen Garrett, slightly peevish that the conversation was drifting onto the gamekeeper's life history instead of her own prize possessions. 'That's what makes his hounds so special. They are crossed with Indian mastiffs and bulldogs from the Transvaal. For a time we toyed with christening the breed "the Transcontinental" – only it sounded rather too much like the name of an hotel.

'I flatter myself that I have improved the breed still further since they arrived at Haydon. When Mr McCrea came over here from America, he was persuaded to bring a pair of dogs from his ranch, which I rechristened Ajax and Cassandra. Sadly a bout of disease in kennels killed Cassie and most of her first litter except Argo and Iffie. Penny and Heckie are Iffie's pups, but we couldn't breed her with her father or brother, so we had to get an outside stud in. They may have ancient Greek names,' she tittered in a way that made me suspect I was about to hear a very well-worn quip, 'but their ways are not *quite* so incestuous.'

I had already lost track of who was who. As subjects for conversation went, I began to wonder whether canine genealogy might be an even more powerful anaesthetic than interior design.

McCrea led Argo back indoors, and at Mrs Garrett's insistence we followed him. The din as we filed inside was deafening – deep bass booms like the presses back at Catcliffe's, accompanied by the rattling of metal – but a word from the gamekeeper and the barking stopped abruptly.

Inside the stable, the line of stalls had been modified with heavy cage doors, behind which the remaining dogs were kept. Argo had a cell to himself – presumably to frustrate any ancient Greek impulses – as did his sister Iffie. The younger ones, Penny and Heckie, were in together. These two were almost as tall as Argo, but leaner, not quite so heavy around the neck, with deeper chests and longer muzzles. One was sleek and tan, the other dark with a broken coat.

These ladies, no doubt, represented the next step in canine perfection, and once Argo was safely contained in his bachelor quarters, McCrea called the lighter-coloured one to the door of her cage, slipped a rope on her and brought her out. Close up, her shoulders were like giant hams. She was obedient to a fault but I still didn't much enjoy being in a confined space with her.

'Since we were obliged to dilute them, we crossed Iffie with a champion Russian wolfhound. I can't tell you how lucky we were to secure his services. His owner only agreed as a special favour to my husband. Heckie's coat has come out wrong so we won't breed from her – which is a shame because she's wonderfully fast.'

Ellen Garret ran a hand admiringly down the flank of the one they called Penelope.

'We're aiming for a bit more bulk with the next generation, so when Penny comes into season we'll cross her with Argo.'

Uncle Argo, I thought. Still sounded fairly incestuous to me.

'Ought to have called them Claudius and Agrippina,' I joked, then regretted it when everyone looked at me with blank incomprehension. All except Wilkie, who didn't get the joke either, but grinned encouragingly because he wanted me to think someone had enjoyed it.

For all Mrs Garrett's mind-numbing talk of bloodlines and attributes, it sounded to me like they'd just got a big thing and kept crossing it with other big things without ever thinking whether any of it was actually a good idea. A chaotic monster laboratory in an old barn, overseen by a dead-eyed career hunter and a would-be lady-of-the-manor with too much money and time on her hands.

Twenty-Four

As we returned through the gardens, I could hear music drifting faintly from the open French doors. A strangled recording of some big Russian with hands like dustbin lids beating the stuffing out of a piano. The dowager's bath chair had been moved outside into the soft evening sun, and Alice was arranged decorously next to her on an uncomfortable-looking wicker seat. From somewhere within, a voice bellowed over the top of the phonograph.

'Salty little beggar wanted a thrupenny tip! Cheek of it. Thought he had me down for a soft touch.'

The voice began to get louder as its owner approached the door. Alice was looking over her shoulder in a rare show of attention, but the older Lady Horncastle had her gaze fixed grimly on the horizon.

'Told him I'd intended tuppence but it had gone down to a penny on account of his manners. Should have seen his face...'

A sort of goblin in evening dress emerged into the open air, and stopped abruptly when he saw the four of us crossing the lawn. He made no move to acknowledge us, just eyed us up and down and took a long pull at the glass in his hand.

'My father-in-law, Mr Piers Garrett,' announced Horncastle when we were close enough for introductions.

‘Piers, darling,’ interrupted Ellen, as if her son-in-law had spent too long getting to the point, ‘these gentlemen are Mr Harrison Catcliffe and the Reverend Peter Wilkie.’

‘Catcliffe?’ said Garrett, pressing my hand perfunctorily and ignoring Wilkie altogether. ‘Steel Catcliffes? Jonas’s lot?’

‘My father.’

Somewhere inside, the cylinder ran out and the music stopped.

‘You’re a long way from home,’ he remarked, without warmth.

‘I am visiting my aunt in Whitby and she recommended I take a week or so to explore the moors,’ I said, smiling. ‘It is a most welcome holiday. London is wretched in this weather.’

‘Each to their own,’ he grunted, then paused and narrowed his eyes as if to let me know he was not quite satisfied with my answer. As the evening went on, I would come to realise that Piers Garrett radiated scepticism in much the same way as his daughter radiated ennui. He had the air of a man who was always trying to catch you out in a lie.

Close up, Garrett looked about as appealing as his reputation. He was flabby without being corpulent, but much of his weight seemed to sit around the neck area. He had a sort of slug of blubber that bulged from his collar, upon which was mounted a reddish face, scrupulously close shaven. His hair was plastered to his skull with lashings of shiny pomade – thinning and grey on top, but much thicker and darker at the back, where it peeled away from his neck in greasy strands.

His manner was not especially welcoming, and as we took our seats for dinner it quickly became evident that he viewed our presence as an almighty bore. His wife and son-in-law were attentive hosts, but father and daughter had the air of being there under sufferance. In Alice’s case, I suspected she might have made herself a good deal more charming if Wilkie or I had possessed a title, but I'd wager the King himself would have got a similarly lukewarm reception from Piers Garrett. He was a man who measured those around him in terms of commercial hunger, and few would match up to his own ravenous appetite.

On the subject of appetites, Garrett was one of those for whom the principal object of a meal was to eat and drink as heavily as possible. He did not trouble himself much in the conversational line – though he would occasionally interrupt whoever was talking to dispute some point or other. Only on the subject of business was he forthcoming.

'Word is your pa's ditching the squareheads for the Poles?'

'Nothing's decided yet,' I said vaguely. 'The Polish steel is cheaper but we don't know enough about the quality. If the thickness is even slightly out then it won't work with our presses. We know the steel from the Ruhr is excellent, and that's worth something.'

He placed two chubby fingers under his eye and dragged his eyelid down in a grotesque sort of gesture that was presumably supposed to demonstrate disbelief.

'You're cracked. Wouldn't catch me paying over the odds, not for anything. The lowest quote is the most you ever pay. Poles can give you the exact same quality as the Germans did, or the Germans can drop their price. None of that's your problem.

'You see, Catcliffe,' he said, taking a swig of his wine, 'your old man and I go way back, and as long as I've known him he's been coasting. One new factory since he took over from Old Jonas! Just one! I don't doubt he's a stolid enough businessman but he hasn't got the bit between his teeth the way our fathers did.'

He paused to reach into his mouth and for a moment I thought it was a symbolic gesture to show me the bit between his own teeth, but in fact he was just picking out a fish bone.

'My father came from nothing,' he went on, flicking the bone under his chair. 'A cobbler's stall in Ponder's End. Methodist, you know – couldn't stand your lot.'

This directed at Wilkie.

'To start with he barely made enough from fixing other people's shoes to mend his own, but he soon started to pull himself up. Left me with a nice big shoe factory doing decent trade, but I haven't sat on my laurels. We're in shoes, textiles, shipping, trade... mark my words, young Catcliffe, you need to buck up your ideas if you don't want to go under one of these days. If you're not getting ahead, you're falling behind – I've always said that.'

I could see he was half interested in trying to hook me into an argument, which was why he was ragging on the old man, but I wasn't going to bite.

'Shipping, you say? I didn't know you were in that line. Makes sense though.'

He paused before answering, because one had to remember he was not officially in shipping. The Mercury line and Paley's Wharf were both owned by the mysterious Mr Amos Patchard from Hull – even if the east coast skippers knew it as the 'Garrett line'.

'I am a shareholder in a shipping company,' said Garrett carefully from behind his wine glass. 'A major shareholder,' he added, presumably because he couldn't resist.

He took more interest in me for the remainder of the meal, and I wondered if, in my eagerness to pick him up on a half-truth, I had showed too much of my own hand. He became particularly attentive when Lord Horncastle, in a good-natured sort of way, enquired about our Sunday afternoon excursion.

'Did you enjoy your sketching trip on the Ernecliffe, gentlemen?' he asked as the servants were serving up the lamb. 'It was a glorious afternoon for it.'

'Truly it was,' replied Wilkie. 'Though I must admit that there may have been more snoozing than sketching on my part.'

'I daresay conducting Sunday services is most fatiguing work,' joked Horncastle, before realising how rude it might sound. 'Mother very much enjoyed your sermon,' he added hastily. 'The fruit and so forth.'

The Dowager Lady Horncastle was absent from the table. Wilkie told me she took her meals in private because she had to be spoon-fed – though I noticed she had wrangled a gin glass pretty competently earlier on. Perhaps she just didn't care for the company.

'You a keen artist then, Catcliffe?' asked Garrett through a mouthful of new potatoes.

'Oh yes, very,' I lied. 'It was my object in coming here. My aunt told me there is simply nowhere like Birkdale for rugged picturesque beauty. And then there are the Reverend's misericords.'

'Funny sort of hobby for a man,' he said. 'Don't suppose you get much chance to sit around drawing in the city.'

'Oh, on the contrary, I have sketched many a... riverscape,' I countered, realising as I did so that I was digging myself into a hole. 'Wharves and rigging and lightermen...' I added vaguely.

'We would very much like to see some of your work,' said Horncastle encouragingly. 'Wouldn't we, my dear?'

There was a short delay while Alice realised some sort of response was required.

'Yes, assuredly, Mr Catcliffe,' she said sweetly. 'Just lately the Reverend Wilkie was good enough to let us admire some of his shell paintings.' This line was delivered in such an innocent manner that – having seen Wilkie's work – I began to wonder if Alice's deadpan façade concealed a bone-dry sense of humour. As it was, she promptly opted out of any further part in the conversation by putting a very small piece of lamb in her mouth and chewing it carefully for at least five minutes.

'I'd sooner you kept clear of the Ernecliffe,' said Garrett sharply. 'Can't have one rule for visitors and vicars and another rule for everyone else.'

He looked pointedly at his son-in-law as if daring him to disagree, but of course Horncastle did not. Ellen Garrett looked smug, while Alice chewed her lamb more vigorously.

'I gather you are trialling new game-rearing methods in the western woods,' said Wilkie brightly.

'What my keepers are doing in those woods is none of your business,' replied Garrett, with such unwarranted rudeness that poor Horncastle had no choice but to intervene.

'Yes, that's right,' he blurted out, avoiding Garrett's gaze. 'New methods, experimental, scientifically grounded and all that. We really don't know the ins and outs of it ourselves – Mr McCrea oversees it all.'

What a lot of rot we were all talking. I wondered if anyone had told the truth the whole night, because I certainly hadn't.

Presently, the ladies left and the cigars came out. I had already decided that Peter Wilkie was a good sort, but I liked him even more when he baited Piers Garrett into a conversation about Garrett Senior's Methodism, leaving me and Horncastle to escape out onto the terrace.

I looked back at the amiable vicar, smiling as sympathetically as if he were visiting a day-old widow, his head resting on two fingers with the cigar dangling so close to his temple that it looked like his woolly hair might flare up at any second. Garrett was giving him what-for, but the stream of invective passed over him without effect, like a spring tide rushing harmlessly through a kelp forest twenty feet down.

It was gone ten o'clock but the sky still held a little light: a fading blush on the encroaching dark. The day had been hot and the night would be close, but somehow as one merged into the other there was a brief feeling of freshness over the terrace and the garden before us. The parched grass and the shrubs that had looked so limp and dusty a couple of hours earlier seemed greener and glossier.

There were a few cane chairs on the scrubbed flagstones, but Horncastle stood and so did I. He took a long, indulgent pull on his cigar, looking as relieved as I felt to have some respite from his father-in-law's humours.

'Does your family firm ever feel like a weight as well as a blessing?' asked Horncastle, out of the blue.

'It will, I think. One day. At the moment my father's generation is taking the strain.'

'In that case I fear you're in for a shock, Mr Catcliffe.' He smiled. 'Sooner or later you end up holding the baby. You have all these people relying on you and you can't just wind the whole thing up and let it die – so you have to do things you don't particularly want to, just to keep it alive.'

'Are we talking about Catcliffe Steel or Haydon Castle?'

What we were actually talking about was the bad-tempered little man sat indoors, and I suspected this was Horncastle's way of apologising for him.

'A bit of both,' replied Horncastle. 'How many generations does the business go back?'

'I'm the third. My grandfather was a veterinarian – realised engines were going to replace horses so he got ahead of the game.'

'Shrewd man. Lots of those in my family, though I'm not sure I'm one of them. My father wasn't either.

'If I might try to explain,' he said, 'imagine the weight you feel as the third generation of Catcliffes – and how you might feel if the whole thing went down the pan. Now consider that Horncastles have had Haydon Castle since the last owners ended up on the wrong side in the Civil War. That's two hundred and fifty years, give or take.'

'I see your point. Don't want to be the one who finally signs the bill of sale.'

'Exactly. I think of all the sacrifices they made, all the things they endured, and if I lose it then that was all for nothing.'

'Hence Piers Garrett,' I ventured, feeling I might safely introduce the subject of our conversation now that we were so far along with it.

Horncastle smirked weakly.

'Hence Piers, yes.'

'We all do what we need to do,' I said.

'He's not so bad when you get to know him,' said Horncastle, his tone suggesting that he didn't believe a word of it. 'And anyway, I have been very lucky with Alice. Of all the girls with rich fathers I could have picked, she is something quite out of the ordinary.'

It wasn't the sort of statement that sought a response, so I stayed quiet and watched the last light leaching out of the sky. Really I ought to have been pressing him for information, but having been questioned at length by the Metropolitan Police on several previous occasions, I'd learned that you often gave up the most when no-one was asking you anything.

'He has his quirks,' said Horncastle, 'and we've had to make various compromises that might not always be immediately apparent, but I have to keep telling myself that Haydon simply won't survive without him. I think of all the people who work here, the people who will work here in the future, the villages around us and the people who will live here generations down the line, and I think to myself that I'm just a custodian. Like a churchwarden, if you like. There are some luxuries of scruple that I simply don't have.'

'I had heard,' I said carefully, 'that fewer people from the villages were working at Haydon Castle than was previously the case.'

Horncastle looked at me curiously.

'Where did you hear that, Harry?'

'The Bull,' I lied.

He laughed at that.

'I haven't been in the Bull for years. Is it as grim as ever?'

'Fairly grim, yes. I liked it. Wilkie was very rude about it.'

'Not quite as mild as he looks, is he, the Reverend Wilkie? Though I'm with him on the Bull, I'm afraid. Partly because if you walk in there as a Mayhew you never get out without buying everyone in the village a drink. My father used to make a habit of it every Christmas. Nearly ruined him.'

'Mostly miners in there now, from Ross and Blayne.'

'Yes, we did have to let a lot of staff go,' he said, realising he wasn't going to change the subject that easily. 'That's one of those compromises I mentioned. But as you say, there was the mine. We'd signed the lease by then, so I knew they weren't going to be out of work.'

He must have known the mine was failing, but I felt instinctively that Horncastle was my only potential ally in that place – and it didn't seem sensible to start picking more holes in his already moth-eaten conscience.

'That's just it, you see,' he said. 'People expect you to be responsible for everyone and everything in the valley. The road needs repairing, the vicar's stipend is too low, the school needs a new coke stove... and have you seen the state of that bloody church?' he said, cracking a smile at the thought of the old girl's heroic dilapidation.

'My aunt Diana greatly enjoyed sketching the misericords.'

'Jolly decent of the woodworm to leave her one or two – and the less said about the roof, the better. In my father's day, we couldn't afford to fix our own buildings, but when the churchwardens come knocking – which they will – out will come my pocket book before you can say Jack Robinson. That's the choice, isn't it? Saying yes to the church and the school and everyone else means saying yes to Piers and whatever comes with him.'

We lapsed into silence and gazed down the lawn. At the other end of the garden, just beyond the hedge line, a man in a cap walked across. He was a fair distance away, but even in the half-light it was clear that he was carrying a rifle slung over his shoulder.

‘Gamekeepers working late,’ I observed.

‘Something like that, yes,’ said Horncastle, his face clouded in cigar smoke and sudden ill-temper – though it didn’t seem to be directed at me. ‘Come on, let’s go inside.’

Twenty-Five

'Not the friendliest of chaps, is he, old man Garrett?' said Wilkie as we followed the lane back through the darkness to Yattonby. It would have been quicker to cut across the fields, but Lord Horncastle had requested in that deprecatingly urgent way of his that we stuck to the road.

'Our staff are very wary of intruders after a number of incidents,' he explained apologetically, 'I'd hate for you to get mistaken for a trespasser in the dark.' It was a thin explanation for some caprice of his father-in-law's, and he knew it well enough.

'I would go further than that, Peter,' I said, watching a rabbit freeze for a moment in our lamplight before pelting off into the hedge. 'I consider him one of the most disagreeable men I have ever come across.'

We were still not far from the castle gates, trudging along the dry earth lane between a hawthorn hedge and a brick wall about seven feet tall that bordered the castle grounds. The night had turned humid and still. The ghostly form of a barn owl floated silently across our path and I raised my lamp to get a better look at it.

As I did so, a violent booming noise on the other side of the wall nearly made me jump out of my skin. I stumbled sideways into Wilkie, who was just as alarmed, and the two of us stood there staring at the brickwork. We both knew exactly what was on the other side of it.

'That's one of Mrs Garrett's monsters,' said Wilkie over the din of the creature's barking.

Men's voices on the other side shouted at the dog to pipe down, but it took no notice, becoming if anything even louder and more intimidating.

The stables and kennels were round the other side of the house, and the part of the estate we were walking past was a garden. Fragrant purple roses with cabbage-like blooms spilled over the top from where they were growing up the other side.

'No wonder Horncastle didn't want us cutting through the grounds,' I whispered, hoping the men over the wall wouldn't hear. 'They're walking the perimeter with the dogs.'

The barking had been joined by an even deeper one further back towards the castle gates – presumably Argo, the big male – and they were making a terrible racket, the barks punctuated by rumbling growls, the shouts of their handlers and the sound of claws scraping down the bricks.

'Bark's probably worse than their bite,' observed Wilkie, though neither of us believed it for a second.

....

'What was he like?' asked Jabez as Wilkie poured out some brandies. He'd switched to a different chair this evening, presumably because he'd cleaned all the lost coins out of Wilkie's favourite one.

'A wretch. Just like my old man said.'

'Thought so. Learn anything else useful?'

'His guard dogs are just about the most intimidating beasts I've ever seen,' offered Wilkie, fetching the brandy to Jabez's chair. I marvelled anew that this entitled little vagabond was supposedly in service.

'We saw.'

Among the beekeepers, armourers and other hobbyists who had scattered their assorted detritus about the vicarage, one former vicar of St Stephen's had been a keen astronomer. The man himself had not lasted long before having some sort of unspecified episode that had seen him removed from the post, but a relic of his incumbency remained in the form of a powerful brass telescope on a tripod. Artemisia had oiled the stuck joints and cleaned decades of grime off the lenses with a pot of vinegar, then earlier that evening – as Wilkie and I set off to our dinner engagement – she and Jabez had carried the instrument up onto the moortop and circled round the ridge until they found a spot with a good overview of the castle.

As the sun sank into the Bronze Age barrows that dotted the horizon, the two of them had taken it in turns to make a detailed survey of the castle and grounds. Missy knew the layout of the place pretty well – since she had grown up around it and both she and her father had worked there. What they were really interested in was what had changed since then.

As Jabez and Artemisia swept the place with their antique telescope, enjoying the spectacle of Mr Harrison Catcliffe loitering nervously right at the back of the group while Ellen Garrett was showing off her prize hunting dogs, they noticed armed patrols that were entirely out of place on such a remote country estate. There were always at least two pairs of men walking regular routes around the grounds, sometimes with a dog and always carrying rifles.

‘Rifles, Jabez? What sort?’

He wiped a drop of brandy off his chin.

‘You mean were they the sort that might fire a .303 like we found in the woods? Most of them, yes.’

‘Easy to come by guns like that?’

‘Well you’re not going to get a cartload off a man on Chapel Market. They were pretty much all Martini–Enfields. That’s a military rifle, and Garrett’s got a lot more of them than any civvy ought to.’

‘There must be men who can get them for you if you’ve enough money.’

‘It’s not so much that,’ said Jabez. ‘Some of his men look like they might have been greybacks in a past life, and I daresay they might know a man who knows a man.’

‘Greyback?’ queried Wilkie politely, opening the window to try and let the sticky summer air out, but actually only succeeding in letting more of it in.

‘Army men, Reverend,’ offered Artemisia from her place on the hearth rug. ‘You know, the grey shirts.’

‘Oh, yes,’ said Wilkie, who presumably didn’t know the grey shirts.

‘I’m not saying they’d be hard to get hold of,’ continued Jabez. ‘I bet the army’s got plenty sitting around going rusty, but they don’t just flog them off on the open market. You’d need very good connections to start buying up that much firepower for use on home soil without someone asking questions.’

He was right. No doubt every anarchist ever to raise a pint pot in the Lamb and Flag coveted a crate or two of military armaments, and you had to hope that someone, somewhere was making sure they didn’t get them. I thought for a moment.

'What if he bought them abroad and shipped them over? Somewhere in the colonies, maybe?'

Jabez grinned.

'Not so many questions asked there, I daresay.'

'You said Mr Garrett has a shipping line,' ventured Wilkie.

'Just a coastal one, I think, but he must have connections in import-export. A crony with a steamship company and connections in Africa or Asia. It isn't especially hard to imagine.'

But it was not just guns, guards and dogs that Jabez and Missy had seen as they glassed the grounds of Haydon Castle. Among the outbuildings, one had caught their attention.

'It used to be the old smithy,' said Missy, 'back in the old days when the estate had its own farrier and blacksmith. But it hasn't been used for that in a very long time. When I worked at the castle it was just a store – dusty old dogwhips and worn-out horse blankets. Food for vermin, really. The gamekeepers used to put a terrier to ratting in there and take bets on it.

'But it doesn't look like a store now. Least not unless they're feeding the rats with baskets of bread and gallon jugs of water.'

As darkness crept over Birkdale, our two amateur astronomers had twice seen a man go into the old smithy and a different fellow leave shortly afterwards.

'Three hours between them. Absolutely on the button. Like they're changing shifts.'

'Maybe it's not what it looks like...' said Jabez, leaving his sentence hanging and looking at me encouragingly as if I were a particularly slow child.

'...But it looks as though someone is being kept prisoner in there.'

Twenty-Six

It rained briefly sometime around dawn. One of those desperate, pelting releases that rattles the windows and fills the room with a sort of pond smell. It woke me up and I couldn't sleep much afterwards. By the time the Reverend's carriage clock struck six, I could hear horses on the road and voices in the fields. Dressing carelessly in corduroys and undershirt, I threw the spare blanket over my shoulder and slipped downstairs through the still house.

The rain had summoned up a plague of slugs, and the vicarage hall carpet was criss-crossed with ribbons of pearlescent mucus. Out in the garden there were hundreds of them, slimy cigar ends littered across the flagstones and draped over the ravaged marigolds. I tiptoed around them in unlaced boots and fetched a mouldy rattan chair from the conservatory.

Even allowing for the molluscs, it was cool and pleasant in the garden, swathed in the blanket, listening to the cows being turned back out into the field next door. The real world was a welcome distraction from the one behind my eyes, where the story of what might have happened to the missing union men was slowly taking shape. In fact, I was so distracted that I didn't hear Artemisia come out of the house until she crunched a snail on the path.

She was holding a tray with a coffee pot, and seemed not to notice or care about my state of general disarray.

'Old habits,' she said, and smiled, looking at the tray, before I could remind her that in this house it wasn't her job to serve breakfast.

'Morning, Artemisia. Will you join me? I could do with an ear.'

I fetched another chair from the conservatory while she got herself a cup. There was a colony of sparrows in the hedge at the vicarage, and their shadows danced around the back wall of the conservatory in the low morning sun.

'Things start early here,' I said as she sat down, wrapping herself in a well-worn black coat that looked like one of Wilkie's. It was a telling little liberty, like falling asleep on the hearth rug.

'Sun comes up, beasts get up, so do you. Not much sleep this time of year. But no-one minds. It's better than winter when you're doing everything in the dark.'

'I shouldn't imagine it's much fun then.'

She warmed her hands on the coffee cup, as if even thinking about it made her feel cold.

'It isn't. The game is to find a nice warm job before someone else does. Griping muck out of a shed, that's a good one on a raw day. Plugging a box out, we call it.'

'You worked on the farms then?' Artemisia was built like a bird – I couldn't imagine her shovelling towering barrows of shit.

'On the farms, in the fields, in the houses. Women's jobs, men's jobs. All sorts. My father took ill so I had to take what I could get.'

'I'm sorry.'

I thought of my own youth. Lazy holiday mornings spent flopped in an armchair, drawing eye patches and snaggle teeth on the pictures in the newspaper. The canine, humanity-stripping world of public school that had seemed at the time simply an ordeal to be endured before you could get on with the business of life – now placed firmly in perspective.

'No need to be,' she said. '"He that tilleth his land shall be satisfied with bread."'

'Sounds like Wilkie talking. I don't think it's true though, is it?'

'No, not true at all.' She smiled. 'Reverend Wilkie has lots of lines like that. He just sort of throws them out with a smile like he doesn't really mean them, to hide the fact that he sometimes does.'

She obviously felt she was talking too much about the Reverend, because she turned her attention to the slugs.

'Where do they come from? There weren't any yesterday.'

I didn't know, and I didn't really want to talk about the slugs any more than she wanted to talk about Wilkie.

'Look, Artemisia,' I said, 'what do you think is going on at Haydon? Because I have an idea, but I can't really believe it.'

She sipped her coffee and thought for a moment.

'If your idea is difficult to believe,' she said, picking her words carefully, 'then maybe you need to think what it would take for you to believe it.'

As usual, Missy Moss still wasn't telling me her own opinion.

'The facts, then,' I said. 'At least the ones that seem likely to be facts.'

I listed them one by one.

'First, that a number of troublesome union men have gone missing in London, several of whom are connected to Piers Garrett's factories.

'Second, that Seamus Dyer, an otherwise inoffensive docker who doesn't fit with the others, disappeared from Paley's Wharf. The wharf is owned by Mercury Shipping, which we now know is mostly owned by Piers Garrett. Mercury operates a more or less direct line with Port Blyth – and by extension Haydon Castle – and on the night Dyer went missing, a boat was leaving on that exact run. Implying that Dyer saw something he shouldn't have.

'Third, that when the crew of the Mercury boat spotted me on the way to Port Blyth, they didn't seem at all pleased about it.

'Fourth, that Duke came here to investigate Haydon Castle, and went missing when he tried.

'Fifth, that as far as I can tell, Piers Garrett basically runs Haydon, whether or not it technically belongs to his son-in-law.

'Sixth, that he appears to be keeping prisoners in one of the outbuildings.'

Now we're getting to it, I thought.

'Seventh, that Piers Garrett loves to go shooting, but lost interest in the usual hedge chickens last September. At pretty much the same time, he suddenly became incredibly secretive. He fired all his gamekeepers and most of the house staff and replaced them with a bunch of outsiders. The grounds are now patrolled by armed men with bloody great guard dogs – which might be understandable if Haydon Castle contained Imperial Russian royalty, rather than low-end Yorkshire aristocracy and a boot-and-shoe man from Ponder's End.

'Eighth, that Garrett and Horncastle have become obsessively protective of the western woods – allegedly due to some new pheasant-rearing practices – and a local poacher, Tom Creedy, recently went missing there.'

I paused.

‘And there was that shell casing in the woods,’ Artemisia reminded me, though there was no need to.

‘Can he?’ I asked her, still not quite believing it. ‘Can he really be hunting *men* over there?’

It sounded even more ridiculous spoken out loud, but Artemisia wasn’t smiling.

‘He could be,’ she said, ‘but it’s a stretch, even with the things you already know. If you called the police in right now, do you think they would get him?’

I rubbed my temples with frustration.

‘No, I don’t think they would.’

‘Why not, Mr Catcliffe?’

‘Because I couldn’t just tell the village bobby. I would need to send word to Whitby or Middlesbrough for some town coppers, and there’s no way I could keep that secret in a place like Birkdale. Garrett would know they were coming a mile off, and by the time they got here, you can be certain any prisoners would have vanished.

‘And really I don’t expect I’d even get them to come out in the first place without a decent level of proof.’

I had dealt with coppers before. It wasn’t exactly that I didn’t trust them, but they had an inconvenient way of seeing what was actually in front of them rather than what you wanted them to see.

‘Then how would you prove it?’

Typically, I had not thought that far.

‘I suppose we would need to look in that outbuilding,’ I said after a pause.

‘If you’ll forgive me, Mr Catcliffe, that seems very dangerous if there’s some other way.’

Quite, I thought. Dogs and .303-calibre rifles and all that. Was there another way?

'The woods?' I said slowly. 'Should we go back to the woods?'

We were interrupted by the sound of the front door opening, and presently Peter Wilkie appeared on the garden path.

'Go to the ant, thou sluggard!' he exclaimed, addressing the slimy creatures through which he picked his way.

'Consider her ways, and be wise,' finished Artemisia, rising to fetch another chair.

Wilkie grinned.

'I like that one. Missy knows all my favourites. According to Proverbs, the ant goes about her work without "guide, overseer or ruler". Authority is dead weight if everyone just knows their job and gets on with it.'

'Ants have queens, Peter.'

He wagged his finger, and I saw I had fallen into one of his little traps.

'Not if you think like an ant. We call her a queen. To them she's just another ant with a different job.'

He sat, and we told him how far we had got.

'I'm glad you've said it,' he said, 'but also I'm not. I suppose part of me wants to think that Piers Garrett is just an objectionable man. The alternative is... well, it's difficult to contemplate in human terms.'

'Maybe we need to contemplate him in terms of something else.'

'I can't,' said Wilkie, simply.

'You've thought it too though.'

'We all have.'

We fell to how we might prove it without risking the castle grounds, and once more the conversation turned to the woods.

'We didn't find much last time,' observed Artemisia.

'But we also didn't know what we were looking for.'

'Then what *are* we looking for?' asked Wilkie.

Someone had to say it, and it might as well be me.

'Human remains, I suppose. Blood, bodies, clothing, anything.'

'There was that cloth cap,' said Wilkie. 'I think I can remember where it was. Maybe we could take another look at it.'

'Hardly conclusive though.'

'The question is,' said Artemisia, 'would they really bury any remains in the woods where any old poacher could stumble across them?'

She waited for me to make the connection.

'Maybe one already did?' I ventured.

Wilkie wasn't far behind.

'Tom Creedy, you mean? Sam's cousin?'

'Took his dog, didn't he, Reverend?' said Artemisia. 'Nosy little snap dog scratching about. No telling what it might have found.'

Poor Creedy. I hoped that wasn't what had happened to him. Set out under a full moon for a bag of bunnies, ended up sniffing out more than he bargained for.

'Well if he did come across something, then that's blown our chances of finding any evidence in the woods. I can't think they would be so careless as to leave anything lying around after that.'

The coffee pot was empty and the slugs were beginning to slink back into the shadows as the morning sun warmed the flagstones. And yet we were still no closer to an answer.

Whichever way I circled around it, there was only one thing that could prove beyond any doubt that Piers Garrett was murdering men in the woods. I needed to see inside that old workshop in the grounds of Haydon Castle.

Twenty-Seven

STRICTLY NO TRESPASSING by order B Chalmers AGENT

Such an unambiguous sign – its excess of capitals admirably balancing out its lack of punctuation – positively cried out to be disobeyed. But perhaps not with the head gamekeeper standing next to it.

Jabez and I were up on the western side of Birkdale, walking across the open moor above the valley. Beyond the fence, a steep, hummocky field dropped down to the edge of the western woods.

McCrea was working on the fence, deftly knotting lines of barbed wire around the posts while another keeper held them tight for him. It was a hot day, but they were working fast. Both men were in shirt-sleeves, their jackets slung over the rolls of wire. As we approached, McCrea straightened up and took off his salt-stained hat to wipe the sweat out of his eyes.

'Mr Catcliffe.'

As before, he was polite but he didn't seem very pleased to see us.

'Mr McCrea,' I said brightly. 'My man Potter and I are enjoying a ramble on the moor. We have some bottles of beer, if you would care to take a break and share them with us?'

He looked at us with a hint of interest, predatory rather than sympathetic. I felt his eye cataloguing my scars, Jabez's walking stick and the blotted tattoos below my friend's rolled sleeves.

'All right then,' he said. 'Thank you.'

Jabez opened up his knapsack and brought out a couple of bottles and glasses, wrapped carefully in a cloth by Wilkie's maid. In a rare show of deference – no doubt for the other men's benefit, not mine – McCrea and I got the glasses, while he and the other gamekeeper swigged at what was left in the bottles.

'No Reverend today?' asked McCrea, leaning on a fence post.

'Alas, the vicar has church business to attend to.'

'Keeps him busy, no doubt.'

'No doubt. Are you perhaps one of his congregation?'

McCrea cracked a rare smile as if I had made a very good joke.

'Not a churchgoing man, Mr Catcliffe.'

Neither McCrea nor his companion were talkative, looking silently across the dark expanse of trees to the Ernecliffe rising out of the centre of the dale. I didn't usually mind gamekeepers – there was always the odd officious one, but most of them could just as easily have been poachers, and they knew it. This man felt different.

'Thank you for showing us the dogs last night,' I said, more because it was something to say than because I was especially interested. 'Mrs Garrett seems most passionate about the further evolution of your new breed.'

McCrea said nothing.

'Those Turkish beasts sound quite the rarity,' I went on airily. 'I remember meeting similar ones on my own travels, only they were shaggier, and not nearly so heavy-set. Didn't look much like yours at all, actually,' I added lamely.

It was a lucky strike. The American snorted quietly to himself.

'With respect to Mrs Garrett,' he said, 'she likes stories better than the truth. Argo's a quarter Turk, that's all.'

'Oh?'

He wiped his mouth with the back of his hand.

'Most of the blood in those dogs is from Boer farm mutts. But she likes the stuff about the "ancient guardians of Asia Minor" better, so that's the way she tells it.'

He mimicked his mistress's voice on the Asia Minor bit. It was surprisingly accurate and would have got him sacked on the spot if she heard it.

'Well I can see why it might play a bit better with her opera set. Not very smart to be a Boer lover.'

'One of the big problems with you British, if you don't mind me saying.'

'You might have to be more specific. We have a lot of problems.'

He liked that.

'You think you're the best at everything, so if someone else does it better – especially if they're your enemy – you just pretend they haven't. But saying something doesn't make it true, and ignoring something doesn't mean it isn't there.'

'You mean we refuse to learn anything new unless we've invented it ourselves.'

'And that's why you're falling behind.'

I took a pull at my glass of beer.

'And what has that to do with Mrs Garrett and her dogs?'

'Those Boer farmers make the best hunting dogs in the world. Only reason I crossed 'em with the Turks was to make 'em bigger. But Boers are the enemy, they couldn't possibly have anything right – right? And those farmers ain't barely been to school, how could they know anything?

'So she changes the story, tells herself and anyone who'll listen that they're ancient Trojans or whatever, starts breeding them like they were bird dogs because that's all she knows. What would a smart man do, Mr Catcliffe?'

I thought for a moment, wondering if it was a trick question.

'Accept the real story, I suppose – and find out how they did it.'

'Even if the answer offends your English sensibilities?'

'Perhaps especially then.'

McCrea settled his forearms lazily on the taut wire fence. I could see the spikes pressing into his skin.

'At six months they set the pups to hunting baboons – just the young ones to start with. When that gets too easy, the farmer catches a baby baboon and holds onto it while it cries out for help until the big male baboon comes. See what the dogs make of that. Hell of a thing, a full-size baboon. Closest thing to bringing down a man, they say. When it's done, the farmer keeps the dogs that fight, kills the ones that don't.'

'And the baby baboon?'

'Gets a clasp knife through the heart. Farmer can't make the dog do all the work.'

'Decent of him.'

McCrea raised an eyebrow.

‘By two years old, the farmer only has the brave dogs left, but he needs to skim out the dumb ones. So he starts them on leopards.

‘First time out, the cat has to be trapped by the forepaw, else the game won’t work. The smart dogs attack from the back, stay behind the leopard until she’s exhausted. The dumb ones come straight at her from the front and get their hides stripped. See, the leopard’s stronger head-on, but it wears out quicker.’

I resisted the urge to pass comment. It was the sort of tall tale that some windbag might tell you in a London pub, only I had the nasty sensation it might be true.

‘And do you know what you’ve got left after all that, Mr Catcliffe?’

‘A lot of dead dogs,’ interjected Jabez, who had managed to hold his tongue this far.

‘And a couple of live ones. And *those* are what you breed from.’

‘Not quite the way it works at Haydon?’

McCrea shook his head.

‘“Heckie’s coat has come out too dull”,’ he parroted in his Mrs Garrett voice, but without a smile. ‘You know, she found that Russian “wolfhound” at Cruft’s Dog Show. Ain’t ever seen a wolf.’

I thought back to the previous evening. The dog they called Hecuba was supposed to be the fastest and the best, but spinsterhood awaited because she was the wrong colour. He had a point – it was just about the most English sort of nonsense you could imagine.

I could see why McCrea enjoyed the story. The hungry new world circling the overfed, ineffectual old one like a pack leader getting long in the tooth. He was more or less the opposite of those bright, naïve Americans that Henry James liked to write about.

‘Don’t like them much, do you?’ I ventured.

He shook his head.

'Nor do I.'

But if I meant to try and build some kind of camaraderie with the fellow, I had misjudged him. He just swirled his glass and looked disinterestedly into the dregs.

'Don't matter either way.'

'Suppose the buggers must pay well then,' said Jabez with a grin.

McCrea drained his beer and stood up straight, flicking the last few drops out into the heather.

'They do.'

'Why? You looking for a new job, shipmate?' asked the other game-keeper. He and Jabez shared a grin. It was difficult to judge whose teeth were worse, but the other man certainly possessed fewer.

McCrea held out the empty glass.

'Thanks for the drink, Mr Catcliffe.'

'You're welcome. Hot day.'

'It is. Wouldn't be up here if I didn't have to be. And yet you are.'

He looked at me pointedly and I felt a sudden twist in my stomach.

'I'm on holiday,' I said, trying for a smile that I couldn't quite pull off.

'We were talking about smart men just before. A smart man would know when it was time to finish up his holiday and go home.'

'A friendly warning?'

'I ain't your friend, Mr Catcliffe. Don't make me show you that.'

He turned away and bent down to pick up another roll of wire.

Jabez and I walked on around the dale head, the joy sapped suddenly from the day. Behind us, we could hear the distant clang of a sledgehammer as the two stick figures with whom we had recently enjoyed a beer and a horrid story set about driving in another fence post.

'Useful stuff, that barbed wire,' Jabez observed after a while. 'They used a lot of it in Africa.'

'Who did?'

'That's what I'm wondering, mate.'

I shot him a sidelong look to see if he was winding me up, but in fact he was just thinking out loud. It was an affectation that would have provoked considerable scorn if roles were reversed.

'Go on.'

'Man knows how to rig a fence in double-quick time, is all. So does his mate.'

'Lots of people do. Farmers, for example. Gamekeepers too.'

'And soldiers, mate. Specifically ones who fought that wire and blockhouse war in Africa. Lot of international volunteers on both sides – Yanks included. Then there was that other lad.'

'What about him?'

'Called me shipmate, didn't he?'

He held up one of his forearms.

'I suppose you're going to tell me he recognised that mysterious blue smudge as an extremely significant regimental tattoo – thus accidentally revealing himself as a military man?'

He narrowed his eyes and thumbed at the faded ink.

'Wreath, globe, bugle, mate. Badge of the Red Marines. Need to get your eyes looked at.'

'I see it now, yes.' Though I didn't. 'If I may say, Jabez, I'm not sure it would take a wealth of insider knowledge to deduce that a rough-looking chap with tattoos and a major injury may once have served in the navy.'

When you thought about it though, he could well have been right. Taken alone, any one of these things might just have been a coincidence, but here in Birkdale they just kept stacking up.

Twenty-Eight

Later that afternoon – when Wilkie had finished his visits – the four of us stripped down to our underwear and went for a swim in Cod Beck, which wiggled along the southern edge of Birkdale. There was another beck that ran down from the head of the dale, passing behind the castle and the church to meet Cod Beck in the centre of the village, but Wilkie cautioned against setting foot in that one.

'It runs past the mine and the Lord above only knows what they sluice out into it at Ross and Blayne. I certainly wouldn't drink it.'

Cod Beck was a different matter, though. The water was clear and stained brown by the peat moor, which gave it the look of bright amber ale, especially where it foamed attractively in the eddies. Artemisia had led us to her favourite bathing spot just below the moor edge. A drop and a kink in the stream had carved out a small pool that was a little over waist deep, with a couple of slabs of gritty rock that served as an entry platform.

'We call it Jenny's Pool. My father and I used to come here when I was a girl,' she volunteered, sitting on the edge of the rock ledge and dangling a bare leg into the water. 'He told me the beck water was full of juniper from the moor and it would keep my skin young when I got older.' She pronounced it 'watter' rather than 'water'. Artemisia's accent had no doubt suffered a good deal of 'improvement' in my aunt's service, but since we arrived in Yattonby I had noticed her beginning to slip back into a broader dialect.

'Is juniper good for the skin then?' I asked.

'It is not,' she smiled. 'But I suppose fathers may tell their daughters little white lies if it pleases them.'

Wilkie floated on his back in the beery liquor, his undershirt removed to reveal an amply-fleshed torso the colour of window putty. His neck, face and forearms were a much deeper brown, giving him the appearance of wearing a white undershirt with the sleeves rolled up.

'I do wish I could talk you out of this evening's plan, Harry,' he said with his eyes closed. 'There are too many men and dogs in that place and only two of you.'

'And only one of us is any use,' added Jabez. He was sitting on the bottom with only his head and neck above water, his leg removed and discarded on the bank next to Artemisia.

I didn't like it either. There is the old saying that life expands and contracts according to one's courage, but my own ration of that particular attribute was extremely modest. I was scared of big dogs at the best of times, and Mrs Garrett's ones made me feel like a baby baboon. That was before we got onto the bunch of professionals guarding the place with large-calibre rifles.

Set against all that was the simple fact that time was running out – especially if Duke was still alive and trapped somewhere.

‘We’ve got to go in,’ I said without much conviction. ‘We’ve followed every other thread we can think of and they all lead into Haydon Castle after dark.’

Fortunately, my apprehension had made me speak quietly, because it turned out we were not alone by Jenny’s Pool. Somewhere just out of view above the lip of the hollow, there was the sound of a horse whickering, and a male voice called out sharply:

‘Who’s there?’

Since none of the others responded, and I couldn’t just at that moment think how I ought to identify myself to the stranger, I called back to him with the same question.

‘Who’s that up there?’

‘Dash it, I asked first,’ the voice replied irritably. ‘Don’t you know this is private property?’

A smile of recognition stole across Pete Wilkie’s face.

‘It’s Reverend Wilkie, Mr Chalmers. How are you today?’

A bit of jangling and a thump announced that the man was getting down off his horse, and presently Mr Chalmers himself appeared at the edge of the moor looking down at us. He had a high forehead, ruddy cheeks, and a face that seemed rather too young for him.

‘This is estate property, Reverend,’ he chided. ‘My permission is required to bathe here.’

While I had not yet been introduced to the Haydon estate’s ‘sharp’ agent, I had seen him out and about in Yattonby several times – and he cut a distinctive figure. In my experience, estate managers tended to fall into two categories: they either considered themselves one step above the tenants or one step below the landed aristocracy. Chalmers was emphatically in the latter group. As he stalked through the village on an expensive horse, his gaze roamed over his territory and its occupants with a faintly disapproving, proprietorial air – as if everyone from the woman hanging out her washing to the man tying his shoelace at the roadside were somehow taking liberties.

That same critical eye now took in the unclothed vicar, two strangers and a disembodied wooden leg, before lighting with especial dislike upon Artemisia.

'My apologies,' said Wilkie with an easy smile. 'I shall be sure to speak with Lord Horncastle directly on Sunday. I am certain it will not be a problem.'

Chalmers must have known that Horncastle would not object, and he appeared all the more irritated at having his authority circumvented.

'You enjoy special privileges here, Reverend – but my concern is that it muddies the waters when the rules are applied unequally. All the other estate workers are quite clear on what is acceptable.'

He looked pointedly at Artemisia as he said this, and she avoided his eye.

Wilkie, however, smiled even more beatifically.

'No estate workers here, old chap. Just your humble parson and his guests.'

Seeing that picking a fight with the amiable vicar was like trying to antagonise the weather, Chalmers muttered something about speaking to Lord Horncastle on the matter, then withdrew. Presently we heard his horse move off.

Jabez spat some water after him and described our visitor in his own sparkling vernacular.

'Not fundamentally a bad man, Chalmers,' said Wilkie, sighing, 'just not a kind heart. But then that's the point of him, I suppose. They call him "Charmless" in the village.'

'Presumably he's good at his job?'

'Extremely. Old Lord Horncastle poached him all the way from an estate in Shropshire ten or eleven years ago. He had his work cut out for him to turn the estate's finances around. Debts all over the shop, half the tenants on peppercorn rents or in arrears, farms barely scraping by. He put a stop to all that, bumped the rents up, booted out the non-payers and made the farmers modernise. Don't like it, sling your hook. There's even a rumour that he was the one who hashed out the mine deal with Ross and Blayne.'

'Is he on the take? I always assume they are.'

'Scrupulously honest, I suspect. One of those who likes power more than money.'

Only Artemisia said nothing, but a few moments later she put her shoes on and set off to walk back to the vicarage.

Somehow her departure broke the spell of the afternoon – or perhaps Chalmers's intrusion had already done it. At any rate, thoughts of the night ahead began to churn up the peace of Jenny's Pool, and it wasn't long before we dried ourselves off and began to descend from the moor. Jabez trailed behind, busy filling his pipe.

'Can I ask you something, Harry?' said Wilkie. 'You don't have to answer if you don't want to.'

'Of course.'

'In that case, I'm curious what you're really doing here?'

I had been thinking about the same thing all afternoon.

'Well, originally I came to solve Abraham Bickley's death and the other disappearances. I know it seems like a long way to come on a hunch, but Duke calls it legwork. Maybe you'll find something, maybe you won't, but you won't know unless you look.'

'And you think you'll find the answer to your mystery in that old outbuilding?'

'Probably not,' I admitted, 'but the situation's changed. Now I would settle for just finding Duke safe and sound. I owe him a very great debt.'

'He saved your life once, you said?'

'Yes, but it's even more than that. Christmas before last, someone laid a trap for me. I knew what it was but I marched Jabez and Duke right into it anyway. Duke's wife, Liza, saved us, but she died doing it. I got tangled up in something that was none of my business, and the Dukanwallas paid the price. They weren't the only ones either.'

'And yet here you are again, old chap,' said Wilkie, not unkindly. 'Tangled up in something that's none of your business.'

He was right, too. When it came down to it, the Bickleys were just some men who worked for my family. They weren't my responsibility and they wouldn't have wanted to be. Yet here I was, three hundred miles from home, preparing to sneak into an armed castle with more lives than my own on the line.

'I don't know why I do it, Peter, really I don't. Because I *do* think things through. I decide they're a bad idea, but I do them anyway.'

Wilkie said nothing, but looked at me expectantly. That old confessional trick again.

'I tell myself I'm trying to do something decent for someone else, but I don't think that's true. I think it's the same impulse that makes men drink or womanise or punt their inheritance on African diamond mining ventures.'

'Well at least you don't have messianic delusions,' said Wilkie. 'So many do, you know. I often think there are few things quite so dangerous as a man with unquestioning faith in his own goodness.'

In that moment, I wanted him to do what vicars were supposed to and give me some sort of well-meaning advice, but he didn't. Perhaps the question had been enough.

'A question for a question, Peter?'

'Go on, old chap.'

'You've asked me why, and I've given you no sort of sensible answer. But what about you? Why are you helping us? Not very priestly to take sides like this – hate the sin but love the sinner, and all that.'

He pushed his damp hair out of his eyes.

'A subtle twisting of Augustine. "Hate sin, love mankind" was more like it. As for the Bible, I'd say it's more like hate the sin but *forgive* the sinner. And the thing is that to be forgiven something, you really ought to be sorry for it first. "If thy brother trespass against thee, rebuke him; and if he repent, forgive him."'

He held the gate for me as we reached the road into Yattonby.

'I'm afraid I can't quite keep up.'

'Trying to forgive people for doing evil things when they don't care that they did them – it isn't an act of love. It's just cowardice, and I've done it far too often.'

'I find that hard to believe.'

'Oh, but I have, old man. And I am tired of it.'

'What about Jesus on the cross – "forgive them; for they know not what they do"?'

'Special dispensation. Son of God's prerogative. Besides, most of the time people know exactly what they're doing. Do you recall your catechism?'

It was a rhetorical question, as he was well aware.

'There's a section in it that I've never been comfortable with. First you promise to love your neighbour as yourself, and to do to all men as you would they should do unto you. All quite reasonable. But then you promise to submit to people in positions of authority – "To order myself lowly and reverently to my betters."'

'Sounds like that bit was added in by the betters.'

'Quite. And it contradicts the part before, don't you see? Sometimes, to love your neighbour, you need to resist your betters. Whatever's going on at Haydon Castle, it has got this far because people like me have submitted reverently to our betters, over and over again.'

I was grinning broadly by now.

'Good for you, Peter. Have you considered setting any of this down on a lavatory door?'

Twenty-Nine

Shortly after one o'clock in the morning, Jabez and I crossed St Stephen's churchyard. As we passed the east porch, we could hear the gentle snores of the itinerant fellow who made his home there. Somewhere among the brambles a fox or cat prowled, its presence betrayed by the stillness of the night around it. Behind us, moonlight picked out the gables of Yattonby. The village was asleep and every window was dark.

We climbed over the wall at the end of the graveyard and passed from the Almighty's domain into Horncastle's. Between us and the castle grounds lay a wide wheat field, at the far side of which was a low stone wall topped with a good deal of barbed wire. On the other side of this, we could make out the dull cluster of outbuildings that contained the old smithy, and some way beyond them was the moonlit bulk of the castle – a few lights still glowing in the windows.

This same group of buildings also included the dog kennels that I had visited the previous evening. In fact, as Artemisia went over the layout of the site earlier on, I realised that I might have been standing within thirty yards of Duke's prison as Ellen Garrett introduced us to her doggies. I had no wish to meet Argo or his harem again, and I fervently hoped that our plan for getting in and out would come off without a hitch.

Jabez and I moved stealthily through the field, keeping low and quiet. I wore stout boots and that same rough old second-hand suit that I put on when I visited the Saracen's Head. A black cloth cap hid my face and an old scarf of Wilkie's covered the white of my shirt front. The moon was high and full, but even so, it would take a keen pair of eyes indeed to spot me in the darkness if I stayed still. For his part, Jabez was an old hand at sneaking around places where he wasn't supposed to be, and he crept softly through the tall wheat stalks in front of me.

About twenty yards short of the fence, we stopped and waited, glancing back at the church. Jabez had one of Wilkie's canvas knapsacks, which he took off and laid at his feet. He began rummaging inside for a set of wire cutters.

Somewhere, not too far off, we heard the deep bark of one of those four enormous beasts. We froze and sank lower into the crop cover, but it wasn't barking at us. In fact, it was right where it was supposed to be, making its rounds with a couple of guards. The other dogs in the kennels picked up the chorus, and we could see the glow of the dog handler's lamp passing through the outbuildings ahead then continuing on into the gardens beyond.

On cue, I spotted the faint light of a lamp in the shadowy face of the church bell tower. It lasted not longer than ten seconds before it was extinguished, and you would not have spotted it unless you were looking for it. Wilkie and Missy were up there with the telescope, and the lamp meant we had a short window between patrols to get in and out.

Jabez clipped a breach in the barbed wire, then swapped his wire cutters for the revolver that he had recently acquired from one Monsieur Magnette in Lambeth. It was a cheap Continental knock-off of a Webley Bull Dog and he was quite pleased with it. The gun was vicious, pocket-sized, and had no doubt been involved in a good deal of crime over the years – rather like Jabez himself.

We crept over the wall, through the cut wire and into the cobbled yard. There was a stable block down one side and a locked workshop on the other, with an old-fashioned water pump in the centre. We slunk round the edge, hugging the shadows and praying that our scent would not carry to the kennels in the next yard across. A few of the smaller gundogs were still making a fuss about the patrol that had just passed, but the deep barks had fallen quiet.

The old smithy was much as Artemisia had described it – with a couple of cobwebbed windows and a set of wide, very rotten double doors that must have stood permanently open in the days when there was a working blacksmith there. The glow of a lamp showed through from where a lone guard sat within. We had watched him take up his post at midnight. I imagined he might be quite bored by now, idly wishing something would happen to punctuate the tedium – which it presently did.

With a grinding screech of rusted hinges, I heaved the door wide open and Jabez darted through with his revolver raised. I heard him make a sharp 'SSSST' noise, and there was the sound of something clattering to the floor inside. Ducking round the door, I found the startled guard standing next to an overturned chair. His rifle was still leaning up against the wall. He had a knife in one hand, and a thin line of blood was beginning to run down the other.

'Put it down,' hissed Jabez.

This ground-floor level was obviously still used as a storeroom, and it was cluttered with dusty tools and piles of old sacking. Along one wall, the long-cold remains of the brick-built forge were obscured by stacks of mangled furniture. There was a single tin hurricane lamp hanging from a nail on one of the beams, and a stone stairwell at the far side of the room.

The watchman was a burly fellow, slightly older than me, and I took care as I bound his wrists while Jabez kept the gun on him. He didn't say a word but we gagged him anyway, then Jabez motioned for him to go down the stairs.

'Dozy bugger was cleaning his nails with his knife,' he whispered to me as we followed with the lamp.

At the bottom of the stairs was another door, much newer and heavier. The key was in the lock on our side, and Jabez reached past the guard to turn it, keeping the revolver pressed against the man's spine while I held the light aloft. Lifting the latch, we pushed it open, and the room breathed out a damp, malodorous sigh of warm air. Jabez pushed the guard inside, and I followed them.

Roughly two-thirds of this dead little cellar was set behind thick iron bars that ran right from floor to ceiling, and beyond them several dark shapes stirred.

'Hello?' I said, holding the lamp to one side so it would illuminate my face.

One of the shadows approached the bars.

'Harry. Have you found my dog?'

....

There were five of them in Garrett's underground gaol besides Duke. A tall man in overalls was Seamus Dyer, the missing docker from Paley's Wharf. Then there was a clicker called Bert Lockwood from Garrett's boot factory, Tom Creedy – the local poacher whose cousin I had met in the Bull – and Jem Clay, the youthful shop steward at Duraweave.

Finally, to my immense relief, there was the familiar face of Timmy Bickley, bearded and hollow-eyed.

'Mr Harrison!'

He thrust his hand through the bars and gripped mine.

Timmy's uncle and brother were both gone, but if I could just get him home again then Arthur Letts would have been right to trust me. Even now – I realised with that sense of detachment that fear brings – I was thinking of myself.

'There'll be time to talk later,' I hissed as I unlocked the cell door. 'For now we just need to get out and away before the next patrol passes.'

'How long is that?' asked Duke. He was dirty and unshaven, but apparently none the worse for whatever ordeal he had been through. He also appeared singularly unsurprised to be rescued.

'Depends how fast they walk,' replied Jabez unhelpfully, 'but between five and ten minutes.'

'What do we do with him?' asked Dyer, gesturing towards the guard. Jabez rewarded him with one of those witheringly impatient looks that were normally reserved for me. We were, after all, standing next to a prison cell.

We locked the cell and then the cellar behind us, and as he reached the top of the stairs, Jabez tossed both keys into the jumble of furniture heaped around the old forge.

'Lights out,' he murmured, and I doused the lamp.

Opening the door slowly and cautiously this time so as not to let the hinges squeak, I peered round. The courtyard appeared just as we had left it. All the dogs were quiet now, and we had entered that dead part of the night where every creature on earth falls silent. I could hear all seven men behind me breathing with what seemed like excessive volume.

'Looks clear,' I whispered, and crept out into the open.

Clinging once again to the shadowy side of the barn, I made for our breach in the fence. The wire tinkled softly as I squeezed through, but I dropped into the field on the other side without incident. Way across on the other side of the wheat field, the dim light came on in the church tower. I felt the first stirrings of relief. We were all right.

But then the light went out and reappeared a second time, and I froze.

'Come on, come on!' I hissed back at the others. 'They've given us the danger signal. Something's wrong!'

Jabez was first over, tearing his coat on the fence. Then Duke, then Clay. The wire shook and rattled, nailed boots scraped on the top of the wall, and one of the dogs over in the kennels began to bark. Soon others chimed in, joined by the bass boom of the two hellhounds who weren't out patrolling. Suddenly we could hear the call of men's voices.

'Run,' said Duke.

I felt like a medieval criminal dashing pell-mell for the sanctuary of a church as the eight of us took off across the field towards St Stephen's.

The tall wheat that had concealed us so obligingly on the way in now clawed at our legs, willing us to trip and fall. Behind us, we could hear shouts among the outbuildings we had just left. Clay and Duke were in the lead, with Jabez and Lockwood lagging some way behind the rest of us.

We must have been about halfway home when two shadows rose suddenly from the wheat stalks about thirty yards ahead of us. Both had rifles already pulled into their shoulders, and there was a flash as the man on the left fired. I heard the two-tone thump of the shot, and Jem Clay's head snapped back like someone had hit it with a bat. What was left of him crashed headlong into the crop cover, and the rest of us followed it, diving to ground.

I lay still for a moment. Around me I could hear rustling and panting but all I could see were wheat stalks and the moon.

'Stand up,' called a calm voice. None of us did.

'Stand up or we send the dogs in,' the voice added, and I realised it had an American accent.

I got up slowly to see McCrea the gamekeeper slotting another round into the breech of his rifle while his companion covered us. Glancing around, I saw the others were standing up too.

'Come on, one more,' said McCrea, and Lockwood the boot man emerged reluctantly from the wheat.

This was presumably what Wilkie and Missy had been trying to warn us about. Two men concealed in the field – and we had done exactly the wrong thing and run straight into them. I looked longingly at the churchyard boundary, then up at the tower where our two friends must still have been watching, powerless to help.

McCrea caught my eye and glanced over his shoulder.

‘Saw the light about ten minutes ago. We were heading across to take a look.’

It was just like a professional hunter to move under the moonlight without a lamp to give him away. He must have seen the warning light come on again, heard the sound of us coming over the fence, and dropped flat out of sight until we were close enough for a clean shot. All the same, it was some marksmanship to have bounced up out of cover and hit a running man through the head at thirty yards. Poor Clay, at least he was dead before he knew it.

More men came from behind and disarmed Jabez before marching us back to the fence.

‘Just to be clear,’ said McCrea, ‘That’s it for rescue attempts. We’ll be paying the Reverend a visit later to get that point across. Firmly, if necessary.’

Thirty

'There were more of us,' said Duke.

'Seven other blokes when I got here,' added Lockwood, who had been down there longest. He was in his fifties with wheezy lungs – and for reasons that were about to become apparent, that had probably kept him alive this far.

It was pitch-black in the cellar, and deathly silent apart from our own voices.

'Garrett hunts them,' explained Creedy, the local man.

It was as we had thought, then. There was a difference between suspecting it and knowing it. I thought of Wilkie's .303 casing, and wondered if the front end of it had put someone in the grave.

'Turns up once a month, stays for a week,' said Creedy. 'Picks a man every two or three nights, then takes them over to the western woods and runs them down with guns and dogs.'

'Was it bodies you found?' I asked.

Creedy shook his head.

'An actual hunt. Bloody full moon. Why I got pinched, you see. I was poaching over that way late one night – just to make a few pennies on the side. Turns out Garrett likes to hunt under a full moon too, only his game is a lot bigger than mine. Ran right into one of their hunts just as the dogs got him. Such screams you never heard. I tried to get out but someone spotted me and I was done.

'Shot my fucking dog too,' he added with bitterness. 'What did he ever do?'

'I met your cousin in the Bull,' I told him. 'He did try asking after you, but Mr Chalmers more or less threatened to evict him if he didn't back off.'

'Sour old Sam.' I could hear the smile in his voice. 'Always told me I'd end up in trouble. If we'd made it out, I don't suppose I'd ever have heard the end of it.'

His quiet implication being that he was never going to make it out now.

'Been going on for months,' said Lockwood, after a pause. 'When I arrived, there were men who'd been here since May. Gone now.' His voice cracked. Poor fellow had been in the bag too long and was close to his limit.

'All union men?' I asked.

'All except Tom and Seamus,' said Duke. 'Wrong place, wrong time for those two.'

'As far as I can tell,' he went on, 'his men in London usually lift their marks on the way home from the pub, or whenever else he can get them on their own. Couple of armed heavies like our friends upstairs will threaten them, usher them into a blacked-out carriage. Sometimes they pose as police. Maybe they even are. Then he runs them over to Paley's Wharf and loads them straight onto a ship.'

'That's how I ended up here.' Dyer's Irish accent came from somewhere to my right. 'I was working a night shift in late June, when the *Clare Kelly* was in. She's one of the Mercury line steamers.'

I remembered the name of the ship. It was the *Clare Kelly* and its mysterious cargo that had led us to North Yorkshire in the first place.

'The crew are in on it, even if they don't know why they've got men locked up on board,' explained Dyer, 'but most of us at Paley's aren't. How could we be? Hundreds of lads working there – you'd never keep it a secret. Not that there weren't rumours. Extra cargo loaded between shifts, armed men on board, but we just assumed someone had black-market business. There's a lot of it goes on and you learn not to notice it if you know what's good for you.'

'Quite right,' observed Duke, who was frequently up to his neck in it.

'So I was working my late shift loading the *Clare* ready for the morning tide, and I heard banging coming from a part of the hold that we didn't usually go near. Thought someone had got themselves trapped – and fool that I am, I went looking. Found a man in there, then Garrett's men found me. I wish I'd wound my neck in.'

I thought about trying to tell Dyer that without him we might never have found any of them. It was his ill-fated curiosity that had put us onto the *Clare Kelly* and eventually led us here. However, given the unmitigated disaster of our rescue attempt, I decided it might not be much consolation.

I learned that the prisoners were brought to Whitby on the big steamship, then transferred across to the *Barbara* – that smaller coastal boat whose crew had given me the evil eye on the way in. The cramped hold on the *Barbara* was designed to take cargo rather than men, and enduring several hours trapped in there with a full load on a choppy sea must have been a special kind of torture. Lockwood had travelled with the missing engineer from Dick Fletcher's sugar factory, and the poor fellow had suffocated before they reached Port Blyth.

At Port Blyth, they were briefly given the use of their arms and legs in order to stagger up the cliff path, before being blindfolded, gagged, and loaded into one of the castle carriages for the final leg of their journey. The transfer from sea to land usually took place at night when the tides were right, but even so, it was hard to believe that no-one at either Whitby or Port Blyth had ever caught sight of the abducted union men.

When I voiced this thought, I could almost hear Duke grinning.

'Not lived in a port, have you, Harry?'

I told him I did not know what he meant.

'I mean that kidnapped factory workers aren't the only dubious cargo coming into the east coast late at night. Whitby's notorious for it, and a little place like Port Blyth is just the kind of spot I'd pick to bring in something I didn't want to pay duties on.

'The people running these rackets aren't jolly smugglers in stripy tops. They're very bad men playing with very big sums of money. Live somewhere like that, you learn to be very selective about what you see and hear.'

I thought of the friendly woman who had served us fried fish and beer in her roadside garden at Port Blyth. Had she witnessed these unfortunate men being brought in? Watched them from her window then gone back to bed?

Eventually, after their long and uncomfortable journey in darkened carriages and cargo holds, the disorientated East London factory workers would find themselves in this dank little dungeon at Haydon Castle, where they might languish for months or be murdered before Sunday service rolled around. Garrett's business concerns kept him in London most of the time, but each full moon he would escape to Birkdale for a week, leaving the gaol cell a few men lighter upon his return. Old Lockwood had survived longer than most because he never got picked. He was considered poor sport on account of his age and his bad lungs.

No-one could say how long it had been going on for, but I remembered Duke had tracked disappearances as far back as March – and I had a sickening conviction that there must have been more victims than the ten missing men on his list.

'What about you, Duke? How did you manage to get snatched up?'

He sighed.

'Just bad luck. Comes to us all sooner or later. I spent a night getting the lie of the land in the pub, then snuck in here to take a look. Timed it wrong and a patrol scooped me up – cornered me with one of those bloody dogs.'

'They are Boer bulldogs, apparently – crossed with Turkish shepherds and Indian mastiffs and Russian wolfhounds and God only knows what else. They're ever so proud of them.'

'Are they? Well, give me old Cap any day. I was glad he got away. Turned tail and ran when he saw that big thing huffing and puffing at him. Did he look all right when you saw him?'

This being a difficult question when a beast was quite so rough-looking as Cap, but I reassured Duke that his lump of a terrier was in clover down at the Bull. Since the death of his wife and the departure of his children for Ireland, Duke's affection was reserved almost exclusively for ugly things like his dog and Jabez Potter.

In the blackness of a far corner, I heard someone rise to his feet and cross the cell. Timmy Bickley had not uttered a word since we had been put back in there, but now he dropped to the floor next to me.

'I'm sorry you've finished up in here, Mr Harrison.'

'It's not your fault, Timothy.'

'It is a bit though.'

Thirty-One

Wilkie told me later that he had let himself down badly that night. The business with the lamp in the church tower he considered simple ill-fortune, or, rather, God's inscrutable plan – which amounted to much the same thing. But he was sorry he could not summon up a suitably pithy piece of scripture when McCrea came for him.

'Forgive me if I do not invite you in, but I have lately witnessed you murder a man in cold blood and kidnap seven others.'

Wilkie had been expecting the knock on his door, and after hours of waiting it was almost a relief when he opened it at three in the morning to find the American and two others standing there.

'Fair enough. We won't take long.'

McCrea peered past the dishevelled vicar to where Artemisia stood in the hallway cradling one of those short fowling shotguns known bluntly as a 'cripple-stopper'. The barrel was full of spiders and there was no ammunition for it, but he wasn't to know that.

'Ma'am,' he said politely.

Artemisia did not reply, and McCrea took the opportunity to light a cigarette. His manner was easy and unconcerned.

'Now listen, Reverend. I don't know what you think is going to happen after tonight. Perhaps you think you'll go to the police, summon the cavalry, ride in and save the day.'

That was, in fact, exactly what Wilkie had planned, but he didn't say so.

'Only when you went round to the village policeman, he wouldn't open the door, would he?'

McCrea let his statement hang in the air a moment.

'He didn't open the door because we were there first and we told him not to. He's not a corrupt man and we haven't paid him off. We've just explained why it's better for everyone that he leaves the castle alone.'

'You mean you have threatened him,' clarified Wilkie.

'In a way. But we've also made it clear that if he did come looking for anyone, he wouldn't find them. And that'll be just the same if you go to Whitby or Middlesbrough and bring some town police out. We'll know they're coming long before they get here, and that old barn will be spick and span when they arrive.

'In fact, the only thing the arrival of the law is guaranteed to do is shorten Mr Catcliffe's life dramatically, so I mean it when I say that the best thing you can do for him – and his little friend – is nothing at all.'

McCrea's gaze fell on Jabez's battle-scarred hazel stick, leant up against a trunk at the bottom of the stairs. Being never really required for mobility except when his hangovers were literally crippling, he had left it behind on the principle that his hand would be more usefully filled with the black-market Bull Dog.

‘And in case you’re cracked enough to try another rescue, we’re going to leave a couple of dogs running loose in that yard from now on. Reckon you can handle those girls?’

Wilkie rubbed his temples. He was extremely tired and thoroughly out of his depth.

‘Didn’t think so. I wouldn’t take ’em on, not if I was made out of steel.’

‘So what will you do with him? With all of them?’

‘None of those men will be harmed, I give you my word.’

Wilkie gave a nervous laugh.

‘After you shot one barely two hours ago?’

McCrea raised his palms in a placatory gesture. He had no obvious firearm but Wilkie couldn’t help noticing the huge knife on his belt.

‘That wasn’t part of the plan. They ran, and I had to stop them. Didn’t want it. Still don’t.’

‘So what will you do with them?’

One of the ex-soldiers behind him shifted impatiently, but McCrea remained polite.

‘Listen, there are things going on here that you have no idea about. But Mr Garrett is a reasonable man. Not a killer – not unless he has to be. We’re on the side of good, I promise you.’

Bad men, as Wilkie was well aware, always claimed to be on the side of good. Usually they believed it, but McCrea sounded unconvinced.

‘Those men there will be kept as long as they need to be, then when things have been done that need to be done, they’ll be released. They will have to make some promises, but I think they’ll play along.’

‘And in the meantime? When people come looking? Because they will, you know – certainly for Harry at least.’

McCrea's tone hardened.

'Well that's the important bit, now, isn't it? You tell them a story, and you'd best think of a good one. He came, he left. Didn't find anything, job done. Set out to walk back to the harbour with his manservant, never heard anything more from him. And anyway you hardly knew him. Think you can do that?'

'And if I don't?'

'He dies, you die, she dies.' McCrea gestured towards Artemisia. 'Just be thankful you aren't down in that cell with them already.'

Wilkie cocked his head on one side.

'Why aren't I?'

'Horncastle wouldn't like it. He doesn't ask questions about the other stuff, but he'd be difficult if we lifted a priest. Old-fashioned like that.'

'If I go back without Mr Catcliffe, there's no story I can tell his aunt that she'll believe,' said Missy.

'Then that's a real problem right there, isn't it? Maybe you'd better come with us for the time being.'

Artemisia shrank back into the hallway and raised her useless old shotgun, while Wilkie expanded his already quite ample frame to block the doorway.

'Easy,' said McCrea with a slight smile. 'It was just a suggestion. You sort it out however you like, but if anyone comes seriously looking for those men, they all die and so do you.'

'I think that's enough threats for one night, don't you, Mr McCrea?' said Wilkie with more firmness than he felt.

'Just one more then.' McCrea dropped his cigarette and screwed it out with the toe of his boot.

‘If I catch you watching us from that belltower again, I’ll shoot you out of it like a jackdaw.’

He tipped his hat pleasantly, then turned and led his men back out into the lane.

Thirty-Two

Timmy Bickley knew already. Duke had told him. He knew about Abe and he knew about Alf. I couldn't see his face in the darkness but his voice was steady enough, considering what he'd been through.

'Alf was just nervous, that's all. We both was.'

'Nervous of what?'

The wall was cold and damp against my back.

'Abe wanted to pack it in at Catcliffe's – go and work full-time for the AATMM. Said the lads running it didn't have the stones. Probably right.'

'And why were you and Alf worried?'

Timmy sighed.

'It was all right for Abe. He was getting old and he'd made a good go of it, got to head shearman. But Alf and me was just starting out. What chance did we stand of getting on in life with an uncle in the union offices?'

'I'm not sure I follow you.' Though in fact I probably did.

'You know how works are. When a good job comes up, it goes to the company men, not the troublemakers. And union men's troublemakers.'

‘I’m sure that wouldn’t have been the case at Catcliffe’s. Your uncle was head shearman, after all.’

‘He was head shearman *before* he got involved with the unions. Even Abe was smart enough not to show his colours before he climbed the ladder. Look, Mr Harrison. I don’t mean anything bad by it, and you’ve always seemed decent enough – but we *do* get blacklisted. No-one can pretend it don’t happen.

‘You might not tell anyone to do it, nor Mr Jonas, but it’s a mark against our name when it counts. Alf and me, we always supported old Abe – believed in what he was doing – but we tried to keep our heads down at the same time. It was hard enough even before he started talking about going into leadership.’

I wanted to argue with him, but he wasn’t wrong.

‘Well I’m truly sorry about that, Timmy. Sounds a pointless thing to say now, doesn’t it? If we make it out of this alive then you have my word that we’ll sit down with Mr Jonas and talk about this.’

‘If we make it out. Not likely, I’d say.’

I waited for him to continue.

‘Alf and me had been chewing it over ever since Abe first told us. We knew he didn’t mean no harm – he just hadn’t thought it through from our side. I said I’d talk to him, but Alf thought he was too bloody-minded to listen.

‘Course, he was right, wasn’t he? I tried to tell it to Abe straight in the Two Brewers and it blew up in my face. It all got out of hand – like things did with Abe. He gave me a whack across the ear, stormed out.’

‘Arthur Letts told me.’

‘Solid old Arthur. “Company man to the soles of his feet” – or at least that’s what Abe used to say,’ he added.

'What Alf didn't tell me, though, was that he'd come up with another plan. He knew Abe wouldn't see sense, so he went to one of the blokes at the union and asked for some advice. Fella told him we was right. "It's an old man's game, union work," he told him, "and I'm sorry to say it but it'll be guilt by association the way the bosses see it," or something like that.

'Alf was courting a girl, looking to settle down, start a family – but still new in the job. He had a lot on the line and he couldn't let Abe scupper his future before he'd had a chance to get started.'

He stopped abruptly, catching himself. Because Alf would never have a future, not now. I heard Timmy swallow a couple of times, then sniff. A wet sound as he drew the back of his hand across his face.

'So this bloke,' he continued, the lump in his throat still audible, 'he tells Alf he's got an idea. Few lads he knows will catch Abe alone somewhere. Give him a good scare, mention that we're next. Just some food for thought. Make him realise it's not just his own neck he's sticking out.'

The way Timmy told it, Alf hadn't liked the plan at all. Abe was, after all, a stubborn sod at the best of times, and his nephew had worried that any attempt at intimidation would descend into violence. Not with these boys, the man at the AATMM had assured him. They would get the message across and Abe would be on his way without a scratch on him.

After all – the fellow had said to Alf – Abraham Bickley was a good man, fighting the fight. He would be a very valuable member of union management one day, but he just needed to keep his powder dry for a few more years until the boys had decent jobs behind them. And really, a bit more time as shop steward at the coal face was bound to help him build his reputation. Alf was doing him a favour, if he was only smart enough to realise it.

'And God love him, Alf says fine. The best place to get him on his own is on the way home from the Two Brewers on a Friday night, when he walks along the riverbank.'

And suddenly I understood why Timmy was growing a beard in a Yorkshire dungeon rather than sleeping off a skinful in his own bed two hundred miles away.

'He wasn't alone though, was he?'

In the dark I could see Timmy, calming down after the fight, going after his uncle to try and make peace with him. Following the route he knew he would take home, running to catch up.

'They were on him when I got there. Three big lads dragging him towards a van. Looked like he'd already had a beating. So I get stuck in, Abe gets free, starts holding his own. One of them goes down, comes back up with a great big spanner, cracks Abe hard with it. Then again. I manage to get hold of him but the other two drag me off. Abe's on his knees and I can tell he's done. Head and face all broken, mouth not working properly. "Run," he says, then the bloke hits him again and he goes down for good.'

Yet somehow, before they could murder him in turn or bundle him into the back of the van, Timmy had wriggled out of their grasp and made a dash for it.

I could imagine him jinking through back alleys, blood thumping in his temples, naked fear keeping him on his feet. Bursting back into the rented room he shared with his brother. Alf's terrible moment of realisation.

'He didn't mean any of it to happen. Really he didn't. Told me what he'd done, what was supposed to happen. But then suddenly, before either of us can say much, there's the police knocking on the door and I'm standing there covered in blood and we both know what it looks like.

'So I tell him, I've got to run. Stay quiet, we'll fix it, we'll get those boys and we'll get Jake bloody Bell but we can't do that with me in a cell.'

'Jacob Bell!' I exclaimed.

Duke's voice came out of the dark.

'Thought you'd like that.'

Jacob Bell. So that was who had arranged it all. The mild little politician who I'd met at the AATMM headquarters, with his gracious manner and his common-sense approach to industrial relations. Striking as a last resort, but abduction and intimidation of comrades gladly arranged at short notice.

'You've met him, then?' asked Timmy.

'I will admit, he didn't seem the type.'

'No, I didn't think so either. Reckon that's why Alf went through with it. Who'd believe someone like that would order a kidnapping?'

I could see why Timmy had run. It would have looked thoroughly damning, following old Abe out into the night after a fight and then being arrested shortly after the murder, bloodied and bruised. He had been frightened and disorientated and just needed some time to think, but unfortunately that was not on the cards.

Because if the men at the door were policemen at all then they were certainly not acting in any official capacity. Rather, they were performing the role of ferrets in a rabbit warren, flushing out the quarry.

As the constables ascended the stairs, Timmy Bickley had climbed out of the window, dropped from the outhouse roof into the cobbled yard, and slipped out of the back gate without spotting the second team lurking in the alley. Before he knew where he was, he had found himself face down on the cobblestones with a rag stuffed in his mouth and some lump of a man kneeling on his back while another bound his wrists and ankles.

Upstairs, Alf Bickley would have been swallowing down his guilt and swearing he hadn't seen his brother since they clocked off work, desperately hoping he was on his way to safety. But alas, Timmy was already in the back of the van that had been meant for Abe, en route to Paley's Wharf and the cargo hold of the *Clare Kelly*.

'Us Bickley boys haven't had much luck, have we, Mr Harrison? Ought to have wound our necks in while the going was good.'

It was the same expression Seamus Dyer had used. I daresay all of us in that cell were wishing we'd wound our necks in.

'I suppose you wish you'd kept your sentiments to the backs of toilet doors.'

There was a confused silence.

'The Porcelain Poet, you mean?'

'He's what brought me here.'

'Did he write something about us?' He sounded surprised.

'It's what he didn't write. When you and Abe went missing, so did the Porcelain Poet.'

Timmy whistled to himself.

'So it was Abe all along. Sly old sod, I'd never have guessed.'

'Unless it was you.'

I heard him laugh.

‘There’d be no point hiding it now if it was. If we get out, though, I’ll have to take up the paint pot. You won’t tell, will you?’

‘It’s the least I can do.’

Later, I heard him chewing over bad limericks in the darkness.

‘*There once was a fella called Abe…*’

Thirty-Three

Generally in life, the temperature you have is always the wrong one. This is part of the Englishman's condition, but it seemed especially true in the old smithy cellar. Outside in Birkdale it would be another baking hot, shirtsleeves and open collar sort of a day and I would have been longing to dip my bare feet in the beck, but huddled on the flagstones in that dank cellar with my head resting against gritty stone blocks, I felt like I might never be warm again. I longed for the detestable heat of Catcliffe's, but would have settled for just thirty seconds with the sun on my back.

At a noise nearby, I lifted my cap and opened my eyes. My vision remained almost perfectly black, but I could tell that someone was feeling their way round the edge of the room. There was a clang as their foot found the bucket that was generously provided for our personal needs, and they enacted their business with it, afterwards retreating as far away as possible from that appalling receptacle. Every life has its highs and lows, but this could well have been the absolute nadir of mine.

I fished out my pocket watch and passed it in vain back and forth in front of my face.

'Mid-afternoon, I'd say,' rasped Jabez's voice about two feet from my ear, startling me by his proximity. I could smell his rich perfume of horses and baccy even over the emanations from the bucket, but this was no reliable indicator of his position since it did tend to carry.

'How do you know?' I asked in hushed tones, though there was no need to stay quiet.

'Not his first time in chokey,' answered Duke from somewhere else in the darkness.

Or yours, I thought.

'I see quite well in the dark,' said Jabez, ignoring him. 'Give that watch over here.'

He took it, unseen, from my hand, then returned it a moment later.

'Later than I thought,' he said. 'Quarter to six.'

'Time flies when you're having fun,' observed Duke.

By 'fun', he must have been referring to a miserable basket of bread rolls and a demijohn of water provided about ten hours earlier, because that was the only thing to have happened to us all day.

'Rotten sods up at the house are probably bathing before dinner,' I said with feeling. 'I would very much like a bath.' The others remained silent, but the bucket answered me in its own way.

I wound the watch carefully in the dark, and only thought what a pointless exercise it was once I'd finished.

Presently, our guard came in and placed a tray within reach of the bars. Six chipped enamel mugs filled with a thin, lukewarm stew. No spoons.

'You've got five minutes, and I want all the mugs waiting on the tray when I come back.'

An undefined amount of time later – after the guard had been and gone again with the empties – someone in the cage began to sing a lewd song in an undertone, presumably to keep his spirits up. Several of the others knew the words, including Duke and Jabez, and they began to pick it up with hushed, tuneless voices. It was about a man who goes out hunting bunnies but ends up having a roll in the hay with some local harpy. Towards the end, as if by universal consent, they suddenly began getting louder,

'Well me powder is wasted and me bullets all gone, me ramrod is limp and I cannot fire on...'

There was an angry jangling and scraping of keys on the outside of the door, but by the time our guard had it open, they had whispered the final line and lapsed back into silence.

'Quiet!' he shouted. His lamp briefly illuminated the cell full of dirty, hollow-looking men as well as his own more substantial bulk. 'No talking, no singing.'

Only Jabez was rash enough to utilise his considerable vocabulary in response. The man glared at him.

'You think they won't hunt you because you won't be any sport with that leg. But that doesn't mean they won't find something to do with you. Very imaginative man, Mr McCrea. He'll fix it so your own mother wouldn't recognise you.'

'Wouldn't anyway,' said Jabez.

Our gaoler went out for a moment, returning with a bucket of cold water which he tossed in Jabez's general direction – mostly over me – then retreated with his lamp and shut us back into darkness. Spirits that had seemed momentarily lifted sank back into the abyss again.

'I wish I'd never heard of Piers Garrett,' murmured Lockwood in despair.

'Might not have made a difference,' said Timmy Bickley. 'I didn't know him from Adam and I'm still here.'

You're right, I thought, and suddenly it hit me that there was something odd about the men who had ended up imprisoned at Haydon Castle. Lockwood and Clay both represented workers in Garrett's factories, so I could see why they had been in danger. Timmy, Creedy and Dyer had all ended up in the bag by accident. But what about the others? Abe Bickley, Dick Fletcher's coal trimmer, or the regional officer from the AATMM that Bell had said was a soak. None of them had anything to do with Piers Garrett. So how was he picking his targets?

Jacob Bell had set Abe up, and while I still couldn't understand why he had done it, it made even less sense that he would be feeding names to Piers Garrett. More to the point, how would they even know each other? Garrett was in textiles and boot factories – in the ordinary course of things he should never have had any dealings with a metalworkers' union.

After a while, there were noises outside again, and the cellar was flooded with light as several men trooped in. There was McCrea, then the guard, and two or three more burly lads. From somewhere among them emerged the squat form of Piers Garrett, wearing full evening dress with some spots of food on his starched shirt front. He cast his lamp around the cell, sizing us up like livestock – which I suppose was roughly what we were.

Seamus Dyer was nearest the door. He had been a heavy-set fellow at one stage, but too long on starvation rations in the cellar had hollowed him out. Behind him, Lockwood coughed into his fist and looked resolutely at the floor. Garrett made a show of shaking his head, and turned to McCrea.

'I'm sorry to say that some of this meat is beginning to spoil.'

He raised the lamp higher and peered deeper into the cell, where he paused on me. His face betrayed a moment or two of indecision. Of everyone in that room I was the only one with the influence to do him any real harm, and so disposing of me was a pressing matter. Equally, though, it was a considerably riskier thing to murder a rich industrialist than any of the working men around me – most of whom were already considered lost and dead by their families. In the event, he decided to put off the dilemma for another occasion.

'You know, McCrea, I feel especially on my mettle today,' he mused. 'I think it is a night for a challenge.'

His head keeper made a show of looking us over with a critical eye, though there could only have been two or three candidates who would give them a good run. For a moment, it looked like he would pick the local man, Creedy, but then he turned to his employer.

'The Indian will be hard to bring down.'

Garrett pressed his jowly face up against the bars and studied Duke with evident pleasure.

'Yes, yes. A big brindle bull lurcher to match my own coursing dogs. Profession?'

'Publican,' said Duke mildly.

'Criminal, ex-sailor, muscle for hire – according to our guy in London,' said the American.

Garrett nodded approvingly.

'A good choice, Mr McCrea. See to it. I shall change.'

He bustled off up the stairs, and the five remaining men prepared themselves to winkle Duke out of the cell. Given the death sentence that awaited, I imagine they usually had to drag the chosen rabbit kicking and screaming into the open air, but Duke rose wearily, and McCrea held up a hand to his men.

'Seen worse, though, haven't we?' said Duke to Jabez, hauling the little man to his feet. Jabez didn't say anything, just shook his hand warmly. Those of the other men who still possessed hats had taken them off.

'I'm sorry you came looking for me,' said Timmy Bickley.

I rose too.

'Good luck, Duke.' It occurred to me that if he had never met me then he might never have ended up here, which was a silly thing to think because with a man like Duke it could just as easily have been something else.

'Hope you get your bath, mate.'

Duke and I were quite good friends, in a way, and what he really meant by the business about the bath was that if by any chance I got out of this, he would appreciate it if I would make sure his children in Ireland were all right.

A couple of McCrea's boys covered us with shotguns through the bars, while they let Duke out of the cell and manacled him. Then he allowed them to lead him out without a backward glance.

'Seen much worse than this!' shouted Jabez belatedly after him. Then the door shut, and darkness returned.

Thirty-Four

McCrea pointed his rifle in the air, and at a signal from Garrett he let off the starting gun. The men holding Duke released him, and he shot from their grasp like a racehorse out of the starting gate. Piers Garrett could barely contain his delight.

They gave Duke a head start of two or three minutes, which seemed quite sporting until you considered that he was trapped in a relatively small patch of woodland, hunted by a team of sixteen men with Martini–Enfield rifles and four dogs, any one of which could have brought down a pony.

Actually the sport was unlikely to be considered a success if anyone except Garrett or the dogs got him. In an ideal situation it would be both in turn, since McCrea would not give the order to loose the hounds unless his employer gave the word.

Twelve of the men were posted in pairs at suitable vantage points covering the edges of the wood, and their jobs were to signal the quarry's position and to stop him escaping into the fields beyond. They were a mixed bag of former soldiers, all excellent shots, and to cross open ground anywhere near them under a full moon was almost certain death. Garrett was accompanied by McCrea and two more armed men who were primarily dog handlers but also doubled as bodyguards and beaters. All of which had been explained to the hunted man before proceedings got underway.

Duke's odds were looking very long indeed as he sprang away through the shadowy tree trunks. At least it was old growth woodland with a dense canopy and there was very little scrub cover to slow his progress. What was more, he had explored these woods a week earlier while he was getting the measure of the estate, and he had an idea how he might just possibly save his skin.

Where the western edge of the woods climbed up onto the open moor, there was a collar of steeply sloping pasture land that he would not be able to cross without getting the stuffing blown out of him by a large-calibre rifle.

The eastern edge, however, was bordered by the sheer cliff that gave the Ernecliffe its name. A fellow gaining the top of that cliff might then run south along the wooded ridge of the Ernecliffe, eventually following the slope straight down into the sanctuary of Yattonby. It was a perilous climb, except if a man had spent many years swarming up the rigging of sailing ships in heavy weather, which fortunately Duke had. He still didn't much fancy his chances, but they were there and he could see no other way. Before he could try it, however, there was just one major hurdle, in that he had no idea which way he was running.

He knew he was in the western woods of Birkdale, but since he had been transported blindfolded on the floor of a carriage, Duke could not tell whether he had been set loose at their northern or southern edge. His captors had left him none the wiser, and the canopy was so thick that he could not make out the stars. After that first sprint into the darkness, which he could not keep up for more than a minute or two, he dropped his pace to a loose-limbed jog that he could sustain for hours. Unleashed, the dogs could catch him at any speed – but until McCrea let them slip, the pursuit party would be travelling at the pace of an overweight industrialist in his fifties. They would need Duke to tire or become disorientated before they gained ground.

As he ran, he tried to see which side of the tree trunks the moss grew on – having once been told it favoured the north – but he could not make it out. An experienced woodsman might have known any number of other telltale signs, but those same decades at sea that had made him a fine climber had also left Duke a poor outdoorsman, and the only trees with which he was particularly familiar were those that stuck upwards from the decks of ships.

The bag over his head and the noise of the carriage wheels had muffled sound as well as vision, but try as he might, he could swear he had not heard the sounds of a pub or church bells. Since the road to the southern edge of the wood went through Yattonby, he took a giant leap of faith and began to curve left, reasoning that he must have been released in the north. He turned gradually, fearful of accidentally doubling back on himself and bounding into the arms of his pursuers. Somewhere behind him there was the pop of another pistol shot, presumably signalling that the game was now afoot.

He stopped dead, just for a second, and in the quiet of the still summer night he could hear them coming through the trees. They were stealthy, and the dogs did not bark, but that amount of human and canine muscle did not move in silence. There was the occasional crack of a branch, the scrape of hobnails on a tree root or the clink of a rifle strap. They had taken his jacket before he set off, leaving him in a dirty white shirt that would show up brightly among the trees. He pulled it over his head, together with his undershirt, and dropped them among the previous autumn's rotten leaves, revealing a wiry-haired torso that was criss-crossed with old scars and poorly executed tattoos. Let them try spotting a dark-skinned man in the shadows.

After a while he splashed into an unseen beck, only shin-deep, and decided to risk the noise of carrying on through in the hopes that it might throw the dogs off his scent. The bank on the other side was steep and soft, and Duke struggled up on his hands and knees, groping through the damp leaf litter to find purchase in the creamy, iron-rich mud that stained his forearms bright orange. It slowed him down and made a mess that a man like McCrea would not miss, but with any luck it might slow them down too.

Wet and muddy, he pushed on, forcing his pace to make up the lost time. His breathing felt deafeningly loud, and he was so preoccupied with trying to quieten it that it took him completely by surprise when he suddenly burst through a rhododendron thicket into an open field that rolled away from him towards the dark edge of the moor up above. There, off to his right, the north star twinkled smugly. He had gone the wrong way.

The moment Duke emerged from the shadows there was the shriek of a police whistle somewhere diagonally ahead. He froze. The moor ahead seemed so close. Could he risk the dash? There was a thump and a muzzle flash from somewhere near the alarm whistle, and a fist-sized clod of turf jumped out of the earth in front of him. In a moment he had disappeared back into the dark of the wood, a rabbit back into a burrow full of polecats.

He knew that by turning back towards the main party he would be doing exactly what they wanted him to, but the snipers out at the moor edge would shred him. An easier end than the one that waited in the wood, but a certainty.

The dogs were barking now, and he could hear Garrett shouting,

'Flank him!'

Duke stopped dead and squatted silently down on his haunches, listening hard and trying to work out which directions his pursuers would come from. There was no sense in moving now until he had to. He was pinned against the rifles at the western edge of the wood, and the only way to the Ernecliffe was through Garrett's party. At least if they had split up to box him in then he might not have to handle them all at once.

As his own breathing recovered, he could hear the approach of at least one group, then the splash as they crossed the beck just ahead of him. This was it. Whoever it was and however many there were, if he could hit them from above as they toiled up that steep bank, it was his best chance.

Creeping forward to the lip of the slope, he peered down at the panting figures clawing their way up, weighed down by their firearms. Two men, one dog – one of the heavier-set ones that looked more mastiff than wolfhound. Lord knew where the others were, but that couldn't be helped. The moment he popped his head up, the beast began barking – a deep, deafening thump of a bark. The men had just a moment to look up before Duke launched himself down, taking two long leaps then cannoning into the nearest man feet first.

Duke's boot connected hard with a head, and he felt his hobnails go through some teeth. There was a moment of stunned silence, then an agonised wail of pain as Duke rolled away down the bank and splashed into the beck, tearing the man's rifle from his shoulder as he went. Before he could get up, the dog hit him like a runaway carthorse, driving him down into the muddy stream bed. With a tremendous expenditure of strength he wriggled frantically out from underneath it, thrashing at its face with his free arm, and as the beast sprang forward to pinion him a second time, it came up short with a jerk. The screaming behind it grew suddenly more intense, and Duke realised that the dog was still attached to the man whose face he had kicked in. Somehow the unfortunate fellow must have got tangled up with the lead and the powerful creature was dragging him down the bank like an anchor.

Duke slipped once, then made it to his feet and made a short dash to put some distance between himself and the dog. As he turned, he saw the uninjured man on the other bank pulling his weapon into his shoulder. It was a rushed shot, and as Duke flung himself away from it he knew it had gone wide. He brought his own rifle up. The dog was struggling towards him, while the man who had just fired was fumbling to get another round into the breech. With a great effort to swallow his fear of the dog and think rationally, Duke swung his sights onto the hunter and drilled him into the bank. He had no ammunition belt, nor enough time to beat man and beast to death with the stock, so he dropped the rifle and ran.

He was through, but the others were bearing down on him, and he could hear the shouting and barking close by. Someone – probably Garrett – took a long shot and missed. Would the mess he had left behind him at the beck hold them up for a moment? They had not loosed the dogs, so they must have been thinking they could still get him. He loped on through the wood, weaving through the trunks. It couldn't be more than half a mile to the Ernecliffe. Something burst loudly out of the bushes to his left, but it was just a pair of startled deer, their white rumps bouncing off through the trees.

He wanted to know if they were still behind him, but he didn't dare stop, not even for a moment, so he ran and ran until he could see the looming black shadow of the cliff up ahead of him. The urgency was too great to start inspecting it for the best route up, and he began to climb at the first opportunity, hauling himself up towards the moonlight.

The first fifteen feet were easy, but then the cliff face began to grow crumbly – a treacherous, gritty mix of eroded sandstone and dry earth that felt solid but disintegrated into powder and pebbles when he put weight on it. More than once he had to scrabble across from a patch of cliff that began falling away beneath him, grabbing woody stems of trailing ivy and praying they held. It was difficult to get a purchase with his heavy boots and he would have preferred to string them round his neck and climb barefoot, if only time had allowed. It was noisy work and he felt sure he must soon start to be shot at, but it looked like he might have been dealt an unexpected piece of luck. Somewhere in the dash across the forest, Garrett and his remaining hunters had got on the wrong track – perhaps following those deer he had spooked. He could hear them a good distance further along the foot of the cliff, shouting with frustration.

Duke began to feel a glimmer of real hope, until a chorus of excited barking told him that they had finally swallowed their pride and released the dogs. He would have to hope the fall killed him if he slipped. He was now high enough that he had to thread his way through the tree branches where they pressed against the face of the cliff. There were few leaves since it was too shaded even in the middle of the day for there to be much light there, but the twigs needled his back and snagged on his trousers.

He was nearly up on the Ernecliffe, but one final hazard remained. Between the threadbare tops of the trees and the lip of the cliff was a band of moonlight that he must cross to get to safety. The branches below him would offer some camouflage from anyone at ground level, but even so he would be lit up like a big dark spider against the cliff face. The gruff barking of the dogs was now directly below him, and the men could not be far behind.

Sure enough, as Duke swung himself up into the light, his hands and elbows bloodied and his trousers torn, he heard them. First there were the low tones of McCrea's voice far below, followed by Garrett's cry of exhilaration as he followed his gamekeeper's arm. To pick him off the side of the Ernecliffe and have him plummet a hundred feet into the leaf litter would be a jolly good end to such a dramatic hunt.

The first shot whacked into the cliff face well wide of Duke. Excitement and the fatigue of the long pursuit had made Garrett's aim unsteady, and as the industrialist slotted another heavy round into the breech his delight was tempered with a sudden sense of urgency. Up above him, Duke was moving fast, pulling himself up on stiff boughs of ivy that had bolted themselves into the Ernecliffe like climbing ropes. There were mere seconds remaining of the pursuit, and if Garrett missed, there was a very real risk that the Indian would escape – something which had never even come close to happening before, and the consequences of which could not be contemplated.

Duke had his hand on the lip of the cliff when it came. There was a fraction of a second where he felt something slice into his ribs, a palm's width below his armpit, and prepared himself for the inevitable tumble, then a moment of sheer joy when he realised he had not been hit but simply winged by a sharp fragment of stone or steel from a shot that had landed a few inches clear of him. With a final aching effort he grasped an overhanging sapling and heaved himself up onto level ground.

'McCrea!' Garrett was screaming on the forest floor. Men were in uproar, shouting and running south in a hopeless attempt to get round the edge of the Ernecliffe and cut him off. The dogs were going berserk.

Panting with exertion, Duke rolled over onto all fours and looked down over the edge of the cliff. Way down below, McCrea took aim through the thin web of tree branches at the dark figure illuminated in the moonlight, and shot him.

Thirty-Five

The first hint we had that anything was wrong was when our gaolers changed shift in the early hours. Presumably there had been a regular old commotion out in the yard as the hunting party came back in, and the man who took over was still full of it. He was keen to talk to someone about whatever had gone on – and since guard duty was a solitary gig, his prisoners would have to do. He brought his lamp and stool down into the cellar, waking us all up with the noise and the light.

'Right carry-on your mate's caused,' he said, as if it was our fault. 'Wouldn't want to be you today.'

Most of the men just rolled over on the stone floor to turn away from the light, so he piped up again.

'A right to-do.' He whistled for emphasis. He was much younger than the others, and obviously possessed that gift for human relations that sees men exiled to lonely guard shifts in the dead of night.

'What sort of a to-do?' I prompted.

'Well,' he said, evidently pleased to be sharing his news. 'Two in the infirmary, for starters. One not like to see the night out, and the other... well you take my word, his old dear's going to have a hard time recognising him with a face like that.'

‘And the prisoner?’ grunted Jabez.

‘What? Your mate, you mean? The Indian?’ taunted the young man. ‘Yeah, that’s right, I know you came here looking for him.’

He paused for effect, and I realised suddenly that he was frightened. His cocksure bravado was all nerves.

‘Nah, sorry mate – didn’t make it,’ he announced suddenly. ‘McCrea blew a right big hole in him.’ He thumped his fist against his chest to indicate the impact of the shot.

We had known, I suppose, that there was no chance, but it still ached deep inside to hear it. I did not dare look at Jabez. All the same, I knew there had to be more. Now that I had sniffed out his fear, the crueller our young guard’s words got, the more scared he sounded. It reminded me of the way a university professor of mine at Leipzig, one F. H. Müller, had imagined that his constant lascivious talk about women masked his lust for his more handsome students rather than emphasising it.

‘Trouble is, though, it was such a long shot that he crawled off into the bracken to die, and they haven’t found him yet. Still out there now, beating about the bush. Got every dog in the place out sniffing about, but no joy so far.’

So that was it. That’s why the lad was frightened. If a bullet-wounded Duke made it back to a town then there would be no covering it up. Garrett’s hunts would be done for, and everyone involved in them would be on the hook – including McCrea, his men, and probably Horncastle too.

Somewhere amid the grief there was just the tiniest flicker of hope. The slimmest of chances that Duke, however badly hurt, might just have managed to get to safety. I risked a glance towards Jabez, but his face was granite, the lamplight making deep black pools of his eye sockets. I didn't need to see his eyes just at that moment to know there was murder in them.

Having unburdened himself of his thoughts, and sensing perhaps that he had given away more than he ought to, our irritating young gaoler picked up his stool and lamp and went out, climbing up into a dawn that was for us entirely abstract.

I rolled over in the darkness, thinking about what he had told us. If they couldn't find Duke, then Garrett's only hope would be to try and destroy all the evidence – and there weren't many versions of the story that ended well for the gaggle of men banged up in the cellar at Haydon Castle. Eventually, somehow, sleep caught up with me – the sort of lurching sleep that feels like drowning and leaves you more exhausted than if you'd just stayed awake.

....

The guard shifts changed; a basket of bread and a canteen of water came and went. I had struck my last match the day before in order to check my watch – and with that option now removed, I found I cared less and less what the actual time was. All the same, I continued to wind the watch, holding it against my ear and enjoying the delicate urgency of the action chuntering away.

We whispered our hopes sporadically to one another – never our fears – but mostly we sat in the cold and the silence, listening for rodents and passing in and out of sleep. There was nothing else to do and it was the only way to feel any sort of peace.

It was during one of these occasional conversations with my cell-mates that Creedy mentioned Artemisia Moss. Except that, like everyone in Yattonby, he used a different name.

‘Why do you call her Missy Richardson?’ I asked. ‘A man in the pub the other night called her that too, but we know her as Artemisia Moss.’

‘Going by Moss again is she?’ smiled Creedy. ‘That was her maiden name. Richardson’s her married one.’

‘She never mentioned a husband.’ When I thought about it, Artemisia hadn’t mentioned much about herself at all.

‘She wouldn’t, I suppose.’ He was obviously not much given to gossip and would have preferred to leave it at that, but even in the pitch-black he could see us looking at him expectantly. After a short silence he caved.

‘She’s never had much luck, Missy. Only child, mother died when she was born. Her father was a keeper on the estate, but he got ill when Missy was twelve or thirteen. Something in his guts. Took him a long time to die and Missy had it hard looking after him.

‘It was about the time Chalmers started as agent and he had a real bee in his bonnet about them living in that cottage rent-free. Fortunately, old Lord Horncastle had a soft spot for Moss and he insisted they didn’t take a penny off him while he was ill. All the same, there still wasn’t enough saved to see them through. Skinny little thing almost wasted away with her father.

‘After Moss died, Chalmers finally got his way. She had to give up the cottage but they took her on as a maid at the castle. Then when she was sixteen or so she caught Richardson’s eye. He was Lord Daniel’s valet.’

‘You mean the present Lord Horncastle?’ Not a man who would be getting a Christmas card from me, as things stood.

‘Aye. Still haven’t got used to calling him that yet.’

'And she married this man Richardson?'

'She did, against everyone's advice. He was a handsome one and he had plenty of charm but the rest of us knew him for what he was. Except Missy. He gave it all the tender sweetheart routine until they were married, but after that it wasn't much of a life.'

Creedy was not the sort of fellow to elaborate, and he did not need to. Men like this Richardson were universal, wherever you came from.

'Didn't anyone do anything?'

'They wanted to. We all wanted to. Everyone felt sorry for Missy. But Lord Daniel thought the world of Richardson. Cross him and you crossed the family.'

'There were no children?' I asked tentatively.

'No,' said Creedy, sighing. 'There was that mercy at least – though there was some as thought that might be part of it.'

'So how did it end? She must have left the castle at least six years ago, for she has worked that time for my aunt in Whitby.'

'Yes, I suppose it would have been about that long ago that it happened. She'd been married to Richardson a couple of years by then. But she didn't leave – she was let go. It got awkward. She never made a fuss but she was showing up at work in a bad way. Lord Horncastle said it couldn't go on, but Richardson put the blame on Missy. Said she wasn't right up top, said she used to go at him with her fists for no reason in the evenings and the injuries were from holding her down. No-one really believed it, but Lord Daniel stood up for Richardson – and Missy wouldn't tell her side of things. So there it was.'

'And I suppose it got even worse once she had no job to go to?' I thought of resourceful Artemisia, hidden away with her split lips and bruises in an estate cottage, dependent on her captor.

'Until she ran away.'

'To the vicarage.' The voice from the gloom was Jabez's.

'To the vicarage,' I repeated. 'To Reverend Wilkie and his sister.'

'Just about the only people who couldn't be bullied into giving her back. He's a funny fish, the Reverend. Seems like butter wouldn't melt, but he won't be told what to do by anyone. Chalmers tried first, then even Lord Daniel went over there, but Parson still refused to send her home. He's not a bad man, you know, Lord Daniel. Didn't mean to make Missy's life hard, just trusted his valet's word over some maid he didn't know. Even by then I think he knew he'd made a mistake. Threatened Parson at the time but he never followed through.'

It was not difficult to work out what had happened next. A short while living temporarily under Wilkie's protection, then finally a bumper dose of luck in a life thus far devoid of it, when two selectively deaf old bats in comical sun bonnets showed up in the village to sketch the worm-eaten misericords of St Stephen's. The persuasive Reverend Wilkie would have given them the hard sell over an exemplary young domestic currently looking for a situation, and a fortnight later Missy Richardson was Artemisia Moss, looking out from Whitby's West Cliff with Aunt Diana's keys on her belt and open water ahead.

'And Richardson? Presumably she is still married to him?'

'Widowed, thank the Lord above.' Not a phrase one often heard, but apt enough in this case. 'He died three years back. Tooth went bad and poisoned his blood.'

Was his the grave I had seen her standing by in the churchyard on Sunday morning? Or had it been her father's? Whatever the case, it must have been harder than I had realised for Artemisia to return to Yattonby.

I wondered what the subject of our conversation was up to while we were languishing down there. In the unlikely event that Duke had got away, the best thing we could hope for was that he had ended up at the vicarage rather than the policeman's house. Wilkie was a good, game chap in his way, but it was Missy who would know what to do.

Thirty-Six

I awoke from a nap to the clattering of the door opening once more, and the scraping of hobnails on flagstones as men with lamps tramped in. How I loathed these visits – even more than the dead time between them.

Blinking in the lamplight, I saw there were four of them, including the lanky, bowler-hatted form of McCrea.

'The old man wants to see you,' he said, holding his lamp up. I looked around to see who he was talking to, and realised it was me.

'No need to worry,' he added, hoping to forestall a struggle. 'He just wants to talk. In the house.'

He made the others stand back against the wall while one of his men poked a shotgun through the bars and the unpopular young gaoler opened the cell door to let me out.

As I stepped forward there was a voice behind me in the gloom.

'You, McCrea.'

The gamekeeper cast his lamplight past me into the cell, and there was Jabez standing a little apart from the others. The man with the shotgun raised it a fraction.

'It true you shot Duke?'

'I did,' said McCrea. He looked at the wonky little man standing there in his cavernous overcoat, but with no real interest in his eyes. 'And I suppose you were old friends and you've all kinds of things you want to say to me.'

'Just that I mean to do something properly horrendous to you if I get the chance.'

McCrea smiled faintly.

'Then I'd better make sure you don't get one.'

With a backward glance at Jabez I followed McCrea out and up the stairs. As we came out into the open air I had to stop for a moment while my eyes adjusted. After nearly two days underground, the warmth and air and light was so wonderful that it bordered on the unbearable.

'Give it a moment,' said McCrea. 'It'll pass.'

Which it did, leaving a warm, clear summer's afternoon in the cobbled yard, complete with the yapping of spaniels and the deep bass boom of the manhunters in the stable next door. There was a horse tied up and a trestle table in the middle of the courtyard with a couple of rifles all stripped down for cleaning. I took my watch out of my waistcoat pocket and it showed ten past five.

Across the yard, beyond the barbed wire and the wheat field, was St Stephen's. It was just about close enough that I could pick out some of the colours in those cracked old windows, but it was in a different world now.

Someone produced a set of shackles from inside the guardhouse, and when my wrists were manacled, two of the guards led me off towards the house. The lad disappeared back inside and McCrea returned to cleaning his guns.

For some reason they took me round the front of the house and we entered through the main door into that imposing great hall, almost as if I were a guest arriving early to dinner rather than a scrofulous prisoner being dragged out of the depths for an audience with a maniac.

The maniac himself was waiting for me in the library, puffing on a cigar in an armchair that had been built for a man with considerably longer limbs. Notebooks, ledgers and crumpled balls of paper were scattered on the carpet around him, though the library books themselves remained unmolested behind plate glass.

Garrett motioned me towards a rough wooden kitchen chair that had apparently been brought in specially for me, then made a sort of hissing noise at the two guards, who promptly took themselves outside.

I sat, and he sucked in a capacious mouthful of smoke, rolling it around his tongue.

'Comfortable?' he asked.

'Not especially. Trouble you for a match? I've run out.'

He tossed me a silver match case from the side table, and I took out my cigarette case. Only three left, as if the day wasn't bad enough already.

'You see why you are a problem, Catcliffe,' he said. His foot was jiggling back and forth, and it struck me that, far from being relaxed with his cigar and his oversized armchair, he was in a state of great agitation. So they had still not found Duke, then. Had that indestructible old lascar really made it out alive?

'Yes, I can see that. Though hardly my fault, I would argue.'

'Preposterous,' he said. 'Little shit. How dare you talk to me like that?'

I smoked my cigarette and waited. This was, in fact, the third time in my life that I had knowingly sat opposite someone who was considering killing me, and I had learned that it was usually better to say as little as possible.

'Of course it's your fault,' he went on. 'All your fault. You come here, messing in my business. What were you trying to achieve?'

'I just wanted to find out what happened to Abraham Bickley.'

He looked at me goggle-eyed through his cigar smoke.

'Bickley? Bickley! Why in God's holy bloody name do you care what happened to *Bickley*? He was nobody!'

I stood up and went over to the ashtray on the huge leather-topped desk. This was presumably the exact spot where the old Lord Horncastle had planned to get one over on the Ross & Blayne Mining Company, and had arranged the disastrous marriage that had seen his son's estate turned into a murder park.

'He was somebody, Mr Garrett.'

'Yes, that's right, he was a sanctimonious bastard, just like you. Why don't you bugger right off and join a fucking convent? Making out you give a tinker's about the men who work for you. Do you want to give them your office? Let them sit around drinking your brandy while you break your back on the factory floor? Let them have your tasty society girls while you go home to their pinched little wives and their fifteen scabby children?'

He looked at me expectantly, angrily.

'No, I don't suppose I do.'

'No, I don't suppose you do either. Little prig. There's an order to these things. Even in a failing old heap like Catcliffe's. They work for us, that's all there is to it – and they should be damned grateful for it. But they're not, though, are they?

'People like Bickley – whingers, blackmailers! Threatening us with strikes and God only knows what else. How... how *bloody* dare they?' He could barely contain himself.

'These men have the gall to try and tell us what to do! And now they're even in Parliament! It's the beginning of the end. It's us that run things, not them. They're parasites. Illiterate, unexceptional, greasy little slum-dwellers trying to do me out of all I've worked for because they're not clever enough to build anything themselves.'

I let him bluster away, because with men like that you just had to let them say their piece. In many ways he had quite a bit in common with the tub-thumpers like Abe Bickley who shouted about social reform in the Two Brewers of a Friday night, except those union boys didn't have quite such a ready supply of money and guns – which was probably just as well for the likes of Garrett and me.

I lit my penultimate cigarette. Somehow it had a slight taste of that appalling bucket in the cellar.

'So you did kill him then?'

'Who, Bickley? Damn right I did. Had my men beat him like a slab of old meat. That's the way to deal with these people. Clean, cold fear. Just a whisper – a rumour – step out of line and one dark night you might just end up being fed your own teeth as a last meal. No-one needs to know who does it or how it happens, just that it does.

'Or you snatch them in the night, like the ones I've been hunting here. They're not fools, these lads, whatever else they are. "What's that?" they'll say in hushed voices as they drink their pissy pots of mild.

"Another man gone, you say? Vanished without a trace? Well, was he a union man? *My God, he was?*"'

His voice had steadily risen in pitch, and he was affecting a hammy Cockney accent.

'You'll see. The working man mostly just wants a comfortable life. Make it dangerous to get outside his box and he'll soon get back in it again.'

He stopped himself.

'Well, I mean, I said "you'll see", but you won't.'

I had more or less known this was coming, but still, to hear it out loud felt like having most of my lower bowel turn to rust.

'I had you brought up here as a courtesy to let you know it's your turn tonight.'

I nodded, trying to swallow down my nausea.

'Fair enough. Duke got away then?'

'The Indian? Probably not, but we haven't found him and I can't take the chance. It's going to be the devil's own mess to sort out, but here's how I'm going to do it.

'I'll shoot you in the woods later – maybe let the dogs have a go if they're lucky – then we'll come back here and put bullets in that little friend of yours and all the rest of them. Reverend and his housekeeper will have to go missing too – which my son-in-law won't like, but he'll have to live with it. Been on the cards anyway. McCrea bought us some time the other night by promising them that you were all going to be fine if they stayed quiet, which *obviously* you weren't.

'Once that's done, you'll all go on the bonfire and what's left will go in the pit behind the barns with the others. Throw in some quicklime and move a nice big muck heap on top of you for good measure. I'll even name it after you, if you like.

'So you see, you really have fucked it for everyone concerned, haven't you, Mr Catcliffe?'

Including you, Mr Garrett, I thought to myself – though it wasn't much consolation.

I wished now that Wilkie had paid more attention to his catechism, but at least he had made a deliberate choice to side with us. Missy had just been minding her own business as a housekeeper for two old ladies before I turned up, and I felt wretchedly guilty at dragging her into it all.

'And if Duke did make it out?'

'If the law does come knocking, we can claim we haven't seen you since dinner on Monday. This place will be squeaky clean by then, and it'll be the word of a darkie criminal against a pillar of industry and a hereditary peer.'

He permitted himself a half-hearted smile for the first time since I'd been brought in – more for my benefit, I think, than because he was feeling chipper. We had, after all, thrown a huge spanner in the works of his leisure pursuits. More to the point, he must have known he was done. Bad apple as I may have been, my family knew exactly where I was, and I could guarantee they would come after me with all the influence new money could buy.

Garrett's number had been up long before I arrived in Yattonby. He had simply racked up too many bodies to get away with it, and now he was proposing to add eight more to the heap in a single night. It was simple insanity – a last desperate play for a man who could already feel the noose chafing at his Adam's apple. Not much consolation to those of us on the butcher's bill for the coming evening, but there was nothing to be done about that.

I stood up, suddenly weary of this wretched little man. My old pa was right, he was a gnome, and it seemed a terrible waste of my final hours to spend any more time in his company – even if the alternative was that dank cellar with its bucket and rats.

'I suppose that's that then. If you might permit the condemned man an indulgence, there's one thing I'd love to know.'

He looked at me wide-eyed as if I were the mad one.

'Who helped you make your list, Mr Garrett? Who gave you the nod about which men to snatch? You may not have liked what Abe Bickley stood for but your paths would never have crossed. So who gave you his name?'

Garrett shook his head.

'Just won't give up, will you?'

'I'll have to soon.'

'So you will. When you put it that way, I'm delighted to disappoint you. You're right, I did have a fellow helping me pick my quarry. A clever man with a good deal of experience managing labour relations. But I'm not going to give you his name because I'd rather you die wondering.'

He didn't need to, I thought. There was one man I'd spoken to who matched that description almost exactly. William bloody Collison from the Free Labour Association.

'In that case, I'll bid you good afternoon, Mr Garrett.'

'Piss off.'

Thirty-Seven

I came out of the library into the great hall, hands cuffed, flanked by guards. Each had a hand on my arm, but despite the fact that I was shaking with fear, I was determined to follow Duke's example and conduct myself with dignity. And then I looked up the stairs to see Lord and Lady Horncastle coming down.

They were dressed for dinner, elegant as ever. Arm in arm, they looked the perfect young couple. Young one on the way, bright future ahead. Except there, ahead of them, was a filthy, manacled man who was marked for death, and by the horror on their faces, they knew it full well.

In a panic, Horncastle pivoted his wife and the two of them hurried back upstairs, Alice stumbling over her long skirts. Perhaps there was a difference between knowing more or less what the old man was doing in the western woods and actually seeing a fellow they had lately dined with on his way to be chewed up by Ellen Garrett's doggies, but it was evidently more than they could bear.

It was more than I could bear too. Somehow it was easier to cope with Garrett's malevolence than Horncastle's weakness – perhaps because I recognised myself there.

'Horncastle!' I shouted. There was the sound of a door shutting hastily. The moment I cried out, my guards seized me roughly under the arms and began dragging me across the hallway, my boot heels scoring wide scars into the pile of the expensive Persian rug.

'Damn you, man, don't bury your head! This is your home, your land, your place! You can stop this! You just have to stand up to him!'

Somewhere in one of the upstairs rooms a woman was sobbing. Everyone in the house must have been able to hear me as the men hauled me towards the door, kicking and struggling.

'He's murdering people out in the woods! For sport!' I raged. 'You know that! You have to make it stop! Don't be a coward!'

Just as we reached the steps, I caught a movement at the top of the stairs, and the last thing I saw before that heavy front door shut behind me was the Dowager Lady Horncastle sitting in her bath chair on the landing, nurse standing at her shoulder, gazing down at me with a blank stare that could have expressed either pity or indifference.

....

McCrea knew why Garrett had summoned me to the house.

'Last rabbit,' he said by way of greeting as my guards manhandled me back into the yard. There was a tinge of regret in his voice, but I daresay it wasn't for me. No doubt by the time the police arrived to clean up, he and the other mercenaries living in the stable block would be long gone.

He looked me up and down, much as he had sized up Duke in the pen the night before – only this time there was much less approval in his gaze.

'Not much of a finish.'

He was an inscrutable fellow, McCrea. I wanted to ask him why he did it all. Was it just about the money? Because he seemed to take no pleasure in any of it. He lied and threatened and murdered, but he did it with a sort of detached apathy that I had only ever seen in men who had lived through too many wars. Jabez had him pegged as an old soldier, but I just couldn't tell.

I turned to him.

'"A year or two here, a year or two there," you said.'

He raised an eyebrow at me. His way of saying 'go on'.

'That evening you brought Argo out of the stables to show us, that's what you said.'

'Lot of demand for my skills. All kinds of clients.'

'You must be a very good shot.'

'Got to find the prey first. I'm good at that too.'

'The prey. Was it mostly human or animal?'

'There's no difference.'

He turned away in apparent disinterest, and went back to polishing the stock of his rifle. It occurred to me that he might shoot me with it later, and furthermore that being shot by McCrea was quite possibly the best way the evening could turn out.

Down in the dungeon, Jabez and the others knew too. Perhaps the garrulous gaoler had spilled it, but more likely they had just worked it out for themselves.

'Sorry, mate,' he mumbled in a voice unaccustomed to sympathy.

'It's worse than that, Jabez.'

'Is it?' He thought for a moment.

'All of us then?' asked a northern voice which must have been Creedy.

‘I’m afraid so. After they’ve finished with me in the woods.’

There was the sound of four men in the darkness breathing out their last dreams for the future into that rank air, but Jabez just whistled.

‘Hope those bloody dogs choke on my leg.’

Sometimes, I considered, it might be nice to be like Jabez Potter. He was probably going to get killed later, but he wasn’t too frightened about it just yet. His was the sort of life philosophy you read about in Epictetus or Seneca, only I wouldn’t share that with him because he was liable to tip a bucket of effluent over my head.

I turned up the collar of the ill-fitting old serge jacket that I’d bought off a bloke at the factory, and considered that I wasn’t even going to die in a decent suit. If I was worrying about that, it wasn’t exactly a ringing endorsement of the life I had lived.

Shifting a little to reach my watch, I held it next to my ear again, listening to the soothing sound of the ticking. I tried hard to think about my family – or even about Agnes, living in her great hall in Surrey and married to the man I hated most in the world. But what I mainly thought about was what time Piers Garrett would finish his dinner.

Thirty-Eight

The sun had dropped off the horizon and distant thunder clouds bloomed purple over the moor as Artemisia slipped through the church gate at St Stephen's. She crossed the churchyard, past crumbling sandstone graves with pitted skulls chiselled into the head-pieces, to the church's western door. There she set down the object she had been carrying, which was one of Wilkie's big glass jars full of shells and fossils suspended in methylated spirit. Eight or nine more of them were already placed there.

She turned and followed the cracked flagstones to where the Reverend Peter Wilkie sat on the wall, legs swinging, looking up at his church. On the way she passed the tramp who lived in the east porch, slowly dragging the small bogey in which his few earthly belongings were stored under an oilskin tarpaulin. He was off to sit out the oncoming storm in the comparative luxury of the Reverend's potting shed, and his grin was even broader than usual.

Artemisia swung her legs over the wall and perched next to Wilkie, but facing the other way, towards the castle and the bruised sky.

'Beautiful, isn't it, in its own way?' he said, gazing at the weathered old building.

‘That it is, Reverend.’ She watched a barn owl skim across one of the fields opposite, wobbling in the breeze. The air was still muggy, but the storm was beginning to reel it in, rippling the wheat with warm gusts.

She shuffled slightly closer.

‘My times are in your hands…’ she began, then let him finish the verse.

‘Deliver me from the hands of my enemies, from those who pursue me.’ Wilkie smiled without taking his eyes off the church.

They stayed that way for a moment or two longer, then Missy straightened up.

‘Are you ready, Reverend?’ she asked. For the first time he turned to look at her, and nodded.

‘Good,’ she said. ‘Give me a quarter of an hour, then get started before this rain blows in.’

She hopped off the wall and set off back down the street towards the vicarage. Wilkie in turn slithered awkwardly back to earth and began carrying the jars inside the building, lining them up along the front pew. The musty cool of the church was a relief after the humid graveyard.

As he ferried his jars down the aisle he instinctively avoided some of the deeper potholes, wondering as he did so how many times he must have walked up and down that gangway. Finally he knelt to say a prayer in front of the altar. There was quite a lot to say, but time was short, so he had to confine himself to the basics, reminding himself that his Lord above knew it all anyway.

That done, he returned to the jars, picked one up, and poured its contents carefully over the choir stalls.

Thirty-Nine

Insulated as we were from the outside world by a good deal of earth and stone, we could hear the faint sounds of shouting filtering down the stairs and through the door. At first I thought it must just be McCrea and his boys out in the yard getting things ready for the evening's sport, but they had not made nearly so much noise on the evening they took Duke away. Though the voices were distant, they had an urgency about them – an indistinct quality of panic that had us all sitting up in the darkness, especially when we heard a popping noise underneath the hue and cry. Suddenly, there was movement on the stairs outside and the grinding of keys in the lock.

As the door swung open, the uproar outside became louder, and the light of a lamp fell across the room, but no-one came in. There was the sound of whispering and shuffling, and the scrape of something hard on the stone floor, then a black shape materialised in the lamplight.

Old Lady Horncastle moved slowly and stiffly, but she was out of her chair and walking of her own accord. She leaned heavily on a polished wooden stick, and her nurse hovered close behind, holding the lantern at shoulder height.

The nurse looked petrified, but the dowager had that twist at the corner of her mouth which I had seen before. I still hadn't the faintest idea what it meant, but I did know it wasn't contempt or pity as I'd thought before. Not that we mustn't have made for a pitiful sight. Six filthy men half-starved and blinking in the light, pressed up against the bars with the acrid reek of the bucket strong enough to make your eyes water.

Lady Horncastle rapped her stick on the floor, and the nurse stepped forward with the keys. Timmy Bickley's hand was first out, and he fumbled to get them fitted into the lock from the wrong side.

'I'm sorry, Mr Harrison,' he said, still using our peculiar mode of address from Catcliffe's that seemed thoroughly out of place here. 'Can't stop my hands shaking.'

Eventually there was a loud click, and Timmy held the door for me.

I bowed to the old dowager as I stepped through, feeling dizzy and a bit ridiculous.

'Lady Horncastle. Thank you.'

Standing up she looked even smaller than in her bath chair. She pointed her stick towards the door.

We did not need telling twice. I climbed unsteadily up the stairs, my limbs still half asleep. Jabez and the others crowded in behind me.

'We'd never have got in without the distraction,' the nurse said breathlessly. 'I've never seen anything like it. Honestly, the way those dogs threw it about...'

At the top of the stairs I pushed the door open and stepped out into a roar of noise and orange light.

....

St Stephen's was on fire. The blaze was furious, with streams of flame running along the gutters and spilling from the broken windows, glowing through the roof tiles and the stonework. At one end the roof had already fallen in and clouds of sparks fizzed into the air on a cushion of smoke. A stiff breeze was blowing towards the castle, carrying molten gobbets of fire into the wheat field. These took root where they fell, and new blazes were springing up all over the field faster than anyone could put them out.

Not that anyone was trying any more because they had more pressing matters on their hands. Through the haze of smoke, spots of light flickered along two sides of the boundary wall, and it took me a moment to work out that they were muzzle flashes from men firing over the walls into the field. I suddenly realised with a surge of gratitude that these were villagers from Yattonby, finally roused to drive out the rot from their valley with whatever bird guns and rabbiting rifles they had at their disposal. The crackle of gunfire and flame mingled with the rolling boom of thunder from the moor above.

Most of McCrea's men were crouched among the wheat stalks trying to return fire, but even an inexpert eye could see that their odds weren't good. A few were trying to withdraw in a semi-orderly fashion to the top end of the field, but the rest were pinned down as the flames drew in on them. Fish in a barrel, like the factory workers they hunted in the western woods.

Just as extraordinary, though, was the scene in the smoke-filled courtyard right in front of us. One of the younger dogs lay dead, her huge grey frame draped over the low wall at the edge of the yard. The barbed wire that ought to have topped the wall had been cut with pliers and hung loose from its posts. Another dog – that dreadnought of a bitch that they called Iffie, was tied haphazardly to the pump in front of the stable, struggling fiercely to free herself. The irate beast was entwined in yards and yards of heavy rope, which was looped and knotted around her limbs, neck and body in an almighty tangle like a giant cat's cradle. She was rolling something large around on the cobbles and making a terrible racket, accompanied by more muted base notes from the two other dogs that were still locked in the kennel block.

Half-hidden by her massive bulk, the object of Iffie's attentions turned out to be a suit of armour. The same suit of armour, in fact, that usually lived at the top of the stairs at the vicarage, only now it was filthy with blood and dust and someone had lashed an old-fashioned sword bayonet to the right forearm. It was curled up in an attitude that reminded me of the way a small mongrel that I kept as a boy used to sleep, its forearms crossed over the back of its neck. Iffie had it by the elbow, her saucer-sized paws pounding on its breastplate as she tried to get her teeth into its arm.

Incredible as it seemed, the suit of armour had presumably clipped the wire open then clambered over the wall and into a confined space with around twenty stone of canine muscle, concocted from some of the most brutal animals on three continents. Whoever was inside that suit must have taken the beating of their life as they lanced one dog and tied up the other. There were no signs of movement now, and I wondered for a moment if they were even still breathing.

They were, though – because as Iffie got her muzzle underneath the tin soldier's body and flipped it over, it suddenly unfurled from its snail-like position and swiped clumsily at the big dog's face with the twenty-inch spike on its fist. Iffie was a good deal faster, but as she sprang back, the suit of armour scrabbled away from her across the cobbles. The dog lunged to catch it up again, but the tangle of rope held her fast to the pump, and she only just managed to get her teeth around an armoured shin.

Given time, I daresay Iffie might have cracked this particular nutshell, but while I was watching the spectacle, Tom Creedy had dashed back into the old smithy and emerged with a long-handled billhook.

'Away, tha' big bitch!' he shouted, jabbing it at Iffie's muzzle and beating her back while Jabez and I dragged the gallant cuirassier well clear. As we retreated, the dog launched herself at us again and again, straining at the ropes and bellowing with impotent rage.

We got our floppy metal scarecrow sitting up against the smithy wall and I knelt down next to it, fiddling around with the buckles to try and get the helmet off. It wasn't easy because it was a bit tight and fitted very closely up against the gorget, but eventually I managed to lift it clear. Close up, I realised Wilkie had been right – it was a very small suit of armour, and I had a good idea who might be in it.

'Loony bitch,' breathed Jabez with admiration.

Some rough edge on the inside of the helmet had bitten into Artemisia's forehead and there was a good deal of blood on her face, mixed with sweat, matted hair and a lot of brown pigment that must have come off the rotted leather lining. All the same, she managed to give us a smile – which came off a bit ghoulish because some of the blood had got into her teeth as well.

'I was just... coming down to get you,' she said without preamble.

Her breathing was all wrong and she had to suck in a couple of quick gasps even just to get through a short statement like this.

'It's good to see you, Artemisia,' I said, almost tearfully, grasping her arm with affection, though I shouldn't think she could feel it much through the plate armour. The metal was covered in blood and saliva and she stank of dog.

Somewhere behind me, Tom Creedy uttered a rich obscenity, half drowned out by the barking of the dogs and the rattle of gunfire.

'Missy Richardson? That you in there?'

She tried to say something but ended up coughing.

'She uses Moss these days,' said Jabez.

'Don't talk, Missy, just concentrate on breathing. Lady Horncastle let us out and now we need to get back to Wilkie's just as fast as we can.'

First we had to get Artemisia upright. Jabez and I hoisted her up between us, an arm around each of our shoulders, but the height difference was too great and so we switched Jabez for Seamus Dyer, the docker.

'Sounds like you've crunched up some ribs,' observed Jabez, no stranger himself to extensive personal injury. 'Get you laid up and you'll mend.' Somewhere between the cellar and the spot where we now stood, he had acquired a broad-bladed shovel of the sort used for heaping up animal excrement – with which he no doubt hoped to murder someone.

I didn't fancy braving the crossfire and the burning wheat field, so we left the courtyard on the path towards the castle, intending to leave by the main gate. It was only just then that I realised the dowager was no longer with us. In a flash of lightning from the oncoming storm I could see her shadowy form some way up ahead, tottering slowly back towards the house through the drifts of smoke with the nurse at her elbow. I called out my thanks to her, but the rumble of thunder drowned me out.

Artemisia was not large and the armour wasn't nearly as heavy as it looked, but our progress was slow all the same. We had just cleared the outbuildings and come to the edge of an overgrown area where the gardeners obviously dumped their grass clippings and other waste, when Jabez suddenly called out, 'Down!' All seven of us dropped into the compost heap and I heard Artemisia inhale sharply with the jolt.

Up ahead, one of the side doors to the castle had opened, and the light from within illuminated two figures – one tall and muscular, the other short and dumpy. They began running towards the courtyard from which we had lately issued, passing the dowager as she made her slow progress towards the house and looking back with puzzlement but without checking their pace. They passed quite close to us, McCrea slightly ahead and Garrett panting heavily, then disappeared into the tangle of outbuildings. Both carried those wretched rifles.

We rose hastily from the rotting grass clippings that had hidden us, just as the first bloated droplets of rain began to fall, plinking off Artemisia's armour. As I helped her up, I saw Jabez Potter set off back the way we had come.

'Jabez!' I hissed. 'Not that way!'

He turned and called back, 'A promise is a promise,' then continued after McCrea and Garrett.

I could have cried with frustration, but I made a grab for Creedy's arm and pulled him into my place supporting Artemisia.

'Keep going! We'll be right behind.'

Forty

I ran to catch up with Jabez – which was not too difficult since one of his legs was made of wood – and by the time I got there I realised Timmy Bickley was with us too. The rain was picking up now, socking into the parched earth and kicking up a rich scent that mingled with the stinking clouds of hot smoke.

Up ahead I heard a wail of anger over the barking of the dogs and the whooshing of the rain.

'No! No! No! No! No!' screamed Garrett. 'The horrid old cow!'

Jabez suddenly pressed himself against the wall of one of the barns, and Timmy and I followed suit. A moment later, Garrett charged back past us, oblivious to everything except the orange-tinted shadow of the old lady and her nurse battling their way across the lawn.

There was a gap of four or five seconds – which presumably represented McCrea pausing to inspect the deceased canine bulk slung over the wall – then we heard his hobnails approaching at a run. The gamekeeper was a good deal more observant than his master, and he registered us the moment he rounded the corner, but he was going too fast to check his pace. Jabez checked it for him, swinging the stolen shit shovel in a wide arc and hitting him tremendously hard with it.

McCrea went down and his rifle sailed through the air and clattered onto the cobbles.

I snatched the weapon up and turned it on McCrea, who was flat on his back in the dirt. I suppose I ought to have killed him there and then, but I have always been a bit soft and I wasn't up to kicking a man while he was down – let alone executing him – particularly since Jabez had him covered with the shovel.

'Harry!' shouted Jabez. 'The old bird!'

I turned to see that Garrett had closed about half the distance between us and the dowager. As I watched, he paused and pulled his rifle into his shoulder. Timmy Bickley was sprinting across the open ground towards him, but he was still too far off to stop him firing.

It was a rushed shot and it went wide but clipped the nurse, who stumbled and sank down onto one knee, clutching her elbow. The inscrutable Lady Horncastle was obviously a loyal sort, or perhaps just a fatalist, because she stopped walking towards the house and turned to face Garrett as he reloaded.

By now I was running too.

Garrett raised his weapon again, but he must have heard something behind him because he spun round suddenly to see Timmy Bickley bearing down on him. There was the sound of another shot, and a good deal of Timmy blew out of his back and across the lawn. His legs kept going a couple of strides further as if they hadn't quite caught up with what had gone on upstairs, then he tumbled forward into the wet grass.

As Timmy fell away, Piers Garrett saw me coming up behind him, and I like to think he may have started to feel especially unhappy when he realised that my rifle was loaded where his was not.

I had never been much of a hand with a firearm – the one and only time I had shot anyone was at point-blank range with a pocket pistol – but this was an easy shot. I pulled the weapon tight into my shoulder, squeezed the trigger with as smooth a motion as I could, and missed.

Now it was my turn to feel unhappy. I looked back over my shoulder with some vain hope that Jabez might be there to get me out of yet another tight spot, but to my horror I saw that McCrea was up, with a knife in his hand, and the two men were circling each other on the cobbles under the glow of the flaming church. The whole of the church roof had fallen in now, and clouds of steam rose off the smouldering field, though there could not have been much left alive in it because the pepper-pot gunfire from the edges was dwindling away.

I turned back to see Garrett fishing another round out of his trouser pocket, and registered for the first time that he was dressed for dinner, his soaked white shirt gone see-through and his stiff collar flapping open but still attached by the back stud. I, alas, had only the one bullet which I had just sent on its merry way to nowhere, so I broke into a desperate charge towards him.

And then a glorious thing happened. Slick with rainwater and gun grease, Garrett's stubby fingers fumbled and he dropped his round. In a moment, it went from the thing which was going to kill me to a nub of scrap metal that the gardener might find next year. More speed, less haste, as my mother used to say when there was a train to catch.

He tried to get hold of another one and his hand was still in his pocket when I got to him, swinging my rifle by the barrel and clubbing him to the ground like a tubby little seal. I tore the rifle from his hands and flung it away into the grass. Blood welled from his nose and eyebrow and the rain spread it across his face in pink rivulets. He looked up at me in terror with his mouth gaping and his pomaded hair plastered lank across his cheek. He obviously couldn't think of anything to say, which was all to the good really because the last time I met him he had talked such an awful lot of rot.

I mentioned just earlier that I wasn't really one to kick a man when he was down, but to my shame I now proceeded to do just that – putting my boot good and hard into a shirt front which presumably still held traces of the rich dinner he had just enjoyed while he looked forward to murdering me. He rolled over and retched a bit, while I reached down to transfer the remaining cartridges from his trouser pocket to my own – keeping one back which I slotted into the breech of the Martini–Enfield.

I risked taking my eye off him for a moment to look back towards the outbuildings. Jabez and McCrea had disappeared into the billowing smoke and steam, but there was a terrible wailing coming from one of the barns and I couldn't tell whose voice it was. I was in a quandary, but whatever the hazards of leaving Garrett unattended, I couldn't very well abandon my old friend on his own against a much bigger man.

I knelt, pulled Garrett's bow tie from where it hung soggily about his neck, and tied his hands tight behind his back with it. His feet presented a problem, but then I remembered his braces, which I unbuttoned at front and back and hauled out like a sort of eel from under his jacket. I wrapped them quickly about his ankles and tied them with a series of very inexpert knots, much as Artemisia had done with his wife's dogs. As an afterthought, I pulled his trousers down, then started to run back towards Jabez.

I paused when I got to Timmy lying face down in the grass, but when I turned him over I knew he was gone. Even in the heat of all that was going on around me, I felt a terrible stab of sadness at the thought of having to take that last straw of hope from Arthur Letts.

As I got to the outbuildings, the screaming trailed off. It had been coming from behind the nearest barn, and I crept nervously towards the corner, my rifle levelled. I could hear nothing over the scrape of my boots on the cobbles, the drumming of rain and the distant shouting of men. We were closer to the fire here, and hissing cinders danced around me in a shroud of churning steam as I squinted down the iron sights of the rifle and swung around the corner of the barn.

'Reckon you might even be able to hit me from there,' said Jabez, his eye about three feet from the muzzle.

And that was the funny thing about Jabez Potter, because he would risk his life for you but he still couldn't bear to be nice to you. There was a good deal of blood and mud on him and he moved a bit more stiffly than usual but did not seem much hurt. Further along the wall I could make out a crumpled form lying next to a water trough. By mutual unspoken agreement, we never discussed the specifics of Mr McCrea's end.

'You all right?' I asked.

'Clawed me a bit. Nothing much.'

He was slurring a little and I wondered if he might have taken a knock to the head.

'Time to go home, would you say?'

Forty-One

As we returned towards the house, we could see that things had developed somewhat, but I was too tired now to run. Piers Garrett had somehow managed to get up, and was shuffling across the lawn as sheets of rain gusted across him, his hands and feet still tied, trousers round his ankles, shirt tails flapping. But he was not alone.

Around him like devils in the swirling smoke stood a circle of sodden villagers, most of them armed with a motley selection of rook rifles and shotguns. I could see the scar-faced pub landlord, and Tom Creedy's cousin, Sam, brandishing some sort of antiquated muzzle-loader. Artemisia was there, still half-upright in her suit of armour, though it was the Reverend Wilkie who now supported her. Dyer and Creedy were close by, while Lockwood was laying his threadbare jacket over Timmy Bickley. Old Lady Horncastle still stood as I had left her, next to where her wounded nurse sat woozily on the grass.

'Are you all right, Lady Horncastle?' I asked as I reached her, and she shrugged stiffly, as if none of this were so very extraordinary.

Hearing me, Garrett turned. I started to raise my rifle, then realised there must be at least five already trained on him, so I lowered it again and laid it on the floor. I would probably only hit someone else anyway.

'Please, don't hurt him!' someone cried from the edge of the circle. 'Daniel, stop them!'

Ellen Garrett was in her evening gown, the lace trimming wilted in the rain and a muddy tide mark climbing the long skirt. Clinging to her daughter's arm, the appeal was addressed to her son-in-law, but the man himself was not paying her any attention. Arriving upon the scene, Lord Horncastle had spotted his mother, and he now rushed to her side. That steely old bird made an economical sweep of her hand that managed to encompass herself, her injured nurse and Piers Garrett. He looked aghast.

'Piers?' he breathed.

'You don't mean to say he has finally crossed a line by shooting at your own mother?' I asked him loudly, though Lord Horncastle would not look at me.

'Drop dead, Catcliffe,' spat Garrett, wiping his bloody mouth on his shoulder. Then to his son-in-law. 'Come on, lad, send this lot packing.'

Only he couldn't, not now, and he knew it. All eyes were on Horncastle, but I do not know what anyone expected him to do. For possibly the first time in his existence, his presence in *Who's Who* and 250 years of deference weren't worth a bean. If he lived until daylight, he might be someone important again, but at that moment he was just a man in the midst of a storm, surrounded by other men who might kill him if he wasn't careful.

Horncastle looked to the dowager, then to his wife where she stood comforting her mother. And it was Alice, the young Lady Horncastle, who acted.

Gently, she detached herself from Ellen Garrett, and crossed to where Piers stood. I couldn't tell whether there were tears mingling with the raindrops that streamed down her face, but she was composed.

'I'm sorry, Daddy.' She stroked his bloodied cheek. 'He can't help you.'

Then she walked steadily to her husband, took his arm in hers, and turned him towards the house.

'Ungrateful little bitch!'

'Alice! Your father!'

Ellen Garrett dropped despondently to her knees, but I noticed she did not make any move to try and protect his body with her own. Piers Garrett wasn't the sort of man you would take a bullet for, even if you were married to him.

Like Horncastle, Garrett found himself in an unfamiliar situation. Power, wealth, and force of character had carried him unscathed through a life of cruelty and excess, but at last it was over. He had gone too far, and was only just beginning to realise it.

I remembered someone – it may even have been Dick Fletcher – once saying that the real monsters in this life see themselves in three dimensions and other people in only two. So it was with Piers Garrett. The regret in his countenance was not on account of the men he had murdered, but only for himself. Now, facing ruin and humiliation, his famous anger surfaced in a gross swell of rage.

'Why don't you blame them?' he shrieked, pointing a trembling finger at Horncastle's back.

'You jealous little people hate me because I earned my money. Grubbed for every farthing. But they did nothing for all this and somehow whatever they do to cling on to it is fair game, is it? Flog your farms off for mines, let Ross and Blayne dump poisonous slag in your river. They snag my filthy rich daughter and turn a blind eye as I hunt you in the woods so long as I keep writing to my bank manager when they want new wallpaper in the east wing? And *I'm* the greedy one?'

Horncastle shrank under Garrett's bile, but Alice continued to lead him slowly away into the fog.

'Christ, we're going to be here all night,' shouted someone in a strong Cleveland accent.

'Just finish him, anyone!'

'Let his dogs have him!'

'You wouldn't dare!' roared Garrett in response.

Ellen gave a gulping sob like a child.

'Enough, please!' cried out Wilkie.

He stepped forward, still supporting Artemisia in the crook of his arm.

'We are not murderers. No-one is going to kill this man. He must be taken to Whitby and given over to the police. The law will deal with him.'

'But we've already killed,' protested one man in grimy miner's leggings. 'Happen we go to gaol instead of him?'

It was true. There must have been half a dozen dead men lying in that wheat field, and self-defence was going to be a hard sell when they had been ambushed and shot from cover.

Another man I did not know stepped forward and levelled his rifle. But before he could make up his mind to fire, the half-armoured hybrid of Wilkie and Artemisia had performed a rather inelegant side-step, deliberately interposing themselves between Garrett and the weapon. The rain clattered noisily off Missy's tarnished steel plate.

'Don't,' she gasped. 'It's not our place.'

'Good idea!' shouted Garrett with withering sarcasm. 'Take me to the police! Drag the Haydon estate through the mud!'

To make his point he tried to kick a clod of mucky grass at his protectors, stumbling because his legs were still tied together.

'Maybe I go to gaol, maybe some of you do too, maybe that coward over there does.' He jerked his chin towards Horncastle.

'Because he knew. Oh, he was thoroughly aware, you must know that! Then one day I'll get out, and I promise you I'll come right back and...'

His speech was arrested by a saucer-sized explosion at the base of his throat. For a moment I thought Wilkie had been hit too, but it was just a considerable quantity of Piers Garrett propelled across the Reverend's sopping white shirt by a .303 Martini–Enfield rifle.

If Garrett had any consciousness of having been shot, it did not register in his face, which was twisted by the impact but still looked as if it might burst into a fresh torrent of invective. He rocked onto his heels then flopped backwards onto the lawn. His trousers were still round his ankles.

At the sound of the shot, Horncastle and Alice spun round. The disbelief in their faces was directed not so much at the dying industrialist gurgling in the grass, as at the elderly woman standing next to him.

'Mother, no,' Horncastle mouthed.

Old Lady Horncastle was clutching the same rifle that I had laid down just a minute or two earlier without unloading it. Quite possibly she lacked the strength to lift the weapon into her shoulder and aim it, but she had not needed it. She had simply walked up behind Garrett, placed the muzzle in the centre of his back, pointing upwards, and pulled the trigger.

And perhaps she had done the only thing she could do. Certainly it was the only thing that could save her son. As I took the rifle gently from her, she looked up at me, and her previously inscrutable face now displayed a single clear emotion. Defiance.

A trial would have ruined both Horncastle and his estate. Several of the brave men ranged around on that bloodstained lawn would have been at risk of prison or worse. And for what? The guilty party was dead now, and his men had either gone the same way or scattered to the four winds. Apart from anything else, Garrett had threatened revenge and he had only himself to blame if the dowager had taken him at his word.

She was a bolder soul than me, and I offered her my arm.

'Lady Horncastle. May I escort you back to the house?'

As we moved slowly away, the scene came to life behind us. Ellen Garrett began wailing loudly, and Alice rushed to her side. Several of the men came out with richly incomprehensible obscenities over a murmur of agitated conversation. There was a hacking cough from Artemisia, and the sound of Wilkie gently soothing her. Horncastle just stood there, stunned.

'Trouble someone for a smoke?' That was Jabez's voice. 'We've got some work to do before we fetch the coppers...'

At the castle's side door, we paused. A footman had been watching the scene from behind the curtain, and at the sight of his mistress he snapped back into his professional self and offered her his arm. She nodded at me as he led her away, her dress dragging a muddy trail across the carpet.

There was a table-lighter on a stand by the door, so I retrieved the last cigarette from my silver case. It was a bit damp, but after a few attempts I got it sparked up. I leaned dripping against the door frame, closed my eyes for a moment, and blew out a long, slow lungful of smoke. I had been down to my last hours on earth, but now life was a mystery again. I might survive another fifty years or my heart might give out before dawn, but for just a moment I savoured the uncertainty with a fresh sense of relish.

I opened my eyelids to see that the rest of the family were approaching – first Alice, supporting her grief-stricken mother, then Horncastle, still glancing over his shoulder in disbelief. Ellen Garrett was in too much of a state to notice me, her cheeks raw and streaked with mud, but for the first time in our acquaintance, the younger Lady Horncastle looked at me with something other than indifference as they passed. Horncastle and I were left alone on the threshold.

'We were trapped, Alice and I – don't you see?' said Horncastle shakily. 'I couldn't stop him once he started – not without losing all of it. By the time I knew, it was too late.'

It wasn't my world and I was too tired just then to think about it. In the distance, St Stephen's still glowed through the steam rising off the wheat field, as the rain pelted down through the darkness and shadowy figures on the lawn began laying out the bodies.

Forty-Two

'The diocese won't be impressed,' observed Peter Wilkie, looking up at the blackened shell of his church. 'Horncastle has offered to fund the rebuild. Jolly decent of him, but I daresay I'm for the chop all the same.'

As far as I was concerned, it was the least Lord Horncastle could do – especially given that he was now a fantastically wealthy man. Alice Garrett was an only child and so the inhabitants of Haydon Castle were in clover for the time being.

'Now I think about it, I could probably have come up with a better plan,' Wilkie sighed, 'but we were all in a bit of a flap and it was the only distraction I could think of that would be big enough. I couldn't just sneak in and torch the field because they were watching me, and they'd have caught me before I got a real blaze going. But with the wind blowing north and the church flinging embers right across the castle grounds, we knew they'd have to set every last man they had fighting the fire.'

He paused, steeling himself for an admission.

'It sounds terrible to say, but I think I rather hoped God might have carried the fire into the castle and taken that too. Cut out the stony heart, and so forth.'

I wondered, not for the first time, whether Peter Wilkie might be slightly unhinged. A sort of good-natured Madame Guillotine in a cassock.

It was nearly a week since the blaze, and Wilkie and I sat on his favourite stretch of wall in the cool of the early morning, admiring his handiwork. It seemed remarkable that his pretty jars of shells and fossils could have caused such carnage.

The east porch had fallen in, and so the tramp had migrated across to a roomy mausoleum at the edge of the graveyard, where he napped in the shade of a pillared stone arch under the gaze of lichen-frosted angels. I was pleased Wilkie had remembered to remove the man to the vicarage potting shed for the evening before he burned St Stephen's down. The immolation of the thousand-year-old church had caused the vagrant some modest inconvenience in that his wheeled bogey now had to sit out in the open air, but otherwise his situation was largely unaltered.

'He'll be off soon anyway,' said Wilkie. 'Always gone by mid-August, and he doesn't return until the next June. I've never discovered his name or where he goes.'

Of Garrett's mercenaries, eight were dead or wounded and the remaining five had made their escape out onto the moors. Two villagers had been injured – both miners from Ross & Blayne – and one had not survived the week. He was part of a crew that had come up from East London the previous year looking for work, and it seemed an eerie coincidence that he should be buried next to Timmy Bickley from Bermondsey. The two men might once have brushed past one another in a pub overlooking Father Thames and never known where they would finish up.

A surprise casualty was Chalmers, the land agent, who had rushed to the castle to try and assert his authority when the fighting broke out. In the confusion, some unknown opportunist had seen the chance to heave a brick at him, with the result that he was expected to be out of action for some weeks at least. It was unfortunate for him, but possibly not for everyone else.

'Lord Horncastle has pledged to hire a more benign agent,' said Wilkie, 'though I fear it's in the nature of the place that such a man will ultimately be supplanted by another Chalmers.'

This being the unpalatable truth of our bright new era, and one that Piers Garrett would have delighted in predicting. The jackals would fall upon the carcass of the Garrett empire, and Horncastle – an essentially decent fellow for all his considerable shortcomings – couldn't hope to defend it against men like Dick Fletcher as they stripped and ruined it. The stored-up wealth and the leftovers from the ailing drift mine would hold out for a while, but Haydon Castle would chew through it eventually, no doubt with plenty of help from the church, the school, the village hall and the odd bad harvest or swine fever outbreak. Sooner or later, Horncastle would need another man like Chalmers to get him back on track, and when that time came, he would do what he had to.

Not that the villagers seemed worried. They were wise enough to take the long view, riding out good and bad luck as it came – whether it was an accident in the mine, a rent rise, a bumper harvest or a loony tycoon from Ponder's End hunting other humans with giant foreign dogs. The uprising against Garrett had been a rare show of defiance, but viewed from a different angle it was also a resounding vote for the status quo.

Speaking of the dogs, there was some suggestion that they ought to be shot, but in the end Yorkshire thrift had won out. It seemed a shame not to make use of such outstanding guardians, and they were given to farmers on some of the more outlying smallholdings. No doubt Ellen Garrett was bitterly upset over their loss, but in truth I suspect she would have been just as happy going back to spaniels, and perhaps that is what she did.

'The strange thing,' said Wilkie, 'is that the servants say Mrs Garrett seems more upset about the dogs than about her husband. I wonder if he was a different man when she met him.'

'Maybe. My old man said he was always a sod.' I had a more cynical heart than good old Wilkie, and I assumed – perhaps unjustly – that Garrett's wife had overlooked his character in favour of his bank balance. We all like to be comfortable.

The detective from Middlesbrough had turned up two days after Piers Garrett's death with a detachment of grizzled town coppers, and if any of them suspected they were being fed a tall tale, they were sensible enough not to say so. In the spirit of politeness, the detective expressed his regret to Lord Horncastle that the old church had caught fire during this spell of uncommonly dry weather, taking care not to notice the line of fresh burials in the churchyard.

As it happened, there were more men in that churchyard than graves. Possibly some pigs and sheep in the mix too. The morning after the assault on Haydon, as the sodden skeleton of St Stephen's still steamed drowsily into a blue summer sky, Jabez had taken a small crew of the least squeamish men in the village and dug up the rubbish pit behind the castle barn. Aside from the skulls and the telltale items like belt buckles and hobnails, it was tricky to tell which of the charred remains in there were human or animal, so they just heaped them all in a cart and buried them in a corner of the graveyard. Wilkie stood over them reciting the *Nunc dimittis*, the burned bones of his church mirroring the ones under his feet. Jabez said he hadn't counted how many skulls they found, but I never believed him.

In a makeshift morgue in the castle cellar, the detective had examined the single gunshot wound that had killed Piers Garrett. Many a vigorous country sportsman killed in such tragic accidents, he observed – though the bruising on his face meant they would not be able to rule out foul play until the fugitive American gamekeeper had been apprehended. Not that he ever would be, because McCrea was in the castle pet graveyard between Hecuba – the dead dog – and a much-loved horse called Whistler. Wilkie would have put him in the churchyard despite everything, but the villagers wouldn't have it. When the local stonemason finally got round to making him a headstone, it was one of those tiny semicircles that usually adorned the grave of an infant, and simply read 'Hunter'.

I have no doubt that the statements taken by the Middlesbrough detective and his men will have matched rather too closely to be truly convincing. I heard he was unable to speak to Ellen Garrett due to her fractured nerves, but that Alice's performance struck the perfect note of brittle dignity. Under insistent questioning, Lord Horncastle admitted that a considerable amount of drink was often taken before his father-in-law set out on a deer stalk.

I was not interviewed. Merely mentioned in passing as an artistic tourist who had come to sketch the ill-fated misericords at St Stephen's and had dined at the castle earlier in the week. Remaining in character, I sat on a folding stool among the gravestones, drawing the ruined church with a stick of charcoal, and nodded at the constables as they passed. I suppose I could have bolted straight back to London – as Dyer and Lockwood had – but I wanted to hang around until certain of the injured were out of the woods, so to speak.

Whatever his private reservations, the detective returned to the Middlesbrough coroner with a wad of evidential notes that strongly suggested accidental death. I wondered if he had picked up some notion of what Piers Garrett had been doing in Yattonby, but perhaps these Teesside policemen simply had a sense of perspective in their work. They came, after all, from a seething 'Ironopolis' where a hundred and twenty thousand people lived and died cheaply among mines and blast furnaces. A single death in an isolated village was scarcely a good use of their time, and perhaps they understood that whatever had happened in Yattonby was over.

From the direction of the vicarage, Wilkie and I could see three figures moving slowly along the road towards us.

Artemisia was back in her work dress and apron, her days of dressing like Sir Galahad presumably behind her. Half of her face was a lurid yellow-green colour and one arm was splinted, but her broken ribs and wrist were healing well enough.

Wilkie had nursed her himself in the days following her tussle with the dogs, and it had not been a very great surprise when, sat in the garden one afternoon, she quietly told me she would not be returning to Whitby with me when the coach came.

'Would you give my deepest apologies to Miss Catcliffe and Miss Wynnster for the inconvenience?' she asked, shifting uncomfortably in her deckchair and cradling a cup of honeyed hot water that Wilkie had brought. 'The doctor says not to travel until I'm mended, and Reverend Wilkie has said I can stay on at the vicarage until then.'

We both knew she would never go back to Aunt Diana's service, but if she wanted to pretend otherwise then I would play along. Wilkie's days at the vicarage were numbered, but wherever life carried him next, it seemed a good bet it would carry Artemisia with him. No doubt marrying a housemaid would be yet another black mark against Wilkie's already sooty reputation, but he was not the sort of man to worry about that.

Loping alongside her was what Piers Garrett had compared to a lurcher in human form, his left arm thrust inside the front of his jacket to take the weight off it. Duke's free hand held a length of rope with his grotesque dog on the end, and his shoulder and neck were swathed in a wad of dressings where McCrea's long shot had just about missed him.

It was fair to say none of us had enjoyed a relaxing stay in Yattonby, but Duke's night in the woods had been a special sort of purgatory. As he turned to look down triumphantly from the lip of the Ernecliffe, McCrea's big .303 round had whacked through the ridge of muscle above his left collarbone, tearing most of it away and creating a sort of firework of flesh that must have looked pretty impressive from down below. Already shaking with fear and anger, he didn't feel very much pain just to start with, but as he raced down off the Ernecliffe he began to stumble. With an odd sense of clarity – as if he were thinking about someone else rather than himself – he realised that he was losing a good deal of blood and was on the verge of passing out.

Having discarded his shirt in the woods, the only thing he could think of to try and staunch the bleeding with was his sock, but once he had sat down to take it off, he found he couldn't stand up again. So he crawled the rest of the way down on his elbows, clasping a filthy stocking to his shoulder. By the time he reached the outskirts of Yattonby, there was not much juice left in him, but he could hear the sounds of pursuit up on the Ernecliffe and knew he had left an obliging snail trail all the way down. He tottered the last few steps down to the bank by the duck bridge then floated himself out into the beck and drifted dreamily down through the village on his back like the Lady of Shalott until a couple of drunk miners spotted him.

It was some wonder rot had not set into the wound, but Duke had the luck of the devil and there was no point judging him by other men's standards. To me, the likes of Potter and Dukanwalla seemed unkillable – they just went through the world becoming ever more scarred and broken but clinging doggedly to life.

He had been nursed that first day by Artemisia, but after her own injuries his luck had finally run out and he had endured the ministrations of his old shipmate, Marine Potter. Jabez could dress a wound well enough but his bedside manner was a thing to behold.

Together with Jabez, Missy and Duke joined us on the wall and I passed my cigarette case along. Wilkie frowned as old Cap scratched at the loose soil of a fresh grave then cocked his leg against the wooden cross.

'Our bags are loaded up,' said Jabez, opening up his pocket knife. 'Coachman says to be there in about a quarter of an hour.'

He cut a couple of coins of tobacco off a length of twist and began shredding them into his pipe.

While we had been causing trouble in Yattonby, the landslides on the coastal line had been cleared and the train was up and running again, meaning that our journey back to town would be a good deal swifter than the way out.

'Whitby by tonight, back at the Saracen's in a couple of days,' breathed Duke dreamily through a haze of smoke.

Jabez and I glanced at each other.

'The stink of piss and carbolic...'

'The tittering of whores...'

'The belching of Polish sailors...'

As the sun climbed through the still morning air, the mist was beginning to burn off the fields. It was going to be a delicious day.

'To hell with you both,' said Duke. 'And to hell with the English countryside.'

Forty-Three

Aunt Diana did not acknowledge the existence of subjectivity. Things were either agreeable to her or they were bad. I, apparently, was bad.

'You have caused a great deal of inconvenience since your arrival, Harrison,' she told me as I sat down to tea. 'And now I find you have put Artemisia out of action. Truly a thoughtless boy, much as I dote upon you. Thank heavens for dear Edith.'

She raised her eyes gratefully to the ceiling – conveniently overlooking that it had been I, rather than the Almighty, who had brought Edie to Whitby – but I was too amazed to be indignant. Even as I mouldered in Piers Garrett's dungeon, I had occasionally cringed with remorse about inflicting Edie on these two cracked but essentially decent old ladies. Yet here was the unmistakeable implication that she had distinguished herself.

'I wonder,' began Clara tentatively from her perch right on the edge of the settee, 'would it be a terrible imposition for you to write to Edith's father asking if she might stay on a while here? Only until Artemisia is well again, you understand.'

She edged even further forward to the point where I thought she might slide off onto the floor.

'Diana has become ever so attached to her, and really good help is so difficult to come by up here.'

The newly indispensable domestic presently entered with an embossed silver tray and three thimble-sized sherry glasses.

'Dinner will be served whenever you are ready, Miss Catcliffe,' she said primly. As she placed my pre-prandial drink on the side table, Edie's usual lemony manner was notably sweeter, and I thought back to my school chemistry lessons. Perhaps she and my aunt Diana were, respectively, a powerful acid and alkaline that had inadvertently neutralised one another.

'Please, Mr Catcliffe, please let me stay – just until Miss Moss is recovered,' she urged later. 'She is a very fair woman, your aunt, though she does like things just so.'

I noticed she had taken to wearing the house keys on her belt, much as Artemisia had done.

And so, the following morning – after a late night getting the third degree from Diana and Clara – I went to the telegraph office and sent three messages. The first, to Edie's father – my landlord – explaining concisely that his most wayward daughter wished to take up a temporary housekeeper position in Whitby, were he amenable. I suspected he would be extremely so, once he conquered his disbelief.

My second telegram was to my father.

BACK TO LONDON TOMORROW WILL EXPLAIN ALL

I had sent him a letter from Yattonby sketching the bare bones of the thing, but really only because I wanted to tell him that Timmy Bickley was dead – and because I knew that news of Garrett's death was bound to make it back to London before I did. And indeed the matter had already been extensively covered in the newspapers by the time we got back to town.

Ghoul that she was, Aunt Diana had preserved several cuttings from the *Whitby Gazette* detailing the accidental death of the celebrated industrialist, along with a very poorly informed obituary that conflated his biographical details with those of a more philanthropic boot-and-shoe man from Wakefield who was still very much alive.

'We didn't believe a word of it,' winked Auntie Clara. 'We knew it couldn't have been an accident.'

'And if it was then it couldn't have happened to a nicer man,' added Diana darkly.

But there were at least two fellows for whom a reckoning still awaited, and it was not something I wanted the old man involved with. So I sent a final message to Dick Fletcher.

GARRETT ABDUCTING UNION MEN STOP BELL & COLLISON INVOLVED STOP GARRETT DEAD STOP RETURNING LONDON TOMORROW

Tangling with labour organisations was a dangerous business for any firm, and I hoped to keep Catcliffe's well out of it. All the same, Collison had fed working men gaily into Piers Garrett's mincing machine, and Jacob Bell had betrayed Abraham Bickley for reasons that were still not clear to me. if there was one man who would know how to get both of them, it was canny old Fletcher.

'I still don't know why you won't let me deal with Bell and Collison,' whinged Jabez over a lunchtime pint. 'Duke can find out where they drink, then I can catch them on the way home for a little word. It's what Bell did to Bickley. See how he likes a taste of his own medicine.'

For an unsentimental man, Jabez had taken Timmy Bickley's death unusually to heart. Perhaps a shared prison cell and the brief possibility of being shot together had awakened some of those old feelings of camaraderie from his days in the Royal Marine Light Infantry.

We were sitting in a public house where Duke was staying, over across the bridge in the old part of town. Aunt Diana – or actually Auntie Clara – had offered him a room, but having spent most of the past week convalescing in a vicarage, Duke had just about had his fill of the English middle classes. He was homesick, and preferred to nest somewhere disreputable within spitting distance of a waterfront.

'You will think me soft, Jabez,' I replied, 'but after so many dead and beaten men I am loath to add two more to the ledger. And apart from anything else, Jacob Bell is the piece that doesn't fit. I understand Collison getting one over on his enemies, but I can't work out why Bell served up Abe.'

'You *are* soft,' said Duke, before Jabez could offer his own opinion. 'But you're not wrong. I've been thinking it too.'

'He struck me as an inoffensive bureaucrat,' I mused out loud. 'Evasive but basically decent. I just can't see him selling his own comrades out to a twenty-four-carat shit like Piers Garrett.'

'Was he being blackmailed, do you think?' asked Jabez. 'Maybe Garrett had something on him. Exotic tastes, hand in the till, that sort of thing.'

It seemed the most likely possibility, but whatever the case, we would get it out of him once we were back in London. Bell had blood on his hands and he would need to answer for it one way or another.

'If we find out what it is then maybe you could blackmail him too, Harry,' suggested Jabez. 'Be useful to have an insider at the AATMM in your pocket, even for a great defender of the working man like yourself.'

He settled back contentedly in his chair and started stuffing his pipe.

'I don't suppose you would consider staying on with Aunt Diana too, Jabez?'

We sipped our pints quietly. I was contemplating the next few days, Jabez presumably the next thirty seconds, but Duke's mind was still back in Yattonby.

'Those dogs,' he said.

'Those dogs,' I agreed.

'What about Missy, eh?'

The ability to take a beating was always impressive to Jabez.

Duke grimaced. He had, after all, come uncomfortably close to the beasts himself. He reached under the table and fondled old Cap's ragged ears.

'I thought they'd have me,' he said. 'All the way as I was crawling down, trying not to bleed out, I thought I'd look up and see one coming out of the trees towards me. I tried not to imagine what it would feel like when they got their teeth into me, but it's a funny thing – now I'm safe, it's all I can think about.'

'I was thinking,' I said. 'Imagine taking a stroll around Birkdale, say, thirty years down the line. You fellows, me, Garrett, Wilkie... we'll all be long forgotten. But the farm collies will be ten-stone bastards and hardly anyone will be able to remember why.'

Forty-Four

Our journey home could not have felt more different to the biblical conditions we had encountered on the way there. At Whitby West Cliff station, the unshaded portions of the platform were bathed in sunshine as Jabez, Duke and I perched on our cases and waited. The station master's terrier strained at its leash, issuing a steady stream of canine invective at old Cap, but neither the little dog's owner nor the subject of its rage seemed at all concerned. Cap lay immodestly on his back, sunning his nether regions and panting so stertorously that it took us a while to distinguish the sound of the approaching steam train.

In Scarborough, the rainswept gables had transformed into an elegant seaside resort, and I felt a pang of regret that we could not stay for a day or two of deckchairs and orchestras. Even just a dip in the grey North Sea would have done me, but there was no time for that. A game little porter humped our baggage through the crowds of West Yorkshire mill workers on their summer excursions, and we were installed on the York train without time for so much as an ice cream.

Jabez wanted to stay too, and I caught him gazing in admiration at a group of coquettish young lasses as they bowled noisily past our train window. He rarely expressed much interest in the female sex beyond lewd commentary, but a fair day makes romantics of us all.

'One day,' he pronounced a couple of hours later as we sat in the station buffet at York, 'I shall find a good woman and we shall move to a place like that and run a boarding house. Just a few rooms, tasteful but inexpensive for the discerning working man and his lady wife.'

Stranger things had happened, I supposed, but not many.

'Where will you find a good woman, Jabez?' I asked. 'I do not think they go to any of the same places we do.'

But he was content in his reverie and even Duke didn't seem inclined to dispel it, so I left him to it and went in search of the lavatories. York was a cathedral of a station, and the noise echoed around the high halls as I threaded my way through a stream of passengers pouring off a newly arrived train.

'Platform three for Beverley!' boomed one voice.

'Drowning at Naburn Lock! Read all about it in this evening's *Yorkshire Gazette*!' squeaked another.

'Catcliffe,' called a third.

I turned abruptly, but there was no-one to be seen. I rose onto the balls of my feet and craned my neck, but not a single face in the departing crowd was turned towards me. As they dispersed along platforms and walkways, I was left alone save for a few stragglers and a railwayman in sooty overalls fishing out a penny for the newspaper seller.

When you thought about it, there must have been a lot of words that could sound like Catcliffe when called out in a crowd, though I couldn't at that moment bring any of them to mind. I was used to being wrong, and it never occurred to me to trust my instincts and make my way back to the protective company of the two seasoned killers currently fantasising about domestic bliss and boarding houses on Platform One.

Instead, I followed my nose to the gents' latrines, where many a Porcelain Poet appeared to have found his muse.

TAX THE LAND NOT THE MAN

NO JEWS IN CABINET

ELSIE BAGSHAW DOES IT ALL

The door swung open and a man in a boater and a smart sack suit sauntered up to the urinal a respectful distance away from me. He looked like he might be on his way to take the waters at Scarborough.

'Nah then,' he observed by way of acknowledgement, twitching a neat moustache and keeping his eyes firmly focused on the soggy cigarette ends at his feet. He commenced his business as I finished mine.

I caught a glimpse of myself in the mirror, and noted with displeasure how much older I was beginning to look. In the glass I could spot flickers of scalp where my oiled hair pulled away from my forehead, and a yellowing at the inner corners of my eyes.

Emerging onto the platform, I moved a safe distance from the miasma of the gents then paused to light a cigarette. The smell of hot tarmacadam always made me want to smoke. The platform was beginning to fill up again and I could see a train some way down the line approaching the platform. I began to weave my way through the crowd, when something hit me hard on the right shoulder, pitching me sideways. I stumbled into a woman, knocking her down, but when I lost my own footing and fell, the ground was not there to meet me.

Instead, there was a dizzying void, then a hard landing on steel and grit.

I was on the tracks.

Curiously, none of my legs and arms seemed to work properly, and there was a sharp pain in my side. The tracks thrummed underneath my body, and it took me a moment to realise that this was because something else was on them apart from me. I rolled over with some effort, not unlike a landed fish, to see the engine barrelling into the station, all shrieking brakes and momentum and looking very different from ground level than they do when you are on the platform. I had that feeling, often encountered during such moments, that I was watching something happening to someone else.

And yet I was not alone on the cinders. A pair of spindly arms like dirty blue pipe cleaners locked round my chest and began to haul me upwards.

'Come on, mate! Get up!' screeched a voice in my ear, pronouncing it 'mett' and 'yerrup'. I flapped my legs a bit then found my feet, tottering a couple of steps forward and stumbling into the platform edge at about chest height. I scrabbled groggily to pull myself up, but there was nothing to grip onto, and the noise of the train was so loud that acceptance of the inevitable began to settle upon me.

But what seemed inevitable to me apparently was not. Next to me, a figure in blue launched itself from the tracks up onto the platform, all flailing limbs, and at the same time several pairs of hands gripped my arms and collar and yanked me forcefully over the lip of the platform. There was a good deal of screaming and shouting and I felt a rush of air as the train galloped past.

The unseen hands dragged me across the floor and propped me up against a pillar, at which point I could see they belonged to a luggage porter and two nicely dressed punters. Behind them, a scrawny young fellow in sooty blue work overalls was on all fours trying not to be sick while a fellow railwayman knelt beside him, slapping him repeatedly on the back in a congratulatory manner that cannot have helped with his nausea. The train had stopped but no-one had opened the doors, so all the passengers were just gaping through the windows. And of course there were crowds on the platform too, all goggling at me and shouting excitedly at my rescuer.

Eventually a couple of railway workers picked me up and bundled me into a little side room where they took their tea breaks. They put the lad in there too, along with the woman I'd sent flying when I fell, and who someone suspected had a broken wrist.

'You hurt?' asked the young chap.

I had pains in various places but everything still moved, so lasting damage seemed unlikely.

'I don't think so. But only thanks to you. I don't know how I can even start to thank you.'

He mustered a weak smile.

'Aw you're all right,' he said. 'Reckon railway company'll give me a pocket watch or summat.'

'He pushed you, you know.' It was another railwayman – the one I'd seen buying a paper just earlier. 'Saw it right in front of me. Good and hard, right onto t'tracks.'

Oddly, I hadn't yet got round to thinking about how I'd ended up in front of a steam train, but I remembered the thump on my shoulder that had sent me reeling across the platform.

'Who did?'

'Smart-looking bloke, straw hat, moustache.'

'Sack suit and a boater?'

'That's him. Know him?'

He might have been describing half the holidaymakers in York station, but I couldn't help remembering the man at the urinals. He must have come out right behind me.

'Not at all. Just said hello to me in the gents, I think.'

'Well 'e nearly did for both of us,' remarked the lad, starting to get his colour back a bit.

By the time I'd been given a cup of sweet tea, the station master had turned up with two constables. They asked pretty much the same questions as the two railwaymen, but took ten times as long to do it and demanded most of my life history as well. By the time they'd finished with me, there was the clear unspoken understanding that they believed me to be a career criminal who had arranged it all on purpose for reasons they would soon get to the bottom of.

Somewhere along the way, the young railwayman melted away, refusing to accept more than the price of a few drinks by way of thanks. One of those quietly decent fellows who hates a fuss.

The constables detained me long enough for me to miss my train, but I was eventually released, with the news that my friends were waiting outside. These 'friends' in fact turned out to be a couple of reporters from the local newspapers, but I soon spotted Jabez loitering by a coffee stand in a cloud of rank pipe smoke.

'State of you,' he remarked as I approached – which was his way of asking if I was all right. I must have looked pretty bad, streaked with soot and ash and the other more unsavoury substances that get sluiced out onto train tracks.

'No permanent damage as far as I can tell,' I said wearily, answering the question he hadn't asked. 'Where's Duke?'

'Duke is as Duke does,' he replied unhelpfully.

We found a pub near the station and I soon discovered that Duke was off making enquiries. He wasn't on home turf but he was a resourceful chap and I felt certain his endeavours would be more productive than those of the constables who had lately interviewed me.

'Old trick,' he told me when he and Cap flopped down at our table an hour later. 'If you don't know someone by sight but you've got a decent description, you can make sure it's them by calling their name out in a crowded place. If they're the only one who turns around then you've got your man.'

By that time I was beginning to feel distinctly peaky. That's the curious, topsy-turvy thing about danger. In the moment, I had experienced paralysis, and in the period immediately afterwards a sort of numb disbelief. Only now, a couple of hours later, was I beginning to feel afraid, and there was a tightness in my chest that was making it difficult to swallow my beer.

'You all right anyway?' asked Duke.

'Sort of. I do just wish people would stop trying to kill me for a while.'

Jabez snorted into his pint pot, and really I suppose his point was a fair one. People had been trying to kill him for most of his adult life and you didn't catch him yarning on about it.

At least the dog was sympathetic. I felt it move across to me under the table and lay itself heavily across my cloth-top boots like a hot sandbag.

'I thought we might be past that too,' agreed Duke. 'And more's the point, I just don't understand why. Payback for someone we killed at Yattonby?'

'But why me? Why not all of us?'

My companions shared a look.

'Well...' began Duke, as if the answer should have been obvious. 'You're, you know...'

'And we're...'

The penny dropped.

'What? You mean I'm just easier to kill?'

My face must have been a picture because both men sniggered unkindly.

It was a good answer, and an even better one for giving them a laugh at my expense, but I did not think it could be the right one. In fact, I was beginning to suspect something I ought to have realised long before.

'Did you find out anything about the man who pushed me?' I asked, offering cigarettes round.

'Nope, and that tells us something in itself. I don't know many people in this city but I've got a couple of decent contacts and no-one knows anything about him.'

'So either he's not local or he's not a known criminal, assuming your sources are decent.'

'I'd say it's more likely to be the first of those. He hoofed you onto the train tracks in front of a dozen people so he wasn't worried about being recognised. And he did it so calm and quick that I'd bet anything he's done it before. Or something like it.'

'If it's the man I think it was, he followed me into the gents just beforehand. Seemed very relaxed for someone about to commit murder.'

I remembered his languid air as he sidled up to the urinal, more like a half-cut holidaymaker than a stone-cold killer.

'Talk to you at all?'

'Just a passing pleasantry. He sounded northern.'

Duke paused a while, deep in thought, then stubbed out his cigarette decisively.

'I think we need to get out of York as soon as we can. We've missed the train to London but we'll go to the station and get on the first train going south of here. See if we can't change a couple of times before tonight, then lie low for a few days somewhere out of the way.'

'If you reckon they'll have another pop,' said Jabez, 'then we'll be better prepared second time around.' Jabez didn't much care for lying low. He had retrieved his black-market Bull Dog from the gun room at Haydon Castle and I suppose he quite fancied firing it at someone.

We're not ready for a fight, I thought. Jabez was – Jabez always was – but I was bruised and shaken and Duke had very recently been shot. He was upright and doing his best, but a child could have knocked him down by flicking a beermat at him, and he knew it.

'Listen,' he said wearily, 'this bloke has all the makings of a professional. He's travelled for the job, but whoever sent him knows all about us because they've used a northern man. If he was a Londoner then I'd have a chance of tracking him down, and someone's thought about that. They've got to have been following us since Whitby, and if they're willing to go that far then I'd bet good money they're willing to have another go.'

Duke fixed his eyes deliberately on his pint pot.

'Don't let on, but If I'm right, then we've probably got someone watching us right now.'

'A professional killer seems a bit full-on for revenge,' observed Jabez. 'And who was he supposed to be avenging? Surely not Garrett. Not a soul alive sorry to see that one dead. Maybe one of the old greybacks in the graveyard at Yattonby has some mates?'

I sighed.

'It's not revenge. Actually, I think it might be something else altogether.'

It had taken me a while to get there, but now I thought back to that sunny lunchtime in my office talking to Mickey Helm, the die-setter who'd tussled with Jabez outside the Two Brewers. Something he'd said.

'A lion become a lamb…'

And things other people had said too.

'There's an order to things, and each man has his part to play…'

'These men have the gall to try and tell us what to do! And now they're even in Parliament!'

'He's different, even in a field of cut-throats and show-offs like ours…'

I saw now, with reasonable certainty, that what we had assumed was one thing was actually a lot more complicated. I also saw that our odds of survival were already lengthening rapidly, and that hiding would not save us.

'We need to get back to London,' I said. 'As soon as we can. I've made a serious mistake.'

Duke raised an eyebrow.

'Bugger off,' said Jabez, but more by way of exclamation than disagreement.

'It's our best chance,' I said, and briefly explained why.

Forty-Five

The following evening, at five minutes to midnight, I stood alone on the factory floor at Catcliffe Steel. The place was silent, cold, and empty of every human being except me. Half an hour earlier, I had sent the baffled night watchman home, then done a sweep of the offices. My cousin Gregory was still in his office poring over a set of tool designs, so I packed him off too.

'Tell you in the morning,' I said, when he asked mildly why he was being evicted. I hoped I would have the chance.

The factory was dimly illuminated by a handful of new electric lights mounted high up on the gantry. I stood in the shadow of the three heaviest presses – Samson, Caesar and Blackbeard – and watched the giant clock on the end wall, much as my workmen did for ten hours a day when they weren't scrawling on the bog doors. Like them, I wondered that it could move with such excruciating slowness.

I rocked back and forth on my heels, the thick layer of dried oil on the floor sticking to my soles. The loose drape of my light summer overcoat concealed the bulge of Jabez's revolver tucked awkwardly in my jacket pocket, but it didn't make me feel any safer.

At two minutes to twelve, I heard the double doors open at the other end of the factory, followed by low voices and the scrape of hobnails. Out of the half darkness, a line of square-shouldered men came into view, striding down the wide alley between the ranks of steel presses.

They passed the racks of clock cards, the banks of dented lockers and the kiosk with the big red-painted alarm bell that started and stopped the working day at Catcliffe's, its one tiny window covered over with newspaper on the inside. I could see them craning their necks to scan the gantry above, peering through the half-full cages of automobile parts and fire extinguishers in search of an ambush that wasn't there.

There were four of them in caps and long coats, with a slighter, more smartly dressed figure left of centre. From a distance, they looked like a gang of Collison's blacklegs turning up on the quiet to work a night shift, or a union delegation from the AATMM come to give those money-grubbing Catcliffes what-for.

But they weren't blackleg labour and they weren't union men, and the figure in the middle was not William Collison. It wasn't Jacob Bell either, because he was already dead.

....

'Can you even drive?' asked Agnes as her chauffeur opened up the garage in the mews behind the house.

'I run a heavy engineering firm.'

'And as usual you never answer the question I've asked. The one thing is no guarantee of the other. In my experience your skills are extremely limited.'

The driver looked at me with apprehension. I had first met Rackley years earlier when he worked for Agnes's dead brother-in-law, the former Lord Halsingham. Like so many chauffeurs, he had started out in the stables, and he loved the vehicle like a favourite horse – his pride amplified by the fact that Agnes's motor car was an exceptionally beautiful one. She had owned it before she married, and if anyone were ever in doubt that Lord Kelverton's middle child was his favourite, then the imported Delaunay-Belleville tourer was proof enough. Its immaculate paintwork was a rich damask red with brass accents that gleamed in the evening light, and the distinctive cylindrical bonnet marked it out immediately as something a bit special. Half the men at my club would have given their right eye for such a machine.

Rackley bent down and gave the handle a practised jerk that brought the engine smartly to life with a bubbling cough like a smoker clearing his throat. It settled down to a steady putter and thump, and he stood up, wiping his hands on his overalls. He wasn't wearing his uniform, because I was.

It was my second disguise of the day. About an hour earlier, I had turned up at the kitchen door of the Halsinghams' London house on Eaton Square, dressed in Dawoojee Dukanwalla's clothes – showing some slight blood residue about the collar where his wound had seeped.

Under Duke's direction, my exit from the York train had been brought off with some considerable subterfuge. Not knowing who might be watching us – but confident that someone would be – Duke had made an arrangement with a young widow three carriages down. During the bustle preceding our arrival in King's Cross station, we had hastily switched clothes in a luggage car as Jabez kept watch. I had then alighted arm in arm with the woman and her children, balancing a snot-streaked toddler on my hip while all eyes were on Jabez picking a fight with a burly Yorkshireman further up the platform.

As I zigzagged across London by way of two cabs, an omnibus and a short ride on the Metropolitan Railway, I nursed three quiet hopes: that Lady Halsingham was in residence; that her husband was not; and that she wouldn't send me packing when I told her what I wanted. Of the first two I was hopeful, and of the third I was rashly confident. However badly our last adventure had ended, Agnes and I had been through the wringer together, and something told me she would do it all over again. Delusional as I might have been, I believed she was, like me, stuck in a dead life that tasted somehow unsalted after what had gone before – not that either of us would ever admit it.

As luck would have it, Lord Halsingham was still abroad on business and his wife was preparing to dine out. Unlike her sister – the previous Lady Halsingham – Agnes rebelled at long periods spent alone out at Halsingham House in rural Surrey, and she was to be found in London quite often. To be found, that is to say, by everyone except me. In the normal course of things I was still *persona non grata* at Eaton Square.

This time, however, my reception was surprisingly warm. Presumably because I had something interesting to offer her, and also because I proposed to place myself in her debt.

'You will admit, Harry,' said Agnes, 'that this is outlandish even by your standards.'

This line delivered as I stood in one of her upstairs bedrooms, straightening the buttons on a smart navy blue chauffeur's jacket. Rackley was a carriage horse of a man and the shoulders were a little on the broad side, but otherwise it wasn't a bad fit. I resisted the urge to ask for a mirror, but she stepped past me and opened the wardrobe door to reveal a full-length one set upon the inside.

People who routinely wear uniforms cannot wait to get out of them, but for those of us who never do, they have the appeal of the dressing-up box. I adjusted the smart peaked cap and thought what a shame it was that you had to commit to a life in service if you wanted one. Agnes stood back to watch me preen. I could see her in the glass, smiling despite herself.

'For your information,' she said, 'a driver stands up straight with his weight on both feet, and he doesn't wear his cap cocked over one eye.'

'Then he is missing a trick.'

'I imagine the idea is not to appear as if he's been drinking beer all afternoon.'

Out in the garage, Rackley did indeed stand square and tall, watching uncertainly as I clambered behind the wheel.

'In case you haven't driven this particular motor car before, sir…' he ventured, and proceeded to show me the various sticks and pedals. It was a kindness, not least because – while I did know how to drive a car – I certainly wasn't very good at it. The gears made some painful crunching noises as we lurched out into the yard, and I could feel Agnes's eyes boring into the back of my neck from the rear seat.

After an uncertain start, the wide, quiet span of Eaton Terrace was easy enough going, lined with immaculate mansions under a layer of gleaming stucco like royal icing.

'Lovely smooth ride!' I shouted over my shoulder.

'Eyes on the road please, driver.'

By the time I reached Ebury Bridge, coasting over the Grosvenor Canal and the railway line, I was really starting to enjoy myself, but alas it was not to last. The nearer I got to the riverfront, the busier the roads got and the fewer rules anyone seemed to be observing. On

Westmoreland Street, distracted by a scruffy canvas-covered wagon that was trying to push me onto the pavement, I nearly mowed down a constable who had stepped out into the road to help some pedestrians cross. The man was obviously sweltering hot in his big coat and he turned angrily to give me what-for, but fortunately the combination of the elegant car and the even more elegant woman in the back persuaded him to wave us on.

I hit the river at Grosvenor Road, where a growling, clattering slug of traffic blocked my way. I tried unsuccessfully to stick my beak into a jostling herd of omnibuses – advertisements for Pear's soap on every single one, as if someone at the bus company might have been dropping their evil-smelling passengers a hint. Since they were all hooting their horns at me, I reached out and honked mine back, and miraculously this opened up a sliver of dusty road between two buses. I thought I was cutting it fine, but in the event, two barrow bicycles crowbarred their way into the traffic on either side of me. These infernal little contraptions were everywhere, the boxes on the front loaded high with newspapers or heaps of rag, pedalled behind by fierce little men in torn clothes.

I daresay it was a beautiful summer's evening by the Thames. Strolling couples in boaters queuing for the paddle steamers, amorous pigeons clattering in the trees, all of that. I saw none of it, so entirely focused was I on avoiding a road accident. My oversized jacket chafed with sweat, and the juddering of the engine travelled up my arms and into my stomach until I felt quite sick. Even crossing mighty Vauxhall Bridge into the south of the city, I couldn't bring myself to look up from the dusty back end of the motor car in front. Chauffeur could keep his bloody cap.

A gloved hand touched me lightly on the shoulder.

'You're doing ever so well, Harry,' said a voice in my ear, clearly trying not to laugh.

Penned in by coal carts and trams, we were swept under the booming railway arch at the south end of the bridge, and I might have glimpsed William Collison's office a hundred yards ahead down Kennington Lane if Agnes hadn't shouted, 'Right! Right!' as we emerged into the light again. I cut across an enraged drayman's wagon to turn down Harleyford Road, then cruised on past the Oval and the shadowy tower of the Phoenix gas works.

The traffic began to ease as we travelled south through Kennington and Camberwell in the golden evening sun, until finally, with an avalanche of relief, I drew up on the terrace off Peckham Road that housed the Amalgamated Association of Toolmakers, Millwrights and Metalworkers.

I turned to Agnes in the back and did not care for her sly smile.

'Don't say a word.'

Forty-Six

It was not the need for a car and a chauffeur's uniform that had led me to throw myself reluctantly upon Agnes's mercy. I required the woman herself.

The reason I needed her was sitting at a desk in the entrance hall, scribbling violently in a ledger and looking as forbidding as ever. I recalled the righteous disdain with which the wire-haired gorgon who guarded the offices of the AATMM had greeted me on my last visit. No doubt she would have seen me off in short order at this late hour, but Agnes was a different proposition.

'Can I help you?' she asked, without much friendliness but also with a degree of curiosity. It cannot have been particularly often that women who looked like Agnes turned up at a metalworkers' union, let alone after eight o'clock at night. For my part, I hid in plain sight, standing smartly behind my temporary mistress in my clammy uniform. The woman barely gave me a second glance, let alone recognised me.

'I do hope you can,' began Agnes, showcasing all the charm of her Swiss finishing school. 'I would like to speak to Mr Jacob Bell, please. It is a matter of the utmost urgency.'

Medusa laid down her pen and shook her head with some satisfaction.

'I'm sorry, ma'am, but Mr Bell has gone home for the night.'

Agnes affected to rub her temples in dismay. I had seen her do it for real and it was a decent counterfeit.

'I feared as much,' she muttered, almost to herself. 'This is really most unfortunate. You see, the matter cannot wait until tomorrow.'

'Perhaps I can be of help?' asked the woman at the desk, in a manner that suggested she hoped not to be.

'I'm afraid not,' replied Agnes. 'The issue is an extremely sensitive one, and I am advised that I must speak only to Mr Bell.'

'Advised by whom, may I ask?'

It was Agnes's turn to shake her head, but she managed not to look too satisfied about it.

'That is a trust that I cannot, alas, betray.'

She paused, as a Drury Lane ham might do to indicate deep thought, then stepped closer to the gorgon's desk.

'I don't suppose you might be able to give me Mr Bell's home address, would you? You must believe me when I say that I would not ask unless it were absolutely imperative that I speak to him without delay. The issue cannot wait.'

It wasn't a bad play, but the secretary was unmoved.

'I'm sorry, that is out of the question. I can't very well go around handing out personal details to any old skirt who comes through the door.'

And here she made her mistake, because the rudeness allowed Agnes to deploy her broader repertoire. Her hazel eyes hardened.

‘I will thank you,’ she said sharply, ‘not to refer to me as “any old skirt”. I am Lady Ackland, and I haven’t been spoken to like that since I wore a schoolgirl’s apron. I have come here – at great personal inconvenience – in the urgent interests of one of your members, only to find myself both obstructed and insulted.’

Tough as she was, the woman quailed a little and began to mumble an apology, but Agnes cut her off mid-sentence, pressing the advantage.

‘Look here,’ she said in a more conciliatory tone, ‘I cannot give you any details, but I can perhaps confide in you a little. I have been approached by a working woman of long-standing acquaintance whom I hold in the utmost regard. Her husband – a member of your union – has found himself in a dire situation, and if the matter is not resolved before tomorrow morning then things are certain to get drastically worse.

‘I am led to understand that the *only* man with the influence and ability to save him is Mr Bell. The husband himself has attempted to go through the proper channels, but they have been too slow to help, and his wife came to me just this evening in desperation, begging me to do anything in my power.

‘Please,’ she said. ‘I cannot fail them. Not after all that good woman has done for me over so many years.’

She dabbed a slender fingertip at her tear duct in a gesture that I thought a bit much, but taken on top of everything else, it seemed to do the trick. The secretary scribbled down an address and passed it across, while telling us sullenly that it was more than her job was worth.

‘I promise you,’ said Agnes, ‘Mr Bell will understand.’

I wasn't sure he would, but that was another matter. I had long ago learned that Agnes was a woman almost impossible to say no to, and I felt a faint glow of satisfaction that someone else had just learned it too.

....

'Lady Ackland,' I said pointedly, opening the car door for her.

'She's a wicked old trout,' said Lady Ackland as she stepped up. 'The real one, I mean. Lives on Chesham Place. Been beastly every time I've met her'

'Not a close resemblance between you then?'

'If I were about four hundred years older and built like a hay wagon, perhaps.'

'We take life's small satisfactions where we find them.'

'Exactly. Drive on.'

Forty-Seven

A couple of streets away from Jacob Bell's residence, I pulled the car over to the side of the road, ignoring a hissing intake of breath as the wheel rim scraped the kerb. If my passenger was piqued at the thought of a scuffed tyre, her annoyance was likely to increase considerably when I asked her to stay in the motor car.

The thing was, whatever business Bell was wrapped up in, it had already killed at least twelve men that I knew of, and certainly a good number more that I didn't. There was no telling what the consequences of this visit might be, and while I had needed Agnes's powers of persuasion, I didn't want Bell setting eyes on either her or the car if I could help it.

As far as the gorgon was aware, Agnes was Lady Ackland – and even when further investigation revealed that she was emphatically not that great personage, I was fairly confident that her true identity would remain a mystery. But Jacob Bell had been an engineer – and if he saw that magnificent vehicle draw up outside his terraced house, he would know full well what a rare machine it was. Tracking down its owner might not prove too much of a challenge.

For a year and a half, Agnes's husband had kept me silently complicit in his crimes by dangling the threat of her death over my head.

After everything that had been sacrificed to preserve her life (and she had sacrificed more than me, without knowing it), it seemed a special kind of insanity to put her at risk now – especially if I didn't have to.

Cutting the engine, I hopped down from the driver's seat. Agnes nodded meaningfully at her own door and raised her eyebrows.

'Agnes, I really think it's better if you...'

'Absolutely not.'

I could see this would not be as easy as anticipated. And I had not anticipated it would be easy.

'You would leave me here on my own?' asked Agnes.

'Just for a few minutes.'

'Sat like a sherbet lemon?'

'As sour as one, just at this moment.'

'And whose fault is that?'

'Please, Agnes,' I wheedled. 'It wouldn't be for long.'

'You are no sort of gentleman.'

'So you are always telling me, but I really think it would be safer.'

Agnes narrowed her eyes.

'Tell me, Harry, does Mr Bell strike you as a violent man?'

'Not especially, no.'

'Is he likely, would you say, to assault, ravish or otherwise lay a hand on me?'

I thought of the careful little politician I had met at the AATMM offices earlier in July.

'He didn't seem the type, I admit.'

She was doing that face where her mouth looked like folded wire.

'So in what world am I safer sitting on my own in the back of a Delaunay-Belleville outside Stockwell Orphanage than I am with you, talking to a trade union official in his own home?'

Put like that, she did have a point, and so I opened the door and gave her a hand down. She was magnanimous in victory – it was one of her few good points – following me wordlessly down a piss-scented ginnel through to the next terrace across. I wondered what state the car would be in when we next saw it. It was a decent enough area and there didn't seem to be anyone about, but all the same, it was a very shiny vehicle.

Jacob Bell's house was a few minutes' walk down the street – a larger end-of-terrace with a small front garden. As we approached, I could hear a piano lesson going on in one of the other houses. The student slowed down at the difficult bits then raced away discordantly when they got to a passage they knew. The effect was that of a sort of drunken automaton, regulated to some extent by a loud female voice saying 'steady' when the music began to gather momentum too quickly. Twice the wheels came off completely, and the cacophony was brought smartly to a stop by the unseen teacher clapping their hands together.

'Did you ever play?' asked Agnes.

'Violin. Badly. You?'

'Yes, pianoforte. About as well as our friend there.'

As we approached the Bell residence, I recalled the last time Agnes and I had made a house call on a man we wanted to interview about a murder. The fellow in question had tried to escape through the back door, only he had found Jabez Potter waiting for him with a bad temper and scabby fists.

'Hold on, Agnes. I've got an idea. I'm going to peer through some windows, get the lie of the land before we knock. Give me a minute or two.'

Bell's house was larger than its neighbours – probably built as foreman's quarters – and its position on the end of the terrace meant that the front and back parlours had large side windows. As usual, the front one was kept empty and immaculate for visitors, with an arrangement of dried flowers in the fire grate and a number of what looked like professional certificates hanging above the velvet mantel cloth. The curtains to the back parlour were closed – presumably to stop any passing Tom, Dick or Harry (Catcliffe) peeping in. I decided I might get a better view from the rear of the house.

An alleyway ran down the back of the terrace, festooned with soot-speckled washing like Himalayan prayer flags. The gate to the backyard was unlocked, and as I slipped through it, the outside privy greeted me with fragrant echoes of that awful dungeon bucket. As I pressed my face to the kitchen window, all within appeared in darkness. Next to it, a second pane might have given a view into the scullery, had it not been completely steamed up.

Stepping over a couple of withered plants in terracotta pots, I peered through the third window into the dim back parlour. By the sliver of dusky evening light that I was partly blocking out, it appeared much more homely than the visitors' room. I could just make out a couple of grubby armchairs and some zoological etchings on the walls. The man's armchair was angled away from me, but the more upright lady's one contained a middle-aged woman who I took to be Mrs Bell. She was fast asleep, with a book across her chest. A bedroom alarm clock sat between the two chairs on a side table. Obviously the Bell household snoozed after dinner. I felt a pang of guilt at disturbing such domestic tranquillity, even if Jacob Bell did have a piper to pay.

Returning to Agnes, I rapped smartly on the front door, setting myself in a steely aspect for the unpleasant encounter that was inevitably to follow. Agnes, in contrast, affected a winning smile – which soon faded when no-one answered the door.

'Fast asleep in the parlour,' I explained, and gave the door another good hammering.

'Both of them?' she asked when there was once again no response.

'I couldn't see. Definitely her, not sure about him.'

I went and tapped loudly on the curtained side window while Agnes set persistently about the door knocker, but to no avail. She followed me round the back and into the yard.

'Oof,' she grunted, holding her gloved hand under her nose as she got her first hit of the privy.

'Agnes, you have no idea,' I said, thinking again of Haydon Castle.

We pressed our foreheads up against the parlour window, budged up together in the corner of the yard.

'Has she moved?'

'I don't think so, no.'

'I think that's his hand on the chair arm, isn't it?'

'Difficult to see in the dark.'

Agnes looked up at me out of the corner of her eye.

'I don't like this,' I said.

She stepped back and put her hand on the scullery door.

'Here's something you're going to like even less.'

She pushed it open and went in.

The humid scullery held a powerful odour of soap and vinegar, but as we passed the copper and moved through into the kitchen, there was a note of something else.

'Do you smell that?' asked Agnes.

I nodded and pushed past her, on through a small lobby full of cupboards and larders, and into the narrow hallway. A set of stairs led upstairs, and a little light filtered through a stained-glass panel above the front door, bathing the hall in a coloured glow. The smell was unmistakeable now, and as I pushed the parlour door open, an acrid, chemical haze assaulted my eyes and lungs.

'Gas!' I gasped.

Behind me, I heard Agnes fumbling with the locks on the front door, trying to get it open.

Inside, the parlour was almost black, save for the weak square of light from the back window. I ducked out into the hallway, took a deep breath, then rushed across the room, stumbling over a low table and tipping its contents onto the floor. There was a clang and the sound of smashing crockery. I flung the curtains wide open, flooding the room with evening light, and fumbled with the sash mechanism, my eyes burning. I felt Agnes next to me, and together we heaved the window up and hung out into the street, hacking and gulping fresh air.

Behind me I could hear the gas jet still hissing from the light fitting by the door, together with the ticking of Mrs Bell's alarm clock. Overlaid from outside were the discordant tones of the piano lesson still going on, and a dog barking somewhere nearby.

'Oh, Harry,' said Agnes, her voice rough and wet like Dick Fletcher's before it caught somewhere in her chest and she dissolved into a coughing fit. I turned back, and saw what she saw.

Both Bells were there, slumped in their chairs, books laid open in their laps – looking for all the world as if they had just closed their eyes for a nap. I crossed the room quickly and pulled the chain to shut off the gas. Agnes was doubled over, retching and trying to catch her breath, and I dragged her out into the hallway where the air was better.

She looked up at me, tears in her eyes, though I couldn't say whether it was town gas or horror that had put them there.

'If that in there was an accident,' I said, 'then I'm a maharajah.'

Agnes nodded, swallowing breathlessly.

'But then why did she set...?'

She never did get to finish her sentence, because several things happened at once. Agnes's gaze suddenly shot across the gas-filled room to the small side table I had overturned on my way in. There, among the scattered periodicals and shards of broken teacup, was the small brass alarm clock, still ticking. With the extra light from the main window, it now became apparent that something was attached to the double-bell and striker assembly on top. From a distance, it looked like a large bundle of matches, and perhaps it was. Anyway, I didn't get a decent look at it because Agnes drove her head into my chest like a bullock, hands on my shoulders, heaving me backwards towards the open front door.

There was a loud pop, then a boom that thumped right through Agnes and into me, flinging us both forcefully down the front steps with a tremendous rush of heat and light. The stained glass burst from the panel above the door, showering down through the fireball that belched out from the hallway.

The force of the explosion spent, the flames retreated back into the house again, where they commenced to take hold of the curtains and upholstery. I blinked, choked, tried to get up and couldn't – then registered that this was because I was lying on my back with Agnes on top of me. She also appeared to be on fire.

I rolled her off, scrabbled to my knees and beat the smouldering parts of her dress out with my chauffeur's jacket. Fortunately she was rich, because your average Cockney sparrow in cheap flannelette petticoats would have gone up like a Roman candle.

Her eyes were wide, one of them was bloodshot, and in general she looked like she'd just drunk fifteen pints of Duke's best Burton ale. There was a reek of burned hair, but it could have been either of us.

'Agnes!' I hissed, taking hold of her soot-streaked face in panic.

She opened her mouth but it took a moment or two for her to remember how to work it.

'Do I…' she began, '…do I look as bad… as you?'

'Just about. Can you move.'

'Maybe. Can't tell.'

I got my arms around Agnes and hauled her upright like a sack of coal. She smelled like one too.

'We need to go,' she whispered in my ear.

And we really did. Already, neighbours were starting to rush out of their houses. One man made as if to dash into the hallway, and I reached out a hand across his chest.

'Don't,' I wheezed in my best Bow Bells accent. 'They're dead already. The gas. Suffocated.' I made sure to drop the 't'.

He looked at me curiously, but then someone started shouting from the open side window, and we took the opportunity to make off down the road.

'Are you all right, love?' asked one woman as we passed.

'Tip-top. Thank you,' muttered Agnes, limping badly and clinging on to me like a toddler.

'*Tip-top*?' I hissed.

We got back down the ginnel to the next road along, and to my delight, the car was still there, apparently unharmed.

'You get the handle,' said Agnes, climbing into the driver's seat. Between us we managed to get it started in short order, then Agnes switched to the back and I set off for Belgravia in the gathering dark.

The roads were a little quieter now, and we didn't say a word as I weaved in and out of the evening traffic. Risking a glance over my shoulder, I saw that she had lain down across the back seat and wrapped herself in a blanket. I felt the same way.

Back in Eaton Square, I turned into the mews behind the Halsingham residence and cut the engine. After what had gone before, the sudden silence was blissful. I sat back in my seat and closed my eyes for a moment. There was a rustling behind me and a smell of something burnt, then I felt Agnes's chin rest on my shoulder. She leaned her head wearily against mine.

'Are you all right, Harry?'

'I'm fine. I think you got the worst of it.'

'I think so, yes.'

'Thank you, by the way.'

'You're welcome.'

I liked that about Agnes. Just about anyone else I knew would have started up about what an awful night it had been, but it wasn't the worst one Agnes had experienced – not by a long shot. Sadness was deep down in her bones, and it made her tough.

The chauffeur must have heard the car, and at the sound of the coach house door opening, she sat back in her seat again. I looked guiltily down at the burst shoulder seam where her face had been.

'He's not going to be happy about his jacket, is he?'

'No.'

'Your dress has seen better days too.'

'At least the car's all right.'

'That's the important thing,' I said.

....

An hour later, I was out of the chauffeur's burned and ripped clothes and back in Duke's slightly bloodstained ones. My cuts had been swabbed with alcohol by a hostile housekeeper who vastly disapproved of my presence in her mistress's house (more accurately, her master's house), and a mirror had revealed that I'd lost most of my eyebrows and a good chunk of the hair that usually sat in a flop above my right eye. I ached like I'd been kicked by a horse.

The summer night had fallen strangely still, and the scrape of my boots echoed down the long, empty pavements of Eaton Terrace. Over in a pub behind Victoria Station, Jabez would by now have arranged a room, a plate and a pint. Whatever repercussions followed me from Stockwell – or, for that matter, from Yattonby – they would not find me tonight.

I wondered if I would ever have questions to answer over the deaths of Mr and Mrs Bell. Certainly, Agnes and I had been seen by a number of people. The car probably had too. And Medusa would report that Lady Ackland had come looking for Jacob Bell on the night he died. I smiled to myself at that.

But whoever had set up Bell's death had made a pretty good job of it. I had seen no obvious marks of violence on the bodies, and the fire would have made short work of what evidence there was. There was the alarm clock, but I couldn't think there would be much left of that after the house went up. The man who I had prevented from entering would remember me. So would the woman who had passed us in the road. Would they make the leap to foul play, or would they simply assume that we were passers-by, caught up in the explosion?

People died from gas leaks all the time, and it would take an unusually diligent policeman to hear the clip-clopping of hooves and start looking for a zebra instead of a horse.

A zebra it had undoubtedly been, though, and I was now fairly confident I could finger the zookeeper.

Forty-Eight

'Good evening, Harry,' said Dick Fletcher, short of puff after his walk from one end of Catcliffe's to the other.

'Hullo, Dick.'

'How's the family?'

'Well enough, thank you. Haven't seen them since I got back.'

'I know.'

He sighed and looked around himself wearily.

'Any chance of a chair in this place? I haven't got your youth.'

'Try that foreman's kiosk over there.'

Fletcher nodded at one of his boys and the man moved heavily off towards a small green-painted hut at the end of a row of presses, a bit like a sentry box. It had windows round three sides, and the desk inside was stacked high with order slips and ledgers.

The fellow returned bearing an oil-blackened wooden chair, not bothering to close the door behind him. It was a small act of disrespect towards a foreman he didn't know, and it annoyed me. Fletcher saw my pursed lips and smiled as he sat.

'You're becoming quite spirited in your old age, Harry.'

'Not something I've ever been called before.'

'No, I should think not. But you've been full of surprises lately. So come on out with it then. Let me know what it is you want.'

'We could start with the truth.'

A wheezy laugh.

'Very dangerous place to begin, that. Start with the truth and there's no telling where you'll finish.'

'I suppose you were hoping we could agree on a lie.'

'I was actually. But if that's where we end up then I don't mind starting with the truth.'

I felt oddly powerful standing over him like that, but I knew it was an illusion. He had just about all the cards, and if things weren't resolved to his satisfaction then those big lads would make sure I didn't leave the factory with breath in me.

'Well, shall we open with Jacob Bell? Since this was all about him, wasn't it?'

Fletcher nodded and looked indulgently at me.

'I'll say it again, you're full of surprises just at the moment. Tell me why, then. Actually, hold on...' He gestured to one of his men to fetch the other chair from the foreman's office. As the fellow dragged it carelessly back along the oily floorboards, I could feel the sand running through my personal hourglass.

'Much more civilised,' he observed as I sat down opposite him. 'Sounds like we'll be here a while, and at my age I'll get a crick in my neck talking up at you.'

It was unlike him to play the age card at all, let alone twice in quick succession, and I wondered if the old crow was rattled in some small way. He fell silent and looked at me expectantly, so I began.

'On the evening Piers Garrett proposed to gun me down like a bunny, he and I had a little chat in Lord Horncastle's study.'

'I imagine that was hard going.'

'Very. But one of the things he said stayed in my mind. He was raging about the unions, and he said, "and now they're even in Parliament". Which they are. And liable to become more of a presence, I would say.'

'I would say so too. Another general election coming up in the not-too-distant – and I'll wager when it's done, a few more members will speak with my vowels and a few less with yours.'

'It strikes me that Garrett's scheme to try and murder or intimidate every union member in London was not an effective long-term solution.'

He laughed.

'Certainly not!'

'But what about if you murder and intimidate selectively?'

'Weed out the difficult ones, you mean?'

'Not exactly. More like weed out the ones who are in your way. Or rather, Bell's way...'

'Now you're talking.'

'Because he was your chosen horse. I thought when I met him that he was a man destined for politics, and so did you...'

I stopped, suddenly realising that one of Fletcher's men had circled round behind me. I glared at him and tried not to look frightened.

'Behave,' croaked Fletcher, flicking a lazy finger to return the fellow to his two companions. They reminded me of Ellen Garrett's dogs.

'I always think people waste a lot of time working against each other when they might just as well work together,' opined Fletcher. 'Jacob Bell saw that too.'

'And so you were busy paving his way to become a candidate for the next election.'

'I was paving his way to win, as it happens. A mutually beneficial arrangement.'

'But first you had to get rid of the competition.'

I thought of clever young Jem Clay, who had made shop steward at Duraweave before he was twenty-six years old. Bert Lockwood, local union secretary and – as he had told me when we were in chokey – respected Methodist lay preacher. And fearless Abraham Bickley, who would go toe-to-toe with tycoons until he got his fellow members what they deserved. How many other potential Labour Party candidates had been shot, beaten or broken at a nod from Dick Fletcher.

'In my defence, they weren't all competition,' said Fletcher, picking at his too-tight collar in that familiar way of his. 'Most of them were exactly what they looked like. Troublemakers who gave us a hard time but were never going to make it past local leadership. Remember, Garrett lifted his own quarry.'

'But you made sure that anyone who happened to be in Bell's way made it onto the list. Garrett told me he had a man helping him pick his rabbits. I thought he was talking about William Collison, but later I realised he could just as easily have been describing you.'

'Piers and I were in the habit of taking a drink together at my club from time to time. I may have made the occasional... suggestion. Couldn't stand the man really, but he was useful in his way, and he sucked up something terrible.'

I thought of Garrett's disdain for me, for Wilkie, even for his own son-in-law. But Dick Fletcher would have been a different kettle of fish. A fellow even more rapacious than the boot-and-shoe gnome himself. Fletcher was all Garrett aspired to be, and I could see why he might have fawned over him, hanging on his words and looking for advice and approbation in throwaway comments.

'Piers Garrett's first hunt was a one-off, last September,' explained Fletcher. 'Started with a vagrant, as you do. But after he'd done it the once, he told me he'd quite lost his appetite for shooting anything else. He organised one in November, another to celebrate the new year, and they gradually got more frequent. Soon realised he couldn't keep lifting his quarry from the local area – plus pickled old tramps on crutches weren't much of a challenge. He wanted his marks fitter and faster, so that's when the abductions started.

'Since May he's been going up there once a month, and it's become quite a business keeping his cellar stocked. By the end he was very grateful for the odd recommendation.'

I had always liked Fletcher, but there was something repellent about discussing those poor lads in the underground cell at Haydon Castle like they were bottles of Club Claret. The disapproval in my face must have been plain to see, because he suddenly became rather defensive, sitting forward in his chair and jabbing his finger at me.

'Look, Piers Garrett was a lunatic. Screaming insane, and he deserved to be fed to those dogs of his. But he was suggestible and he fulfilled a purpose. I saw an opportunity and I took it, same as I've done ever since I was a shipping clerk at Mulligan's.'

He softened a little.

'I just made out that I was all on board with how much he loathed the working man. I may even have contemplated out loud how he could combine it with his other passion for killing things that couldn't kill him back,' he added in a self-deprecating manner that made it clear this was exactly what he had done.

'Sometimes,' he added, 'all it takes to make a mad idea seem reasonable is to talk about it like it is.'

'Extraordinary to have managed it without getting your own hands dirty at all,' I said with grudging admiration.

'Oh, well, you know, I did soil them just a little bit. He wasn't completely soft in the head. Pushed me to commit a morsel of crime – an "act of good faith" if you will. I imagine he thought it would mean he had something on me if he needed it.'

These rich old men were all about leverage, but Garrett had been an even bigger fool than he looked if he reckoned he could try and get one over on Dick Fletcher.

I thought for a moment. My own voice drifting back to me from Peter Wilkie's study. *A crony with a steamship company and connections in Africa or Asia*.

'The guns. Those bloody Martini–Enfields. We wondered how he had got hold of so many.'

'Well, there are a few more where those came from.' He gave me a wicked smile. 'I got hold of a job lot in Melbourne a few years back. Rainy-day purchase – squirrelled away for darker times.'

Occasionally in life, you come across an incidental piece of information that will one day become quite important. At the time, I simply wondered how many ex-military rifles constituted a 'job lot'.

Fletcher waved his hand dismissively.

‘I let Garrett have a handful – made out I’d sourced them for him specially. He was delighted. Made him feel like he was one of the big boys.’

And when it came down to it, he never had been. Families like the Garretts and Catcliffes were middle-grade industrialists at best. High up above us, tooting their trumpets in the firmament, were Dick Fletcher and his fellow Olympians. Creatures of almost unimaginable wealth and influence. Gods of their own making. America was their natural habitat, but a handful still roosted in the old world.

These men weren’t monsters of excess, like Piers Garrett. They were careful and quiet, and their schemes were years in the making. I could imagine Dick Fletcher already had half the Conservative Party and a decent fistful of Liberals up his sleeve, but now Labour was on the rise, the Lords were getting their teeth pulled, and there was no knowing where it might all end. A shrewd operator would be spread-betting.

Like all good businessmen, Fletcher also knew when to cut his losses, and it had come as a shock to me – sitting in the pub in York with Jabez and Duke the previous afternoon – when I realised that he had sent me to cut them for him.

Forty-Nine

'I will admit, I feel a bit of a fool,' I said. 'You sent me to Yattonby with the express purpose of bringing an end to Piers Garrett's hunts. Even gave me Duke to help me along.'

'Actually,' he corrected me, 'I gave Mr Dukanwalla *you* to help *him* along. If you remember, I already had him working on it before you strolled into my office.

'Though I'll say this, I was highly delighted when you did. And quite lucky, all things considered. I thought Dukanwalla would be able to shut Garrett down on his own, but as it turned out, he might have struggled without you.'

'Garrett started getting careless?'

'Piers was sloppy from the start. It's amazing that he managed to carry it all off as long as he did. He had a few coppers on the books, which helped – but paid hands like that will only stick their necks out so far, however much you tip them. There's been a crop of incorruptibles springing up at the Yard, and there are only so many missing person reports your average desk sergeant can lose before the busybodies start taking an interest.

'He was out of control, and it was only going to get worse. More and more men every month. Factory owners like your old man starting to take an interest. Cock-ups like the Bickley debacle and that extra bloke he had to snatch at the docks...

'And God knows people must have been starting to talk in those villages up north. Told me over a drink that he'd put a local poacher in the bag – as if no-one was going to pay it any mind when he took one of their own. The wheels were coming off, most of the men on Bell's list were out of the way, and it was time to wind it up.'

I jabbed my thumb at my own chest.

'Mr Harrison Catcliffe, at your service.'

He liked that. Grinned, shifted in his chair, picked at his collar again.

'Garrett's not the only suggestible fellow about,' Fletcher said, winking. 'You Catcliffes are quite easily led too. Did your pa tell you it was me who talked him into sending you all the way up to deepest, darkest Yorkshire?'

Not an entirely accurate description of drowsy Birkdale in high summer, but I let it pass.

'He did actually – though only in passing, and I didn't think anything of it at the time.'

It was a secret that I would never tell the old man. He was basically a good-hearted soul – so long as you weren't asking him to part with money – and the idea that he had been duped into sending his eldest son on a near-fatal errand would haunt him for the rest of his days if he ever found out.

'But then why did you try and warn me off?'

The old boy frowned.

'I didn't, lad.'

'Twice, Dick. The kicking after the funeral then the chap in St Wulfram's.'

'Not guilty. Why would I put you off when I wanted you up in Yorkshire doing my dirty work? If someone was leaning on you to back off, then my money's on Piers Garrett.'

Actually, if it wasn't Fletcher then Jacob Bell seemed a better bet. I thought of the hobnailed boots in my side, the Cockney accent telling me to keep my nose out and the attempt to make me walk home barefoot. I don't suppose one would have to look very far at the AATMM for someone willing to put the boot into a Catcliffe.

'Was I supposed to die at Haydon Castle?' I asked. It sounded peevish when I said it out loud, but truthfully I did feel aggrieved about it.

'Now really, Harry, after all the years we've known each other? I remember you when you were nothing but a stripling, clinging to your old pa's coat tails.'

'No you don't, Dick. We didn't meet until I was in my twenties.'

'Didn't we?' He tapped his temple to indicate fictional senility.

'Well, anyway, sentiment's there. And I really didn't mean you any harm. It would have served my purpose just as well if you'd been killed, but it certainly wasn't my plan. If you must know, I didn't expect things to end in quite such a lot of blood. I thought you or Dukanwalla would just uncover what was going on and take it to the police.

'Garrett would be arrested, there would be some terrible headlines – "Shoe-t to kill", "hang him with his own bootlaces" and so forth – and a line would be drawn under the whole thing. He might have tried to bring me into it, but it would never have stuck. The missing men would have been killed at random by a lunatic, and no-one would trouble to look into it any further.

'*Then* look at how it might have played out. Piers Garrett gets a nice rope necktie and is mourned by precisely no-one. Young Harrison Catcliffe returns to London a hero. Jacob Bell continues to rise at speed through the Labour movement and is in due course elected to Parliament, where he makes sure not to forget the man who put him there.'

'Was he really that cynical? Bell, I mean.'

Fletcher pressed his lips together and shook his head slowly, indicating no doubt that I was young and still had a lot to learn.

'Not at all. Quite honourable in his way. The truth you won't want to hear is that Jacob Bell had the same ideals as Abraham Bickley – only he would have actually made a difference.'

I could feel a lecture coming on.

'It's my feeling that there are three kinds of politicians. The rarest type are the pure idealists. Almost always extremely wealthy and largely incorruptible. Waste of time trying to reason with them, in my experience. Then there are the ones who are on the make. Plenty of those about. Easily bought, willing to do or say just about anything for money or power. But they're flaky. Turn their back on you if they get a better offer – plus everyone knows who and what they are.

'The third kind are the ones you can really work with. The pragmatists. Deep down, most politicians have got principles of some sort or another, but they know that ideals aren't worth a brass farthing if you're not in the room when the deals are made. So they make whatever alliances and compromises they need to get themselves into that room. Bell was one of those. He was using me, I was using him. He'd have made a good MP, fought for the working man like he promised. But he won't now, will he?'

I rubbed my eye in frustration.

'Because I sent that bloody telegram.'

Fletcher spread his hands as if to say, *well what could I do?*

'You forced my hand. Now it was you that was out of control. So I sent a telegram of my own to a man I know in Leeds. Very professional, used him before.'

'Told him to shove me onto the tracks at York station.'

Sitting there chatting for so long, I had almost forgotten that he'd tried to have me murdered the day before.

'Not in exactly those words, but yes. And not without regret, Harry.'

I heard a noise at the far end of the factory floor, and a fourth man came sauntering out of the darkness to join his comrades. Where have you been? I thought.

At the sound of his approach, Fletcher glanced over his shoulder and the man shook his head.

'So why kill Bell too?' I prompted him. 'When you thought you'd already taken care of me.'

He shrugged irritably.

'By then, there was no telling who'd heard about Jacob Bell and how far it might have spread. The two blokes who got back to London a few days ago might already have talked. Then there was Dukanwalla. And your little terrier – we'll get to him, by the way.

'The secret was out. I had to get rid of Bell, and I had to get rid of you too because I knew you wouldn't let it go until you had the full story. And I was right, wasn't I – because we're sat here now.'

Maybe he was. I wanted to tell him that the reason I was still pursuing the truth even with Bell dead was that he had made it about my survival. I was there that night because someone had tried to kill me, and they would keep on trying until Fletcher and I put this business to bed.

But was that really true? I had a long history of picking at loose threads just because they were there, and who was to say I wouldn't have picked at this one.

'How did you get that first whiff of shit off Bell, by the way?' Fletcher asked. 'Did he give himself away when you visited him at the AATMM?'

'Not at all. Didn't suspect a thing. I was distracted by William Collison, especially after I saw your motor car outside the Roaring Meg. It was yours, wasn't it? The Belsize? What were you doing there?'

Fletcher looked delighted.

'Gone down a blind alley there, I'm afraid. I was there for the same reason as you. Lining up some manpower in case the Sailors and Firemen's Union voted for a strike.'

'Nothing more?'

'Nothing more. Honestly, lad, not everything is a conspiracy.'

'But Collison lied to me. He pretended he didn't know Abe Bickley.'

'And wouldn't you, in his position? Someone starts asking you about a murder victim, you're hardly going to come right out with it and say you never liked the bugger anyway. As it happens, Collison's as straight as they come. Not a popular man, but I'd suggest he's a good deal more honest than many of his friends on the other side of the picket line.'

'Abe was honest.'

'Maybe, but Bell wasn't. So go on. How did you get onto him?'

'Timmy Bickley told me, down in that prison cell at Haydon Castle. His younger brother, Alf, was the one who told Bell he could nab Abe Bickley on the way home from the Two Brewers. Bell must have passed it up the chain to you, then I suppose you gave Garrett the wink.'

Fletcher nodded, gratified to have discovered the cause of his undoing.

'It was a mess, that,' he observed.

'Just one of those things that will happen if you push your luck, Dick. If Timmy hadn't fought with his uncle in the pub and followed him home, then Abe might have gone in the van without getting his skull cracked open and perhaps we'd still be none the wiser.'

'If it had been up to me, I'd have killed the younger Bickley then and there. Rub the witness out. But Garrett's lads bagged him for the larder. Sent him up to Yorkshire in place of his dead uncle. Used their initiative – I wish muscle wouldn't do that.'

He glanced at the four bored-looking lumps behind him.

'Why did he do it, the younger brother? Give Uncle Abe away like that? Bell said he wanted Bickley out of the way and told me where he could be got on his own. Said the information had come from his own flesh and blood, but he never said why.'

'Alf was young and scared for his future. He was only just starting out at Catcliffe's and he wanted to work his way up the ladder. Thought he'd get blacklisted if his uncle went into union leadership in a big way.'

'He might have been right.'

I sighed, not really wanting to believe it. Sat there among the sleeping steel presses, I wondered how many casual injustices were meted out in that place each day. Not because we meant to do anyone harm, but because we didn't notice.

'He paid a high enough price anyway.'

I thought of Alf there, strung up in the lav.

'He nearly did more than that,' said Fletcher.

There was an implication in there somewhere, but I couldn't quite reach it.

'You didn't kill him, did you, Dick? It looked like suicide, cut and dried.'

'It was, but let's say he chose it based on a slightly skewed version of the facts.'

'He was just a lad.'

'Oh, save it for Jacob Bell, won't you?' he said irritably. 'He did it, not me.'

'I thought you said Bell was arm's-length from it all?'

'He was, but Jake Bell learned the same lesson Piers Garrett did. The same one you might have to learn in due course. That once you start spilling blood, you have to keep on doing it, over and over for the rest of your life.

'You started poking Bell, and he knew there was only one man at Catcliffe's who could connect him to what happened with the Bickleys. So he went to Alf and force-fed him a ten-ton guilt pudding. Told him Timmy was dead, even though he wasn't. Gave him some really nasty story about how it had happened. Reminded Alf that it was all his fault, his own brother.'

I thought back to the day after they'd found Abe's body. Alf Bickley standing on that same factory floor trying to warn me off. In the afternoon when we made the appointment to meet on Monday, he had told me Timmy was still alive – and I was sure he had believed it. So what had happened over the weekend to change his mind?

Abe's funeral, that was what. Bell must have got him on one side after the funeral tea. I remembered Jacob Bell's unaccountable grief in the Anglican chapel at Nunhead Cemetery. Had he been distraught at what he had done to Abraham Bickley, or what he was about to do to the man's nephew?

'Bell told me he was just trying to get the boy to keep quiet, but I don't buy that. He must have known the lad couldn't cope with the weight of it. Not for long anyway. And there was you waiting in the wings, letting Alf know you weren't going to leave it alone. I'd say his options just dwindled away until there was only one left.'

'Don't you dare try that.'

I knew enough of murder to know that the real killer wasn't always the man who pulled the trigger. Indirectly, my curiosity had almost certainly led to more than one death in the past, but I was beginning to get very tired of people like Dick Fletcher, Piers Garrett and Agnes's husband trying to pin their own crimes on me simply because I had asked some questions.

Why did you do it here, Alf? I thought to myself. With all weekend to think on it, why had he waited until the Monday morning at exactly the hour when he was supposed to be meeting me? I knew what I wanted the reason to be, but we would never know now.

FIFTY

There was a long pause, then Fletcher sat forward.

'And so here we are.'

He reminded me more than ever of a magpie, his head cocked and his gnarled fingers gripping his knees like birds' claws.

'You wanted to start with the truth, and we have. So now shall we get onto the lies?'

'All right.'

'Before that, though, Harry – bearing in mind your recent unpredictable nature – would you tell me where your terrier is?'

'You mean Potter?'

'I do. You see, Dukanwalla is at his pub, surrounded by drunks and whores, recovering from a gunshot wound. We know that because we've been watching the place. You are here with me. But Potter is unaccounted for. Suspicious as I am, I assumed you might have him up on that walkway above us with a weapon, but my man here has just gone looking and, well...'

He gestured to a wheeled cage full of steel blanks, waiting to be pressed into shape the following morning.

'Drawn a blank,' he quipped, pleased with his joke.

I remained tight-lipped.

'Harry,' he said cautiously, 'I sincerely hope you're not about to do something rash. You can't think I'm stupid, and I don't think you are either. After what happened yesterday, I don't for a moment believe you'd have come here tonight without some sort of insurance policy – and I'll wager your terrier is holding it.'

I nodded.

'Fair enough,' I said. 'Yes, then, I have him taking care of something for me, but you won't find him. So let's finish our discussion and we can decide whether Jabez has an interesting night or not.'

'Cocky little bastard,' he said with approval. 'But all right, let me tell you what happens next.'

He took a leather cigar case from his inside pocket and offered me one, which I declined.

'Suit yourself,' he said, lighting his own then taking a moment to get it going.

I waited, trying to look calm, my shirt stuck to my back with sweat.

'First option,' began Fletcher, 'we both leave here in one piece. You tell the old man all about Piers and his loony manhunts. The rumours will spread, and in time it'll become common knowledge in the pubs of the East End, however much his people try to pass it off as a hunting accident. Notably missing from the story will be any mention of Jacob Bell or yours truly – except, of course, as a benevolent industrialist who paid Dukanwalla to investigate the case.' He inclined his head and twirled his hand in regal manner.

'Second option: my men cut your throat right here, we bundle you in the back of my car, and you're never seen again. Can I just say that these options are in descending order of preference as far as I'm concerned.'

'Third option?' I asked tentatively.

'My least favourite. It involves you choosing the first option then going back on your word and trying to expose me once you get clear. It might seem like a good idea, but before you choose that path, I'd like you to consider my position in society compared to yours, and how little proof you really have. I'd also like you to think about some of the people you love. If it gets ugly, I probably can't incriminate myself by coming after you directly, but the others are fair game – and some of them are within particularly easy reach.'

With a twist of my insides, I realised that he was talking about Agnes. The Halsingham estate neighboured Fletcher's own country house out in Surrey, and his wife was on pally terms with Agnes despite their age difference. Bitterly, I reflected that this was the second time she had been used against me in this way.

'Not just her,' said Fletcher, reading my mind. 'And I like her very much, so you can see why I'm not in favour. There's Dukanwalla, Potter, your family... those two sapphic aunts in Whitby. If I have to defend myself then I'll do whatever it takes – and history would tend to suggest that you won't.'

That smarted, but it was true. I wondered how much he knew about the pact I had made with Captain Robert Edlington – now Lord Halsingham. And, for that matter, how he knew about it at all. The deal had been that if anything happened to me, Halsingham's crimes would be exposed. If he were ever arrested, on the other hand, he had arranged that Agnes and others would be murdered by a third party. Mutual destruction, only kept off the table by mutual inaction.

But if I didn't know better, I'd say Fletcher was referring to the third choice Robert had given me back in his drawing room on New Year's Eve 1907. The wildcard. You see, his hired hands had been given express instructions that Agnes should not be harmed in the event of Robert's own death – however it occurred. I had only to kill him and all bets were off. Only I wasn't brave enough, and he knew it. I could hear his voice again now:

'You will choose to sacrifice Agnes's future rather than your own, and I will enjoy that thought.'

I looked at Fletcher again now.

'How did you know?'

'Doesn't matter. Knowing is my business. And it was the right choice. Practicality over pride. Your way, no-one else died.'

'What about those who were already dead?'

'Nothing you do will make a blind bit of difference to them. You have to carry on moving forward. Keep looking back and the dead will drag you under.'

I was no longer clear whether we were talking about my own mistakes or his.

'Remember what I was saying about pragmatists?' said Fletcher. 'You choose the first option on my list, and you haven't just saved lives, you've also made an alliance. You've put yourself in the room next time round. The world is changing and you can adapt to it or you can help dictate how it changes.

'Consider that this past fortnight you've been banged up in an underground cell, thrown onto railway tracks and nearly shot for sport. You're like one of my steamships getting bashed about on an Atlantic crossing, all hands on deck just trying to survive. Wouldn't you like to be the weather rather than the ship?'

'Why be Odysseus when you can be Poseidon.'

'If you say so, lad. I started work at twelve so I must have missed out on my ancient Greek lessons. What I do know is that those three choices I've given you are all there is. There's no other path, and you might as well get used to it.'

He was right, and I knew it. As usual, I was hopelessly out of my depth.

Fletcher's cigar had gone out, and he applied himself to relighting it while I stood up wearily.

'You wanted to know where Jabez is.'

Fletcher glanced over his shoulder at his boys.

'It would be a gesture of good faith,' he suggested.

I pointed down to the far end of the factory floor, where the little kiosk with the giant red alarm bell stood. It must have been sixty feet away, but even at such a distance, I fancied I could see the sheet of newspaper covering the inside of the window give a slight twitch.

'He's in there.'

Fletcher nodded at his men. Two of them peeled away and began walking briskly towards the bell hut.

'What's the little chap doing in there then?' He chuckled, placed his cigar in his teeth and drew in a deep lungful of smoke.

I raised my hand to wave at the window. Then took the decision and closed my fist.

The piercing clamour of that alarm bell was a source of both despair and delight at Catcliffe Steel – depending on whether it was telling you to get to work or to down tools and scramble for the Two Brewers.

It could last for up to ten seconds if Norman in the kiosk was in a sour mood, which he often was because he had an old war wound that played up in hot, cold or temperate weather.

Today, the clanging only lasted for about three seconds. It was long enough for me to see Dick Fletcher's eyes widen through the tendrils of cigar smoke. The two men heading towards the bell hut broke into a run, and the other two stiffened up, reaching inside their jackets.

Then, way off in the boiler room, Arthur Letts heaved down the black rubber handle that shut off the electricity, killing the bell and plunging the whole factory into darkness and silence.

In front of me, the tip of Fletcher's cigar glowed in the blackness. I drew Jabez's little Bull Dog revolver from my jacket pocket and placed the muzzle about three inches above the cigar.

The fourth option.

'I'm sorry, Dick.'

I closed my eyes but the muzzle flash still flared through my eyelids.

The shot was deafening in the sudden silence. I felt the pistol jump in my hand, and as I opened my eyes again I saw the cigar snap away to the side, scattering sparks like a firework.

Remembering the plan, I dropped flat to the floor, as more revolvers flashed in the dark. Some were firing at me, others presumably at Jabez in the kiosk, but they couldn't hope to hit us except by the most outlandish luck. Something that felt like warm water flicked across the back of my neck and I realised one of the shots must have hit Fletcher's body, slumped in the chair.

The shooting stopped, and the men began shouting instructions to one another. They called out to Dick, and I could hear the edge of panic in their voices when he didn't answer. After the dazzling muzzle flares, the blackness was absolute – like being submerged in a bottle of ink. Now was my moment.

I crawled to my left until I touched the cold steel footings of the nearest big press. It was Caesar, the middle one. Rising quietly to my feet, I felt my way round the back. Then, placing heel to toe, I set off into the dark, a pace at a time.

Catcliffe paces – that convenient, shoe-sized unit of measurement upon which the whole factory was laid out. Now I just had to remember my counts. Fifteen paces until my outstretched fingers came up against the oily surface of Samson. The men were quiet now, straining their ears. Blind but still dangerous. I reached for the small spanner I'd left inside the back strut of the press, and pitched it underarm down the aisle between the presses. There was a low thump as it landed on the oily floor, followed by the flashbangs of revolvers.

Heel-toe, heel-toe – revolver in one hand, the other feeling around in front of me like an antenna. Fifteen paces to a row of five smaller fly presses, then a ninety-degree left turn and a gap of twelve paces to the tall stacks of sheet steel where the shearmen worked. In the blackness, I couldn't help but feel the Bickleys there. Alf bare-chested and hungover, wracked with guilt; Abe white and bloated as I had seen him in the police mortuary. Timmy with that big hole in his back, a dead man running. I thought of him, sitting next to me in another dark room not long ago. *Us Bickley boys haven't had much luck, have we, Mr Harrison?*

I groped my way around the stacks of steel, the cages of blanks and the machines. Low voices away among the presses and the scrape of hobnails. Someone risked sparking a match, and the shadows converged on it before it was quickly shaken out. I resisted the urge to fire at the light. They weren't hunting me any more – they were trying to regroup, find their way out.

Forcing myself to move slowly despite the screaming urge to run, I lined myself up with the edge of the last press. This was it, twenty-two paces in a straight line to the bottom of the gantry steps.

Halfway there, I heard the muted flap of a rubber swing door at the far end of the factory floor. Jabez was out, then. He had a line to follow, like Theseus in the labyrinth – a skein of Mrs Letts's knitting yarn, thoughtfully laid by Arthur before he disappeared into the cellars to wait for the alarm bell. He had wanted to lay one for me too, but Fletcher and his men would be closer to me, and I couldn't risk anyone spotting it and smelling a rat.

Distracted by thoughts of Jabez's escape, I must have miscounted, because I reached twenty-two paces and there was nothing there. Had I got turned around somehow, set off in the wrong direction? I risked three more heel-toes, feeling around at arm's length until I got hold of the underside of a metal step. I was off, but not far.

I felt my way back to the bottom of the steps, then pocketed the revolver, knelt down and slowly removed my boots. The thick coating of oil on the factory floor meant I could move silently with a bit of care, but the cast iron stairs would need to be tackled in stocking feet.

I crept up to the gantry, then followed the rail along. Below me, the men had struck another light, and were using it to find their way back down the main aisle towards the door they had come in through. They were dragging something heavy, and I realised it was Dick Fletcher.

Presumably, the perilous nature of their situation was beginning to dawn on them. They were, after all, four armed men in an empty factory with a murdered corpse. For all they knew, Jabez and I were long gone, and if the police were to turn up, they would have a hard time explaining their way out of it.

I felt a pang of despair at the concept of Dick Fletcher as a murdered corpse – since I had made him that way – but I shut the door on all that for the time being, continuing my passage along the gantry to the glass-panelled doors that led to the offices. But instead of going through, I took a smaller wooden door a little further along the wall. I shut it after me and left the black cavern of the factory floor behind – mercenaries, dead bodies, gods, ghosts and all.

I was in a cramped brick stairwell, used mostly by the maintenance men. The stairs led me to the roof, and I emerged into the dim light of a sticky summer night under a half-moon. Streetlights glowed below, lamps glimmered in windows, and there was the distant sound of hooting and thumping from the river that never slept. Jabez and Arthur were already there, sitting with their backs against the parapet at the foot of a bare flagpole.

No-one said anything until we had watched the headlights of Dick Fletcher's big Belsize limousine move off down the street past the darkened windows of the Two Brewers. No lock-ins tonight, apparently.

'What will they do with him, I wonder?'

I realised I was crying, and it took me quite by surprise. But then I had liked old Dick Fletcher. It wasn't lost on me that I had lacked the courage to kill a man I hated, but found it in me to murder one I didn't.

'You had to, mate,' murmured Jabez, as usual answering a different question to the one I'd asked.

‘It wasn’t revenge,’ said Arthur quietly. ‘God knows I wanted that, Mr Harrison, but that wasn’t what it was.’

I thought of that muzzle flash after the lights went out. If old Fletch had fancied himself a god then I was a sort of ersatz Prometheus, condemned by those sparks in the dark. At least in my case the punishment was to spend whatever remained of my life looking over my shoulder, rather than having my liver ripped out once a day by an eagle. There was that to be grateful for.

‘He wasn’t wrong, you know,’ I said, wiping oily fingers across my eyes and smelling the cordite on my left hand. ‘His way worked. It was just the cost that was too high.’

Fletcher’s play had almost got him a tame MP, but it had killed half of Arthur Letts’s family. It had killed Jacob Bell and Jem Clay, six mercenaries, the miner who had died in the assault on Haydon Castle, and the unknown numbers of factory men who had met their horrifying ends in the Birkdale woods. It had even killed McCrea and Garrett, not that the world was much the worse for that. Murdering Dick Fletcher closed the tab, and it had to be done. Justice delayed – as the quotable Mr Gladstone once said – is justice denied.

All the same, there was the feeling that I had shut one ledger and opened another.

Fifty-One

I fully expected someone would come for me sooner or later, but it was a surprise – and a sort of relief too – when the man sat down opposite me at a coffee stand in Green Park. More so because I recognised him.

It was the following Sunday afternoon, and my sense of foreboding had achieved a steady crescendo throughout the week, despite the fact that everything seemed to have gone to plan. Under Arthur's careful direction, Jabez and I had spent most of the night cleaning up the mess at Catcliffe's. We had mopped the floor carefully and burned the blood-soaked chair in the yard. We found the disc of one bullet where it had pancaked into Samson, another one in Norman's desk in the bell kiosk, and a third that had gone through a wooden crate and embedded itself in a car headlamp. The others we couldn't place, but it was a steel factory and no-one would think twice about the odd slug of metal lying around. Spent cases might have been more distinctive, but no-one had emptied their revolvers to reload.

The only real damage had been to the bell hut, where a gunshot had put one of the small windows out. We broke the rest of it out of the frame and boarded it over until Arthur could get some more glass. Jabez's pistol went off Waterloo Bridge on the way home.

'What were you up to in here last night?' Gregory had asked when I saw him the next day outside his office. 'I still had work to do, you know.'

'Shooting practice on the factory floor with some of the chaps,' I whispered. 'Don't tell, will you?'

'Sounds good fun. You might have invited me along,' he said sniffily.

As for Fletcher himself, he had simply disappeared. According to the papers, the Belsize had gone too. I wondered where you disposed of a car like that without anyone finding it.

My old man was bothered about it, and I pretended to be too. I hated lying to him almost as much as I hated the truth.

'I'd have faked a suicide,' I told Duke over a pint in the Saracen on the Wednesday. 'As it is, people will be looking for him forever.'

'And that's why they're professionals and you're not. Where there's a body, there are clues. So long as no-one ever finds the body or the car, everyone's in the clear.'

Duke had been in an unusually pensive mood that afternoon. In fact, he had not been himself since that night in the western woods. He talked about it every time I saw him, poring over every detail of the night again and again, and the memory preyed on his mind in a way that none of his previous brushes with death had done.

I supposed being hunted like an animal would do that to a man, but it turned out to be more than that.

'I had something I wanted to tell you, Harry,' he said gruffly. 'Well, two things really.'

He swilled the dregs of his pint around without drinking them off.

'I've been thinking, and I'm going to bring the kids back from Ireland.'

We sat in silence for a moment while he let the news sink in. Because if his own children were returning to London from the safety of his sister-in-law's cottage in County Clare then that meant Thomas Edlington was too. I thought of the frail little boy – who would be seven years old by now – and the danger he would bring with him.

Thomas was heir to the Halsingham estate. Both his parents had been murdered to put his uncle in Halsingham House, and his life had been the only thing I had salvaged from the whole ghastly affair. If Robert found out that Thomas was back in England then there would be blood – his, Agnes's, Duke's, and maybe even mine.

'I know what you're going to say,' said Duke. 'But hiding him in Ireland was never going to work forever. One day, sooner or later, it'll have to be dealt with. I want them back, and I can protect them.'

'It could get rough.'

'It probably will.'

I thought I understood. Dawoojee Dukanwalla had never been the same since his wife had been killed. He had sent the children away, ostensibly for their own safety, and kept moving forward in a valiant attempt to dodge his grief. For a year and a half he had tried to bury everything that reminded him of Jane, but somewhere in Birkdale, faced with his own grisly demise, he had decided that those were the only things that mattered to him.

I nodded.

'And the other thing?'

Duke shrugged.

'You know the other thing.'

And I did. Because the only way to give Thomas Edlington any chance of living beyond his next birthday was to kill Agnes's husband.

'Just that,' he said, 'and then I'm finished with this life. If you've any sense, you'll finish with it too.'

Fifty-Two

The Sunday afternoon following the murder at Catcliffe's – much as I struggled to call it that, even in my mind – I took coffee with Agnes. Green Park was her choice, and she had managed to pick a locale that was famous for both execution and assassination. Even when she didn't mean to, she had an uncanny ability to eviscerate my conscience.

She told me Robert was returning from Africa within the next fortnight. I sipped my coffee and wondered whether I ought finally to get round to murdering him – save Duke the job. In for a penny, in for a pound.

'So I suppose I shall not see you for a while,' I said instead.

'I suppose you shan't.' Then, because I didn't say anything. 'Oh, don't look at me like that.'

'Can you tell me something honestly, Agnes?'

'I don't see why I should. You are almost never honest with me, and when you are, I usually wish you weren't.'

'All the same?'

'All the same, you can ask.'

'Are you glad you married him?'

She picked at her high collar irritably in a manner that reminded me of Dick Fletcher, but then I saw him everywhere these days.

'Why could you possibly want to know that? And what right have you to ask?'

'Tell me and I'll tell you.'

Agnes looked at me and narrowed her eyes.

'Something's happened to you, Harry. Something even more horrid than the other night. Part of me wishes I hadn't come.'

'And the other part?'

She peered into her half-full cup of coffee, as if the two remaining slurps of tepid brown water were justification enough to stay a little longer.

'I'm right though, aren't I? Something *has* happened.'

I nodded.

'Tell me about it?'

And so, because I knew she was expecting me not to, and was really looking forward to getting worked up about it, I told her.

Much of it she knew already, but I'd deliberately kept my suspicions about Dick Fletcher out of what I'd told her before. I went through the events again, stitching it around him to make a substantially different story than the one she thought we'd been caught up in. Bell's pact with Fletcher, Garrett's abductions, Abe's murder, the madness of Birkdale. Finally, I ended up at Catcliffe Steel in the dark with a revolver in my hand, and I told her all about that as well.

I expected disapproval – horror, even – but in the event it did not materialise. She said little during my story, her half cup of coffee cold and untouched.

'Poor Harry,' she said when I was done. 'The price was too high, wasn't it?'

'That's what I've been trying to tell myself. All those men.'

She smiled, but her eyes were glistening.

'That's true, but it's not what I mean. I mean you've gone too far, changed yourself too much.'

I nodded mutely. Tried a smile myself but I couldn't carry it off.

'Will they catch you?'

'As far as I know, they're not even looking. But that doesn't mean they won't one day. It'll always be there.'

Agnes was quiet for a long time then. Finally she sat forward in her chair, chin on her fist.

'I'm not.'

'Not what.'

'Glad I married Robert.'

'I see.'

'But I don't want to talk about it. And now I don't want to know why you asked. I've spent so long being cross with you because you never tell me the truth, but that was suddenly an awful lot of it.'

'It was. I rather surprised myself.'

'I don't think I can take any more, not just now.'

I felt something under the table and was about to move away when I realised it was Agnes's gloved hand seeking out mine. I let her find it.

'People think you're harmless,' she said. 'But they're wrong, aren't they?'

It wasn't an accusation, just a statement of fact.

'What will you do?' she asked.

'Live a safer life.'

'Starting now?'

'Starting now.'

'That shouldn't be hard,' said Agnes. 'No doubt there's a circus somewhere that needs a chap to put his head in a lion's mouth. I can see you now, grinning blithely at the crowd as the feline saliva drips down your cheek.'

I sat there for a few minutes after she had left, thinking to myself that it would almost certainly be better for both of us if I never saw Agnes again.

For some reason, my mind drifted to Peter Wilkie and Artemisia Moss. A happy, fanciful vision. Missy snoozing on the hearth rug, Wilkie sketching her from his chair, the portrait in his lap resembling an injured greyhound. I wanted badly to believe that when the wreckage washed up, you could somehow end up in the right place.

I took a deep breath and prepared to stand up. At which point a man in a light summer duster dropped heavily into the chair lately vacated by Agnes. He barely fitted in it.

'Moment of your time, Mr Catcliffe?'

It was a rhetorical question.

I looked across at the great ape of a man who had threatened me that afternoon some weeks earlier in St Wulfram's church. At the time, I had assumed he worked for Piers Garrett – something which now seemed unlikely.

'Not thrilled to see me, then? I did try and warn you off.'

The fear and dislike in my face must have been plain to him, but mainly I was just tired. Tired of people threatening me or trying to kill me or expecting me to be better or worse than I was.

'Bet you wish you'd listened now,' he said when I didn't reply.

Had he been Fletcher's man? Dick was dead, but the fellow might have come to hold it over me, feather his nest now he was without an employer.

'What do you want?' I asked coldly.

He reached into the patch pocket of his duster, withdrew his fist and tapped something down on the tabletop with a hairy forefinger. It was a penny, of course it was. He began trundling it across the cloth towards me until it got halfway, where he stopped and took his finger away. The coin fell flat and settled.

'Penny for them?' he asked.

What an annoying man he was, I thought. The café was busy, and I considered myself safe enough to reply with one of Jabez's more anatomical one-liners.

The fellow smiled.

'Good. Tight lips is what we're after. You listen to what we have to say – and do as we say – and we'll return the favour and stay tight-lipped about what happened at Catcliffe Steel last week.'

So that was it. Blackmail. It hit me then how impossibly naïve I'd been to think I would ever get away clean.

'I wish you'd do us both a favour and get to the point,' I said. 'All this business with pennies and such is a frightful bore. I suppose you have a sum in mind?'

'You mistake me, Mr Catcliffe,' he said, wagging that furred forefinger at me. 'I've only ever been your friend.'

'Threatening me and having me beaten up are the telltale signs, I suppose.'

'Some gratitude I call that. After I stopped those two lads giving you a kicking off the Queen's Road.'

I recalled the deep, Cockney voice that had warned off my two assailants after Abe Bickley's funeral. The brisk, brutal way they had been dealt with.

'That was you? Then who were they?'

'So many loose ends in this world, aren't there? I did try to tell you; you brought that one on yourself.'

'Garrett?'

He shook his head.

'Some of Bickley's mates from the AATMM. The radical lads on the fringes with their syndicalist pamphlets and "end the employer" slogans. You can't blame them for getting the wrong end of the stick. They thought management had a hand in Bickley's death, then you played right up to it by taking a stroll through Lambeth in broad daylight with the general secretary of the Free Labour Association. Afterwards, you turned up all humble-as-you-like at the funeral and I suppose it stuck in their craw.'

'But if you were protecting me then why did you threaten me afterwards?'

'Because you were making a mess on our patch, dragging your little murder into something much bigger.'

'Murders plural,' I said, exasperated. 'What could possibly be bigger than that?'

'This is about guns, Mr Catcliffe. An awful lot of guns.'

'A "job lot" of guns?' I asked cautiously, beginning to realise that this was not going where I thought it was.

'Is that how Mr Fletcher described it?'

'Those Martini–Enfields. Said he got them from Melbourne.'

The man raised his eyebrows.

'Job lot is about right. About four hundred of them, give or take. And he got more than just the rifles. The reason I tried to warn you off going after Piers Garrett wasn't because we gave two hoots about some lunatic mounting manhunts in the provinces, or an industrialist trying to set himself up with a tame politician – as if that's never happened before.'

'I suppose a bit of murder is neither here nor there to you.'

'Nor to you, apparently.'

He pointed two fingers at me, cocked his thumb as if it were a hammer, and 'shot' me across the table. He was right, I suppose. People in glass houses.

'Last year,' he went on, 'there was a slip-up at an Australian arms depot.'

'A "slip-up"?'

'Bit more than that, actually. An unknown party got their hands on enough toys to have every anarchist and republican in Europe dancing on the tables. So far they've been clever, biding their time for the right sale. Then in the spring we got lucky checking a steamship at Hull. A handful of rifles with the right serial numbers, destined for Piers Garrett at Yattonby. First ones we'd come across. Ship was Fletcher's.'

He rubbed the top of his bald head where it was burning in the sun, then put his cloth cap back on.

'Wasn't any point sounding the alarm bells over a box of ten Martinis, so we nailed the lid back on, placed men on Fletcher and Garrett, and waited for one of them to lead us to the rest of the guns.

'Only now,' he went on, 'they won't.'

'I suppose not.'

'Because some fucking idiot has killed them both.'

I couldn't quite believe what I was hearing. Not only had my whole appalling summer been completely inconsequential as far as he was concerned, but I now appeared to be getting a telling-off.

'So we're back to square one. Worse than that, with old man Fletcher gone, his associates might start to get twitchy about all the iron they're sitting on. Might not be quite so choosy about who they flog the guns off to. What do you think about that, eh?'

Truthfully, I felt relief mixed in with the apprehension. I wasn't going to hang and I wasn't being blackmailed. I still didn't have the faintest idea what was actually happening to me, and I told him so. The gorilla smiled.

'I think the least you can do now is help us find those guns, don't you?'

'Gladly, but I don't see how.'

'You've got some connections that we need, so you'll work for us until we tell you otherwise.'

'What connections?'

'You won't like it.'

I looked at him expectantly. The man extended a fingernail that was the size and colour of a lump of barley sugar, and tapped the empty coffee cup in front of him. The penny dropped.

'These connections...' I asked. 'Is one of them currently on his way home from business in Africa? Because if it is, then I can tell you right now that I am the very last man for the job.'

'We'll be in touch.'

'May I ask,' I said as he rose to leave, 'who you mean by "we"?'

'I don't believe even *you're* that slow,' he replied, and shambled off towards the park gates. He stood a good head taller than the crowds pouring in and out of the park on a sunny Sunday afternoon, and I watched him until he disappeared around the corner onto Piccadilly.

Fifty-Three

Eight o'clock on Monday night, and the last of the presses had fallen silent. At the scream of the bell, the men had peeled off their oily overalls, punched out at the clock card rack and hurried to the Two Brewers for a quick pint that most of them wouldn't mention to the wife.

Only a couple of boys from the maintenance crew remained behind to finish up fitting the pane of glass that some clumsy oaf had knocked out of the bell hut.

I stood on the porcelain toilet bowl, one boot balanced on either edge of the pan. My initials, 'HFHC', were still there, scratched into the paintwork up by the hissing cistern, and I was busy with my penknife adding the letters 'RIP' above them.

Strangely, I felt all right about it all. In the space of a couple of weeks, I had been imprisoned by a deranged boot-and-shoe tycoon, narrowly avoided being torn apart by dogs, and – if I wasn't very much mistaken – had also been recruited by some shady arm of His Majesty's government looking to exploit my friendship with Agnes. On the subject of Agnes, I couldn't decide whether I had built bridges or burned them, but I had at least put her at the scene of a double-murder and nearly got her killed in the process.

On top of it all, I had lately executed a defenceless old man – a crime made even more brilliant for having been committed in a building that had my surname written over the front gate in four-foot letters. There was a sense of having passed so far beyond the limits of what a decent man ought to be that it almost didn't matter any more.

What did matter was that I was alive and at liberty. Still in play, despite everything.

The curve of the 'P' was tricky. The paint kept flaking, dropping into the yellowish water between my feet. Really I was just killing time before I put the last outstanding mystery to bed.

There once was an angel called AbeTo Heaven two fingers he gaveHe went up to GodAnd said you tight sodI want overtime after me grave

It was written on the door behind me, and had appeared the previous Wednesday morning. The script was unmistakeable, and unless a master forger lurked somewhere among the workers at Catcliffe Steel, it meant the Porcelain Poet was alive and well.

I brushed away the last loose scraps of paint, and climbed down off the pot to admire my work from below. A fitting memorial for the Harrison Catcliffe who had first carved his initials there three years earlier, now long gone. I leaned against the wall of the cubicle and resisted the urge to light a cigarette, in case the smell might deter the great man of letters. I already knew who it was, but I wanted to catch him in the act.

I didn't have to wait long. After about fifteen minutes, I heard footsteps approaching. Hastily, I climbed back onto the toilet and squatted on my haunches as the main door to the gents creaked open and the steps drew closer. There was a rustling sound from his overalls as he dropped to his knees to have a quick look under the doors, see if anyone was in. Satisfied they weren't, he entered a cubicle two doors down and locked it behind him.

Innocent until proven guilty, I thought to myself, and waited a minute or so for the telltale sounds of legitimate water closet use. There were none. Just the sound of him breathing through his nose, his lips no doubt pursed in concentration as he began to transcribe his latest verse onto the pale green paintwork.

At the sound of my boots landing on the tiled floor, the breathing stopped abruptly. I left my cubicle, walked two doors down to his, and rapped on the door.

'Open up, Arthur.'

There was a click as the bolt drew back, and the door opened to reveal the maintenance chargehand holding a little pot of black enamel paint and a pointed paintbrush.

He smiled guiltily.

'Another secret for us to share, Mr Harrison.'

'As if we don't have enough already.'

He came out of the cubicle and placed his paint pot in the sink with the brush balanced across the top.

'I hope you don't hold it against me.'

All things considered, I did a bit. He'd suckered me in good and proper, but I knew why he'd done it.

'You didn't think we'd be in any rush to look for Abe and Timmy – but you reckoned we might just make more of an effort for the Porcelain Poet.'

'Something like that.'

He took his hat off and scrunched it in his hands nervously, the way he had in the pub on the day they found Abe's body.

'It was a way of making the point that they were missing – getting you all to take notice. Up until then it was just two men who hadn't turned up for work. And one of them not very popular neither.'

'But then you made it so that it was the Porcelain Poet missing – and suddenly you'd drummed up enough interest to get half the management of Catcliffe's down to the gents.'

Arthur shrugged.

'I got the job done with the tools I had, same as any good workman.'

'And I ended up murdering someone because of it. Nearly died myself.'

The little chargehand drew himself up defiantly.

'Someone had already killed Abe. Why did he matter any less?'

I sighed.

'I don't suppose he did. All the same, you played me – even if I can't summon up any anger over it.'

'I'm sorry, for what it's worth, Mr Harrison. If I knew how it would go, I might not have done it.'

Careful wording from a careful man, and it made me smile despite myself.

'Which means you still might have.'

I still couldn't reconcile the deferential middle-aged fellow standing opposite me with the sweary joker in the pack, daubing his limericks on the bog doors then painting over his own work twice a year and starting all over again.

'Have you always been the Porcelain Poet, Arthur?'

He grinned, and for the first time I saw the poet instead of the man I knew.

'Since my first week on the job.'

'And no-one's ever rumbled you?'

'Almost no-one. Why would they?'

He made a sweeping vertical gesture that took in his neatly clipped moustache, the clean collar poking out of his overalls and a pair of paint-splattered boots that nevertheless obviously saw regular applications of polish. He looked just about as respectable as any fellow could.

'Company man to the soles of me feet,' said Arthur proudly.

'Abe knew,' he added. 'And he kept quiet because it tickled him so. It would, wouldn't it? Everyone giving him a hard time for stirring the pot, and little old me doing it just as bad without anyone giving me a second look.'

I shook my head slowly.

'Remarkable,' I said, 'how a fellow can be two completely opposite people and get along with himself just fine.'

'With respect, Mr Harrison, you would know.'

That was the poet talking for sure.

I reached round to the sink, picked up his paint pot and brush, and held them out to him.

'Want a go?' he asked.

Acknowledgements

I'd like to begin with a huge thank you to everyone who read my last book, *The Tin Face Parade.* A little bit of support goes a long way with a first novel, and I had a lot of it. It's thanks to you that *The Porcelain Poet* has made it out into the world, and the regular pestering from certain quarters kept me writing when I might have run out of momentum.

Thank you once again to my excellent editor, Richard Sheehan. It was a pleasure to work together again, and it goes without saying that any remaining mistakes are all mine. The handsome cover is the work of Jane Dixon-Smith.

As usual, I'm grateful to everyone who scattered little crumbs of inspiration or knowledge on my metaphorical fish pond, mostly without having any idea they were doing it. You should always be careful what you say to writers – just ask the character who died an unhappy death as a result of a passing conversation in Whitby Co-op car park.

The Porcelain Poet himself was inspired by an anonymous Sharpie-wielder operating in Hunslet in the early noughties – known by a more profane nickname that I couldn't put on the front cover of a book. I've since been reliably informed that bog door poets are fairly widespread across British industry, so I tip my hat to all of them, whoever they may be.

Lastly, many thanks to my friends and family, especially to Gwubba, Ian, Popy and Helen.

Joly Braime

Joly Braime is a writer, editor, cartoonist and occasional long-distance bimbler.

He's written on everything from Sherlock Holmes, moorland dialect and home-brewing to international hiking trips and bee-related etiquette. He lives in a cottage by the sea with a lurcher, a poodle and a tortoise.

His first novel, *The Tin Face Parade*, was shortlisted for the 2018 Bridport First Novel Prize.

jolybraime.co.uk

Also by Joly Braime

The Tin Face Parade

October 1907, East London. A mask maker works painstakingly to rebuild injured faces out of painted copper alloy, until he is brutally murdered at his workbench. The police suspect a burglary gone wrong, but when a much more high-profile killing shocks the city just weeks later, one man is convinced the two crimes are connected. Somehow it falls to Harry Catcliffe, a dissolute young industrialist with a gift for being in the wrong place, to try and discover the truth. Reluctantly paired with an unhinged ex-marine on a quest for revenge, Harry's investigation takes him from the great country houses of Surrey to the carbolic-scented back alleys of Limehouse, as he realises that the masks he really needs to watch out for are the ones made of flesh and blood.

Shortlisted for the Bridport First Novel Prize in 2018, this darkly humorous historical crime novel is set in a vividly grimy Edwardian London, with a twisty storyline that'll keep you guessing.

Harrison Catcliffe and his friends will return...

Printed in Dunstable, United Kingdom

75400886R00221